Poisoned Arrows
By Paul M. Berry

Prologue

Walton Prison, he could just make it out from their parking spot halfway down the narrow street. Only a section of the outer wall was visible; dark brown brick, like it was made out of shit. Cameras and security lights surrounded the structure, projecting their glare inwards and emphasising to the rest of the world exactly what was concealed within. It made for an intimidating sight, even more so for Kev Lloyd, now that he knew he was likely to spend the next 3-6 years inside it.

The cold November rain hammered down onto the roof of the black Range Rover with increasing ferocity, outside a scattering of golden leaves were pounded into the pavement by the incessant downpour, and Kev felt a shiver run through him that had nothing to do with the weather.

The large figure in the driver's seat shifted uncomfortably, Kev flashed him a cold look and then turned away before their eyes could meet. Begsy was a big fucker, with a large bald head, a muscular build and an old scar that stretched across his right cheek. He had a crooked nose where it had been broken at some point in the past, though it must have happened a long time ago, Kev had never heard of Begsy walking away from a fight with so much as a scratch. Whoever had managed to do him must have been one tough bastard, or at the very least a lucky one.

The right side of Kev's face felt numb, he ran a finger over his lip to see if it was still bleeding but the wound finally seemed to have closed up, even without looking he could feel Begsy smiling. What he'd give to put two into the big ape's head, but the bastard had taken his piece off him earlier that night, right after slamming a fist hard into Kev's stomach.

His trigger finger twitched at the thought and sent a wave of pain straight up his right arm, sharp enough to make him wince. In amongst the catalogue of injuries he'd received from Begsy were a broken thumb and two fingers on his right hand. Most of the beating had been focused on the body, places where Kev's boss would never see them, but a few times the big goon had gotten carried away with himself; one such occasion resulted in his busted face, another the broken fingers, they were the ones that hurt the most. The ones that, in the end, had made him talk.

Now that he'd given the bastard what he wanted he wondered what they were going to do with him. Begsy had made no effort to hide his face, a sign that hadn't been lost on Kev even in the beginning, and though there had been a promise of payment before the violence began, it was good practice not to trust a word that slithered out of Begsy's mouth, every villain in Liverpool knew that much.

Still, it wasn't as if he could go crying to his boss, even if he wanted to. In the end Kev had given up everything he knew, and if he'd had it he would have given up even more just to make the beatings stop. Tony Miller wouldn't suffer that kind of betrayal from one of his own, especially one as senior as Kev. If word ever got back to the boss that he'd cracked then he'd be looking at a beating ten times worse than the one Begsy gave him, and it'd be the kind you didn't wake up from.

It was his own stupid fault, Begsy and his boys had grabbed him coming out of Mandy's house far too easily. With the court case less than a week away, and everything else that had come with it, he had taken his eye off the ball, and now he'd well and truly paid for it.

Lately he'd spent more time at Mandy's place than his own, if they'd been watching him for any length of time then they'd have had no problem sussing out his schedule. He'd made it simpler for them then it had ever needed to be, that was the most frustrating part.

He'd been there every night this week, but then what else was he supposed to do? The filth had a solid case, everyone said so; GBH, maybe even intent with a deadly weapon if they pushed for it, and if he went down what happened then? He had to keep Mandy sweet if he was going to have any chance of keeping her loyal. That was the problem with screwing a twenty three year old when you were pushing forty; the kid was impulsive, frivolous and gorgeous, if there was a more uncontrollable combination then Kev hadn't come across it. The previous day she'd dyed her hair pink just because she was bored of being a brunette, what happened when she got bored of being alone? Bored of having no money? Kev knew he had more than a few so called friends who'd be happy to cure her of those afflictions.

He'd been thinking about all those things as he'd walked out of her front door, his eyes looking past the blood red lingerie they'd just finished christening, to what was underneath. Horny old git that he was, he hadn't even realised Begsy was there until the man was standing over him, asking for a quick word.

Instinctively Kev had reached for his gun, but that was the worst decision he could have made. Begsy sucker punched him right in the gut and dragged him towards the waiting car, the last thing he'd seen before the bag went over his head was one of the others wrestling Mandy back into the house and closing the door behind him. Right now he had too much going on to even consider what might have happened when they got inside.

Begsy lit a cigarette, illuminating his coarse features within the darkened confines of the car, before leaning back in his seat. It was still hard to believe this was really happening, with this prick of all people. Begsy had been a fierce villain, back in his day, but that day had been over a decade ago. When Stephen McSharry had been top dog in Liverpool, Begs had been his second in command and probably the most feared gangster in the city, but things had changed a lot since then. Tony Miller's crew ran the majority of Merseyside now, and the parts they didn't were controlled by Wayne Caddock and his boys, though to a lot of people on the outside that was practically the same thing. While his boss rotted away in prison Begsy had been left to keep the remainder of their troops in line, while McSharry's dumb fuck of a nephew ran the firm into the ground.

Begsy had been given a wider birth than he ever should have been allowed, and it was his reputation that had convinced the major players to let him earn around the edges while his boss wasted away inside. There was a long running debate amongst Tony Miller's crew that said the big fucker should be taken out whilst his stock was low, but the debate always came back to the same point; why risk starting a war with someone as fierce as Begsy, especially when he'd dropped to the periphery of things, happy to earn a little while Tony Miller and Wayne Caddock chipped away at McSharry's empire. As another stab of pain made its way up his arm, Kev couldn't help but wish that his boss had shown a bit more balls.

As far he was concerned that was the problem with Liverpool these days, people cared more about reputations and perceptions than they did about what was genuinely good for business, but then that was how it went when things ran smooth, it was the curse of the fucking affluent.

The city was seeing more drug money than it ever had before, second only to London in the business of importing narcotics. Recessions came and went, but their industry had been growing unchecked for as long as Kev could remember, year on year it seemed Liverpool sank deeper into a sea of smack, coke, dope and ex. It was a boom that had made a lot of villains rich, especially guys like Tony Miller, and after fourteen years with his firm Kev Lloyd had been seeing a tidy little chunk of it himself, enough to make him untouchable, or so he'd thought before tonight.

The dashboard clock flashed, announcing that midnight had finally arrived. Begsy instantly extinguished his cigarette and turned off the engine.

"Time to go, move your arse"

Kev bit back a sarcastic reply. The last one had cost him a tooth on the right side of his mouth and a swollen jaw. There was a look in his captor's eyes that said he would hurt him at the slightest provocation, and Kev didn't see the need in making it any easier for the prick than he had to.

Pain shot up his arm as he fumbled with the lock on the door but in the end it opened, bringing with it a blast of rain that made him flinch. As soon as his legs touched the ground they buckled and Kev had to put a hand on the roof just to keep himself from falling. It took another couple of seconds before they found enough strength to continue, and by then Begsy was smirking at him like a bloody Cheshire cat. They started slowly down the quiet residential street, the big man keeping close, all the while his right hand was buried deep within the confines of his overcoat, watching Kev's every move.

Despite the cold he could feel the sweat building all over his bruised body. Begsy hadn't told him where they were going but it seemed pretty obvious, everybody knew this was coming, but the word from their people in the Prison Service was that it would be another week at least before all the paperwork was done. Miller wouldn't be happy when he found out, he wouldn't be happy with a lot of things that were happening lately.

They reached the end of the side street and carried on across the main road until they stood directly in front of the nick. Walton prison was in full view now, its high brick walls running parallel with the street for as far as Kev could see.

In front of the main entrance was a small staff car park, and in front of that was a white plastic hut with two guards stood inside. Kev noticed as he crossed the road that both men were having a good laugh, but as soon as Begsy ground to a halt ten feet from their station all the smiles had disappeared, and their faces had taken on a look of stern concentration.

One of the guards glared at Kev contemptuously, his hand gravitating towards the truncheon on his belt as he surveyed his bruised face. For a brief moment he considered fleeing from Begsy's side and throwing himself at their mercy, telling them he'd been abducted and beaten by the maniac standing right in front of them. The thought of freedom was almost enough to send him on his way but he knew it was a no-goer almost as soon as he considered it. Even if he could beg for help from the men who might soon be his keepers, what would people think of him when word got round about his cowardice. Not only that, but the filth would surely want a word once they found out who he was, and Kev was going to have a difficult enough time explaining the nights transgressions to Tony Miller, without throwing a police interview into the mix.

So instead he just stood there in the rain, focusing on the different sensations as the water struck the part of his face that was numb, and the part that wasn't, until a large creak echoed throughout the night sky, and the main doors of the prison slowly started to open.

It was a good few minutes before a flicker within the opening finally caught his attention, looking passed the small hut Kev watched as a shadow made its way slowly towards the light. At first it was just a small movement, but it steadily grew larger and larger until eventually a man stepped out into the rain.

By now even the guards had turned around to look as the older man, somewhere in his fifties, marched forward leaving the prison in his wake. Kev watched him closely, as he moved under a streetlight the flickers of grey invading his black hair near the temples suddenly became clear, as did the patches of grey stubble protruding from his chin, beneath the sallow olive skin and sharp features that in youth had probably been handsome. He wore a brown suit that looked like it had seen better days and hung loosely from the man's frame. Kev may have only met him a dozen or so times, but it seemed like ten years in prison had taken a hell of a toll on Stephen McSharry.

Begsy tensed as McSharry's eyes locked on them for the first time. The whole thing was all a bit cloak and dagger for Kev's taste, sneaking him out in the middle of the night and all that, but it was how Her Majesty's Prison

Service liked to do it sometimes, particularly if they felt that the inmates release was likely to be of interest to some of Liverpool's more dangerous personalities. Kev knew first hand that their fears were definitely justified in this case.

As McSharry shifted his trajectory and started towards them Kev saw the jaw clench and the back straighten, a focus appearing in his eyes that seemed to grow more prominent with each free breath. The barrier beside the small white hut opened and McSharry passed through it without breaking stride. Not once did the man look in Kev's direction, instead his eyes remained locked on Begsy until he stopped just in front of them, buttoning up his suit jacket and drawing his arms closer to his chest.

"It's fucking freezing" the older man complained, scanning the road in front of him with a cynical eye.

"Welcome home, boss" Begsy replied, the same low growl that had pressed Kev for information.

For the first time McSharry let his gaze drift towards the small white hut, the two guards were still watching but where before there had only been contempt, now there seemed to be a hint of caution in their faces.

"Ten years inside and they sneak me out the door when no one's looking, like a god dam invalid. Fucking vermin" McSharry spat on the floor and turned back towards Begsy "Where's my nephew?"

"We've got the sit down arranged for Tuesday, he's back at the house, getting the boys up to speed. He said something about keeping a low profile" Begsy paused and looked at Kev, a cruel smile touching the corners of his mouth "some people want to know where we stand"

"That boy never could stomach this place" McSharry continued "only came to see me when he absolutely had to. My own blood for God's sake, my heir, and I get obligation where I should get devotion. Is everything set?"

"Almost"

"What about the kid?"

A look that could almost have been concern flashed across Begsy's face. For a moment he seemed unsure whether to answer but then a subtle nod from McSharry encouraged him to continue.

"Making progress"

"Good" McSharry replied, before finally turning his attention on Kev "so this is the guy?"

"Kev Lloyd" Begsy announced, a hint of menace in his voice as he moved close enough for Kev to smell his breath.

McSharry regarded him carefully, looking him up and down like you would a battered old motor. It was a while before he spoke, instead he just stood there, the rain soaking through his old brown suit and matting the grey hair to his head.

"I think I remember you" McSharry said eventually "from back in the day. Miller Senior brought you in, had you running that garage out in Kirkby. That was a good little service you ran, new paint job and new plates before you know your car's been stolen. That was you, right?"

Kev nodded. Tony Miller's old man had brought him in, just a couple of years before McSharry had had him killed, that was if you believed the rumours. Kev definitely did.

"That was how I started out"

"I hear you've fallen on some hard times" McSharry pointed a thumb over his shoulder towards Walton nick "maybe you'll be taking my old bunk in D block"

"Maybe not, the lawyer thinks there's a chance he can still get me off"

McSharry flashed him a condescending look and then shook his head, droplets of rain falling onto the shoulders of his brown suit "That's what lawyers always say, it's the tender word in your ear while they bend you over, think of it as good practice for your time inside"

Begsy sniggered in his ear but Kev kept his focus on McSharry, who was again pointing over his shoulder at the high brick walls "Over the years I made some good friends in there, friends who owe me more than a few favours. People I like do ok behind those walls, people I don't... not so much"

Kev knew he should be scared, but after the beating he'd taken he was finding it difficult to feel anything other than defeat "I already answered all your man's questions" he said, the response sounding meek even to his ears.

McSharry took a moment to consider the answer before he nodded towards the way they'd come "Let's walk"

A nudge from Begsy sent Kev off in the lead and he started walking back towards the car, crossing the deserted road without even looking.

"He give you what you need?" he heard McSharry ask Begsy as they reached the other side.

"Names, addresses, imports, everything but their fucking star signs"

Kev was thankful he was walking ahead, at least that way they couldn't see him cringe. He was an old school villain, he'd been around the block more times than most, and he'd given up everything he knew about both his bosses suppliers, and their friends suppliers after only a couple of hours of torture. He was disgusted with himself.

"Good" McSharry said, his voice maintaining the same even tone that it had throughout "and has Begs given you your money?"

Fifty grand, that was what Begsy had promised him. Not much, but it might be enough to keep Mandy loyal, a depressing thought on so many levels. Kev didn't look back, but carried on straight towards the Range Rover "Not yet"

"It's in the trunk" Begsy replied, though it sounded like the answer was more for McSharry's benefit than it was for Kev's.

When they were only a few feet away from the car a hand gripped Kev's arm and pulled him round until he was face to face with Liverpool's newest ex-con.

"You'll have to forgive Begs if he was a little rough, the man doesn't like to

7

ask the same question twice, it reduces his already short temper. Still, there's no reason why this has to be looked back on as a bad experience for anyone. You got your compensation to make up for any excesses on his part, if your lawyer gets you off you can treat yourself to whatever you want, if he doesn't then you can use it to keep your interests happy while you're away. Either way, I think it's best we keep this conversation between us, your boss would only overreact, and let's face it; neither of us would come out too well in this one, would we, son?"

Though the tone was friendly McSharry watched him closely the entire time he spoke. Kev saw something in that moment, a glint in the eye that told him beyond a shadow of a doubt; this prick was going to cause a lot of trouble, for a lot of people"

"I appreciate your generosity, Mr McSharry" Kev told him, suddenly overcome with the urge to get away from the two men as fast as possible "I won't be saying nothing"

"Good man, but before you go I had another quick question I wanted to ask you, and I'm going to need a straight answer, I'm sure Begs has been through what happens if I don't get it. Now, what kind of thing has your boss been saying about me since he heard I was getting out?"

Kev hesitated, he didn't know why, he'd already grassed up enough of Tony Miller's operation to get himself hung from a tree with his balls stuffed into his mouth, but there was something about talking about the boss himself that set him on edge. He considered playing dumb, and denying ever hearing the old man mentioned, but before he could speak Begsy was at his side, and when he nudged Kev in the shoulder all courage evaporated in an instant.

"Talk" the big man demanded.

"He says that you can't be trusted and that you need to be watched"

If McSharry was angry or surprised he did a good job of not showing it, he just kept watching Kev with that same careful look.

"What else?"

Kev swallowed hard "That it's safer to have you as an enemy than to have you as a friend"

It felt like a very long time before anyone said anything, and then eventually Stephen McSharry turned his focus back to the prison and waved dismissively in Kev's direction.

"Take your money and get out of here"

Kev hesitated briefly before he hobbled towards the car, making his way past a smirking Begsy who moved past him to stand by his boss's side.

"Have you had the boys doing what I asked?" he heard McSharry say in a low voice.

"They've been on them for three weeks" Begsy replied as Kev reached the Range Rover "the pricks haven't been able to scratch their arses without us knowing about it"

This time he used his good hand to work the lock on the trunk. When it popped open it took his eyes a few seconds to adjust to the darkness within.

As the shadows stared to transform into solid objects, Kev's first thought was to wonder why they'd packed his money into a pink bag. It was a few seconds more before he was able to make out the plastic sheet that lined the entire trunk, and the figure lying across the bottom with pink hair and a red hole in her forehead.

Mandy, Jesus fucking Christ, it was Mandy. He felt himself retch; it was like the base of his stomach was being pulled upwards, pushing every organ out of the way in its haste to burst free. He leaned forward in preparation for the sickness that could only be seconds away, and as he did he felt the cold hard metal as it was pressed fiercely against the back of his head.

It was the last thing Kev Lloyd ever felt.

Chapter 1

Rob Thomas was woken by a sound; a sharp intake of breath, it was only when he jerked upwards and peered into the darkness that he realised he'd made the sound himself.

The nightmares began to fade from the forefront of his mind as his eyes roamed around the small studio apartment, slowly adjusting to the limited light. The terrors in his head continued to fade and in its place he was left with a dull resignation; ghosts made way to badly chipped walls, horrors replaced by cheap furniture. This was what New York meant to him, it had been home for a long time now, but ten years since leaving England it existed as little more than a cramped apartment in a rundown Manhattan building. All the rest was just dressing.

Rob took a deep breath and used the back of his hand to wipe the sweat from his brow. He felt his pulse racing, unlike the dreams it showed no sign of retreating with the onset of consciousness, taking another deep breath he glanced at the clock on the wall; 6.10, the same time as every other morning.

To his left he heard a small moan, he turned and took in the petit body lying next to him, and the thick head of auburn hair that almost lit up the darkened room. Jo hadn't moved, she seemed strangely impervious to the noise of his nightmares, with their increasing ferocity he was growing more thankful of that fact by the day. Leaning in close he stroked a strand of hair away from her face and listened; it didn't take long for her breathing to regain its gentle rhythm, when it did he leaned back and sucked in another deep breath.

Echoes of the nightmare continued to haunt his conscious mind; a scream, a gasp, a plea, they were all present, just like they always were. A woman's voice, Rob looked down again at the peaceful body beside him, another time, another place and another woman, but still the echoes made him ashamed to lie next to her, damning indictments of a half forgotten past that refused to relent.

Slipping out of bed he crossed the room to the kitchen area. Taking a mug from the top shelf and a bottle of whisky from beneath the sink he poured himself a heavy measure and forced it down in one gulp. He felt the warm sensation at the back of his throat, then a moment later as it reached the pit of his stomach, not long after his pulse began to slow and the echoes grew quieter still. Another quick shot and Rob returned the bottle to its resting place under the sink before, flicking on the kettle.

Tiredness gnawed at every muscle in his body, as the noise from the kettle grew louder Rob washed out the remnants of whiskey from the bottom of the mug and dropped three heaped spoonful's of instant coffee inside, the water boiled just as Jo began to stir beneath the sheets.

"Tea?" he asked as he filled the mug with boiling water, he took the carton of milk from the fridge before deciding against it, black coffee always jolted him that little bit quicker.

It took Jo another minute to untangle herself from the sheets and stumble to her feet.

"That'd be grand" she muttered, the tired slur doing nothing to diminish her thick Belfast accent.

Rob took in the sight as she made her way towards the kitchen counter that separated them. The underwear he'd bought as a Christmas gift highlighted her figure perfectly, not that it needed much highlighting. She may have been twenty eight, five years his junior, but her body showed no signs of following her towards the big 3-0. That wasn't to say she didn't work for it, four gym visits a week made sure of that. Rob admired the discipline, though he wasn't stupid enough to think it was all for him. He got that working full time as a barmaid meant that a large part of her wage depended on men finding her attractive, he might not like it but long ago he'd learned to accept it. Christ knew, he'd done a lot worse for money over the years, he'd be the last person on the planet to judge a low cut top or a flash of leg.

His eyes made their way down towards the four leaf clover tattooed on the right side of her stomach, when they made their way north he caught the sympathetic look a second before she opened her mouth.

"Nightmares?"

Rob nodded, tossed a tea bag into the second cup and filled it with water. Though his eyes were on the counter he could feel her looking over at him, it made him uncomfortable, annoyed even, he didn't deserve her sympathy and he didn't want it, all it did was make him feel like an insect beneath a microscope.

Jo twirled a strand of hair around her finger and cautiously opened her mouth, it was a few more seconds before she finally decided to speak.

"Maybe, if you tried not to drink so much?"

He poured the milk into her tea, slamming the carton down harder than he needed to.

"We've been through this before, I don't have nightmare because I drink, I drink because of the nightmares"

He fished out the tea bag and dropped it into the bin before sliding the cup across the counter, once again he saw the caution in her face, it grated worse than the sympathy.

"I know but you could cut down, that's all I'm saying"

"I'll think it over" the words sounded blunter than they had in his head.

"I'm only trying to help"

"Yeah"

Jo let out an exasperated sigh and put her hands on her hips, dressed in just her underwear the gesture looked almost comical.

"You know, you never tell me what they're about. I understand, I know it's hard for you, but you have to give me something"

Rob put the milk back in the fridge and slammed the door shut.

"I have to give you something? Like what?"

"I don't know, anything to stop me feeling like a useless spectator, maybe if you went to see a psychiatrist? Just so I knew you were trying to get some help?"

Jo was almost pleading, her voice took him back to his nightmares, it was like someone had suddenly turned up the volume of the echoes inside his head. He rubbed at his eyes and tried to control the swirling muddle of guilt, anger and resentment.

"I could *tell* you I was going to see a psychiatrist, would that make you feel any better?"

"Why are you being like this?" he caught the hurt in her voice and for a second it stopped him in his tracks, then he made his way around the counter and towards the bathroom.

"I'm not being like anything, I need to get ready for work"

Rob locked the door behind him and rested his hands on the sink, glaring into the mirror above it. He looked tired, sleep hadn't been coming easily, over the last few months the nightmares had been growing steadily worse, and he had a pretty good idea why that was. Large bags rested beneath each bloodshot eye, exacerbated further by the wrinkles around both. Thirty three and he looked closer to forty, on examination of the thick mane of black hair he found more greys than he'd expected, he needed to do something with it, it was far too long for a man his age anyway.

The onset of silence gave him time to organise his thoughts, he felt bad for taking his frustration out on Jo, but that emotion was far outweighed by his need to avoid delving into those frustrations any deeper. Openness wasn't in his locker, and at thirty three it wasn't likely to ever be, but he'd have to find a better way of dealing with that fact if their relationship was going to survive.

He doused his face with cold water and quickly brushed his teeth, unlocking the door and stepping out he was surprised to find that Jo was no longer in the apartment. On the kitchen counter was a hastily scribbled note *'Gone for a run, I'll see you tonight x'*, he picked it up, as if holding it might give him more insight into the mood in which it was written, then scrunched it up and tossed it into the bin.

It took five minutes for Rob to finish his coffee and get dressed before he was out the door. He wanted to stay and clear the air with Jo, he knew he was out of line and was willing to admit it, but if he didn't leave soon he'd be late, and the new foreman had a real hard-on for timekeeping.

The cold wind bit at his skin as soon as he stepped out onto E 5th Street. It was one of those days when he knew he should get the subway, forty minutes in the cold instead of fifteen in the warm didn't make an awful lot of sense to the logical part of his brain, but he'd always liked to walk, and it was very rare that he listened to the logical part anyway.

The cold urged him on at a frantic pace as he made his way towards the end of the street and turned north onto Avenue B. Novembers in New York were always so much colder than they were back at home, or at least that was what he told himself. It was the little things like that, the day to day stuff, which he'd found it hardest to adjust to.

The forty minute walk passed by in one big haze, his thoughts bounced back and forth between Jo and the nightmares, his nightmares and Jo. It was all connected, he passed through Tompkins Square Park wishing he could share his secrets with her, by the time he hit E 10th Street he was wondering if he could ever align the two, when he finally reached Fourth Avenue he wound up back at the same place he always did; compartmentalise, keep her safe, and preserve the love she still has for you.

Rob made it to the site with five minutes to spare, as he walked past the scaffolding he could already hear the conflicting sounds of drilling and hammering echoing around the large building as if they were vying for supremacy. He said his hellos to the rest of the crew and made his way directly to foreman Bill, who was already perusing a set of plans on a small wooden table while adjusting his hard hat every couple of seconds.

Foreman Bill wasn't one for small talk, he gave Rob his instructions; demolish the southern wall of the master bedroom to make way for a walk in wardrobe. On another day Rob might have argued the point, explaining to the so called boss that the new plans would put them two weeks behind schedule, but after the morning he'd had he kept his mouth shut and took the updated plans without a word.

The work was hard. Hard and exhausting, but it was exactly what he needed to keep his mind free of distractions. Despite the cold air seeping in through the house's many holes and gaps the nature of the work had him sweating profusely. He spent most of the morning trying to establish whether or not it was a load bearing wall, and then installing a header when it became apparent that it was. Getting started on the deconstruction was the fun part, but even that was tiring. As the afternoon began to creep on Rob found that his lack of sleep was beginning to dull his senses. His legs moved slower, his arms couldn't carry as much and it felt as if his eye lids were being weighed down. He started to wonder how much longer he could go on like this. The nightmares always came in waves, usually at the same point in the year, but this was different. They were longer now, more vivid, and more terrifying. He was worried that they would never stop, but then worried further that they would; he didn't want to think what that would mean.

As the day drew to a close Rob's frustration continued to grow, he was annoyed that he hadn't gotten as much done as he'd hoped. Most of the trim had been removed, and a section of the drywall, but he still had to make sure there was no plumbing or electrical lines back there, and then the studs and the bottom and top plates would have to come. He knew none of the other lads on the crew would have done any better, but he also knew that by his own standards, this simply wasn't good enough.

He clocked out by six thirty and started to make his way home. Jo's shift didn't start until seven, he'd already decided to head to McGlinchey's and make his apology there, but that didn't mean he couldn't make his way home slowly, stopping off at a bar or two on the way.

By the time he reached McGlinchey's, it was pushing nine o'clock, three large whiskeys had succeeded in numbing him from the chill but it hadn't done anything to halt his tiredness. Despite that he felt a certain excitement about seeing Jo again, the exchange that morning had been weighing on him all day, she was the only thing he had in the world and when it wasn't working it left him feeling detached from everything else around him.

He pushed open the door and made his way towards the bar. McGlinchey's was a small Irish tavern just off E 7th Street that had succumbed to every Celtic stereotype imaginable. Everything from four leaf clovers on the bar sign, to pictures of leprechauns on the walls were on display to make any Irish native blush with embarrassment. Jo was definitely in that category, but she hid it well when she was at work. If Ireland was so great, she argued, then why were so many of them in New York? Rob always reminded her that the same argument could be made for a hundred proud nationalities that called New York home.

Scanning the room he found the usual mix of local residents and engaged tourists, he recognised a few familiar faces who offered casual hello's or slightly interested nods, his eyes found one guy who'd been drinking there the last time Rob had come across some trouble, though his gaze remained firmly fixed on his bottle of beer.

Jo was working the shift alone, an occurrence that was becoming common enough to warrant a word with the owner sometime soon, though that was a conversation he would have with her later. Not that it seemed to be bothering her, he watched as she talked with the customers, exuding the same effortless charm that always blew him away. She wore a small, black tank top that showed off both her breasts and her stomach. Rob guessed it was probably good for at least twenty five dollars in tips, and a tight pair of denim jeans that showed off her ass. Probably good for another twenty.

He sat down on an empty stool and waited, Jo glanced in his direction mid conversation and continued without bothering to acknowledge him, Rob fished some notes out of his pocket, it was the least he deserved.

It took another few minutes for her to finish the conversation, after that she served two waiting customers and eventually made her way towards his end of the bar. She took a deep breath as she got closer, planted her hands on the opposite side of the bar and looked at him expectantly.

"Hi..." he began

"Hey"

"Listen, about this morning...." his mind went blank, he'd spent half the afternoon thinking about what he would say, now he was here; nothing.

"Well?" Jo asked impatiently, she glanced behind her to make sure no one was waiting to be served.

"I'm sorry. I shouldn't have been so short with you. I know you're only trying to help. I'm just not very good with this kind of thing"

"I'm sorry too" Jo said, her face seemed to have softened, he could tell it had been playing on her mind as well "I don't want to push you, but it'd mean a lot to me if you saw someone"

"Listen" he could sense the early tingles of frustration build in his chest, he did his best to stifle it before it had a chance to cause any more trouble "Can we talk about this another time, I don't really feel up to it tonight"

"Is everything OK?

Jo had reached over and put her hand on top of his. The intimacy felt good, he was already looking forward to getting her upstairs.

"Fine, it's just, it's been a long day"

"You look tired, maybe you should head back up to the apartment. Get some rest?"

"I don't think so" Rob said, massaging the bridge of his nose "Anyway I feel better when I'm with you. These days it's the closest thing I get to rest"

She smiled at him "That's so corny"

"You used to like corny"

"I used to be twenty-three"

"I didn't know romance had an expiry date" Rob told her.

"Maybe it doesn't, but corny definitely does"

"Go get me a beer, will you"

"Fine" Jo replied with a smile, she skipped off to the fridges at the other end of the bar and Rob felt a weight released from his chest. Maybe this was going to be a decent day after all.

Two hours passed and Rob didn't get to see as much of his girlfriend as he would have liked. A steady stream of customers kept her pacing from one end of the bar to the other, at sporadic intervals she managed to fit in a few brief conversations, but for the most part it was just him, his beer and his thoughts.

As he reached the end of his third bottle and gestured to Jo for another he caught a sound from a table close to the door, over the noise of the crowd he could barely make it out, but it was the tone more than anything that drew his focus; cold, angry and on edge.

"The limey fuck's got a lot of balls"

The voice was Irish, he dropped his head to the side and strained to hear more; there was a second voice, that was Irish too, though he couldn't make out any specific words over the voices that surrounded him.

He shifted on his bar stool until he caught a reflection in the glass frame of a Guinness poster; two men, late twenties, both in leather jackets. Rob felt a familiar, almost soothing calm wash over him as he assessed the two men in the piece of glass, one had their back to him, gesturing profusely at his pal, the other was staring at Rob's back, with a look of pure loathing etched upon his face.

It wasn't the first time he'd crossed paths with a stoutly devoted republican, and if Jo kept working in McGlinchey's it wasn't likely to be the last, what had him curious was how the two men even knew that he was English, Rob guessed they must have heard him in conversation with Jo, not that it really mattered, it was what it was, he was more interested in how it would turn out.

Jo dropped a bottle of beer onto the bar in front of him, the smile that had been spread across her face disappeared as soon as she looked into his eyes.

"Oh no, what is it?"

Rob supressed a wry grin "There might be some trouble brewing"

"From you?" she asked accusingly.

"Not from me. From you're two kinsmen in the leather jackets"

Jo pulled a cloth from her apron and began wiping down the bar, diverting her eyes every now and then to the two men near the door.

"I'll ask them to leave" she suggested, keeping her voice low.

"Not a good idea"

"Why?"

Rob took his first sip from the new bottle and returned his attention to the image of the two men in the glass "I think you'd probably end up compounding their grievance if you force two Irish lads to leave an Irish bar because of an Englishman"

"Jesus, we're back to this again?" the frustration in her tone seemed to match the ferocity with which she continued to wipe at the bar.

"Looks like"

"Couldn't you just talk to them, try that 'scousers are practically' Irish spiel you used on me when we first met?"

Rob kept his eyes on the glass and shook his head "I don't think that would work"

"I don't want any trouble" he heard the pleading in her voice, for the briefest of moments it took him back to his nightmares.

"Neither do I, but if it comes to it, I'll make it quick"

Jo shook her head and tossed the cloth into the sink below. Further down the bar a queue of customers was starting to form, she glanced over and then back towards Rob.

"What do you want me to do?"

"Don't worry about it. Go back to work. Be charming"

"Yeah, ok" she said, planting a kiss on his cheek before turning away. Rob could have done without the show of affection, if the two paddies were pissed that he was in their bar, he couldn't imagine that they'd take his involvement with the Irish barmaid any better.

For the next twenty minutes nothing much happened, with one eye on the glass reflection he slowed down his alcohol intake and every few minutes fought the urge to antagonise the two men with a quick look or a cheeky wink.

The more time went by the more Rob could feel it building inside him, it was a primal urge deep in his gut, an inherent violence that called to him, yearning to be embraced, it was only the occasional glances at Jo that kept the emotion from overpowering him. Since their conversation she'd kept away, busying herself at the other end of the bar, only moving in close when people around him were waiting to be served. It didn't stop her sending him worried, nervous glances at every opportunity, he did his best to respond with a warm, casual smile, but the more the anger radiated upwards from his gut the more difficult it became.

He tried to focus his attention on Jo, on the rational side of his brain that wasn't consumed by violence, that hadn't seen what he'd seen. He'd tried and tried but in that moment it felt alien to everything that he was. Looking down he realised that he'd finished another beer, he didn't even remember starting it.

It was a moment later when Rob caught a flicker of movement in the glass, the mick who'd had his back to Rob was getting up, without looking towards the bar the man made his way through the crowd, towards the men's room in the back. Rob tried to get a look at his face but with the other guy still watching he had to be careful not to make his interest too obvious.

Almost without thinking he gripped the empty glass bottle in his hand, a walk across the bar at a swift pace and he could halve his problem in a matter of seconds, even if paddy number two caught on to his intention Rob was still confident he could take out the one in the men's room before his buddy even got close.

Before the idea had a chance to grow into anything more Rob heard the groan of a chair leg scratching against the floor, he knew where the sound was coming from and watched in the glass as the second mick pushed himself to his feet and started moving forward.

Rob swivelled round to face the oncoming problem. Looking directly at him he noted a few details which had been hidden by the glass; the guy was well built, six one, with a cold hard face that looked like it had seen some time inside. Not only that but he was drunk, the slight shuffle of the feet and the way he carried his arms said that he'd been drinking for a while, and his reaction would be all the slower for it. As the paddy got closer Rob stood up and steadied himself, the empty bottle was well in reach if he needed it.

"You've got some fucking nerve boyo" the man said, a slight slur infecting each word.

"How's that?" Rob asked evenly, he felt his muscles tense and the taste of adrenaline in his mouth. His arm gravitated closer and closer to the empty bottle, almost of its own accord.

"This is our bar, for our people. My old man was killed fighting fucks like you, you think I'm just going to sit here and watch you drink our beer and fuck our women?"

Rob gave a disinterested shrug of the shoulders, the movement allowed his hand to move even closer to the bottle, while the paddy pressed in close enough for Rob to smell the whisky on his breath.

He heard the bar descend into silence behind them, Jo would be amongst those watching, he pushed the thought from his head, it was a distraction he didn't need. He watched as the paddy sucked in a deep breath and looked him up and down, Rob knew the moment for what it was; a brief flash of indecision, and his hand moved naturally towards the bottle without him even needing to think.

It was only when his fingers brushed the glass that Rob heard the quick, heavy sound of footsteps, before he knew it the second man was between them, pushing his pal backwards towards the door.

"What did I tell you?" the second man was shouting "Get the fuck outside"

He'd pushed his friend halfway to the exit before he turned back towards the bar, when he did Rob recognised the man's face, he'd been drinking in McGlinchey's the last time Rob had gotten himself into a scrap, his antagonist that night had been carried out half conscious, and the peacemaker before him had been one of the men to lift him up and dump him on the street.

Rob maintained his focus until his rival had been pushed out the door, a moment later his friend came back in, bringing the cold with him.

"Sorry, pal. He didn't mean anything by it, he's just had a wee bit too much to drink"

Rob kept his face even "Keep him out of here"

The paddy gave a solemn nod, then disappeared into the night. Rob's body remained on edge, he felt an emptiness that he was almost embarrassed to admit to himself, something inside his body yearned for violence, and it remained unsatisfied.

Slowly conversation started to return to the bar, by the time Rob returned to his stool and looked over at Jo it was like the entire incident had never even happened. As she walked towards him he noted the relieved look upon her face and all thoughts of violence scurried to the back of his mind.

"That went better than expected" he told her.

Jo let out a long breath "I guess"

Rob held up the empty bottle "Thanks, I'd love another beer"

It was well after one when Jo kicked out the last of the stragglers and started locking up. Rob offered to lend a hand but she assured him that she had everything under control, sliding on his jacket he gestured towards the door and stepped outside.

The cold hit him as soon as he stepped outside, rubbing his hands together he took in the symphony of New York sounds that filled the air; a dog balking, the wind rattling against a trash can, the sound of a police siren a few blocks away. At some point in time they had all become peaceful noises, as Rob closed his eyes and sucked in the cold air he started to think that for once he might just be able to sleep, if the cocktail of exhaustion, alcohol and adrenaline couldn't get the job done then he didn't know what would.

His eyes were still closed when he felt Jo's warm fingers slide in between his own, he turned towards her and planted a kiss on her forehead.

"Ready to go?" she asked softly.

"Absolutely"

Jo rested her head on his shoulder and they walked the next few blocks in silence, every now and then her hand would give his a gentle squeeze, he could tell she was happy, or at the very least relieved.

"I was thinking," she said when they were nearly home "I've got tomorrow night off, why don't we head uptown and grab some dinner, maybe catch a movie, we haven't done that in a while"

They reached their apartment and building and he held open the door "Sounds good"

Rob watched Jo as she walked in ahead of him, her hair had been tied up in a bobble for the duration of her shift, but at some point since she'd let it drop down. It suited her, she looked younger, less troubled.

He met her at the bottom of the stairs, flashing that familiar coy smile she took him by the hand and led him up to their apartment. When they reached the front door she leaned in and kissed his neck, Rob fished around for his keys as the kisses came harder, and with more urgency. Lightly, she began nibbling at his ear while her hands moved to his chest. Eventually he found the keys and managed to slide them into the door. Pushing it open he heard the phone next to the bed ringing. Jo stepped back, surprised by the interruption, and gave him a curious look.

"Who's calling us at 1am?"

Rob walked over the threshold and towards the bed. He stood over the phone and let it ring a few more times, hoping whoever it was would give up and leave them alone.

But it didn't.

After two more rings he picked it up.

"Hello?" he said cautiously.

"Alright, lad" said a familiar voice "It's time to come home"

Chapter 2

The phone call didn't last long. Conversations with Charlie never did, in the ten years since he'd left Rob had spoken to his younger brother less than twenty times, birthdays, Christmas's, the occasions when family was supposed to be important. Passed that they had no contact, New York might as well have been another planet.

"You know what time it is here, Charlie?" it came out like a reprimand, Rob was too busy jostling with the impact of the previous statement to care.

"Six am?"

"It's one am"

His brother let out a laugh and whistled down the phone, he looked towards Jo as she closed the door behind her, she didn't look back.

"Sorry lad, I never know whether I'm going forward or backward"

"I know the feeling"

"Did I wake you?"

"No, it's fine"

"Good, good" Charlie paused, it was a nervous pause. Rob could see his brother clearly, as clearly as if he was standing in front of him. He could already hear the words that he knew were coming "So listen, you've got to come home"

"Why?"

"They want to see you"

Rob swallowed hard, he felt a weight press down on his chest. Jo sat on the opposite side of the bed, staring at the floor.

"He's out?" Rob asked

"Yesterday"

"When?"

"When what?" Charlie said

"When does he want to see me?" Impatience was getting the better of him already.

"In a couple of days"

Something about the situation bothered him, it took a few seconds to detach the feeling from the overall sense of misery that Charlie's phone call had brought with it. As soon as he figured it out Rob realised that it had the potential to be just as big of an issue as the order to come home.

"What are they doing going through you?" he asked with more than a hint of suspicion.

Charlie sensed the tone and let out an amused laugh "Showed up at my house, didn't they? You know the one, the big ugly fucker with the scar? He told me I needed to get a message to you by the end of the day, I told him that I'd do my best, that you move around a lot but he said it was in my best interest to get it done quickly, I got the feeling I should believe him"

Begsy, Rob had no doubt that Charlie's instincts were right on the money.

So this was it, it was really happening, if he was honest with himself he'd always thought that someday it would, but why did it have to be today? He closed his eyes for a few seconds and took a deep breath

"OK"

"You're coming?" Charlie asked "I can tell them?"

"I'll jump on a flight tonight"

"Alright, sound lad. Drop me a line when you know what time your flight gets in, I'll come meet you at the airport"

"Thanks, Charlie" Rob said "I'll see you soon".

Rob hung up and sat down on the bed. Jo had maintained her position across from him, her eyes still focused on the floor. He waited for a few seconds, trying to think of the right words to break the silence, but none came. He reached out a hand to touch her back but thought better of the gesture, it was a few seconds more before Jo finally spoke.

"You have to go back?" her voice was even, he could tell she was holding in the anger, or the fear, it was too soon to tell which.

"Yeah"

"Why?"

"Jo..."

"No, tell me why" she stood up and marched angrily towards the window "Tell me what reason you've got to leave me, to leave New York, to go back to the place you ran away from a decade ago?"

"Because the thing I was running from" Rob said, standing up and following her towards the window "it just caught up"

"It can't be that bad. Just tell them no, tell them you have a life here and that's what's important to you. You can't go flying halfway around the world just because you got a phone call, I mean Jesus, it's ridiculous. Just tell them that you're sorry but you can't do it, and that will be the end of it"

Rob envied the luxury she had of not knowing, of not understanding. She turned back from the window to face him looking hopeful, as if her idea was new to him, as if he hadn't considered and dissected it a million times before.

"I can't" he told her.

"Why?"

"Because it will put people in danger. My family, your family, people we know, neighbours, friends. If I don't go back I put all those people at risk" Rob felt himself losing control. He was having enough trouble dealing with the reality of having to go back. He worried the process of spelling it out for her might be more than he could handle.

"Rob, what the hell is going on?" She was exasperated, gesturing with her arms more than usual. The look on her face was one of complete incomprehension "I know you have your past, you have your secrets. I understand that some bad things have happened to you. I never asked you to tell me, it has no bearing on us, on our relationship and the life we've built together. But honestly, is it that serious?"

Rob held her gaze for a few moments before he answered.

"Yes"

"And you're just going to run back to it?"

As he watched her trying to hold back the tears an overwhelming sense of guilt washed over him. It jostled with the fear, the anger and the frustration already vying for control of his head.

"I don't have a choice"

"Yes, you do" the tears began to flow, streaming down her face as if the delay had only made them more determined "you can tell them no, you can stay here with me and we can keep on living our lives"

"Joanne you have to trust me on this, there is no choice. I have to go"

"No, Rob" she declared stubbornly "The demons you live with, what that place did to you, I know you think I don't notice but I do. Please don't go back there"

Her shoulders were shaking in time with her sobs, he watched her valiantly try to hold them back, but he had nothing left to say. He walked over and put his arms around her. She was receptive to his touch, melting into his arms and resting her head on his shoulder. He brought a hand up and slowly stroked her hair. Soothing phrases passed through his head but each one sounded clichéd or juvenile. He continued stroking her head, because it was the only thing he could think of to do.

It must have been a few minutes before one of them spoke. Minutes Rob didn't want to end. The apartment was quiet, only the faint noise of a television next door, and the weakening sound of Jo's sobs filled the air. Rob didn't want it to end, because he knew things could only get worse from then on. Eventually Jo spoke, it was only a whisper but Rob heard it clear enough.

"Please..."

"I have to" he said.

Jo lifted her head and pushed him away. She turned to the window and looked down onto the street. Her shoulders weren't shaking now, and the sobs had disappeared just as quickly. She was hardening, the sadness was making way for anger.

"When will you be back?"

"I don't know"

"But you are coming back?"

"I don't know"

There was a pause before she spoke again. Her eyes remained locked on the street below, he didn't know if there was something down there to focus on, or whether she just wanted to look at anything but him.

"Are you leaving tonight?"

"Yes"

She still didn't turn from the window. Rob waited for a few minutes, hoping that she might come back to him. But she didn't.

"I'm sorry"

He made his way towards the bathroom, Jo didn't say a word.

Rob closed the door behind him, flicked on the light switch and looked at himself in the mirror. Another long day had made him look even worse, and the bright lights weren't helping. The bags under his eyes were more pronounced, his skin looked even paler than usual, and his hair; long, greying and chaotic, it just wouldn't do for where he was going.

He turned around and went to the cabinet on the opposite wall. On the bottom shelf, untouched for five years was his old electric razor. Before he could change his mind he plugged it in and went to work.

Shaving his head was a strange sensation that brought back a string of forgotten memories; he remembered doing it himself for the first time when he was fourteen, letting Kelly do it when he was twenty. He remembered the first time the army had shaved him and all the complex emotions that had been passing through his head then. He felt a very strong sense that removing all his hair was somehow linked to his youth. It felt natural.

Rob watched massive clumps of black hair tumble from his head. It seemed to take longer than he remembered, his hair was full of knots, tangled and undisciplined, too many years of neglect, not like the old days. He felt the cold around his ears and at the back of his head, an old sensation that he maybe even missed.

When it was over, Rob saw someone different looking back at him, someone he didn't necessarily want to remember. He ran his hand through and felt the small bristles brush against his fingers. He'd been twenty six the last time his head was shaved, two years before he met Jo.

The razor returned to the shelf and Rob stepped into the shower. He pressed his head against the tiled wall and watched as tiny hairs fell from his head, disappearing down the drain. The warm water felt good, like the embrace with Jo he didn't want it to end, everything he had to come just seemed so hard. But there really was no choice.

He quickly dried off and opened the door. He saw Jo sitting at the table, already halfway through a bottle of wine. She looked him straight in the eye, but made no effort at acknowledgement. Rob held her gaze for a second, until the cold look won out. Defeated, he moved towards the bedside table and began calling major airlines.

It took twenty minutes. The only flight leaving New York for England in the next twenty four hours was going to Gatwick, leaving in five hours from JFK. If he waited for two hours in London he could get a flight to Manchester, which would be faster than driving North, even with the wait, and he could get Charlie to pick him up. He told the operator to book it, waited five minutes for his confirmation and hung up.

Jo sat listening from across the room, Rob tried to catch her eye but she was too immersed in the contents of her glass.

Time was suddenly so short, he made his way towards the wardrobe and pulled out a large shoulder bag, grabbing the nearest few t-shirts and jeans he bundled them in and dropped it onto the bed.

Jo kept working on the wine as if she was alone, like he was nothing more than a ghost.

From the back of the wardrobe Rob pulled out an old shoebox. Placing it gently on the bed he lifted the lid and took out one of its two contents; his lucky cross. The cross was faded gold on an equally faded chain, it didn't seem too damaged and the clasp opened easily as he put it around his neck. He remembered taking it off ten years ago in JFK just after he'd landed. He'd been filled with paranoia that day, every police officer that came close, every person who flashed him a look put him on edge, filling him with certainty that his number was up. He remembered untying the chain and sliding it into his pocket just after the final passport check, and he hadn't worn it since. He adjusted the small cross so it rested in the centre of his chest. It felt heavy, like it was merging with the weight inside, he told himself it was all in his head, like most things it seemed.

He took the box and put it in front of Jo, it was only when he sat down across from her that she relented and looked him in the eye. He tried to flash her a gentle look as he reached into the box.

"Something to remember you by?" Jo asked coldly, Rob watched her eyes widen as she pulled out the 9mm pistol and placed it on the table "Oh Jesus"

"You need to take this. And I need you to be extra careful"

"Careful about what?" Jo asked, not taking her eyes off the gun.

"I don't know yet" Rob said with a frustrated sigh "someone hanging round the bar, asking questions, someone you start seeing on the street more than usual, anything suspicious. I don't know how much they know about you but I don't want to take any chances, you're going to have to be vigilant, keep your eyes open"

"And you actually want me to use this?" she said in surprise, lifting her eyes from the gun to look into his.

"I hope not...but maybe. If something happens to me, or if I do something to make these people unhappy they might try to come at me through you. If anyone tries to break in here, if anyone tries to hurt you, use this. Don't worry about the law, it'll be on your side, and if something does happen... well they won't expect you to be armed. You'll have to use it to your advantage.

She shook her head "I don't think I can"

"Yes, you can" Rob said, he put his hand on top of hers and felt it flinch "You're strong and you're brave. And if they do come after you, you have to trust me, this is the best possible way it can end"

"Rob, who is they? What is this?" she was getting agitated again, he

24

squeezed her hand and tried to smile.

"Baby, believe me when I say you don't want to know. Suffice to say they're bad people, and whatever you have to do will be justified"

"I always knew...I always knew you had a past...but Jesus"

"I know, and I'm sorry. I'm sorry I dragged you into this mess"

Rob gave Jo's hand another squeeze as they sat in silence, a few seconds later she returned the gesture. Hesitantly, she raised her other hand, and ran her finger down the barrel of the gun, then she moved the hand on top of his and flashed him a sad smile.

"I guess we're not going to see that movie tomorrow night"

"I guess not" Rob returned the smile.

"How do I use it?" she asked hesitantly. Rob removed his hand from Jo's and gripped the weapon.

"It's easy, you just push this latch down here to check the safety's off, and then you squeeze"

"That simple?" she asked, pushing down on the safety and hearing it click.

"That simple" Rob agreed, using his thumb to push it back on.

He put the gun down and caught Jo assessing his new haircut, she ran a hand across his head, flinching as the bristles touched her skin, then traced a route down the side of his face until she was stroking his stubble.

"You can take the boy out of Liverpool..." she said sadly, "How are you coping with this?"

"I'm ok"

He caught her concerned tone "Are you lying to me?"

Rob nodded. They smiled at one another, which seemed strange under the circumstances. Maybe they'd just reached their limit.

"I wish you'd tell me what's going on" she stroked the side of his face, he took her hand and wrapped it back in his.

"You really don't" he assured her.

"When do you have to leave?"

"Now, I guess"

She stood up, Rob followed a moment later. Even before he was vertical she had wrapped her arms around his neck in a fierce hug. He slid his arms around her waist and returned the gesture.

Rob had no idea how long he stood there, savouring the moment. However long it was, it wasn't long enough. He was aware enough to realise that the moment signalled the end of one life, and the beginning of another. Eventually he released his grip, and a few seconds later Jo released hers.

"Promise me something" she said, the smile gone from her face.

"What?"

"Promise me you'll come back"

Rob didn't know whether he had the strength to lie. He reached onto the table, picked up the gun and placed it back inside the box.

"I promise" Rob muttered as he put the lid on the shoebox and pushed it across the table, he felt Jo's fingers against his chin, pushing his face up, when their eyes met she looked as serious as he'd ever seen her.

"Promise me" she repeated, staring deep into his eyes. Rob paused for a moment as he considered how best to answer her.

"I promise" he lied, staring into her eyes.

Jo reached in and kissed him, it was a deep, slow, loving kiss and one that, for the slightest of seconds, helped Rob forget his troubles. But it was only a second, then she pulled away with tears in her eyes.

"I love you" she said, wiping her cheek dry.

"I love you too"

Grabbing his bag from the floor he made his way out, against his better judgement he turned back to look at Jo one last time. She had a hand clasped over her mouth as she tried to fight back the tears. Rob felt his heart breaking, he opened the door and stepped into the hallway.

It took ten minutes to get a cab, but once the journey started it went by faster than he'd expected. The bright Manhattan streets seemed to whiz by in a blur of colour, and before he knew it he was watching the rusted metallic arches of the Williamsburg Bridge bearing down upon him. Rob starred out the window in fascination, he studied the lights, the architecture and the beauty that at some point he'd learnt to take for granted, until it began to disappear behind him in the rear view mirror.

He thought of Jo, sitting in their apartment, crying, scared and alone. He wondered whether he'd done the right thing; warning her and giving her the gun. It was a lot to take in, she'd need a week or two to properly digest it and even then there were no guarantees. He'd seen people disappear within their own fear when confronted with this kind of threat, paralysed by the realisation that their safety was only a myth, a glass barrier that was liable to shatter at any moment. No, Jo was tough, she always had been. She'd struggle with it for a few days, like anyone would, she'd be careful, but she'd be ok. She had a good head on her shoulders; it was one of the many reasons why he loved her.

Maybe he was being too careful, they might not even know she existed, the only people who knew he had a girl were his mother and his brother, if he couldn't trust his family, well, Rob didn't want to think about that.

He considered the possibility that he may have worried and then armed her for no reason other than his own paranoia, his problems were on the other side of the world after all.

Still, if the worst thing to come out of the situation was that he scared Jo into being a little paranoid for a while, then it would have gone a lot smoother than he feared.

The bright lights of New York City disappeared behind him, Rob noticed he was twisting the cross between his finger and thumb, an old habit long forgotten. He took one look back at the home he was leaving and vowed to do whatever was necessary to ensure that trouble didn't come this way, looking for Joanne.

The cab drove on through the night, Rob glanced at his watch, three hours till take off, he began to feel something stirring in his chest.

The sense of panic began to set it soon enough, it had been ten years since he'd lived in the world he was returning to, and he wasn't sure whether he could handle it again. Physically he was in as good a shape as he had ever been, but mentally, that was a different story altogether. He'd spent so long running away from the person he had been, though he knew deep down inside that if it wasn't for that guy he wouldn't be alive. Rob wondered which he would prefer; becoming that person again, or dying as he was. Time would tell.

What bothered him just as much was that he didn't understand what was happening around him. So the old man was out, trouble in and of itself, but what did that mean? And what part did Rob have to play?

Going in blind was a bad idea and he knew it, but then what choice did he have? He did his best to get inside the old man's head and predict what was coming, but it was impossible, he'd had ten years to fester, to hoard information and to plot for the future, how could Rob predict anything when he didn't even know what kind of future Liverpool had embraced.

When Rob had left his old employer had control over the whole city, even in prison that kind of control could be maintained, but if it had then what need would they have for him? It was all just too much to think about, unfortunately for Rob he had nothing but time on his hands, eight hours of obsessing and he was liable to drive himself crazy.

The cab pulled up outside JFK, Rob fished his wallet out of his jacket and paid the driver, he gave a big tip, he wasn't entirely sure why.

The queue at the British Airways desk was bigger than he'd expected. A long line of tourists wearing Giants jerseys or 'I heart New York' t-shirts were intersected sparsely with businessmen. Rob took his place at the back, listening to some dick in a cheap suit as he bitched down the phone about a lost file, a lack of professionalism and the threat of legal ramifications. The arrogance in his tone was palpable four queues over. Rob felt vaguely envious of the kind of man for whom a misplaced file could be the cause of such distress.

Eventually Rob reached the front of the queue. The woman checking him in was a Geordie, it was an accent he hadn't heard in a long time. She checked his bag and ushered him on his way with a smile. With an hour and a half to kill he took a seat at the airport bar. Rob looked at his watch, it had only been a few hours earlier when a drunken scrap had been the most pressing thing in his life, he could hardly believe it was the same night. The stress of the last few hours had completely cancelled out the intoxication of the nights booze, but he hoped that lightning wouldn't strike twice. When the waitress made her way over he ordered a whisky neat, and tried to get his mind to stop racing. In a little over eight hours he'd be home, and there was nothing to be done about it. The waitress returned moments later with a glass on her tray, she laid his whisky on a napkin and flashed him a smile.

"You look glum pilgrim" she said "business or pleasure?"

Rob took a sip of the whisky and let it slide down his throat, it went some way to quieting his mind. He thought of Liverpool, he thought of murder, he thought of misery, he thought of betrayal and he thought of impossible decisions.

"Business" he said "Definitely business"

Chapter 3

The large house felt cold and empty. Anywhere was likely to seem large after a decade locked in an eight by ten cage, but it was the emptiness that kept him awake at night, and framed his bad mood from the second he woke.

Stephen McSharry had purchased the nine bedroom Victorian house in 1974, he'd paid a little over sixty grand for it back then, it was worth one and a half million now. In his absence Begsy had paid a string of cleaners to keep it in top condition, but all the attention in the world couldn't detract from the fact that it had been empty for ten years, it was the kind of thing that seeped into the walls and defined a home's ambience. Something would have to be done.

A large, gold framed mirror came close to consuming an entire bedroom wall, it was a far cry from the handheld shaving mirror which had housed his reflection for the ten years previous. As Stephen McSharry stood before it, buttoning up a new, crisp white shirt, he started to feel more like himself, like the nasty bastard that he used to be.

Prison changed a man, did things to him that were difficult to quantify. It robbed them of more than just their health, though the food in Walton Prison had certainly stripped a few stone off his frame, it robbed them of their will. Stephen McSharry planned to take his back, no matter the cost.

He picked a black tie from a collection of seven and slipped it around his neck. It was the one item of clothing that a man in his business could never have enough of, testament to a life spent at other people's funerals; friends, enemies, often times one and the same.

The promise of the day's events filled him with anticipation, only his second day of freedom and already the major players of the Liverpool crime scene were convening to embrace his release. Ten years was a long time, but evidently it wasn't long enough to erase the name of Stephen McSharry from the streets of the city. That name was written in blood, and it would outlast them all.

He pushed the knot tight against his throat and lowered the collar. As he reached into the wardrobe and removed his suit jacket a flash of colour caught his eye. It was only after he'd opened the door on the other side of the wardrobe that he realised what he was looking at; hanger upon hanger of greens, pinks and yellows, they were Julie's clothes.

His wife had been dead for more than eleven years, he'd let the clothes hang there for over a year before he went down, to this day he couldn't explain why. Whatever the reason he was past it now, one of the boys could dump it all in the morning.

He allowed himself a quick scan of the dresses, picking out a few of his favourites. His wife, if nothing else, had been an unparalleled beauty, looking at her clothes he could almost see her before him; that disarming smile, the curvaceous body, her beautiful eyes.

The door slammed shut with a bang. Best to forget such memories, his wife was long gone, no good would come from enhancing her memory. He suddenly regretted the decision to turn away the two whores on his first night home. Begs had paid for them out of his own pocket, a welcome home gesture, and an expensive one by the look of them, but McSharry hadn't been in the mood. It was all linked, if he didn't feel like himself then how could he fuck like himself? The time would come, and when it did all the whores on the planet wouldn't be enough to satisfy his cravings. Until then there was only one thing that mattered, and that was progress.

The time was fast approaching, he made his way out of his bedroom towards the staircase, listening to the old floorboards as they creaked underneath his feet. He headed down the stairs and towards his study. As he got closer he heard the sounds of conversation, he felt the hairs on his arms stand upright, this was what it was all about, a General leading his troops into battle.

The mahogany door opened easily, conversations halted mid-sentence. By the time Stephen McSharry stepped through the door all eyes were focused on him. He counted eleven men, they were packed tightly into his study, despite that, they'd found enough room to split into several factions. McSharry approached the one he knew best, smiles greeted him as he approached their half circle.

Handshakes and salutations went around the group, he said a brief hello to each of the four men. Back in the day they had been the core villains of his organisation, just looking at them filled his cautious mind with optimism.

The first two were Mercer and Macca, both men had been twenty five when he went down, they looked exactly the same as they had then; big, nasty bastards with bald heads, the only difference between the two was that Macca had a goatee. McSharry remembered rescuing them from the doors of a city centre nightclub, where a hustling scam was on the verge of landing them in trouble with some much bigger fish. Spotting potential had always been his gift, he took the two men out of the firing line and turned them from bouncers to gangsters in a matter of months. From what he'd heard on the inside that progression had continued throughout his absence.

The next man to welcome him back was Ads, the tangled dark hair and bushy beard may have had a hint more grey than he remembered, but other than that the image fit perfectly with his memory. Ads was ex-armed forces, despite his forced removal from her Majesty's Service he still fulfilled the role of soldier impeccably within his organisation, there were few men McSharry trusted more to get a difficult job done. Yet what interested him most about the man, was his extracurricular activities, chiefly his revulsion of Heroin addicts. Over the years Ads' hobby had evolved to the point of actively seeking out nests of smack heads in his spare time. Once he located them the story generally ended with a baseball bat and a string of fractured skulls.

Never one to miss a trick, he always made sure to sell the smack on to a local dealer, thus the circle of self-abuse continued. While he was inside Begsy had kept well on top of it, McSharry was all for a relaxing pastime so long as it didn't turn into anything more. The word from Begs was that the boy had lost a girlfriend to smack, too much of the nasty shit in her veins and she eventually OD'd, sometime after Ads developed a hard on for badly beaten smack fiends. The boy was free to continue as long as it didn't interfere with his work, if he got his jollies knocking around junkies and making a profit in the process, McSharry was happy for him to indulge.

The final member of the quartet was the one who amused him the most. Nikolai, the little blond man with horned rimmed glasses was by far the strangest, and the most dangerous, of the men before him. His diminutive figure looked almost comically out of place in a room full of heavily muscled, tattooed gangsters, but then that was part of his charm. Nikolai had a solid reputation across Liverpool as a first class knife merchant, people instinctively feared knife men more than their gun carrying counterparts, such choices implied an interest in causing pain. Nikolai defiantly had one of those. His reputation had spread even faster due to his quiet, odd disposition. As a child his Russian immigrant parents had settled in a council flat in Kirkby. Living his formative years as a spectacled, short, immigrant in one of Liverpool's roughest areas was at least partly responsible for creating the nasty little bastard he was today. In spite of his humble beginnings McSharry would go as far to suggest that, aside from Begsy and himself, Nikolai was the most feared villain amongst the group. He smiled at the small man and patted him on the shoulder, a simple nod was all he received in return. McSharry laughed and patted his shoulder once more.

The other guys chuckled and shook their heads. McSharry felt movement behind him, he turned and saw Begsy waiting, a step behind was his nephew George McSharry.

Begsy shook his hand, it was all ritual, Sunday night had been their reunion. George followed suit, another handshake.

McSharry analysed his nephew, the years had transformed him into a carbon copy of his father, the same receding hairline, the same rounded face, the only difference lay in their clothing. Where George Snr was a suit and tie man, his boy stood before him in a stripped jumper and a pair of tracksuit bottoms.

Looking at George was like looking at a ghost, it evoked a kind of strange feeling that he'd never known before. George Jnr was thirty six, his father had died at forty, victim of a car bomb planted by some particularly ungrateful and particularly malevolent underlings. The things he had done to those men when he caught them, they'd lived for over a week before he finally allowed them to die. Neither before nor since had he dissembled a living creature as completely as he had with those two, it hadn't brought his brother back, but it had kept his grief at bay.

George had been fifteen when his father died. The boy's mother had been little more than a drunk prior to her husband's death, afterwards she blew across the line into full blown alcoholism. McSharry had never approved, his brother had been too easily enchanted at a time in his life when he should have known better. Pretty, dumb sluts were two to the penny in this town, but there was no use telling his brother that. When George Snr wanted something, he wanted it bad.

After George died he had taken the boy in, he gave his sister in law just enough money to drink herself into oblivion and that had been the end of it, George Jnr had been under his wing ever since.

In his enforced absence George had taken care of the business. It was a steep learning curve for the boy, trying to run his Uncles drug empire at the age of twenty six, but McSharry was a firm believer in allowing talent to sink or swim. If truth be told there hadn't been much choice in the matter, the only other man he completely trusted was Begsy, and his enforcers talents lay more on the physical side of the business.

"It's fucking good to see you back amongst it" George said eagerly.

McSharry clasped his nephew on the shoulder, and gestured for Begsy to follow him across the room.

The next group were all Begsy recruits, the big man had been busy. The initiative was impressive, the crew needed soldiers and Begs had kept them well stocked. Assessing their value would come later, for now it was a case of quantity over quality, especially for today.

Begsy had briefed him on all three the night before, he knew who was who the minute he laid eyes on them.

The tall, skinny one was Sie, the kid was close with some connected people in London, Begsy's chief reasoning for bringing him on board. Passed that he'd proved to be a solid little worker, somewhere in his mid to late twenties the kid had plenty of time to develop. He gave a respectful nod when McSharry laid eyes on him, just before he moved on to the next man.

Caffers had a lot more of Begsy about him, he was a large, vicious looking bloke, who wasn't too pretty on the eye. From what he heard Caffers had Begsy's gift for brute violence without the sensible business head to go with it. That wasn't necessarily a bad thing, every serious crew needed a couple of bruisers, McSharry just hoped his enforcer wasn't trying to groom the ape as some kind of protégé. He sensed disappointment in Begs future if that was the case.

McSharry didn't need a briefing on the final man, he knew him from the old days. Rico Wallace had been a fixture of the Liverpool boxing circuit for what seemed like an eternity. McSharry remembered watching him when he first went semi-pro, his right hook damn near decapitated a couple of top rate fighters. That was before the booze and the coke had taken its toll, from there his career had fizzled and Rico Wallace became the poster child for unfulfilled potential. At thirty nine his boxing days were done, but a man like that still had value. Begsy deserved credit, it was a smart catch, Rico's reputation was still strong enough to provoke both fear and cooperation from the degenerate elements of the Liverpool underworld, most of whom had seen first hand the kind of damage that right hook could do. If someone was needed to beat the shit out of dealers and junkies then Rico Wallace ticked all the boxes, and the boy knew at thirty nine that his best chance of a solid income was hooking up with the right people, it was the definition of win-win for all parties involved.

McSharry cleared his throat and addressed the three men.

"Begs has been my top dog for a long time. He knows what we need around here, and exactly what it takes to make it. He brought each of you in because he sees a use for you, Begs has my full confidence so if he trusts you then I trust you. Now, this warning only comes once, the trial starts here, give me your best, your loyalty and commitment to the cause and things will work out well for you. Fail to give me any one of those things and life will turn pretty nasty pretty fast. We're going to make a good living together, pretty soon we're going to own this town, keep your eye on the ball and we'll own it a damn sight faster. You understand?"

He heard universal agreement, behind the bravado and the posturing he also sensed a hint of fear. That was good, it showed they were smart, he felt his ego inflate that little bit more. Piece by piece, he was slowly finding himself.

Huddled in the corner he saw the final two men in the crew; Berger and Will, his nephews boys. Something about them struck him as off, they had a sly edge about them, like the kind of blokes who would sell their own mother for a knife with a good blade. He decided not to approach them, it could wait until later, and he thought about talking to George about his choice of company. His nephew liked a bit of violence, that much he knew. Stories found their way back to him about attacks on bouncers, a few vaguer ones about beating women. McSharry didn't put too much stock into them, like all things it was only relevant if it interfered with business. Still, he was back now, it was his business, and he would decide who would be a part of it.

He shook the thought from his head, domestic matters could wait until later, they had somewhere to be.

He nodded towards Begsy "Round them up"

It didn't take the big man long to coordinate the group, each man had a space in one of the three cars outside, McSharry watched them disappear out the door as soon as they got their orders.

McSharry buttoned up his suit, by the time he was done only Begsy and George remained in the room, the two men watched him expectantly.

"Let's go change the world boys" he said to them.

George smiled.

Begsy nodded.

McSharry led the way out.

Three shiny new beamers greeted him as he stepped outside. Jet black; his favourite colour. Cars one and three where both full, McSharry made his way towards the middle vehicle and climbed inside, George took his place next to his Uncle, Begsy slipped behind the wheel and not long after they were on their way.

George fidgeted with the sovereign on his finger, McSharry sensed an edge to his nephew, he wondered whether young George was having difficulty stepping back.

"How's Martin Cassidy doing these days?" McSharry asked.

The question shook George from his daze, he took a moment to consider the question, then shrugged.

"He's doing alright"

"Martin's a solid bloke. Me and him go way back, he used to run with your father, back when we were first staring out. The man's been at the top table for well over thirty years now, in this game, that takes some doing"

George quit fidgeting and shifted his body until he was facing his uncle.

"His wife died a couple of years back, he's been less involved since then. He still shows up to all the meetings, keeps his fingers in plenty of pies, but it's like he's stepped back a bit, you know?"

McSharry nodded "She was a dependable woman, not many of those about. I'll bet it hit him hard"

He remembered their wedding day, he'd been little more than an ambitious kid back then. It riled him that he'd been unable to make the funeral, an old friend like Martin Cassidy deserved that kind of support, the money they'd made together over the years necessitated a deeper level of loyalty. Deeper than the kids on the street could understand. Aggression only got you so far, passed that there were only two things that made you great; brains and fidelity.

The thought took him in a different direction, he tried to catch Begsy's eye in the rear view mirror.

"What's the news on the boy, Begs?"

"Got on a plane last night" the big man's tone was blunt, ten years had done nothing to dull his sense of hatred.

That was good news. He had some questions for Rob Thomas, questions he needed to ask directly. The kid skipped town within days of McSharry being sentenced, it was a move that never sat entirely right with him, nor did the fact that he left without a trace. It was only now, all these years later, that his family claimed to know where he was. The boy had some explaining to do, that was for damn sure. Aside from that, another weapon in his arsenal couldn't hurt, particularly when the time came to make his move.

"What boy?" George asked, looking from his Uncle to Begsy and back again "Who you talking bout?"

McSharry gave a dismissive wave of the arm "Don't worry about it. Tell me what I can expect today"

"Not much, everything's been ticking over nicely. I had dinner last week with a couple of Miller's people; Crowley, Jordan, Woody, we went through a bit of profit distribution stuff. They're all pros, you'll like working with them, it's like I was telling you Uncle, there ain't that much to do, the machines running smooth"

Stephen McSharry lit a cigar and cracked a window.

"Tony Miller wasn't there?"

"Miller? No"

"Why not?"

"I don't know. He doesn't get involved in those meetings. What's the problem?"

The open window brought a chill into the car, he liked it, the cold helped him focus, it kept him on edge. George was waiting for an answer, his body language was offended bordering on belligerent. He took another pull of the cigar and blew in his nephews direction before he chose to reply.

"Let me give you a piece of advice. When you're running a firm that's as renowned, and as involved as we are, you don't take meetings and you don't barter with the mid-level guys. When you negotiate you negotiate with the top brass, or you don't negotiate at all. You get what I'm saying? Your decisions start getting influenced by nobodies, pretty soon you get labelled as a nobody and not long after your crew gets tarred with the same brush. I've worked my whole adult life to create something real, something tangible, I don't want it cheapened by amateur moves. Perception is as important as substance in this business, I thought you would have learnt that by now"

George looked out the window and went back to fiddling with his ring. He gave the kid a few minutes to pout and then resumed his questioning.

"When was the last time you saw Tony Miller?"

"Six weeks ago"

"Tell me about it"

George gave a sigh "Not much to tell. I met him for a drink, we talked a bit of business, shared some contacts. He seemed pretty interested in you I'll say that much, had a bunch of questions about when you were getting out"

McSharry turned and looked at his nephew. Now that was interesting, Tony Miller. According to Begsy he was the man who was seeing more drugs and more money than anyone else in the city, what interest did he have in Stephen McSharry?

"What kind of questions?"

"I dunno, questions. How long you'd been in, how you'd coped, whether you were looking forward to getting back into the game. There was nothing sinister or anything like that, he just said he was looking forward to doing business with you, he said his father was full of respect for you"

Respect was right, in the days before Tony took over McSharry and Christian Miller had proceeded over millions of pounds worth of smack deals. Christian Miller had been full of respect right up to the point that McSharry

35

had Rob Thomas blow his head off.

"When was the last time you met with the heads of the other three families?"

George exhaled, like he was struggling to keep up with the questions. They'd keep coming until McSharry was happy with the picture before him, Tony Miller, Wayne Caddock and his old friend Martin Cassidy headed the three other major drug traffickers in the city, if his nephew hadn't been meeting with them then his nephew was well and truly out of the loop.

"About three months ago" George answered.

McSharry tossed the cigar out the window and gave George his undivided attention.

"Fill me in"

"Same as always, business is business, isn't it?" McSharry glared at his nephew, George soon clicked on "Alright well you head about that new kid, right? Duffy? He was causing problems, muscling in on some of our territory, trying to go to war with the big dogs. This was before the police did him for that murder charge obviously, we met to talk about how we we're going to handle it, who'd have guessed the filth were about to do us a favour, right? On top of that, well I've got a good little connect with a couple of Wayne Caddock's boys. We got the ball rolling on a scam with some of the swankier bars in town, supplying them direct with coke and E, on top of that we got a couple of the waitresses on the payroll, they clue us in to any big spending yuppie types who might be ripe for a little exploitive taxation. I do love those yuppies, they'll pay through the nose for the same shit you can get on any corner in Bootle so long as it's served on a bit of sterling silver. Anyway we agreed at the meeting that I'd take point on the job, I'm linking in every week or so with some of Caddock's lieutenants"

McSharry caught Begsy's look in the mirror, he didn't have to say a word, they were both on the same wave length.

He turned back to George.

"So, no business with the top brass?"

George shook his head "It's pretty quiet at the minute"

McSharry felt the need for another cigar, they were still a few minutes out. He lit the Cuban and slid the lighter back into his pocket.

"So paint a picture for me, the mood at this meeting, what exactly are we looking at?"

George paused to think the question through; the answer came slow and deliberate.

"We've got a lot of respect with these people. I think their impressed with the legacy you bring to the table, I think they like dealing with me, they know what I'm about, and with guys like Begs here I think they know we've got some of the hardest bastards around in our ranks. Truth be told I think we're in a good place, I can't wait for you to see just how good"

The words rang hollow in McSharry's ears, the constant looks from his enforcer weren't helping. The car was drawing steadily closer to the city centre, on a day like this he didn't have time for bullshit.

"Begs," he said, looking into the mirror and catching the big man's eye "you share young George's optimistic appraisal?"

The response came instantly "Not exactly boss, no"

From the corner of his eye he caught his nephew flinch.

"Why not?" McSharry asked.

Begsy shrugged his shoulders "I've been hearing things from some of our people, worrying things. A couple of gangs we use have been on the receiving end of some nasty beatings over the last few weeks, the lads have had their stashes nicked, a couple of them ended up in hospital, in every case the descriptions fit the same couple of wankers in Tony Miller's crew"

McSharry watched George for a reaction; his nephew played the surprise card well, a little too well.

"How many of these attacks have there been?"

"Enough to make me think it's more than just a coincidence, not enough to warrant a full blown response"

It was food for thought, no question there. He didn't like that he was just hearing about it now. George didn't interject, McSharry took the opportunity to press further.

"Anything else?"

Begsy gave another shrug as he made a sharp left turn "Just petty shit really. A couple of scraps in boozers between our peddlers and Miller's mostly talk, there's not a lot to it, but I don't like the trend"

The car stopped on North John Street, McSharry looked ahead and saw Nikolai, Ads and Rico Wallace emerging from the first car. He turned his attention towards George.

"What do you make of all this?"

His nephew gave a solemn shake of the head, more disappointed than worried.

"If there's some kind of covert assault going on against us then this is the first I'm hearing about it. I honestly don't know what to tell you, maybe the guys Begs is bringing in just don't play well with others. If you're asking me my opinion, I think its way off the mark"

McSharry caught the look in the mirror, he hadn't seen that kind of menace in over a decade, it radiated from Begsy's grey eyes in waves.

He opened the door and stepped onto the street, the other two cars emptied fast, McSharry waited until both George and Begsy were standing in front of him. Tossing the cigar into the road he let his gaze pass from one man to the next.

"Well boys, at least one of you is going to be wrong"

They were stood in front of a large Beatles themed hotel, McSharry eyed stone gargoyles of John, Paul, Ringo and George on each corner of the building. To his left, where the hotel met Mathew Street, he clocked the gift shop, Asian and American tourists buzzed around like insects.

The hotel was new, he tried to recall what had been in its place before he went down, his memory came back with nothing concrete; shops, bars, distinctly average enterprises in a distinctly average town. The things he was seeing before him was something entirely different.

The group amassed on the street, McSharry gestured for Nikolai and Ads to lead away, as they began to move George and Begsy fell in either side of him. The electric doors slid open, McSharry watched the bouncer shrink back and pretend to watch something further down the street. The rigidness of his shoulders told the real story; he didn't want any part of the men currently passing through his door.

They made their way up a small flight of stairs and across the marble floored reception. McSharry eyed three crystal chandeliers above him and caught the sullen tones of Hey Jude playing somewhere in the background.

Nikolai and Ads made their way straight to the elevator, the doors opened as the rest of the group caught up and McSharry stepped inside with George, Begsy, Mercer and Macca for company. He pressed the button for the penthouse himself.

Hey Jude reverberated from three separate speakers; he listened to the song for eleven seconds before the doors reopened. A narrow hallway separated the elevator from the penthouse door; Begsy led the way with McSharry a few steps behind. The door opened without a key.

The penthouse was kitted out high roller flash, marble fittings, floor to ceiling windows and a fully stocked mahogany bar in the corner. McSharry heard his footsteps echo off the wooden floor, his eyes were attracted to the windows, they gave a first class view of the Albert Dock, with the River Mersey lingering peacefully behind it.

Six men lingered in the far corner, one of them stood and slowly made his way over. Age had taken its toll but he still recognized the beaming smile on Martin Cassidy's face as he extended his hand.

"Now there's a sight for sore eyes" Cassidy said, up close the man looked every bit of his sixty years "How are you my boy? It's good to see you again"

McSharry clasped his hand and returned the smile, his eyes passed over the heavily set wrinkles and the wispy grey hair before settling on the hazel eyes that seemed as sharp as they had ever been.

"How've you been Martin? It's been a long time"

"Too long" Cassidy said with a regretful nod "Still you're out now and that's all that matters. Back where you belong, it must feel good?"

McSharry took a moment to take in the room before he responded. Being surrounded by the class and elegance of the suite did make him feel good, in spite of himself he was still comparing the outside world to Walton Prison, he urged himself to put that hell behind him, it was easier said than done.

"You have no idea. Ten years is a long time, ten years locked in a cage is a hell of a lot longer"

He saw the sympathy in his old friends eyes "I can only imagine, all on account of one rat bastard shyster"

The boys had settled against a nearby wall, McSharry caught Begsy's eye and smiled.

"The prick got what was coming to him in the end. Begs hooked him up to a car battery and fried his bollocks to a crisp. I made sure the little bastard suffered before he was clipped"

A small smile at the corner of Begs mouth told McSharry that he'd caught the comment, Martin Cassidy looked towards the big man with admiration before returning to the conversation.

"That boy of yours certainly knows his trade"

"He certainly does. I was sorry to hear about Margaret, she was one of the good ones. After all you've done for me I should have been there"

Martin Cassidy gave a weary shake of the head, McSharry noticed for the first time that the man didn't only look older, he acted it. His movements were slow and labored while he spoke with a hesitation that seemed almost defeatist in its tone. He tried to keep the disappointment from his face as he looked down at his old friend.

"She was always fond of you Stephen. It was best that she was released from her burden. Towards the end the cancer had eaten away at so much of what she was, all that she wanted was for the pain to stop, I was grateful when she finally found that peace. The honest ones shouldn't have to suffer like that, even as a professional quick and painless was always my preference, though as we just discussed with the lawyer there are always exceptions to that rule"

McSharry looked around the room, he glanced through an open door, inside he clocked a conference table with ten chairs.

"You're the first here then, Martin?"

Cassidy looked around the room and took a deep breath, flashing a relaxed smile in the process.

"I like to get to these things early, it gives me a chance to enjoy the calm before the storm"

Begsy's warning came back to him in an instant.

"You're expecting a storm?"

"My boy, when you get to my age all of these negotiations and debates begin to feel like a season of storms. I find the vigor of youth more exhausting by the year, at the same time I don't know what I'd do if I ever walked away from it all"

McSharry clasped his old friend by the shoulder "There's no walking away for men like us Martin, you know that. We grind until we drop, our kind don't know how to live any other way"

Cassidy considered the comment for a few moments before he gestured towards the bar "Let's grab a drink"

He followed as Martin Cassidy made his way behind the bar and removed two tumblers from the top shelf. The sound the whiskey made as it pooled in the glass brought back a thousand sweet memories, he took the glass and pressed it to his lips. The taste was familiar; Johnny Walker Blue, it had been a long time since he'd tasted whiskey that good.

"What can you tell me about these new kids?" McSharry asked after another sip "Do they run their businesses like their fathers?"

Cassidy took a sip and studied his glass "I'd have thought George and Begsy would have had you fully briefed"

McSharry looked towards his huddle of men. George had decided to stay with the group and was currently deep in conversation with his lackey Berger, it was good that his nephew was taking a back seat of his own accord; power could be a difficult habit to kick.

"I want to know what you think" McSharry said, turning back to his old friend.

The men shared a few more sips of whiskey before Cassidy finally decided to respond.

"Wayne Caddock is smart. His father knew how the game was changing and taught his son to be a businessman first and a gangster second. He's calculating, diplomatic and entirely ruthless. Tony Miller is everything you remember from when he was a boy, magnified tenfold by age and power. He's short tempered, paranoid, inherently violent and prone to assaults on anything he deems threatening. He seems to have inherited all of his father's ambition with none of the prudence. Personally I find him coarse, unpleasant and uncooperative; professionally I believe he possesses the perfect combination of psychotic tendencies to maintain his place at the top of the Liverpool drug trade"

It took another sip of whiskey before McSharry felt as though he'd absorbed the entirety of his old friend's tirade.

"That's quite-" the ding of the elevator cut him off mid-sentence, McSharry turned back to Cassidy as the movement outside the door grew louder "That's quite an assessment"

A moment later Wayne Caddock breezed into the room, followed closely by eight of his employees. McSharry remembered him vaguely as a boy, on occasion his father had brought him to business meetings, plans had been afoot for Wayne to inherit the business long before Gary's unexpected death.

Caddock made his way towards the bar, the man was in his early thirties, good looking with meticulously styled blond hair. He wore a tailored grey suit that looked as expensive as the entire penthouse with a pair of sunglasses that probably didn't cost much less.

As he approached the two men he slid the glasses into his pocket and extended a hand towards Cassidy.

"Good to see you Martin, how have you been?"

Cassidy shrugged his shoulders and let out a long sigh "Can't complain Wayne, at my age you take every day as it comes. I'm sure you remember

40

Stephen McSharry?"

"I do" Caddock said, shaking McSharry's hand "We met a few times when my father was still alive. I'd say congratulations but I'd guess you're probably sick of hearing that by now"

McSharry reached for his whiskey as soon as they broke off the handshake "I can stand to be reminded a few more times"

Caddock smiled and slipped his hands into his expensively tailored pockets "My father used to say that a stretch inside was nothing more than the filths way of trying to break you, but the bastards never understood that all it really does is make you stronger"

"A wise sentiment" McSharry said.

"My father was a wise man"

Gary Caddock had been a wise man, right up to the point that McSharry had Rob Thomas blow his head off.

McSharry returned the smile "I hear you've done some good things with the business since his death. I always enjoy working with smart men, in this game there's always new ways to make money, the switched on guys are the ones who make the most of it. There's a lot of opportunity for our kind, I'm looking forward to getting into it"

A look of apprehension flickered across Caddock's face; it was the kind of look that made McSharry nervous.

"I'm sure we'll have a lot of opportunity to work together in the future, though I imagine we'll get to that later. If you'll excuse me I need to talk to a few of my boys before we get started"

Caddock made his way back to his troops, stopping to exchange a brief handshake with George. When they were done McSharry motioned for George to come join him, when he did he leaned in close to his nephews ear and kept his voice low.

"How close are his ties with Tony Miller?"

George looked over his shoulder "Who, Caddock? They're pretty close. Miller shares his smack supply coming in from South America, Caddock hooks him up with some of his E shipments he gets from Holland. The last I heard they were trying to set up some kind of deal in Afghanistan for poppy cultivation"

McSharry nodded and crossed the room towards Begsy, as he eased around the table he found himself close enough to a couple Caddock boys to able to hear them conversing in hushed tones.

"You hear what happened with Kev Lloyd? Bolted, didn't he? He was looking at five years and the little shithouse did a runner with his bird, I hear Miller's raging"

The smile that he felt never touched his lips, instead he continued on towards his enforcer, whose own face looked like it was made out of stone, and gestured for him to lower his head.

"Keep your eye on the Miller and Caddock crews, I want to know just how close these guys are, ok?"

Begsy nodded and refocused on surveying the room. McSharry made his way back towards the bar, noise in the hallway stopped him in his tracks and he found himself standing in the middle of the room as Tony Miller entered. Ten nasty looking bastards followed close behind him, the man's eyes took in the whole room before they finally settled on McSharry.

"Well fuck me, Stevie McSharry" Miller said, moving slowly towards him "Made it out alive did we?"

They shook hands, Miller's grip was overly firm, like he was trying to make a point.

"Certainly looks that way Tony"

Tony Miller looked just as McSharry remembered, though ten years had given him a rougher, more arrogant edge than before. The man was in his early forties, well built with a shaved head and a jet black goatee. He wore an expensive suit that looked wrong on his broad frame and did nothing to hide his classless demeanor. His two small eyes where too close together and held a constant look of contempt, as if Tony Miller found offence with the whole world and every creature in it.

"Ten years, right? At your age I thought looking at those kind of years that would've finished you off. This is a nice place though, right? They keep it on reserve for me whenever I need it. It must be a lot bloody nicer than what you're used to" Miller stretched his arms as far as they would go "Look at that, I'm nowhere close to touching both walls, that must blow your mind"

McSharry kept his face indifferent, inside he fought the urge to grab the pricks shady little face and slam it through a nearby glass table. Miller read the urge, even if he couldn't see it. He read it because it was exactly what he would have wanted to do. A big, shit eater grin spread across the man's face, pressing his beady little eyes even closer together. Options stalled in McSharry's head; too soon to initiate conflict, too late to accept that kind of insult. He could feel the gears in his head slowly grinding back into action, ten years out of the life had left them rusty, he wasn't finding his stride as quickly as he needed to.

The response eventually came to him.

"Never done anytime, have you Tony?"

Miller sucked at this front teeth and shook his head, his spiteful little eyes taking in the roomful of people in the process.

"Never have, never will. The fuckers aren't smart enough to put me in bracelets; I see them coming from a mile away. Anyway, most of the filth know not to fuck with me now, the smart ones at least. A lot of people have learnt that lesson while you've been gone. You hear what I'm saying?"

The beady eyes made their way back to McSharry, he held the gaze.

"I'm sure they have"

The staring contest continued for a few more seconds, Miller blinked first, clapping his hands together and turning to face the waiting masses.

"Alright let's get this fucked thing started," he shouted, pointing towards the room with the conference table "big dicks, follow me"

Tony Miller crossed the main floor and entered the room, Wayne Caddock took a moment to utter a few final words to one of his men and quickly followed suit. Martin Cassidy wandered over with two refilled glasses of Johnny Walker Blue, McSharry accepted his with a smile and gestured for George to follow.

Someone closed the door behind them, McSharry made his way towards the large oak table and sat down, Martin Cassidy and George sat either side of him, directly across sat Miller and Caddock, the symbolism of the moment wasn't subtle.

Tony Miller stood up first, he scratched at the suit like it was giving him an itch, court cases aside, McSharry suspected it didn't get much use. He clapped his hands together and looked at the four men one by one.

"Alright lads, let's get to it. We've got a lot of shit going on at the minute so the faster we plough through the faster we can all get back to our day jobs. I dunno bout the rest of you fuckers but I've got plenty of drugs that need selling, plenty of birds that need fucking and plenty of mugs that need beating, so let's get started"

Miller took a moment's pause, McSharry took the chance to gauge the mood of the room; Caddock was pure calm, Cassidy looked morose, his nephew looked nervous.

Miller continued "Top of my list is all this SOCA bollocks. Ever since the coppers set this thing up I've had the filth up my arse like a fucking queer on heat. My lawyer tells me their mandate is every big dog they can get their hands on. I've got on-again-off-again surveillance teams following me and a few of my boys around, the bitches have tried putting the heat on people we work with. They're hauling in my boys with the slightest hint of probable cause and then trying to get them to roll over. These cunts are rolling out every dirty little trick they can think of, makes me fucking sick"

Wayne Caddock leaned forward in his chair and took in the three men sitting opposite.

"It's going on across the board, they're a couple of steps behind on every bit of business we do, asking questions, hassling people. Sooner or later the bastards are going to get lucky, that's not an opinion, it's hard fact"

Stephen McSharry took a sip of his drink, Johnny Walker warmed his throat and urged him to speak.

"What about getting someone on the inside?"

McSharry directed the question to Caddock, Miller was still standing and took the lead.

"Nah, not with these 'Serious Organised Crime Twats" he answered, scratching even harder at his shirt "they're vetted two years in advance and once they're in trying to get info on them is like trying to catch a fart in the wind. These jokers know our whole fucking lives back to front and we haven't even got their names"

"How close have they got?" Cassidy asked.

Miller exchanged a glance with Wayne Caddock before he replied, the look told a story; these two were close, equal partners close.

"Two weeks ago they caught one of my guys coming back from Manchester with two kilos of H. Those SOCA boys got a crack at him, offered to let him walk on a fifteen year stretch if he turned grass. The ungrateful fuck rolled over on us, luckily the whole scene played out at Huyton station where we've got some guys on the payroll. They gave us a heads up, by the time the little grass made bail we had a couple of guys waiting to round him up. The coppers found his body the next day, all's well that ends well"

Miller sat down and leaned back with a self-satisfied grin, Wayne Caddock took his queue and cleared his throat, like a lawyer preparing to deliver his final statement.

"We have to keep an eye on this thing. The closer they get the more money these political types down South are going to pump into it, keeping ahead of the curve will only get harder"

Miller nodded his agreement "That's why everyone needs to keep their ears to the ground. These sneaky little bastards seem to be floating around everywhere, so I want every dealer, enforcer or user with the slightest link to any of our crews to keep their eyes and ears open. The slightest hint of a grass I want it coming straight to the top. We deal with this like we would any infestation; complete fucking eradication. Ok, what's next?"

Wayne Caddock pulled a bundle of papers from the folder in front of him "The chincs in Kensington are starting to cause us some real bother"

McSharry took another sip of whisky and glanced at George, the gaps in his nephews briefings where beginning to look more like chasms "What's the issue?"

Caddock caught the look and gave George a once over as well, his nephew was fidgeting with his sovereign ring and missed the whole thing. Caddock glanced at the papers before answering McSharry directly.

"Cigarettes. They're packing terraced houses in Kenny with upwards of 20 Asian immigrants and producing very cheap, very nasty cigarettes"

"Nasty is fucking right," Miller added "I got a few of my lads to try them out, the cigs swelled up their throats to double the size, the poor bastards couldn't eat solids for three days"

Caddock nodded and pulled a piece of paper from the pile "I got a list here of some of the shit they're filling them with; arsenic, glass fiber and rat shit. It says here they're filled with 60% more tar and 130% more carbon monoxide" he dropped the piece of paper back on the pile and shrugged "I don't know what any of that means but it sounds pretty fucked"

Miller slammed a fist on the table, the mood of the group went ice cold in double quick time.

"Something needs to be done before this bollocks starts affecting our cig profits coming in from the Costa del Sol. What punters going to pay three quid a pack from us when they can get them for one fifty from our commie competitors?"

Wayne Caddock took over immediately, it was like watching a duet "Not only that, but its bringing down more heat from the filth. They're so concerned they're talking about setting up a dedicated alcohol and tobacco unit to sort this shit out. Once they do you know where there first stop will be when they want some answers"

McSharry waited; when neither George nor Martin Cassidy spoke he took his opportunity.

"I served with a few of those Asians in Walton. I was under the impression a lot of them had Triad ties?"

Miller flashed him a cold stare "What the fucks that got to do with him?"

McSharry's passive face held "I'd have thought quite a lot"

The silence that followed put everyone on edge. Wayne Caddock broke it with a typically diplomatic response.

"Obviously and Triad links are a concern, but the way we see it if we coordinate a combined assault; all four of our organisations attacking at the same time then the message will get through loud and clear, that should be enough to close this chapter before the busies even get a chance to open the book"

"What kind of combined assault?" Martin Cassidy asked. He seemed as keen to know the details as he was to keep the dialogue going, the sour twist of Tony Miller's mouth hinted that problems still lay ahead.

Wayne Caddock handed out a sheet of paper each to McSharry, Cassidy and George; a quick glance confirmed it was a detailed map of Kensington with seven streets circled in four different colours.

"We know this is where the shit is being produced," Caddock began "from what I've seen each house has a few well-armed men and the rest are half starved immigrants. Half a dozen tooled up soldiers should be more than enough, if we each take two houses each and go in hard we can shut them down fast. My advice would be to send in villains with solid reputations, if they know they're up against all the major players that should be enough to veto any kind of reprisals"

Tony Miller's eyes brightened, the prospect of imminent violence pushed all belligerent thoughts out of the man's mind "The slanty eyed pricks know they haven't got the numbers to go toe to toe with us but I wouldn't put it past the crazy bastards to try. If they do then we paint Chinatown red, plain and simple, I'm more of a curry man myself anyway. What's next?"

Miller and Caddock looked expectantly across the table, McSharry turned towards his nephew, after a couple of seconds George got the hint and stood up, nerves had the boy breathing fast.

"Well, as you all know, the big man here just got out of the nick. I've been babysitting our interests in his absence but now my Uncle's back he's gonna be taking-"

Miller cut him off mid-sentence "Hold on their G. Before we go any further I had something I wanted to raise with you"

George kept his face relaxed, but the way he fidgeted with his ring was a dead giveaway.

"Well," Tony Miller began, confidently brushing a hair of his suit jacket "I was hoping you'd explain to me why you and two of your boys out there were spotted delivering a kilo of pure coke to a house in Huyton. It's a bit of a problem for me when people start selling large amounts of drugs in my part of town, I get this paranoia thing going on. But you know, seeing as how we're business associates and all I thought I'd give you a chance to explain"

George scratched at his nose, the colour seemed to drain from his face "I'm glad you brought it up Tony, it isn't what it sounds like. I don't want you to think I was dealing in your backyard, cos you know I'd never disrespect you like that"

George's nerves seemed to be fueling Miller's assault, McSharry kept a close eye on the assailant; he watched every malicious flicker in those beady eyes.

"I'm hearing a lot of noise, G, but I'm not hearing any explanation"

"It was just for some friends. We have a few associates living in Huyton who were running low, they asked if we could sort them out, that's all it was, just a personal supply"

Miller looked unconvinced, McSharry could see anger masked behind confidence, he hoped his nephew could see it too, for his own sake.

"Personal supply? One kilo? G either they're lying to you, or you're lying to me because those associates of yours stepped on that package as soon as you dropped it off, a day later they were punting it round like those chinks with their blag DVDs"

George shook "No, Tony, they said-"

Miller slammed his fist on the table "Are you calling me a liar? They've been selling your package in my pubs and on my streets for over a week, and if you're too dumb to believe it then you can ask them yourselves. I'd wait a while though; you won't be getting much out of them till their broken jaws have healed. The bastards shouldn't have made me ask twice"

"I didn't know Tony, they said they wanted it for a party they were planning"

Miller looked livid "I don't care if they bought it to give to their grannies for Christmas, if it's on my turf then it goes through me. I took their stash and I gave them a beating, just this once I'll leave it at that, but you make sure those stupid little fucks know if they ever try to sell their product on my turf again it'll be the last thing they ever sell. The same goes for anyone who supplies them"

George was losing his composure, he fiddled with his ring so frantically it looked like it might come off, McSharry took another sip of whiskey and stepped in, he'd given his nephew enough of a chance.

"Maybe I'm missing something," McSharry said to Miller "but wasn't Huyton McSharry run when I went down?"

Miller flashed another cocky as shit smile, McSharry gripped the tumbler tight and kept his poker face secure "Times have changed, Steve-o"

The edgy silence returned in force, it was so quiet they could hear the men talking outside, this time it was Martin Cassidy who stepped up to play facilitator.

"I think the points we discussed earlier about increasing our cooperation against the efforts of the police is hugely important. I wanted to discuss specifically how we can work more closely to ensure our shipments coming in through the docks are free of any police interference"

Miller kept his eyes locked on McSharry, he granted Cassidy the courtesy of finishing before resuming his antagonistic assault.

"Martin, I think before we discuss this any further we should decide whether it's wise to be talking about these kinds of sensitive subjects in front of a man 3 days out of the nick. We don't really know what kind of deals he's made or where his heads really at after so long in the cage. I want some kind of assurances that this bloke isn't working with the filth"

McSharry laughed.

George mumbled "Bollocks"

Cassidy shook his head an exhaled "That's one hell of an accusation Tony"

Wayne Caddock adjusted his tie and wadded in "I'm not so sure that it is Martin. Ten years is a long time, long enough for a man to have a lot of desperate moments. What assurances do we have that deals weren't made to keep his stretch smooth, or simply to keep it down to ten? We're all taking a risk here"

McSharry took another sip of whisky and addressed his accusers "I don't need anyone's help to keep my stretch smooth, and I've got more reason to despise the busies than either of you kids can ever imagine. Now, it's becoming increasingly clear to me that the empire I left behind has been incessantly gnawed away at by the two of you. I'm here today, in the spirit of cooperation which began with myself, Martin and your fathers to see what we can do about that, and what we can do about the money, influence and territory that's been stolen from me in my absence"

He caught the look of pure hate on Miller's face before he spoke.

"That spirit didn't keep my old man from getting popped in the back of the fucking head, did it? It didn't stop Gary Caddock taking a sniper shot to the temple. Why the hell should it help you get your money back?"

McSharry feigned outrage "If you're implying that I was complicit in either of those murders then you're way out of line boy. I lost people in that chaos too"

Miller scoffed "People? A couple of power grabbing lieutenants and a few incompetents? Our crews lost their heads and their whole fucking high commands. It always seemed to me that you came out of those hits stronger than anyone else, but then what the fuck do I know, right? I'm sure it's just a coincidence that you and your old pal were the only two heads not to get buried"

The poker face had lost its value, McSharry let some of the anger in his chest seep through "I don't like what you're accusing me off"

"I don't give a shit" Miller replied "The old days are gone, we own what we own, if you have a problem you know where to find us"

Martin Cassidy leaned forward in his chair and tried to smile, it came across forced "I'm sure there's a compromise that-"

Miller's fist slammed against the table for the third time and cut Cassidy off "No. What's done is done. You should be thankful I left you with what you have, if I'd had it my way you'd be on the fucking street selling the Big Issue. As it is my business partner here believes in appeasement, to a point I'm willing to listen"

McSharry turned towards Wayne Caddock "So you agree with your 'partner' here then?"

Caddock had looked out of sorts since the comment about his father's execution. The question hung in the air for a few seconds as he gathered himself and looked McSharry square in the eye.

"My organisation has made some exceptional strides in the ten years you've been inside. I have no interest in downsizing my operation and I'll meet any attempts to do so with aggressive resistance"

Half gangster half lawyer, Martin Cassidy's description was right on the money. Miller stood up and buttoned his jacket.

"What's done is done, I suggest you enjoy the extortion racket we've allowed your nephew to run. Hustling toffs is about as good as it's going to get for you Steve-o. I'd advise that you keep your head down, maybe someday we'll find out what really happened to my old man, but until then; welcome home.

Tony Miller didn't wait for a response, he marched across the room and slammed open the door. Wayne Caddock took a few seconds to collect his things and followed his associate out, McSharry listened to the noise as the two men and their entourages left the suite.

He took a moment to think things through; eventually the ideas in his head organised themselves and made their way towards the obvious conclusions. He stood up without a word and made his way out of the room, on their way out he grabbed Begsy and whispered into his ear.

The drive out of town was conducted in pure silence. Begsy drove, McSharry and George sat in the back, he watched the other two beamers through the rearview mirror, they kept close, as per their instructions.

McSharry watched the city pass by his window and tried to remember what it had been like before. Everything seemed so different, new buildings had sprouted up at every turn, clouding the image of the home he thought he knew. The city disappeared behind him; Tony Miller's city. Wayne Caddock's city. He vowed to tear the whole thing down and return Liverpool to its former glory, to his glory.

The car continued on. McSharry enjoyed the silence, twenty minutes later they turned down a dirt road in Formby and stopped in a green field surrounding by trees. McSharry stepped out first, George followed close behind, the change of scenery seemed to provide him with the confidence to speak.

"I know it seems bad, but I think a lot of that shit back there was just posturing and bravado" his nephew said, McSharry turned to face him as the other two cars began to empty "Some bad bloods still there, but in a few months, when the dust settles, these guys are going to see the advantages of working with us"

McSharry's eyes bore into George while he spoke, when he was finished he glanced over his nephews shoulder and nodded to Begsy.

The speed with which the big man moved surprised him, it only took a second for Begs to pull the sharp metal wire free from his pocket and wrap it around George's neck. McSharry heard a small whimper emit from his nephews throat a second before he was dragged to the ground. Begs used all his strength to squeeze the wire tightly around George's throat, the boy flailed helplessly for a few moments before his movements were suddenly still.

In front of the second car the rest of his men pounced. Berger and Will hadn't even figured out what was wrong before Caffers and Mercer nailed one each on the back of the head, they both fell to their knees simultaneously, the rest of the crew swarmed into a half circle in front of them. McSharry made his way towards the action as Ads and Macca both pulled their pieces.

"Stop" he shouted.

When he reached the group he extended his hand, Ads gave him his silver Glock, it felt heavy, he hadn't held one in so long.

Stephen McSharry only took a moment to enjoy the feeling; once that moment passed he turned towards the two little shits waiting on their knees and put two shots into each of their heads. Berger tumbled forward, Will fell to the side, McSharry kept his eyes on the corpses as he handed the gun back to Ads.

Now he was really starting to feel like his old self.

Chapter 4

Facts and figures jumped out at him from the piece of paper. He tried to memorise as many as he could but the statistics blurred into one, the noise in the coffee shop wasn't helping.

David Walker took a sip of lukewarm coffee and reread his notes, every now and then he looked away from the papers towards the car park across the street and then to his watch, their meeting was due to start in around ten minutes, and there was still no sign of Chris Railton.

He rubbed at the bridge of his nose and tried to will more energy into his weary body. Chris Railton was a good kid, and he was a good police officer. He needed to be, with the pressure Walker had coming down on his team it was imperative that he could call on the best to support him, filling the role of his number two had been an important a decision as any he'd made, and he was still confident that with Railton he'd gotten his man. The only real issue was the young officer's casual relationship with time. In the two years since David had plucked him from the Anti-Social Behaviour Taskforce he had arrived late to three meetings with senior management, four presentations on resource allocation and seven senior staff teleconferences. David glanced at his watch again; John Barry was not a man who liked to be kept waiting.

Meetings with the Regional Director were always a big deal, but lately they'd taken on even more importance. In fact, in the four years that David Walker had been with the Serious Organised Crime Agency he'd never known a period as tense as this, at least not in this particular part of the world.

Ever since SOCA had come into being with the passing of the Serious and Organised Police Act their mandate had been set in stone; reel in the Mr Big's of Great Britain and disrupt the drug trade from the top up. The philosophy was simple; cut off the snakes head and the body will stop moving. It was a nice idea, but one that didn't take into account a crucial principle; these kinds of snakes didn't often show their heads.

While London inevitably bore the brunt of SOCA's focus it was the North West that got the second closest look. An estimated three billion pounds worth of illegal drugs made their way into the country via the North West of England on a yearly basis, from there it flooded the whole of the North with some supplies even making their way to the already overstocked capital. Almost all of those drugs were funnelled through Liverpool, and the city had a criminal fraternity capable of managing that demand, as well as keeping people like David Walker and his SOCA unit permanently busy.

They'd snapped him up from the Merseyside police force four years earlier, at the time David Walker had been a Detective Constable in the Major Incident Team, on the verge of making Detective Sergeant. It was unusual for the agency to approach an individual direct and offer them a post, but David's stock had been steadily rising since he put away a couple of big time villains six years earlier. SOCA was in need of a marquee name to boost their dwindling profile, for a shot at the big time David was happy to be that name.

Since then his career had continued along a steady path, three major convictions in four years wasn't a bad return, but he was still nowhere near the four major firms that ran the city. What frustrated him most of all was that the one truly senior villain he'd put away back in his days as a DC was now back in play. It was the one truly great thing he felt he'd done with his career and a group of incompetent solicitors meant that it only lasted for a fraction of the time that it should have.

That was where today's meeting came in, with his old target Stephen McSharry back on the streets David had convinced John Barry that he would need a monopoly on SOCA's North West resources to manage the ensuing fallout from the man's release. That meant sole use of the Dedicated Surveillance Team, and unlimited overtime for every one of its twenty two members of staff.

Prior to his request the DST had been split amongst five other major cases in the region on a rotational basis, the Regional Directors acceptance of his proposal had called a halt to all surveillance on those enquiries for a four week period. The decision hadn't gone down well, either with his fellow officers or the DST, but David was willing to take the hit if it meant keeping one step ahead of Liverpool's major players. With Chris Railton as his number two on top of the 24 hour surveillance detail he had more resources than he knew what to do with. On the flip side of that coin he found himself constantly having to justify how he was utilising them. John Barry gave him sole control of the Surveillance unit for four weeks, one week into that arrangement and he was about to go into the Regional Directors office and tell him that so far he had nothing.

He finished off the last of his coffee and glanced across the street just in time to see Chris Railton's blue Ford speed into the car park and into one of the empty spaces. David glanced at his watch again; they were going to be late.

He bundled the papers into the folder and made his way across the street, reaching the car park just in time to see Railton casually climbing out, sliding on his suit jacket and reaching into the back seat to remove a folder.

As the two men met David couldn't help but note the appearance of his number two; untucked shirt, buttons not fastened and messy, uncombed blond hair. It was four in the afternoon and Railton looked like he'd just dragged himself out of bed.

David shook his head "You're twenty minutes late"

"Sorry there was traffic" Chris Railton replied, buttoning the top of his shirt and adjusting his tie.

"There's always traffic" David said impatiently "or an emergency, or an unforeseen circumstance, or-"

"There was traffic ok? What do you want from me?"

"Punctuality Officer Railton, not a lot"

"You sound like my mother" Railton said, returning the shake of the head in the direction of his superior officer.

"Well if grounding you and docking your pocket money will get it done" David said, taking the opportunity to glance through his file one more time.

"She tried that once, I stole a tenner from her purse and snuck out the back window"

David closed the file "What a remarkable advertisement for law enforcement. Did you bring the stats?"

"The plea bargain stats? Yeah I brought them"

"Good, let's go. And tuck in your shirt for God's sake"

As they made their way towards the twelve story glass building David tried to put the best possible spin on the information he was about to present. So far the DST's additional assistance had offered nothing in the way of tangible evidence, at this point all he'd gotten from his request for extra man power was more pressure hanging over his head on a daily basis. Something told him that wouldn't be the best way to present it to the RD.

He pressed his ID against the sensor and the reflective doors parted, stepping through they were greeted by two armed guards either side of a metal detector. They both passed through without incident and continued on down the corridor.

"I really don't understand why we have to do this" Railton grumbled as they reached the staircase and started their ascent towards the fourth floor.

"Report to our superiors?" David asked, recognising the hint of condescension in his own voice.

"We already report to our superiors, we have twice weekly meetings with the head of division, we speak by phone every couple of days to the Senior Special Investigator and the Detective Chief Inspector is in constant touch with our office, why have we got the Regional Director crawling up our ass every day of the week?"

"Because he directs the region, and he sees a certain degree of importance in the work we're doing here"

"Well he should see the certain degree of importance in not bothering us all the time so we can do our work"

"In a perfect world Officer Railton" David said as they reached the fourth floor "In a perfect world"

They stepped inside the Regional Director's office, the size of the room always surprised him, he estimated it was bigger than the Designated Surveillance Team's twenty man bullpen. Across the room John Barry was sat behind his desk, instead of bothering to stand the Regional Director gestured towards two chairs positioned in the middle of the room. He was a large, round man in his mid to late fifties with a bright red face, made all the more noticeable by the contrast with his white hair and moustache. He had the usual look of discontent plastered across his face that David had come to associate with his superior, in all of their conversations he had yet to see it waver.

"Good afternoon, sir" David said as he took his seat.

"Afternoon, sir" Chris echoed sitting down to David's right.

With an effort John Barry pushed himself forward and rested his elbows on the desk. Taking a sip of coffee he shuffled some papers and cleared his throat.

"The two of you are late" he said in a deep, bellowing voice. David often wondered what it would have been like to hear that voice so many years ago, when Barry was an energetic and ambitious young policeman. It was a shame, the man in front of him seemed to have lost the ability to do anything other than scold with it "I'm a busy man, don't like to be kept waiting"

"Sorry about that sir, won't happen again" David said, throwing a quick look towards Railton. His deputy glanced back out of the corner of his eye, and pretending not to see him, resumed his focus on John Barry.

David looked around the room. Plaques and commemorations filled two of the four walls, many signed by the Queen or the Prime Minister, a few by both. The wall behind Barry's desk was made entirely of glass, filling the room with bright afternoon light.

"Talk to me about your progress" John Barry said, distracting David from his analysis of the room.

He took a deep breath "Well as you know sir, we've been having a difficult time as of late. Our efforts have focused primarily on attempts to extract information from within the closed ranks of the major organised crime syndicates. Due to this sensitive period of time, what with Stephen McSharry being released, obtaining information has proven extremely difficult. Even reliable informants are failing to hand over solid tips. We've been conducting extensive surveillance on low level players to uncover suitable candidates to assist us. We've interviewed known associates of these groups, specifically KAs currently incarcerated on sentences of ten or more years and we have utilised our plea bargain powers to strike deals with a number of these incarcerated informants. Officer Railton would like to present you with the stats that plainly indicate that the plea bargains we have negotiated have a higher ratio of criminal convictions per deal struck than any other unit in the country"

Railton leaned forward and prepared the papers in his file, but a swift wave of John Barry's hand halted him in his tracks.

"I don't want to talk about plea bargain statistics, and I don't want to talk about interviewing prisoners" John Barry growled, pushing himself up he walked around the desk and leaned against its edge only a few feet away from the two officers "Three weeks ago a young man working part time in his local corner shop was shot and killed in a hold up. The assailant was a known associate of Tony Miller's crew and the gun was almost certainly smuggled into the UK from the Republic of Ireland on their dime. One week ago a twenty seven year old newlywed was stabbed in the chest four times when he tried to break up a disagreement between two men in a city centre bar. The two men have significant ties to the Miller and the McSharry organisations respectively, the young man died in hospital that same night leaving behind a twenty four year old widow who is two months pregnant. So Officer Walker, Office Railton, I'd like to talk about what it is you're doing to get these people of my streets because the last time I checked you weren't working for the serious statistical agency you were working for the Serious Organised Crime Agency".

David exchanged a look with Railton, who raised his eyebrows in surprise. When he looked back at John Barry he caught the expectant stare.

"We're doing a lot. Conducting arrests, surveillance, interrogation, the information you just recited you have because the men who committed the crimes have been brought to justice by us. But honestly sir these people, the top people, are where they are for a reason and unless they slip up, which they're not likely to do, are hands are tied. Criminals, even the fearless ones aren't willing to indite them and those that are don't last long enough to help us, as we saw last week in Huyton"

John Barry crossed his arms and readjusted his position as an angry look spread across his face, it was clearly a subject he had intended to reach and he looked keen embrace it.

"You were the one who made the deal with these men?" he asked David.

"Yes sir"

"So what the hell happened?"

"We arrested them, on the back of surveillance conducted by the Dedicated Surveillance Team and offered them a deal. They were carrying two kilos of H, they knew the score. They took the deal but before we could get it approved from the Director General the two men were released on bail. They were picked up in the car park and executed soon thereafter"

Walker chose to leave out the part where the station captain had refused to hold them overnight, tying the hands of David and his SOCA jurisdiction. He also missed out the fact that the captain had been the only other man in the room when the deal was made, yet somehow Tony Miller's men were waiting when they left the station. He'd sent four memos with that information and been told to drop it every time, the station captain was a highly decorated officer who'd earned his stripes in the Toxteth Riots, the department had no intention of dragging his name through the mud unless proof of bribery was put on a plate for them. Bureaucracy made him sick.

"What about the killers?" Barry asked.

David shook his head "The DC who caught it's got nothing sir, no leads to speak of. From the look of it though they were butchered before they were killed, badly, I wouldn't be surprised if the top man was in on it"

Barry sighed "What have you got on the current activities of the four families?"

"There was a meeting yesterday. No doubt timed to coincide with the release of Stephen McSharry. We've been unable to obtain any information as of yet about what went down, but word should start filtering down to our people in the next few days. From what we can gather there appears to be some tension between certain factions but other than that" David hesitated for a moment, unsure if he should go on. Speculation wasn't appropriate when you were addressing the Regional Director. He caught Railton's subtle nod, then continued "We've been getting reports that McSharry's top enforcer has been recruiting, but it's difficult to tell to what ends. With Caddock and Miller as strong as they are it'd be foolhardy to start a war, and they must know that".

John Barry jolted forward from the desk in alarm "Officer Walker, I want assurances it won't get that far".

"It won't"

Barry stood from his perch and wandered towards the window in silence. The two men waited patiently until the Regional Director had considered whatever was playing on his mind and resumed his position on the edge of the desk.

"Good" he said slowly "I have a budget meeting in five minutes, Officer Railton would you mind waiting outside for a moment"

Railton stood up and made his exit without a word. When the door closed behind him Barry took the vacated seat, positioned it directly opposite Walker and sat down. There was a serious expression on the RDs face, it was the same one he used when he went on television.

"The reason I asked him to leave was because I wanted to gage for myself your current mental state, in light of recent events"

"I'm sorry, sir, I don't quite follow" David looked into John Barry's eyes as they watched him intently. He felt like a lab rat, being studied for some purpose beyond his own comprehension.

"Stephen McSharry's release" John Barry said, not breaking eye contact with his subject "I understand you're the man who sent him down".

"Yes sir" David said, intrigued to hear what would come next.

"You haven't worked for me for very long, and I'm afraid I don't know you as well as I would like. Such is the unfortunate nature of the beast when our political masters chose to form new agencies as frequently as they form new loyalties. Often times David," he noted it was the first time Barry hadn't called him Officer Walker and speculated on what the shift in tone might mean "men like yourself, men of principal, men of character, can become obsessed when the term of their greatest successes are spent. I wanted to ensure that you weren't becoming preoccupied with the re-emergence of this criminal, and to warn you of the inherent dangers to your career were you to become so".

David ran a hand through his hair as he tried to think of the best response "Sir, Stephen McSharry is a killer, and his presence on our streets is a threat to every man, woman and child that walk them. But sadly he is not alone in that category, and I intend to diligently pursue him and every other criminal like him to the best of my ability without bias or prejudice until they are all at her Majesty's Service".

"Good" Barry said, standing up from his chair and extending his hand "Type up a list of your ongoing cases for the next two months and send them over to me ASAP"

"Yes sir" David said, standing up and shaking his hand.

"Thank you"

"Thank you, sir"

When he stepped out of the office the first thing he noticed was Railton, leaning against the opposite wall, his tie already removed. Though the young copper was twenty seven he gave off an air of someone considerably younger, not that it affected his performance, the boy was natural police. He stood up straight as David approached and fell in alongside him on the way to the staircase.

"What was that about?" he asked as his eyes followed a young female officer travelling in the opposite direction.

"He wanted to know if I was becoming obsessed with McSharry" David bluntly replied.

"Are you?"

"Don't be ridiculous"

"It's a fair question, Guv" Railton said as they began their descent down the four flights of stairs.

Walker kept his voice firm "Drop it, ok?"

"Sure thing..." they covered another two floors before Railton continued talking "What a waste of time, we couldn't have just had that conversation over the phone?"

"He likes to see the guys on the front line face to face" David said impatiently, he was conscious of the fact that he'd been more disrupted by Barry's line of questioning than he'd initially realised "he thinks his powers of perception are so efficient that if he looks into your eyes he can deduce whether or not you're losing it".

Railton scoffed as they reached the bottom of the stairs and walked towards the exit "What a load of shit. How these people get so high up the ladder is beyond me. Want to grab a beer?"

"Can't" David replied, passing the security guards and stepping out onto the street "I have to follow up some leads"

"Now? Haven't you been on the clock since four am?" Railton looked at his watch, David looked at his, it was now four thirty.

"Two am actually" he corrected.

"Jesus Guv, give it a rest"

"I'll pick you up at 7am tomorrow morning to meet with the surveillance detail," David started towards his car "I'll call you at 6am!"

"I can wake up on time!"

"I'll call you at six!" David repeated.

"Fine, go get some sleep will you!" his young deputy shouted.

David reached the brown Vauxhall Cavalier, opened the door and slid into the front seat. He felt exhausted, like something was sucking away at his energy, reaching under the seat he pulled out a metal flask and poured himself a cup of coffee.

So far his informants were coming up short, it was a worrying trend, even an increased slush fund for potential talkers wasn't doing the job of loosening their tongues. The development was a problematic one, but not entirely unexpected, people always tended to clam up in times of great upheaval, it was a self-preservation thing. Right now it was too early to tell how the game was going to play out, and no one wanted to bet on the wrong horse, he sympathised with the dilemma, the problem was he couldn't use it, so it was on to plan B.

He'd been out that very morning to the home of the first magistrate to answer his calls with ten freshly typed warrants detailing a number of questionable characters who were suspected of concealing narcotics. Each one had been signed, which meant he knew ten scumbags who would be getting a nasty wakeup call in the early hours of the morning. All he needed to do was procure himself a couple of uniformed officers in the mood for a rouse and his night would be all set. He could see it already; shakedowns on cold streets and intimidation on decrepit council estates, the very concept left him weary but he banished the feeling with a quick jolt of caffeine.

No one forced you into this Walker he reminded himself *this is the life you chose.*

He drank as much of the black liquid as he could, tossed the rest out of the window and thought about John Barry's warning. They were afraid he'd become obsessed with McSharry, there was no doubt putting him away had been the highlight of his career. It had speeded up his promotion by at least five years and it was a major reason why he was heading up his own unit in SOCA at the age of thirty five. He thought about his answer, seeking justice without bias or prejudice, what a load of bollocks. The McSharry case had been his coming out party, it had signalled to everyone in the department that he wasn't just another rookie, that he was a policeman to be reckoned with, and an officer destined for great things. The very thought of that piece of shit back on the streets made him want to hit something. He turned on the engine and recalled his vow that Stephen James McSharry would rot in a prison cell for the rest of his life. If it took a hundred cold, lonely nights chasing down leads on council estates then that's what he would do. He pulled out of the car park, took a deep breath and prepared himself for night number one.

Chapter 5

Charlie Thomas hated coming into Manchester.

He avoided it in all but the most extreme of circumstances. Every time he made the trip he found himself overrun by the same horrible little bastards, and every time he vowed it would be his last. But it never was, there was always some stupid reason, some niggly little job that drew him back, with any luck this would be the last time, and maybe he might just get through it without any hassle.

He'd only parked the car twenty minutes ago but already he was at breaking point, people eyed him suspiciously and every time he opened his mouth he saw that same look of comprehension on their faces *ah, he's a scouser* it said, ignorant fucking bastards. Manchester Airport was a big place and whoever designed it clearly hadn't done so with convenience in mind. Three separate terminals and it was just Charlie's luck that the last one he checked would be the one that received Trans-Atlantic flights. Despite Manchester's best efforts he'd still managed to beat the flight by half an hour, which was half an hour more than he wanted to spend there.

Charlie wandered over to the music shop directly opposite the arrivals lounge and tried to kill some time. The security guard clocked him as soon as he stepped through the automatic doors. Suspicious eyes gave him a once over, locked in on his tracksuit, and a few seconds later the chubby, middle aged git had positioned himself next to the exit, arms crossed and eyes alert. Charlie felt his blood boil, he was half tempted to nick something just on principle, give the chubby old boy a decent work out, but then what would be the point in that, he was here to pick up his brother.

He headed towards the CDs and flicked through the racks of new releases. Nothing but a load of shite from start to finish. Picking up a CD he glanced at the price; £11.99, he knew a guy down The Old George who could copy any CD you could think of for £2.50, what kind idiots were wasting this kind of money? He put the CD back and headed for the exit, the security guard stared at him and Charlie stared back, feeling a swagger come into his stroll. He flashed the guy his best 'fuck you' smile as he left, and headed back towards the pick-up point.

As he reached the barriers, surrounded by chauffeurs and excited looking relatives, he spotted two girls passing through with a trolley full of suitcases. The golden colour of their skin hinted at a return from tropical climates, the blond one in particular was showing enough skin to make it clear she wanted everyone to know it. He turned as they passed behind him, and whistled in their direction.

"Alright, gorgeous" he called to the blond in the mini skirt.

The girl kept her head down and continued walking, her brunette friend turned and flashed him an evil look. Charlie stuck two fingers up at the ugly bitch, no way was anyone talking to her.

He turned back towards the doorway through which Rob would soon be walking and thought what it would be like to see his big brother again. As kids they'd spent all their time together, hanging out at the local park and playing football whenever they got the chance. Being out of the house and away from the old man had been the best scenario for everyone involved back in those days, especially when he was drinking. Even after the selfish prick bailed, when Charlie was nine, they'd still spent all their time together, finding some excitement to keep them amused, some stupid little adventure that made them feel like big shots. A smile came to Charlie's lips as he thought about all the tight spots his brother had helped him out of, as a teenager he'd never developed the ability to walk away, come to think of it he still wasn't sure if he'd ever learnt that lesson.

Through the fabric of his tracksuit pocket Charlie ran a finger over the scar on his right thigh. He'd fallen at fifteen, climbing over a fence as they tried to get out of the park after closing time. The spike had sliced through his thigh all the way to the bone, he didn't remember the pain but he remembered screaming at the sight of all that blood. When he'd woken up he was in the hospital, the story they told him was that Rob had walked for two miles with Charlie on his back to the nearest A&E. The story hadn't touched their mother quite as much as they'd hoped; she'd still delivered one of the hardest beatings she'd ever given them. Charlie remembered the dual pain like it was yesterday; the dull throbbing in his leg and the flailed skin on his back.

His thoughts drifted to what Rob was going to be like, after all it had been ten years since the last time they'd seen each other. He had to remind himself that the fun, high spirited Rob he remembered had been a much different creature to the one that got on the plane just over a decade ago. His brother had been solemn for a good couple of years before he'd skipped town, not that he didn't have reason to be, but Charlie still missed the guy he grew up with.

They talked a couple of times a year, it was hard to gage a person's attitude in those kind of circumstances, but he definitely seemed happier since he met this Joanne bird a few years back. Hopefully that would tell when he got off the plane.

Charlie glanced up at the monitor, his flight landed twenty minutes ago, Rob should be coming through the doors sometime soon. He hoped so; his parking ticket expired in another twenty minutes.

He pulled the mobile phone from his pocket to kill a couple more minutes, only to be greeted by three missed calls from the wife. He wondered what was so urgent, probably something that needed picking up for the kids, sliding the phone back into his pocket he looked up towards the arrivals screen. He got the impression more and more that Vicky thought he was made of money, he didn't know why, a dole cheque didn't go far these days, particularly when you had three mouths to feed on top of your own. He had his work on the side, but selling a bit of ecstacy and a bit of coke down the pub was hardly likely to put them in the fortune five hundred. Still, as work went, Charlie could imagine plenty of duller ways to earn some cash. He got his supply from Leroy Tate, a fairly well connected dealer in the Bootle area. For a 40% cut he gave Charlie enough class A's to get himself round five or six local pubs, business was usually slow during the week, but once Friday came he easily brought in five of six hundred by the end of the weekend, tax free. Leroy could be a bit of a tit, but all in all he wasn't a bad guy to work for, on top of his government benefits he was actually seeing a fair few pennies. If it hadn't been for the wife and kids he might have gotten to spend some of it.

It wasn't long before people started filtering through, families and couples mostly, batteries recharged after a couple of weeks in the states. Eventually Rob made his way through, a navy bag thrown over his right shoulder.

The first thing he noticed was how much his brother had beefed up over the years, he'd never been skinny, but with the extra muscle he had a bit of an edge to him. The look was intensified by the shaved head, though the tan line on his forehead suggested it was a new look. He circled round the barriers and found himself face to face with his older brother.

"There he is" Charlie said, unable to hold back the beaming smile, he opened his arms and hugged his brother tight, lifting him up in the air to keep it from looking too sentimental.

"Hey Charlie, how you doing?" Rob asked as he patting him on the shoulder, the two disengaged and took a step back to look at one another. Rob was a couple of inches taller than Charlie, that was the first thing he realised he'd forgotten.

"I'm good lad, I'm good, you look..." he squinted and gave Rob a closer inspection "old"

Rob laughed "Curse of the genes matey, it'll be you in a couple of years"

His brother seemed happy to see him, but there was an unmistakable sadness in his eyes, unmistakable at least if you had the same eyes.

"Not a chance there, lad" Charlie said, flexing his arms "see this Adonis-like body? Sculpted on beer and kebabs alone this is, my friend. Loving the hair by the way, the Thomas boys with matching skinheads, just like when we were kids".

"Without the matching outfits though, right?" Rob asked.

"Yeah"

"Good, cos once was bad enough"

Charlie gestured towards the exit and the two brothers started walking, falling in side by side after a couple of seconds.

"Listen I should warn you" Charlie said "Vera wants us round for dinner"

Rob's shoulders sagged, Charlie watched him give a disappointed shake of the head

"What are you doing to me, little brother?"

"Sorry mate, but you know what the woman's like. Honestly, how long did you think you'd be able to keep yourself out of her claws?"

"Long enough to catch up on a night's sleep, do you know how big of a bitch this jet lag is? Dealing with her in this state's going to be..." Rob let out a sigh "It's going to be a real fucking mess"

They exited the airport and crossed the road towards the elevator for the multi-story car park. Rob seemed to be taking everything in, his eyes wide and childlike; it was as if he'd never seen England before. Charlie imagined how strange it must have been, remembering the familiarity of another lifetime. Eventually Rob turned back towards Charlie and focused his attention on his brother.

"And so it should be" Charlie continued "you've left me to deal with her for the past ten years, do your duty as a son and share the bloody burden"

"She was bloody hard work. Any chance she's gotten better?" Rob asked as the elevator doors opened in front of them. They stepped in and Charlie pressed the button for the fourth floor.

"Worse"

"Brilliant. When?"

"In a couple of hours, right after I introduce you to your sister in law and your two nieces"

"Little Zoe and Alexis?" Rob asked, a warm smile creeping onto his face.

"Correct, two points to you. They're very excited about meeting their uncle Robbie"

The smile on his brother's face grew even wider, then he looked down towards the ground and seemed to check himself.

"Listen Charlie, I'm sorry I couldn't get back for your wedding. I should have been there, mate".

The elevator reached the fourth floor and Charlie led the way out into the busy car park. "That's alright mate, I understand your reasons"

"Still I should have been there" Rob said, lightly jogging a couple of steps to catch up "to make sure you didn't cock it up"

"Hey I did alright, but thanks bro"

"So how's married life treating you?"

"Can't complain" Charlie said, finally catching sight of his red Volkswagen "Can't say the same for her, you've never met a woman who can moan this much"

"You can't blame the girl; you are a pretty big pain in the ass"

They reached the car, Charlie slid his keys into the door and swung it open, leaning on the roof as he spoke "Nah mate, you wouldn't believe it; this, that, the other, don't go out with your mates, pick this up for me, pick that up for me, I swear to God, put a ring on their finger and they turn into a completely different species"

Charlie lowered himself into the car and reached over to the passenger door, Rob climbed in with an amused grin plastered across his face. Charlie gave a disapproving shake of the head and slid the key into the ignition.

"My little brother's all grown up" he said, tossing his bag into the back seat "I guess that's the price you pay for making an honest woman out of her"

"I know" Charlie nodded, started the engine and reversed out of the space "I'm cursed by the purity of my morals"

"Quite the weight on your shoulders" Rob let the sarcastic comment hang in the air, when he spoke again there was a seriousness to his tone "What did they say about the meeting?"

The mood in the car took a nosedive, Charlie swallowed hard and thought about how to answer, he'd hoped to have a little more catch up time before they'd brace their one taboo subject. If they could just ignore the reasons for Rob's return, even for a couple of hours, then it would give them enough time to get reacquainted, but when he glanced across and saw the look in Rob's eyes he knew that wasn't going to be possible.

"He wants to see you in the morning"

Charlie hated being the go-between, and it wasn't even like it was his idea. The feeling when he passed on the information felt like he was piling heap after heap of shit onto his brother's prone body. It made him feel awful, like he was responsible for Rob's misery, though in a sense that was entirely true.

"Where?" Rob asked, staring straight ahead like he was in some kind of trance.

"They didn't say. They're going to give me a call in the morning and then I'm supposed to pick you up and take you where they want" Charlie's conversations with the bruiser called Begsy had been blunt to say the least, the man wasn't telling him anything more than he absolutely needed to, which seemed to Charlie to be a pretty bad sign.

"OK"

"What do you suppose he's going to ask you?"

Rob didn't respond, he just kept looking straight ahead, Charlie felt a pang of guilt in his chest as he realised how the stupid the question had been.

"What's your answer going to be?" Charlie asked after a few more seconds, Rob's silence was starting to worry him.

"An answers something you give when you have a choice, Charlie" Rob replied bluntly.

"I guess"

The two sat in the car for a few minutes in deft silence. Every now and then Charlie glanced over but his brother was unmoving, his gaze focused directly ahead, his jaw clenched tight. Charlie tried to concentrate on the road but every couple of minutes he found his eyes glancing back towards Rob. Eventually his brother let out a deep sigh and turned his head to face him.

"Tell me about my nieces"

"Ah mate, they're a right little pair" Charlie said, relieved to be given a chance to talk again, silence drove him crazy "Alexis, she's four and a half now, she's starting to grow into a real little person, right in front of your eyes. She won't listen to anyone's opinion except her own, just like her mother, she's one of the smartest kids in her class though, and she's got those big, brown Thomas eyes. Zoe turned one last month, lad she's got a pair of lungs on her, I tell ya. She can scream so loud, no word of a lie, they can hear her four houses down when she gets going. She loves her bottle though, you put it in front of her and that's it, she's quiet for the night"

"Just like her dad" Rob said with a sad smile.

They drove on for twenty minutes more before Charlie pulled into his street. Lynwood Avenue was a long road of old Victorian terraced houses in the middle of Bootle. He wasn't wild about the area, there was always a gang of kids on at least one corner, and if you got through the weekend without a single drunk husband yelling at his wife from the street, then you considered it a success. He and Rob had hung around the area for a while as kids, mainly because back then the corner shops weren't too picky about who they served alcohol to, but it wasn't a place that was close to his heart. Still, it was a stone's throw from Vicky's mums house, and she wouldn't be able to look after the kids without her. Charlie would be happy enough to live out the rest of his days without seeing the old hag again, but she was a big help to Vic when the two little ones got out of hand.

Parking the car and turning off the engine he tried to look at the street with a critical eye, to see what Rob was seeing. They'd bought the place five years earlier and at some point he'd started to take the place for granted, it was home, that was all he saw. Yet looking at it through unbiased eyes, at the faded paint jobs, the graffiti and the bundles of litter, he suddenly found himself feeling a little embarrassed. Reaching into the back seat he grabbed Rob's bag and climbed out of the car.

"I know this street?" the tone of Rob's voice implied it was more of a question than a statement".

"The Dixon girls used to live down here" Charlie said, remembering the sisters they'd hung out with for the duration of a summer holiday.

"That's right, Lauren Dixon, she was as fun fourteen year old"

"We sure could pick them, couldn't we?" Charlie said, sliding his key into the front door and forcing the rusty hinges with a thrust of the shoulder.

He stepped into the hallway and picked up the bundle of post that lay on the floor. Skimming through them quickly he ushered Rob inside and closed the door behind him. Bills, notices, second notices, it seemed like the only reason anyone used the postal service anymore was to try and get money out of him. He walked into the living room and dropped the letters onto the coffee table, surveying the room as he did so, it was a tip. Kid's toys littered the floor, the coffee table had an equal number of mugs and baby bottles spread out across it and the bin in the corner was overflowing with newspapers and takeaway wrappers. Charlie let out a sigh and started picking up toys while he gestured for Rob to have a seat. It took a few minutes but he'd piled most of them in a corner by the time he heard footsteps from the floor above, making their way towards the staircase.

"Charlie! Is that you?" came an angry voice.

"Yeah"

The footsteps thundered down the stairs as Charlie left the toys in the corner and moved to the middle of the room. Rob stood up as well and Charlie sent him an inquisitive look, his brother responded with a shrug of his shoulders and the two men turned their attention towards the doorway.

"Where the fuck have you been? I left you five voicemails asking you, if could handle it, to pick up some nappies. It's bad enough you didn't even come home last night..." her voice trailed off as she made her way into the room and saw that her husband wasn't alone.

"Vic, this is my brother Rob" Charlie said, putting his hands in his pockets and nodding towards his brother "Rob, this is my darling wife, Vicky"

"Hi Vicky, it's good to finally meet you" Rob said with a smile, leaning forward and extending his hand.

The anger on Vicky's face evaporated in an instant, replaced a moment later by an awkward embarrassment as she wiped her hand on the back of her jeans and shook Rob's. She didn't look at her best, her light brown hair was tied in a bun with a couple of stray strands falling across her face, self-consciously she tried to brush away after shaking Rob's hand.

Her skin looked pale and fatigued, sleep had been a rare thing for both of them since Zoe was born, but since Charlie brought home the money it was Vicky who handled the midnight feedings. On top of that she still had half a stone of puppy fat on her, which she hadn't shifted since the birth, all things considered it wasn't the impression he would have wanted his wife to make. Charlie suddenly wished he'd given her more of a warning about Rob's arrival, if he had maybe she'd have been able to make a bit more of an effort. His wife could really turn it on when she wanted to, but after two kids, the number of times she wanted to seemed to decrease by the week. Charlie watched her take a couple of seconds to compose herself before she responded.

"Rob... yeah you too. I was beginning to think he'd made up this big brother of his, Charlie talks about you all the time!"

"Really?" Rob raised his eyebrows in his brother's direction, Charlie felt his face go a little red, he gave his head a slow shake from side to side.

"Nah, only when I'm ripping the shit out of you"

Rob sent him a cynical look and turned back to face Vicky, she seemed very uncomfortable, like she didn't know what to do with herself. He wondered whether Rob had noticed.

"Charlie didn't tell me you were coming home, this is the first time in, what? Fifteen years?"

"Ten" they both said at the same time.

"What's the occasion?" Vicky asked, put off a little further by the synchronised response.

"I've got some business I've got to take care of" Rob said, this time it was his turn to speak a little awkwardly and again Charlie found himself trying to discern whether Vicky had picked up on it.

"Charlie says you're in construction?"

"That's right"

"Well this is the place to be" Vicky said, looking at Charlie and attempting to smile. He could tell she was still pissed at him, but she was putting on a show for Rob's sake, no doubt he'd get an earful later "We've got plenty of that going on around here haven't we?"

Charlie nodded.

"Well, that's why I'm here" Rob replied.

An awkward silence descended on the group for a few seconds, both Vicky and Rob threw Charlie a look before he realised they were urging him to speak. He took his hands from his pockets and clapped them together.

"Sweetheart, where are the girls, I wanted to introduce Rob to his nieces".

"Oh, well Alexis is out with my sister and I just put Zoe down for the day" she squinted "Don't take this the wrong way but I don't want to risk waking her up. She had me up most of the night and since I was here taking care of her by myself"

"Don't start" Charlie warned, hearing the anger in his own voice. It was bad enough she looked like an unkempt mess and embarrassed him in front of his brother, the last thing he needed was her causing a scene as well.

"No listen, its fine" Rob said, interjecting himself into the conversation with a sense of urgency "We'll do it some other time, right? I should be home for a while anyway, I think"

Charlie tried to swallow the bile that was building in his throat. He looked at Rob, whose eyes were pleading not be caught in the middle of a domestic dispute, he let out a sigh and turned to face Vicky.

"Listen, Mar wants us to go round for dinner, so we're going to head over now, you alright for food?" he considered for a moment inviting her along, but the mood she was in he just didn't have the patience.

"Fine" she said bitterly "so does that mean you're coming home tonight?"

"Should do, but it'll probably be pretty late" Charlie replied, calculating that another night long absence would put him in the dog house for more days than he had on this earth "I might have some business tonight, couple of people I need to see. Here's some money though, for nappies and stuff" he said pulling a wad of twenties out of his pocket and holding them in front of her.

"I've got money" Vicky said, crossing her arms and looking away.

"Take it anyway" he said, holding the cash closer to her face "treat yourself to something, a new dress, pair of shoes or whatever"

With a sigh of resignation she reached forward and took the role of notes out of Charlie's hands, stuffing them in her pocket "Are you as chivalrous as your brother then, Rob?" she asked sarcastically.

"There's no one quite like our Charlie"

"Don't I know it" she said bitterly. Charlie leaned in to kiss her but she made a sharp movement and pulled her head away, causing his lips to brush against her cheek. He moved away and looked at Rob.

"We should get going," he turned to his wife "don't wait up for me"

"I never do"

The ride to their mother's house passed in almost total silence. Charlie was still seething with Vicky's attitude, and he could tell that Rob was apprehensive about seeing Vera again.

Their mother had never had the smoothest of relationships with her eldest son, after a ten year hiatus the odds were high that there would be a good deal of backdated animosity for her to catch up on.

The car ride from Bootle to Kirkdale took ten minutes. Charlie spent the time imagining all the things he could have said to Vicky, he suspected Rob was conducting a similar exercise in preparation for what was about to come.

They pulled up outside their childhood home, both stepping out of the car at the same time. The house hadn't changed much since their father had bolted over twenty years earlier. Like most of the houses in Kirkdale it reeked of working class dilapidation, aside from an extension here and a satellite dish there, he guessed the houses looked identical to when they were first built at the turn of the century. The closest their Mother came to refurbishing her house was every couple of years when Charlie got roped into applying a new lick of paint to the outside walls, though it was always the same colour as the one that greeted them when they first moved in. He patted Rob on the back and made his way towards the front door, the prodigal son following a few steps behind.

He took his key, and put it in the lock. This one was much better oiled than his own and opened easily without the use of his shoulder. He breathed in the same musky smell that always reminded him of his first home and made his way through the immaculately clean hallway, into the living room. Like everything else in the house, the room hadn't changed much since they were kids. The bird pattern wallpaper which had been put up at some point in the eighties still covered the four walls, though it was fraying considerably in a couple of the corners. Charlie continued on into the dining room, there was no sign of their mother.

"Mar" he shouted, hearing his voice echo around the room "You here?"

"In the back" came the shout from the kitchen.

They walked into the small room and found their mother bent over the oven, inspecting a steaming dish. When she saw them she stood to her full height of five foot two, and looked them both over. Charlie took in the wrinkled, blond haired creature standing in front of him and tried to remember how he'd lived so long in fear of the woman. After a moment he dismissed the question and pointed towards Rob.

"Look who I found!" Charlie said

"Hey, mum" Rob's words came out a little awkwardly.

"Hello Robert" she replied, shuffling towards him and giving him a hug. Neither of them seemed to put their all into the embrace "You're looking well"

"Thanks, you too" Rob said, stepping away and looking around the room "The house looks spotless, as always"

"Cleanliness is next to godliness" she uttered, a statement that was etched upon his brain from a hundred different childhood memories.

"I remember" Rob said, sharing a look with Charlie that confirmed they were both reliving the same experiences.

"Oh you do, do you?" Vera replied in an antagonistic tone, Rob pretended like he hadn't heard her.

"Mar, how long's dinner going to be, I'm starving" Charlie said, slipping back into the role of peacemaker before he'd even realised it.

"Ten minutes, I'm making beef stew" she ushered them out of the kitchen towards the dining table. Rob and Charlie both took seats opposite one another but their mother remained standing, Charlie got the impression that she didn't want to concede the height advantage, it was one she so rarely got to utilise these days "You do still eat beef don't you Robert? I find it difficult to recall after so long"

Charlie watched his brother suppress a sigh, he couldn't resist throwing a smile in his direction. Vera made no secret of her displeasure at Rob's defection over the last ten years, but it was still pretty amusing to watch her passive aggressively torture her eldest son, especially when Charlie got a front row seat.

"I still eat beef"

"Good. Heaven knows that nasty eating habits you've adopted from those Americans"

"Well it was a close Mar, but somewhere between chewing tobacco and roasting buffalo I have managed to find enough room in my diet for beef" there was a determination in Rob's eyes "but thanks for asking"

"I see living over there's done nothing to cure that smart mouth of yours" she said, her voice scalding, it was the same voice she'd used when they spilt things on the carpet "Are you back for long or is this just a flying visit?"

"Too soon to tell" Rob mumbled, looking away and fidgeting with his hands.

"Well I guess we should enjoy your company while he have it, shouldn't we Charles?" Charlie cursed under his breath and kept his head down; he'd spent enough of his life stuck in the middle of their battles "I might not be alive the next time you show your face"

"I wouldn't worry about that" Rob replied "You'll outlive us all!"

"Oh somehow I doubt it" Vera said as she hobbled off into the kitchen, he heard the clattering of plates coming together as she shouted into the other room "Charles, I haven't seen my Grandchildren for nearly a month, is there something I should know?"

Charlie waited for her to return before he answered. When she did she was carrying three plates; he watched as she placed one in front of him, one in front of Rob and one before an empty seat.

"Sorry about that mar" he said finally "It's been a bit manic, we'll try and get them down this week, ok?"

"Good, at my age there are so few joys left" Charlie glanced at Rob and saw him role his eyes, he tried his best to hold the laugh inside "I do look forward to seeing my granddaughters, ever so much. Can I expect my eldest to give me any in the near future?"

"Not yet, no"

"Oh well, odds are I'd never see them anyway" she said, making her way back into the kitchen "And where is this Joanne of yours? I was looking forward to meeting her"

"She couldn't make it this time, she had to work, she sends her love"

A few seconds later she returned with a pan full of beef stew, it smelled fantastic. He saw Rob make a move to help her with the pan that looked almost as big as she was, but Vera ushered him away and rested it safely on the table.

"To think, my son has been in a relationship for five years with a woman I've never even met, incredible" she took Charlie's plate and filled it with stew, as she handed it back she looked at him with inquisitive eyes "How is Vicky, Charles? Are you helping her out with the little ones?"

"You know me, mar" Charlie replied, a mouthful of stew doing nothing to delay his response "I'm not one to shy away from my responsibilities"

"No, just tasks, duties and ambitions" Rob said, the mischievous smile that he remembered from childhood plastered across his brothers face "he never shies from responsibility though"

"Your face will be shying away from my fist in a minute"

His brother grinned back at him as he dipped a piece of bread in the thick, brown stew.

"Do you think it's your passive nature that makes you such a good father?" Rob asked, shovelling the bread into his mouth.

"Probably, I'm pretty fucking cool as well"

"Don't forget modest"

"Damn, I always miss that one out" Charlie said, slamming his fist down on the table in mock annoyance. He heard his mother sigh, messing around at the dinner table had always been one of her pet peeves, luckily they'd passed the age where it was punishable by a crack around the ear.

"So Robert, where are you staying while you are home?" Vera asked, trying to shift the conversation towards a more polite topic. He glanced at Rob and caught the nervous look; like a dear caught in the headlights. Charlie contemplated rescuing him now, or letting him sweat for a while. He knew which was more fun, so he stabbed another potato with his fork and devoured it in one.

"I haven't had a chance to give it much thought, really. This whole trip happened pretty quickly" Rob threw his brother a pleading glance, Charlie just laughed and went back to eating his food.

"Well, your rooms all made up if you want to stay here" Vera said, lightly nibbling at her meal.

"Thanks-"

"Actually mar" Charlie interjected, his conscience getting the better of him "I know a guy who owns a couple of flats, the gentleman in question is inclined to do me a favour, he said he can give Rob a place for however long he's in town"

The relief on Rob's face was blatant, but if Vera had noticed then she was doing a good job of pretending like she hadn't.

"I think that would probably be easier" Rob said, frantically nodding his head like a parakeet, "I'll be in and out at all hours, you know, with business stuff"

"Oh, well I wouldn't want you waking me up in the middle of the night, Lord knows I had enough of that when the two of you were boys"

Her voice gave of a slightly offended edge, not that she was likely to admit it. Charlie felt a pang of guilt sucker punch him side on, the old girl was probably just looking forward to a little bit of company. He made a mental note to bring the kids down a couple of times during the week and focused his attention back on the stew.

Vera stayed quiet for the rest of the meal. It was difficult to tell what she was thinking, but her silence, combined with the brutal manner with which she stabbed her potatoes, suggested it was somewhere between upset and angry, if not both.

After they finished Charlie and Rob went into the kitchen to clean the dishes, their old routine returning in an instant; Rob washing, Charlie drying, just like the good old days. Their mother sat on a small stool in the corner, smoking a cigarette while she inspected the job they did with each plate. The sense of déjà vu from the whole episode kept a smile on his face for the remainder of their visit.

Once the dishes where done Vera made herself a cup of tea and moved into the living room, her soaps were due to start in only a few minutes and it would take more than a returning son to make her miss an episode. The two brothers collected their jackets and shared a relieved look before following her through.

"I'll come see you in a couple of days" Rob said, giving Vera a hug "When I'm settled"

"You better" she said, patting him on the back, her voice bore no hint that she was angry, but that didn't necessarily mean that she wasn't "The same goes for you Charles, don't think you're getting off the hook just because your brother's home"

"I'll see you in a couple of days, mar" Charlie said as she moved away from Rob and gave him a hug.

They made their way outside as Vera settled down on the couch; Charlie was surprised to find that as they stepped onto the street it was dark. Their mother's house seemed to exist in a state of timelessness where the curtains were always closed and the walls were strangely void of clocks. It was one of the many oddities that resided in their mother's character, and one he never quite got used to. Anxious to get out of the cold night air he clambered inside the car and opened the passenger door for Rob.

They drove for another ten minutes to their next destination. Jimmy Smith had a nice little three bedroom gaff just outside of town; his inability to pay his debts obviously hadn't stretched as far as his mortgage. Jimmy's indebtedness was annoying, but the two of them had a system that worked; whenever Jimmy's debts got too high he'd hook Charlie up with one of the flats he owned, Charlie repaid the favour in Cocaine, everyone was a winner.

He left Rob in the car and headed towards the house to collect the keys. It took three knocks before Jimmy's wife dragged herself off the couch and answered the door. She was a pretty rough bird, an observation he'd made on each of the five previous occasions he'd met her, but as she opened the door in her pyjamas looking at Charlie like he was something she would wipe off the bottom of her shoe, he couldn't help but note the same observation one more time. Jimmy was out, he and some mates had gone to the dog track, a social outing that she clearly didn't approve of. Charlie looked at the scowl, which seemed to be as consistent an occupant on her face as those green eyes, and wondered if there was any form of outing, social or otherwise, that she did approve.

He told her his name; she stomped off into the hallway, grabbed a pair of keys from a nearby table and tossed them in his direction. She'd slammed the door before Charlie could even say thanks, not that he had much intention to.

Through the window he saw her march back into the living room and collapse on the couch, turning the TV up several notches as if to cleanse herself of the experience. Charlie shook his head in sympathy for Jimmy Smith and made a mental note to buy the poor sod a pint the next time he saw him.

The car ride from Jimmy's place to the flat took fifteen minutes more, by the time they reached their destination Charlie could tell that his brother was getting frustrated, not that the constant sighs and glances at the watch were difficult to interpret.

"Here we are"

Rob's new pad was a ground floor flat on the edge of Bootle, twenty minutes' walk from Charlie's place. The street wasn't a pretty sight, at least half the houses were boarded up and those that weren't didn't look much better. As they stepped from the car, a gang of teenagers eyed them suspiciously from the corner, as did their two Dobermans.

At least the flat above was occupied, which suggested that the area wasn't entirely uninhabitable, a theory he might have disagreed with a few seconds earlier. He looked over at Rob, who seemed to be taking it all in without much emotion. Charlie guessed that for a guy who would be living out of a shoulder bag for the foreseeable future, sleeping here wouldn't be too much of a stretch.

He took the keys from his pocket and opened the front door. He stepped into a narrow hallway with a small bedroom to his immediate left, he followed the hallway onwards until he reached the living room, straight through led to the kitchen, which in turn led on to the bathroom. Compact was a good word for it, it was probably best that Rob hadn't brought his girlfriend.

The furniture looked pretty old, large chunks of fabric pushed out from a couple of exit wounds in the couch, elsewhere the wallpaper was frayed and smoke damaged, while the curtains dangled half loose in front of the back window. Charlie turned as Rob entered the room; his brother's face was still impossible to read as he tossed the bag on the floor and ran a hand over the wallpaper.

"Well here it is, Casa del Thommo!" Charlie said "I know it ain't the Hilton but it's yours for however long you need it. What do you think, lad?"

"It'll do fine, cheers Charlie" Rob said, taking his eyes off the room and looking at his brother for the first time since they came inside "Who is he, the guy who owns this place?"

Charlie took a seat and spread his arms out along the back of the couch "Just a customer. He's in with me for a couple of grams of coke, and he's having a bit of trouble paying it back, what with the current economic downturn and all. He's a good lad so I let him hook me up with a flat or two when I need them and I keep him nose deep in the good stuff"

Rob nodded his head slowly, they'd never talked about his "career" over the phone, but Charlie always got the impression that his brother knew where he was getting his money. The fact that they were talking about it seemed to help a few things click into place for Rob, but there was still a curious look on his brother's face.

"What are you using these flats for Charlie?"

"Nah, nah big brother" Charlie said, smiling and shaking his head "You'll have to stick around longer than a day before I fill you in on all my dirty little secrets"

"Fair enough"

Charlie jumped up from the couch and followed Rob into the kitchen. There was a gas cooker that looked like turning it on would be tantamount to suicide, and a sink which started producing brown water as soon as Rob turned the tap. Charlie didn't dare continue the tour on to the bathroom, instead he retreated to the living room and waited for Rob to return from that particular adventure.

"Listen, I've got a bag of nose candy if you want to do a couple of lines?" Charlie said, starting to feel a little guilty for the state of the flat "We could head down the boozer, remind you of the real Liverpool that you left behind?"

"I quit that stuff mate" Rob said, avoiding eye contact, Charlie noted that his voice was a little solemn "Long time ago"

"Alright then, kidda" Charlie continued enthusiastically "Just the pub then, couple of jars, bit of a catch up. What do you say?"

"The jet lags catching up with me to be honest" Rob said, he did look tired, and the glazed look in his eyes seemed to have worsened since they left their mothers "I think I'm just going to get some shut eye, we've got a big day tomorrow"

"Alright lid, no bother" Charlie said, he didn't want to cause Rob anymore stress than he was already under "You've got your mobile, I'll give you a call in the morning... Rob?"

"Yeah?"

Charlie tried to frame the words to explain how he was feeling, he'd never been good at expressing himself, doing had always come easier to him than talking. Rob raised his eyebrows and watched him expectantly, eventually Charlie felt like he'd found the right words.

"Try not to go too far into your head, ok? I know what you're like. Just get in, do whatever the fuck he wants you to do, and get out. Don't dwell, it'll just make the whole thing ten times worse"

Rob looked a little surprised, maybe he wasn't expecting anything quite as deep from this joker of a brother. A little smile crept into the corners of Rob's mouth

"OK, Charlie"

"Good, and listen if it all gets a bit too much" Charlie reached into his pocket and pulled out the small bag of cocaine "Dr Charley's got your prescription all made up!"

"Sling your hook!" Rob ordered with a smile, pointing towards the door.

"Alright lad, I'll call you tomorrow. Take it easy" Charlie shouted making his way down the hallway and closing the front door behind him.

He stepped out onto the street and glanced at his watch, it was 10:30. Time for one more stop before he'd have to get back. He surveyed the rest of the street as he got closer to the car, the teenagers had departed to cause mischief someplace else, and in their absence it was eerily quiet.

Charlie was pretty thankful he didn't have to stay in that dive, but he felt bad that his brother did. Still, it was cheap, and Rob didn't seem to mind all that much, he reminded himself that if anyone could handle a couple of nights in a dodgy street; it was his brother. He circled the car, just to make sure the kids hadn't left their mark, then climbed in and sped off.

He turned the stereo up full blast as the car turned out of the street, sucking in a deep breath that he inexplicably felt like he needed.

What a day, his brother was back, it was strange but on some level it didn't even seem real. There was no doubt that Rob was struggling with coming home, Liverpool had been a hard place for him, and Charlie knew he took a big chunk of the blame for that. The waves of depression seemed to hit him just like they did before, but there was still a bit of his brother left in there, New York seemed to have helped preserve at least that much. It was only now that he realised just how worried he'd been about seeing Rob again, worried about not recognising his own flesh and blood, of having to call a stranger 'brother'. But that wasn't how it had turned out. Sure Rob had his problems, and sad as it was more were likely to come his way in the next couple of days, but he'd never let them beat him before, and that would be the key again. He'd do what needed to be done, he'd head back to New York, and who was to say, maybe Charlie would have a chance to get his foot in the door with the major players before he left. Everyone needed their big break and maybe it was selfish, but ever since he'd gotten the call he couldn't help but think that maybe this was his. One way or another something needed to change, Charlie was only a couple of months shy of thirty one, selling coke by the line to scrawny little shits wasn't what he'd call a career that was going places.

He found himself thinking more and more about what it would be like to get himself a reputation, to have everyone know his name, to be the big dick around town. The Thomas boys deserved a rep. After everything that Rob had done, if word got out he would be the biggest name in Liverpool. But that wasn't how he'd wanted it; in fact he'd told Charlie explicitly that it would be the worst possible outcome. Charlie didn't get that, what was the point of doing the things he'd done and seeing the things he'd seen, if people weren't going to respect you for it. He vowed that if he ever got a crack of the whip like his brother had, he'd do things a hell of a lot differently.

Snapping out of his daze he realised that he'd reached his destination. Charlie parked up and got out of the car, checking his breast pocket as he locked the door.

He crossed the street and knocked on number 78; the green door. He waited for a few minutes, nothing, then knocked again. Eventually he heard footsteps, the door led to an upstairs flat and he recognised the thud of bare feet dropping down the stairs one at a time. The latch clicked, and then the door opened, ever so slightly. After a few moments it opened a little bit further and then a head popped around the door, the first thing he noticed was the cheeky grin.

"Sorry lad, we don't buy the big issue round here. Jog on sunshine"

It had been nine months, and Charlie still forgot how gorgeous she was, every time. Her blond hair was curled to perfection and that cheeky grin showed off a set of pearly white teeth that looked even better in contrast to the golden colour of her skin. And then there were her eyes, those deep blue god damn eyes. He took a second to catch his breath and smiled, reaching into his pocket he pulled out the small see through bag and waved it in front of her.

"A little Charlie from your Charlie?" he offered, trying to match her cheeky grin.

She swung the door wide open and leaned against it, as Charlie took in the view. It was incredible, she was wearing a tight white halter top with nothing underneath, showing the perfect swell of her breast and the flatness of her stomach in the same instant. South of that it got even better, nothing but a black thong, her long golden legs, perfectly shaped, were crossed at the ankles and seemed to go on forever. Charlie's eyes eventually found their way back up to her face, she was smiling a self-satisfied smile, she knew what she did to him, he knew the hunger on his face was impossible to hide, and he had no desire to. He pushed her roughly into the hallway wall, pressing his mouth against hers. She responded with a moan as her arms went around his neck. His weren't so easily satisfied, they started on her back and spread quickly, trying to touch every part of her with an urgency that boarded on the fanatical. As his fingers found her hair and pulled hard, Steph moaned again, letting her hands drop from around his neck and move towards his groin. He pressed her harder against the wall as she pulled at the chord on his tracksuit bottoms, Charlie squeezed at the nineteen year old flesh and let her scent fill his nostrils, then he remembered something. His left hand found her breast, his right found the door, and slammed it shut.

Thirty minutes later and Charlie lay naked on the couch with a spliff in his hand, and a naked teenager dozing on his chest. Steph lay on top, her blond hair ruffled, covering half her face as she struggled somewhere between asleep and awake. Charlie took another drag and blew a couple of smoke rings towards her golden skin, taking in the sight.

His brain swirled with excited memories, she'd come into one of his locals just under a year ago, not many girls that looked like her drank in those kinds of places, if a woman was under thirty that usually made her the most attractive thing on display. But Steph was something else, put her in any bar in the country and she would stand out. Luckily for him; she liked her coke, she liked her pills, and she liked her weed. She'd spurned his advances for the first couple of weeks, some jealous old git had spread the word that he was already married, so the only time he got to see her was when she was looking for some party treats. But let it never be said that persistence was not a virtue of Charlie H. Thomas, after a couple more weeks, a shit load of freebies and a sizeable chunk of his charm he'd found himself sitting on this very same couch enjoying the best sex of his life.

He ran a hand over her skin, she shivered and let out a little laugh. Charlie remembered back to when he first met Vicky, she'd never been this hot but she'd been close. It upset him to look at her now, two kids had destroyed a lot of what he loved, it upset him even more when he saw Steph in the same night.

She pushed herself up onto her elbows and threw him the same smile that always ruined him, she gestured for the spliff and he handed it over without protest.

"You staying here tonight?" she asked, taking a long drag and releasing it into the air.

"Nah"

"Running back to the old ball and chain, are ya?" Steph said with a smile, she'd come to accept his responsibilities, but it hadn't been easy.

"You sound a little jealous there, love" Charlie said, yanking the spliff from between her fingers "My brother's back in town, we've got ourselves a big meeting in the morning with some pretty nasty villains"

"You trying to impress me?" she asked cheekily, jumping up from his chest and leaning against the back of the couch. Sometimes Charlie couldn't help but laugh, she might look the part but when she opened her mouth, she was as scouse as they came "I've seen the kind of people you deal to; dole-ites and pissheads, there ain't a dangerous fucking wanker amongst them! This is some good bloody weed, leave the bag when you go, ok?"

Charlie took in the living room of the one bedroom flat, it was nicely decorated, a new paint job on the walls, there was a good size TV and best of all; the floor wasn't littered with toys. Being a nail technician didn't bring in any real money, but it brought enough to pay the bills. Charlie calculated that her weekly pay packet was stretching at least twice as far now he was paying for her drug habit. From his side he barely noticed the mark it left on his profits, and as he greedily stared at her naked body he knew for certain that it was a financial hit that was worth taking. When his eyes finally worked their way up towards her face, he saw she was looking at him with a look that bordered on mocking.

"Times are changing darlin" Charlie said with all the arrogance he could muster, which if he was honest, was quite a lot "Got a meeting tomorrow with Stephen McSharry, you know who he is?"

He caught a look of surprise flicker across her face, before it made way to a smile.

"Isn't he the gangster that just got released?" she was looking at him differently now, it was a look of admiration, she licked her lips seductively "How'd you get hooked up with him?"

"You kidding? Him and our Rob go way back" Charlie said, he couldn't stop the words flowing from his mouth, already he was feeling like the made man that he so fiercely wanted to be. What was even sweeter was that she felt it to, the look in her eyes willed on his ascension "I'm telling you Steph, this is my chance to really make a name for myself, forge some contacts, really start bringing in the big money"

Steph leaned forward on her hands and knees and started nibbling on his ear, he could feel her breath coming in short, sharp bursts "Hmm, I've always wanted to be fucked by a proper gangster" she whispered.

Charlie made a dismissive sound with his lips "You already are love" he said, feeling the confidence of tomorrows promise coursing through his veins.

She let out a little giggle and ran her tongue across his neck "So when you start bringing in all these big bucks, you gonna spend them on me?"

"Course" Charlie said, running fingers lightly down the curve of her spine, she shivered and giggled again.

"What you gonna get me, Charlie?" she asked, returning her attention to his ear.

"What do you want?" he asked, his hand now making its way up her inner thigh.

"Diamond necklace? A beamer? Oh, we could go on holiday? A week in the sun, just me and you?"

"Done" Charlie said

"Have you got time to fuck me one more time before you go?" Steph whispered as her lips moved towards his, he wrapped his arms around her and forced her backwards, landing roughly on top of her.

"Always" he muttered as his lips found hers. Today had been a good day, tomorrow would be even better.

Chapter 6

In the beginning there was silence, darkness. A tranquil sense of calm that engulfed all things. But it was tainted, tainted by a sense of foreboding that warned of worse times to come, the winds would rise, the storms would descend, and it was right, just as it always was, just as it always would be.

The silence was pierced by a scream. A scream as familiar as his own reflection, that would never leave, that was synonymous with all that he was. No, it wasn't a scream, it was never a scream, it was a plea. A plea so filled with fear, desperation and passion that it could be mistaken for a scream, but as the sounds began to turn into words, like strangers in the fog moving closer and closer, each step a step towards recognition, it became clear what it was; it was a prayer for life.

The words came clearly now in the darkness, so clearly that he wondered how he ever could have got them confused, they were barely a whisper, yet they were loud enough to blow houses clear off the ground.

"Please. Please don't kill me, I'm so sorry please, I'll do anything, just don't kill me"

The words were repeated in the darkness over and over again, he tried to shut them out but he couldn't. Somewhere, deep inside, told him to enjoy it while it lasted, for that place knew what was coming next. As he tried to catch up to whatever it was that was warning him, he was caught off guard. He saw it, and knew then that it was always coming, of course it was, why couldn't he have seen it before?

The eyes, they were the most amazing eyes, he had never seen anything like them, they were enough to make a person lose themselves. Fascinating, intriguing, incomparable, they seemed to change colour by the second, flickers of orange, of green, or blue existed in those eyes and merged in a fashion that even the most gifted oil painter could not dream of replicating. They were the most beautiful eyes in the world.

No, they were the ugliest eyes in the world, made infinitely uglier by their capacity for beauty, how could they ever be beautiful when they looked like that? Wide, petrified, grasping for the life that was slowly slipping away. The fear, obvious in every flicker of colour that existed in those eyes screamed at him until he could hear nothing else. He tried to shrink back away from those eyes, but they were everywhere, they were everything.

Suddenly, there were no longer just eyes. Now there was a face. It's emergence had done nothing to lessen the mesmerising power of those eyes, yet the face itself was still beautiful, at least it would have been had it not been infected with the same desperate fear that permeated every aspect of her being. Her light brown hair that had once been so perfect was now matted and scattered across her face, her lips that had once been seductive and voluptuous now bled onto her dainty, pale chin.

There was something else, somewhere in the background, something important. He yearned with all his being to discover what it was, but it wouldn't come.

Hands, that was it hands, but they weren't a woman's hands, they were rough and powerful, they were his hands, and they were around her neck.

Then it hit him like a wave of ice cold water. He was leaning on top of her, the weight of his body holding her down, her dress was ripped, but only from the struggle. His reactions had been slow, the defiance of his subconscious to engage in such a despicable act. His gun was gone, he had no idea where, what did it matter? It had to be done, it was the only choice. But she wouldn't understand, how could she? He was holding her down, his hands pressing harder and harder around her windpipe, he felt himself force with all his might, just to end it, to stop the begging in those eyes. Her breath was almost gone, but what she had left she was still using to plead.

"Please don't kill me, I'll do anything" she whispered.

He felt his eyes well up. "I'm sorry" he tried to say, but the words got caught in the back of his throat.

She tried to speak again, but no words would come. Her eyes went wider and the fear intensified as she realised there was nothing left she could do, for the first time he felt hatred, mixed in with the fear projecting from those eyes into his head. He prayed for her to hate him, the hatred he could handle, but almost instantaneously it was gone, leaving nothing but the primal need to live. He swallowed his tears and pressed down as hard as he could, it had to be done.

The eyes stared at him, and pleaded for his mercy. But now there was no mercy to be granted, the eyes were hollow, but they were still beautiful. The look hadn't changed, not in the eyes, they still prayed for mercy, and even though she was dead, they would never stop praying.

Rob woke to the sound of his own screams. He toppled out of the bed onto his hands and knees, panting desperately, as if he hadn't taken a breath for hours. He pressed his head to the carpet as a small whimper escaped from his mouth, they were getting worse, he didn't know how much longer he could handle it. For a while he didn't move, perched on his hands and knees, with his forehead touching the floor he tried to catch his breath and work out where he was.

He looked around the badly decorated room, with the faded paint job, the water damage in each of the four corners and he remembered what had brought him there. With a pang of pain he remembered leaving Joanne, and with a pang of dread he remembered what was planned for the day ahead.

After a few more minutes he found the courage to stand, his legs were a little shaky but they got him to the door, and he took the six steps from the small hallway into the living room. His bag was where he had left it the night before.

Rob felt exhausted, whatever sleep he'd managed hadn't come close to cancelling out the jet lag of a Trans-Atlantic flight, combined with the sleeping problems he had been having before and it was a wonder he was even vertical. He realised he was wearing nothing but a pair boxer shorts. His body was covered in a thin layer of sweat that seemed to be protecting him from the cold, but he felt a numbness in his hands and feet that reminded him that it was still November. He went to run a hand through his hair before he remembered there was none there; scratching at the bristles instead he wandered around the small flat.

The curtains on the living room window were only semi functional, a number of the hooks from which it hung had snapped off but it was still effective enough to hide him from the outside world. Carefully, so as to not cause any further damage to the fabrics precarious existence, he pushed it to one side and looked out into the small, bricked backyard. The frost on the floor told him that it was a cold morning, though the sun was bright overhead and there wasn't a cloud in the sky. He wondered what the weather was like in New York, whether Jo had gone for a run when she woke, and who would finish rebuilding the wall in the Fourth Avenue master bedroom. He shook the thoughts from his mind, it did him no good to think about that life, until he got back on the plane it didn't exist for him, and distractions would do nothing but get him killed.

Absentmindedly he made his way towards the kitchen to make a cup of coffee, before his sleep deprived brain realised there wouldn't be any there. Stifling a curse he ran the tap for a glass of water, but when he saw the colour of the liquid it secreted he abandoned that idea as well.

Letting out a long sigh he went back into the living room and decided to do some exercise. Fifty push ups wouldn't wake him up the same way a cup of coffee would, but it would get the blood flowing and maybe pump a bit of adrenaline in to his weary body.

As he lowered himself down he started to think about the dreams, they were bad in New York but being back in Liverpool seemed to make them so much more real. He'd never known one as vivid as the one he'd had that morning, being back here was already starting to do strange things to his head. Maybe that was the difference; in New York they had always just been dreams, memories, shadows of a forgotten life, but it was here where all those nightmares were born, this world was his nightmare and living in it was intensifying his dreams.

He wondered how long he would be able to go on if the dreams maintained their ferocity, the speed of the press ups increased as he tried to shake that pessimistic feeling; it was just the shock, the last two days messing with his head. Things would settle down, and his dreams would go back to normal, it seemed almost perverse to think of that as a positive result.

His mind drifted towards the upcoming meeting with McSharry, he had no idea what to expect. He remembered the last conversation between them, the morning before McSharry had been arrested. He had no idea what ten years inside had done to his old boss, but if the man wanted a meeting with Rob Thomas, then he had a certain type of plan in mind. The thought occurred to Rob that maybe McSharry just wanted to kill him, it scared him that in a lot of ways that would be the easiest solution, but he doubted it. Even in New York, if Stephen McSharry had truly wanted Rob dead he could probably have gotten it done.

Rob suddenly realised that he hadn't been keeping count of his press ups, he had no idea how long he'd been going but the dull ache in his arms told him that the target of fifty had been easily surpassed.

He stood up feeling even sweatier than he had before and made his way to the shower. The temperature of the water was lukewarm at best but after the long flight he was in no mood to complain, the sweat on his body felt like an embodiment of his nightmares and he scrubbed frantically to remove it. He ran a hand over the stubble on his chin but decided it could wait for another day, there was no one he would be seeing who he wanted to impress.

Stepping from the shower he heard a loud thumping noise coming from the front door. He made his way into the living room, threw a pair of boxers and jeans over his wet body and stepped lightly towards the door. Moving fast he cursed the fact that he didn't have a gun and vowed to make it one of his top priorities if he survived the mornings meeting. He reached the door and tentatively put an eye to the peep hole; his brother was rocking on his heels and rubbing his hands together to fight off the cold. He swung the door open irritably and shook his head.

"What the fuck are you doing? You said you were going to call"

"Chill out, lad" Charlie said, following Rob as he headed back towards the living room "I was in the neighbourhood so I thought I'd just pop round, when did you get so bloody high strung?"

Rob turned and took in his little brother, when he'd left Charlie had still been a kid, he was having some difficulty accepting that the man before him was the same person. He'd have never thought it growing up, but Rob could see the similarities in their appearances now, especially given that they both had their heads shaved. Charlie was of a lighter build than Rob and his face had a constant look of mischief that he'd kept from childhood, extenuated by his sharp nose and narrow chin. It was the eyes that were most familiar, though Rob wished he could keep his as buoyant as his brothers seemed to be. He grabbed a towel and started drying down his body, realising as he moved that his jeans stuck uncomfortably to his wet legs.

"You were banging on the door with a little bit of urgency, wouldn't you say?"

"Was I? I guess I don't know my own strength" Charlie said bashfully before glaring inquisitively at Rob's chest "Hey, isn't that the cross I got you for your Twentieth?" he asked with a smile.

"Yeah, yeah it is" Rob said, grabbing the cross between his thumb and forefinger, he'd forgotten that he was even wearing it.

"That's good mate, that you kept it and all, I must have pretty good taste"

Rob felt his face go a little red and gave an awkward nod. He didn't want to tell Charlie that he had took the cross of as soon as he had landed in New York, that it was a symbol of everything he had been trying to escape. He turned away from his younger brother and dried the rest of his body before throwing on a black t shirt and sliding into his thick black overcoat.

"Let's go" he said cautiously "No use dragging this out longer than we have to"

Charlie gave him a sympathetic smile and made his way out. Rob checked his appearance in the mirror, more out of habit than anything else, and followed him to the car. By the time he climbed into the passenger seat Charlie was playing some dance/ hip-hop nonsense, seemingly to be oblivious to the enormity of what was about to unfold. He envied his brothers naivety; he seemed to be enjoying himself.

"So, where we off?" Rob said, trying to keep the nerves out of his voice as the car pulled out of the street.

"Town, the Anglican Cathedral"

"He wants to have the meeting in a Cathedral?"

"No. In the cemetery outside, not sure why"

"That's where his brother's buried" Rob said.

Charlie tried to make conversation a couple more times but Rob didn't feel much like talking, he gave Charlie a couple of one word answers and eventually his brother got the hint.

He couldn't stop his mind from racing, he was anticipating every possible reason for why McSharry might have wanted this meeting, and then tried to counter every one with an answer for why he should be allowed to go back to New York. He knew the futility of it all, this wasn't a man who listened to reason, especially at the expense of his own desires, but Rob didn't know what else to do. He suddenly felt very vulnerable going in without a weapon; if only he'd had another day or two to get hold of a piece his negotiating position would have been a lot stronger. He wondered what ten years inside had done to the man, he'd been ruthless enough before, it was worrying to think what he would be like now.

Before he knew it the car had stopped and Charlie was saying his name, Rob snapped out of his daze and looked around, they were at the front entrance of the Anglican Cathedral. He stepped out of the car and took in the large brick structure. He remembered coming here on a school trip when he was a kid, he had been too young to appreciate the beauty of the building back then but as his eyes surveyed the bell tower, the stained glass windows and the wonderfully carved brick arches he felt perfectly positioned to appreciate it now. He remembered being told once that it was the largest

Anglican church in Britain, Rob didn't know whether or not that was true but if it wasn't he wanted to see the one that surpassed it.

Across the city he saw the two Liverbirds peeking above the skyline, he was enjoying the sight when a hand on his shoulder brought him back and urged him on. Reluctantly Rob tore his gaze from the city and followed Charlie towards the cemetery.

The morning was cold and the frost on the ground made it difficult to walk, he tried to convince himself that was why he was moving so slowly. They made their way down the narrow path, ancient grave stones protruded from either side of the walls, surrounding them and making the path seem more claustrophobic. He read the names of the deceased here and there, half expecting to recognise some of them as his victims.

As they took their first step onto the burial ground he felt his stomach churn, there were only two people standing in the graveyard, he recognised them as clearly from fifty yards as if they were standing right in front of him.

Rob took a deep breath "Let's do this" he said, stepping in front of Charlie and walking towards the two men. McSharry and Begsy eyed them the whole way, neither man diverting their gaze until they stood no more than a few feet apart.

Stephen McSharry spoke first, the look on his face seemed jovial, even vaguely amused.

"Rob Thomas. It's been a long time"

Rob looked long and hard at McSharry, ten years didn't seem to have changed him all that much, he was a little greyer and a little skinnier, but the strength of his spirit seemed undiminished. Rob took a deep breath and tried to keep his voice steady.

"It has" he said evenly, Rob's gaze made contact with Begsy's and he saw the look of sheer hatred staring back at him from those cruel grey eyes. Rob felt his own gaze grow darker as he returned the stare, he hadn't missed looking at that ugly psychopath. After a few seconds Rob turned his focus back to McSharry, annoyed that he'd been so easily distracted, so long as McSharry kept him on a tight leash Begsy was as harmless as the corpses beneath their feet.

"Who's this?" McSharry asked, pointing towards Charlie.

"The brother, the mouthy one" Begsy said, his tone little more than a growl, Rob noticed that the look he flashed Charlie was only slightly less intense than the one he'd shown him.

"Alright, Mr McSharry" Charlie said leaning forward and extending his hand "I'm Charlie Thomas, we never properly met"

McSharry glanced dismissively at the outstretched hand without making a move to grasp it, he turned to Begsy, stood a little behind, and then back at Charlie.

"You got young Robert back here then, did you?" McSharry asked a half smile on his face that reeked of vague indifference "Well done. Now on your fucking way, the grown-ups need to talk"

"You what?" Charlie said angrily, taking a step forward, Rob grabbed him by the shoulder and pushed him backwards. Out of the corner of his eye he saw Begsy reach for his inside pocket, Rob put his hand up, gesturing him to stop, the big enforcer relaxed and dropped his arm back to his side.

"It's alright Charlie" Rob said, looking his brother in the eye "Go wait in the car"

Charlie stared back at him, as if waiting for the internal conflict between his temper and his common sense to conclude, Rob maintained eye contact until he saw the shrug of Charlie's shoulders.

"Alright bro, I'll just be over there" Charlie said taking a step backwards and throwing an angry look first at McSharry, then at Begsy "You just shout if you need me"

With that Charlie walked back the way they'd come, Rob waited until he was out of sight before turning back to face the two men. McSharry still had that same amused smile, Begsy's face was like stone.

"That's better, isn't it?" McSharry said, looking at Rob then Begsy "Just old friends. So... ten years, it's almost hard to believe isn't it?"

Rob took a step forward and slid his hands into his pockets "Seems like a lifetime ago"

"Indeed, I remember our final conversation as if it was yesterday" McSharry's face seemed to darken "I've thought about it a lot over the years"

"I'll bet you have" Rob said, finding himself being drawn into a stare with McSharry. His heart was beating twice as fast as normal but he felt a calmness come over his extenal features, a cockiness he hadn't felt in a long time.

"It wasn't often I gave you an order that you didn't follow, and then Begsy tells me you fled the country. What were you running from, Thommo?" McSharry's voice was even, but Rob could sense the resentment somewhere beneath the surface, it crossed his mind seriously for the first time whether they had brought him there to kill him. He looked at Begsy whose steely gaze was focused solely on Rob, when he looked back at McSharry there was an impatient look in the old man's eyes.

"What was I running from? You'd just been convicted to a fifteen year sentence, who knew what the hell they had on me, was I supposed to wait around and find out?"

The muscles in McSharry's jaw clenched "The lawyer had nothing on you and you knew that, so what are you saying, exactly? You thought I was going to turn grass?"

Begsy seemed to shift on his feet, he looked agitated, like the very suggestions might be worthy of a shot between the eyes. Rob tried to pick his words carefully, with these two there would be no second chance if he said the wrong thing.

"That's not what I'm saying, but they raided your house, they seized all of your papers, how did I know there wasn't anything in there to expose me?"

"I'm more careful than that" McSharry said, his words were slow and deliberate, his eyes had narrowed significantly since the start of the conversation "there was no need for you to run, maybe if you'd been here to give Begsy your...expertise, we wouldn't be in the position we're in. Still that's all in the past I suppose, let bygones be bygones and all"

With that McSharry's suddenly seemed to relax, and he knelt down at the tomb near his feet, scooping up a bundle of long deceased flowers from the marble headstone and tossing them aside. His face took on a sombre, retrospective look and Rob found it difficult to imagine that the dark disposition which covered it seconds before had ever even existed. He glanced over at Begsy who's face had remained the same; resolute and hateful. He found it odd but after the sudden shift in McSharry's mood there was a strange comfort in the consistency of Begsy's demeanour, it was easy to know where you stood with a man who's disgust was too strong to be hide.

"In my absence it seems as though my brother's final resting place has fallen into disrepair. Such a shame, a man's tomb should be a shrine, a testament to all the great things he has achieved in his life, don't you agree?" he asked, looking up at Rob for the first time since he'd turned his attention to the grave.

Rob gave a shrug of the shoulders "I suppose..."

"In the end, all that's left of a man is his legacy and even that lasts for too brief a time, when our blood fails and the future disappoints..." he stopped and stared at the grave, losing himself for a few moments in another world, before snapping out of whatever daze he was in and looking at Rob, when he did there was a darkness that had returned to his eyes "You'd do well to remember that kid. Anyway, down to business, I imagine you're wondering why I summoned you"

And there it was, Rob swallowed hard and got ready for the conversation he'd been dreading for the past two days. He felt his outer calmness continue to hold strong but inside his heart was racing.

"I have a pretty good idea"

"Really?" asked McSharry, pushing himself up from his knees and standing face to face with his prey, Rob felt uneasy every time those calculating eyes fell upon him "I must confess I expected a greater degree of resistance when Begsy called for you"

Rob let out a small laugh and shook his head "Did you think I've forgotten what you're capable of? What he's capable of?" he said nodding towards Begsy "I think we both know how that would have ended, so what do you say we just get on with it?"

A flicker of surprise flashed across McSharry's face, but was gone just as fast, Rob felt a small pang of pride that he's been able to catch the old man off guard, but it was a small victory in a much bigger war.

"It's good to see your years across the Atlantic haven't dulled your senses, you always were a bright boy" McSharry said, looking impressed. Rob tried to hide his concern that they knew where he had been, he wondered what else they knew "You say you haven't forgotten what me and Begs are capable of, but that's not really why we're here, is it? The real question is: Have you forgotten what *you're* capable of?"

Rob saw a smirk from Begsy out of the corner of his eye and did his best to ignore it.

"I remember" he said.

"But is it just a memory?" McSharry asked inquisitively "I saw this kind of thing a lot on the inside, years of inaction can dull a man's senses, reduce him to a shadow of his former self, that hasn't happened here, has it?" The man's eyes were questioning, searching, as if he was looking for the answers in Rob's head to the questions he asked. Rob tried to maintain his external calmness, give nothing away, that was always the first rule.

"Would it matter to you if it had?"

McSharry shrugged his shoulders and let out a sigh "Not really. My role in your life has never been to protect, simply to unleash. Anyway, you were always too modest"

"And that's what this is about?" Rob said, equal parts relieved and scared that they were finally getting to the core of why they were there "You want to *unleash* me?"

McSharry flashed him a self-satisfied smile "Do you know much about Greek mythology?"

"Not especially, no" Rob answered impatiently.

"I read a lot of it when I was locked up" McSharry said, running a hand over the top of his brothers tombstone "You read what you can get your hands on, anything to keep your mind active. At first I thought it was a load of old bollocks, but overtime it gets to you. Those Greeks really knew their shit, they understood ideas like morality, and revenge, and they knew how to utilise them. There was one that always made me think of you, it's the story of Niobe, do you know it?"

Rob shook his head, he had no idea where the old man was going.

It's an interesting tale. Niobe was a Queen, married to a powerful King. She had everything she could have wanted, but she fancied herself for more than what she was. She resented the honours that were reserved for the Gods, and in her foolishness she insulted the God Leto. She ridiculed the yearly celebrations and she mocked the Gods ability to only produce two children where she had produced fourteen, she thought the people should worship her instead. Now, if there is one thing that infuriates the Gods, it is those who don't understand their own fate, who consider themselves more powerful than the Gods that watch over them. Leto took his revenge, all fourteen of Niobe's children were killed by poisoned arrows, her King was murdered and she was sent out into the wilderness to rot"

"That's a great story" Rob said sarcastically "What's it got to do with me?"

"It seems the world is not as we left it, my young protégé, a few wrongs are in need of being set right. In our absence a few have risen to power who suppose themselves to be more than what they are. You are the poisoned arrow I intend to strike them down with. Begsy!" Rob watched as Begsy stepped forward and placed a red file in McSharry's outstretched hand. McSharry glanced at the papers inside before passing them on to Rob "Two targets, that's the first, have you been keeping up on your Liverpool underworld trivia?"

"I can't say that I have"

Rob took the file and opened it. Inside were a collection of surveillance pictures featuring a well-dressed, blond haired man, only a few years older than Rob. A few pages in was a three week record of his movements and on the final page was a mug shot with the man's name at the bottom. Wayne Caddock, shit, it was Gary Caddock's son.

"Our old friends; the Caddocks and the Millers, have taken advantage of our absence with some, shall we say, aggressive expansion, I expect they were motivated at least partially, by the untimely deaths of their fathers, though I'm sure you don't need reminding of that" Rob looked up from the file and threw McSharry a disgruntled look, the old man paused for a second until Rob's gaze returned to the papers "Anyway the two pragmatists in question appear to have grown above their station, they fancy themselves for Gods, can you imagine? They don't understand their true place, they're a cancer on this city, we need to cut them out before there's nothing left to save"

Rob slammed the file shut, he felt that hollow feeling inside his chest.

"Why me? Why not him?" he said, pointing with the file towards Begsy "You didn't need to drag me halfway around the world to do a job that heartless bastard would do in a second!"

"What the fuck did you just call me?" Begsy said, taking a step forward. There was murder in his eyes, Rob wondered whether he could keep out of the way of those massive arms long enough to get a decent hit in.

"Settle down, Begs" McSharry ordered before the big enforcer had made it five steps, he ground to a halt immediately, crossing his arms and awaiting further instructions as McSharry turned back to Rob "My boy here has a lot of admirable talents but let's not kid ourselves, you bring something quite unique to the table. Murder is your gift; you know that as well as I do"

Rob had trouble taking his eyes off Begsy, the big man was standing so close and looked liable to pounce at any second, eventually he forced himself to look back at the man who had brought him here.

"Maybe before, but that was a long time ago. It's not who I am anymore"

"A talent like yours doesn't just disappear" McSharry said, he sounded so assured it made Rob want to throw up "It's in the blood, in the soul"

"I don't have a soul" Rob replied "you saw to that"

"Oh, how dramatic" McSharry said with a smile, he was acting like Rob was a petulant child refusing to eat his vegetables, the man had just ordered him to murder two people "All the more reason to do as your told, I've heard a burdened soul is a heavy weight to bear, you're lucky you don't have to worry about such things. It's time to repay your debts Robert. Don't think I've forgotten whose job it was to clip the lawyer, and whose failure allowed him to testify. That failure cost me ten long years"

The anger was back in McSharry's eyes, stronger than ever. Rob recognised the danger but he was too far gone to care about appeasement, he felt himself getting sucked deeper and deeper into a black hole and he would do anything he could to get out of it.

"You knew that job was impossible the second you gave it to me. I got as close to the rat as anyone could but the guy was under lock and key twenty four fucking seven. What else could I have done?"

"You could have killed him!" McSharry said, the anger in his throat giving his voice a sharp edge "Now's your chance to make it up to me. Be grateful, many don't get that chance"

Rob was running out of ideas, his arguments weren't working and he had no idea how to get out of this corner without endangering the people he loved, he hadn't expected reason to work but it was the only card he had left, he may as well give it a go.

"I rebuilt my life, I changed. I can't do it"

"Of course you can" McSharry said

" I won't"

Rob watched Begsy's hand move inside his coat and grip the gun, there was no way he'd be able to find cover before the first shot was fired, Begsy might be big but he definitely wasn't slow.

"Is that your final answer?" he caught a hint of resignation, maybe even disappointment, in the old man's voice. Rob nodded and McSharry shook his head "It won't end here you know, that brother of yours will be next then whoever else we can find that you care about, how many are on your list so far Begs?"

"Four" Begsy said, his hand still positioned inside the coat, waiting for the order to withdraw it "Give me the word boss and I'll wipe this little shits memory off the face of the earth" the vigour with which Begsy uttered the words surprised even Rob.

"Last chance?" McSharry said, raising his eyebrows expectantly.

His mind flashed back to when he was nineteen, something about the moment reminded him of being stationed in Bosnia with the Cheshire Regiment. He remembered patrolling through the bullet ridden city of Mostar, he and two other soldiers had stopped a group of men from looting an old woman's shop, she spoke a little English, to thank them she'd given them each a shot of grappa. She looked frail, and weary, all that she'd wanted was an end to the fighting. He remembered the words the civilians had lived by, the lesson they had learnt;

It is better to eat dry bread once a day than to go to war

Those words had touched him, though it would be years later before he truly understood them. He wanted to share the experience, but he knew they would mean nothing to the men before him. Resignation swept through his body like a poison, there was no way out now, all he could do was hope for the best possible deal.

"Two hits? That's it?"

"Two hits" McSharry agreed "Hits against two very dangerous criminals for which you will be generously compensated"

"How much?"

"A hundred grand"

Rob had to concentrate to maintain his composure, the last hit he'd done for McSharry had earned him fifteen grand, but then that had been over ten years ago. He didn't know why but he found it an odd occurrence equating inflation to the business of murder. He lifted his hand from his side so the red file was at head height.

"Have you looked at this? It's not going to be easy. A minimum of six accomplishes, no easy locations, and if you're giving me Caddock first that means Miller's going to be even tougher. I haven't done this kind of thing in over a decade" Rob may have been resigned but he was still trying every last way out he could think of to get McSharry to change his mind.

"I have confidence in you" McSharry said assertively, like a father telling his son he could get an A in his next maths test.

"They're going to know it's you" he said, refusing to give up "Before... it was different, the circumstances made sense, but two high profile hit's a couple of days after you get released, of course they'll know it's you"

"Certain people may have their suspicions, but with you pulling the trigger there'll be no tangible evidence to link us to the hits, it will be as if Caddock and Miller were executed by a gust of wind, by a shadow. Anyway as will come to light in the next few days, my family is not immune to assassinations, my young nephew George should be discovered any time now, that should deflect enough attention for you to get the job done, don't you think?"

He remembered meeting George a little over ten years ago, though Rob had been introduced under a fake name. He'd been an enthusiastic kid, a little on the naive side but with good enough intentions, his worship of McSharry was obvious even then, desperately following him around and trying to please him. Rob thought, with a pang of regret, that he obviously hadn't succeeded.

It sickened him to think McSharry would murder his own family just like that, and from the glint in Begsy's eye Rob knew exactly who it was who'd carried out the order.

"You've only been out a couple of days, don't you think it's worth trying a little diplomacy with these guys before you decide to take them out?" Rob knew he was pleading but he was down to the last card in his deck.

"There is no diplomacy in our world" McSharry said impatiently, fire burnt in his eyes "there are the weak and there are the strong, nothing else. So, do we have a deal or not?"

Rob took a deep breath, he had exhausted all of his possibilities, every door had been closed, there was only one left walk through.

"Two hits, then that's it, I'm out. I get to walk away with my hundred grand and you never come near me or my family again.

"You're an exceptional asset Robert, I don't know if we could just let you walk off into the sunset"

Rob knew he was toeing a fine line, but it was the one ace he refused to give up. If he lost it, it would be the end of him and he would never make it back to Jo, he knew that for certain.

"That's the deal" he said, summoning every bit of resolve he had "I take out these two for you, cripple both the Caddocks and the Millers and it's done, the city is yours and I'm gone. Shoot me if you have to but that's the deal"

McSharry eyed him suspiciously and Rob heard the small click inside Begsy's jacket as the safety was switched off. He took a deep breath and prepared himself for the what might be about to come, it felt like the three men had stood for an eternity before someone finally spoke.

"Done" McSharry said eventually "I suppose once these two pretenders are out of the way, there will be little need for your particular kind of skill. Two hits and you're finished"

He felt a flicker of relief, though it was nothing more than a drop in his ocean of problems he still heard the change in his voice "When do you want it done?"

"In four days" McSharry said.

"When do I get the money?"

A nod from McSharry was enough for Begsy to finally remove his hand from the pistol, Rob didn't realise until Begsy moved away how tense he'd been. The big man walked a few feet and picked up a navy blue sports bag from behind a headstone, when he returned he tossed the bag at Rob with more force than was probably necessary. He looked inside at the piles of notes bounded together.

"Ten grand now" McSharry said "The rest when it's done"

Rob placed the red folder inside the bag and closed it, tossing it over his shoulder he took in the two men one last time.

"Anything else?" he asked, when neither of them responded Rob began walking back the way he'd come.

"Robert, one more thing" McSharry shouted after he had covered less than ten feet, Rob turned back to face them "The last time you failed me it cost me ten years, fail me again and it will cost you a hell of a lot more. Do you understand?"

Rob held McSharry's gaze for a few seconds before he responded "I'll call you when its done" he said finally, and continued on with his journey.

By the time he reached the car the gravity of what he would have to do was already weighing heavily on his mind. Charlie leant against the boot of the car looking expectantly at his watch as Rob turned off the path.

"How'd it go?" he asked, pushing forward excitedly from the car, Rob let out a deep sigh as he reached the passenger door, throwing the sports bag into the back and sitting down.

"Fine" he muttered impatiently as Charlie took his seat. Rob didn't feel up to replaying the whole conversation for his brother, especially given the level of excitement Charlie seemed to have for the whole thing.

"What did they want you to do?" Charlie asked, starting the engine and speeding out of the car park, as if he expected heavily armed men to start chasing them any second.

"He wants me to kill two men, Wayne Caddock and whoever's running the Millers" Rob said reluctantly.

"Tony Miller?"

"If Tony Miller runs the family then it will be Tony Miller, if someone else runs the family it will be someone else"

Charlie was nodding his head as if Rob had just told him he'd got a promotion, he tried to stifle the anger that he felt just by watching him. He knew he was taking out his frustration on his little brother but he couldn't help it, it was like Charlie had no comprehension of the situation, like someone celebrating at a funeral. His face felt red, he looked out the window and tried to focus his mind on Jo, he was doing this to keep her safe.

"They must be paying you well for that lad, they're too big time fuckers"

"A hundred grand"

Charlie whistled through his teeth and continued to nod his head "Fuck me that's a good little payday, I'll come with you if you want, drive the car or something, I'll take a 5% cut"

"Stop the car" Rob said angrily, feeling something snap inside. Charlie finally stopped nodding his head but he didn't stop the car, he looked over at his older brother as if trying to discern whether or not he was joking, Rob raised his voice to emphasize the point "STOP THE BLOODY CAR!"

The car swerved hard and pulled against the side of the road, accompanied by the sound of angry horns. Rob noticed they were on a dual carriageway with the river Mersey just to his left. If he followed the river back to Bootle he would be at the flat in a little over an hour, and a walk was just what he needed to calm his head.

91

Charlie looked through the back mirror and then through the front, confusion etched across his face "What's going on?"

"I'm walking" Rob said bluntly, reaching into the back and grabbing hold of the sports bag "I'll give you a call in a day or two but until then don't get in touch, I need some time to think"

Rob didn't wait for a response, slamming the door shut he slung the bag over his shoulder and began the long walk to the flat. For a few minutes he was very aware that Charlie's car hadn't moved, he could hear the engine humming in the background but his brother seemed to be just sitting there. Rob felt a quick twinge of guilt for being so short but repressed it just as quickly, he had enough problems to contend with at the moment, there was simply no room left in his head to feel bad for Charlie. Eventually the car started up and gave a beep as it passed by, Rob gave a wave, hoping that would do as repentance for his temper. Then the car was gone, and Rob found himself facing much bigger problems. He stopped for a second and leaned over the railing that separated him from the River Mersey.

He was definitely in it now.

Chapter 7

Stephen McSharry strongly believed that a man's life came down to a handful of key decisions. Looking back he was certain that the day he met Rob Thomas had been one such occasion, and as he watched the kid take his final steps out of St James cemetery he felt an overwhelming sense that the job they'd just agreed would be another defining moment.

So much of his plan was based around the boy, but their meeting left him with a seed of doubt in the back of his mind; to place so much importance on the success of a reluctant partner was a risky proposition, his gamble could prove to be a precarious one to call.

He leaned down and ran a hand over the engraving of his brother's name, readjusting the flowers so that they stood front and center, putting all the other graves to shame.

He said his goodbyes, stood and buttoned up his coat against the crisp morning air. As he walked towards the car, with Begsy a few steps behind, he found himself analysing why he'd chosen to have the meeting here. Stephen McSharry wasn't the sentimental type but he felt he owed his brother a visit; for both the ten year absence, and the other thing.

As they reached the car he spotted the first wave of grievers, an elderly couple gave Begs a peculiar look, the big man glared back and slid behind the wheel.

The first five minutes of the journey were shrouded in silence. Begsy knew better than to disturb him when he was thinking, and there was a lot to think about. The last few days had left Stephen McSharry frantically trying to keep up with the pace of his own ambition. There was so much to do, more than once he'd wondered whether it was too much for a man of his advancing years. It was only when they exited the city that McSharry's gaze shifted from contemplative to alert, and his enforcer dared to share his thoughts.

"You really think he'll get it done?" Begsy's voice failed to hide the disdain with which he held Rob Thomas.

"I do" McSharry replied bluntly. Rob Thomas and Begsy had never seen eye to eye, even in the old days, but McSharry found their interactions fascinating; two men so incredibly different yet in many ways very much alike. Both were valuable weapons and they were his favorite two to wield.

"I don't trust him, he's soft, always has been, he's a weak fucking sister" Begsy uttered the words with disgust, like he wanted to spit them out. McSharry grinned as he watched the big man, irritably scratching his scar every couple of minutes.

"That might be true Begs, but do you know anyone who's got the gift for the kill like this one?"

Begsy didn't respond, it was the closest the big man would ever come to giving Rob Thomas a compliment and his shoulders shook with the strain.

McSharry laughed, his enforcer would need to hit something pretty soon, and pretty hard.

"Me neither" McSharry continued "We're going to need him, even if he hasn't got the stomach for it"

Begsy shifted in his seat, there was an agitation in his demeanour that McSharry hadn't seen since his release, it surprised him just how much the Thomas kid got under his skin. Begs was too much of a pro to openly oppose McSharry's moves, but he was sure of his opinion and wasn't letting it go lightly.

"I think it's a mistake boss. Did you see the look in his eyes when you told him what you wanted, he's weak, he'll fuck it up".

The conversation was growing more tiresome by the second, good leadership was about making tough decisions and sticking by them. He had no intention of admitting to Begsy that he had his doubts about the kid as well, but the more he was reminded of the risks the more he questioned his own judgment. Enough was enough, the dye was cast and there was nothing to be done, it would play out how it played out, McSharry's attention needed to be elsewhere.

"Relax" his tone was crystal clear; it was an order, not a suggestion "He'll get it done. In the meantime, we have enough to be doing without worrying about him. Talk to me about what's next"

"All the boys are ready, in the next couple of days we pay a visit to a few of the top suppliers" Begsy's response was encouraging; he seemed to wholly embraced the change of topic to the point that his shoulders were looser and his voice was less strained. He started to think maybe Rob Thomas should come with a health warning

"Who have you decided on, and where are the shipments coming in from?"

Giving Begsy the authority to choose which suppliers to squeeze had been an important part of his plan, it showed his enforcer that he had the boss's trust and reinforced to the crew just exactly who was the number two. Since George's death it felt like a point that needed to be made.

"The Caddocks have boatloads of Ecstacy coming in from Rotterdam" Begsy replied, subtly puffing up his chest, he looked it he was enjoying the opportunity to show off the info he'd squeezed out of Kev Lloyd "the shipments are brought in by two cockney brothers who have their own fleet of freighters, they have a couple of ports along the Mersey bought and paid for. The Millers are bringing in Heroin from South America, to the Costa Del Sol and then through to Ireland"

"That's a lot of different borders to be passing through" McSharry said sceptically.

"Yeah, but they're corrupt as fuck. The hardest part is getting them in to England, but the security is at its weakest point on the Irish border. That's run by a guy called Samuel Ho, he has his own people in Spain and Ireland who get it to him here, and then he sells it on to Tony Miller. Ho in particular may take some convincing".

He liked the sound of everything he was hearing; both avenues were lucrative, both had the added bonus of being taken from the pricks who disrespected him. If the Cockney twins and Ho got on board with his operation then it would mean a lot of money and a lot of influence would be immediately redirected to where it should be. All he needed to do first was topple a couple of empires. McSharry looked over at Begsy, who caught his eye, and gave a small grin.

"I'm sure you can persuade him Begs. What do you predict in terms of retribution?"

Begsy squinted and shook his head from side to side as if the shifting weight of possibility was constantly moving inside his brain, he let out a sigh "If we time it right, who knows, there might not be any" he seemed far from certain, it was the answer McSharry had expected.

"I was thinking the same, but we'll have to time it just right. There'll be Caddock and Miller on one side, the filth on the other, and a very small gap for us to squeeze through before it disappears"

"Speaking of the filth..."

McSharry caught the apprehensive tone "Yes?"

Begs scratched at his scar "We've gotten word that the cunt who put you away, that Walker fucker, he's been asking questions about you. Our guys say he's been waking people up in the middle of the night questioning, threatening. The bastards got the bit between his teeth, you remember what he's like, he doesn't tire easy"

Stephen McSharry remembered him; it was hard to forget the prick who stole ten years of your life. Over that span of time his recollection of many things had become a little hazy, but there were two occasions that served to perfectly crystallise that particular copper in his mind. The first was when the pointy nosed prick stormed into his house with a warrant, the second taking the stand at his trial, both times he had the same smug, self-satisfied look plastered across his pale, skinny face. McSharry knew that kind of face all too well, it was the kind of face that received regular beatings at school, the kind that suffered constantly at the hands of an alpha males like him. McSharry understood people like David Walker better than they understood themselves; he knew that their every action was motivated by a need to gain retribution against the kind of men who had tormented him his entire life; hard men, men who chose to make their living outside the boundaries of his safe little world.

The man was an annoyance, nothing more, it had been his own carelessness that caused his downfall the last time. He should have realised that the lawyer was going soft before the filth had a chance to pounce. Distractions had blinded him, he'd been over confident, and the scrawny little copper had been in the right place at the right time to take advantage of that fact.

But it wouldn't happen again.

This time he was alert, this time he was keeping on top of everything, and everyone. If he maintained his concentration then David Walker would be chasing shadows until the end of time; an outcome as rewarding as any other aspect of his success, all McSharry had to do was pull it off.

He knew Begsy was aching to kill the little bastard, he shared the sentiment himself. But killing police officers was more hassle than it was worth, the only time you ever felt the full weight of the Metropolitan Police Force was when they were united by the death of one of their own. Best to let them just buzz around in the background, killing one bee wasn't worth bringing the whole hive to your doorstep.

"Well, we expected that didn't we?" McSharry said returning to the moment. He tried to hide the annoyance in his voice, he could hear that he'd failed "Keep an eye on him. For now he can wake up all the small timers he wants, what the fuck are they going to tell him? So long as we keep our own counsel, he's no kind of threat"

"What about when it's done? No one knows shit now, but we can't take over the rackets of two major crews without letting the cat out of the bag, word will hit the street"

"We'll worry about tomorrow's problems tomorrow Begs"

Begsy recognised the tone "No problem"

The car resumed its earlier silence, McSharry's brain immediately returned to the overwhelming obsession that monopolised his thoughts. He found himself thinking about it first thing in the morning and last thing at night, it was like a thorn in his paw, and maybe he was just about ready to discuss it.

"What did you take from the meeting the other day?" So far the subject had been pure taboo; he could see it in their eyes, no one wanted to face the brunt of the boss man's fury.

"In what way?" Begsy asked tentatively.

"You know what way"

The big man scratched the scar on his face and took a pack of cigarettes from his coat.

Lighting up, he opened the window and cleared his throat. The crisp November air swarmed into the car "I dunno, the same as you I suppose. Tony Miller's the wildcard, he's a nasty bastard and that's been the driving force that's led us all to where we are now. Caddock's ambitious but he's just riding the wave of Miller's warpath. You take Tony M off the board and I don't think Caddock's got the balls to go to war"

"You think we should be taking out Tony Miller first?" he hadn't sought any council before making his decision. He sensed Begsy's frustration, but sometimes that was just the way it went.

"Nah"

"Why?"

"Miller's going to be well protected either way," Begsy began, his tone was assured enough to suggest that he'd been considering the issue since McSharry announced his decision, probably even before that "and with his temper, he comes after us with no proof that we we're behind Caddock and it gives us a justifiable reason to wipe him out. Not for nothing, but if you have to send that little pussy after them both, I'd rather his first hit for ten years wasn't Miller. If he bottles it and Tony gets hold of him, he'll torture the bastard until he gives us up, which won't be long with that little fuck"

He ignored the prejudice and focused on the enforcer's content. The first move could prove to be the biggest, if things went badly wrong it could prove to be the last. Every decision brought with it a hundred possible repercussions, sorting them into any kind of order was beginning to give him a headache. McSharry watched the world pass by his window, so many choices to make, so many factors to consider.

"I don't like that Miller gets a warning, I want him dead before he has a chance to bring a shitstorm down on our heads"

"You think there's any chance he'll go into hiding?" the cigarette at Begsy's lips obscured the words.

"No, not Tony Miller. He doesn't have enough going on upstairs. To villains like him hiding is tantamount to cowardice, he couldn't bear the thought of anybody, anywhere thinking that about him. Sometimes in this business Begs you have to be smart enough to swallow your own pride, we'll put him in the ground before he learns that lesson"

He caught the approving smile on Begsy's lips, a second later his own face was mimicking the look.

A sharp turn later and McSharry suddenly found himself staring up at his home. The three storey Victorian mansion truly was an impressive piece of architecture, the older he got the more he respected the elegance and the timeless beauty of such things. It seemed in every walk of life the new was sprouting up in all directions, piss poor imitations of the past, cheaper, lazier and less effective than what had come before it, his home was the perfect metaphor for the decaying newness of the world.

He stepped out of the car and took in the external beauty of the property. He'd done the same thing on his first night of freedom, and every day since. Green grass ran either side of the drive, grass that had been tended well in his absence. Two black beamers sat ahead of him in the driveway, negating the rustic Victorian feel of his home. He did what he could to block them out. The house itself seemed to glow with class; the faded reddish brown brick looked more beautiful now for its wear than it ever could have new. Four old trees stood proudly along the front of the house, partially obscuring the view from two of the windows either side of the front door. How old those trees must be, how many generations of men they had seen come and go. Patriarch after patriarch tending their branches, claiming them as part of their property only to expire and pass into the ownership of another man, a man whose expiration was just as certain. As McSharry watched the trees, swaying so slightly in the wind, silently guarding his home, he found they reminded him a little of Begsy. Stoic, unmovable, resilient, they were qualities that were desirable in all aspects of existence, it comforted him to know they were also embodiments of his home.

His gaze passed over each window in turn, nothing stirred, but he knew people were inside. He climbed six steps that led to his front door, wrapping his hand around the ice cold rail in the process. Behind he heard Begsy's footsteps, his number two was halfway up the drive when the door swung open and Mercer stepped out into the cold.

Mercer was slightly more muscle than fat, a thin t-shirt and a pair of jeans did nothing to protect him from the cold. McSharry caught the flinch when the weather hit him, it was amusing to watch the boy try to pass it off as a stretch.

He ignored the reflex and gave Mercer a curt nod while waiting for Begsy to catch up. He made up the ground in a few seconds and followed McSharry into the house.

The warmth engulfed him immediately, discarding his jacket and scarf McSharry handed the bundle to Mercer and rubbed his hands together.

The hallway was quiet, bright sun seeped in where it could though darkness held its ground for the most part. McSharry had to remind himself that it was only two days earlier when he'd followed his soldiers across that space on their way to a crucial meeting. So much had already changed in that time, Stephen McSharry contemplated just how much more would have to change before his plans were complete.

He felt a small pang of regret for the death of his nephew, but suppressed it before it had a chance to settle. Weakness encouraged extermination, if he wasn't strong enough to live with the decisions he'd made then he may as well give up now.

McSharry saw Nikolai step lightly through the kitchen door and into the hallway, the little blond man's face was as unreadable as ever. Over the last few days McSharry had noticed that Nikolai's right arm never left his side, it took a while to figure out the reason; close proximity to his knife. There was something almost sexual between the man and his machete, the way he stroked the metal left McSharry feeling occasionally disturbed, the rest of the time he was just relieved that the weird little bastard was on his side.

Nikolai leaned back on the wall, his body seemingly relaxed as his spectacled eyes methodically scanned the hallway.

McSharry turned on his heels and started up the stairs, Begsy and Mercer followed without being told, routine was coming back to the crew.

"Good meeting?" Mercer asked "You gonna tell us who it was with now?"

His men were showing too much interest in aspects of the business that didn't concern them. In the old days they knew better than to ask about specifics that he hadn't chosen to share, Mercer especially had been around long enough to remember how it worked. He knew they were interested in events that went on outside the crew, especially when a string of unsolved murders seemed to engulf the majority of their enemies. McSharry understood the curiosity, it was human nature, but he'd made the decision long ago to keep Rob Thomas out of sight. It was a decision that had reaped massive rewards over the years, and it was a decision he was willing to kill to protect.

"Easy with the questions, lad" Begsy responded "you know what curiosity did to the cat, don't ya?"

McSharry glanced at Mercer; there was a tightness to his face. The memory of George McSharry was still fresh in their minds, it reminded them just how quickly a man could lose his value. Mercer had been around long enough to know that if Begs intended to carry out the threat he wouldn't get a hint of warning, but the mere suggestion seemed to unnerve him nonetheless.

Mercer gave the slightest of nods and lowered his head, McSharry caught Begsy's eye and smiled.

"Easy Begs, the boys just exorcising a little curiosity"

He slapped Mercer on the back. It brought a small grin to the man's face, but the guarded look in his eye suggested he would be watching what he said for the next couple of days.

He was halfway up the stairs when he heard Ads voice calling him from the hallway below.

"Boss, you've got someone here to see you!"

McSharry leaned over the bannister and looked down, Ads was stood with his arms crossed while his right hand stroked his beard. Even a casual pose like that betrayed the man's military background; his body language possessed a level of poise and a discipline that never seemed to wane.

"Who?"

"Martin Cassidy" Ads replied "I put him in the bar"

McSharry glanced at his watch, it was eleven in the morning. He wondered what kind of urgent business would bring Cassidy to his home at such an early hour. A wave of concern flooded his mind, did Martin know about his plans? Did he somehow know about Rob Thomas? It seemed too coincidental that his old friend would show up the same morning that McSharry put the wheels of his plan in motion. He searched through his memory for another time, however long ago, when Martin had come to see him at such an unsociable hour, and found none.

One glance at Begsy's raised eyebrows told him that his enforcer was thinking the same thing. He looked around, first at Mercer, then at Ads, neither seemed to have found anything suspicious in Martin's visit, or if they had they were keeping it to themselves. McSharry ushered Begsy and Mercer aside and descended the stairs, when he passed Begsy he caught his eye.

"Get the lads together, make sure they know the plan for the next couple of days, I want everyone prepared"

"We've already been over it-" Begsy began, McSharry didn't give him the chance to finish.

"Go over it again!"

Begsy grunted an acknowledgement.

McSharry began down the staircase, by the time he reached the bottom Begsy and Mercer had already disappeared onto the floor above.

He followed Ads through the house, their journey took them through what had previously been the dining room. When Julie was alive it had been the centre of the house, guests were received there and expensive paintings had covered the walls, as he passed through he watched Rico Wallace and Macca while they dismantled and cleaned a pair of 9mm semi-automatics. The men nodded as he passed, McSharry watched oil drip from one of the gun barrels onto Julie's five grand mahogany dining table, he definitely preferred the room this way.

"Carry on lads" he muttered. To one side he clocked another six pistols waiting to be cleaned, already he was looking forward to the time when his men would get to use them.

Ads led the way across the hall and held the door open, McSharry made his way inside and closed it behind him. He didn't need to tell the ex-soldier what to do; he'd stay in the hallway and make sure they weren't disturbed, the man was vintage pro, he needed more guys of that ilk.

The room was large enough to fit three leather couches, a pool table and a wooden bar that stretched ten feet. A coal fire roared in the corner, conveying ever changing shadows onto the brown wallpaper. There was no window in this room, this was the room where serious discussion took place.

Sat on the couch nearest the fire was Martin Cassidy. Seeing McSharry enter the room he stood up and walked towards his host, the two men shook hands.

"Martin, what a pleasant surprise" McSharry said, taking the hand and giving it a firm shake.

He looked his guest over, his face seemed as warm and honest as ever, not a hint of suspicion existed in those old eyes. He analysed his old friend and found himself making the same old preconceptions; that Martin was friendly old man, a grandfather figure whose kind leathery face would do anything to help. McSharry had to remind himself that the old man standing opposite him was a cold blooded killer, a man who had done as many despicable things on this earth as he had, if not more. To live at the level Martin had for as long as he had, a man needed to be a lot more than just smart, he needed to be ruthless.

McSharry recalled a dozen gruesome murders that Cassidy had either ordered or committed. The memories hazed the image he saw in front of him and brought the old man into a different kind of focus, he made a conscious effort to keep them at the forefront of his mind. A friend was a friend but it was naive, to say nothing of dangerous, to think of him as something he wasn't.

"Hello my boy" Martin said, the warm smile was familiar "I just stopped by to see how everything was, after the other day"

His tone was sincere, and concerned. McSharry wondered whether he was already becoming paranoid, this was a man, the only man outside of his crew, who had gone out of his way to ensure Stephen's prison sentence had passed as smoothly as possible. An old friend whose loyalty had never been brought into question, even in the crazed few years before he was sent down.

"Would you like a drink?" McSharry asked "Johnnie Walker Blue? I just got a case of it delivered yesterday"

"Please, it's never too early for the good stuff." Martin replied.

McSharry walked behind the bar and picked up the crystal decanter. Removing the stop he put his nose to the rim and took a deep breath. The scent filled his nostrils, it smelled like success, he allowed himself a moment to enjoy the aroma before he filled two tumblers. Carefully, he put the stop back on the decanter and removed two cigars from a nearby draw. He handed one to Martin along with a glass and gestured for him to take a seat. McSharry joined him on the parallel couch and for a few moments the two men sat in silence, eventually it was Martin Cassidy who spoke first.

"So my boy, as I was saying, the meeting..."

Martin looked at him expectantly, McSharry kept his face from betraying anything. He held his old friends gaze for a few seconds, before turning his attention towards lighting the cigar.

"What about it?"

"I was hoping to have more of a chance to talk to you, at least before the others arrived, I wanted to explain a few things" Martin's tone was apologetic, the look in his eyes expressed a need to explain "Times have changed, I'd be lying if I said it was for the better, but nonetheless, they are different. The days of our two organisations dominating proceedings in these parts, they were glorious times but... you have to understand the new generation have come through the ranks, cutting a path through all before them. They're ambitious, smart, energetic, it's difficult to compete. Especially after all that we have seen, you know, you reach a certain age and all you want in life is a little peace and quiet. You'll let an awful lot slide under the carpet to maintain that quiet, more than you may have realised when you look back and try to discern how you ended up where you did"

It occurred to Stephen McSharry that he had never seen Martin look quite as old as he did in that moment. He looked like a man bled dry of his youth, bled by the things he had seen and the things he had experienced.

"I understand Martin, there must have been some difficult times"

Martin Cassidy let out a little chuckle, a chuckle that told McSharry he didn't know the half of it and took a long sip from his glass. For the first time

McSharry noticed that the old man's hand was shaking.

"Oh, I weathered some tricky storms, but it wasn't all bad, there was a time when I struggled, I'll admit, but once you can accept that things have changed, well it becomes a much lighter burden to bear"

He couldn't help but study his old friend, and the way that Martin's eyes would not meet his. He wondered whether it was shame that kept his gaze lowered. To speak aloud about his loss of influence seemed to weigh heavily on the old man, he seemed unable to raise his eyes higher than the half empty glass in his hand, and even then they lingered just for a moment before returning to the carpet.

McSharry tried to keep his voice low and supportive, it felt wrong to pander, that wasn't what he did, but if anyone in his life deserved his patience then it was Martin Cassidy.

"How did it happen? This change I mean, when I left everything was so secure"

Cassidy finally found the strength to look up, he couldn't be sure but he thought he caught moisture in the man's eyes, before he could be sure they had returned to the carpet and Cassidy was sucking down more liquid courage.

"I've been asking myself the same question, it's amazing how easy it is to put ones head in the sand, it took you coming back for me to appreciate just how much things have changed. It was a confluence of events I suppose, when Margaret passed, I... and then there's your nephew. I mean no disrespect to George, he's a good boy, but I sense the family interests will be a lot more secure with you back at the helm. There were a lot of factors, I'm sorry my boy, I never meant to let you down"

McSharry considered filling him in on the fate of his nephew. Word would be out in a few days anyway, the boy's body had been rotting in Formby woods for quite a while, it was only a matter of time before some unlucky dog walkers stumbled upon the corpse. He played with the idea for a moment and then dismissed it, Cassidy's emotional state seemed precarious enough as it was, admitting to executing his kin was unlikely to stabilise it. It was best for the old man to think he'd been killed by an enemy, should he then need to call on Cassidy's muscle for support he still had the avenging uncle card to play.

"Don't be ridiculous, Martin" he said, moving towards the other couch and sitting next to Cassidy "Tell me, how are your interests these days, have they left you with much?

Cassidy let out a long sigh and took another drink, his hand was still shaking but less noticeably than before, the whiskey seemed to be having at least some effect.

"They're acceptable. We run protection for a lot of the clubs in town, hijack the occasional lorry, a small area to deal to in the North of the city, enough to make a living but, compared to what we used to run..."

"Do you meet with the other two often?" McSharry asked, he'd noted at the meeting the lack of communication between Cassidy and his two major headaches.

"Not especially. Now and again the four heads will get together, but I sense it's more out of habit than anything else" As he spoke Martin's tone grew increasingly more melancholy "Tony and Wayne keep most of their business in house, I only really hear about their plans when they want something doing from my men. It's strange, you say it out loud and it's much more difficult to hide the truth of what you've become"

The moment felt right, he took a large gulp of whisky and made his decision. So much of what he intended to do relied on timing and instinct, both of which seemed to be merging at that moment. He stared at Martin Cassidy until eventually the old man forced his eyes from the carpet.

"Martin, how would you like the chance to take back what you've lost?"

Cassidy gave him a quizzical look, before a small smile appeared at the corners of his mouth "I remember that look, my boy, what have you got in mind?"

McSharry reached over and grabbed the glass from Martin's hand, his old friend released it willingly.

Stephen McSharry smiled.

"Let's have another drink"

Chapter 8

Bright lights filled the small room, reverberating off the white walls to give the impression that they themselves were lit. In the centre of the room, bathed from all sides by the piercing light were the fifteen officers who made up the Detailed Surveillance Team, every pale face and bloodshot eye amongst them was accentuated by the condition of the room. They sat alongside one another in front of a long metallic table, standing on the other side was David Walker, absorbing every angry look and returning his own with ten times the force.

David glanced behind the seated officers towards the corner of the room, leaning against the back wall with his leather jacket slung over his shoulder was Chris Railton, the man's body language as he yawned against his closed fist was in stark contrast to the group sat between them. It was the same relaxed demeanour that seemed to encompass every aspect of Railton's existence. David wondered whether being stood in front of fifteen angry stares would do anything to alter his disposition, somehow he doubted it.

Steadying himself David Walker returned his gaze to the DST officers seated in front of him, one by one he focused his attention on each individual, staring hard with a forcefulness that surprised even himself. Some shirked away and looked elsewhere, others angrily returned the glare until David moved on, one or two seemed vaguely amused by the entire process. Reaching up to his neck he pulled at the tie until there was enough space to undo the top button. The room was warm despite the freezing temperatures that awaited them outside, it was the kind of cold that he could still feel in his bones.

David stifled a yawn of his own, three hours sleep had been enough to see him through most of the day but now it was starting to catch up with him, exhaustion it seemed, was an inevitable by-product of spending half your evenings hustling lowlifes. A steady supply of coffee had kept him alert up until now, but he knew it wasn't a bottomless pit, he would have to sleep sometime.

It was the second time in twenty four hours that he and Railton had stood in that room. The first instance had come at 8am that morning when they were due to be briefed by the senior officer on the unit's recent progress. When they arrived they were met by a Junior Analyst with nothing more than a message that the unit had been unsuccessful, and so far had nothing to report.

Walker had been livid, even Railton's calm exterior seemed to have been ruffled by the contemptuous manner in which their meeting had been disregarded. David's order to the Junior Analyst had been simple; all fifteen officers present for the quarterly shift change at ten pm, anybody who couldn't make it wouldn't need to come into work the next day, they'd be facing an immediate suspension.

Only four of the individuals present were involved in that changeover, the others were missing out on valuable free time, and if the pale faces and bloodshot eyes were anything to go by; valuable sleeping time as well. He noted without surprise that it was those eleven officers who stared at him with the greatest degree of contempt.

Eventually David's eyes settled on Marcus Roberts, Senior Officer of the unit, who sat in the centre of the group. Marcus was a small, spectacled man in his mid-fifties who had been transferred straight in from a desk job at Customs. While he was an efficient and competent individual he had nothing that singled him out as an effective leader of men. The man was a long way from being a true copper, and Walker doubted his ability to ever become one, a bean counter with some high placed friends seemed like a much more accurate way of describing him.

Roberts had already made his displeasure clear at being superseded by an officer from another department, even if that officer did outrank him. Despite all the talk of interdepartmental co-operation there was still a significant degree of tension that existed between the Intelligence section of the agency and David's Enforcement division. For his part, David knew that he hadn't helped that divide, particularly when it came to Marcus Roberts and his team, but David was a man who knew what he wanted and had trouble hiding his displeasure if he didn't get it on time.

"Well, I'm sure you all know why you were called in" David said, his voice firm and full of conviction as he addressed the whole group.

A few of the officers shared a confused look, the others just stared back at him with the same angry glare as before. It only took Marcus Roberts a second to answer his rhetorical question.

"Officer Walker, if you had a concern over the progress of this unit, the appropriate thing to do would have been to discuss it with me. Hauling in my entire team at ten pm is a thoroughly unprofessional move and a blatant abuse of the powers you have been given"

"Those powers, Officer Roberts" David replied slowly "were given to me to ensure that every possible action was taken to ensure this case is tackled with efficiency and competency, that includes dealing with actions that are being missed within this agency"

Roberts narrowed his eyes suspiciously, he looked liable to burst at any second.

"What exactly is it you're accusing us of?"

The rest of the officers were watching the exchange with interest, most seemed to have sided with their boss, but there were a few who were enjoying the sight of their superior being publicly scolded. A quick glance towards his deputy confirmed that he was enjoying himself as well; his eyes were wide as he flashed an amused smile in David's direction.

"A lack of progress" David eventually replied "is that an accusation you're willing to refute?"

Under the bright lights he was able to see just how quickly Roberts cheeks turned to a dark shade of crimson.

"These things take time. If you had worked in intelligence before, rather than just showing up and demanding results, you would realise that hours upon hours of manpower are needed for the kind of information you're demanding"

"You've had hours upon hours of manpower, how many more do you need?"

"Surveillance isn't an exact science. You can't just give us a list of queries and a schedule and expect us to have all the questions answered by the time you fit us in to your timetable, it's just not possible. There are factors that need to be taken into consideration, not the least of which is that we can't make these people talk about the things they don't want us to hear"

He could already feel the frustration start to build, he had enough on his plate without having to go twelve rounds with the surveillance officer every time he wanted something done.

He took a deep breath and tried to look at the bigger picture, below him he caught Marcus Roberts checking his watch and sighing impatiently.

"Ok, so what's the good news, what can you tell me?" Walker asked, trying to make his voice sound slightly more affable.

"I'm afraid at this stage, not a lot" Roberts answered bluntly, he spoke through gritted teeth as though the very words embarrassed him.

"You've been tailing Caddock, Miller, McSharry and Cassidy people?" David asked. It was a rhetorical question; he knew they had because that was what he'd told them to do.

"When we can, but our manpower doesn't stretch to anywhere near the level we would need to have them under constant surveillance, maybe if we had more resources..." Roberts trailed off, his tone was belligerent enough to suggest that he held David personally responsible for the lack of said of manpower.

"Officer Roberts, I swear to you if it was in my power to give-" David began before he was cut off mid-sentence.

"But it's not, I understand. As I was saying we don't have nearly enough staff to keep them under constant surveillance but even when we are able to pursue them, their drivers are experienced criminals, more often than not they're able to shake their tails"

"And what's being done to rectify this?" David asked, placing his hands behind his head and fighting the urge to stretch. The tiredness was beginning to seep into every part of him now, every muscle in his body screamed out for rest but David kept his attention focused unequivocally on Marcus Roberts.

"What can we do?"

"I want you to send your people on the 3 week surveillance driving course as a matter of urgency"

"They've already done it," Roberts protested "and the two week navigation course"

"Then they'll do it again!" David said, raising his voice to emphasise the point "and anything they have encountered that isn't covered on the course they can bring up at the end. I'm not kidding around, we're not going to miss a step if we can help it. Ok, what's next, I asked you to get a bug into McSharry's house, what's the news there?"

David felt the tension within the room intensify, he caught a few of the officers looking towards Roberts with trepidation in their eyes.

"Again, not a lot. McSharry has men watching the house twenty four/ seven and we've had absolutely no window in which to get inside. From everything we've seen of him since his release I'd say he's being extra careful in everything he does"

"I know" David said, letting his voice soften. Once in a while he had to remind himself that they were all on the same side, he may have disagreements with their policies but at the end of the day the DST wanted to bring these people down just like he did "He's not missing a step, and he's smart enough to keep operating like that consistently. Is there anything positive we can take forward? Anything we can focus our attention on?"

"Sir?"

The voice came from the end of the row, David followed the sound until he came upon the source. It belonged to a young woman, probably no older than twenty five or twenty six. In his focused rage he hadn't taken in any of the officers when he'd scanned through them earlier, but now that he did he couldn't fathom how he'd missed this woman. Her short brunette hair was cut to just above her shoulders and her face looked young, certainly younger than the age he had attributed to her. It was the eyes that gave away her years, big, brown eyes that spoke of a maturity at odds with the rest of her features. David tried to focus on the woman, he was suddenly aware of the fact that a few seconds had passed and he was yet to respond.

"Yes, Officer?"

"Saunders sir, Rachel Saunders" she spoke with a confidence that bordered on the arrogant but it seemed almost natural, although she held herself with poise there was a glimmer of nervousness in her eyes, once again they betrayed the front that the rest of her features carried so well.

"You have something you want to contribute?" he tried to keep his voice even, the way he would speak to any junior officer, but when he looked over her shoulder and caught sight of Railton's grin he knew there was at least one person he wasn't fooling.

"Sir, we've been getting snippets of conversations, not from the top but from mid-level guys. It's been nothing concrete, but you get the sense that something is coming, there's a lot of animosity on the streets that could boil over at any second. I wouldn't be surprised if what we're seeing now is the calm before the storm"

"The Regional Director will be delighted to hear that" David sighed, forgetting her beauty and returning to earth with a bang. His gaze was drawn back towards Marcus Roberts, leaning forward and looking at Rachel with anger in his eyes.

"Rachel, this is no place for idle intuition, if you have something to contribute back it up with suitable evidence, if not keep your opinions to yourself. Officer Walker has no interest in your predictions"

The rant reminded David of a teacher scolding his star student for embarrassing him in front of the headmaster. He noted the derogatory tone and the hungry way Marcus Roberts glared at her body, he got the overwhelming sense that the spurning of his advances at some point in the past had led to their current dynamic.

David caught the steely determination in her eyes as it was flashed first at Marcus, and then at him.

"It's more than just a prediction!" she insisted.

"Rachel, is it?" David said, stepping towards the young woman "I agree with you, the things I've been hearing, they suggest the same thing. But Officer Roberts is right; speculation isn't going to get us anywhere. I want you, all of you, to keep your ears to the ground and any information that has even the slightest chance of enhancing this investigation; I want you to pass it on to your superiors. With a bit of luck, maybe we'll be able to get a jump on this thing before all hell breaks loose. Until then we all need to remain vigilante, and hope for our slice of luck. Ok, thank you everyone, you can go"

David stood back against the wall as one by one the officers stood up and filed out of the room, he noted unsurprisingly that Railton had been the first one out the door. Running a hand through his hair he saw that Rachel Saunders was one of the last ones to move, before he knew what he was doing he had shouted her name and moved towards her.

"Rachel, thank you for your contribution, it's important to speak up, I know that wasn't the most hospitable environment in which to do so"

If it was possible she was even more beautiful when she smiled, it was only a half-smile, David found himself immediately craving to see more of it.

"Well, this is important stuff, isn't it?" she said "Sometimes you have to say 'what the hell' and take your chances"

"I agree" his voice was a little too eager, he hoped she hadn't noticed as he reached into his pocket "Listen, here's my card, it has my mobile number on it. You hear anything that we can use, that you think is too important to go through the usual chain of command, give me a call"

She eyed the card suspiciously and when she looked back up at him the smile was gone, she stared at him for a few seconds more as if she was working something out in her head.

"Too important? That's not what you mean is it?"

"No"

"You mean illegal"

So she was smart too David thought, a small smile formed on his own face but it was not mirrored in hers, she still seemed suspicious.

"Like I said, I've been charged to bring this case in, whatever it might take"

A small smile appeared at the corner of her mouth, but was gone so quickly that it left David wondering whether he'd actually seen it.

"Ok, thank you sir"

"Thank you" Walker responded with a nod, watching her leave the room.

He waited for a few seconds, buttoning the top of his shirt and redoing his tie, before exiting himself. Stepping out into the DST bullpen he walked over to the makeshift desk where he'd left his paperwork, Chris was sitting on the edge of the table watching people pass him by.

"That was inspiring stuff" Chris Railton said as David approached "Looks like I'm not the only one who thought so. You get yourself a date, Guv?"

"Excuse me?" David asked, glaring hard at Railton until his deputy was left in no doubt as to whether or not he found him funny.

"Sorry" Railton muttered as David leaned onto the desk and begun signing the pile of order sheets that were waiting for him "It's been a long day, I thought it was time to relax"

"What time are we speaking to the families of the Huyton prison station victims?" David asked, half distracted by the documents he was signing.

"I guess I thought wrong" Chris muttered

David tore his gaze away from the papers and looked up at his deputy "What time?"

"Eleven, tomorrow morning"

"Ok, I'm going to head back the office and get ready for that"

Finishing with the order sheets he placed them in a steel tray two desks down, as he walked back to where Chris was standing a member of the clerical staff marched over and planted a piece of paper in his hand. Clearly word of his scalding had already made its way around the unit.

"Officer Walker" the woman said, a belligerent tone evident in her voice "the Regional Director left a message, he asked you to call him back with an update"

With that the women turned and marched back the way she had come, David watched her go for a second before the piece of paper was yanked out of his hand by his deputy.

"What are you doing?" he asked impatiently.

Railton held the piece of paper in front of him "I'll take that, you need to go home and get some rest. Don't worry I can deal with Barry, I know plenty of professional jargon that translates to 'we've got dick all'"

David took a step towards Railton, who in turn took one step back "You're not taking care of it ok?" he said, feeling his temper shorten by the second "I have to speak to him"

"Why?"

"Because I do!" David said, raising his voice higher than was probably appropriate.

"Look at yourself, you can barely stand" Railton said, matching his tone "If you keep going like this you won't be able to stop a school kid knocking over a corner shop. Go home, get some rest, I'll deal with Barry and get the stuff sorted for tomorrow.

David suddenly became aware that most of the Detailed Surveillance Unit were watching the exchange. He looked around the room and every time his gaze caught curious eyes they turned away and busied themselves with whatever anonymous task they could find. All except for Rachel Saunders, who stared back looking quite amused by the entire exchange. He raised his hand as if preparing to grab the piece of paper and Railton took another step back.

"I should do it" David repeated. Railton flashed him with a sympathetic look and he felt a pang of guilt for being so short.

"Guv, you're working yourself into the ground, and that's just going to mean more work for me when I have to cover your nervous breakdown. So please, for me, for the investigation and for the love of God, yourself; go home, get some sleep and I'll see you in the morning"

David was finding it harder to argue with Railton's point. He did feel exhausted, and he knew he wasn't operating anywhere near a hundred percent because of it. Shaking his head he resigned himself to defeat "Fine, but don't be late, ok?"

"You have my word" Chris replied, placing the hand that held the note over his heart.

As if on cue a wave of fatigue washed over David's body, he looked for Rachel one last time but she was already back at work, typing at a keyboard and talking on the phone. He let himself look at her for a few seconds more before turning away and heading towards the car park.

By the time he stepped through his front door David had put all thoughts of sleep to the back of his mind, the car ride home reminding him that he still had too much to do before that particular indulgence could be embraced. He walked swiftly down the hallway and made his way into the kitchen, hanging his jacket on the banister en route. The house was cold, he hadn't spent much time in it over the last few weeks and the November chill was beginning to seep into the walls. Hurriedly he switched on the electric fire and snatched a bottle of red wine from the nearby rack; it would do an acceptable job of warming him up until the heating kicked in. Taking a glass from a half empty shelf and a corkscrew from a half empty draw David forced the metallic device into the cork and surveyed the kitchen of his two bed roomed, semi-detached house. It had certainly seen better days, he could remember deciding a couple of years ago that it was due to be redecorated but it was a job, like many around the house that he could never find the time to begin. He glanced towards the sink and noticed it was half full of dirty dishes, he didn't want to think about how long they'd been sitting there.

He wrapped his hand around the base of the bottle, gave a firm tug and heard the familiar *pop* of success. Slowly pouring the red liquid into the glass he left the kitchen and made his way towards the living room on the other side of the hallway. The room was just as cold as the kitchen had been; taking a sip of wine he repeated the process of switching on the fire and settled down on the cream couch.

Directly in front of where he sat was a low, wooden coffee table, strewn with police records and criminal files. Carefully placing the glass away from the most important documents, he surveyed the files in the order in which he'd left them.

Mostly, the documents in front of him consisted of criminal files relating to known associates of Stephen McSharry. Mug shots were strewn here and there, loosely attached to the appropriate file, but David no longer needed them, he had already memorised the faces of every man in those photographs. Scattered amongst the files were criminal reports, most of which were unsolved, that had the smell of McSharry's boys about them. He'd studied them for hours, trying to find a pattern, an insight into their intentions, but so far he was coming up short. He needed something to swing his way. A lucky break.

Taking another gulp of wine David felt the warm liquid radiate outwards from somewhere inside, all the way to his face. Pushing the reports to one side he rearranged the documents so he had each of the men's files and mug shots in a line before him. The first one that caught his eye was Nikolai Kornikov, the little blonde man looked more like a computer programmer than a multiple murderer, but one glance at his criminal record was enough to dismiss any such preconceptions: assault with a deadly weapon, seven counts of grievous bodily harm and a suspect in five unsolved stabbings. The man had served a total of eight years inside and every time he was released he committed a crime more heinous than the last, that was until he met Stephen McSharry. In the years since his recruitment they had been unable to pin a single job on him, that wasn't to say there weren't crimes that had the look of Nikolai Kornikov about them, if anything there were more. But there was no evidence, he was more careful now, they all where. That was the devastating secret of Stephen McSharry, that was why he had to be taken down.

Next along the line was Adam Croft, the distinctive wild black hair and shaggy beard were recognisable a mile away. Croft was ex-military, over the last five years they had hauled him in twelve times over the murders of heroin addicts, and every time he had an alibi. The circumstances of the attacks were almost always the same, three or four dead, severe haemorrhages to the skull most likely caused by a baseball bat, and all of their drugs stolen. It was of considerable embarrassment to both David and the Merseyside Police Force that after five years they still hadn't managed to make any inroads into solving what was effectively a drug addict serial killer. Unfortunately the rights of heroin addicts didn't count for much when it came to the majority of police officers, he even knew a few who considered the murders an act of community service.

Next along the line was Mark Mercer and Jeff McCoy, a thuggish double team that went back a long way with Stephen McSharry. Six months ago he had a tip that the pair were involved in the kidnapping and ransoming of an upcoming drug dealers family. The incident was never reported to the police, one of David's informants later confirmed that the pair cleared a cool hundred K from the episode, and the dealer's wife had walked away with a broken jaw and two fingers missing.

With a sigh David pushed the file aside and leaned back until the top of his head touched the wall behind him. He'd been over the files a hundred times and yet every spare moment he got he found himself staring at the same information that was already etched upon his brain, looking for something new, something he might have missed. His eyes closed for the briefest of seconds and he felt the tiredness he'd been holding back flood forward, immersing every inch of his body. With a groan he pushed himself upwards and opened his eyes, it wasn't time to sleep, not yet.

Reaching for the glass of wine he ran his free hand over the fabric of the couch and lamented its comfort, it wasn't what he needed when he was working. With a jolt of surprise, he realised that it had been the final purchase that Karen had made before she left. He'd been divorced for six years now, on a normal day it wasn't something that played on his mind, he was too busy to dwell on such things, but there were odd occasions where something would set it off and he would be reminded of what he'd lost.

Twelve months ago he'd come across a friend of Karen's who told him that his ex-wife had remarried and was expecting her first child. That had been the last time he'd felt something like this, and the memory of that revelation ignited the dwindling flames of his melancholy. He took a long sip of red wine in the hope it would douse the fire and wandered into the kitchen for a refill.

When he returned he felt himself viewing the house with a critical eye, everything was how Karen had left it; the furniture, the wallpaper, the accessories, except now after six years it all looked worn and dated in a way that she would never have allowed. Karen had always been such a home bird, but then she had to be.

Even in their honeymoon period it was rare if David's workday consisted of anything less than fourteen hours, and that only increased when they started having problems. It was the house that had kept her content with that life, for a time. David had found early on, earlier than he liked to admit, that married life didn't suit him, marriage to your job meant one wife too many and in retrospect it was always obvious which of his two brides was going to come out on top, it was just the way he was built. He tried not to remember the fights, the tears and the accusations but they filled his head nonetheless, other banished memories came too, none of which he wanted. The worst one that he could not escape, that haunted him to this day, was the simple truth that he loved succeeding more than he had ever loved her.

Sitting down he was almost surprised to realise that he genuinely hoped she'd found contentment in her new home, with her new family. She deserved a better life than the one he could offer her, if there was any kind of justice in the world then she would have found it. Taking another drink he tried to turn his attention back towards the present.

Shuffling papers on the cramped table he located his notes from the previous night, his evening excursions had started promisingly be he was still yet to obtain any truly useful information. The kind of people he was waking, small time dealers and the like, dealt only in rumour, but that was what made them useful. In the world they lived fact was the rarest of all commodities, decisions, deals, even lives rested on the strength or weakness of a rumour. Already word was making its way higher up the food chain that David was making a nuisance of himself and that was exactly how he wanted it. The more they knew about him skulking in the shadows, nipping at their heels, the more likely they would be to make a mistake, and David Walker had every intention of being there when they did. Tomorrow night he would be out amongst them again, making people nervous, getting his face noticed.

He took another gulp of wine and let his head drop onto the back of the couch, his body was preparing another assault to push him towards sleep and he doubted his ability to withstand a second onslaught. Closing his eyes he let the exhaustion take him, tomorrow it would begin all over again and he needed to be ready, that was what he lived for, it was who he was.

And he would not be denied his glory.

Chapter 9

Rob waited patiently in the dark alley, his gaze fixated on the six storey building across the street. He looked at his watch; 5:30. It was the first time in forty five minutes that his eyes had left the main entrance of Buckland, Treadgold & Gardner, and within a second they were back on the large revolving glass doors. In the time he'd been waiting twenty seven people had exited through those doors, but there was still no sign of the one he was waiting for. He was familiar with the company, Buckland, Treadgold & Gardner had a law firm in downtown Manhattan, on a few occasions he'd even heard that the bosses had done business with them, but that was about as much as he knew. As a rule the construction crew weren't briefed on the legal side of the business.

Rob wondered whether it was strange for an American Law Firm to have an office in Britain, he'd never heard of it before, but then why would he? It was hardly his area of expertise. Two more people left the building, a man and a woman both in their early forties, neither was the person he wanted. Rob took a step back, deeper into the alley to reduce his visibility. Darkness had already claimed the early evening sky and streetlights lit the pavement in front of him, but not his alley. He knew he would be invisible to anyone on the other side of the road, even someone glancing in from his side of the street would have to do a double take to confirm there was someone there, and people weren't too eager to look twice at a lone man standing in the dark.

Then it happened; two men pushed their way through the revolving doors out onto the street. The first was a large man who looked like he was probably in his mid-fifties, receding grey hair exposing a large, pale forehead. The man he was speaking to one step behind was younger, probably in his mid-thirties, he wore an expensive grey suit and his dark hair was cut short and styled. Rob squinted to make out the face but the distance was too far in the current light, standing at about 5'10 the man was certainly the right height. Taking a step forward he kept his eyes on the man. They were walking past Rob's alley, but on the other side of the street, Moorfields train station was five minutes away and he had to confirm it before then. As the two men passed Rob's position they stepped under a streetlight that illuminated the man's features. Rob recognised the young looking face immediately, boyishly handsome with those same small, calculating eyes, he pulled up his collar and stepped from the alley, crossing the street he fell in ten paces behind the two men.

Rob walked fast, as fast as he could without drawing too much attention to himself, overtaking a couple of people in the process. Within a few seconds he found himself staring at the two men's backs, able to overhear their conversation, he stopped where he stood and put his hands in his pockets.

"Matthew!" he shouted.

The men kept walking but the younger of the two turned his head, when his eyes settled on Rob they went wide and he stopped in his tracks. For a few seconds the older man kept going, until he realised he was talking to an empty space at his side. Taking a few steps backward he asked his colleague a question Rob couldn't quite make out, he doubted whether its recipient could hear it either, such was the focus with which he was staring at Rob.

"Sorry Frank, old client I need to have a word with, I'll see you tomorrow, ok?" the younger man muttered, his friend gave a quick look at Rob, shrugging his shoulders he continued on his path to the train station.

Tentatively, Matthew took a few steps forward, buttoning up his suit jacket in the process. As he got closer the speed with which he walked seemed to slow, by the time he stood in front of Rob he was moving at a snail's pace.

"Hello, Matthew" Rob said evenly.

Matthew stared back for a few more seconds, Rob was surprised how young the man looked, although they were close to the same age he felt about five years older.

"Fuck" Matthew said eventually "I thought you were dead!"

"I am" Rob replied "I'm done haunting all of the people that I like, so I thought I'd move on to you"

A large grin spread across Matthew's face as he took a step forward and the two men hugged.

"It's great to see you again, Thommo" Matthew said "This place hasn't been the same without you"

"You too mate" Rob replied as the two men disengaged "You too"

The smile on Matt's face had vanished by the time he'd taken a step back, his old friends small eyes were darting along the floor, as if he was trying to put something together in his head. By the time he looked back at Rob his face had tightened and there was concern in his eyes.

"I saw in the paper he just got released" Matt said "and now you're back in town. Is this what I think it is?"

Rob held his gaze for a few seconds before he began to nod "I'm going to need the stuff, Matt".

It took half an hour to reach Matt's place, his home in Maghull was deep in the suburbs of the city and required a twenty five minute train ride followed by a ten minute walk. As walks though Liverpool went it definitely wasn't a bad one; large oak trees covered the pavements of quiet streets and green patches of well-tended grass offered a refreshing contrast to the environment in which Rob was currently living. In the smallest of ways it reminded him of being back in New York. The two men didn't talk much on their journey; it didn't take a genius to see that Matt looked a little shell shocked. On top of that he seemed on edge, Rob didn't like the idea that his oldest friend might be scared of him, but he understood why it might be the case. For his part Rob wasn't too eager to talk either, trying to find the right conversation for a friend he hadn't seen in ten years wasn't what he needed when there were so many distractions swirling around in his brain, but at least it wasn't an awkward silence. Both men seemed content enough with the quiet, as if they feared the conversations they would inevitably need to have.

Eventually they arrived at Matt's home; it was a big place with a large grass lawn that looked bigger than Rob's entire apartment. They stepped through the front door and Matt led him straight up two flights of stairs, when they reached the second floor Rob watched as his host pulled at a rope attached to the ceiling. With a deep thud the set of stairs descended from the roof leading towards the loft.

He followed Matt up the steep wooden steps until they reached the top, the first thing that struck him was the old musky smell, so thick that it was almost overpowering. He took a few awkward strides forward to avoid hitting his head on the ceiling and followed Matt to the corner of the room. His stomach lurched when he spotted the familiar black bag, half hidden by a couple of books and a box of old clothes.

"I'll be honest with you, the first few weeks after you gave it to me I was a paranoid wreck," Matt said with a shaky laugh "Every time I heard a car stop outside I thought it was a police raid, but after a while I forgot it was even up here"

Rob ran a hand over the length of the bag, and took a deep breath to calm his nerves. He had no desire to open the bag, he'd hoped he would never lay eyes on it again, but such hopes had long been abandoned. It was Friday now and they had disappeared on Monday.

"I appreciate you keeping hold of it for me, I don't know what I would have done if you'd said no"

Rob caught a gesture out of the corner of his eye that he took for a shrug of the shoulders "Yeah well" Matt said "What are mates for?"

Composing himself, Rob reached for the zip and pulled the bag open. Pushing the sides of the bag apart so he could see within he surveyed the items; a kevlar vest, two silencers, a pair of binoculars, a baseball cap and two Smith & Weston 1911 pistols with patchmayr grips. Rob's heart began to race as his eyes settled on the two jet black guns with the golden trim. Tentatively, he reached into the bag and lifted one of the weapons. It was heavier than he remembered but at the same time it fitted into his hand naturally, like an appendage that had been severed and then somehow reattached. Rob pressed the side of the gun against his forehead and exhaled a long breath as the memories of what he had done with that piece of metal came flooding back. He saw the faces of every person he had killed with it, the terrified looks of so many men, staring back at him in their final seconds, with nothing more than the simple piece of black metal between them. Reaching into the bag Rob took the other Smith & Weston and held them outwards either side of him, feeling the balance on each of his arms. He thought he heard Matt take a step backwards but the emotions that were flooding his head didn't leave room for him to be sure.

The guns had been a gift, from Stephen McSharry of all people, imported from the States as a reward for his first hit, Rob didn't like to remember that. The guns had been a part of him, no matter how hard he fought it he knew somewhere inside they would always be a part of him, he had done too much with those two pistols for them to not occupy some place of importance deep within his very being. The guns were part of him because they defined him, he hated them much like he hated himself but at the same time he loved them, he was one with them. The guns were simply agents of his will, and no matter what he told himself on many of those occasions his will wasn't simply to follow orders, it was to kill. As he moved the weapons in his hands he was amazed at how natural it felt, had it always felt this right or had ten years of absence made his body crave the very thing that his mind would never condone?

It was idiotic to keep using the same guns over and over again, if the police ever caught him the ballistics alone would be enough to put him away for a hundred years. The smart move was to use and dispose, minimise the evidence and avoid slipping into a pattern, but in a city like Liverpool going through that many weapons would eventually attract attention. Besides which the two Smith and Weston's meant too much to him, like a married couple who'd shared so much history they were one, for better or for worse.

Rob shook himself from the daze and placed the two pistols back in the bag. He pushed the vest aside to confirm there was enough ammunition in the bag, there was. He saw enough clips for fifteen hits, two wouldn't be any kind of a problem.

"I really thought I was done with this" Rob said, he wasn't sure whether he was talking to Matt or the bag.

"So be done with it" Matt said bluntly, there was still a nervousness in his voice "Put the bag down and leave, you don't have to go back to all this Thommo"

Rob reached inside and fingered the Kevlar vest. He'd worn it for every hit and yet it had never been punctured by a single bullet, no one had ever been fast enough to hit him. Suddenly he felt very slow, and very old.

"And what would you suggest Matt? Leave, let them kill Charlie and my mum?" Rob was getting tired of having this conversation, with Jo, with Matt, with himself.

"They can leave with you" Matt said, it was easy for him to suggest this, he was completely off their radar, Rob had made sure of that.

"Can you see Vera or Charlie leaving Liverpool?" Rob said with a laugh that was void of humour "They're scouse to the core, leaving here for them would mean death all the same, just much slower"

He heard Matt sigh but Rob's eyes were still focused on the bag, he couldn't take his eyes off it.

"All I know is I remember what it was like before, I remember you" Matt said angrily.

"I don't know what you mean" Rob said only half listening.

"Morose, coked out of your head, I don't think I saw you sober for six months before you left. Walking around in a daze of death, drugs and god knows what else, and what you did to poor Kelly. Do you know how hard that was for her, watching you destroy yourself like that, dragging her deeper and deeper with you. You fucking nearly ruined that girl"

For a second Rob's focus on the bag wavered, he blinked and turned to face Matt.

"I didn't want that, I didn't want any of it, you know I didn't. It just all got so fucking... I don't know..." Rob's gaze was back on the bag now, he was staring at the guns, and in a strange way he felt that the guns were staring back.

"Chaotic?" Matt suggested, there was sympathy in his voice that hadn't been there before "This place was chaos, with the murders and the vendettas and the blood feuds. This city was in chaos, and these sadistic manipulative bastards put you right in the middle of it. You absorbed more than you should, because you're a good lad" Rob felt Matt's hand on his shoulder "Come on, let's go down the pub and forget all this shit, it'll keep until the morning!"

Rob tore his eyes away from the bag and stood as much as he could under the sloping roof. "The pub? You buying?"

Matt's local was situated at the end of the street. It had the feel of typical English country pub, the kind of place Rob hadn't even realised he missed until he stepped through the door. The patrons ranged from teenagers in tracksuits to old age pensioners, but they seemed to coexist amicably enough. Rob followed Matt to the bar and became aware of the fact that his friend was still wearing his expensive suit, it made him feel a little underdressed in jeans and a t-shirt. Matt ordered two pints of larger and the two men took a table in the corner of the pub out of earshot of the other customers. The first mouthful of lager felt good, the adrenaline from seeing his old guns was beginning to wear off and in its place he could feel a headache coming on.

"So, where've you been hiding all this time?" Matt asked.

"New York City" Rob said while he surveyed the room for trouble. Most of the time he didn't even realise he was doing it, but after the episode at

Matt's house he was suddenly very aware of every action he made.

Matt whistled between his teeth "Not a bad place to go into exile, lucky you weren't a communist, the best Trotsky ever got was Kazakhstan"

Rob smiled, Matt had always been the academic type, even when they first met back in high school. They both came from the same kind of working class, catholic families but their lives had taken very different courses. Rob had joined the army at sixteen while Matt had gone to college and then to university to get his law degree. They had always stayed close though, no matter where their paths took them, at least until he left. By then it was just too dangerous to have friends.

"Trotsky didn't work construction with his uncle for four summers" Rob said, glancing at the bag under the table. He'd decided to bring it with him, whatever surprises came his way it couldn't hurt to be prepared.

"You got into construction?"

"Yeah"

"Under the table?"

Rob took another sip of lager and nodded "Yeah, it's actually easier than you'd think. Go to the right bars, talk to the right people, there are always jobs that'll need to be done off the books, it's just about being in the right place at the right time"

"Well, you always had a skill for that" Matt said. Rob wondered whether he was being sarcastic, being in the wrong place at the wrong time had been responsible for his current plight, but Matt could have been talking about any one of a hundred different memories from when they were growing up. These days he was finding it difficult to focus on anything but McSharry and the road that led him there. He had to remind himself that it wasn't always the case for everybody else.

"What about you, Matthew?" Rob asked, trying to push such thoughts from his mind "the big time barrister for the international law firm? When I left you were giving free legal aid to those less fortunate, what the hell happened?"

Matt leaned back in his chair and adjusted his tie, Rob thought he caught a hint of embarrassment flicker across his old friends face "You know how it is mate, sold out didn't I? There's only so long you can resist the lure of the Yankee dollar. The money's good but it's not as glamorous as I thought it would be, cutting deals and filling in paper work takes up most of my days" Matt reached for his drink and Rob saw the same look flash across his face, at the second glance he realised it wasn't embarrassment, it was disenchantment "That's the easy part, spending the rest of your time defending people you know to be guilty definitely has its.." Matt paused as he searched for the right words "Moral pitfalls"

"So does killing people!" Rob said with a sympathetic smile.

"Between us we've got quite the warped sense of civic duty haven't we? How proud do you think our old teachers would be if they could see us now?"

"Pretty proud" Rob said with a laugh, Matt was laughing too but there was a sadness to his eyes that Rob suspected was mirrored in his own, he took another long look around the room "You know what's worrying, I've only been back in Liverpool for four days and already it's starting to feel like I never left"

Matt gave a nod, the sadness remained in his eyes but they took on a more pensive look "It's your home Thommo, there'll always be a place for you here, whether you want it or not"

"McSharry wants me to kill Wayne Caddock and Tony Miller" Rob said, suddenly blurting it out. He hadn't intended to bring the details up, the less Matt knew the safer he would be, but it had just felt like the natural thing to do. There weren't many people Rob could talk to openly about that part of his life and the words tumbled out of him as if afraid the opportunity would disappear before he had the chance to say them. "That will make two generations of those families I'll have wiped out, can you imagine what kind of damage that will do to their wives, to their kids for god's sake!"

Matt let out a sigh and leaned forward in his chair, in that instant he had the look of a lawyer who was counselling his client, like a man had gone through this kind of thing a million times before. Rob thought with a shudder that his current predicament could very well lead him to that exact scenario. He wondered how good Matt was, and whether he would be able to afford him.

"It's not worth doing this to yourself mate, it'll be the end of you if you keep going over it in your head. You remember how we used to solve our problems in the old days? You've got the weekend off from the base, my student loans just come in, there didn't used to be problem in the world that we couldn't solve in the pub. They say the old solutions are the best solutions!" Matt was smiling but Rob could tell that it was only for his benefit. He tried to muster up the good will to smile back.

"Sounds good" Rob replied, lightly nodding his head, Matt slapped his hands on the table and made his way towards the bar.

While he waited for Matt to return Rob kept one eye on the rest of the pub. No one seemed to be watching them, but that may just have meant that if someone was, they were very good. Rob shook his head, whenever he found himself alone lately his mind always went back to the question of whether or not he was being followed. He was fairly sure that he wasn't, every time he left the flat he was being extra careful, often diverting great distances to ensure he didn't have a tail, but ten years of inaction made him nervous, maybe he was just an easy target now. He tried to suppress the feeling of dread in his chest. If he was being followed then just being in the pub together put Matt in all kinds of danger, danger that he'd tried so hard to keep off his friend's doorstep. Rob drank the remnants of his pint and told himself he was being paranoid. He'd been careful, extra careful. If McSharry was having him followed then there was no way he could have kept up without Rob noticing, and who was to say that he was even important enough to be followed. To McSharry Rob was just a tool, a means to an end, and nothing more. If he succeeded in killing the two men then all the better, but if he didn't, well there were a hundred other guys who could take Rob's place. It also hadn't escaped his attention that should he die there would be no way to link him back to the old man even if people did have their suspicions.

A coarse laugh came from the other side of the room, breaking Rob's concentration. A group of middle aged women sat with a collection of wine bottles in the middle of their table making increasing amounts of noise. Rob noticed a number of other patrons eyeing the women with disdain, he wondered what those people would think if they knew the kind of things Rob had done, and was about to do. But that was the funny thing about most people, they didn't mind what you got up to, just so long as you were subtle about it.

He looked up and caught sight of Matt making his way across the room. He passed the table of middle aged women and raised an eyebrow in Rob's direction just as another chorus of laughter filled the pub. As Matt got closer Rob vowed to make more of an effort to keep his thoughts off the job, he hadn't seen his old friend for so long and he was determined not to waste it.

"So, Matt" he said as his friend sat down "Nice house, fancy suit, your own little slice of suburban paradise. It sounds like you've got this thirty-something life down to a tee, where are the wife and kids to finish it off?"

Matt let out a laugh that implied the suggestion was too absurd to be taken seriously. He waited a few seconds to see if Rob actually expected an answer before he gave one "Not for me matey, commitment never sat well on these shoulders, I'm more the free and easy type. What about you? Got yourself a family back in NYC?"

Rob shook his head "No, just a girl"

"She special?" Matt asked.

"Very" Rob told him as a picture of Jo appeared in his mind. He'd spoken to her twice since he'd been back in Liverpool, but on both occasions it hadn't really felt right. Rob was remiss to tell her too much about what he had to do, particularly over the phone, and she seemed to take that as a sign of distrust. He got the impression that she spent half of her time worrying about him to the point of making herself ill, the other half being angry at him for leaving. Regardless of which half was driving her when they spoke it was still impossible for them to click and talk like they normally would. That frustrated Rob most of all, the one thing he needed more than anything else was to be able to listen to Jo talk to him like she usually would, he could forget all of his problems if the chemistry was right between the two of them, but he had no idea how to make that happen.

"Good lad, good lad" Matt said before pausing, a look of hesitation flashed across his face "Listen, I'm not sure if I should be telling you this, after so long I don't even know if it matters, but maybe I should..." Matt trailed off as if he was having second thoughts about whatever it was he was going to say.

"What is it?" Rob asked, suddenly he was alert, had McSharry's men made contact with him, did they know about Matt, about where he'd kept the guns?

"I was in town the other week, just doing some shopping. Anyway before I knew it I was face to face with... I bumped into Kelly, she told me where she was living, I thought, you know, you might want to pop round there or something?"

Rob felt his face flush, he had thought about Kelly a few times since coming home, but whenever he did he quickly banished the idea from his head. She was probably married by now, husband and kids, the whole nine yards, and seeing her again would just drag up memories that were best left to rest.

"Kelly? No I don't think so mate" Rob said, trying to sound casual "Better to let sleeping dogs lie and all that"

Matt gave a shrug of his shoulders "Fair enough"

Rob thought about what Matt had said earlier, about how he had almost destroyed Kelly before he left. His goodbye to her had been brief, he hadn't even told her he was leaving town, just that it was over for both of their sakes, and then he had gone. She hadn't even had time to shed a tear, he heard her voice calling him as he got back in the car, a voice that had more than a hint of desperation in it, but that was all he had to remember. His childhood sweetheart, on and off again for eight years and that was how it ended. Rob cringed as memories flooded his head of how he had treated her. Thousands of pounds worth of cocaine had made him a monster of a boyfriend, it had shielded him from the pain of killing but it hadn't shielded her from his moods, from his temper, from his cruel tongue. They were memories Rob had fought hard to repress but as they came forward they made him question who he was. He held the picture up in his mind of being coked to high heaven, yelling at Kelly for some stupid petty reason and smashing up half the kitchen while she yelled back, then he set it next to his memories of Jo, a quiet happy life of love and contentment. The two memories contrasted one another to such a degree that even Rob couldn't believe it was the same person. He owed Kelly an apology, but it was more than that, for his own sake he wanted to show her that he had changed, that leaving was the best thing for both of them and that he wasn't the bastard that she almost certainly remembered.

"Actually mate, you know what, give me the address"

"Yeah? You sure?" Matt asked hesitantly.

"Yes"

"38 Church Road West" Matt said "Just off County Road"

Rob knew the street, for a time he had drank round that area, he didn't remember it being a particularly pleasant place.

"Next to the Black Horse? It used to be a bit rough round that way" Rob said

"Still is" Matt replied taking another sip of lager and turning round to glare at the table of cackling middle aged women, Rob was waiting for him when he turned back round.

"So how is she doing? Did she seem different?"

"She's...you know Thommo, it's been ten years, a lots changed, we're all pretty different. Don't expect it to be the same girl you left behind"

"Yeah, I guess" Rob said, trying not to remember her how he did, young, beautiful, five foot three with light brown hair and big blue eyes. Ten years had altered them all, it would be foolish to expect the twenty three year old he left behind "Do you think it's a mistake, seeing her again?"

I don't think so, no" Matt said after a seconds hesitation "After all you went through why wouldn't you want to see her again, anyway who knows the next time you'll be back, right?"

Rob took another sip of lager and looked around the room, if all things went to plan, never. But then when did things ever go to plan.

Chapter 10

Charlie pressed his hands against his ears, desperate to block out the noise for just a few seconds. It didn't work, he scrunched up his eyes and took a deep breath, that didn't work either. When he opened them again and let his arms drop to his sides he was greeted by the same high pitched sounds; Vicky yelling and the baby screaming.

He leaned back on the couch and stared at his wife, his brain was still half asleep and he desperately tried to assemble his thoughts into some kind of logical order. She seemed to have paused her tirade, at least that was something.

Zoe rocked back and forth in her mother's arms, eventually the screams turned into cries, and not long after that they downgraded to moans. He watched Vicky as she cradled their baby girl; every movement she made was full of motherly affection. Not her eyes though, they were trained exclusively on Charlie and projected nothing more than undiluted anger.

"For Christ's sake Charlie" she whispered, anxiously glancing at the bundle in her arms "I ask you to do one thing, one fucking thing"

There was hatred in her voice, so much of it that she sounded like she might be on the verge of tears. Charlie stifled the yawn was slowly creeping up his throat, it would only get him into more trouble and the way it stood he was in the dog house for the long haul anyway. She'd left him an hour ago to pick up Alexis from her mothers, even then her mood hadn't been the best, it never was these days. He gaged it as being somewhere in the 'icy-hostile' region, when she went out he'd been happy for the peace. The previous night on the town had been a heavy one and his body was still recovering from the narcotics cocktail that was working its way through his system. It was around that point that his evening had gone to shit; Vicky asked him to feed Zoe while she was out, but his weary mind had fallen asleep before the door had closed behind her, and trouble had started to brew from there.

The next thing he knew she was standing over him with the baby in her arms, each of them screaming at the top of their lungs; mother and daughter united in trying to make his come down as painful as possible.

"Look, I forgot alright? I said I'm sorry" he stood up and extended his arms to take Zoe "I'll do it now"

Vicky took a step back and motioned him away with a flick of her head "Don't fucking bother I may as well do it myself" she was still rocking the baby as she spoke "How the hell didn't you hear her crying?"

Charlie sat back down on the couch. He hadn't seen Alexis since Vicky had brought her home, but the creak of the floorboards above told him she was upstairs. He tried to lower his voice, he hated fighting with Vicky when his daughter could hear, it reminded him too much of his own childhood.

"Cos I didn't, I was asleep, I've been knackered all week" Charlie told her, he couldn't keep the irritation out of his voice, it seemed like all he did these days was defend himself "you're not the only one who works hard around here you know, do you think the bills just pay themselves?"

Vicky gave a harsh laugh and shook her head, the trip to her mother's house had given her cause to make a bit of an effort. Her hair was combed and she was wearing a bit of make-up, a rarity in itself these days. She wore a top that showed off her breasts but the puppy fat still clung to her face and her hips. Charlie found himself thinking about Steph.

"Don't even try and swing that one with me Charlie, I know what you do to make your money, and working hard doesn't come into it"

Charlie recognised the familiar wave of indignation, provoked by his wife's dismissive tone. He tried to keep it in check, for the sake of Alexis, when he spoke it was through gritted teeth "I don't hear you complaining when you're spending it"

When Vicky looked at him she did so with such contempt that Charlie thought she was about to reach out and slap him, if she hadn't been holding Zoe maybe she would have.

She looked down at the baby in her arms and then back at Charlie, as if debating which of the two were going to influence her mood. Eventually her eyes settled on her husband while she continued to gently rock the baby.

"That's neither here or there. I asked you to do one thing; feed your daughter and you even managed to fuck that up. I swear to god Charlie, sometimes I can't believe just how worthless you can be"

When she spoke her voice was slower and more methodical than it had been before, all that confirmed was that she meant what she was saying. The heat of the moment wasn't influencing those words, they came from the heart.

Charlie stood up, the physical action served to keep him from shouting. He paced the length of the small living room, dodging the toys scattered across the floor "Worthless?" he said, emphasising the word "Why don't you try feeding yourself for a week, then we'll see how worthless I am!"

Vicky's eyes widened, she looked stunned, but then that had always been the case with his wife; if she needed to be silenced money was always the card to play. Slowly, the disbelieving look made way to an angrier one, Charlie kept his eyes moving around the room, he had no desire to meet that gaze.

"You'd actually do that, wouldn't you?" she asked incredulously "You'd starve your own children just to make a point?"

Charlie didn't like where she was leading him, she had a way of turning his words against him so that he always looked like the bad guy. Resentment built in his chest, he tried to compose himself but he could feel his self-control waning.

"They're you're kids too, if you don't want them to stave then why don't you get off your fat arse and find yourself a job. Maybe then you wouldn't spend all day thinking about all the ways I've let you down"

He recognised the hurt look instantly, for the briefest of seconds he regretted calling her fat, but then her face hardened and the look of contempt returned to her eyes. Charlie suddenly wished he'd said something worse.

"You're not letting me down, Charlie" she said, the methodical tone of voice was at odds with the fierce look in her eyes, he wondered whether she was speaking the way she was for the sake of the baby "You're letting your kids down, you're letting yourself down. You're the one who has to live with being a bad father"

Charlie felt something snap inside him, he paid the bills, he looked after his family and this was how he got to spend his Friday night, when he could have been out having a laugh with his mates. Taking a couple of quick strides he grabbed a jacket from the back of a chair, muttering "Yeah, whatever" as he moved.

"Where are you going?" Vicky demanded, there was shock in her voice.

"Work" Charlie said, reaching into the pockets of his coat to make sure the few grams of coke and a bag of pills were still inside, they were "someone has to feed you and the kids"

"You can't go out" Vicky shouted, all pretensions of civility had left her voice for good, Zoe stirred at the increase in noise "I still need to bath both of the kids and feed Zoe, how am I supposed to do that all by myself?"

Suddenly Vicky's shoulders sagged, her eyes imploring him to compromise. In that moment his wife looked vulnerable, almost defeated. Charlie looked at her for a second, maybe in different circumstances he'd have felt sorry for her, but after the things she'd said he took nothing but pleasure from her dejection. "I'm worthless, remember?" he told her, hearing the smugness in his own voice "I'm sure it'll be easier with me out the way"

Charlie brushed passed her and made his way into the hallway, as he reached for the front door he heard her voice behind him, there was no anger in it now, just sorrow.

"You're a bastard Charlie, a real fucking bastard"

Charlie looked around and saw her standing at the other end of the hallway; Zoe made a few unhappy moans as Vicky continued to gently rock her back and forth.

He opened the door and looked back at her one more time. Behind her at the top of the stairs he saw Alexis peeking her head around the banister, trying not be noticed. He held her gaze for a second and gave her a wink before focusing back on his wife.

"Watch your mouth will you, I don't want my daughters growing up sounding like a couple of cheap tramps. It's bad enough they're being raised by one"

Before she had time to respond he'd stepped out onto the street and closed the door behind him. He took his phone out of his pocket and looked at the time; 8:30 on a Friday night. He tried to put his wife out of his thoughts, there was plenty of fun left to be had tonight and he had no intention of letting her ruin it.

Charlie tore his eyes away from the crowded room to check the time; it was 10:00, and already he'd made a hundred and fifty quid. The *Stag and Bull* was busy, but then it always was on a Friday night. Scattered amongst the crowds were old men, grouped in twos and threes with pints of bitter in their hands. Charlie knew from experience that a visit to the old pub on a Sunday, Thursday or any night in between would guarantee those same elderly men and little else. Yet come Friday and Saturday the *Stag and Bull* served as the ideal watering hole for locals under the age of thirty, stopping by for a few drinks before making their way into town, where whatever debauchery they craved awaited them.

Charlie watched a few of the old men, eyeing their young invaders suspiciously and muttering under their breath about today's misguided youth. Charlie noted, with a smile, that their condemnation extended only as far as the men, when it came to the girls in their slutty little dresses, the old geezers seemed willing enough to tolerate their presence.

His eyes took in another quick survey of the room, he was careful these days, more careful than he used to be. The busies had nicked two guys he knew in the past eighteen months, possession with intent had been the charge on both occasions, and he had no intention of completing the hatrick. Charlie took the crowd in, they seemed normal enough. Groups of young men crowded around the pool tables and fruit machines that took up half of the room. On the other side of the pub girls in miniskirts sat at wobbly, wooden tables seeing off bottle after bottle of rose wine. Charlie for his part felt pretty inconspicuous amongst the crowd, on a few occasions he found eyes settling on him from across the room, but only from people who had bought from him before. He knew those people well enough to be able to trust them, to a point.

The old pub hadn't changed in fifteen years, which was one of the major reasons why he kept coming back. The entire decor screamed nineteen-eighties, from the worn pool tables and outdated, dark green wallpaper, to the rustic bar and substandard bathrooms. In fact, if it wasn't for the three flat screen TVs that were scattered across the room it would be difficult to tell that twenty years had passed since the pub first opened. Despite its decadence, the pub always seemed perfectly suited to the young people who occupied it. If it had been located in the city centre then Charlie had no doubt that the smartly dressed twentysomethings currently residing inside would avoid it like the plague, but because it was their local they just accepted its faults until they didn't see them anymore. People would accept all kinds of shit so long as it was part of their routine, Charlie suspected it was

127

that metaphor which kept him coming back to the old place time and time again.

He was stood at the bar with two of his more consistent customers. Benny and Glen never missed a weekend on the town and they were always looking for a couple of class A's to take the night up that extra gear. It was easy money as far as Charlie was concerned, getting himself to the *Stag and Bull* between 9:00 and 11:00 on a Friday or Saturday almost always meant a hundred quid of theirs in his back pocket. On top of which they were both top lads to hang out with. It was a habit of Charlie's to always do a couple of lines with the guys he was selling to, though his body was still recovering from the night before he managed to push through and keep up with them line for line. He sipped at the pint they'd bought him and spared a thought for the next day's hangover.

As he put the glass back down on the bar Charlie noticed the landlady eyeing him suspiciously. It wasn't a new occurrence; she'd been giving him that same look every time he came in for the past five months. So far tonight she'd saved her sharpest looks for when the three men returned suitably buzzed from the toilet, paying particular attention, Charlie noted, to him. Since then he'd made a special effort to order plenty of drinks and tipped heavily whenever she'd served him. It did nothing to thaw the frosty look, but he hoped it would be enough to keep her from taking any further action.

Flashing his best innocent smile, which admittedly wasn't very convincing, Charlie excused himself and made his way outside. A few smokers stood huddled in the cold, indulging in their own drug addictions which were becoming as strictly admonished by the government as his own. Taking the phone from his pocket he dialled Rob's number, padding his pocket to make sure the remainder of his stash was still there. The call went straight to voicemail and Charlie hung up before the beep. He hadn't heard from his brother in two days, ever since the meeting that had culminated in Rob walking home in a mood.

As the night had improved and he'd made a bit more money the idea of getting his brother down the pub had been building momentum. A couple of pints and a bit of a laugh sounded like just the thing Rob needed to sort him out, but wherever he was he obviously didn't want to be disturbed. Sliding the mobile phone into his coat, Charlie stepped back inside the *Stag and Bull*.

He returned to the two men who were propped against the bar deep in conversation. Glen was the taller of the two, although he was in his early thirties the grey head of hair made him look a few years older. Benny was shorter than his mate, though he was of Asian descent Charlie had never pried into the specifics. He sounded like a scouser so he was a scouser, at least that was how Charlie saw it. They were both about the same age, and wore a similar style of shirt, though Glen's was black and Benny's was blue.

"Alright lar, thought you might have fucked off on us" Benny said to him as he picked up his pint "Glen was starting to get worried he'd have to talk to the birds with nothing but lager in his stomach"

"Don't worry, lad" Charlie replied, aiming his response at Glen "I wouldn't let you go and do something that stupid, we'll make sure you're bouncing off the walls by the time you start breaking out those shapes"

The two men grinned, Glen was a good bloke but he wasn't the sharpest knife in the draw, and his inefficiency with the women was legendary. Charlie might have felt sorry for the guy if watching him get rejected wasn't so funny.

"I did alright last weekend" Glen said in a disgruntled tone "Got well close to this one bird, managed to get her tits out in the club and everything"

"That was a strip club, soft lad!" Charlie said, Benny gave a loud chuckle, drowning out Glen's grunts of denial.

Benny gave a casual look around the bar and then turned his attention back to the others, he had the look of a coke fiend gagging for another couple of lines, but before he could speak a shout came from somewhere behind him that grabbed the attention of all three men.

"There's my fella!"

Charlie spun around and saw Steph sauntering towards him. Within seconds he'd caught sight of at least four pairs of eyes watching her cross the room. He forced himself to stifle the pangs of jealousy that erupted in his head. When he looked back at her all such thoughts disappeared from his mind. She was wearing a tight fitting green dress that clung to her body in all the right places, her long legs seemed to move in slow motion as they made their way towards him. After what seemed like an eternity she reached him, wrapped her arms around his neck and slid her tongue into his mouth.

"Alright sweetness, I didn't know you were out tonight" Charlie said, releasing her from the embrace.

"It's my night out with the girls, I told you about it the other night" Steph said, an expectant look on her face.

For the first time he realised that she wasn't alone, standing behind her where two of her best mates, whose names had long since slipped from his mind. He nodded in the direction of the two, one was blond, the other brunette. Looking them over he noticed they were wearing dresses as revealing as Steph's, but not receiving anywhere near the same amount of attention. Charlie wasn't surprised, they were good looking women and all, no question about it, but when they stood next to Steph it was like trying to appreciate the beauty of a new Range Rover when it was parked next to an Aston Martin.

Before Charlie had a chance to respond he heard Benny's voice from over his shoulder offering to buy the girls a drink. The brunette's eyes lit up at the very suggestion, but Charlie noticed the blonde's seemed to be focused in on him. He smiled; she reciprocated with her own bashful grin before following her friend to the bar. Steph was rummaging through her bag and missed the exchange, it was probably best, he didn't know what it meant but he imagined she would have some pretty strong ideas.

Taking Steph to one side Charlie looked back towards the bar, Benny already had his claws into the brunette who was laughing along to every other word he said. The blond was talking politely to Glen but every couple of seconds her gaze flickered over to Charlie. Taking a deep breath he looked down at Steph, even in heels she was a good five inches shorter than him.

"Jesus love, you take it up a gear when you doll yourself up, don't you?"

She blushed, ever so slightly, she was used to compliments but every now and then he could still embarrass her.

"Thanks. Is that what you brought me over here to tell me?"

Charlie looked down at the floor, he'd been thinking about what he was about to say for the last few weeks, but even more so after his interaction with Vicky earlier that night. For a second he questioned whether the coke and alcohol in his system was making him bolder than usual, but dismissed it out of hand. This was something he wanted to do, that he'd wanted for a long time. Hesitantly he cleared his throat.

"Listen love, I know we've talked about moving into our own place for a while now, and it always gets put on the backburner, but it's starting to feel really right, I think we should do it, like in the next couple of weeks, what do you reckon? You fancy moving in with me?"

Charlie caught the twitch of her mouth as she stifled a smile, but her eyes had an inquisitive look. She tilted her head to the side as she looked at him, as if it would help her efforts to figure him out.

"What about your kids?" she asked "You always said you couldn't stand being away from them?"

"It'll be hard" he agreed, preparing the line he'd been rehearsing most of the night "But not as hard as living without you"

As soon as she smiled Charlie knew that her mind was made up, it was a smile of such complete affection he was almost surprised that she was capable of it. Leaning in she gave him a long passionate kiss, though it felt like a second it must have lasted for at least five minutes. She was still smiling as they pulled apart, brushing a strand of curled blond hair away from her face.

"I'd love to move in with you" she said.

Hand in hand they walked towards the bar, the half full pint glass he'd been drinking earlier sat where he left it, but he pushed it to one side and ordered a new one. In his line of work he knew better than most about the kind of shit people could put into your drink when you weren't looking.

Once he'd paid for their drinks they headed towards a booth in the corner where Benny, Glen and the girls were already downing a couple of shots. He clocked Benny's hand on the brunette's thigh in double quick time, from what he could see she seemed quite happy to let it stay there. After a few minutes of conversation the three men went to the toilets for another line.

"She's a bit of alright that Yvonne bird isn't she?" Benny said, taking his house key, dipping into the bag and drawing it up to his nose. Charlie did a line himself before responding, he could only assume that Yvonne was the brunette, he still hadn't thought to ask Steph.

"Yeah lad, she's tasty" Charlie replied, running a finger over his nostrils and licking the contents clean. Glen had been at the urinal for the duration of the conversation, once he was done he re-joined them, snorted a line before the three of them returned to the girls.

The pub was slowly starting to empty out as people made their way into town. Charlie sold a couple more pills to a few of his regulars and two more grams of coke, which made him another eighty quid in total. Since he was feeling generous he gave Steph the remainder of his coke to share out with her mates. Evidently she wasn't feeling quite as charitable; for every line her mates saw she was nailing another three on her own.

As he watched a girl in tight jeans leave the pub his eyes made contact with a young lad walking through the same door. The youngster halted in his tracks when he caught Charlie's eye, not sure whether to go on or turn back the way he came. After a few seconds of indecision he swallowed hard and stepped over the threshold, taking a place at the bar. Charlie knew the lad well enough; Ross McIntyre, a local runt who was about as sure to fail in life as anyone ever was. He must have only been about twenty, but already he had a reputation around the locals for being a down and out loser.

Only a few weeks earlier Charlie had been drinking in the *Blue Bell*, where the barmaid told him how the kid waited around until last orders and drank the dregs of pints that people left behind. Charlie had never liked him, but against his better judgement he'd sold the little tit three grams of coke, it was a hundred pound he was yet to see four weeks later. He stared at Ross for a few seconds, the runt knew Charlie was glaring at him, but he tried to pretend like he didn't. Just looking at the guy made Charlie angry, his blonde hair was ragged and looked like it had been cut with a pair of hedge clippers, while his t shirt and jeans were both three sizes too big. Finishing off the remainder of his pint Charlie stood up and walked towards his client.

With every step he felt himself getting more and more pissed off, after only a few paces he had to clench his fist just to keep himself under control. It wasn't that he hadn't been paid the money, it was the insult. The little dickhead knew Charlie dealt in the pub, and unless he was a borderline retard he must have considered the possibility that Charlie might be working on a Friday night. Yet here he was, standing at the bar without a care in the world, while Charlie sat in the corner a hundred quid light. He wondered whether or not it was an intentional slight, was the little runt trying to make a point? Was he trying to tell people that he didn't respect Charlie Thomas enough to pay him back on time? Was he trying to embarrass Charlie in front of his girl? As he got to within a few feet of Ross McIntyre the possibilities were swirling around inside his head and he didn't know which one was the truth, but he knew they all reeked of disrespect. Whoever the git thought he was he was going to find out that Charlie Thomas was no mug; he *would* get his money back.

A few seconds later and he was staring at Ross McIntyre's back. He threw his right hand into the runts shoulder, pushing him forward into the bar. The kid's ribs smashed against the wooden frame as he keeled over. He heard the air rush out of McIntyre's lungs, but his body was only bent for a moment. He bounced straight back up and turned to face Charlie, there was fear on the kids face as he tried to pretend like it hadn't hurt. He only held Charlie's gaze for a second before his eyes moved towards the floor.

"Alright Charlie, mate" Ross said, scratching his head. The casual words were at odds with his trembling voice "how you doing?"

Charlie moved forward until Ross's face was inches away from his own. Sweat filled his nostrils and he caught the scent of stale beer on the kid's' breath, but the eyes remained glued to the floor, refusing to meet Charlie's.

"Don't fucking mate me you little twat" he glared at Ross, projecting every ounce of anger that was filling his head "where's my money?"

Finally Ross' eyes lifted from the stained carpet and looked at Charlie, he wet his lips, Charlie wasn't sure if he had the courage to speak.

"Listen mate, if I could just get a little more time-"

Charlie cut him off before he had a chance to continue "More time?" he said in disbelief "We said two weeks, it's been four. I don't know what fucking game you're playing but I want my money and I want it now. You push me any further I might decide to split your little head right open"

Charlie was surprised by the words that fired out of his mouth, he felt fuelled by the righteous anger that coursed through his veins. It was a good feeling, and he enjoyed watching the skinny little kid shrink back before him.

"I'm not playing any games lad, swear down" Ross stammered, he was looking around the bar in the hope that someone would help him out, but no one seemed to be paying the two men any attention "It's just... I just got binned from my job the other week; I've got nothing at all coming in"

"Not my problem" Charlie said bluntly, shaking his head from side to side.

"Mate, I've got nothing, I can't even afford to buy food right now" there was a desperation in Ross's manner, his voice was going higher and Charlie caught a couple of heads turning towards them to see what was happening.

"But you can afford to be in the pub on a Friday night, you cheeky little shit" during the course of their conversation Ross had taken two steps back, but Charlie pressed forward again, the kid was more nervous when Charlie was close, and that was how he wanted to keep it "are you trying to embarrass me?"

"Nah Charlie, course not" Ross protested, he was looking at the floor again and rubbing his nose. Charlie clenched his fists even tighter, he fought the urge to hit the little shit right then and there.

"How much have you got on you, right now?" he asked.

The question brought Ross's eyes back up to meet his, there was a look of confusion on his face, like he didn't understand the question. McIntyre was either stoned or pissed but either way he wasn't all there.

"What?"

Charlie pushed him hard in the chest and watched him stumble backwards, he heard a few gasps around the pub and felt a whole host of eyes upon him but he pressed on, resuming his proximity to the kid.

"How much money are you carrying right now? Come on, get your wallet out" Charlie demanded.

"Charlie lad, don't do this" Ross pleaded, from the look in his eyes Charlie thought the kid might cry at any second. The weakness only spurred him on, he'd been insulted and an example had to be made.

"Get your fucking wallet out, now!" Charlie growled, giving him another push in the chest and following the runt as he stumbled backwards.

Ross reached into his pocket and fumbled around inside, a few moments passed as he tried to find what he was looking for. With a look of relief that lasted for the briefest of moments he pulled the wallet from his pocket and handed it to Charlie.

He opened the leather wallet, with his eyes firmly on Ross his hand delved in and searched for reparations, only when he felt the familiar texture of notes did his eyes move down. Charlie pulled three twenty pound notes out and held them in front of Ross's face.

"Sixty quid? You stand here telling me you've got nothing and you're coming into the pub on a Friday night with sixty quid? You've got some fucking nerve you have, lad"

Charlie could hear his voice reverberating around the pub, it had already quietened down significantly from the earlier peak, but he knew that the people who remained were watching his exchange with Ross in silence. He could only assume that Steph was watching him as well, though she was somewhere behind him so he couldn't be sure. Ever so slightly Charlie puffed up his chest, eager to show his woman how much of a force her man could be.

"Come on Charlie, that's got to last me for the whole of next week" Ross pleaded, he was trembling now, and Charlie wondered whether all the eyeballs that were focused on the two of them were making the runt even more nervous. Being embarrassed was one thing, but having it done in front a room full of people would make it ten times worse, not that Charlie felt any remorse, he was too far along to cut the wanker any slack. He had him on the ropes and it was time to finish the little shit off. He lifted the three twenty pound notes, folded them in half and slid the money into his pocket.

"Well not anymore" Charlie said firmly, he thought he saw a tear appear in Ross's eye but he couldn't be sure "That's sixty, if I see you in this pub, or any other before I get the rest of my money I'll beat the fucking shit out of you"

Ross gave a nod of his head and Charlie threw the empty wallet over the kid's shoulder, it landed a few feet from the door.

"On your way, you little prick" Charlie said.

Ross stood where he was for a few seconds, almost afraid to move. He glanced around the room, Charlie thought for a second that the runt might try and attack him as a means of trying to preserve some pride. Charlie waited but eventually Ross's shoulders dropped and he scurried away with his eyes glued to the carpet, picking up his wallet on the way and stepping out onto the street.

Charlie let out a deep breath and surveyed the rest of the pub; half of the eyes where still on him, the other half had returned to their own company but still no one spoke. For a few moments he stayed where he was and listened as the silence was occasionally interrupted by a cough or the scrapping of a chair leg. Reaching into his pocket he took the sixty pound and walked towards the bar, by the time the glaring landlady got to him a few people had resumed their conversations. A few seconds after that the room was bustling with noise.

"Six shots of Sambuca" Charlie said, deciding to forgo the usual smile he reserved for the middle aged woman.

"I don't want that kind of nonsense in my pub again, do you hear?" the woman said angrily. Charlie held her gaze for a second before looking over to Steph's table, they were all watching him expectantly, only Steph's blond friend was smiling.

"Six shots of Sambuca" Charlie repeated. The woman glared at him for a moment longer before storming off to pour the drinks. A few moments later she returned with the six shots on a tray and Charlie handed her the money.

He felt the awkwardness as soon as he sat down, Steph gave his shoulder an affectionate little squeeze and Benny nodded his thanks when Charlie placed a shot of Sambuca in front of him. When he'd positioned a shot in front of each of them he sat down and waited for someone to speak. After a few moments Steph leaned forward.

"Do you guys want to come clubbing with us tonight? It's ticket only but I know some people who can get you in"

Charlie looked over at Benny, he caught the smile and the nod of the head. Charlie felt a smile spread across his own face and suddenly everyone around the table was grinning. The tension from the McIntyre incident seemed to seep from his body within seconds, and Charlie suddenly felt on top of the world. Glancing around the pub he wondered how many people were talking about him at that moment, how many of them would go home and recite the tail of Charlie Thomas, that nasty piece of work who shouldn't be messed with. Sliding an arm around Steph's waist he pulled her towards him and moved his other hand towards his drink.

"Sounds like a plan" Charlie said lifting his sambucca in toast. The other five lifted theirs and after a clink of glasses they all downed their drinks in one.

Chapter 11

County road was a long winding street, made up of shops and takeaways, sustained largely by its proximity to both Goodison Park and Anfield. Unlike other parts of the city it didn't seem to have changed much, Rob noted one disheartening alteration; that the sports shop where he'd bought his first ever Liverpool kit was no longer there.

He stepped off the bus and started walking. The weather on the Saturday afternoon was the warmest it had been since he got back and though the sun was barely visible in the clouded sky, the numbing chill that had tinted the air all week seemed to have temporarily abated. Considering his chief mode of transport these days seemed to be walking, it was a small mercy for which he was thankful.

Pedestrians passed him here and there, hurrying in and out of the small shops that littered the long street. Rob noticed that every parking space was full. Goodison Park was only a few minutes away where Everton would have kicked off twenty minutes earlier, it was things like that, the little intricacies of the city, which he was still trying adjust to.

As Rob reached the corner of Church Road he spared a glance for the pub on the opposite side of the street. He'd been a regular patron of the *Black Horse* when he was a teenager, but looking at it now he had no desire to go back in, it housed too many bad memories, and too many bad people. With one last glance he turned down Church Road and made his way towards the address that Matt had given him.

From what Rob remembered from the old days, Church Road and its surrounding area had been seen as something of a stain on an otherwise adequate stretch of North Liverpool real estate. It wasn't that the surrounding area compared to the Upper East Side or anything like that, but it had always been a couple of rungs above where he was currently passing through.

The last time he'd walked these streets he remembered them being home to dole-ites, single mums and scam merchants, as he took in the first three houses he got the quick sense that little had changed in that regard.

Matt had told him that Kelly lived at number 38; a quick glance at the nearest door told him he was currently outside 362, perfect. Somewhat discouraged he slid his hands into his pockets and continued walking.

One of the first things that hit him was the number of windows that were bordered up. The small houses on the terraced street were crammed in together so tightly that it took no time at all to pass fifty of them and by that point he'd noted at least seven that were derelict and a few more that could have gone either way.

His hand went instinctively to the bulge at his belt, running a hand over the Smith and Weston to make sure that it was still there.

He'd gone back and forth over whether or not to bring it; after all it wasn't

135

as if he was expecting an assassination attempt from an ex-girlfriend, but with the planned hit on Wayne Caddock only two days away Rob didn't fancy taking any chances. Who knew what kind of games were being played in the background, while he was preparing to do his part.

He heard the familiar crunch of glass beneath his feet, with a sigh he glanced down and saw what remained of a car window scattered across the pavement.

The empty parking space next to the glass hinted that someone would be walking to work on Monday morning. He wondered whether it had been done overnight, or if some poor Evertonian would be getting a nasty surprise when he left the game.

He continued walking, both impatient and apprehensive at the same time. The street was largely deserted; the only people he passed were two sets of kids in hoodies, though both groups seemed too preoccupied with their own conversations to pay him any more attention than they did to the shattered glass or the bordered up windows. On the whole it seemed like a quiet street, especially for a Saturday afternoon. It was only the occasional house blaring R'n'B music from one of its upstairs windows that overpowered the sounds of the rustling wind and distant traffic that otherwise seemed to hold sway over the area.

The further Rob got down the street the more he began to wonder whether he was making a mistake. Kelly had always been temperamental, he'd met her in the midst of hormonal adolescence and it seemed to him that she'd never really grown out of those feelings of stubborn aggression and irrationality that defined the age group, even when she was well into her twenties.

For his first few years in New York, Rob had woken up every day half expecting to see Kelly waiting on his doorstep, ready to deliver a cuff around the ear and a return ticket to Liverpool. That impression was fuelled more by her stubbornness than any love she may have had for him, he couldn't imagine that she was the type to react well to a ten year absence.

But then surely her life would have changed a lot in that time too, a beautiful young girl with a fiery personality, he had no doubt that men much better than him would have been seeking her affections as soon as he was gone. With any luck she might see him leaving as the best thing that ever happened to her. A dozen different scenarios and outcomes played out in his head, but the one thing they had in common was that they all made him nervous. He was nervous about Jo too; he wondered whether she would read anything into the fact that he was going to see her, if she had known. Rob had decided not to mention it, for the simple reason that things were unstable enough as it was, going to see an ex-girlfriend, even with the best of intentions, couldn't possibly help his position, particularly when the re-emergence of his past had given her reason to be both suspicious and angry with him.

Halfway down the street he passed a group of kids in matching tracksuits, he watched as they screamed obscenities at a middle aged man before darting away down an alley in the hope of being chased. Rob tried to imagine what kind of men those kids would turn out to be when they grew up, with a self-conscious grimace he found himself thinking perhaps they would end of making money exactly the same way he was.

A few minutes later and Rob found himself outside the door of number 38. One of Kelly's neighbours had their front door open and from within he heard a child screaming at the top of its lungs, just like at the other end of the street the occupied houses were broken up by a scattering of abandoned counterparts, though Rob was surprised to see a middle aged man exiting one of the houses he'd previously designated as derelict.

There was a small porch that separated the gate from the front door of Kelly's house. Littered across it were children's toys, amongst them a plastic tricycle and a doll, both of which looked like they belonged to a child under the age of five. Rob ticked off a box in his head, she definitely had kids, but that was all he would know unless he stepped forward and rang the doorbell. Taking a deep breath he put a hand to his head to check his hair, his fingers made contacted with the short bristles as he realised the mistake, looking like a thug was proving hard to adjust to. He pushed open the metal gate, listening as it creaked, and stepped onto the porch.

He knew someone was home as soon as he reached the door, the realisation sending a small flutter of panic through his chest. Through the window he caught the flickering lights of the TV and his ears picked up the sound of people moving around inside. Slowly he raised his hand and rang the doorbell; it was a few seconds before he heard a pair of footsteps crossing the wooden floor.

The second the door opened Rob knew it was her; the diminutive figure and light brown hair were exactly as he remembered, but as his eyes took in the rest of her features he realised that a lot of things about Kelly Thompson had changed in ten years. The first thing that struck him was the cigarette that hung from the side of her mouth, she'd started smoking casually towards the end of their relationship but for some reason he'd managed to block that memory out. Her eyes seemed different too, the sparkling blue he remembered that had been so bright and full of life now looked duller, as if they were fading and he saw no sign of the intensity that had always lived within them, replaced instead by a morose acceptance.

It wasn't just her eyes that had changed, her face seemed too thin for her features and the wrinkles at the corners of her mouth and her forehead looked like they belonged on a woman closer to forty three than thirty three. Her skin was dark but it was the familiar orange-brown of a tanning salon rather than the natural golden tint of sunlight. He noted that her hair was tied back, which seemed to draw more attention to the wrinkles on her forehead, finishing it off she wore a pair of grey jogging pants and a white jumper that both seemed a little too big for her small body.

Yet underneath all of the changes Rob could still see the woman he had loved. She still stood with the defiance that seemed to challenge the world in front of her, and the eyes that weren't quite as bright as before still took everything in with a sharpness that was easy to overlook. Those eyes stared at him now as she took the cigarette from her mouth, but neither her eyes nor her face betrayed the slightest hint of emotion.

"Well" she said ostentatiously "back from the dead!"

Kelly had always been a hard one to read but Rob had forgotten just how unsettling it was to be on the receiving end of that uncertainty, the calmness of her face left room for it to either explode in anger or rejoice in happiness, and both seemed equally likely at this point. Now that the door was open Rob could hear the noise from the TV and was sure that whoever was inside was watching cartoons.

"I've been getting that a lot lately" Rob replied, trying to smile without showing his disappointment at what the years had done to her "It's nice to see you again, Kelly"

To his surprise she smiled at him, it wasn't the warmest smile he'd ever seen but it was a tolerant smile, which was about as much as he could hope for in the current situation.

"You want to come inside?" she asked, her face still the picture of well-maintained calm, she took a step back, allowing him to cross the threshold.

Rob nodded and stepped forward. It didn't take long to get his bearings; the front door led straight into the living room with a kitchen at the back of the house, straight ahead of him were a set of stairs that led up to what could only be two bedrooms, the house was too small to contain any more. The living room seemed basic but nice. He caught sight of the two kids sat in front of the TV on the wooden floor; a boy and a girl, neither turned away from the cartoons until Kelly spoke their names.

"Matilda, Stevie, this is Robbie, one of Mummy's oldest friends, say hello" Kelly said, her voice was firm but affectionate, a mothers voice.

"Hi" Stevie said, briefly turning to acknowledge their visitor, before his attention returned to the TV. He had golden blond hair and a large face that bared very little similarity to Kelly's. The little girl was another story, when Rob looked at Matilda he had no doubt that she was Kelly's daughter; the child had the same light brown hair and bright blue eyes as her mother, it was like looking at a miniature version of the woman he remembered.

"Hello, Robbie" Matilda shouted enthusiastically. Grinning she stood up and walked towards him, extending her hand and shaking his, throughout the process she watched her mother keenly, like she was seeking approval for her attempts at social etiquette.

"Hello" he said to Matilda. Vicky smiled and stroked the side of the child's face, a second later she followed her brother's example and turned back to the TV "Cute kids, you always wanted to be a mum"

138

Kelly shrugged her shoulders and gestured him towards the back of the house "Come into the kitchen" Rob followed her into the small room and watched as she made her way directly towards the kettle "You want a cup of coffee?"

"Please" Rob said, taking a seat at the small table. He shifted a little uncomfortably as he tried to adjust the gun in his belt, the first effort failed and he wound up jabbing himself in the leg. Quite the natural born killer.

"You still take two sugars?" Kelly asked almost rhetorically, busying herself with the cups and spoons.

"No actually, just milk these days" the response caused Kelly to pause for a second, before continuing what she was doing "This is a nice place you've got here"

"Thank you" she said, her back was to him as she filled the cups with boiling water. Rob tried to imagine the sexy young woman he had known but from behind it was almost impossible "We moved in about ten months ago, after Matilda's father left we couldn't afford our old place. It's taken a little while but it's starting to feel like home, how did you find out where I was?"

"Matt told me, he said he saw you a couple of weeks ago"

"I should have known" she said as she slid the milk back into the fridge and placed the two cups of coffee on the table. She took a seat directly opposite him, pulling a pack of cigarettes from her front pocket "It really caught me off guard when I saw him; fancy suit, expensive briefcase, it looks like the lads doing ok. Good on him I say, it's nice to see at least one of the old gang doing well for themselves. What about you, straightened yourself out yet?"

When Kelly spoke there was a wry twist to her mouth but Rob knew that whatever humour she was injecting was meant to disguise her cynical opinions of him, opinions that in her mind seemed to have long since hardened into fact.

"I thought I had" Rob said ambiguously, Kelly looked at him as if she expected more but when it wasn't forthcoming she looked away and let the moment pass "I thought you'd be more surprised to see me"

"I suppose I'm not" she said, lighting a cigarette and looking out into the small garden at the back of the house "I always had this feeling that you were going to come back, I didn't know when or how but there was always this sense inside me that wherever it was you'd gone, I wasn't quite finished with you yet. I'm glad I was right. I tried hard for a while to find out you know, I harassed your Charlie for about three months"

"Charlie didn't know" Rob said, remembering those early days "I was away for a year before I told him and Vera where I was, I wanted a few things to blow over first"

"And where were you?"

"New York"

Kelly nodded, she looked a little sad as she stared at the table. After a few moments she looked up at him and smiled "How are the family?"

"Good, good. Our Charlie's married now"

Kelly laughed "No way!"

"With two kids" Rob replied, taking a first tentative sip at his coffee before realising it was still too hot.

"Charlie? Married with kids? I can't imagine that, he was such an irresponsible little fuck up when we were kids, I wouldn't have fancied him looking after a house plant, let alone a family" she was still laughing as she took another long drag from the cigarette.

"He's still a fuck up" Rob said bluntly "Now he's just a fuck up with a family. He's a good lad, he just has a bad habit for getting himself in trouble"

"It must run in the family" Kelly said with a knowing grin "So how's Vera?"

"Same as always" Rob said with a sigh "still trying to put the world to rights in her own disapproving fashion"

"I always thought it was just me she disapproved of" she said standing up and peeking her head into the living room. Rob leaned in his chair to follow her gaze; she was watching the two kids, both still sat in front the television. It struck him how different she was, not only in looks but in personality too, she was a mother now, that seemed to take up more of her attention than he'd ever known her to give.

"No, she liked you" Rob said, talking to her back "I think more than she liked me to be honest"

She turned away from the kids and sat back down "Well that doesn't mean much, people usually do"

Rob didn't rise to the bait "Let's talk about you, two kids?" he thought about his two nieces "seems to be the fashion these days, Matilda's the spitting image of you"

A softness came over her fiery features that, for a second, reminded Rob of the old Kelly. It was the softness that used to change her when she was most in love, when she was truly content, but the look she had now was so much stronger than it had ever been looking at him.

"Yep, they're my babies" she said, her eyes glistening slightly "I didn't think I could ever love anything as much as I love those two, but I guess that's what all parents say, right? They're great kids, but Matilda's having a tough time, she's taken my break up with her dad pretty badly"

As Kelly spoke he tried to connect his memories to the woman before him. A dozen images flashed across his mind, memories of snorting cocaine off her naked stomach, of dancing until 6am, of living in a bubble of sex and drugs. He remembered the times when they would get so high there would be nothing left in the world but the two of them. Sometimes, not often, but sometimes those moments would help him forget the terrible things he was doing. They weren't real, not really, the next day would come and so would the fights, and the guilt, but those rare moments shone out amongst the other memories like a lighthouse amongst a clouded coast, but try as he might he couldn't relate those memories to the single mum sitting in front of him.

"What about Stevie?" Rob asked, trying not to let his thoughts project onto his face.

"Jeff wasn't Stevie's dad, just Matilda's" she looked pensive as she gazed into the small back yard, Rob wondered if she was thinking about the same memories as him "he was always good to Stevie but his father…well he doesn't keep in touch"

He felt a jolt of fear as a possibility he hadn't considered came to life in his head; was she talking about him? The cruelty of his abandonment suddenly cranked up a notch; he imagined leaving her pregnant and all alone. Tentatively he opened his mouth, unsure as to what he was going to say "How old are they?"

Kelly seemed to read his mind, taking her gaze from the window she looked at him with an amused smile while smoke rings floated away from her mouth. She let him stew for a couple of seconds before turning away and looking back into the garden.

"Six and four" she said, still smiling.

Rob felt the relief wash over him. Glancing into the living room he realised how irrational his fear had been, the kid was obviously nowhere near ten years old, and his bright blond hair was the exact opposite of Rob's dark features. Subtly he tried to let out a breath without letting Kelly know that he had been holding it in.

"And this guy just ran out on you and his four year old daughter?" he asked, returning the conversation to less embarrassing territory.

"Jeff wasn't really the family type. Don't get me wrong, he did his best for a while but I guess if I'm honest, I had my doubts for a long time about whether or not he was going to stick around. One night he just came home from work and told me he couldn't do it anymore, that the whole thing was just too much commitment for him. He says that he loves Matilda but the poor kid is lucky if she sees him two days a month. It's strange but when we first got together I thought Jeff would make a great father, he reminded me of you a little; slightly erratic but with a good heart, he could be incredibly sweet when he wanted to be, I guess my taste in men hasn't improved with age"

As Kelly finished speaking started to nibble on her bottom lip with a playful look in her eyes. Rob remembered the habit from the old days, he used to think she was at her sexiest when she bit that bottom lip, but looking at her now he felt none of those old feelings. He looked away to avoid making that impression obvious.

"How did you meet this Jeff guy?" he asked, surprised at how interested he was in her life.

Something about her years without him stoked his curiosity; it felt strange, like his interest was morbid in some way, like watching a traffic accident on the motorway. Perhaps it was because she'd changed so much in the time that had passed. Charlie and Vera were effectively the same, the only thing that was different about Matt was that he was successful, but with Kelly he needed to understand how it was she'd changed, and what had happened to the woman he knew.

"He was the manager of a club not far from here, where I was working for a while" she said stubbing out her cigarette, Rob raised his eyebrows and she nodded in response "I know, I know, a barmaid, but what else was I going to do? Stevie was only just born and I needed the money. There aren't a lot of jobs in this city for a single mum with no qualifications, especially one who can only work nights, so that was where I ended up. It wasn't so bad, chart music till three or four am and there were always stay behinds, Jeff would buy me a couple of drinks. I was there a few weeks before he asked me out. He was a really nice bloke back then, always offered me a lift home and that. You know, it's not easy to meet good men when you've got a six month old baby at home; it kind of kills the mood for blokes. But Jeff was different, we started going out and he seemed really interested in Stevie, buying him presents and stuff. He had a bit of a reputation as a player but he knocked all that on the head when we started going out. A few months later he moved in, then I got pregnant, and before you know it he'd done a runner"

Kelly had grown progressively more solemn the longer she spoke, when she eventually finished she let out a long sigh, staring at the ash tray in front of her. The sound of cartoons in the other room masked the awkward silence as Rob took another sip of his coffee and took the story in.

Slowly Kelly lifted herself up and offered an awkward smile. He watched her as she walked into the other room and kneeled next to her two children. In a low voice that was bursting with love she asked the two what they wanted for dinner, as the conversation went back and forth Rob could hear her voice brightening with each exchange. When she returned she was free of the sadness that had threatened to consume her.

Kelly went straight to the overhead cupboard and removed a number of tins, he knew he should let it go but there was a part of him that craved more insight into her life.

"Is he paying you, for Matilda?" Rob asked.

Kelly took a knife from a nearby draw and slammed it onto the work service "What's with all these questions Robbie?" she asked irritably. Her frustration was palpable as she opened a can of tuna and sliced at a loaf of bread in silence, not once looking in Rob's direction. It was the same angry, silent treatment she had given him in days gone by and it brought forward another string of memories, most of which were unpleasant in comparison to the ones that he'd just remembered. Once again he found himself tentatively searching for the right thing to say.

"Just interested, Kel. A lots happened in ten years"

Once again she slammed the knife down but this time she left it where it was and turned to face him. With her arms folded she looked like she was quickly losing whatever patience she had mustered in the last few minutes.

"Can I ask you a question?" When Rob nodded she took another cigarette from her pocket and lit it "Why did you come here?"

It was a question Rob had asked himself more than once and as he looked around the small kitchen he realised he didn't have a satisfactory answer to give her. It wasn't to confide in her about McSharry, even in the old days he had kept that part of his life as separate from her as he could, and it wasn't to reignite any old flames, it wouldn't have mattered if she had still been the hot little twenty three year old he remembered, doing that to Jo was unthinkable, especially after what he had already put her through. Finally, he met her gaze, he had exhausted every other possibility in his head and as far as he could see it left him with only one possible answer.

"Redemption" he muttered. For a second he thought it was too quiet for her to hear but the confused way in which she scrunched up her face told him that she had "I suppose I wanted to show you that I'm not the same as I used to be, and to tell you that I was sorry. I was awful to you, and it wasn't on"

Rob felt his face blush, he didn't like giving apologies, it wasn't something he did very often, but if anyone in his life deserved one then it was Kelly. Her face seemed to relax a little and there was a hint of surprise in her eyes. Moving away from the work surface she resumed her seat on the opposite side of the small table.

"You weren't awful to me Robbie" she said with a sympathetic smile "the truth is we were awful to each other, we were just too young and too stupid to realise it, that's all"

The way she smiled made him believe her, it was a sad, sympathetic smile with more than a hint of warmth. Rob didn't think he had ever seen that kind of smile on her face before, just another change that ten years had made. A shout came from the other room, the kids were demanding their dinner.

"I should probably go" Rob said, standing up from his chair, Kelly did the same and wrapped her arms around him. There was a familiarity in their embrace that Rob hadn't expected, even after all this time their bodies still recognised each other. Giving her a light squeeze he let go, and a second later she did the same.

"Can I come see you again?" he asked before he even had time to think it through, his interest in her life continued to play on his mind, it was a curiosity that hadn't been satisfied by their conversation. It occurred to him that he hadn't thought about McSharry or the hits since he walked through her door. Nothing else had managed to keep them at bay for longer than five minutes since his return, but Kelly had, Rob was encouraged by the thought.

"You know where to find me" she said, giving him a light kiss on the cheek. Rob could feel her proximity reviving long forgotten feelings; he did his best to suppress them and tried to remind his subconscious of everything that had changed over the years.

143

"Alright, then" Rob said, reciprocating the kiss on the cheek and making his way through the living room. He said goodbye to the kids, whose hunger had left them significantly less hospitable, and made his way out of the front door. By the time he closed the gate behind him Kelly had already disappeared inside to quell the mounting rebellion from her two children.

Making his way back up the street Rob felt the familiar anxieties waiting for him, he looked up at the sky and said a silent prayer to the God he wanted to believe in. Two more days and it would start all over again.

Chapter 12

A strong breeze from the Irish Sea swept across the Liverpool waterfront, scattering pieces of litter to all four corners of the deserted car park. Large, silent warehouses loomed in front and behind, the early Sunday morning sun casting dominating shadows over the concrete landscape. Overhead seagulls called out in frustration, desperately searching the contaminated river for any source of food. Their calls only brought more companions to their plight, circling overhead in the bright morning sky.

Stephen McSharry surveyed the docks and breathed in the fresh air. Huge cranes and metal containers lay as dormant as the warehouses, giving the place a serene sense of calm. He was happy to have an excuse to come back here, the Liverpool docks had been the setting for some of his finest moments, particularly in his youth. Back in the late sixties and early seventies they'd been the perfect home for a young gangster trying to establish himself in the overpopulated world of organised crime.

Container ships from all four corners of the earth were arriving on his doorstep with an endless supply of goods; alcohol, household appliances, clothing, anything that the people wanted was sitting in containers waiting to be stolen by men with the stomach for greatness. Men like him and Martin Cassidy had made their names in those days, hijacking whatever they could get their hands on to sell to the punters of Liverpool. In those days scousers were still struggling to banish the memory of the blitz from their consciousness, embracing the luxuries of capitalism was a popular way to achieve that aim, and Stephen McSharry was happy to help them achieve it at a slightly lower price.

They had been the good days, the golden days. On the shores of the River Mersey container ships unloaded the products that would fuel the North of Britain, and on those same shores Stephen McSharry had found himself.

It was here that he learnt he would never be happy to follow the rules they laid down for him, or live his life the way they wanted. Here he discovered what it was like to be a King, and it was a life he couldn't resist.

But those days didn't last, in hindsight it was clear to him that they couldn't have lasted. As Thatcherism took its toll and unemployment soared upwards people's needs began to change; whisky, expensive suits and electrical appliances were no longer what the people needed from their underworld suppliers, they needed drugs, hard drugs, to numb the pain of a hard world. The docks dried up as quickly as the jobs and the city because awash with narcotics. Heroine took its hold on the streets, Liverpool became known across the nation as scag city, and Stephen had to live with the part he had played in the deconstruction that followed. He bore no regrets from those days, he held no responsibility as his home degenerated around him. He was a businessman, and a very good one at that, he knew what the people wanted and he gave it to them. If blame was to fall at the feet of anyone then it fell to those who sought his products. Supply and demand; the governing force of capitalism.

Despite his indifference a part of him was relieved to see the back of those days. Profitable they may have been, but smackheads were a filthy breed, desperate, misshaped addicts who would steal from their own grandmothers just to get another hit. The drug world, like the economy, had recovered from its eighties blip and was much the better for it. Drugs weren't about poverty, or desperation anymore, they were about recreation. McSharry's dealers sold to everyone from dole-ites to multi-millionaires. Liverpool was awash with cocaine and ecstasy and everyone was in on the act, class A's were just a part of life now, and the longer it took the governments and the lawmakers to realise it, the more money people like him were going to make.

Pressing engagements shook him from his thoughts and redirected him to the task at hand. He looked towards the car ten feet ahead and the three men who surrounded it, his eyes instinctively drawn to the two large figures of Rico Wallace and Macca as they lent against the bonnet. They made for an intimidating image, both around the six foot two mark, though Rico was slightly bigger. The ex-boxer with his cropped red hair had a physique that could have been crafted from stone, in contrast Macca toed the line between fat and brawn. Both had their talents, both were handy in a scrap, hence their presence.

The two men only held his attention for a moment, his real business was with the young man stood at the boot of the car.

Sie was one of Begsy's recent acquisitions, McSharry had been free just shy of a week but with so much going on finding time to assess the new recruits simply hadn't been a priority. Rico Wallace was the exception; he respected the man as a fighter and had made a special effort to incorporate him into the group. He liked the guy, over the years the ginger behemoth had always gone down when he was supposed to, McSharry warmed easier to people who made him a quick profit.

That left Begsy's other two recruits: Sie and Caffers, as the only unknown entities remaining in his crew. The two had proved to be respectable villains so far. Every job that had been asked of them they'd done efficiently, which included disposing of George and his groupies, but he was still waiting for that flash of something different, a skill that made them indispensable. Today was Sie's chance to put himself in that bracket.

When Begsy's car arrived they would be walking around the corner to pay a visit to the Drake brothers, principal drug runners for Wayne Caddock and his crew. McSharry didn't know much about the Drake's, but what he knew intrigued him. Cockney born and bred, they'd cut their teeth in the London Underworld before inexplicably shutting up shop and moving North. Liverpool was a good place for business, if your business was drugs, but it didn't compare with the kind of money that could be made in the capital.

McSharry wanted answers, and that was where Sie came in. According to

Begsy the kid had a lot of friends in the capital, including a few vague links to some of the major players. When Stephen McSharry conducted business he made it a rule to know as much as possible about the people he was dealing with. He needed to know what the two men were about before he stepped through their door, shit house drug runners were ten for a penny but if he wanted their cooperation then he needed to press the right buttons. If Sie led him to those buttons then the kid might just cement his place in the new world order.

He called the kid over, a hurried walk put Sie in front of him in just under five seconds. He caught a determined look in the kids' eyes, he was pleased to see that the youngster had an appropriate understanding of the opportunity before him.

Sie was the youngest in the crew by some distance. McSharry wasn't too interested in specifics but he knew the kid was in his late twenties, though he was tall he had a slim build and dark enough skin to suggest that there was some Indian in his parentage. Wavy jet black hair stood out along with two bushy eyebrows and a strip of facial hair that resided on his chin. He was rubbing his hands together and rocking on his heels while he waited to be addressed. Eventually McSharry lit a cigar and began to speak.

"These contacts of yours down South, I want to know how you got hooked up with them"

Begsy had already filled him in on the basics but McSharry wanted to hear the story direct, he trusted the big man's judgement but he needed to be certain that the kid was right for his inner circle. This time around there would be no mistakes, he would not allow it.

Sie nodded and began to speak, his words had a rehearsed vibe to them, like he'd been up half the night preparing for his part "I used to run with these two black lads out of Toxteth, they started heading down to the big smoke about nine years ago to run smack and guns up the M1. They worked with a few crews out of the West End, respectable villains like, the lads shipped the stuff up and I made sure there was someone waiting to buy it when it arrived".

"Your boys were the go between, you stayed up here?"

Sie realised where McSharry was headed and shook his head.

"At first they were but two years in they got pinched for armed robbery, daft bastards got picked up trying to hijack a post office van, after that I dealt with the cockneys myself"

The kid looked nervous, he flashed him a smile to put him at ease.

"Must have been a nice little payday?"

Sie nodded and smiled back "Top dollar boss, those southerners know how to make a profit"

McSharry took another puff at his cigar and checked the time. Begsy and the rest of the crew were due to arrive soon, he wouldn't have as much opportunity to grill the kid as he originally hoped.

"Who ran the crew in the West End?"

"Tommy Sway was in charge, he used to come up every couple of months to oversee everything, make sure it was kosher and that. You know him?"

McSharry nodded "I know Tommy, we did some business in the old days, he's a respectable gangster, one of the old school" The kind of old school that would gun down a man's entire family if he felt he'd been insulted, but he kept that to himself, it wasn't strictly relevant "So let's get to it, what do you know about these two brothers?"

Sie focused in a heartbeat. Sie knew what was expected of him. Sie spoke slow and clear and showed the boss exactly why he was useful.

"I've been over it with a few different sources and every time the story comes back to me it comes back the same. The word is they were doing major business with some big players in the East End running drugs from Europe and South America and seeing a lot of cash. They kept this up until they were big enough to invest in a legit shipping company, and funnelled all the drugs through that business. They made good money running the ships but they made real money bringing the drugs in on them"

The same questions came back to him, what were they doing hauled up in an office on the Liverpool docks.

"How'd they end up here?"

"This is where it gets interesting," Sie said, excitedly rubbing his hands together "the blokes I spoke to who were around back then all say how smug these cunts got, I mean these fellas were getting peoples backs up left, right and centre. This is London, down there they all fancy themselves as the next Reggie Kray so to be making so much noise in those parts you know it had to be bad. Anyway, it all comes to a head one night when they start arguing in a club, bottle the manager and call some boys to come down and trash the place. Turns out the club was only run by some proper villains in the West End and the manager they hospitalised is a cousin to one of their main boys. After that the whole thing kicks off, these West End lads are talking about going to war, the East Enders show some sense and decide against tearing up the capital over a couple of drug runners. They cut the brothers loose and before they have a chance to pack a suitcase Keith and Johnny Drake are chased out of London. The West Enders burn their business to the ground and a few days later the two fellas rock up in Liverpool with a thick wad of insurance money. Next thing you know they've hopped into bed with Wayne Caddock and it's like the whole nasty incident never even happened"

McSharry listened with interest, he saw a hazy strategy become clearer with every word the kid said, by the time he'd finished McSharry had tossed his cigar and gestured for Macca and Rico to join them.

"What ever happened to their problems down South?"

"Once they got an agreement in place with Caddock he took himself down to the West End to get the price taken off their heads" the other two approached, their arrival seemed to knock Sie off his game and he mumbled

148

the next couple of words "I heard he's got some business with a few of them, he paid them off and the West Enders called of the hunt, so long as Keith and Johnny keep themselves away from London that is"

McSharry shook his head and whistled through his teeth "Hats off to Caddock, the boys twice the opportunist his father ever was. He must have thought it was Christmas when these two international drug runners stumbled into town, hat in hand, begging for protection. What kind of reputation have they made for themselves in our neck of the woods?"

Sie flashed a reluctant look, he glanced at the other two in the hope that they'd answer for him, when they didn't he shook his head and looked apologetic.

"I know them by sight but not much more than that, they don't ride in the usual gangster circles. They like to think of themselves as above it, as legitimate businessmen, though you wouldn't think it the way they flash the cash"

"What does that mean?" his tone came out harsh, vague comments pissed him off.

"They think they're pretty fucking flash, they go around acting like they're two big fish in a shitty little pond, that kind of thing"

McSharry looked to the other two for confirmation.

"Is that right? What do you know about these cockney jokers?"

Macca shook his head and gave a disgusted look "Wankers. They've got big mouths that get them into trouble, but they know they're connected so they get away with it. They think being in Caddock's back pocket puts them above the street so they mouth off and let their muscle deal with the consequences"

McSharry looked at Rico and waited.

The ginger monster shrugged his shoulders "Gobshites, ain't no question about that, but they're no gangsters, not by a long shot"

"That right?" McSharry heard the hint of excitement in his own voice.

Rico nodded and continued "Fellas aren't comfortable with the physical side of business" he crossed his two huge arms, the temperature was dropping into minus territory and still the man didn't wear a coat "scares the shit out of them, they like to leave that to Wayne Caddock and his boys while they pretend to be the shit, flashing the cash and bedding the tarts. They look like they're for real but get them near a good bit of old fashioned mayhem and I'll bet money they'll show their true colours quick enough"

The strategy was almost fully formed, Keith and Johnny Drake began to feel like the kind of men he'd known his whole life, the kind of men he knew how to handle. The Sunday morning sun was bright in the sky, despite the cold, in that moment it seemed to shine down only on him. Ten long, frustrating years were quickly coming to an end and McSharry could feel the excitement building in his chest. He felt like a child at Christmas.

He kept his outer features perfectly calm. To his men he was the picture of controlled authority, but inside he felt like a twenty year old again. It was as if the last thirty years had never happened and he was still just a young criminal, standing on the Liverpool docks, preparing for another big job.

Over Sie's shoulder he caught sight of the other beamer as it turned into the car park. Begsy was behind the wheel, with Ads in the passenger seat. Even from this distance he caught the resolve in their faces, they were both ready for business, just like they should be. He diverted his attention back to Sie. One final query, to ensure they were all on the same page.

"You agree with what they're saying?"

The kid didn't hesitate. He was nodding his head before he'd even started to speak.

"Absolutely"

The thud of car doors echoed in the morning air. Begsy Ads, Nikolai and Mercer made their way towards the others, each one alert for any kind of unexpected movement. He could sense the undercurrent of excitement flowing through each of them, he was surrounded by blank, serious faces, but he felt it nonetheless. This was as much their time as it was his, the men before him had given a lot to the cause; they had given years, and they had given loyalty. He yearned to reward them the success that their sacrifice deserved, a General was only as good as his troops, and Stephen McSharry felt privileged to lead the group of men before him.

"Just in time" he told the new arrivals, he waited until the four men had settled before he continued "You all know what you need to do, today we make our business pitch. We show these little cockney pricks that this crew right here is the future. You're a bunch of mean looking bastards, you do what you do and they'll be in no doubt that we're the way forward. Every step is critical boys, we fuck up once and we're done. Remember that"

Nods and grunts echoed around the group, without another word he walked out of the car park and up the street. The rest of the crew followed suit; Begsy on one side, Rico Wallace on the other.

They turned a corner towards another set of warehouses, where the last ones were white these were blue, though the same rusted metallic shutters protected both sets. Behind him the click of metal signalled that the men were checking their weapons, if everything went to plan there would be no need for them. Violence was part of the plan, but not this early in the game, for now he needed to tread lightly and keep the body count low, but it never hurt to be prepared.

The group turned off the street and walked through the car park that would lead to their destination. Four security cameras caught them on arrival, whether they were being monitored was another issue entirely. From the car park they had access to five warehouses, Begsy gestured towards the far corner. The men never broke their stride.

The shutters were already open. Two men busied themselves unloading a delivery from a transit van, so engaged in the task that they didn't even see

McSharry and his crew approaching. He repressed a smile, that was one hurdle out of the way, getting access to the brothers was going to be even easier than he'd expected.

The group reached the open shutters, McSharry led the way inside, the others followed close behind. The two men unloading the delivery threw them a quizzical look and for a moment they looked like they might start asking questions, but one fierce look from Begsy was enough to send them scurrying back to their van.

Inside the warehouse stacks upon stacks of boxes stood almost high enough to reach the ceiling. Some had the names of multinational businesses stamped on their sides, others looked more discreet. A scattering of men in overalls littered the large room though none were brave enough to raise their eyes from their clipboards. McSharry watched as the majority of them hurried away to the furthest corners of the building, where some urgent business appeared to monopolise their attention.

All seven of his men were surveying the room with guarded expressions. Now they were inside their next task was to find Keith and Johnny's hideout, as if on cue a shout from the opposite end of the warehouse grabbed everyone's attention.

Drake muscle made its way towards them, two large, bald men in different coloured tracksuits marched the length of the warehouse, shouting obscenities as they covered the distance.

It brought an amused grin to his face. He turned towards Begsy but the big man had already slipped into his battle trance.

"What the fuck do you lot think you're doing just walking in here?" said meathead number one.

"On your bike faggots" meathead two added "you lot got a fucking death wish or something?"

No one spoke, it was quiet enough to hear Rico Wallace cracking his knuckles. He felt the collective tension amongst them, it made his arm hair stand on end, this was what it was all about; us against them, the part of the life that he'd missed the most. His hands slid into his pockets as the two men drew ever closer. He sensed Begsy's eagerness and shared the sentiment.

"You lot fucking deaf?" the first meathead asked "get moving"

"If you boys want to leave this building conscience you better turn around right now"

Meathead one caught sight of Begsy and changed direction to meet him, McSharry nearly cringed at the man's poor choice of target. His associate moved towards Rico, staring up at the ex-boxer who stood at least three inches taller. His decision making skills weren't much better.

"You heard the man, you ugly piece of shit" the first man said to Begs, pulling a Stanley knife from his pocket "He said now"

It happened so fast he almost missed it. To his right Begsy's arms darted up like two vipers and grabbed the hand holding the Stanley knife, before the prick had time to react Begsy had forced the forearm down to his knee with such velocity that the snap of the arm echoed around the warehouse. The scream followed a second later.

To his left Rico stepped forward, drew his arm back and swung a fist at the jaw of his aggressor. The connection was perfect, both the crunch of bone and the ripple of flesh confirmed it, during the moment of impact he was sure he saw the jaw bone press so hard against the flesh that it nearly tore right through, a second later the man was falling backwards. He hit the floor hard and didn't move.

McSharry turned back towards Begsy, his enforcer twisted the broken arm behind his victims back, using his strength and his momentum he bounced the imprudent man's head against the concrete floor.

Once.

Twice.

Three times.

Begs hauled him up by the broken arm, blood poured from a wound on his forehead and his eyes looked glazed. McSharry leaned in and gave a closer inspection; he was conscious, barely, his eyes moved back and forth like that of a confused child's.

McSharry slapped him. They eyes tried to focus, they failed, they tried again.

"You brought this on yourself. Now, where are the bosses?"

He waited for a response, when it wasn't forthcoming he nodded to Begsy. The broken arm was bent further back, the eruption of pain brought their suspect back from the brink of unconsciousness and elicited a cry that echoed off the walls.

The few remaining workers flinched at the sound. McSharry raised his eyebrows impatiently at Begsy's victim, the man reluctantly nodded in the direction he had come, towards a glass window on the first floor. Three men stood behind it, watching the proceedings with interest.

"Bring him with us" he ordered, Begsy nodded and pushed the man forward, keeping a tight grip on the broken arm. The eight men and their hostage started towards the office, stepping over the unconscious villain as they passed.

They crossed the warehouse and climbed the stairs to the first floor office. When they reached the door it was locked, a glass pane at head height gave him a clear view of everything inside; he saw five men spread out, each one looking more worried than the last.

He wrapped his knuckles gently on the door and smiled through the glass. He played it polite and civil, the mugs inside didn't know what the fuck was going on; was it a shakedown? Was it a hit? Maybe they're just a particular nasty and particularly persistent set of Jehovah's Witnesses?

Three of the five men paced back and forth like caged animals, of the other two one was sat behind a desk while the other sat on a couch against the wall, the familial similarities were immediately apparent.

The buzz came faster than he expected, the door opened with a gentle push and they made their way inside. The room was long and narrow with a wooden desk at the far end. The five men kept themselves as far away as possible, huddled close to the desk like moths to a flame. Varnished wooden furniture was scattered around the room in any place it would fit and he counted at least a dozen paintings on the walls, the ship theme was consistent throughout them all, if he had to guess he'd have said mostly Napoleonic.

It wasn't hard to make the Drake brothers, the other three were pure hired muscle, though they'd given up pacing each one looked towards the man behind the large oak desk for instructions that never came.

There was something about the man at desk that interested McSharry immediately. He wasn't good looking, and there was an inherent sordidness to his character that was obvious even after a couple of seconds. His face was too thin, emphasising the cheekbones in a way that resembled a corpse, an effect exemplified further by the tiny brown pupils that resided in his overly large eyes and the greasy brown hair slicked back across his head.

Slouched on a couch in the corner was a man with similar characteristics, the only immediate difference seemed to be that he had a few less wrinkles around his hollow eyes and his greasy hair looked decidedly more unkempt.

McSharry paused at a painting of an old wooden ship in a storm, when he turned back he noticed that the right hand of the man behind the desk was hidden at his side. The only sound was the heavy breathing of the man in Begsy's custody; it drew the attention of his five associates.

McSharry cleared his throat "I like your office, it has a Nordic ambiance to it, it works" he paused and pointed at the two brothers, one at a time "I'm curious, which one is Keith and which one is Johnny?"

The Drake behind the desk watched him suspiciously, his gaze occasionally drifting towards Begsy and his broken armed employee. His stare was intense, the man seemed to think he could deduce their names and their intentions simply by glaring hard enough.

"I'm Keith," he said eventually "who the hell are you and what are you doing in my office?"

The broad cockney drawl was unmistakable, but it couldn't hide the hint of fear that resided in every word.

"You don't need to worry yourself. I'm here to talk business, there's no violent intent, so I'd appreciate it if you removed your hand from that gun"

Keith Drake glanced downwards and shook his head.

"No violent intent?" the cockney nodded towards Begsy, his right hand still hidden "What do you call that?"

"These two had a private disagreement, I'm not telling you how to run your business but you should teach your men better manners, at the very least you should teach them better judgement, though I suppose such a thing can't really be taught, can it? I'm here to talk business with you Keith, with you and your brother. I've got plans, and I want you to be a part of them, my name is Stephen McSharry, now, for the final time; take your hand off that gun"

The demand caused one of Drake's boys to take a half step forward, a few of his men mirrored the action. The tension in the room cranked up a notch, McSharry was only vaguely aware of it, his attention was focused on Keith Drake and the flicker of recognition that crossed his face at the introduction. Drake's right hand moved slowly up to the desk and rested on top of his left.

McSharry smiled, like he would at an obedient child.

"Good"

The brother on the couch pushed himself up and brushed a few strands of greasy hair away from his face.

"What the fuck is this? You think you can just walk into our office and start giving us orders? Do you know who the fuck we are?"

Johnny Drake spat the words with a belligerence that pushed at McSharry's patience, behind him he sensed a similar current running through his men. Johnny was tall and skinny like his brother, the kind of physique that could be snapped in half like a toothpick. The urge to give the order was almost overwhelming, but he was remiss to let his negotiations degenerate into such anarchy.

Johnny stood rigid on the other side of the room, the little prick didn't have the balls to stand face to face, but from a safe distance with three of his soldiers close by he thought he was the hardest man alive.

McSharry looked at the little prick and laughed.

"I know exactly who you are"

Johnny's lips peeled back in a snarl "Don't laugh at me you old git. You're playing with some major players here, have you got any clue who we run with?"

Johnny took a step forward, there was still a considerable distance between the two men, but the move seemed to be meant as some sort of threat.

A sound that was something like a low growl escaped from Begsy's throat, McSharry looked towards the big man and shook his head. He looked back towards the man behind the desk, Keith Drake watched the exchange with both intrigue and concern, if the whole thing went south he wondered whether the kid would know how to use the gun behind his desk.

"I know who you run with. I know who you run with now, and who you ran with way back when. I'm assuming you're the big dick that got the Drakes chased out of London? It's a good job you've got that Caddock protection isn't it? I bet you'd have many a sleepless night if that man was ever out of the picture"

Johnny Drake took another step forward, his eyes went wide with disbelief, making the corpse-like resemblance even stronger. Keith shifted uncomfortably in his chair, though he was smart enough to keep his hands in plain view.

"You threatening me?" Johnny shouted, his eyes locked on McSharry like he was the only man in the room "You hear this Keith? We're being threatened by an old age fucking pensioner. You're messing with some serious fucking people here granddad, this little stunts gonna bring a whole load of problems your way"

Keith shifted in his chair "Johnny-"

His brother cut him off.

"I'll personally see to it that Caddock's people give you a proper going over before they put you down. Not that an old git like you could probably take that much, but these guys are professionals, they're gonna squeeze every last inch of you before you pack in"

McSharry felt the smile return to his face "You really do talk too much. I'm glad to hear it, I hate it when a man's reality doesn't live up to his reputation"

"Oh you'll find out about my reality" Johnny spat "You don't need to worry there"

Begsy hit breaking point. Without a word he pushed his prisoner forward, in one smooth motion stepping on the man's ankle with his left foot and driving his right knee into the centre of the arched lower leg. Once again the snap of bone sounded around the room as the guard collapsed, weeping to the floor. A stomp on the back of the head finished the job, the man's face connected with the maroon carpet, instantly knocking him unconscious.

McSharry turned away from the action, Johnny Drake took a step backwards as he stared at the crumpled mess on the floor. Those corpse eyes were larger than they'd ever been, though any hint of anger or belligerence was long gone.

"Could you repeat that? An old man like me has trouble hearing sometimes?"

Johnny swallowed hard, his eyes darted from McSharry to the man on the ground, back and forth, back and forth.

McSharry took a couple of steps forward.

"No? You're finished? Good, sit down"

Johnny obeyed the command without protest. The remaining Drake muscle looked agitated, they didn't want to back down, but then they didn't want to end up like their unconscious pal. Eventually the three receded back against the wall, McSharry blocked them out, his business was with Keith and Johnny Drake.

He pulled out a chair from the desk and positioned it so he was equal distance from the two brothers. Sitting down he let out a sigh and brushed the warehouse debris from his black trousers.

"I'm told you have a deal with Wayne Caddock for shipments of ecstasy, I'm told the price you have agreed is fifty pence per pill and that your last shipment was for ten thousand pills, please correct me if any of my information is incorrect"

The brothers exchanged a look.

Keith Drake fidgeted in his chair "How do you know that?"

"It's my business to know"

Keith scratched as his face, he tried to keep his cool and play it out like any normal meeting but Begsy had shaken both brothers up, they were out of their comfort zone, exactly where McSharry wanted them.

He looked at one and then the other, they both looked nervous.

"I'm willing to offer you the same deal"

The two brothers shared another look, he caught a hint of the old belligerence come back into Johnny's face. Crippling another one of their boys might be the only way to keep the prick quiet.

Keith ran a hand through his hair, he took his time responding, as if he was picking his words very carefully.

"I'm not sure I see the benefit of your proposal. We have a situation here that works, why would we want to jeopardise that when there's no obvious gain in it for us?" he talked slowly, as if by reciting the words in a clear fashion it would make the flaws of the argument obvious.

McSharry smiled "There will be gain, in the long run. You see I'm looking to expand my business much further than Liverpool, I'm thinking the entire North West, out into Yorkshire, maybe even the North East. When that happens you're looking at triple or maybe even quadruple the numbers you're bringing in now. If you get in on the ground floor there's going to be a lot of money to be made"

The anger seemed to slowly be returning to Johnny's face, his brother was decidedly more diplomatic, he held McSharry's gaze and kept his tone respectful.

"We've no interest in turf wars. We're businessmen, we supply a product to a consumer, that's it. If this 'larger operation' you're talking about includes eliminating your competition then I'm sure you can understand that it wouldn't be in our interest to be associated with you when the retaliations began, would it? We have a good set up the way things are. If we agreed to your proposition then we would be positioning ourselves as a target for anyone who comes into conflict with you"

"You're already a target for anyone wanting to fuck with Wayne Caddock. If I wanted to disrupt their operation this warehouse would be the first place I'd come. I think you've seen today that if someone did come for you two, that so called protection you have wouldn't keep you alive for five minutes. Not only can I offer you more security, I can offer you a bigger piece of a bigger pie and if you're worried about upsetting people or getting dragged into something nasty let me assure you right now; there will be no war. Now, I'm told you're due another shipment within the next couple of weeks, is that right?"

"It is" Keith Drake said, leaning back in his chair. The man looked impressed with what he was hearing, McSharry suspected he could do a lot of solid business with a man like this, all he needed to do was curb the brother. Standing up he buttoned his thick overcoat and smiled at the two brothers.

"I don't want your answer today. Take the rest of the day and tomorrow to think it over, call me Tuesday morning with your decision. I must insist, as an act of good faith, that you don't discuss this offer with anyone else until that deadline has passed. It wouldn't be in the interest of anyone in this room for that to happen, I hope you understand what I'm saying"

He was about to give the order to leave when Johnny Drake rose from the couch and took a couple of steps towards him. All of the pricks previous animosity had come flooding back, maybe it was because he'd been left out of the discussion, or maybe the courage that had abandoned him so quickly had somehow rallied itself for a second assault. Whatever the reason when Johnny Drake stepped over the body of his unconscious employee and squared up to McSharry the mood of the entire room turned in an instant.

"Before you go I've got a quick question. What's to stop me calling Wayne Caddock the second you leave and telling him everything you just told us? Or maybe I should tell him that you beat up a couple of our guys, maybe I'll tell him to send fifty guys round to your house to cut the lot of you up into little pieces. What would happen then?"

"Johnny…" Keith began, with a weariness that said he'd found himself between his brother and danger more times than he could count.

"No, I'm just asking Keith, what would happen?"

For a second he played with the idea of having Johnny taken out right then and there, not only would his men be aching for some action, but he had no doubt that Keith would be easier to negotiate with alone. Then he thought of his own brother, and what he'd done to the men who killed him. There were some things that a man just could not forgive, even if it was good for business. If he wanted their drugs he was going to have to tolerate the little prick. For now.

"You've never heard of me before have you? There's a look people get, when they know who I am. Your brother has it, you don't. Your brothers look says that he's heard some pretty nasty stories, he's heard the name and he knows it's a name that shouldn't be fucked with. Names have a lot of power, why don't you ask your brother what he's heard about mine, and I'll expect the hear from you on Tuesday"

Johnny smiled. The anger was still there, but it had been downgraded, caution diluted it and kept him quiet. He looked at his brother, Keith gave a subtle nod and they both looked back towards McSharry.

Without another word he turned around and ushered the rest of his crew towards the door. A couple of them looked disappointed, a couple more flashed pissed off looks in the direction of Johnny Drake, but they all did as they were told.

The point had been made and the purpose of their visit had been achieved. There was nothing left to do on the docks of Liverpool today.

After all of his men had made their way towards the staircase he turned back to face the brothers one last time. Johnny, his skinny shoulders hunched, was looking at his brother, who in turn seemed lost in thought while he stroked his chin. Only the three remaining heavies kept their eyes on Stephen McSharry, all still troubled by the possibility that something could kick off before he and his men were out of the building.

"Tuesday, and not a word before" he said for the final time. Keith looked up, as if awoken from a deep sleep and nodded in his direction. With that McSharry stepped out of the office and joined his men on the staircase.

The boys were in high spirits for the entire journey back, the last few years had left them so starved of success that even a morsel of a victory against a couple of empty shirts like the Drake brothers had them feeling on top of the world. Even Begsy took a brief break from his stoic demeanour to smile, though with his scarred face and cruel grey eyes it looked more like a perverted distortion of what happiness was supposed to be.

He felt the optimism, the first real step had been taken that would lead them to where they needed to be, and it had come off without a hitch. The brothers wouldn't talk, he was confident about that, the second they left Keith Drake would be telling his brother that Stephen McSharry was not a man to be messed with.

If Keith was as connected as it seemed then it was likely he'd have a few stories about Begsy as well, and those wouldn't be backdated ten years like his own. Recent shit would scare them more; it would let them know that they still had influence, and that his plan could work.

His original plan had been to brace the brothers after Caddock had been clipped, but it was too much a risk. The size of their operation and their need for immediate protection meant there was no guarantee that the brothers wouldn't run straight to Tony Miller when they heard their business partner had been killed. This way they knew Stephen McSharry was back on the scene, and in a little over 24 hours they would know he was for real.

For now the success of the plan was out of his hands, it was time for Rob Thomas to step up and play his part. As the days passed and the date for the hit grew closer and closer his concern over the kid had been growing exponentially. There was no way of telling whether his hitter was up to it until he tried, and if he wasn't it would be too late.

Begsy was right, the kid was soft, it was an unfortunate coincidence that he was also the best.

Rob Thomas could put a bullet through a man's eye from thirty yards, that he was also too deeply entrenched in social dogma to take any joy in his skill gave McSharry all the proof he needed that there was a God, and that he had a sick fucking sense of humour.

Maybe that was why he always went back to the kid, because he was fascinated by his moral turmoil. Usually it was an amusing sideshow to a necessary action, but this time it was different, there was too much at stake for it to be screwed up by a pussy with a conscience.

With a sigh he pushed the kid from his head and tried to focus on the days success. There was no sense dwelling on the negative when there was so much positive, but one glance out of the window as they approached his home blew all such thoughts out of his mind.

The first car was stopped at the foot of the drive, Ads, Rico, Sie and Mercer had all climbed out and seemed to be gesturing angrily at something in front of them. It was only when he opened the door and stepped onto the street that he saw the problem for himself; a police cruiser parked diagonally across his driveway.

Leaning against it were two uniformed Bobbies and that little prick David Walker.

McSharry shook his head in disbelief and marched towards the obstruction. David Walker watched him the whole way, he looked like he'd aged a hell of a lot more than ten years. He recognised that same smug look, the same pointed noise sharp enough to draw blood and the same superior air. The only immediate difference was the coppers receding hairline, and the expensive dark blue suit he wore to offset his rat like features.

The two constables were young, somewhere in their twenties, and both held themselves fiercely rigid. Their eyes darted from one gangster to the next, exposing both inexperience and nervousness. The crunch of autumn leaves confirmed that the rest of his crew had followed him forward and were standing a few paces behind.

Walker didn't take his eyes off McSharry.

"Welcome home"

He fought hard to keep his face neutral, worry and annoyance he could control, but the sheer depths of hatred he felt for the man in front of him did its best to force itself to the surface. He reminded himself of all the important things he needed to do, of how irrelevant this copper was in the midst of it all, when he spoke his voice was pure calm.

"Constable Walker. Is there a reason you're blocking my drive?"

He felt eyes on his back, some of them would never speak to the filth, it was drilled into them since childhood. Others places had their allegiance to God, Liverpool had its allegiance to silence. It was a code strongly adhered to by the new generation of villains, but one McSharry had never truly embraced. It was petulant, to say nothing of naive, a man should always know his enemies. A few of the boys wouldn't understand, but they'd have to live with it. The smug little prick would be hanging around whether he spoke to him or not, it made sense to get a clearer understanding on the man's intentions, something told him he was likely to need it.

"I came with some news. I offered to wait inside but your butler didn't seem too enthusiastic"

McSharry looked past the coppers and saw Caffers stood in the doorway with his arms crossed, contemptuously glaring down towards the intruders. A quick glance behind him confirmed that the rest of the boys wore similar looks.

"He's very particular about the kind of people he lets in. You know what it's like, you let one rodent in the house and the next thing you know you're infested"

The two uniforms shifted in annoyance, Walker's only reaction was a conceited smirk as he assessed the rest of the crew. McSharry remembered the look, it was the same one he'd had on his way to the stand.

"I'd have thought after ten years inside you'd be well acquainted with all kinds of rodents. Maybe another ten would finish the job?"

McSharry shook his head dismissively "I don't think so, I've done my time. I'm a free man ready to live a free life. Now, did you come here for a reason, or are you just stopping by to illegally block my drive?"

The two boys in uniform glanced at one another, he got the impression that they didn't really know why they were there. He suspected if the pointy nosed prick had sold it to them under the guise of rousing a couple of ex-cons they were probably wishing they'd asked for more specifics. Walker pulled a piece of paper from his breast pocket and started to read.

"At approximately nine pm last night a Mr George McSharry was found murdered along with two known associates. Their bodies were located in Formby woods, George was strangled while his two mates were both shot at close blank range. We've had no joy trying to locate Mr McSharry's mother which makes you the poor bastard's next of kin"

McSharry knew exactly where George's mother was; drinking herself to death in some dive on the East Lancs road, the same place she'd been for the last five years. Walker folded up the piece of paper and put it back in his pocket. The prick waited patiently for a response, every now and then his eyes drifted over McSharry's shoulder towards Begsy. The copper knew who killed George, he could cast a lot of aspersions on the man but being dumb wasn't one of them. He played along anyway, just for the fun of it.

"Murdered? Terrible news. I suppose it's too much to hope that you people have any suspects?"

"Funny you should mention that. Would you mind confirming your whereabouts on Monday 18th November between the hours of one and four pm?"

Walker's two lapdogs raised their eyes in interest, their nerves had settled and they seemed to be enjoying their front row seat to McSharry's interrogation. He wondered why Walker had employed two street bobbies to accompany him on the trip, did he think the uniforms would be enough to scare him, or did he not want the people in his department to know that he was harassing an ex-con. He smiled a gentle smile towards Walker, the man would have to work a lot harder than that if he wanted to pin a murder on Stephen McSharry.

"I was inspecting a factory I own in Preston; the twenty five members of staff should be able to verify it. I can tell you there will be CCTV footage from the premises as well, but you can take that up with my lawyer"

"Preston, right" Walker's tone sounded less than convinced "If you could just give the name of the warehouse to these men then we can verify-"

"You can take it up with my lawyer" McSharry repeated.

For the first time in their conversation he caught a look of annoyance flicker across the cops face, it gave his eyes a petulant, more determined look as he continued his questioning.

"Right, and you wouldn't know of anyone who would want to kill George, would you?"

McSharry heard a cough from over his shoulder and knew it to be Begsy's attempt at humour, Walker's eyes darted towards the sound and gave him a long, knowing look. He was surprised how amusing it was to watch the cop's frustration build, he made a mental note to ensure it wasn't the last time.

"My nephew was a young man with a lot of enemies. I blame the absence of a strong male role model over these last ten years. Being locked up and all I wouldn't be able to give you any specific details on his friends or lifestyle, but suffice to say that he was a kid who got himself into more scrapes than he needed to"

"What kind of scrapes?"

"I don't know," McSharry said, shrugging his shoulders "general scrapes, I was speaking metaphorically"

Once again David Walker directed his gaze over McSharry's shoulder, he kept his eyes focused on Begsy while he spoke.

"You know what's interesting; the cause of death for George is remarkably similar to that of your old lawyer James Ploughman after he was put in protective custody. Garrotted, most likely with a guitar string, I'm assuming you heard about his murder?"

Walker finally broke the stare with Begsy, the coppers impotent rage was practically radiating off him, and it seemed to be increasing by the second. It was like a red flag to a bull.

Stephen McSharry had dealt with his own feelings of frustration bore from the name of James Ploughman. When the lawyer turned it had ruined the years of hard work and planning that had led him to the pinnacle of the Liverpool underworld. He still wasn't sure what the police had on Ploughman to convince him to roll over, but whatever they had it was enough for him to give up nine years of privileged information on a variety of dealings. Luckily they had never been able to make murder, the lawyer hadn't been privy to that kind of information. But he had enough knowledge and enough paperwork on drug shipments, gun caches and armed robberies to send Stephen McSharry down for ten long years.

At least he could take comfort in Begsy's drawn out execution of the rat. His enforcer had succeeded where Rob Thomas had failed two weeks before the trial, but it had taken him three and a half years to track the bastard down. The witness protection programme was not an easy one to infiltrate. He wished he could have been there to see the look on Walker's face when news came through of Ploughman's death, when he heard the details of the torture. Walker was the architect of the lawyers deal; it came out in court that he'd been the one who approached him. He was sure the beady eyed policeman blamed himself for Ploughman's death. Knowing that fact brought almost as much pleasure as knowing that the lawyer was dead, it was the very definition of a win-win scenario.

"That's a tragic coincidence" McSharry said, the lack of sincerity in his tone mocking the three policemen "and what a horrible way to go. I doubt it's got any better for Mr Ploughman in the ninth circle of hell. You're a catholic, aren't you Constable? Did it feel good sending that man to join Judas?"

Walker's eyes flashed with righteous anger, when he finally spoke his breathing was ragged "You're talking about a good man. It takes a lot of courage to stand up to a thug like you"

He knew it wasn't smart to antagonise the man, but he could feel ten years of repressed aggression bubbling up inside him. He glared at the man who had stolen a decade of his life. That the lawyer was a sensitive subject just urged him on, and with his men at his back it was impossible to resist.

"How much courage does it take to make up lies in a courtroom?" McSharry sneered "It's irrelevant, clearly there was someone out there who didn't think the shyster was as courageous a man as you did!"

Walker pushed himself away from the car and moved towards McSharry, his eyes were wide and his jaw was clenched, making the man look almost paralysed with anger.

"You're scum, you know that" Walker roared, spitting the words in a flurry of pent up aggression "You're a cancer on this city, and I swear to God I'll make sure you spend the rest of your days in a dark room with a locked door. If I have to spend the next five years of my life personally following you around until I catch you in one of your shady little deals then that's what I'm going to do, you hear me you piece of shit? The next time you go down, you won't come back up"

Stephen McSharry didn't even try to hide the grin as it spread across his face. The filth had nothing, they were desperate, and this petulant little copper was the embodiment of that failure. There was a part of him that burned to strike out at the man for daring to speak to him like that, but the urge was outweighed by the part of him that knew the situation for what it was; victory. The last futile attempt of intimidation by a desperate man with nowhere to go. If he didn't hate the bastard so much Stephen McSharry might have felt sorry for him in that moment; his face red with rage, his eyes bulging erratically and his small jaw grinding hard enough to shatter teeth. The prick was the very picture of a man at the end of his tether.

"I've been out of prison for six days" McSharry said calmly, addressing all three of the policemen in front of him "I'd like to enjoy my first free Sunday without this cheap show of police harassment. Thank you for notifying me of my nephews death, if there's nothing else, get off my property"

He spat at the feet of David Walker, the two uniforms took offence and made a forward movement. It was a bad choice, the crew at his back stepped forward in response and the two kid policemen were forced to slink back under the gaze of seven angry killers.

Walker glanced down at the substance on the pavement, then up to McSharry, the look on his face suggesting that he held the spit at his feet and the man before him in a similar regard. For a moment he seemed caught between two minds, his face was still red, his eyes were wide and full of anger, and then he blinked and let out a small sigh. The hatred suddenly evaporated from his face, within seconds he looked like the calm, pretentious little rat that McSharry remembered from his trial.

With a wave of his right hand he gestured for the two officers to get into the car, glared at McSharry one final time and opened the driver's door.

He watched with the rest of his crew as the patrol car turned across his lawn and out onto the street. When it reached the end of the road and disappeared out of sight a few men started to speak, Begsy made his way forward and leaned in close.

"I'd love to put a bullet in that pricks head"

McSharry let himself think about the police for a second longer. In that second he remembered what it had been like to be their prisoner, he embraced all of his hated for David Walker, and any other man who tried to thwart his ambitions. He envisaged all the unspeakable things he would do to whoever got in his way, he thought about the bodies he would pile up to get what he wanted, and then he turned towards the house and focused his mind on business.

Chapter 13

Rob stood on the cobblestone street facing the Albert Dock, his heart was beating so fast that he thought it might explode out of his chest, but to the outside world he was the picture of calm. He leaned back against the metal rail, vaguely aware of the body of water that lay behind him, and surveyed the large brick complex. The Albert Dock had always been his favourite part of the city, even before the millions had flooded in from the European Capital of Culture success. In the old days he'd loved it for its rustic, eternal beauty, a last standing relic in a city that was slowly dying, but now it was the crown jewel of a new tourist hotspot, what a difference a decade could make.

He glanced to his left and saw the large, white, domineering shape of the Echo Arena. When he'd left that space had been nothing but a car park for weekend shoppers, now it was a 10,000 seater stadium. If he strained his ears he could hear the noise from the on-going gig, some forgotten rock band from the eighties on a comeback tour, it was far from the ideal location for what Rob had to do, but he had no other choice.

A shout from over his right shoulder tore Rob's attention from the docking complex; last orders had passed at the local pub and two drunken middle aged men were yelling at the barman as he ejected them from the premises. The men continued their tirade until the front door was bolted shut, defeated they grumbled complaints to one another and headed off into the city in search of a fresh watering hole.

Rob looked back towards the expensive bar in front of him. *The Blue Café* was one of a string of new, upper class bars that seemed to have taken hold of the Albert Dock. Even from his position on the opposite side of the street he could see blue and purple neon lights within, accompanied by the deep rumble of R'n'B music.

The window gave him a clear view of the main seating area at the side of the bar, though from what he could tell it was only half full, populated by men in suits and women in short dresses, all chasing one thing on a cold Monday in November.

It had been fifteen minutes since Rob followed Wayne Caddock and his men to the bar, he was confident he hadn't been seen, but decided to play it safe nonetheless. Another few minutes and then he'd make his way inside, so far he was conducting the job with an extra degree of caution, he hoped it would compensate for any potential rustiness he might be likely to suffer.

McSharry's file had been scarily accurate; Wayne Caddock had entered his favourite restaurant in Chinatown bang on 7:30, just like clockwork, then it was straight to the *Blue Café* for a few drinks. If Caddock's three previous Mondays were anything to go by, then he would be leaving in around an hour.

Cautiously, Rob checked his outfit for the final time, he knew this was the only place for the hit to go down, and planned his attire accordingly. He wore brown shoes with a pair of denim jeans, and a leather jacket over a black t-shirt. He'd bought the t-shirt a size too big so the Kevlar vest beneath wouldn't be too obvious, to the average passer-by he just looked like a guy in his mid-thirties who was carrying a bit too much weight. Tucked into the back of his jeans and hidden by the leather jacket where the two Smith and Weston, while the pockets of his jacket were filled with extra clips just in case he wasn't as efficient as he used to be.

With a deep breath Rob started off towards the bar, circling around the building and heading towards the front entrance. The two bouncers eyed him suspiciously as he approached, though neither said a word as he nodded in their direction and marched through the open glass doors.

The room was dark, though not quite as loud as he'd expected. Despite the fact that it was only half full Rob failed to spot his target on a first sweep of the crowd. He made his way straight to the bar and ordered a glass of coke, the fast pace of his heart cried out for a shot of alcohol but he fought off the urge, booze made men slow and clumsy, he'd lost count of the number of guys he'd killed where the difference had been a seconds reaction time. If it slowed him down a fraction of a second then it wasn't a risk worth taking. A fraction might be all it came down to.

Rob sipped at the drink and spotted an empty table in the corner, making his way towards it he sat down with his back to the wall and surveyed the room. There was no sign of Wayne Caddock.

He blocked out the first hints of panic. McSharry had been very specific about his deadlines, after what had happened with James Ploughman he was reluctant to make it two failures in a row; that might just be enough to convince the old man that Rob wasn't worth keeping alive.

Just then he caught sight of a large, tattooed arm protruding from a doorway on the other side of the bar. The rest of the clientele all had the look of legit businessmen about them, Rob felt a twinge of excitement that such body art could only belong to one group within the place.

He gave it another two minutes before he moved to a table on the opposite side of the room, sitting down and perusing the menu as he did so.

From his new spot he could see through the entrance into a smaller room in the back, Caddock's tattooed doorman partially blocked his view. Luckily the man's attention was focused exclusively on two tramps at the bar; dancing provocatively and throwing him suggestive looks whenever they got the chance. Rob used the distraction to look past the meathead and see what was going on within the small room. The darkness made it difficult to distinguish individuals, but every now and then a flash of blue light would illuminate the private area, giving him a clear view of his target.

At the restaurant there had only been Caddock and three of his boys, all of who had been easy to distinguish. The boss, with his blonde hair, handsome face and expensive suit stood out like a sore thumb against the backdrop of oversized thugs dressed in black, but here the situation was getting murkier.

In the few minutes he'd lost them Caddock had hooked up with a few more members of his firm; Rob eyed two new blokes in suits, each accompanied by an extra soldier. That upped his number of targets from four to eight, maths might not have been his strongpoint but he could still figure out that the job just got twice as hard. Another flash of blue light confirmed the worst of it; six girls had found their way into the back room and were scattered in amongst Caddock and his men, a blonde in a pink dress and a brunette in green had made an impression on the boss; he had one either side, plying them with booze while he pawed at their exposed flesh.

Rob felt his determination waver. It wasn't the possibility of more killing that phased him, if the new arrivals were associated with Caddock then there was a good chance they'd earned their execution, but Rob had vowed long ago never to take the life of another woman. He didn't think his sanity could take it if he crossed that line. Not again.

With the guard still distracted by the girls at the bar Rob was able to focus his attention on Wayne Caddock; he and his target were about the same age, though the benefits of a privileged lifestyle gave the other man a younger look. Rob noted the expensive haircut and the nice suit, it pointed towards a vanity that was rare in gangsters. On looks alone Caddock seemed better suited to the groups of businessmen in the main room, sipping cocktails and flirting with waitresses, watching him sitting in amongst a group of murderers was a visual that just didn't seem to fit.

His memory flashed back to Caddock's old man, he'd tracked him for nearly two months before he finally felt comfortable enough to complete the hit. He remembered him as an overweight, surly bloke whose dependence on booze had left him purple and bloated long before Rob had gotten to him. He had to wonder how attractive Mrs Caddock had been to offset the physical shortcomings of the boy's father.

He continued watching as Caddock worked his magic with the pretty little things either side of him, he was still having trouble picturing the man as dangerous. Rob tried to visualise Caddock standing over the dead bodies of his victims, when that didn't kick him into gear he tried to imagine the dead bodies of Vera and Charlie. That would only be the start of it if he didn't get the job done.

He took another sip of coke, it tasted sickly sweet without the tint of whiskey to balance it out. Pushing the thought out of his mind he turned his attention towards the supporting cast. Of the five men who made up the muscle Rob caught the unnatural bulges on three that confirmed they were carrying, past that the distance and the lighting made it impossible to tell what their arsenal was.

After a few minutes he became aware that Caddock's man on the door was watching him, Rob turned towards the bar, the two tramps were still dancing but they were doing so with a couple of suits who'd appeared from across the room. Pissed off by the snub the villain on bouncer duty was scanning the crowd intently, looking for anyone he could use as a punching bag to vent his fury.

Rob kept his eyes off the doorway for a while, looking from one woman to the next in the hope that the pissed off soldier would interpret his interest in Caddock's crew as that of a drunken lad eyeing up the talent.

He gave it a few minutes before he tested the water and looked in the direction of the back room. Caddock's spurned muscle had put the two girls well out of his mind while he surveyed the room before him, as his gaze passed over Rob it lingered for just a second longer than it needed to, and then continued on.

He knew instantly that it was time to go. Finishing off the last of the coke he moved towards the exit with his shoulders hunched. If Caddock's boy thought that he'd scared Rob off with a look then it was pretty unlikely he was going to consider him a threat; just another civilian easily subdued by the vaguest hint of violence.

Rob would be amazed if he stayed in the man's mind for more than five minutes.

He watched his own feet the whole way out. Once he was outside he snuck a quick look at his watch: 10:15, if Caddock kept to his usual routine he would be leaving within half an hour. The problem was that in forty five minutes the crowd from the Echo Arena would empty out, flooding the cobbled streets of the Albert Dock depriving Rob of his only chance.

He circled around the outside of the docks and walked along the section of the Mersey where he knew there were no cameras. Quickly he took the old baseball cap from his pocket and slid off the leather jacket. Stuffing the spare clips into his jean pockets he disposed of the coat in a half empty bin and slid the navy blue cap onto his head. It wasn't much of a change but it would do.

Picking up speed he walked back around the docks and resumed his position at the back of the bar, the same position he'd watched from earlier. Without the jacket he was worried that the Kevlar vest would be visible under the t-shirt, he shook his head and dismissed the thought as paranoia, he'd checked himself in the mirror a dozen times, it was just nerves.

Rob looked over his shoulder, the bay of water was all that separated him from the busy dual carriageway fifty feet away. He didn't think he could have picked a more precarious location for a hit if he'd tried, but it was too late to worry about that.

In spite of the adrenaline pumping through his body he began to feel the first twinges of fatigue niggling at his muscles. No sleep had come the night before, his mind had been too busy analysing every possible outcome and predicting the repercussions for the worst of them. Not that it made much difference; the frequency and intensity of the nightmares had him down to a couple of hours sleep per night as it was, and if he had to choose between fatigue and reliving those dreams, he knew which one he'd pick.

By four in the morning he'd abandoned his paranoia and put himself to

167

more productive use. He knew a heavily wooded park close by, taking the two silencer fitted guns he hopped the fence and found a well shielded area to practice his shooting. After ten minutes he was glad that he had. He was a member of a shooting range in New Jersey, but over the years his interest in reliving his former glory had rapidly deteriorated, it was only when he started practising that he realised the same thing had happened to his aim.

Having something to focus on helped Rob pass the remaining hours a little easier, he stayed in the park until after six, practicing until the cold had numbed his hands beyond all use.

His chest tightened when he thought about what might have happened if he hadn't found the time to practice; he'd have been lucky if he clipped one of Caddock's boys before they took him down, though he reminded himself that was still a very real possibility.

Rob glanced at his watch, 10:25; he was fast running out of time. He moved his hands towards his lower back to ensure that the guns would be easy to reach. He gave each of the grips a firm squeeze, checked that the silencers were still screwed on and moved his arms back to his sides.

A few seconds later two taxis pulled up between him and the *Blue Café*. The first driver didn't even glance in his direction; he knew who he was picking up and it wasn't a guy in a baseball cap.

Rob heard their voices first, then as they made their way around the back of the bar he recognised them as the girls with Caddock, more by their legs and their cleavage than anything else, particularly the two who had been draped all over his target.

Walking behind them was one of Caddock's crew, his face was all business as he ushered three of the girls into the first taxi and climbed into the second with the others. He watched him closely, his hand hovering over the gun as he waited for the gangster to spot something suspicious in Rob's loitering.

After half a minute he let his hand relax, Caddock's muscle seemed so preoccupied trying to shepherd six drunken girls back to the after party, that he probably wouldn't have noticed a police riot squad if it had been waiting for him. With a shake of the head he growled a command at the driver and the two taxis sped away, one after the other.

Rob breathed a sigh of relief, at last a bit of luck. Not only were the women out of the equation, but Caddock was one guard down. That still left six to get through before he reached his target, but at this point any drop in the odds was welcome.

The next two cars showed up a couple of minutes later, but where the women got private hire taxis Caddock and his boys rolled in a Jag and a Mercedes. He glanced into the front of the two cars and realised that his lucky streak had ended as quickly as it had begun; both drivers were pure muscle, and both had clocked his presence immediately. Rob fought the urge to swear as the two men watched him cautiously, he leaned back against the metal barriers and tried to glance at his watch with an impatient look; just a guy on a night out waiting for his friends, nothing unusual there.

He'd barely had time to account for the new arrivals when he caught sight of his target coming around the side of the Blue Café. Two men led the way but from where he was Rob could see the blond hair of Wayne Caddock just over one of their shoulders.

There was still twenty feet to cover before they made it to the cars, Rob took a deep breath and looked over; one of the drivers had already forgotten about him as he leaned over to open the passenger door, though driver number two was still keeping tabs.

His heart pounded in his chest, only fifteen feet until they reached the cars, he felt the sweat on the palm of his hands and worried about how he was going to grip the pistols.

Rob confirmed the count as they kept moving forward; Caddock, two lieutenants and the other four were muscle, excluding the drivers. He needed to hit them fast, surprise would be the only thing that would get him through it, he wasn't willing to rely on luck, at least not yet.

Ten feet, time to make his move.

Rob took two steps into the street, as he moved he slid his hands behind his back and gripped the two pistols. In the same instant that his fingers wrapped around the cold metal, his eyes locked with the soldier at the front of the entourage, he recognised him immediately; it was the one on bouncer duty.

His arms froze for a split second, but it was a split second too long. The soldier's eyes widened and he screamed out in alarm, Rob tried to move his arms but they were too slow, all he could hear was the beating of his own heart as the man squeezed off a shot from a 9mm, hitting Rob square in the chest before he had a chance to aim his weapons.

He felt the pain engulf his lunges as the bullet made contact with the vest. A strange feeling washed over him, it was as if time had slowed down and sped up in the same instant, it was a feeling he had forgotten, but somewhere inside it felt entirely natural.

As he fell backwards he instinctively raised the guns towards the first two men, even though he was falling he knew as soon as he pressed down on the triggers that they were dead, a fraction of a second later he watched their heads explode as the bullets connected with each of their foreheads.

Pain reverberated up Rob's spine as he landed with a crash, but he paid it no more mind than he did the hurt in his chest. Rolling onto his side he pushed himself up into a kneeling position. He didn't remember raising the guns for a second time but somehow his outstretched arms where facing the remaining men. The two suit wearing lieutenants had dropped to the floor and the other two guards were pushing themselves in front of Wayne Caddock as they aimed their weapons.

Before they had a chance to fire he had squeezed off another two shots, the first hit a soldier in the throat, he fell backwards clutching the hole in his neck, the second went through the other man's left eye, he dropped to the ground in a crumpled mess, like a puppet whose strings had just been cut.

As he watched the two men die, he became vaguely aware of car engines roaring to life. The sound redirected his attention towards the drivers; he watched Wayne Caddock dive head first into the passenger seat of the first car and in that moment the calm precision that had carried him this far evaporated into the air.

Rob pushed himself up urgently and fired six times from each gun in the direction of the two drivers. He had no idea how many connected but by the time the guns where empty neither man was moving.

Reflex memory took it from there, basic training from eighteen years earlier kicked in before he had time to think. Rob dropped to one knee, limiting his visibility and making him a smaller target, while he ejected the empty clips and replaced them with new ones.

From the corner of his eye he saw Caddock and one of his lieutenants scramble away from the car and sprint down the street towards the Echo Arena.

Pushing a clip into each gun he stood up and aimed the weapons at the Merc and the Jag, he was only a few steps away from the first driver's bloody remains when the other lieutenant jumped out from behind the car, with a 9mm in his hand

The man had the crazed look of someone fighting for his life, but his inexperience with a gun was obvious immediately; the arch of his arm was slow and clumsy, while his grip was loose. Rob had squeezed off two bullets into the man's expensive suit before he'd come close to firing. The lieutenant fell backwards, dead before he hit the ground.

He surveyed the bodies and confirmed what he suspected, the muscle all had Kevlar vests, but Caddock and the lieutenants were unprotected. Pausing long enough to finish off the gangster who was choking to death, Rob started off in pursuit of Caddock and his lieutenant, they already had a head start of about twenty feet.

The pain in his chest threatened to halt him after every step, but Rob did his best to put it to the back of his mind, he chased them for thirty feet until he felt the throbbing began to overwhelm him.

He dropped to one knee and let the gun in his left hand fall to the floor, gripping the other with both in the same movement. His two targets had increased the distance between them to thirty yards now and they were closing in on the end of the street. Once they passed that point they would no longer be restricted by the water on their left and the Docks on their right, which would make catching them so much more difficult.

Rob tried to focus on Caddock, but his view was blocked by the lieutenant running a couple of steps behind. Whether he was intentionally providing cover for his boss or not, Rob couldn't say, but there was only one way to get to him out of the equation.

He took a few seconds to get his aim just right, but as soon as he shot he knew it was good, the bullet caught the lieutenant high in the shoulder and sent him crashing to the ground at high speed. Caddock slowed for a second as he turned to look at his fallen colleague, then shot off even faster than before. Rob aimed again but before he had time to fire Caddock had turned right and followed the outer wall of the Albert Dock towards the Mersey.

"Fuck!"

Rob stood up and ran faster than he thought his weary body would allow. When he reached the fallen lieutenant he used his foot to push the man onto his back; still alive and bleeding heavily, the bullet had gone right through the shoulder. They were both of a similar age, and the fallen man's auburn hair reminded him of Jo, for a second Rob found himself looking into the mans terrified eyes and wondering what the hell he was doing. He found a grim determination somewhere in his gut and used it close off that part of his brain, a second later he fired twice into the man's face. The lieutenant took a few moments to die, once he was gone Rob took a deep breath and continued his pursuit.

As he turned the corner he realised with surprise that he'd made up some ground, with a grunt he pushed himself even harder and followed Caddock along the outside of the Dock towards the Mersey.

He felt the ache in his legs and burning in his chest as he tried to reduce the gap further. In that moment he was vaguely aware of the Echo Arena to his left, it couldn't have been far away, he just hoped that the darkness would do a good enough job of hiding them before anyone could see what was going on.

Rob was gaining ground fast; the distance must have been no more than fifteen feet as Caddock closed in on the metal barrier that separated the dock from the river. He had no idea where the man was planning to go, but he didn't intend to find out, dropping to one knee he repeated the procedure that took out the last lieutenant. His heart was racing as he took aim, it was harder to focus and his hand was ever so slightly shaking. Caddock was only a few feet away from the River.

With a final concentrated effort Rob aimed and fired. The bullet connected with its target somewhere in the back and Wayne Caddock collapsed forward, by the time his body hit the ground he'd stopped moving.

Rob slid the gun in his hand into his belt and picked the other up from the floor, jogging cautiously towards the fallen body. The energy it had taken to reach Caddock suddenly seemed to catch up to him, and the light jog started to feel like the most strenuous physical activity of his life.

He waited for the sound of screams but none came, if he was lucky he still had a few minutes before someone discovered one of the bodies.

As he got to within a few feet he trained his gun on the fallen body, there was no movement. The bullet had hit him somewhere in the middle of the back but the circle of blood soaking through the expensive suit was too wide to tell precisely where. He reached the body and kneeled down to make sure that there was no pulse; he'd done the hard part, he didn't intend to make a mistake now.

As soon as his fingers touched Caddock's neck he felt the body convulse and rise from underneath him, before Rob had recovered his bearings Caddock had slammed the gun out of his grip. A second later the man's free hand emerged from inside his suit holding a knife.

He'd been caught off guard, and before he had a chance to regain the initiative Caddock had pushed him back against the metal barriers that separated them from the Mersey. His hands frantically tried to get a grip on Caddock's arm, but the suit sleeve was too slippery with blood to get a firm hold, it was only a matter of time before Rob lost the weak grip he had and Caddock sliced the blade through his windpipe

He looked into the eyes of Wayne Caddock and found himself staring at the killer he had previously been unable to imagine, those handsome features were distorted in rage, his smooth skin was scrunched into a snarl of pure hatred and his pearly white teeth looked like those of a rabid dog ready to bite. Rob stared into the face as the knife made its way closer and closer to his throat.

The blade was less than an inch away from his throat when Rob heard a loud clatter as the large metal doors of the Echo arena were thrown open, the unexpected sound was enough to cause Caddock to pause for a second, but a second was all Rob needed.

Forcing his knee into the man's groin Rob gripped Caddock's wrist and twisted the knife inwards, with the momentum now on his side Rob forced Caddock's body back into the barrier as he began to push the knife towards his targets chest.

The look of hatred disappeared from Caddock's face as soon as he lost the initiative, he fought desperately to keep the knife away from his heart with a look of desperation etched upon his handsome features. Rob found it difficult to believe that just a few seconds earlier such uncontained hatred had been staring back at him.

As Rob pushed the knife closer to Caddock's heart he heard the sounds of voices as thousands of people began to empty out of the arena.

"Please, don't!" Caddock gasped, the look on his face had moved to fear now, blind, terrified fear, Rob looked at the man and almost lost the strength in his arms.

"I'm sorry" he muttered, not sure if it was loud enough to hear, and with one final push forced the knife into Caddock's heart.

Fear gave way to shock as blood sprayed out over the knife and onto Rob's hands, a second later the shocked look was crystallised in death.

Rob stared into Caddock's hollow eyes for a second longer, then with a mighty effort he lifted the body up and tossed it over the railing into the river below.

172

He turned quickly to face the arena, it was emptying by the thousands but everyone was heading in the opposite direction, and no one appeared to have seen him dispose of the body. Picking up the gun and tucking it into his belt he slid the bloody knife along with his bloody hands into the pockets of his jeans, and hurried to join the crowds heading home.

Walking as fast as he could he worked his way cautiously through the crowd until he was somewhere in the middle, by the time he was out of the Albert Dock he could hear police sirens getting closer and closer. None of the crowd seemed to have any idea of what had happened, all the conversations he heard consisted of either discussions about the gig or ideas about where to go for a post-concert drink.

Rob stayed amongst the crowd until it began to thin out, with his gaze still focused on the floor he darted down a side street and made his way across the city.

By the time he reached a payphone his body was shaking uncontrollably, his left hand was warm and sticky where it gripped the bloody knife. He was sure he could smell the blood; it made him want to vomit so badly that he had to stop himself from throwing the blade away every time he passed a bin.

His right hand was mostly dry, he'd found a puddle of water on the floor where he washed off most of the blood, there hadn't been much on that hand, not enough for the police to trace anyway.

Picking up the receiver with his clean hand he cradled it between his head and his shoulder while he tried to dial. It took a couple of attempts; his hand was shaking too badly to find the right numbers. Eventually he got the sequence he wanted, after five rings she answered.

"Hello?"

The sound of Jo's voice shook him from his daze and brought home the severity of what he'd just done. Thanks to him there were nine corpses scattered around the Albert Dock tonight, nine bodies that innocent people would stumble across, nine mothers who would have to be told their sons were dead, nine fathers who would never again see their children, nine funerals, nine autopsies. The need to vomit rose up into Rob's chest but he pushed it back down.

"Babe, they made me do it" Rob said, into the receiver "I had to"

"Rob?" the concern in Jo's voice made him feel even worse "Are you ok? What happened?"

Rob tried to find the words, but his head was spinning out of control, he stumbled as his legs gave way beneath him, propping himself up against the side of the phone box.

"I had to do it" he repeated "I didn't want to, I never wanted to, but I had to, it's not me, not really, but it's what I have to do!"

"Rob, I don't understand, what are you talking about?" Jo's voice was close to panic, he thought he heard the beginning of tears "Tell me what's happened, are you ok? Are you hurt? Jesus Christ baby, you're scaring me here!"

Rob slid his right hand underneath the t-shirt and fingered the cross around his neck, it all happened so fast; he didn't think he remembered it all. Images flashed in front of his eyes, the splattering of blood, the glazed look of the dead, it felt like waking from an awful dream and slowly remembering all the horrible things he'd seen.

Rob took his left hand from his pocket and stared at the bloody fingers holding Wayne Caddock's knife, he was vaguely aware of Jo talking on the other end of the line, but he couldn't divert his attention away from the blood stained skin. It hypnotised him, held him in a trance he couldn't break. With an almighty effort he forced his hand back into his pocket and closed his eyes, pressing his head against the cold metal of the phone box.

When he opened them again he felt like he'd regained some semblance of control, not completely, he'd need something more significant than a few seconds of darkness to take care of that, but he was calmer, more together.

"No, it's ok, I'm fine" Rob said into the phone, responding to Jo's increasingly frantic pleas "I'm sorry, I didn't mean to scare you, I'm ok. I have to go, that job I had to do, well it isn't finished yet, but I'm close darling, I promise you, I'm close"

It took Jo a few moments to respond, Rob wasn't sure if she was weighing up his words and deciding whether or not she believed them, when she spoke he knew that she'd been crying.

"Come home baby, I love you!"

"Me too" Rob said, he didn't have it in him to say the words, after the things he had just done he had no right to profess love to anyone, he was a monster, and a monster didn't deserve the comfort of intimacy, not even for a moment "I'll speak to you soon"

He hung up quickly, before his courage failed him. He'd hoped calling her would distract him from what he was doing, but the truth was that killing again had infected him too deeply, he couldn't disengage. There would be no segregation in his head until the job was done, and even after that he wasn't sure if he could ever go back to what he had been. Jo may have been able distract him from his memories when he was in New York, but here, in the heart of it all, there would be no peace until it was done. Checking left then right to ensure no one was following him, Rob stepped out onto the street and headed to the nearest pub. The memories would keep speaking to him, no matter what he did, but if he drank enough then he might just be able to drown them out.

Chapter 14

David Walker woke to the sound of his mobile phone as it vibrated against the bedside table. Gingerly, he looked across to the alarm clock and tried to make sense of the flashing numbers; 1:07, that couldn't be right. Still half asleep he shuffled across the bed and answered the phone.

"David Walker"

"Officer Walker" said a firm female voice "We have reports of a multiple homicide that took place at the Albert Dock within the last few hours, the Regional Director has personally requested for your presence at the crime scene"

"When?" David asked, rubbing slowly at his left eye.

"Immediately"

He dropped onto his back with the phone still pressed to his ear and tried to organise his thoughts. Sleep had only come an hour earlier and his body resented the interruption, he fought the urge to wrap himself in the covers and with an almighty effort pushed himself back up into a sitting position.

"Are you sure he requested me? I think you need someone in the Major Incident Team, MIT deals with homicide investigations, not me, I left that team years ago"

"I'm aware of who investigates murders, Officer Walker. The MIT have been at the scene for over an hour" the resentment in her voice made each word sharp and cold "I am acting on the directive of the Regional Director John Barry, who personally asked me to contact David Walker from the Serious Organised Crime Agency and to tell him to make his way to the Albert Dock immediately"

He didn't need this right now, the lack of sleep over the past few days had put him in a near permanent state of irritability, being woken up after an hour by a pedantic secretary with a cryptic message was a hassle he could do without. He tried to keep the irritation from reaching his voice, but he didn't like his chances.

"Why does he want me there?"

"The Director asked me to inform you that one of the victims was Wayne Caddock, he said you would know who that was"

He closed his eyes as soon as he heard the name, there was no tiredness waiting to take him when he did, sleep had been pushed to the furthest reaches of his mind. With a sense of dread he climbed out of bed in nothing but his underwear, the cold hit him instantly but he was only half aware of it. Stumbling towards the small desk he eyed yesterday's suit strewn across the top, it would have to do.

"Tell the Regional Director that I'm on my way"

By the time he reached the Albert Dock every entrance was cornered off by

175

police tape and guarded by uniformed officers, to David's eyes they seemed both watchful and resentful at the same time. A small crowd had gathered near the main entrance made up of concerned local residents, journalists and drunken clubbers distracted by the commotion as they made their way home. Every one of them remained undeterred by the light drizzle that was soaking them through.

David pulled up to the barricade and presented his ID to the young officer guarding the entrance. The rookie sniffed contemptuously at the SOCA badge and silently pulled the barricade aside, ushering David's car through with a casual wave of the hand.

The small cobbled streets were already littered with vehicles; police cruisers, forensic vans and the expensive cars of the higher ups confirmed that there would be a full cast list on display tonight.

The distinctive glass ball streetlamps projected white light in all directions, giving the docks something of a dream like ambience. The impression was made all the more profound by the hazy drizzle that seemed to dim the features of the brick buildings around them.

He scanned the area for Chris Railton's car, he'd called him just before leaving the house and arranged to meet him here. David didn't know why he expected Railton to be on time but on this occasion he did, there was something in the air tonight, a feel of significance that promised the events of the early morning would be felt for a long time to come.

He stepped from the car and made his way towards the huddled mass a few buildings down from Granada Studios. Every officer he passed had a look of deep concentration etched upon their faces that told its own story, he knew a few well enough to talk to, but no one seemed willing to engage in chit chat tonight, this was all about business.

Before he'd taken a few steps he felt a tap on his shoulder and turned to see Chris Railton standing behind him. He was wearing a red jumper with a pair of jeans and black shoes, a little casual for David's liking, but then it was one in the morning. He looked like he'd been standing in the rain for a long time; the red jumper stuck to his body and his blond hair was matted to his head. There was something in his face that betrayed a nervousness, after a few moments Walker realised that it was the way his deputy's gaze would meet his for a brief moment before turning away at taking in the crime scene.

"You're here" Walker said, unable to hide his surprise "Have you seen anything of the bodies?"

Officer Railton shook his head "No, I thought it would be best to wait for you, I've just been standing around"

Walker eyed him suspiciously "Ok, have you seen anything useful, what about from the police side? Many famous faces?"

"One or two, I guess, maybe" Railton muttered, looking towards a group of police officers who seemed to be examining a body "The mayor's here, I saw him but I don't think he saw me. MIT, Anthony Lewis as well, they all look fucking pissed! Really, just, you know…"

"What's wrong with you?" David asked bluntly.

Railton shifted on his feet and let out a sigh "I, nothing, nothing's wrong with me, I'm just, you know, a bit tired and that. It's half one in the bloody morning"

Walker stared at him for a few seconds longer, Chris seemed reluctant to meet his gaze but when he did he let out a sigh and quickly looked away again, it was only after he had repeated the action three times that David finally deduced what was wrong.

"Are you drunk?" he asked in disbelief.

Chris looked around nervously and put a finger to his lips "It's my night off, ok? I went out to a couple of bars with some mates, let off some stream. How was I supposed to know a gangster was going to be massacred in the docks? I've got the worst fucking luck!"

David shook his head "Jesus Christ! Just keep your mouth shut and try not to embarrass yourself. How much have you had?"

His number two stifled a burp hand and winced "A fair bit"

"Jesus Christ" David said again, flashing another reproachful look before marching off towards the growing huddle. Railton followed a step or two behind.

As he covered the distance between himself and the mass of police officers he began to recognise a few more faces; he spotted two forensic scientists he knew from the old days, competent men whose names were on the tip of his tongue. Next he caught sight of a constable from the MIT who he'd met a couple of times, but the one that really caught his eye was the man in charge; Detective Sergeant Carl Drysdale. He looked much the same as David remembered, it had been a little over two years since he'd last crossed paths with the man, and his thick grey beard was still the most striking thing about him. As he got closer he took in the other features; the bald head with a patch of dark hair on each side, the large nose and large forehead that made his face seem fatter than it was, and the burly frame, quite impressive for a man in his mid-fifties. As soon as DS Drysdale saw him coming he issued a number of swift orders to the group and waited with an amused smile for Walker to reach him.

Situations like this always made him slightly uncomfortable. As a former DS with the Major Incident Team his first instinct was to wade knee deep into the crime scene and involve himself with the investigatory process as a matter of urgency, he always had to remind himself that it was no longer his job. As an Officer of the Serious Organised Crime Agency he was a guest on the crime scene run by the Merseyside Police, he was there to observe but in no way interfere, it was a requirement that went against every one of his natural instincts. Often times the grey area between the two organisations paved the way for some pretty brutal confrontations, not with Drysdale though, they went too far back to resort to such territorial nonsense.

"Officer David Walker, welcome to my humble crime scene!" Carl Drysdale uttered with a grin, extending his arms like an artist showing off his newest painting.

David ground to a halt just before his old colleague. The two men had worked side by side on the Major Incident Team for eight years, before SOCA had been formed and David had been handpicked by the Regional Director to lead his own team. Over the years he'd developed a great degree of respect for Carl Drysdale, and for what he could do on the job. The man's skills as an investigator were without question, in David's eight years at the MIT no one had ever amassed a murder clearance rate to compare with Drysdale's, it made him a legend around the place. He wasn't sure what it was that made the man so effective, perhaps it was instinct, or luck, whatever the secret he couldn't help but feel a slight sense of relief that he was in charge of the investigation.

McSharry was behind it, he knew it without looking at a single body, he could feel it in his bones. If they wanted to put together a conviction that was going to stick then they would need as many heavyweight officers as they could get their hands on, luckily Carl Drysdale was in that bracket.

A familiar feeling niggled at the back of his mind, memory recognised it instantly. In spite of his respect for Drysdale he'd never been able to truly warm to him as a person. He might have been one of the best around but the DS had a blasé, almost amused attitude towards murder that never quite sat right with him, even in a job like theirs. It was that feeling that whispered to him now.

He couldn't deny that working in the MIT for any significant length of time would have a desensitising effect on anyone, but there had been times when Carl Drysdale had acted around a crime scene the way a carpenter would act around a beautifully crafted chair. A sense of perspective on the job was essential, especially in a city like Liverpool. David had seen too many officers overwhelmed by the sheer weight of the atrocities they'd been forced to investigate, but a man who was fascinated by the sight of a bullet riddled body was the kind of man David Walker could never truly trust.

"Hello Carl" he said, looking over the shoulder of DS Drysdale to gage the crime scene behind him "what have you got?"

"Nine homicides" Drysdale said, moving aside to give David a clear view of the dead bodies scattered across the cobblestone street "for starters we've got eight shootings, with 45 ACPs taken from each of the bodies, and for the main course the stabbing of one of Liverpool's most famous underworld scumbags, not bad for a Monday night, is it?"

As soon as Drysdale moved aside Walker made his way towards the bodies, as he took in the first corpse he felt his stomach try to jump out of his mouth. It was a familiar feeling by now, he'd embarrassed himself on his first couple of cases by throwing up all over the crime scenes, but eventually his gag reflex had matured and he'd trained himself to deal with it. There was even a part of him that appreciated feeling the urge to vomit, it told him that he still hadn't turned into a man like Chris Drysdale, no matter how cynical he may have felt at times.

The first body he saw was behind the wheel of a Mercedes Benz. There were bullet holes in the windscreen and the side window on the passenger door was completely smashed. The victim had fallen on the gear stick at an awkward angle, David counted five bullet holes in his face and neck.

"Fuck me" he heard Railton mutter behind him.

He felt sorry for the lad, seeing a corpse was enough of an ordeal for a young officer, but seeing one when you were half cut ranked as the toughest stomach test he'd ever heard of.

Behind the Mercedes was a navy blue Jaguar, again it looked like driver was the only one inside and he'd been taken out in a similar fashion. The only immediate differences seemed to be that the dead man in the Jag was still sitting up straight, and he had four bullet holes in his face.

David walked around the car to the other side and felt his stomach give another uncomfortable lurch. Five corpses were littered across the floor and the breeze from the Mersey was already blowing the smell of decay in his direction. Defying every urge in his body he knelt down and examined the first corpse. When his eyes studied the bullet hole in the forehead something Carl had said struck him like a slap in the face, he looked up towards the Detective Sergeant.

"Did you say .45 ACP's?"

"That's right" Drysdale said, nodding his head as if he had expected the question sooner.

He felt a light-headedness to go with the sick feeling, it wasn't a good combination.

"It's been a while since we've seen those kinds of bullets in this kind of murder"

Drysdale unwrapped a piece of chewing gum and jammed it into his mouth "I'd say going on ten years"

The dizziness didn't seem to be going anywhere, he took a couple of deep breaths and looked at the other corpses that surrounded him.

"It could be a coincidence, there not hard to come across over in the states" he said the words more for his own benefit than for anyone else's.

"Could be, the fact that it was Wayne Caddock could be a coincidence too"

David moved on to the second corpse, this one was as heavily built as the first but where that man had just the one hole in his forehead the second had one in his head and one in his throat. The way the hands rested inches from the neck told him that the victim had taken the shot there first, the shooter would have finished him off at some point later, probably once all the others were off the board.

He took a few seconds to watch Railton inspect the first body. The boy wasn't getting too close but the concentration on his face implied that he was taking it all in, even if he was just trying not to throw up.

He turned his attention towards Drysdale and caught him surveying the corpses with a disapproving shake of the head, like the seven dead men had just spilled a glass of milk on his carpet.

"Wayne Caddock? It's definitely him?"

Drysdale nodded "Certainly is my friend. Though I'd guess he's a little wetter and a little more bloated since the last time you saw him. It's definitely your man though, as I live and breathe" he looked towards the corpses with a wry grin "No offence, fellas!"

"Is he here?"

He moved onto the third corpse, this man was smaller than the others and wore what had probably been an expensive suit before the blood and the rain had soaked it through. Walker recognised him; Johnny Tate, Caddock's number two. He was the kind of gangster that didn't like to get his hands dirty, who sent over people to handle his problems. There were two bullets lodged high in his chest, David guessed that both lungs had been punctured; he was dirty by the end, just like the rest of them.

"No, mainly muscle this lot. Your boy made a run for it before he was dropped, either that or the shooter killed him here and dragged his sorry arse round the docks to chuck him in the Mersey. Doesn't seem likely though, not with so many potential witnesses, I guess it could have been a message, like the old Sicilians; Wayne Caddock sleeps with the fishes and all that"

David stood up and brushed the water off his forehead.

"How many shooters?"

"They're still cleaning up the CCTV footage" Carl said, stepping over a few of the corpses as he moved towards Walker "It should be ready in a few minutes but from what I caught it looks like it was just the one"

"One man?" he said with surprise "Did all this?" he looked at the bodies on the floor and noticed that the rain was mixing with the blood, creating pools of pink water all around him.

"I know, reminds you of the old days, doesn't it? Haven't had one like this since the last time these fuckers tried to shoot up half the city... fucking gang wars" Drysdale breathed with contempt "If it was up to me I'd lock all the bastards in a sealed sports hall with a dozen shot guns and let them be done with it. I'm just relieved no civilians got caught up in this mess, otherwise the whole city would be in an uproar"

"You're sure? There are definitely no bystanders in amongst them?" David asked, he looked off towards the main entrance of the Docks and saw that the crowd had grown again by half.

"Oh yeah, no doubt" Carl Drysdale said, shovelling another stick of chewing gum into his mouth "They're all carrying wallets, we know who they are. Each of these slabs of meat has a criminal record as long as your arm, this hit was a hundred per cent professional"

David swallowed hard, the whole scenario was beginning to sound way too familiar "Any witnesses?"

"Not one, can you believe it?" Drysdale delivered the information with an incredulous smile and a shake of the head "Five bars in the area, a 10,000 sell out gig going on across the road and no one sees a bloody thing. We've got one couple who say they thought they saw two men running down towards the Mersey but when we pressed them for descriptions they didn't have a fucking clue"

Walker moved towards the last two corpses, another pair of heavily set men. Everything about them screamed muscle, each had a bullet hole in the middle of their foreheads.

"These two weren't murdered" David said solemnly "They were executed"

Drysdale nodded "No two ways about it, like a fucking Nazi firing squad. Do you want to see the main event?"

He led Walker and Railton to an ambulance on the other side of the Docks, as they walked David gave his deputy a reassuring pat on the back. The young man looked liable to throw up at any given moment, though he was doing an admirable job of keeping his face straight and emotionless, just like David had taught him.

When they reached the ambulance Carl climbed into the back and took a seat. The corpse was plum centre in the middle, laid out on a gurney beneath a white sheet. Drysdale waited until they had both taken their seats before he pulled it back, revealing the wet, bloated body of Wayne Caddock.

It took David a few moments to confirm the identity of the corpse. He'd spent years glaring at the man's features, both in photographs and in person, he was used to linking them to the unshakeable calm and the arrogant demeanour that Caddock always seemed to possess. Walker's eyes took in the damage, Caddock had carried himself with a professionalism too; the expensive suits, the styled hair, the handsome face that never betrayed a hint of worry, but trying to equate those characteristics to the rotting flesh on the gurney felt like an impossible task in that moment.

Caddock's suit was covered in a mixture of dirt, blood and seaweed, his skin was pale with purple veins protruding gruesomely from the cheeks, and the look on his face was one of shock mingled with fear. Of all the corpses he'd seen tonight, this was by far the most disturbing.

"Bullet through the shoulder" Drysdale casually pointed towards the exit wound, before moving his finger towards the centre of Caddock's stomach "but it was the knife to the abdomen that finished this flash wanker off. The first men on the scene spotted the body floating off towards the Irish Sea. You want to give me a couple of tips on who I should be looking to for? Your boy Stephen McSharry, maybe?"

David took a closer look at the wound in the abdomen; the knife had gone deep into Caddock's stomach and the entire bottom half of his shit was caked in blood. He wondered how long he'd had to bleed out before his body made contact with the water, once he hit it the cold would have numbed his already dwindling senses. The smell was in his nostrils, death mingled with dirt, he'd fished bodies out of the Mersey before and couldn't imagine a worse way to go.

"It's a possibility, definitely" Walker said, pulling his eyes away from the corpse and looking at Carl "It was either him, or it was someone using the hype of his release to settle some old scores, looking to sneak under the radar while everyone else was watching McSharry. Whoever it was, Miller will assume that McSharry had something to do with it, you and I may find ourselves standing over a few more bodies before this is done"

Carl flashed him a sadistic smile "That's fine with me, the more of these parasites we put in the ground the better off this city will be, and I could do with the overtime"

The three men stepped out of the ambulance, David hadn't realised how much he was enjoying the shelter until he was back in the rain. He looked at Railton, whose face was etched with concern, at first he thought it was a combination of the booze and the corpse, but after a few moments he realised it was something else.

"You really think he'd make a move like this?" Chris Railton asked "So soon after getting out, before he's hand a chance to acquire the muscle or make the contacts? It's a pretty ballsy play, I'm not sure I buy it"

There was condescension in Railton's tone, like the other two men were missing something obvious. Drysdale's gaze jumped from Walker to Railton and back again.

"Has this little shit been here the whole time?" Drysdale asked Walker "No wonder he keeps his bloody mouth shut"

Walker tried to supress a grin as Railton glared at the DS, his deputy was fond of taking the piss out of other people, but with a bit of booze in him he obviously didn't take kindly to the roles being reversed.

"Do you think it was him?" Railton asked, turning on David.

He looked into the distance and saw the brightly lit Liver Building watching over the entire crime scene, he considered his answer, it was starting to feel just like the old days.

"I wouldn't be surprised. McSharry and his boys never shied away from the contentious move, sometimes it seemed like they went looking for it"

Drysdale spat out the chewing gum and scratched at his dark grey beard.

"But back then they had the influence to go looking for trouble. They're nobodies to these new kids, if they tried half the bollocks they got away with in their heyday we'd be fishing Stephen McSharry out of the Mersey by the end of the week. He's got to know that, a ten year stretch can change a man but it doesn't turn him into a complete fucking idiot, does it?"

David Walker hoped that it did, but there was a certain logic to Drysdale's point, he ran a hand through his thinning hair and felt the wetness on his hand. The dizziness remained, despite this distance from the corpse.

"Ok, so let's look past McSharry" Railton said eagerly, David didn't think he'd ever seen him this enthusiastic about police work, maybe coming in drunk was the way forward "if the order didn't come from him, then where would it come from?"

Drysdale scoffed dismissively, drawing another glare from Railton.

"Get yourself a phone book, a blindfold and a pin son, that'll give you as good a chance as anyone of figuring it out. Wayne Caddock was bringing in a lot of money, we're talking millions. If you're looking for a likely motive then you won't to need to go further than that. Any crew in the city could have thought that the time was right to take a swipe at the established order, smack around one of the four families and redirect a bit of that drug money into fresh pockets. Someone gives it a go every couple of years"

"That's assuming it's even a crew" David interjected, looking towards Drysdale "if your one hitter theory is right then it's just as likely that our guy is a player with a grudge. Maybe ex Caddock muscle or someone who had a run in with the man and decided to act"

Railton's shoulders sagged; the enthusiasm that had come out of nowhere seemed to have abandoned him just as quickly. He shook his head slowly and looked into the ambulance, towards the corpse of Wayne Caddock.

"So we're looking at a probable motive for half the city? Brilliant!" he muttered.

Walker's attention was diverted towards the cobbled street, where four forensic scientists were beginning to load the dead bodies into the back of a second ambulance. He looked over to the main entrance and saw that the crowds had further multiplied, still being held at bay by the one young officer and his barrier. David grimaced when he imagined what would happen when the press got hold of the story, he wondered how long would it be before the Albert Dock opened its doors to the worlds tourists again. For the foreseeable future it would be nothing more than the home of a gruesome murder, an embodiment of the violence that was strangling the life out of the city.

Drysdale, who was watching the growing crowd as well, seemed to be thinking the same thing, when he looked back at David there was an apprehensive look in his eyes.

"We need an arrest before this gets out of hand" Carl was saying "We need to show people that we're in control of this shit. You're watching these guys, have you got anything for me? A soft spot where I can hit the fuckers?"

David took the mobile phone from his pocket "We've got a car on McSharry round the clock, I'll check it out and see if they have anything, when do you make the time of death?"

"Eleven" Drysdale replied "But see if you've got anything a couple of hours before that too, the shooter may have gone there first for his instructions"

David walked away to make the call as Carl Drysdale slid another piece of chewing gum into his mouth.

A few minutes later he hung up the phone, the news from the DST was much as he'd expected; the two officers conducting the night shift had been parked across the road from McSharry's house since 6pm, the target was still inside, and no one had come or gone in that time. That was unusual enough in itself, on an average night Stephen McSharry had at least half of his crew hanging around the place. If he went out then he always left one behind on guard duty, but he was never alone, particularly not without his pet thug. David asked how they knew McSharry was inside, the officer told him that every hour, on the hour, the target stood outside and smoked a cigar. He queried whether it was a usual routine, they told him it wasn't.

The son of a bitch was playing them, of that he had no doubt. He knew Wayne Caddock would be assassinated tonight and he knew there was no better alibi than one provided by a police surveillance unit. His blood boiled when he thought about the other reason for McSharry to show himself; to goad them, and to goad him. The bastard wanted him to know that he was behind the murder, why else would he break his routine so drastically when he knew he was being watched, it was his own subtle way of giving the finger to David Walker and to everyone else who was trying to put him away.

He took a deep breath and tried to calm himself, he'd never really expected McSharry to lay low for long, but he didn't think the man would do anything quite as explosive as this. He tried not to think about the repercussions that would follow the nights events, if another gang war was about to devour the city then he would just as soon not waste time worrying about it beforehand. He feared there would be enough time in the future to fully embrace that emotion.

A shout from across the docks tore David from his thoughts; he turned to see Carl Drysdale gesturing for him to return. The DS and Railton were already following a uniformed officer to a nearby police van, he put the phone back into his pocket and walked towards them as briskly as the damp cobbled street would allow. By the time the other two reached their destination he was only a few paces behind.

"Any luck?" Drysdale asked hopefully.

Walker shook his head, the look of disappointment was conspicuous on each of their faces, he tried to think of something constructive to say but nothing was forthcoming. After a few moments he looked towards the police van and raised his eyebrows.

"They've tidied up the CCTV footage" Railton explained as Drysdale climbed into the van "Time to find out who our guy was, you got any predictions?"

"None I'd care to share" David told him, following after Drysdale.

The inside was probably slightly bigger than that of a standard riot van, though the contents within bore very few resemblances. Built into one of the sides were six large screens with a patchwork of CD drives and keyboards below it. Operating it all from a terminal was a skinny, young man in his early twenties with thick milk bottle glasses and a curly black perm that made him look like a soiled Q-tip.

"This is John Abbot, David; he's the best guy we've got for putting this kind of thing together"

"Alright John, appreciate your help with this"

Muttering something inaudible, John Abbot typed frantically at the keyboard and pushed a CD into one of the drives, the smile and the shrug of the shoulders they received from Drysdale said that was about as deep in conversation as they were likely to get.

He dismissed the strange behaviour and turned his attention towards the screens. If the oddball could give them a positive ID on the shooter then he'd bloody marry the bastard, with or without the weird mumblings. All things considered it would be a small price to pay to get hold of something he could use; the evening was leaving him more frustrated by the second.

John Abbot mumbled another inaudible sentence and shook his head, though David couldn't make out the words he knew the tone to be belligerent. Another flurry of keyboard activity culminated with an image appearing on the largest screen, he knew the location immediately, the back entrance to the *Blue Café*; the space now littered with bodies.

The image was far from clear, John Abbot seemed to have zoomed in from a camera that took in a much wider space, but as he watched two cars pull up outside the bar, he saw it was clear enough to make out the driver in each of the vehicles.

"Here we go" Drysdale said, rubbing his hands together "Let's get to the good stuff!"

The rest of it seemed to happen too fast, as if the recording had been speeded up. To the right of the camera a man came into view, medium height, medium build, no obvious tattoos, no telling marks, with a baseball cap hiding his face. Before David had time to properly digest the image he saw a flicker of gunfire from the left knock the capped man to the ground. A moment later another group of people came into shot, amongst the bald heads and muscle he managed to make out Wayne Caddock diving for the floor.

Walker searched the screen frantically for another hitter, if the first one was killed before he had time to take a shot then there had to be a second one somewhere close by, who took his friends body with him. He only had time to play that scenario in his head for a moment as the man with the baseball cap was suddenly on one knee with his arms outstretched. The speed with which he moved was incredible. Every time his arms changed direction a body on the other side of the car seemed to drop, and a second later he was chasing after two men, one of them Caddock, leaving behind the collection of corpses where Walker had found them several hours later.

Watching the man move he realised how familiar it all seemed, like a twisted sense of *déjà vu*. Before he had time to think the camera had shifted to the walkway by the Mersey, where it focused in on a struggle between two men, each trying to push the other into the water.

By the time the man in the baseball cap had forced Wayne Caddock over the barrier and into the river the only sound David Walker could hear was the beating of his own heart. The sound was fierce in his ears, it grew fiercer still as he watched the killer pick something up off the ground and walk away out of shot, not once did he look up high enough to reveal his face.

"It's happening again..." David whispered to himself. The bad times were back.

Chapter 15

Charlie got the call at 2:30 am, by 2:45 he was out of the house and in the car. The conversation had him worried; even by Rob's typically stoic standards it had been brief.

"I need you to come round now our kid, bring everything you've got".

He'd left Vicky in a frosty mood, though that hardly seemed worth drawing attention to these days. It was like reminding yourself that the sky was blue, as if there was even an outside chance of it being anything different.

Spending the night at home hadn't done a damn thing to help, he'd thought that his decision to forgo making money in favour of spending some time with her and the kids would have thawed the ice a little, but if anything it just seemed to make her madder. For hours he'd given the girls his full attention; feeding them, bathing them, playing with them, every job she'd slated him for not doing he did, and still at the end of it his wife looked at him like a worthless piece of shit, like a senile old dog who had long ago outlived any usefulness. She acted like he was constantly under her feet, as if his mere presence in the house was enough to disrupt her routine and make her life more difficult.

His grip on the wheel tightened as he thought about the way Vicky treated him, even in bed she seemed to be trying to punish him, positioning herself on the very edge of the mattress so she was as far away from him as possible. He had no doubt that if they had a spare room she would have slept in it tonight. And then the call from Rob had come through, making a bad situation that little bit worse.

It only took two rings of his mobile to set Zoe off; he hadn't even deciphered the sound when he heard her wailing at the top of her lungs from across the hallway. The one thing he could say for his baby girl; she had the ears of a hawk. Up to that point she'd been as quiet as a mouse, though judging by the velocity of her screams she intended to make up for lost time.

Charlie wanted to stay and get her back to sleep, after all the work he'd put in it only seemed right to finish the job, but the tone of his brothers voice had him worried. He knew he wouldn't be able to live with himself if Rob did something stupid while Charlie was busy rocking his kid back to sleep, but none of that seemed to matter to Vicky.

"Are you kidding me, Charlie?" she had screamed "You wake the baby up in the middle of the night with your bloody mobile and you're just going to run off and leave me to get her back to sleep, do you ever stop to think about anyone but yourself?"

That had been too much for Charlie, the passive aggressive nonsense had been one thing, but as soon as Vicky started yelling at him for being worried about his brother he'd put on his clothes and stormed out of the house. The look of disgust in her eyes as he left the bedroom told him everything he needed to know.

He was starting to wonder why he even bothered, his wife had nothing but contempt for him these days, she ridiculed the way he made the money she lived on and he was an unwelcome guest in his own home. All the while he had a hot little nineteen year old waiting across town, looking at flats every day, giddy with excitement over the prospect of moving in with him. Charlie scratched the sleep from his eyes, why was he was even trying to make things right with Vicky? She treated him like that and yet he was still jumping through hoops trying to make her happy, it just wasn't right.

He flicked through the radio stations trying to get a heads up on whatever had gone down that was so urgent. It reminded him of the old days; picking up the Echo the day after one of Rob's hits and reading about how many men his brother had killed, he never admitted it but he always felt proud after reading those stories, the busies and the journalists didn't have a clue what was really going on or why it was happening, but he did and it felt good to be in the know. He checked every station until he was back where he started, nothing, not even a hint of a shooting. Maybe his big brother didn't have it in him anymore, the thought had passed through his head a couple of times since Rob had come home, but he hoped it wasn't true.

Charlie pulled up outside Rob's flat, the gang he remembered from his first visit no longer occupied the street corner, though the empty bottles of White Lightning told him they hadn't been gone long. He guessed they'd probably headed home for the night, suppressing a yawn he fought the urge to do the same.

Stepping from the car he stretched his weary arms and slid on his jacket, the drugs were hidden in the inside pocket of the grey coat, he gave the area a light pat to make sure it was all still there and made his way towards the door.

Before he had a chance to knock Charlie realised that the door was already a couple of inches open, lightly he pushed the wood, hearing it creak as it opened the rest of the way. He stepped into the hallway and closed the door behind him, leaving it open in the middle of the night was not a smart move, particularly in this part of the world. As the latch shut behind him Charlie realised that maybe he'd been too hasty in assuming the gang on the corner had gone home.

Walking into the living room he was relieved to see the sight of Rob, sitting alone on one of the worn, green, sofa chairs. The relief only lasted for a second as he took a closer look at his brother's dejected state.

The first thing Charlie noticed was the empty bottle of Jack Daniels residing in Rob's hand, he was shaking it lightly from side to side in a trance like movement, as if hoping the motion would somehow refill the empty piece of glass. His eyes seemed glazed and there was a resigned, melancholy look etched upon his face, like a man who knew his time was up and could do nothing to change it. Charlie only looked at his brother for a few seconds before a flash of colour on the coffee table caught his eye. At first he couldn't tell what it was, his initial thought was that perhaps it was a piece of clothing or the remnants of a Chinese takeaway, but as he took a step closer Charlie realised bright object was a blood stained knife, dripping lightly onto the table.

Charlie took a step back, more in shock than anything else "Christ lad!" he said, slowly composing himself "You need to get that hidden, what if someone tips of the filth and they search the place? That's you down for a ten year stretch at the very least, use your head"

Rob glanced at him with a look of mild indifference, the glazed expression made Charlie feel as if his brother was looking right through him, he was only able to hold Rob's attention for a moment before it returned to the empty bottle of Jack Daniels, still shaking lightly in his hand.

"So, how'd it go?" Charlie asked, pulling another of the green sofa chairs into the middle of the room and taking a seat.

"Not well" Rob replied, even the drunken slur couldn't hide the panic in his voice.

"But you killed the guy, right?" Charlie asked, he was looking towards the bloody knife without even realising it.

"Yeah. Yeah. I killed him, but it wasn't clean. I made a real mess of the thing" Rob replied, his voice was uneven and full of nerves, Charlie was suddenly relieved that he hadn't waited around to get Zoe back to sleep.

"Ah well, at least the bastards dead, right?" Charlie said lightly, his efforts to brighten the mood had no effect on his brother, he just continued to stare at the empty bottle in his hand. A few moments of silence passed before Rob suddenly dropped the bottle to the floor; the unexpected sound gave Charlie a start, though he did his best to hide the reaction.

"Yeah, at least he's dead" Rob echoed, though his morose tone suggested he thought nothing of the sort "It's just, there was just so much blood, I forgot what it was like, I think I forgot a lot of things"

"Like what?" Charlie asked curiously, leaning forward in his chair.

"There was just so much blood" he said again, now the bottle was no longer in his grasp Charlie noticed that both of Rob's hands were shaking "I cleaned myself five or six times, scrubbed myself raw but I can still feel it on there. It's so sticky, nauseating, suffocating, I don't think it's ever gonna go away"

Charlie tried to keep the worry out of his voice, he'd never seen Rob this bad, not even at the worst of times "Course it will lad, it's just in your head that's all"

Rob let out a laugh that was void of amusement, when he caught sight of his hands shaking he rubbed them together furiously "Well if that's true then it definitely won't be going away. The stuff up there doesn't do that, it never leaves, just swims around, reminding me it's up there until I can't close my eyes for longer than ten minutes. I'm running out of space up there for shit like this"

189

Charlie leaned in a little closer; he eyed thick beads of sweat soaking Rob's brow and dry blood caked across his black t-shirt. The small room was eerily quiet save for Rob's heavy breathing, Charlie realised he had no idea what to say to sooth a man who had just murdered someone.

Reaching down he picked up the empty bottle of JD from the floor and placed it on the table behind him.

"Are you ok, mate?" Charlie asked "You seem a little... you know"

With an almighty sigh Rob pushed himself forward in his chair. Resting a palm on each knee he focused his concentration on Charlie with a clarity he'd seemed incapable of summoning a few moments earlier.

"You knew Wayne Caddock, right Charlie? I mean you knew who he was, saw him around town, that kind of thing?"

"I knew the fucker" Charlie told him, his brother was staring at him intently now, while small beads of sweat continued to trickle down his forehead "piece of shit if you ask me, flash little fuck deserves what he got, and don't you think anything different"

"Did he have kids?"

"What?"

"Kids, a wife" Rob's tone was loud and impatient "Did he have a family?"

"What kind of questions that?" Charlie asked, but his brothers stare made him revise his answer "Well, I know he liked the birds, always saw him round town with a different piece of ass. He wasn't married but yeah I think he had himself a woman. A kid too come to think of it, I'm sure I've heard it mentioned, a little girl"

Rob sank back in his chair and let out a long breath. Slowly, as if every action was suddenly a chore, he closed his eyes and massaged the bridge of his nose with a thumb and forefinger.

"A little girl without a dad" Rob said quietly to himself "Another little girl without a dad"

"Yeah well, shit happens doesn't it?" Charlie said bluntly, he suddenly got an image what it would be like for Zoe and Alexis, growing up without a father, but he pushed the idea from his head before it had time to settle.

"There was another guy..." the desperation in Rob's voice was conspicuous "reddish-brown hair, grey eyes, about my age. You know him? Did he have kids?"

Charlie gave an exasperated shake of the head, he didn't know why Rob was doing this to himself, but it wasn't doing him any good.

"I think I know who you mean, he was close to Caddock, but I didn't know the guy, not by name"

Rob stood up and began pacing the small living room, his hands kept moving to his head as if to grab his hair, but when he realised there was nothing there they dropped impotently to his sides. The agitation of his body seemed to increase with every lap of the room.

"What about his muscle, you know any of them? Big blokes, ugly, you know any of those guys?"

"Rob you need to stop this" Charlie told him, standing up to confront his brother.

"There was a guy with a tattoo of a dragon on his arm"

"Rob-"

"JUST TELL ME!" he shouted, stopping dead in his tracks. As Charlie looked at Rob's wide eyes and red face he suddenly felt as if he was looking at the killer who had lived inside his brother for so long "Did you know him?"

"No"

There was a pause. Once again Rob's hands leapt towards his head, and then dropped uselessly to his side a second after they'd reached their destination. He looked like he was out of ideas, like he'd been painted into a corner.

"You bring the stuff?"

Charlie was relieved to finally be asked a question he knew the answer to. Reaching inside his jacket he found the hidden pocket and began removing the small cellophane bags, placing them one by one on the old wooden table.

"Course" he said, his back to Rob as he laid out his products a couple of inches away from the bloody knife "I wasn't sure what you wanted"

"What have you got?" his brother asked, looking over Charlie's shoulder like a curious shopper at the market.

"I got some E, weed, coke and a bit of H" Charlie let his hand rest over one bag at a time while he announced its contents "What's your poison?"

He could sense his brother's hesitation, for more than a few moments Rob just looked down at the bags like he expected them to make the decision for him. When he finally spoke the desperation was still in his voice, but it was altered slightly by something else, Charlie thought it might have been resolve.

"Give me the coke. The whole bag, there's money on the side"

Charlie picked up the bag of coke and held it over his shoulder. Rob didn't take it right away, choosing instead to stare at it, tensed like a wild animal ready to strike. When he finally reached forward he did so eagerly and snatched it from Charlie's grasp in one smooth motion. Further across the table was the familiar navy blue sports bag that McSharry had given Rob as a down payment, reaching inside Charlie took four twenty pound notes from one of the bundles and slid it into his pocket, along with the rest of his unsold products.

"Cheers, lad" Charlie said, returning to his perch on the green sofa chair "Just think; one more job and then it's all over. Nice bit of De Niro in your sky rocket and you're off back to the New World, nothing to worry about"

He watched Rob move towards the table and sprinkle a healthy dose of coke onto the wooden surface. Slowly, his brother took a credit card from his back pocket and arranged the powder into five separate lines. Charlie watched him with fascination; his actions were slow and laboured, as if doubt was creeping into every facet of his being. The steely resolve on his face told a different story to that of his lethargic body, Charlie wondered which one bore a closer resemblance to the truth.

Satisfied with the similarity of the five lines Rob pulled what looked like a business card from his back pocket and rolled it up into a straw. His hands were shaking more than before and the problem only intensified as he lowered his body towards the table. Charlie suddenly felt the urge to call his brother off, there was something about Rob's demeanour that said he was profoundly uncomfortable with what he was about to do, but nonetheless his body eased closer and closer to the white powder. He wet his lips to speak but when he tried nothing came that would have made any sense, running his thumb over his own nose he continued to watch.

The hand holding the makeshift straw was only a few inches away from the first line and shaking badly, Rob closed his eyes and swallowed hard as small beads of sweat dripped past his temple and onto the table. With a flash of resolve he let out a deep breath, opened his eyes and lowered himself the rest of the way. In one swift motion Rob devoured line after line until all five where gone, the entire episode couldn't have lasted more than a couple of seconds.

Rob took a while to compose himself, his body remained hunched over the wooden table but as he dropped the business card his breathing began to steady and the shaking in his hands slowly subsided. Standing up to his full height Rob ran a hand over his face, the stubble that had covered his chin when he arrived was now well on its way to becoming a full grown beard, absentmindedly he scratched at the thick black hair while he made his way back towards the chair and collapsed with a small groan.

"You ever killed a man, Charlie?" Rob asked after a few minutes, the calmness of his voice was in stark contrast to what it had been before, Charlie also thought he caught a hint of arrogance in his tone. His brothers eyes were still wide but they no longer portrayed the panic that had haunted them earlier, instead Rob seemed to be taking Charlie in with an increased intensity that made him a little uncomfortable.

"Nah mate, can't say that I have"

"Did I ever tell you about the first man I killed?"

Charlie flashed his brother a concerned look and gestured for the bag of coke. With a smile that only just touched the corners of his mouth Rob handed the bag back and looked towards the ceiling. Charlie wanted it for two reasons; for starters he didn't like watching people hit their high when he was stone cold sober, it was depressing, but mostly he was worried that Rob was pushing himself too hard too fast. Keeping an eye on big brother he fished around in his pocket and pulled out a set of house keys.

"I was there Rob, remember?"

Rob let out a small laugh and shook his head with smug disregard. Keys now in hand Charlie reached into the bag and heaped a pile of coke onto the metal point, moving it to his nose he closed his eyes and snorted.

When Charlie opened them again his brother was still regarding him with the same amused look.

"That wasn't my first"

"So who was?" Charlie asked belligerently, a little annoyed that Rob had let him think otherwise for so many years.

"I think he was a farmer, or a shepherd...something like that" Rob said, looking towards the wall with a pensive expression on his face "It was when I was stationed in Bosnia with The Old Two-Twos. He shot one of our unit when we were on patrol, only in the shoulder, nothing fatal, but I didn't know that did I? All I saw was a flash of blood and the guy who had the bunk next to me had suddenly collapsed on the floor, the next thing I know I'm unloading a whole rifle clip at the poor sod. We were on his land and the crazy bastard didn't like trespassers. I remember watching him fall, and just being consumed by this blinding panic, the panic never goes away but over time you learn to ignore it. I ran over as fast as I could and tried to resuscitate the guy, but he was good as dead by the time I got there. I still remember what it was like the first time, that all-encompassing sense of guilt. It feels like the whole world knows you ended a man's life and they'll never forgive you for it, that one second of panic has made you an outcast for the rest of your life"

Using his index finger Charlie wiped stray particles of coke from his nose and rubbed them against his gums. He felt the back of his throat go numb, the snow he was getting in these days was top dollar stuff, whoever was bringing the package in wasn't stepping on it too much, a bonus that was getting harder and harder to find in Liverpool.

Rob's confession had left him feeling a little pissed, no matter what may have happened to them in their past he'd always felt closer to him for going through that first murder together. It was a bond they shared that was rarely spoken about, but it remained an important part of their relationship. Now, as it disappeared into the ether Charlie couldn't help but wish that Rob hadn't told him, it cheapened their bond, and it left him feeling a little bit like a mug.

"What happened..." Charlie asked cautiously "...with the farmer?"

Rob let out a sigh "My Sergeant bailed me out, he was a good bloke, we buried the body and no one ever came asking about it. I guess he was the kind of guy who had a lot of enemies, and back then in Banja Luka it wasn't uncommon for people to just disappear. I got lucky, a different place, a different sergeant, I'd probably still be in a prison cell, or maybe I was unlucky, I don't know"

It was strange to hear Rob talk so openly about his past, his normal reaction was to treat it like an unfaithful lover, like a cold shadow that was never to be acknowledged let alone discussed. Listening to him now it seemed his brother was maybe even enjoying the chance to talk about the things he'd kept bottled up for so long.

"Why are you only telling me now?" Charlie asked evenly, he was angry at Rob for keeping it from him, but at the same time it was interesting to see his brother open up.

"I don't know" Rob shrugged his shoulders "I don't like to remember it, I've done a lot of killing but I guess it's like anything else, you never forget your first"

In the silence that followed it seemed to Charlie that Rob was reliving every act of murder he'd ever committed, not with the irrational panic of earlier, but with a passive reflection that said the coke was doing its thing. In spite of his wide eyes the bags underneath were becoming increasingly prominent.

"What are you doing to yourself, lad?" Charlie asked, waking Rob from his daze "So you killed a gangster, it's not like he didn't deserve it, I mean he wasn't a boy scout or anything was he? Have you got any idea how many people out there wish they could do what you do. I mean come on, how many guys did you clip tonight?"

"Nine" Rob told him coldly, he looked as though he was only just tolerating his little brothers tirade.

"Nine professional criminals" Charlie continued "and there's not a scratch on you. Do you appreciate how few people could do what you did tonight? You got a fucking gift lid, you should be more grateful"

He could feel the coke in his system, giving him a brassier edge than usual, not that Charlie Thomas ever lacked for self-confidence, but he could always take it up a gear after a line or two. Dipping his key back into the bag he prepared himself for another hit, but when his eyes drew level with Rob's the stare looking back made him stop in his tracks.

"Have you got any idea how naïve you are, Charlie" Rob said calmly "father of two and you're coming to me with bollocks like that? Killing changes you little brother, it's not like it is in the movies and it's not about being the baddest cunt in town, it's about extinguishing a life, ruining a family, and hating who you are. I swear to God, I hope you never have to go through it. It changes you mate, it really does. I don't know how I can go back to the life I've made, and I don't know if I can look Jo in the eye, not after this"

Listening to him speak, he found Rob's cold, calm voice more disturbing than when he had been on the fringes of madness. Putting the coke heaped key to his nose Charlie took another snort and handed the bag back to his brother, Rob took it without a word and rested it in his hand as he had the JD bottle before it.

"Of course you can look her in the eye" Charlie told him "it isn't like you wanted to kill them was it? You're not some crazed homicidal freak looking to satisfy a blood lust or something are you? You got pushed into it and you did a dirty piece of work for a good days pay. You're no different than a bill collector or a fucking traffic warden. You did what had to be done to pay the mortgage and now you move on. Never take your work home with you lad, that's rule number one"

Rob shook his head, allowing the smallest of smiles to creep onto his face.

"You've got a twisted outlook, anybody ever tell you that?" there was a hint of affection to Rob's words as he dipped his little finger into the bag.

"Coming from a serial killer I'll take that as a compliment! Caddock and his boys were all scumbags anyway"

Pushing his little finger to the rim of his nostril Rob snorted the small pile of coke and shook his head from side of side. Lightly, he placed the bag on the floor and let out a sigh.

"I need to get my mind off this shit"

There was a moments silence, not an awkward silence but a peaceful one, and then it shot out of Charlie like a bullet.

"I'm leaving Vicky"

He didn't know who was more surprised, Rob or him. He hadn't planned on bitching about his domestic troubles, but sitting across from his brother and talking about the kind of shit that had always been too taboo to mention, he suddenly felt the need to be honest with him. Family was family; if you couldn't talk to them then who could you talk to?

Rob looked back at him with raised eyebrows, but there was no judgement in his face.

"Yeah? When did you decide this?"

He tried to condense the deterioration of his marriage into a handful of points, but there were just too many to mention. A million small things that when taken alone meant nothing more than a petty little annoyance, but when added all together made a life of misery and unavoidable mutual destruction. He'd never thought of his marriage in terms of a Cold War before, but that was exactly what it was. The only difference was that his White House and her Kremlin had already unleashed their nuclear bombs, and everything was turning to shit around them because of it.

"It's been coming for a while" Charlie said "all the bitch does is complain. I'm seeing someone else, nineteen year old, tidy little bird, her names Steph. She wants me to move in with her, what do you reckon?"

"Me?" Rob said in surprise, Charlie half expected a moralistic talking down from his big brother, he noted the irony of the man with the bloody knife being the voice of his conscience "I don't know mate, it's your life. If you're not happy then you need to something but, I don't know"

"Go on" Charlie said cautiously, he resented the idea of being preached to by Rob but at the same time he knew it was something he needed to hear.

"Running out on your kids... do you really want to be that guy?"

Charlie knew that had been coming, it was the most unforgivable sin in the eyes of the two brothers, to end up like their old man, to become the kind of coward who abandons his own family. It was the only reason why he hadn't left Vicky a million times already. He loved the way Alexis looked at him and he didn't want to stop being her hero, or Zoe's when she got older. Vicky was doing her best to chip away at that image, she hated the fact that his little girl adored him, and she wanted Alexis to see him for the same useless fuck up that she did. Every day that she yelled at him in front of the girls Charlie knew that his status in his daughter's eyes was a little less secure, but if he chose to leave then it would be gone forever, and the only memory his girls would have would be the same one he and Rob had of their father; a selfish bastard.

He tried to tell himself that it didn't need to be that way, things had changed since the days when he and Rob had grown up, he could still see the girls on weekends, they could come and stay with him and Steph, he could still be their hero. As soon as the thought passed through his head he saw the flaws; Vicky would never make it that easy, she would try to hurt him through the girls and she was smart enough to make it work. At the end of the day they would live in her house, and the mother of his children would use that to poison their minds against him. He felt the sinking feeling in his chest that told him leaving Vicky would mean losing the girls as well, and he wasn't sure whether he could do that.

"Pass me the bag, will you Rob?"

Rob handed it over with a sympathetic look, watching him while he buried his key into the bag and did another line.

"Do what you need to do, Charlie" Rob said after he had passed the bag back "what the fuck do I know about raising a family anyway?"

"Yeah, alright"

The two brothers sat in silence for a few minutes, each searching for answers to their own impossible questions, wondering how it was they ended up where they had. It was Rob who finally spoke first.

"McSharry's going to call you soon, he's going to want to set up the meeting for the second hit. When he does, I want you to tell him that I insist you come along with me, for protection. Tell him I've demanded that you're there for the duration of the meeting and that the issue is non-negotiable. If he can bring that fucked up psycho with him for these meeting then I can sure as hell bring you. That cool?"

"Sure thing, bro" Charlie said, putting his family life to one side. This was the chance he was waiting for, a glance at the inner circle. He tried to keep his face from showing his elation but when Rob looked at him he couldn't help but smile.

"I appreciate it" Rob said with a sad smile "Now get the car, your big brothers in need of some Jack, big time!"

Chapter 16

David sat in the small meeting room with Chris Railton by his side, John Barry's office was only a few doors down the hall but after ten minutes of waiting they were still yet to see any sign of the Regional Director.

The small room was sparsely decorated, a cheese plant withering in the corner and a health and safety notice where the only distractions from the white walls and simple wooden desk that marked it out as a place of business, devoid of comforts. John Barry liked his meeting rooms decorated in that manor, he liked to remind his people that work was their focus, that they were there to conduct serious business for a serious cause, nothing would be permitted to get in the way of that goal.

To his right Chris sighed and ran a hand through his unruly blond hair, his deputy looked tired and dejected, though David could hardly blame him for either. There had been no rest for the two men, not since they saw the bodies in the Albert Dock the night before. Leaving separately they'd hit every source of information they had in preparation for this meeting. Informants, dealers, junkies, anyone with their ear to the street were tapped up and if they didn't know anything then they put the officers in touch with someone else who might. It was a gruelling night's work but one that had to be done quickly, before the shock had been absorbed and the street once again closed its ranks.

Despite the difficulty Walker had been happy for the distraction, he knew that with the thoughts currently swimming through his head there would be little chance of sleep, at least doing something productive would keep him from dwelling too deeply on what he had seen.

For Officer Railton on the other hand, as the fruits of his night off slowly matured into a hangover, well it was hard to imagine the night getting any worse for his young protégé. Railton lightly brushed at the creased grey suit he'd changed into only an hour before and flashed a rueful grin at Walker.

"How pissed to do you think he's going to be?"

"Remember the shoot up in Croxteth last year?" David asked, the case had been a major headache for the higher ups; four dead, two of them teenage girls.

"That bad?"

"Worse"

Railton shook his head apprehensively and buried it in his hands, David ignored the show of dejection and tried to keep his mind focused. He wished they had something concrete to bring to the Regional Director but right now all they could offer him was speculation. He cringed when he thought about the last meeting with Barry, the RD's reaction to the prospect of all-out war had been little short of terror, and David had assured him that he would keep it from happening. Now they stood on the brink of a gangland free for all that would engulf the entire city, and he had little doubt who Barry would blame if they took that final step. Stephen McSharry had played this one beautifully so far, but there was a long way to go to the finish line and David Walker had no intention of being left behind.

Officer Railton raised his head and lightly slapped himself on the cheeks, David wished that he could give him the day off, but there was just too much to do. He suspected that the next few weeks would push them all to their limits, yet he'd have been lying if he said he wasn't exited by the prospect. Going up against the Mr Big's of the world was why he joined SOCA in the first place, and they didn't get much bigger than his current prey.

"How's the hangover?" he asked, with just a hint of mockery.

"When you going to let that go?" Railton replied irritably, David had been quick to bring it up whenever they'd spoken throughout the night, but only because he didn't want his deputy making a mess of an important nights work.

"No, I'm really asking"

"I could do with a greasy fry up" Chris said, rubbing his stomach "But the headache's finally subsiding".

Behind them David heard the door open, as both men stood up he flashed Railton a sympathetic grin.

"We'll see about that!"

John Barry burst into the room like a tornado, walking surprisingly fast for a man of his size. His red face had moved closer to purple since the last time they'd met, and he seemed to be blowing at his moustache in silent rage as he made his way towards the table.

Behind him was a face David had not expected to see, Geoffrey Lincoln strolled into the room and quietly closed the door behind him, with the same look of calm politeness that David remembered so well. His wispy grey hair fell across his head in thin strands and his perfectly round reading glasses gave him the comforting appearance of a librarian, or an academic of some kind. He was a slim man in his late fifties but in the seven years since Walker had last seen him he didn't appear to have aged at all. Lincoln was the Detective Chief Inspector of the Major Incident Team, a position he'd held even before the start of David's spell there, some coppers joked that he'd been locking up murderers since the Nazi's were dropping bombs. He found himself pleased to see his old boss, even more so when the DCI gave him a warm smile and a gentle pat on the back as he made his way towards his seat.

"Officers" Barry said impatiently, reaching his chair and slamming a blue folder onto the wooden table "what in God's name is happening in my city?"

Despite the resolve of his spirit Walker couldn't help but swallow hard when he heard John Barry's tone. Some men got the best out of their charges by showing them trust and inspiring confidence, others liked to scare their way to their goals, there was no doubting the Regional Directors entrenchment in the latter camp. Walker had his doubts as to whether or not

198

it was the best way to inspire men.

"Morning sir" he returned, immediately regretting the meekness of his response.

"I assume you both know Geoffrey Lincoln" Barry continued, ignoring David's response "We felt an MIT presence would be beneficial for all involved"

Geoffrey Lincoln smiled at both men and nodded politely "Good morning, Officers" he said, the mild southern accent betraying a Cambridge upbringing.

"What I have in my hand is an early addition of today's Liverpool Echo" Barry waved the newspaper in Walker's face, his voice seemed all the more harsh in contrast to Geoffrey Lincoln's soft whisper "the first three pages of which are monopolised by last night's shooting, this is just one of the choice quotes I've picked out, you can peruse the rest once I'm finished with you, 'Last night one of the city's most illustrious landmarks played host to an act of crime so gruesome it has not been seen in Liverpool for many a year. The murder of nine men, all known criminals on multiple police watch lists, is set to ignite a gang war that could yet engulf the entire city in a swarm of revenge killings. The shooting, which has left police baffled, threatens not only the commendable progress the city has made over the last few years in shaking off the undesirable tag of urban war zone, but also the safety of its citizens. Just how an act of such grotesque butchery could happen five minutes away from a major police headquarters is a question that will no doubt be asked at every level of the Merseyside Police force today, but perhaps more pressing is the question for the population of Merseyside is this; when was our city lost to these gun toting drug barons who seem to control it?' Poetic, wouldn't you say?" Barry said scornfully, dropping the newspaper contemptuously onto the desk "By six o'clock tonight almost every household on Merseyside will be reading those words and demanding a response from us. Officer Walker, when I put you in place, when I charged you with the task of uprooting the major players in the Liverpool drug trade, is this not precisely what I spoke about avoiding? Did I not tell you that all-out war on my streets wouldn't be accepted?"

He felt John Barry's gaze burning into his skull, the suggestion that he was to blame hurt his pride, even more so since the accusation came from a man who hadn't even bothered to visit the crime scene or look at the bodies. Walker had gazed into their dead eyes, and he knew unequivocally that blame did not lie at his feet. He tried to keep the anger from his voice when he spoke.

"You did sir, but with all due respect what exactly is it you wanted me to do?"

Barry slammed his hand down hard on the table, causing the other three to flinch "Lock these animals up! Get them off my streets and away from my citizens!"

"And how do you expect me to do that sir?" David protested "We've been over this before, these men aren't drugged up street dealers, they're highly organised meticulous professionals"

"I don't care if they're Al Bloody Capone!" Barry shouted back, his face seemed to be turning darker by the second "they shot up the Albert Dock last night and that will not be tolerated under any circumstances, they need to be dealt with!" the firmness of his voice brokered no argument.

From the corner of his eye he saw Railton shifting uncomfortably, he tried to think of a response but every one that passed through his head was tinted with acrimony.

"I think what the Director is trying to say, David" Geoffrey Lincoln interjected, he spoke calmly and with a quiet authority that David had always admired "is perhaps we could adopt a more proactive approach to our respective investigations, with regards to this particular matter"

"Proactive, sir?" David said, making sure his voice possessed none of the previous hostility.

"You and Officer Railton are to assist the police investigation in any way you can, whatever Geoffrey's detectives need you are going to give them, am I clear?" Barry asked.

Walker adjusted his suit jacket and reminded himself what was at stake, taking a slow deep breath he responded to the Regional Director in the most professional tone he could muster.

"Of course, I have a relationship with the lead detective sir, we go back to my days at MIT. We're currently working on a couple of angles to try and get this thing cracked"

The answer seemed to go some way to pacifying John Barry, with a nod of the head he pushed the newspaper into the blue folder and leaned back in his chair "Good, good" he said slowly.

"Thank you, David" Lincoln added with decidedly more sincerity than his counterpart.

"We need results fast on this one gentlemen" Barry continued "The Director General has let it be known that time is not a luxury we will be afforded. He and the Chief Constable expect an arrest within 72 hours. The city demands a decisive response and to appease the media we need to put a tangible arrest in front of the cameras by Friday, or heads will roll"

He knew it was coming but he still had to fight the urge to shake his head, a 'tangible arrest' could mean a lot of things in this kind of scenario, but from the way Barry was speaking it sounded like anyone with a link to organisd crime would be good enough for Friday. Instead of investigating the actual murder of Wayne Caddock and his men they would waste time arresting anyone for whom a conviction would be likely to stick. The press would take their photographs, the Chief Constable would talk about how it was a major spanner in the works for organised crime, and then David and his team could actually get on with the business of building a case against Stephen

McSharry, PR games they made him fucking sick. He wondered how these bureaucrats managed to look in the mirror and still call themselves police. As if sensing his cynicism Geoffrey Lincoln leaned forward and fixed David with those calm, confident eyes.

"The chief constable is already getting calls from the Prime Minister and his lackeys" Lincoln told him "Merseyside has some vulnerable seats in Parliament, if this is allowed to drag out and our bosses get tagged with soft on drugs or soft on crime, we could all be looking at some damaging repercussions. We need to put this to bed by Friday, one way or another we need a man in front of the TV cameras in bracelets. You follow David?"

He could feel the bile itching the back of his throat "I follow sir".

"Good, good" Barry said again, David couldn't be sure but he thought he saw the Regional Director breath a small sigh of relief.

"So.." Geoffrey Lincoln began, looking from David to Chris and back again "John tells me you've had your eye on Wayne Caddock and the other major players for well over a year now, what can you give me to push this investigation forward?"

He hated that question

"Unfortunately sir, not a lot" he said regrettably "We heard nothing to suggest that this was coming and as of now no one's taking credit for it, not on any level. A few old grudges have risen back up now that Stephen McSharry is back in the fold but nothing of this proportion, not even a hint"

To his right he heard Railton clear his throat, the sound distracted him for a moment and it gave his deputy the chance to lean forward and begin to speak.

"Not to mention, excuse me sir," he looked cautiously from Lincoln to Barry, and when no one objected he continued "not to mention we know that they all met up last week, Caddock, McSharry, Miller, all those guys. What's the sense in calling a massive drug conference if you're just going to start blowing each other away a couple of days later?"

"Maybe some people weren't happy with the outcome of the meeting?" Geoffrey Lincoln suggested.

"That's a possibility, sir" David interjected, in his opinion it was the most likely option but he didn't intend to embarrass his number two in front of the bosses.

"So paint me a picture, gentlemen" Barry began, interlocking his fingers as he spoke "What happened down there last night? Was it retaliatory? Was it opportunistic" he narrowed his eyes at Walker "was it your man?"

With all of his heart David wanted to answer yes, but he knew he couldn't "Sir, if you're asking me if Stephen McSharry was behind the hit I'd bet the house on it, but if you're asking me if he or any of his known associates were at the docks last night then I would have to say no"

It pained him to give that answer but at this point it was the only one he had.

201

Geoffrey Lincoln looked at him inquisitively "What makes you so sure?"
"Instinct"

It was more than that, but Walker liked to keep his cards close to his chest, a little knowledge could be a dangerous thing. The CCTV footage had shown their man to be about six foot and average weight which was pretty much all the information they had on their mystery suspect. The most dangerous of Stephen McSharry's men were far too heavily built to have been the shooter, and the other guys in his crew didn't have the kind of skill required to pull off that kind of hit, though David had come across very few men who did.

"The years haven't changed you, have they, David?" Lincoln asked with a wry smile.

"Well sir, I have a little less hair"

Geoffrey Lincoln gave a light chuckle "What about alternatives? What if Stephen McSharry wasn't involved?"

"We've given DS Drysdale everything we have on a Marcus Hamilton, Micky Trevors and Bryan Davis, three known gun runners with clear ties to Wayne Caddock. We have photographic evidence of all three in possession of illegal firearms with intent to distribute, or should I say DS Drysdale has that evidence"

"You're happy to give this up?" Barry asked sceptically.

David almost laughed at the absurdity of the question. Only minutes earlier the Regional Director had ordered them to give as much support to the Police investigation as possible, yet as soon as SOCA surveillance intel was being handed over to the police, for which they would take the credit, John Barry suddenly seemed like a less vocal exponent of interdepartmental cooperation.

"Yes sir" David told him "the DST caught it about three weeks ago. We sat on it in the hope that we'd be able to use it to build a case upwards, but now Wayne Caddock's out the picture there's nowhere we can go other than to straight arrest. Best case scenario; Detective Drysdale gets them to roll over and maybe fill us in on why their boss was killed, worst case scenario you've got three gun runners off the street and a nice little gun cache to display on the evening news. I'm sure that will suitably convince the public that you're cracking down on crime"

"Not a bad scenario in itself" Geoffrey Lincoln said, looking hopefully towards Barry "maybe even enough to pacify the media?"

"Maybe" Barry agreed, the small eyes in his large head seemed hard at work "but I'd feel a lot better about the whole thing if we were close to putting chains on a famous face" Barry's busy eyes suddenly focused in on David "you're convinced it was Stephen McSharry? Getting anything on him a week after his release is going to prove incredibly difficult"

Before David had a chance to respond he heard the sound of Railton's voice, his deputy's nerves were noticeable, but he retained the effortless confidence that seemed to embody everything he did.

"Sir, if I may, word on the street is that this is far from a lock as to who was behind it" he looked towards David with guilt in his eyes before he continued "I've been talking to informants ever since we surveyed the crime scene last night and for every time I hear a junkie or a dealer tell me it was Stephen McSharry I hear two of three other theories just as likely, and with just as much credit out there"

Geoffrey Lincoln shook his head "We all know how much this city loves a good rumour"

Barry nodded and returned the weight of his attention to Railton "Indeed. What have you heard?"

"I don't know where to start," Railton tried to smile, only Geoffrey Lincoln returned the gesture "four days ago a small group of Caddock's muscle led by Darren Crowder, he was one of the lieutenants who was killed last night, were spotted taking apart a triad controlled house in Kensington. We have two dead China men in the coroner's office that back this one up. Some people in Kenny are saying last night was retaliation from the chincs"

John Barry raised his eyebrows, it was a simple gesture, but on a man like him it carried force.

"Pardon me sir" Railton continued "There's another rumour making the ` rounds that Caddock was due to send his London associates a cache of guns; ex IRA, at the beginning of last week. The shipment was halted in Belfast and the crew were taken into custody. Some people think Caddock was holding onto his partners money and they weren't best pleased about it. The last rumour I got was that Tony Miller took Wayne Caddock out himself, they're saying he wanted total control of the drug trade and saw the unrest after McSharry's release as a chance to solidify his power. They're all just rumours, but right now we have as much reason to follow them up as we do the McSharry angle"

"I don't think that's true" David said coldly, allowing his gaze to linger on Officer Railton for the briefest of seconds before focusing his attention back on Lincoln and Barry "follow them up, of course, but our primary focus has to be McSharry"

"Why?" Railton asked "Because of your instinct?"

There was a hint of petulance in his voice. Walker understood his deputies frustration, he wanted results as much as anyone and after a full night on the streets he'd earned the right to his opinions, but David didn't have the patience to go twelve rounds with a subordinate officer in the presence of both the Regional Director and the MITs Detective Chief Inspector, not today.

"Because it's precisely the kind of move he would make" David said firmly, directing his answer to the two men across the table "Come on, he's been locked up for ten years, he's had to watch Caddock and Miller eat away at his empire, the one thing you can never do is underestimate Stephen McSharry, this has his fingerprints all over it!"

"All the more reason for someone else to try their luck" Railton continued, stubbornly fighting his corner "think about it, the spotlights on McSharry, everyone's waiting to see what his first move will be, what better time to settle some old scores than when everyone is looking the other way?"

"That's enough" Barry grumbled impatiently "speculate on your own time, that's not what you're here for"

The two men went quiet; he gave Railton a reproachful look and then turned to face the senior officers.

"David, what happens to Caddock's empire now that he's out of the picture?" Lincoln asked, pushing his spectacles up from the tip of his nose.

"Well there's going to be a big change that's for sure. The guys they have left don't possess anywhere near enough muscle or influence to hold on to their interests. Maybe one of his lieutenants would have been able to do it but Johnny Tate and Keith Crowder both got taken out in the hit, whoever was behind it made sure no one survived who could fill Caddock's shoes"

John Barry grunted irritably "Well that fits in with just about every theory we have so far"

"Yes sir" David continued "there's definitely going to be a power shift but until we know for sure who ordered the hit its going to be difficult to predict which way it's going to go. The major factor will be the drugs, Wayne Caddock brought a lot of narcotics into the city and with him out of the way his suppliers are going to need quick access to a lot of money and a lot of protection"

John Barry leaned forward in his chair, his hopeful expression almost catching David off guard "Could that be our way in, Officer Walker? Watch the drug men and maybe we see who's reaping the rewards?"

Walker shook his head "Sir, I'm afraid we haven't got that kind of intel, our information on the major drug traffickers is hearsay at best"

Barry's hopeful look quickly made way to an irritated one, Walker found himself feeling a little more comfortable with the Regional Directors in his default position

"Why is that?" the RD asked grimly.

"They're careful sir, they don't drop bodies, people aren't scared of them, they just deal with the high command of the major players, to the street dealers and the users they don't even exist. It's not in their interest for the world to know who they are, we'd need someone deep on the inside to bring us that kind of information"

"Which we don't have" Barry said with a sigh, it was more of a statement than a question, but David suspected it would be prudent to respond nonetheless.

"Not by a long shot sir, no. I'm afraid the likely hood is we'll see a few more shootings before the landscape settles back down"

The Regional Director ran two hands over his large, red face before resting them palms down on the wooden table.

"That's not what I wanted to hear, Officer"

"Constable Lincoln" Railton chirped in, before anyone else had a chance to speak "I think you need to push for your detectives to bring in anyone and everyone we can get our hands on; Tony Miller, Stephen McSharry, Martin Cassidy, all the famous faces and give them a grilling"

Geoffrey Lincoln regarded him for a few seconds with an even face, when he didn't respond David took his chance to jump in.

"What good will that do?"

"It will show people that we're taking this seriously" Railton said defensively, his eyes were darting around the table from one man to the next, holding each of their gazes for only a few seconds "that we're not prepared to be messed around, let the city know that we don't intend to be bullied by these animals"

David recognised the look of intrigue on the Regional Directors face "A show of force?" he said, half to himself, David grimaced, he knew just how much John Barry loved a good show of force. Geoffrey Lincoln was still regarding the group with an expressionless face, the odds were high that the DCI hadn't yet made up his mind, and was weighing the pros and cons behind those sharp eyes. David chose to direct his response towards John Barry, once the large man started rolling down the hill his momentum would make him impossible to stop.

"Sir, if you haul those men in with no probable cause their solicitors will have a field day, we'll get tagged with police harassment and that will just make it harder when we try to move on them for real"

He watched John Barry's surly red face as a silence engulfed the table, it was Geoffrey Lincoln who spoke first.

"David's right"

"Well your unit needs to move on to something" Barry shook his head from side to side, causing jowls of fat to flap against his face "No offence constable, I'm sure your detectives will do a solid job of solving this case, but when Officer Walker's unit was put together they were told to make these gangsters the be all and end of all of their existence. Surely there's another avenue we can explore to run parallel with the MITs investigation?"

Once again Railton was the first one to respond, the boys initiative was there for all to see and Walker couldn't hide his surprise at how profoundly the case seemed to have affected his typical blasé attitude.

"We could redirect our surveillance detail towards the remaining Caddock infrastructure, see what their next move is, maybe it might tell us where to go" It was an eager suggestion, Railton was grasping at straws and from the looks around the table the other two men knew it too. It was a boundless enthusiasm that every officer had experienced, but it was a dangerous commodity if left unchecked, and Railton with his insistent pleas was overstepping his bounds.

"No" Walker said firmly "The units making good progress where it is, I don't want to disrupt it on a whim. Sir" he said, turning his attention to Barry

"I promise you the Caddock boys are done, if we want results we need to keep our eyes on the factions with the most to gain"

He tried to keep an angry look from finding its way to Railton, if the Detailed Surveillance Team was going to catch anything concrete then it needed to stick with Stephen McSharry, he knew that with a certainty that he wished he could express to the others, wasting good police on a gang of muscle whose days were numbered was not a part of his game plan.

John Barry regarded him for a few moments as he made his final decision, eventually he nodded but when he spoke his voice was the same humourless growl.

"I'm not going to tell you how to run your department Officer Walker, but this one is on you. Follow the course you need to but if you can't make progress at a time when we need it the most then I may have to take a closer look at your current position. Understood?"

David took the warning on the chin "Yes sir" he replied evenly.

"In the meantime I want you to give the Major Incident Team whatever they need to get this done, the clock is ticking" Barry pushed his papers and the copy of the Liverpool Echo back into the blue folder, David considered reminding him of his promise to let them read it after the meeting was through, but thought it best not to antagonize him further.

"Actually sir," Walker said tentatively, there was just one more concern that was playing on his mind, and it was only after he heard the sound of his own voice that he realised he'd decided to raise it "Detective Drysdale aside my experiences working with the MIT since joining SOCA have been, well, less than productive. I know from my time there that, to put it bluntly; progress is kept in house. I'm not sure how valuable we can be if we aren't getting the full picture from DCI Lincoln's detectives"

Once again Lincoln flashed him that warm, sympathetic smile "Don't worry David, my men know to be on their best behaviour for this one"

When no one else spoke John Barry stood up from his chair "Ok, thank you gentlemen, dismissed"

David and Chris watched as first Barry, then Lincoln made their way out of the room and into the hallway.

The two men remained seated for a few minutes longer. Eventually Chris heaved himself from his chair with a groan; either the meeting had taken a lot out of him or the boys hangover was still getting worse. His eyes were as thin as slits and he seemed to be moving gingerly, like he doubted his bodies capacity to cope with any kind of swift movement.

"You... a word" David said, halting Railton in his tracks.

The younger man turned around, dejected that his attempted escape had failed, and shuffled back towards the desk until they stood face to face.

"Yeah?"

Walker tried to remember how it felt to be a young man on a big case, to feel both the buzz and the sense of self assurance that came with it, he made

206

sure his voice was sympathetic

"Look, I know you're frustrated"

"I just want to solve this thing, that's all"

"I get that" David told him "But you can't let one murder get in the way of our objective. Our targets needs to be all the major players, not just the one who ordered the shooting last night. If what we think is going to happen happens, then we're perfectly placed to play a major part here, we can't be distracted by one twist because you can bet your arse there are going to be more. Our job is to keep our eyes on the big picture, I need you to understand that"

Chris looked at the floor and nodded "I do" he said, with a hint of embarrassment.

Walker gestured towards the door and the two men started moving forward, he wanted to put the discussion behind them, there wasn't time to be dwelling on reprimands and repercussions, not with John Barry's Friday deadline fast approaching.

"Alright, I want you to liaise with Drysdale and go with him on the raids for the gun runners, since it's our lead I want a SOCA presence all the way, make sure you're involved in the interrogation as well"

"Ok" Chris nodded enthusiastically, his embarrassment quickly forgotten "What are you going to do?"

They stepped into the hallway, the RD and the DCI had long since departed, he felt restrained when he was in their presence, now he was free to get back to the job at hand. It felt good.

"I have a couple of leads I need to follow up. I'll be in touch when it's done"

"Ok"

Railton flashed him a half apologetic, half embarrassed smile and made his way towards the staircase on the opposite side of the building, Walker let him get a few steps before he called out to him.

"Officer Railton" he said sternly.

Railton turned to face him, when he saw the snarl on David Walker's lips the smile quickly disappeared.

"If you ever disregard the chain of command, or try to go over my head again you're out of my team, understood?"

Railton swallowed hard as the remaining colour drained from his face.

"Yes sir" he muttered.

David nodded and a second later Chris Railton had disappeared down the hallway. Suddenly he was left alone with his thoughts, it didn't take long to realise how dangerous a place that could be. Fishing in his pocket he found a couple of coins and decided to buy himself a copy of the Liverpool Echo, if the case was about to turn into a media war then it made sense for him to be familiar with the enemy.

As he made his way towards the lift David slid the tie from around his neck and put it into his pocket, the dread over what came next began to build in his chest and Walker found himself recalling the image of Rachel Saunders as a distraction. One day soon maybe he would find the time to do something about it, but before then he needed to return to a dark place in his past, he realised now that it was the only way to get what he needed.

He only hoped he would have enough self-control to make it back again.

Chapter 17

There was nothing to do but wait it out. Stephen McSharry was good at waiting, ten years of practice had made him a professional, he was an expert in patience. The dark pub was unnaturally quiet, a ray of sunlight forced its way through the dirty window at the opposite end of the room and offered enough illumination for the men to see their surroundings. The main room still smelt of the night before, the stale aroma of lager and the sweet scent of sweat filled McSharry's nostrils in a manner that wasn't entirely unpleasant. It was an old smell, the smell of memories, all that was missing was the obligatory scent of smoke that the cigarette ban had stolen from every public house in the land. In defiance he took a cigar from his breast pocket and lit it.

Most of the small wooden stools were perched upside down on tables around the room, he and his men had taken enough down for themselves but there were only six men with him today, the rest of the chairs lay untouched in preparation of the coming evening. The pub was one of many around the city that he owned, not officially, the landlords name was on both the mortgage and the license but Stephen McSharry provided the place with its protection and that meant, in all but name, it belonged to him.

Ads had sent the landlord out for the day, the man knew enough about the people he paid to know that it was in his best interest to quietly take the day off. From what McSharry had been told the man hadn't been a hint of bother since missing a payment five years ago, ever since the scar above his left eye had served as a poignant reminder to pay on time.

With his right hand he took the cigar from his mouth and with his left he scratched lightly at his groin. His first fuck for over a decade had come the night before, he could still smell the little tart on his skin, he'd forgotten what he'd been missing. Locked up he'd been like every other man, night after night spent dreaming of a woman's touch, a woman's smell, a woman's moan, but as soon as free air had touched his lungs the craving for success easily overpowered any kind of sexual desire he may have had.

There were other reasons as well, he'd been surprised just how much he thought of his ex-wife now that he was free. In prison she hardly ever crossed his mind, but in that big old house she seemed to linger like a ghost, hiding behind every piece of furniture, drifting amongst the rooms she had decorated five times over. He knew he probably idealised her memory but still he found it impossible to find a woman who compared to his deceased bride.

Julie had been the kind of beautiful that only came along once in a generation, like a Monroe, he'd hoped to find her equal in the new flock of women who had flourished during his incarceration but amongst the many beauties not one could hold a candle to his Julie.

That wasn't to say that the previous night's entertainment hadn't been enjoyable, it had.

She had talents, the twenty year old stripper whose name had already slipped from his mind, and she knew how to give a man what he wanted. Not only that she was a pretty little thing as well, with red hair and green eyes, but like most women she talked too much. He'd sent her packing not long after, her incessant jabbering was not only annoying, it was distracting. He'd decided in that moment that she would strictly be a one-time thing, he had plenty more to sample, and maybe the next one would know when to keep her mouth shut.

He credited the demise of Wayne Caddock for his new found sex drive. Prior to the man's death McSharry had found it near impossible to focus his attention on anything other than his grand plan. It was only after the first blow had been struck and Wayne Caddock's body had been hauled from the Mersey that his sexual urges had returned, he planned to have a whole troop of whores waiting on the night he put Tony Miller in the ground.

A few of the men shifted uncomfortably on their stools, the meeting had been due to begin at two, and the clock above the bar confirmed that it was already 2:15. He wasn't surprised, at least no more than he had been when the meeting was originally set up. A reaction from Tony Miller had been expected, after the death of his closest ally it was a necessity, but to call a meeting within forty eight hours of the man's death wasn't what he'd have predicted. McSharry had prepared himself for at least a few petulant retaliations, Tony Miller was not a man to think things through. A quick response; maybe a firebombing of one of his clubs or a raiding of one of his warehouses seemed like much more his style, but so far there hadn't been a hint. Perhaps he'd underestimated the man.

All he could do now was wait, he had to admit, it was mesmerising trying to predict how his rival might react to the events of Monday night.

Miller would have his suspicions over who ordered the hit, like most people in the life his first guess was bound to have been Stephen McSharry. But by now the coppers he had on the payroll would have confirmed that none of McSharry's people matched the ID of the shooter. That would be enough to plant a seed of doubt in the pricks mind and that was all McSharry needed to push forward with his plans.

He was pragmatic enough to know that if Miller went to war there would only be one winner, and he'd either be in the ground or in the nick before he could protest his innocence.

He needed Caddock's killer to remain obscure, and he needed Tony Miller to waste time chasing down dead ends. Liverpool was a connected town with an active rumour mill, Miller's own arrogance would convince him that there was no way a secret like that could be kept from him in his town. He'd waste time, he'd look for that confirmation, and Stephen McSharry would have the time to finish what he'd started.

Miller might have been a hot head but until he knew for sure he wouldn't risk the losses associated with all-out war, especially when McSharry had nothing the man wanted. Other than his life.

Whatever Miller's thinking he'd called the meeting and McSharry had little option but to accept. At this point he was willing to let the chips fall where they may, the excitement of the unknown brought a small smile to the corners of his mouth.

Ads, propped on the corner of the bar, impatiently took the gun from his belt and checked the clip. The other men looked equally on edge; Rico Wallace sat cracking his knuckles as his eyes watched the room, Si spun his mobile in his hand, Mercer scratched at the table while Macca had his arms folded tight. Only Nikolai seemed at ease, leaning against the back wall he slowly removed his glasses and cleaned them with the front of his t shirt. When he was satisfied he slipped them back on and dropped his right hand closer to the knife in his jacket. McSharry wondered whether he would need them before the day was out.

It was Begsy's absence that unnerved them, though none would admit it. While McSharry was inside it had been his number two who led the crew, and he knew that their survival over those years was in no small part down the big man, and the reputation that preceded him. His enforcer offered them reassurance, one look at his snarling scarred face was enough to put fear into his enemies and confidence in his allies, it was that confidence which they missed today.

McSharry had been loath to lose his number two, particularly on a day like this, but there was important work to be done.

The call from the Drake brothers came in less than twelve hours after Caddock was clipped. They accepted the deal, it wasn't unexpected, but it was another important piece in the puzzle.

He took their agreement with a pinch of salt. It wasn't like the old days, when he'd been coming up the ranks a man's word was like rock, there was respect in negotiations. With the new generation it was never that simple, their word meant less than shit and the only way to ensure loyalty was to ensure fear. That was where Begsy came in,

At that very moment he would be in the docks; confirming their agreement with the brothers, finalising the details and making it clear what would happen to them if they failed to hold up their end.

McSharry still wasn't certain he would keep them around even if they did. The acrimonious attitude of Johnny Drake had riled him something fierce, in the old days he would have just killed the man where he stood, but these weren't the old days, and for now he needed the two southern bitches to get back on top.

Once their shipments came in and his people could put their product on the street then the landscape was likely to change awfully quickly. Perhaps then he'd be in a better position to punish those who disrespected him, but for now he was in bed with Keith and Johnny Drake and his pride would just have to get used to it.

He picked up the paper that lay on the table and perused the headline: NINE DEAD IN ALBERT DOCK SLAUGHTER. He'd read the article seven or eight times yet it still brought a smile to his face. He loved the buzz words that were littered throughout to try and entice the average punter; phrases like 'gang war', 'drug fuelled shooting' and 'senseless massacre' gave the events described a sense of dramatic impetus. He checked the name of the writer; James Webb, maybe he'd send him a bottle of champagne.

The article pleaded for the quick arrest of those responsible, Mr Webb cited the Merseyside drug lords who he claimed were strangling the life out of the city. In truth it was people like him and the business he did that made Liverpool the party town that it was.

People tried to tell themselves that the tourists came for music, or the culture, but that was all bullshit. People came for the drugs, and party ethos that they spawned. That was the truth of the matter, but truth like that wouldn't sell a lot of newspapers.

Mercer gave an agitated shake of the head "This is bollocks. Where is the gobshite? I'm telling you, this whole thing just doesn't feel right"

Macca sniggered "Don't be such a shithouse"

"Go fuck yourself, Mac"

Ads watched the exchange and then turned to McSharry. The man's arms were crossed and two thick biceps stretched the fabric of his t-shirt.

"You think he's trying to make a point?"

"Maybe"

The truth was he didn't know what games Tony Miller was playing, and it unnerved him. Being in this kind of vulnerable position felt completely unnatural, but at this point he had no other choice. He cursed George's memory for letting it get to this point, Tony Miller shouldn't have been anything more than a stain on his shoe, yet here they were. For now the coarse little fuck had the power, until that changed him and his men would be walking on eggshells.

Mercer stood up and started pacing back and forth "I don't like it. How do we know these geezers aren't waiting outside with half a dozen assault rifles? Maybe he's planning on torching the whole place while we're inside. That'd be a fuck of a way to go"

Macca gave another snigger. The two went back twenty years; the more he saw of them the more they reminded him of an old married couple.

"What you being such a pussy for? Getting scared of dying or something?"

Mercer flipped him the finger and shook his head "Did I say that? I can just think of better ways to go than a barbeque"

McSharry took a long drag on his cigar and savoured the taste. He blew the smoke out loud enough to get the entire groups attention.

"You shouldn't be in this game if you haven't got the balls to lose"

The words sobered them all up, he gave them each a stern look and then returned to his cigar. He wanted them focused, and he wanted them alert, bitching on about possible ways to die wasn't going to do them any good.

Rico cracked his knuckles and leaned forward eagerly "That's not going to happen though, right?"

The boxer tried to sound confident, but his nerves betrayed him in a dozen subtle ways. All he needed was some reassurance from the boys who'd been there before, but that wasn't how it worked. Either he faced his fears head on, or he wasn't facing them at all.

"We'll see" McSharry answered evenly.

Mercer stopped pacing and sat on a wooden table. It creaked under his considerable weight but held strong.

"He's fucking nuts that Tony Miller, though. You ever hear about that lad who stiffed him on a few grams of smack? He hacked the poor bastard to pieces and planted the head outside the boys house"

Sie nodded "I heard that one. Peter Rizzie, wasn't it?" his face was solemn, it was the kids first contribution of the day.

"He was a sound lad" Mercer agreed.

Macca flashed him a dismissive snarl "A fucking dumb lad"

Ads scratched at his thick beard and sighed "How you supposed to do business with a bloke like that? I mean how the fuck do you account for that kind of thing? He wouldn't be so dangerous if he wasn't so nuts" though he directed the question at the room McSharry knew he was only expecting an answer from one of them.

A thought took him back to Catholic school. In that moment he saw nuns with canes and priests with unholy intentions. The words came easily, almost fifty years later.

"Job 5:2; Wrath killeth the foolish man"

The room went quiet, a few of the boys exchanged puzzled looks. Eventually Ads was the one to cautiously speak up.

"One more time?"

McSharry laughed at their ignorance and took another pull of the cigar "It means that idiots who can't control their emotions are the easiest pricks to see off. You just press the right button at the right time and watch them go"

He let the silence wash over the room as the men considered his statement. Eventually it was the quiet, firm voice of Nikolai that broke the stillness.

"He'll come for blood. One way or another"

It was a matter of fact statement completely void of concern. McSharry smiled, Nikolai amused him, he uttered his opinions on retribution and death like most people talked about the weather. A few of the lads exchanged looks. They weren't used to hearing the little man speak, they were even less used to hearing him offer opinions in group discussions.

Sie squinted and looked at Nikolai, his face was etched in concentration, as if he was all of his brain power to try and figure the little Russian immigrant out.

"What makes you so sure?"

Nikolai gave a disinterested shrug of the shoulders "It's what I'd do. We're a problem he doesn't need"

Ads looked towards McSharry for direction but he kept his face even, he enjoyed watching the exchange, particularly as they all tried to figure out the little knife merchant. When Ads failed to get a response he turned to face Nikolai and ran a hand through his shaggy black hair.

"So why arrange a sit down?"

Nikolai gave another shrug, he seemed bored of the conversation already "It's easier to knife a friend than it is an enemy"

Ads glanced at the others and raise his eyebrows "I'll remember that" he muttered.

A few of the boys sniggered, it hadn't amused Mercer, who was up and pacing again "What are we wasting time on all this speculating bollocks for. Why don't we talk about something real, since we're stuck here and all"

Sie was still smiling "Like what?"

Mercer looked towards McSharry with a mischievous look in his eye, he knew what was coming before the ex-bouncer even started to speak.

"I dunno, like who really clipped Wayne Caddock. How about it boss, any ideas?"

Every ear in the room pricked up at the delivery of the question. The entire group had been hassling Begsy for days, gossiping like housewives and speculating like schoolgirls. Begs had eventually subdued the questioning with one of his patented threats but it had clearly only been a short term reprieve. They all wanted to know who the nasty bastard was who'd clipped nine players, whether it was awe, jealously or simple professional curiosity that drove them he couldn't say, whatever it was they weren't letting it go easily.

Ads, Rico, Macca and Mercer each looked intently in his direction, Sie focused on the mobile phone he was spinning in his hand, though the tilt of his head revealed there was more interest there than he was letting on. Only Nikolai looked genuinely unconcerned, his eyes locked on the front door waiting for movement.

McSharry let a small smile touch the corner of his lips. He kept his eyes on Mercer as he took another pull on the cigar and slowly expelled the smoke.

He kept them waiting for a moment longer, then he spoke.

"None I'd care to share boyo. How bout you?"

There was a part of him that wanted to tell them. They needed to know what was coming and they needed to know what might come back to haunt them, it was their battle too, they deserved to know. More than that he wanted to share his success, the cities second largest gangster was in the ground, and he had orchestrated the entire thing. It was a victory that deserved to be shouted from the rooftops, but pride was a dangerous sin and he knew all too well that some victories needed to be kept private.

When it came right down to it the facts were very simple; Rob Thomas was the best kept secret he had. While that secrecy was still valuable he would continue to use it

Mercer pressed a hand against his chest like he was offended.

"You don't even trust your own boys? That's a sad state of affairs that it is, boss. I understand you don't want this bunch of gossiping wankers to know, but at least have a quick word in my ear"

A few heckles came up around the room, the mood felt lighter, he let them run with their bullshit.

Macca pointed a thumb at himself and winked at Mercer "I know"

McSharry turned his smile to Macca, inside a slight flicker of worry passed through his chest. He kept his tone light and amused "Really?"

Macca nodded "Yozzer. Had his name written all over it"

He heard a couple of scoffs, the feeling in his chest passed and his smile became more natural, a second later Ads was leaning forward in his chair.

"Yozza's serving four to six on a rape charge, genius"

Mercer laughed and sat back down "My moneys on Ritchy Batkiss. He was always fond of a bit of carnage"

Sie dropped his phone on the table and gave a shake of the head "Nah, Ritchy's a strict shotgun merchant, isn't he? I hear Mark Jones is a good fit for the Docks though. He's got a solid reputation for that kind of thing"

Ads scratched at his beard and leaned back in the chair "He did have. The cunt took a .45 to the face up in Manchester last month"

Sie looked surprised and went back to twirling his phone. No one spoke for a few minutes until Mercer looked towards McSharry with a cheeky grin plastered across his face.

"Whoever it was, maybe the boss wants to look a little bit closer to home next time. No use bringing in an outside contractor when you've got the skills in your own backyard. I wouldn't mind getting a crack at a couple of these gobshites"

McSharry extinguished his cigar and picked up the newspaper. He quickly scanned the article for the information he was looking for and turned towards Mercer, sceptically looking him up and down.

"You think you're up for it? According to this the alleged perpetrator 'executed nine men in quick succession, limiting his victims to only a handful of wild retaliations, before chasing down two more and murdering them at close blank range'. Sounds like your kind of job Mercer?"

The boy gave a cocky nod and flexed his muscles "Damn right"

The suggestion was universally dismissed. Mercer looked around the room as if he couldn't believe what he was hearing, it was Ads who scolded him the loudest.

"A fat prick like you couldn't chase down a milk float"

The boys laughed, even McSharry found himself joining in. Before they had a chance to add anything else he caught a sound from outside and raised his

215

hand in alarm. Silence followed a moment later.

They all listened to the sound of multiple cars pulling up outside. He gave one slow nod, the men understood; those who were carrying took the guns from their belts and checked the clips. The next sound they heard was the slamming of a car door, first one, then two, McSharry listened closely and kept count, it stopped at ten. He pushed himself up straight, his boys mirrored the action, he glanced around the room and let out a long breath.

"Game time, boys"

Tony Miller led his men into the dark pub and surveyed the room with a contemptuous scowl. It was the first time McSharry had seen him since the hotel sit down, he clocked the difference in appearance instantly.

Gone was the ill-fitting suit, suggesting that the guise of civility had been well and truly cast off. In its place he wore a grey tracksuit with a thick gold chain at his neck, much more suited to his bulky frame and hard face. He seemed more at ease in his new attire, moving with a natural determination that had been lacking just over a week ago.

McSharry kept count as Miller's entourage filed into the pub; he counted ten to his six, with no way of knowing what they had left outside. He considered whether he may have miscalculated and led his men straight into a trap, logic broke through and dismissed the idea quickly, if that was Tony Miller's plan he would have implemented it from a safe distance. That he was here himself, leading his men in, told a different story. It said violence was low on the agenda, that this was a time for talk, it didn't fit with the image he had of Miller. Once again he considered the possibility that he may have underestimated his opponent. His eyes skimmed over Miller's nine soldiers, they all look primed. If it kicked off none of his people would be walking out alive, but if it came to that they'd be sure to take a fair few with them, starting with the boss.

Satisfied with his appraisal of the pub Miller made his way forward. McSharry watched the man who had told him he was finished, who had tried to call time on his professional ambitions. Now that man's closest ally was dead, he could only speculate what was going on inside his brutish head.

Miller stopped just in front of the group and turned his derisive scowl towards McSharry, there was anger in his hard face that Miller was struggling to control.

"Alright, lad. Been waiting long?"

McSharry shook his head. There was no mistaking the arrogance in Miller's tone, it was the same arrogance from before, the kind that demanded a swift execution. Only this time he seemed to lack the confidence from their last meet, in its place was a cold cynicism that suggested he saw an enemy in every face.

"Sound, have a seat" Miller said, sitting down and gesturing McSharry to a

216

stool on the opposite side of the table "so, you can probably guess what this is about, yeah?"

"The Wayne Caddock killing, I imagine"

The mere mention of Caddock's name brought about the narrowing of Miller's brow. There was hatred in the man's heart, it was impressive to see how well he controlled it.

"That's right"

Miller uttered the words though gritted teeth. The tension was thick, it filtered through every one of them and left a presence in the room that you could practically touch, they all knew it; the situation was one wrong word away from total carnage.

Miller stroked his jet black goatee and watched McSharry for a reaction, eventually he continued speaking.

"Some sneaky little shit jumped him and his boys outside the Albert Dock, blew them all away one at a time, but I see the Echo sitting there on that table so I'm going to assume that you're as clued up on the thing as I am. He was a friend of mine, a good friend, and a solid business partner. I'm going around doing what I do, talking to anyone with their ear to the ground, trying find out what was what. Now I've found my way to you. So... what do you know, kidda?"

Miller glared at him, but his poker face held strong. He wondered how sure Miller was of his guilt, that look suggested he was almost certain, but maybe that was just how he was trying to play it. Scaring people into giving up what they knew was the kind of tactic he expected from the man, with a look like that it probably worked more times than it failed.

Thoughts jumbled and compartmentalised, he reminded himself that if Miller was so certain there would be no way he'd be sitting across the table from him. Caddock's death may have vibed gangland hit, but in their business things were never that simple. The fact was Miller's presence signified the meetings importance, the man didn't hold court with just anybody, if he was here it was because he thought he had something to gain.

"Just what I read in the paper Tony, sorry"

Miller breathed in deeply through his nose while he considered McSharry's reply, the hatred in those eyes showed no signs of abating, but equally it didn't seem set to erupt. Instead it just lay there, waiting, like an animal ready to strike.

"Fucking tragic though, innit?" Miller said, shaking his head in disgust "I mean he was a good lad was Wayne. Credit where credits due, it was a ballsy fucking move. I mean whoever killed him must have known I had his back, they must of known I'd see it as an act of war. Who in this city is that stupid? They don't want to go to war with me Stevie, I'll bury ever last one of the fuckers"

The menace and anger in Miller's tone had steadily increased throughout, by the time he'd finished speaking his face had turned a dark shade of red.

The threat of violence seemed to grow in the air, he saw hands on both sides gravitate towards their weapons. He kept his face relaxed and tried to speak in a slow, calm voice.

"I'm sure you will. Like you said; it's a tragedy, you can't just sweep this kind of thing under the carpet"

Miller shook his head "No chance. I heard someone killed your nephew and all?"

"Strangled" he replied solemnly, giving his best impression of a grieving uncle "horrible way for a young man to die, maybe it was the same prick who clipped Wayne? We might have a common enemy on the loose?"

"Maybe" Miller said, not giving anything away "I'll ask around"

"I appreciate that"

Something in Miller's body language said that he was relaxing, maybe it was the casual manner in which he sat, or the curious way he was now viewing the room, but McSharry got the impression that the burning hatred was slowly ebbing away. Not the suspicion though, his beady little eyes confirmed that emotion was still going strong.

"Where's Begsy? Not like him to miss a sit down?"

The mere mention of Begsy's name caused a few of Miller's men to instinctively draw their hands closer to their weapons. Miller tried to ignore the movement, but there was a clear hint of irritation in his cold, grey eyes.

"I sent him on holiday, thought he could do with a week off now that I'm back"

"Where's he gone?" the question came quickly, as if Miller was trying to catch him out.

"I didn't ask"

Miller took a few moments to digest the new information. The longer he sat, staring across the table, the more McSharry got the impression that the man was analysing their previous conversation while he tried to decide his next move. McSharry waited patiently as Miller looked through him with an almost contemplative expression, on his hard face it looked unnaturally gruesome. Eventually something clicked and he shifted forward, leaning on the wooden table with his broad arms.

"You know Wayne Caddock had a lot of interests in this city" Miller began, that suspicious tint returning to his eyes "Played a big part in how it was run. The boy had a lot of fingers in a lot of pies; drugs, security, property, stolen goods, someone's going to have to take them over now that he's gone"

"I know all about his interests" McSharry told him "A lot of them were mine before I went down"

Miller nodded, he didn't argue the point.

"I'm willing to give you forty per cent of those interests to run. I'll take over the other sixty, call it a gift for the fact that I couldn't do anything for ya last time out, but before we agree to anything I'm going to need some assurances"

"What kind of assurances?" McSharry asked cautiously. The offer was more than he'd expected and it caught him slightly off guard. Where McSharry had prepared for retribution Tony Miller had come at him with appeasement, it was an unexpected move and he was annoyed that he'd failed to anticipate it.

"What happened to Wayne Caddock was unnecessary" Miller went on "Whoever it was who wanted him dead may still have grander ambitions. No one wants all-out war, especially not at your age, for one thing it's too fucking expensive. I want your help to find the fuck that put Wayne Caddock down and if, by some stroke of ill fortune we can't find the bastard, then I want your assurances that you'll do everything in your power to keep something like this from happening again. We don't need it Stevie, it's bad for business, it's a fucking ball ache and it keeps us all from doing what we're in this to do; make money"

McSharry understood the implication; if it was you, take the extra money and knock that assassination shit on the head. If it wasn't, help us find the bastards who did it. He read between the lines as well as the next guy, and the lines felt very wrong. It was too out of character, McSharry found it hard to believe that this was the same villain who had so thoroughly dominated their meeting the week before. While he'd been strong and decisive then all McSharry saw now was weakness and compromise.

He struggled to keep the disgust from his face as he thought about how long Miller had ruled Liverpool in his absence, a jester calling himself a king. He reminded himself not to get too overconfident, if things went to plan then his rival's decision to compromise would be his undoing, but for now the man still had the muscle, and he still had the power.

Nodding humbly he smiled, the image of Rob Thomas putting a bullet between those suspicious grey eyes sent a shiver down his back.

"I agree, of course you have my assurances"

Miller nodded and glanced over his shoulder towards his men, the answer seemed to relax him and the sentiment slowly spread around the room. McSharry took two cigars from his pocket and offered one across the table, Miller declined with a shake of the head and left it where it lay, McSharry slid the other into his mouth and gestured towards Mercer for a lighter.

"Nice one" Miller said calmly "Wayne had some big business going on with drug shipments, I'll get in touch with his suppliers and see what we can sort out"

Mercer lit the end of the cigar and McSharry took a long drag, ejecting the smoke into the air between him and Miller "Are you talking about the Drake brothers?"

The surprised look on Miller's face was worth a thousand dead Caddocks. "You know them?"

"They came to me," his voice was firm, it wasn't an apology, Miller knew it as soon as he started speak "after news of Wayne got out, they seemed nervous. They said they needed protection, I couldn't turn the poor lads down, so I did the Christian thing and gave them a new home. They're with me now, signed and sealed"

The surprise gradually made way to anger, the whole process couldn't have taken more than a couple of seconds, and when it reached its conclusion Miller looked ready to reach across the table and grab McSharry by the throat. Heavy breathing seemed to echo around the quiet room, McSharry's eyes were drawn to the two hands resting across the table, clenched into fists so tightly that the knuckles looked bone white. Suddenly this was the Tony Miller he had expected to see; hot headed, rash, out of control. When he spoke his voice was a low growl.

"That didn't take long. The man's not even in the ground yet and you're picking at his remains like a fucking vulture. Where's the bloody respect?"

"They came to me" his reply was unapologetic.

Miller stared with those cold eyes "Maybe they did, maybe they didn't. I should probably pay them a visit and find out for myself. While I'm there I can give them my sales pitch, it's only right that they make an informed choice, right? Nothing wrong with a competitive market place, it's what makes us better than the communists"

Suddenly the tension was back, increased tenfold and coursing through every man in the room. Nervous hands moved closer and closer to their firearms, urged on by the heavy breathing of Tony Miller that seemed to project hatred with the exhaling of every breath.

"You know I can't allow that" McSharry replied, drawing on all his years of experience to keep his voice even.

"Allow?" Miller repeated incredulously, his body was almost shaking with anger "You talk to me and you use that word? In my fucking city? You don't 'allow' a god damn thing, this is my world, Liverpool doesn't exist unless I 'allow' it, you don't exist unless I 'allow' it. You'd do well to remember that"

McSharry sensed the situation was beginning to spiral out of control, but he knew that backing down was not an option. Extinguishing his half smoked cigar on the table he fixed his eyes on Tony Miller and spoke in a slow, calm voice.

"It might be your city, but the Drakes are part of my crew. You know I can't give you access, if you were in my shoes there wouldn't be a chance in hell"

McSharry held Miller's stare for what felt like an eternity, around them the tension held each man where he stood. Once again it seemed like Tony Miller was weighing up his options, the spectators watched with bated breath. Just before he spoke McSharry caught the smallest sigh escape from Miller's lips, and right then he knew; for the second time in a row Miller was going to side with caution.

"Keep the cockneys, for now" his tone was surly "I've got enough product to shift as it is, but this comes out of your share. I'll juggle some things around and we'll see what's what"

"Sounds fair" McSharry replied.

Miller finally relaxed his clenched fists and started fidgeting with the thick gold chain around his neck. "I've got places I need to be. I'll give you a bell in a week or two and we'll thrash out the details"

McSharry nodded "I'll wait for your call

The two men extended their hands, Tony Miller leaned in and he felt that overly firm grip once again.

"You let me know, if you hear anything about that thing" Miller whispered, clenching McSharry's hand one final time with even more force.

McSharry nodded and the two men separated. One wave of Miller's hand and slowly his men began to file out of the pub. Miller waited until they were all outside, anger bubbled away under the surface, itching to be released. Flashing one final contemptuous glance at McSharry and his crew he made his way out into the daylight.

No one spoke, not when they heard the car doors opening, nor when they heard the revving of engines. It was only after the sounds had faded and the men had stood in silence for more than two minutes that McSharry decided to speak.

"Mercer, get a couple of boys and take them to the Drake brothers right now, tell Begs what was said. I want a few of our people around them at all times, I don't know what Miller might try but I want to at least be prepared for it"

"Sure thing boss" he was already halfway out the door with his mobile in hand.

Taking a deep breath he removed the handkerchief from his suit pocket and dabbed it at his head. The adrenaline was pumping through his body faster than it had in years, it felt good, like being alive again.

He left his men where they were and moved towards the storeroom door at the back of the pub. It was already partially open, he pushed it the rest of the way and stepped inside. The cold hit him instantly. Sat on a stool near the door was Martin Cassidy, his old face looked weary, like the events of the last week had taken a greater toll than they should have. He sat with a small glass of whisky he'd taken from the bar, McSharry wondered just how much his old friend was drinking these days, though he decided not to ask the question.

"So you heard?" he asked instead.

"Oh, I heard my boy" Cassidy replied, taking a mouthful of whiskey "I heard"

McSharry closed the door and leaned against the wall, raising his eyebrows at the old man "And?"

"Well, you've got his attention, I don't think there's any doubt about that" Martin flash him a weak smile.

McSharry replayed the meeting in his head and tried to decipher Miller's offer of peace, the words still didn't seem to make sense "He offered me a seat at the table. I killed his closest ally and he offers me a seat at the table. What is that?"

"He recognises the threat. At this point whether it came from you is irrelevant. With Caddock out of the picture he's lost a big slice of his support, the landscape is changing and he knows it. He needs to shore up some backing and reaffirm his control before someone can move to disrupt it. He brings you to the table he gets a formidable ally with a lot of muscle, maybe that's enough to scare off any bold scallies who might want to try their luck. It's a smart move"

"It's a weak move" McSharry snapped, Martin's passive attitude stoked the flames of his hatred, Tony Miller was their enemy, he deserved no praise "weak and stupid. If he isn't man enough for the fight then this whole thing will be that much easier"

"You intend to press on then?" Cassidy asked reluctantly.

"Of course I do. Everything is falling into place, why would we stop?"

"You got what you wanted" Cassidy told him, his voice was almost pleading "Tony Miller has yielded, you're back inside. Is it really necessary to go on another killing spree?"

He felt the tingle of adrenaline as it ran through his veins, it gave him more energy than he knew what to do with, in contrast he looked down at his old friend with pity, the tired old man who had maybe lost the stomach for the fight.

"Tony Miller can't be trusted" McSharry told him flatly "He may want a truce while he's weak but he won't forget. When he gets his house in order he'll come back on us, without doubt. You know what his kind are like, he could never let this kind of thing slide, if I let him live I'll be watching my back for the rest of my days"

Martin Cassidy's wrinkled face seemed to grimace "But if you waited, at least until the business with the Drake brothers has produced some results, perhaps then you'd be in a better position-"

The old man didn't have time to finish, his words stopped suddenly as McSharry kicked a crate of lager bottles onto the floor. The smash brought a look of alarm to Cassidy's face as McSharry turned on him angrily.

"MILLER DIES!" he shouted, surprising even himself with the vigour of this declaration "The way Miller and Caddock talked to us at that meeting, the way they treated us? We built this city, we made the world they know and for what? So these kids could come along and take it all from us the minute our backs are turned? They think they can take our throne and kick us to the curb, you want me to let these men live? Not a chance Martin, they die, all of them"

The alarm in Cassidy's face made way to fatherly affection "You always were headstrong, my boy" he said with a smile, though McSharry suspected he uttered the words more in regret than anything else.

"Let me worry about Tony Miller. You just worry about how we absorb his business once he's out the way"

Cassidy took another sip of whiskey and nodded dutifully "It's all in hand, though it would help if you could tell me just how long I have to prepare"

McSharry watched a stream of lager from the smashed crate as it made its way towards his feet. Slowly, he stepped out of the way of the golden liquid and watched as it disappeared down a grate a few feet from the door.

"Not long. Not long at all"

Chapter 18

It was Friday, his flight had landed on the Wednesday of the week gone by, he'd been back in Liverpool for nine days. Rob double checked the math, had it really only been nine days? It felt like so much longer, weeks maybe even months. Facets of his old life were resurfacing at every opportunity, more and more he was beginning to feel like his old habits had never really died. Instead they'd just been hiding within, lying dormant until they had a chance to resurface, like a terrorist movement, or a disease. The coke, the killing, the way of thinking, despite what he wanted to believe his relapses weren't an entirely unpleasant experience, in a sense it felt like a weight was finally off his shoulders. The guilt was still there but it was offset by the comfort that came from confronting who he was. Ten years of denial would have a serious effect on any man, and Rob hadn't realised just how much damage was being done until he stopped pretending.

Yet in spite of it all there was one thing that kept him anchored to the life he had tried to create, and that was Jo. Imagining himself through her eyes was almost enough to make the lie worthwhile, if she could believe he was that man then there was no reason why he couldn't be. Meeting her had been the catalyst that made his life in New York real, before her it had been more like a dream; the one night stands, the drink, the repression, it was only when he fell for the girl with the auburn hair that he really started to live in New York, to embrace it. What worried him most was that after only nine days his memories of that world were already beginning to fade. He could still see Jo, her smile, her laugh, but it was hazier than before. When he closed his eyes and concentrated he could still smell her, but it was no longer the all-encompassing, heart stopping smell that he remembered from New York, now it was faint, like running passed the kitchen of a restaurant.

He found that he was thinking about her less as well, more often than not he was too preoccupied with replaying the Caddock's hit over and over in his head, and when the past wasn't monopolising his attention then worry about the next hit was always waiting for its turn to gnaw away at his nerves. Jo was becoming more and more of an afterthought, an oasis in the desert sands of his depression, but the deeper he waded into his nightmare the harder it was to happen upon the tranquillity of her memory.

Liverpool was changing him in a number of ways, Jo was just the most prominent. What concerned him almost as much was the arrogance that was slowly creeping back into his demeanour, the overwhelming confidence that he felt after a kill. It was a primal emotion, one that in his darkest moments he feared might push him to a place from which he wouldn't return. He knew he wasn't the first man to be intoxicated by the lust of the kill, he just didn't want to be the latest. The spring in his step, the assurance in his tone, they were the by-products of his complete victory over Wayne Caddock and his men, while the act of murder had made him physically sick he was too self-aware to deny that it had also made him feel powerful. He was ashamed to embrace the rush of the kill but he couldn't hide from the fact that it was there, simmering in the back of his mind.

Suddenly the car ground to a halt, and Rob broke free from the daze in which he had found himself.

"Shape up, fella" Charlie said, turning off the engine "we're here"

Rob let go of the thoughts that had been swirling around his head, Jo's smiling face shone brightly in his mind's eye, reluctantly he forced himself to push it down into the depths of his consciousness. Until the job was done he needed to be hard and he needed to be cold, her memory made him weak, and that was the one thing he couldn't afford to be.

Rob looked out of his window at the extravagant, three storey Victorian house that stood before them and remembered his only previous visit to the property. The first meeting he'd ever had with Stephen McSharry had taken place inside that house and the day was crystalized perfectly in his memory, forgetting the day your life began to spiral out of control was no easy thing to do. It was the only time McSharry had allowed Rob into his home, that day it had been for some twisted kind of audition, he wondered after his sloppy effort with the Wayne Caddock hit whether he would have to prove himself all over again.

"Rob…"

"Yeah?" he answered, taking his eyes away from the house and turning towards his brother "Sorry mate, miles away"

"No kiddin" Charlie said, reaching into the back seat to grab his jacket "The amount of conversation I get out of you, I may as well take a drive with the wife"

"What do you expect with that bollocks you've got blasting?" he gestured towards the radio "It numbs the brain. I'm starting to understand why you're such a bloody retard"

Charlie gave an offended shake of the head "This is good shit old man, but if it means that much to you we can pick up some Chuck Berry for the ride home"

"Don't knock the Chuck young'un" he replied, reaching for the door handle "the man was a genius"

Rob pushed open the passenger door and stepped out onto the clean, middle class street that Stephen McSharry called home. It was a far cry from the depraved, poverty stricken Bootle estate where he rested his head, and Rob felt an overwhelming sense of repulsion that the man who had caused him so much strife actually got to live in such a place, whoever said crime didn't pay clearly wasn't familiar with Liverpool.

Rob looked around the street cautiously, when Begsy called Charlie the day before he had given him assurances that by the time they arrived the house would not be under surveillance, but then Rob had never been inclined to trust Begsy before, he saw no reason to start now. Taking a few minutes he meticulously studied the surrounding area, from the look of the houses most of McSharry's neighbours were probably bankers, lawyers, maybe even the odd footballer, but there was nothing suspicious about the affluent street to put him on edge. Conducting one more sweep of the area he satisfied himself that no one was watching them, police or otherwise, and turned to face his brother.

"Now, remember" Rob said, moving to Charlie's side and speaking in a hushed tone as they made their way up the long drive towards the house "when we get inside try and keep your mouth shut. I know it'll be hard for you, but these guys are fucking trouble and I don't want you making this any harder than it has to be, let's just get in and get out as fast as we can"

"You worry too much" Charlie told him "you need to learn to enjoy this kind of thing, embrace mingling with the big dogs, you might get into it"

Rob leaned in closer to Charlie as they reached the halfway point of the driveway "They ain't dogs Charlie, they're wolves, don't underestimate them, mouth shut, eyes open"

"You a wolf too there, Robo?" Charlie asked with more than a hint of mockery.

"Me?" Rob said with a smile "Nah, I'm a lion"

Charlie laughed and nudged his brother in the shoulder "You fucking smell like one"

Rob held on to the smile until they were a few steps from the front door, then he steadied himself and prepared for business, a quick glance at Charlie told him that his brother was doing the same. He hoped his kid brother was sensible enough to do as he was told. Rob didn't know how many problems he could juggle but if Charlie presented one in a place like this then it would probably be enough to bring them all crashing to the ground.

He glanced at him one last time as they continued up the drive, he was angry with himself for resorting to cocaine at the first sign of trouble but more than that he was embarrassed that Charlie had been there to see it. His little brother had always looked up to him, from the time he was old enough to stand, and Rob felt a strange sense of regret that he'd allowed his brother to see how weak he really was. The morning after the hit he'd flushed what he hadn't snorted down the toilet, and every day since he'd missed the numbing sensation it had brought him. He remembered the cycle, the time when he needed the drug just to be able to function, to forget the images that plagued his mind, but just as quickly he remembered the type of person that routine had made him and he vowed never to relapse again. If his fate on this earth was to be haunted by the ghosts of his past then so be it, it was a punishment he more than deserved, but he refused to become that monster again. Maybe that was the one terrible act he could still choose not to commit.

Reaching the front door Rob straightened himself up and knocked loudly on the brown oak, he felt the confidence of days gone by filling his chest and did his best to control it. He knew with a worrying certainty that violence was as addictive as any drug he had ever encountered, and being around men like this; it was like putting a junkie in a crack den.

After a few moments the heavy door opened and Rob found himself staring at Begsy from the other side of the threshold, though they stood on an even footing Begsy towered over the two brothers by a good four or five inches. His large face was scrunched in a scowl, distorting the scar on his right cheek into something like a wave as his grey eyes regarded both Rob and Charlie for a few seconds each, then he stepped aside and allowed the two men to enter. Rob had no trouble understanding why the man had such a brutal reputation, but at the same time he felt a sadistic urge to test himself against the larger man, just to know who was the best. He was sure Begsy had thought the same thing on many an occasion, he suspected that was the major reason for the thug's continued hostility, that and the fact that his boss trusted Rob with the most important of jobs. For someone like Begsy that was the kind of snub that would really sting.

Without a word Begsy began down the large marble hallway and the two men followed silently behind. They passed three doors; two on the right, one on the left, before Begsy reached the one he wanted and pushed it open. Rob stepped through after him with Charlie bringing up the rear.

It only took a couple of seconds to figure out that Begsy that brought them into McSharry's office, the room was a decent size, able to comfortably fit around fifteen people and was filled with expensive looking furniture, including a ceiling high bookcase that covered the entire width of the room.

On the back wall was a large painting of a battle, Rob guessed maybe from the War of the Roses. The scene depicted two groups of men in bright, shining armour riding to meet in battle, with swords raised against the backdrop of a gloriously green field. He imagined Stephen McSharry saw the war he was currently waging in similarly chivalric terms, and realised that in a lot of ways the world hadn't changed much in six hundred years; the Generals still believed in the necessity of their cause, while it was left to the common man to cope with the horror of the slaughter.

Just below the painting was a large desk, and sat behind it was Stephen McSharry, leaning back comfortably in his thick leather chair. He looked to be gaining weight fast, already there was a substance to his face that had been absent upon his release. The long years of incarceration that had been embedded in his features seemed to be disappearing at an alarming rate, leaving a man younger, fitter and probably more dangerous than the one Rob had met a week ago.

McSharry took his time getting to the men as he intently studied a piece of paper amongst the pile on his desk. Rob took the opportunity to survey the large bookcase that dominated the room, he recognised a lot of the authors; philosophical, historical, classical fiction but found more than a few that he'd never even heard of. He felt a wave of anger course through him as he took in the guise of civility his employer was trying to create, the gangster who fancied himself for an intellectual, it made him sick.

Eventually McSharry rested the piece of paper back on the desk and turned towards his guests, a warm, genial smile playing on his lips. Standing up he moved towards the large bookcase and ran his hand over a set of the old, leather covers.

"So you're still with us?" McSharry asked rhetorically.

"Where are the rest of your boys?" Rob said quickly, getting the question out in the open before McSharry had the chance to steer the conversation towards a more gruesome area.

"I sent them on an errand, they're leading the surveillance team on a merry little dance around the Wirral, I'm a very popular man these days, and I felt it would be more rewarding for us both if we keep our little arrangement as quiet as possible"

"Not just from the police though, right?"

"The people I work with are good men" McSharry said, taking a book from one of the shelves, flicking through it quickly then returning it to its resting place "but it never did a man any good to be too trusting"

"I don't think anyone would accuse you of having that problem" Rob told him, earning a reproachful look from Begsy. McSharry seemed to ignore the comment, turning his attention towards Charlie he moved slowly in his direction, like a predator stalking its prey.

"and your name again?"

"Charlie" he told him, with a little too much enthusiasm.

"Right" McSharry replied with a simple nod of the head before turning his attention back to Rob "So. A little messy wouldn't you say? Bodies scattered all over the place, that never was your style. Used to be, if you paid Rob Thommo for a job, you got what you wanted and you got it done quietly, efficiently and professionally. That's what I pay you for kid, it's why I kept you around a lot longer than most of the men in your field; Professionalism. None of this chasing men down the street nonsense, just quick, uncomplicated murder. You know how lucky you are that the police couldn't make an ID?"

"It wasn't luck," Rob said sternly "and I got the bastards didn't I? Just like you asked"

"By the skin of your teeth" the reproachful tone stirred the anger inside Rob's chest "I saw the video, Wayne Caddock very nearly dumped your sorry arse in the Mersey"

"But he didn't" Rob said, trying hard to control his anger. He could feel Begsy moving closer behind him as he left his position by the door, any act of force against the armed man would almost certainly end with the two defenceless brothers' dead, taking a deep breath he tried to take the sting out of his voice.

"Not the work of the man I remember" McSharry continued, doing his best to goad Rob into a reaction "I'm starting to worry that you've lost your touch"

Rob brushed off the efforts with a shrug "Maybe you're right" he told the older man "I guess me and my brother will be on our way then, go find someone a little bit more professional to finish the job"

McSharry smiled, it was a cruel smile full of malice, as Rob met the stare he felt his heart beating faster in his chest. His old employer's actions were becoming harder and harder to predict, at the height of his power that had been one of his most terrifying traits, a man never knew he was on Stephen McSharry's shit list until he felt the cold metal barrel rest against the back of his head. Eventually it was Begsy who broke the silence.

"You think if we pay you for a job and you don't finish, it you get to just walk away?"

Rob turned to face the big man "Yeah?"

Begsy shook his head, the look on his face was one of pure derision "Think again sunshine. You try something like that and maybe the boss won't look too kindly on it, maybe he'll stop being so insistent that I let you live"

Rob closed his hands into fists as he took a step towards Begsy "'Insistent'?" he mocked "Big word! Give it a go, if you think you've got it in you". His heart was beating faster than ever, but it was an enjoyable sensation now, he could feel the taste of adrenaline in his mouth as he stared up at Begsy's daunting figure, the challenge called to him, it must have been how climbers felt when they laid their eyes on Everest.

"Enough!" McSharry's voice bellowed, the force of the command caused both men to turn even without thinking, slowly he raised his hand and pointed towards Rob "You, get over here"

Rob followed the order in spite of himself, while Begsy took a step back towards the door. As he made his way to the wooden desk he spared a glance at Charlie, his brothers' face had turned a light shade of red and there was perspiration on his forehead. He wanted to smile at his little brother, to reassure him that everything was going to be ok, but he couldn't afford to show that sort of compassion in front of these people, it would have been a lie anyway; there were never any guarantees when Stephen McSharry was involved.

The old man waited until Rob stood on the opposite side of the desk before turning towards the painting on the back wall. Giving the canvas a firm push Rob watched as the left side of the painting came out, while the right edge remained connected on a hinge, behind the painting was a large, silver safe. Keeping the metallic, circular lock hidden by his body McSharry began the process of entering the code as he spoke "Just like the old days, isn't it? Never backing down, ready to kill rather than take somebody's shit!" with the last word the safe clicked open, McSharry glanced over his shoulder "You miss it, boy?"

Rob looked at Charlie, and then back to McSharry, he had no intention of answering the question, he might not have a choice when it came to killing but what was going on in his own head was nobody's business but his own. McSharry gave Rob a few seconds to answer, when he didn't he turned back towards the safe and drew a light yellow folder from atop the pile of papers, casually tossing it on to the desk "To business then"

As McSharry turned back to close the safe Rob allowed himself a quick glance inside, it took a second for his eyes to adjust to the dark interior before he realised that the pile the folder had been resting on wasn't made up of papers; it was money. Bundles and bundles of money. The safe slammed shut before he could see anymore but he was certain there was at least a couple of million inside, quickly he diverted his eyes towards the yellow folder as McSharry pressed the painting against the wall and turned back towards him. After a moment he raised his eyes towards the gangster and McSharry gestured for him to pick up the file, hesitantly he reached forward and lifted it off the desk.

"Contestant number two" McSharry said smugly.

He opened the folder and quickly glanced through it, the format was much the same as the last one; surveillance pictures revealing a vicious looking man in his forties with a shaved head and a goatee identified by the corresponding information as Tony Miller. Additionally there was a record of recent movements, glancing at the dates he turned his attention towards McSharry.

"These reports are over two weeks old" he said incredulously.

"And?"

"You don't think he'll have changed up after his business partner was killed?"

"No, I imagine he will" McSharry said, sitting down behind his desk "that's why I hired a professional, and that's why I'm paying you a professional wage"

Rob shook his head in amazement, he glanced at Begsy who was smiling sadistically, evidently he didn't rate Rob's chances of getting the job done either.

"He had more guys than Caddock before this all started" Rob said, reading through the information in the file "If he's got any sense he'll have a small army guarding him by now"

McSharry gave Rob a knowing smile as he interlocked his fingers "Probably, you won't be afforded the luxury you had with Wayne Caddock, another sloppy performance like that and your winning streak will come to a very messy end"

"How do you even expect me to find him!" Rob demanded, throwing the file onto the desk in frustration, McSharry's eyes hardened as the paper slammed against the table, but Rob was unfazed by the gangsters calculating stare.

"The pattern may change" McSharry told him after a few moments "but the details wont. Miller conducts most of his business at the Old Oak pub, I

230

doubt he'll uproot a routine all of his people are familiar with on the back of one little murder, the prick is a creature of habit after all"

Before Rob had the opportunity to protest further he was caught off guard by the sound of his brothers' voice.

"The Old Oak, that's in Wavertree, right?" not waiting for McSharry to respond Charlie turned towards Rob "I know the place; it's on the outer corner of a little cul-de-sac with seven or eight semi-detached houses. You pin them in there Rob and they'll have nowhere to go, numbers won't mean shit then"

Rob looked towards his brother in surprise, raising his eyebrows he tried to make his voice as firm as possible "Don't, Charlie" he said simply. When he turned back towards McSharry he noticed the older man watching them with interest, a wry smile touched of the corners of his mouth. It was a small smile, but it was big enough to fill Rob with worry.

"No, no, your brother's right, Charlie is it?" McSharry asked, Charlie nodded eagerly "You should listen to your brother Thommo, he's giving you good advice. What is it you do again, Charlie?"

"Me?" Charlie pointed to himself in surprise "I sell a bit of product, you know, round the way".

"Product?" McSharry repeated, the slightest hint of mockery infecting his tone "Round the way? And what way would that be?"

"Bootle"

Rob had been watching McSharry intently since the exchange with his brother began, and as Charlie spoke the last word he caught the older man flash a look over Rob's shoulder towards Begsy. It was a quick glance, lasting no more than a couple of seconds, but Rob knew it meant something. His stomach lurched with worry when he realised he had no idea what that was.

"Wayne Caddock used to run most of Bootle, the major boozers at least" McSharry began "It's a good little earner. The natives like their drugs and they like a lot of them. Since your brother's little escapade last week, well, let's just say its ownership has come under dispute. You ever have any dealings the Caddock family?"

Charlie shook his head "Never, I heard it was their territory but they didn't have much of a presence"

"Who supplied you?" McSharry probed, Rob knew from experience that he was testing Charlie, prodding his brother to discover whether or not he was aligned to one of his enemies.

"Leroy Tate" Charlie told him, "Black lad, big fucker"

McSharry looked towards Begsy and narrowed his eyes, Rob turned around just in time to see the big man nodding.

"We're on him" Begsy said "He goes way back with the Caddock boys, stuff he sells is grade A bollocks, steps on his shit too much, may as well be snorting rat poison straight from the box" he uttered the last words with a sneer and directed his gaze in Charlie's direction.

"I've had complaints" Charlie said lightly, shrugging his shoulders "but you know, ain't a whole lot of alternatives in the area!"

"Maybe not before, but times are changing, a new dawn you might say" McSharry smiled at Charlie, it wasn't the cold, vicious smile Rob knew, but a warm smile, one of friendship that told Rob he needed to end the conversation as quickly as possible.

"Your new dawn can wait" he said, protectively stepping between Charlie and the seated McSharry "let's get back to business"

McSharry fixed Rob with a cold stare "This is business"

"Our business" Rob said sternly "that's the only kind you have with my family"

"Remember who you're talking to" the warning had more than a hint of a threat in it.

Rob repressed the urge to deliver an antagonistic response, somewhere along the way the meeting had slipped out of his control. He tried to focus on the next job; Tony Miller, his golden ticket out of this world. There was only one problem with that hopeful scenario: it meant trusting Stephen McSharry to keep his word.

"The Miller job, I get it done, then when do I get my money?"

"Once we get confirmation that he's dead, my able deputy here," McSharry said, gesturing towards Begsy "he'll take your money to Manchester Airport and send you on your way with a handshake and a pat on the back"

"And then we're done?" Rob asked suspiciously "For good?"

"For good" McSharry agreed "Your debts will be repaid, you'll be free to crawl back under whatever rock you call home, living out the rest of your days in peace"

"What about you?" Rob asked, in spite of himself. It was a morbid curiosity but it still needed to be satisfied "You just going to keep on killing till there's no one left?" there was hostility in his tone that he hadn't planned on expressing.

"What do you care?" McSharry asked "I thought you wanted out?"

Rob looked around the room; Begsy was still guarding the door, an ugly smirk plastered across his face no doubt inspired by talk of Rob's imminent departure, while Charlie was stood rigid to his right, wide eyed and expectant. Rob recognised the look of intrigue in his brothers' eyes; it was the same look he'd possessed when he was first introduced to this dark and sinister world. But he knew the look would never last, the horrors he would be subjected to would make sure of that. Slowly, he turned back towards McSharry.

"I do. Forget it" holding the yellow folder forward he tapped it lightly "I'll be in touch, let's go Charlie"

The two men turned towards the door, Rob only made it a couple of steps before he heard the sound he was dreading; McSharry's voice.

232

"Actually, I'd prefer it if you stuck around"

He turned quickly, noticing that McSharry had stood up, his face was expressionless but Rob could still see the mischief in his eyes. He spared a glance towards the door, quickly making sure that Begsy hadn't moved, before taking a step closer to the older man.

"Why?" he asked impatiently.

"No," McSharry said coyly "I was talking to your brother"

One glance at Charlie's stunned face told Rob everything he needed to know, his mouth was agape and the colour seemed to have drained from his complexion, but the wide eyed look of expectation was still there, and it burned brighter than ever.

"What for?" Rob asked, he spoke slowly, struggling to keep the anger from his voice,

There was a brief silence as McSharry circled around the desk, he saw the look of triumph etched upon those leathery features, Rob had failed to disguise his weakness, and the old man was exploiting it with relish.

"I need to talk with the boy, like I said; business. It's none of your concern, you have your own job to worry about" the voice was a mixture of both mockery and menace.

"No chance" Rob replied resolutely, he swallowed hard as he felt the implications of the meeting weigh heavily on his shoulders. Steadying himself, he prepared to make a move for the door, and its guard, when Charlie's words stopped him dead.

"Rob its fine, I'll stay"

The statement hit him like a blow to the face, he stared dumbly at his little brother and tried to think but his brain was suddenly incapable of cognitive thought, paralysed by two gut wrenching emotions; fear and betrayal. Eventually, when he managed to compose himself he directed his response towards McSharry, the man pulling all of their strings.

"I need a word with my brother, in private"

McSharry nodded, seemingly unperturbed by Rob's request and gestured to Begsy to stand down from his post "The hallway" the older man said "you have two minutes"

In the time it took to leave the room Rob's emotional state had evolved from worry to seething anger, following Charlie out and closing the door behind him he fixed his brother with the most irate stare he had.

"What the fuck do you think you're playing at?" Rob snarled, causing Charlie to take an involuntary step back "I told you; keep your mouth shut, don't get involved. What was that in there?"

"Chill out, lad" Charlie replied, his face distorted by a defensive scowl "I was only trying to help"

"I don't need your help!"

"That's not what it looked like" Charlie said, he was growing increasingly angrier himself "I'm just trying to do my part, giving my brother a helping hand!"

"Yeah?" Rob asked taking a step closer to Charlie "and who are you helping now".

For a moment the two brothers stared each other down, flashes of anger bouncing back and forth from one pair of brown eyes to the other, eventually it was Charlie who looked away. Rubbing at his nose he looked towards the varnished wooden staircase for a few seconds, and when he looked back Rob could see that the anger had passed from his brother's face.

"Look, the man just wants to talk a little business with me, I don't see what the problem is?"

Rob shook his head and let out a frustrated sigh, he suddenly wished that over the years he'd been more open with his brother. If Charlie knew half of the horrors he'd committed on the old man's behalf then there would be no need for the discussion, but Rob hadn't been honest, and now his little brother wanted to get into bed with a psychopath.

"You don't know him" Rob said, hearing the desperation in his own voice "and you can't trust him, you go down this road and it'll bring you nothing but trouble".

Charlie let out a joyless laugh "Right, and I've got such a good thing going on now. Come on Rob, you think this is how I want to spend the rest of my life; selling coke in the toilets of some scrubby little pub? I want a change mate. I need a change"

Looking at his brother, Rob saw a sadness in Charlie that he'd never known before, a resignation that his life had not been what it could have, and it broke Rob's heart to see it. For a second he felt himself wavering, and then he remembered what waited on the other side of the door.

"Well, you can't get it this way" Rob told him bluntly.

As soon as the words left his mouth he saw Charlie's vulnerability induced sadness disappear into the ether, in its place was a cold steely gaze that Rob suspected was all the more determined by the weakness that had preceded it. His little brother was embarrassed, and that would make it all the more difficult to reason with him.

"Why not?" Charlie asked, it was a petulant question and one that reminded Rob of how his brother would act as a child when he was refused money for sweets.

Rob was fast losing his patience with the conversation and with his brother. When he spoke his voice was low, but the ferocity of his words could not be mistaken "Don't ever forget how I ended up here Charlie, why I had to do all the things that I've done"

The vehemence of Rob's words checked Charlie immediately, all he could do in reply was blink three times as a low breath escaped from his mouth.

"I remember" Charlie said a few moments later, in a voice that was barely more than a whisper. The look on his face seemed to be trapped somewhere between fear and regret.

"But you'll piss it away all the same?" Rob asked, angrily pushing the advantage.

"Look, I appreciate what you're saying, but…"

"But what?"

"Buts it's my life! And I don't need anyone standing over my shoulder telling me what to do, least of all a guy who solves his problems by running away" Charlie stopped himself, for a second he looked embarrassed by his outburst and then he settled himself, when he continued to speak his voice was even "look he just wants to talk, trust me ok, I know what I'm doing"

"Since when?" Rob asked, he could sense defeat and he knew it was etched upon his face.

Charlie flashed his brother a sad smile "I've managed fine for ten years Rob, I don't need looking after. He wants to talk business, and this is my business"

"You're making a big mistake"

"But it's my mistake to make bro, maybe you should spend a little more time worrying about your own problems and a little less time worrying about mine"

Rob looked around the marble floored hallway, it hadn't changed much since his first visit all those years ago and he still remembered the sense of awe he had felt upon first sampling the affluent surroundings. The rush of being initiated into a secret world where men could become Kings was still fresh in his mind, and he understood the appeal for Charlie, at that moment he also understood that he couldn't protect him any longer. When he looked back at Charlie, Rob thought he saw more of himself in his brother than he ever had before. Time would tell whether that would be a blessing or a curse.

"I can handle myself" Rob told him

"So can I" Charlie returned, reaching into his pocket he pulled out the keys to his car and held them out. Rob hesitated for a second before he found the courage to take them, giving his brother a final regretful look he made his way towards the front door and slammed it shut.

From the second Rob's foot touched the accelerator he struggled with the urge to turn back and rescue Charlie, by force if necessary. His mind raced with a hundred different possibilities of what the men might be talking about, each guess worse than the last. He felt a weight in his chest as he played out every argument imaginable that he hadn't made. Maybe if he'd tried harder, if he'd said the right things, if he'd been more prepared, he could of convinced Charlie to leave with him, as it was he felt an overriding sense of guilt that he had all too easily abandoned his brother in a pit full of vipers.

The car turned onto the duel carriageway and Rob shook his head, no, this was what Charlie wanted, and it would have happened one way or another. Stubbornness was a Thomas family trait that they had both inherited, and Rob knew even if Charlie had left with him today, it would only have been a matter of time before he found his way back there alone, and then Rob would have no way of knowing what they were doing.

He tried to convince himself of Charlie's argument, his brother wasn't a kid anymore, he was a grown man with a family who was capable of making his own decisions. While Rob was working construction in New York Charlie had been selling drugs to less than reputable people on the scouse bar scene, and he'd been doing it without the protection of his big brother. Why did Rob assume he was more disposed to survive in that world than Charlie? If anything his little brother had more right to be involved with McSharry and his people than he did, though that wasn't a thought that provided him with any comfort.

Rob glanced at the yellow folder lying on the passenger seat; that was the key, once Tony Miller was dead he would have his money and the link between him and McSharry would be broken. Who was to say, maybe Rob could use some of the money to convince Charlie to come with him, he knew enough people to get his brother a job in New York, and getting him away from his life in Liverpool, drugs, mistresses and all, might just be enough to save his marriage. Rob knew the pain of a broken home and had no desire to see his two nieces subjected to that kind of life.

It was just then, as he turned off the dual carriageway, thinking of his nieces that he saw it; the green Vauxhall Astra. He'd first noticed it ten minutes earlier, taking in the cars behind him, more out of habit than anything else, but as his car moved closer to Bootle he realised that the green Astra was almost certainly following him. Tentatively, Rob turned left down a quiet residential street, left again down another and then right onto another main road. All the while his pursuer continued behind, keeping at a distance of about thirty feet.

Desperation clawed at his mind, he was defenceless and the flat where the guns were hidden was still five minutes away. Even if he could get in there before his pursuer had a chance to cut him off he still had no way of knowing whether or not they would be waiting for him, maybe the whole thing was a trap. He didn't seem to have a whole lot of options.

Pulling the car to a stop on the busy main road, Rob slid the yellow file under the seat and stepped out; if his pursuer wanted to kill him they could do it in the open with plenty of witnesses. He watched the green Astra pull slowly to a stop twenty feet away. Rob squinted in an effort to identify the driver but it was still too difficult to tell. For a moment nothing happened, it seemed as if his pursuer was unsure whether or not to leave the safety of their vehicle. Eventually, the driver's door opened and a man stepped out from the car. He walked towards Rob slowly at first, increasing with speed until he was only a few feet away. Rob looked at the man's familiar face and knew that his troubles had only just begun.

"I really hoped you were gone for good" the man said evenly, there was neither hate nor affection in his voice.

"Sorry to disappoint" Rob said, staring back into David Walker's eyes.

Chapter 19

Two days straight, cooped up in a small car with no company other than your own imagination was more than any man should have to endure, but it was a price David Walker was more than happy to pay, right along with the blisters and the 3 bottles of piss that were rolling around next to his feet.

The dull ache of sleep deprivation gnawed incessantly at his tired brain yet somehow he found strength in the sensation, like the stale smell of his grey suit it imbued him with a feeling that his task had value, and there were no limits to what he would sacrifice to obtain his goals.

In forty eight hours he'd left his post only three times, and even they had been brief excursions to replace his vehicle with one of the other four he had scattered around the neighbourhood. The attention of McSharry and his troops had been quite rightly focused on the less than subtle two man surveillance detail parked on the opposite side of the street, but David knew that they would still notice a second vehicle parked further away, especially if it remained inactive for an extended period of time.

Just as difficult as trying to avoid his target was trying to avoid his colleagues. The two man rotational team spent most of their time watching the house, but they were well trained and their sporadic patrols of the street proved just as troublesome to sidestep as the watching eyes within the house.

It was a strange sensation, cautiously watching his team like he would an enemy, but it was an unavoidable necessity. No one could know what he was doing, too much at stake, and he knew they wouldn't understand. Hell, he wasn't even sure he understood. As far as his team were concerned he was on a trip down South, chasing up an informant who'd gone AWOL, and he'd be back in a couple of days, he could only hope he would have what he needed by then, the alternatives didn't bear thinking about.

As the hours wore on he began to dwell on the flaws in his plan. As of yet there had been no movement of note, the occasional comings and goings of McSharry's closest men but nothing that hinted at what he needed. Worry began to build in his chest that maybe he'd been wrong, his hope that history would repeat itself and events would play out as they had ten years earlier suddenly seemed naïve and obtuse. An overwhelming sense of impotence washed over him as he sat in his rented Green Astra and tried to formulate a new plan, but nothing would come, nothing but doubt and a nagging voice that said he wasn't fit to lead one of the biggest investigations in the city's history.

It was then that the worry suddenly began to subside. As if on cue the front door of the large Victorian mansion swung open and McSharry's group of thugs piled out of the house, obliterating the peaceful, afternoon silence that had previously held sway.

Amongst the killers and arsonists Walker caught a sight that immediately aroused his suspicion; in the middle was a man draped in Stephen McSharry's long overcoat with a flat cap the old gangster had occasionally been known to wear. His head was buried within the confines of his upturned collar and he moved in the slow, rigid style of a man past his prime.

Walker only had a moment to take in the scene before they bundled into two waiting BMWs, a second later the engines were starting and the two cars began to move out. Reaching the end of the driveway they pulled out onto the street, passing the V8 Land Rover Discovery that housed the two DST officers and continuing on to the main road, but David had long since stopped watching.

His attention was focused on the memory of the man in the cap and trench coat, though he possessed the same height and build as Stephen McSharry there had been something missing, a swagger that could only be spotted by someone who had studied the man to the point of obsession. He looked up and saw the V8 Landrover follow in pursuit, it was a decoy and his men had taken the bait hook, line and sinker. A pang of disappointment passed through him as he realised how easily two of his team had just been duped, but professional disenchantment was only allowed a moment as he realised what was about to happen next, and he felt his chest tighten in preparation.

It was twenty minutes later when the red Volkswagen Golf pulled up in front of the house and David Walker caught sight of a ghost for the second time that week. Rob Thomas stepped from the car, the same guarded, intuitive look plastered across his dark features that he'd possessed a decade earlier. A thin beard covered his face making him look older than he probably was, and gave his strong features a slightly unhinged look.

Walker watched him anxiously as he waited for a second man to step from the driver's side, though his accomplice was younger and thinner his facial features marked him out immediately as Thomas' brother, a judgment made even more obvious by their matching haircuts.

Within moments the two men had disappeared inside the large house leaving David with no choice but to wait. Playing the image of Robert Thomas over and over in his head he found his hand instinctively move towards the gun concealed in the glove box. It was an old thing, a black revolver that was as ugly as it was dated. Its previous owner had been a small time drug dealer who believed that the gun would act as an instant equaliser against a more dangerous breed of predator. He'd been wrong, and David had easily lifted it from the crime scene four years earlier. Tampering with evidence wasn't a habit he was prone to indulging, but as the years counted down to Stephen McSharry's release he'd felt the urge to prepare for himself, and thank god he had.

Cautiously, he lifted the gun from its resting place and sat it next to him on the passenger seat. Having it so close was an uncomfortable sensation but he knew he needed to harden himself to the reality of what was happening. Murder was not in his blood, but if that was the only option then he would have no choice but to do it. The picture of Rob Thomas was firm in his mind, made all the firmer by the sense of betrayal that surrounded it. He wondered how long the man had been back in league with Stephen McSharry and cursed himself for not predicting this turn of events. There were so many angles to cover, so many backdoors to watch, he'd let the most dangerous threat of all slip past him and now the whole town was on a knifes edge. Rob Thomas was the spark that could ignite the city of Liverpool and if extinguishing him was the only way to extinguish the threat then so be it, David would do what he had to, or at least that was what he told himself.

The next ten minutes felt like the longest of his life, a light drizzle began to fall from the grey sky as afternoon grew closer to night. Doggedly he continued to shift his focus between the house and his rear view mirror, if McSharry's guys returned and caught him lingering then he might miss his only chance to get close to Thomas, and he didn't want to think about what would happen if the DST boys caught sight of him.

After what seemed like an eternity the front door swung open and Rob Thomas marched towards the car, Walker was encouraged to see that he had left alone, and the clenched jaw and determined march suggested he hadn't left on the best of terms. Gently, he eased the car out of its space and fell in twenty feet behind his target, more than once he had to stop himself from pressing down on the accelerator to close the gap, if he fell too far behind and lost the Red Volkswagen who knew how many people would die before he found it again.

It didn't take Walker long to realise he'd been made, pulling off a busy duel carriageway Thomas's car began veering left then right down a series of residential streets in such a nonsensical pattern that eliminated all possibilities for Walker's car to follow other than pursuit. Instinctively he nudged the black pistol on the passenger seat closer towards him. Thomas knew he was being followed, and yet he wasn't trying to escape. When the red VW pulled to a halt on the side of a busy street David took a deep breath and stepped out to meet him.

"I really hoped you were gone for good" David said as he reached him.

He'd slipped the pistol into his belt before leaving the car, he wondered whether it was secure as he ground to a stop only a few feet away. The rain was falling heavier now, the clothes on both men were already beginning to stick to their bodies.

"Sorry to disappoint" Rob Thomas retorted.

Seeing the man up close brought a string of memories flashing to the forefront of David's mind, he remembered the fierce brown eyes and recalled with a sense of embarrassment the fear he'd felt when first looking into them. He demonised the young policeman he had once been and reminded himself how he had grown. Looking into those eyes once again he saw there was more control in them now, the man he remembered was a half-crazed drug fiend, pushed to the edge by the horror of his own memories, this man was different. Angry and cold like before, but less volatile.

"Why did you come back?" David asked disapprovingly, even as the words left his mouth he knew them to be inadequate, hollow, yet he couldn't bear to ask anything else, not until he knew the answer.

He watched as Rob Thomas considered the question, his eyes narrowed, losing some of their anger in the process, he seemed to be searching for deeper meaning in what David had asked.

"Why do you think?" Rob replied, his response was filled with scorn, as if having to explain himself was an inconvenience he could do without.

David fought back the indignation, he took a deep breath as he stared back at the man he had trusted and chose his words carefully "I've seen the footage, I examined the crime scene. You turned the Albert Dock into a bloody graveyard, not quite as mechanically gruesome as I remember but unmistakably Rob Thomas. No, I know what you're doing here, you live through that kind of chaos once and you don't easily forget it. I'm asking why? After all we went through, why?"

Rob shook his head and looked away, anger and impatience shone fiercely from his face as he returned his gaze to David "I don't have a choice" he muttered in a low growl.

"You always had a choice"

"Don't give me that bollocks"

"You think you know better!" David shouted back, already he was losing his self-control and he cursed himself for it, but it was too late to pull back, the floodgates had already opened "You tell yourself they forced that gun into your hand? That you were an innocent victim in all this? You think you're different, but in the end you're just like the rest of them, judging yourself by one set of rules but living by another, bending your logic to suit your needs. Being weak isn't tantamount to being trapped, we all have a choice, you just need to be strong enough to make it"

"Like the lawyer?" Rob asked, angrily taking a step forward "Like Ploughman? He made a choice, look where it got him!"

David felt a heavy weight of guilt descend upon his chest at the very mention of James Ploughman's name, his mutilated body flashed violently in his mind, strangled to death with a guitar string after hours of torture. Burns, stab wounds, crushed fingers and toes, the image alone was enough to make him want to vomit, even without the sense of blame that came with it.

"Ploughman was... it was a mistake" he offered feebly.

"A mistake?" this time it was Rob's turn to explode with anger "You talk like he was a statistical error, a fucking blip on the radar screen. A mistake? I gave him to you on your word that he would be safe. You looked me in the eye and you swore to me. He was..." Rob's voice trailed off as the anger made way for regret "the guy was a civilian, he should never have been done like that. What fucking use are you people if you can't keep one man safe"

David swallowed hard as the weight of the accusation hit him, it was nothing new, nothing he hadn't condemned himself for a million times over, yet hearing it from another mouth somehow made it so much less excusable, suddenly collateral damage didn't sound like such a satisfactory explanation.

"There was a leak, somehow McSharry's people got hold of his new address" David said, remembering how hard it had been to convince Rob to give him that information "What do you know?"

Rob let out a sigh and looked into the distance "I know he sent Begsy, so I know it couldn't have been quick"

"It wasn't"

"Mother fucker" Rob muttered, another burst of anger erupting to the surface. David watched as he took a step backwards and rested the palms of his hands against his head "And why is he even out? Twenty five years, wasn't that what you said? What the fuck is ten years to a man like that? If I'd have known how badly you were going to screw this up I never would have helped you in the first place"

"There were complications in the case" David said defensively "some of the evidence couldn't be disclosed because of legal professional privilege and the Judge threw it out, these things, they're not an exact science, we did the best we could with what he had, and that came to ten years"

Rob fixed him with a cold stare "You seem to be talking a lot about your best, and it never seems to be good enough, does it?"

The urge to reach for the gun was almost overpowering, for a moment David stared into the other man's eyes, feeling his body shaking with anger, it took a few moments but eventually he found the self-control to speak.

"Then let's talk about you" David replied, his voice thick with rage "Who's next? Who've you got on that list? If you tell me now maybe we can warn all those wives and children, let them know there are going to be a few more fatherless families in the next few weeks. I won't let you kill again, not this time. This town has come too far for that, I won't stand here and watch you and your lot burn it to the ground"

Rob scoffed dismissively "Stay out of my way, ok? For your own good" the certainty of the threat sent a slight shiver down David's spine "Take a week off, look the other way and you'll never have to see me again. Trust me, I don't plan on staying here any longer than I have to"

David nearly laughed at the prospect of trusting the man before him, he'd trusted him not to come back and that had been the biggest mistake he'd made so far.

"Or I could just run you in?" David offered threateningly "Right now, suspicion of murder. I find those Smith & Westons in whatever dive your resting your head you'll be going down for life, and I'll have one less killer on my streets to worry about"

A small smile touched the corner of Rob's lips but it didn't hide the flicker of concern that flashed across his eyes "You wouldn't do that" Rob said confidently.

"You sure?"

"You have as much to lose on your side as I do on mine" Rob began, there was an edge to his voice that said he was trying to convince himself as much as he was David "That nice suit, those expensive shoes, how much of that is because of me? You were a nobody when I came to you, you'd still be busting down doors in crack dens, but when I left you were the next big thing. What happens when your bosses find out you worked with a perpetrator of multiple homicides and let him walk away just to further your own career? And I didn't just give you McSharry, what happens to those other convictions when they find out where the information came from? They've got a word for that, don't they, inadmissible? You take me in and that's your career, you willing to pay that price?"

The truth of Robs words rang true in David's head, for a few moments he didn't speak as he tried to convince himself that he was capable of such a sacrifice, but the reality of who he was proved impossible to ignore.

"No" he admitted reluctantly. Slowly he pulled the revolver from his belt "So maybe I should just kill you now"

The rain was falling heavier still as David studied Rob's reaction, and he was surprised to find that there wasn't one. Slowly, Rob's eyes moved towards the gun, stared for a second at the black metal resting in David's hand, and then moved back to his face. There was no fear in those eyes, just resignation. David wondered whether a part of Rob Thomas truly wanted him to pull the trigger, to end his pain once and for all. He squeezed the grip as the thought of giving it to him built up speed in his mind.

"If that's what you have to do" Rob told him nonchalantly.

Looking at the killer before him, without an ounce of fear in his eyes, David saw his threat for what it was; empty. With a sigh he returned the gun to its hiding place and brushed a strand of wet hair away from his forehead.

"We don't have to go down this road" David told him "You can help us cage McSharry again, he won't last another ten years. We can protect you, you and your family"

"Like you protected Ploughman?" Rob asked evenly "Just stay out of my way a little while longer and you'll never have to see me again. You can trust *my* word"

With that Rob turned away and started moving towards his car, filling David with the overwhelming urge to reach for the gun and shoot this particular problem in the back. It surprised him how simply the concept came to mind, how easily a major threat to his career could disappear. As quickly as the thought arrived it had passed, he was not one of those people, and he had no intention of becoming one. He reminded himself of all the good things he'd done, even if they had come about with the help of a murderer, and he promised himself that they would not be the only good things he would achieve. This time he would do it right.

"Rob" David called as the driver's door of the Red Volkswagen swung open "Do you see his face when you close your eyes?"

There was a look of surprise on those cold features as Rob Thomas leaned against the roof of the car, then slowly, unable to take his eyes from the floor, he nodded.

Walker swallowed hard, feeling a surge of adrenaline pump through his body.

"Get out now" he barked defiantly "If you kill again I will take you down. I don't care what price I have to pay. I will"

Rob raised his eyes from the floor and regarded Walker thoughtfully. The rain was hammering heavily against the ground and both men were soaked through, staring at one another, each knowing there was nothing left to say. Eventually Rob nodded, shifted his gaze towards front seat of his car, and moments later he was gone.

Chapter 20

The thick musk was almost overpowering, it was a stale smell, impossible to escape with so many men crammed into the back of a transit van. A bump in the road caused the occupants to knock into one another, sending a wave of grumbles all the way down the van, from one man to the next. It had been a bumpy ride most of the way back, but that wasn't why Charlie's hand was shaking.

He held his right hand up to eye level. There wasn't much light but what there was showed the appendage to be unstable; frantically shaking like a small fox surrounded by hungry blood hounds. After a few seconds his eyes looked passed the hand to the figure sitting opposite, he regarded Charlie suspiciously until he had slid his hand back into a jacket pocket, and then the spectacled face broke out into a leer as he wiped the streaks of blood from his machete.

Charlie wanted to look away but found that he couldn't, the man who they had said was called Nikolai refused to relinquish his gaze, holding it firmly as he casually cleaned the blade with a handkerchief.

Eventually the man's gaze moved on and Charlie took the opportunity to focus his attention on the floor. His breathing was ragged, in his ears it sounded like the loudest noise in the van. The rational part of his brain told him that the laughter must be louder, even if it sounded like it was coming from a few miles away. He tried to keep his face even but knew immediately that he wasn't doing a very good job, he tried to focus on the way Rob looked when he didn't want to give anything away, to make his face like stone, unreadable, but he could feel his mouth twitching into something halfway between a smile and a grimace. Clearly that particular skill wasn't genetic.

As Charlie continued watching the floor, hoping no one would notice his reaction he caught sight of a red splash on his left hand, he examined it closer and realised with a shudder it was blood, definitely not his blood. He felt a gush of vomit rush up his throat and fought violently to push it back down again, he hadn't done too bad so far, but throwing up would be a massive set back. Breathing through his noise Charlie tried to think of something, anything that would take his mind of the claret substance staining the back of his hand.

With an effort he started thinking about what had happened to him earlier in the day, it seemed almost impossible to think that only two hours ago he had stood in Stephen McSharry's hallway watching his brother storm out. He knew the memory had come to him because of how good he'd felt such a short time ago, the euphoric sense of possibility had washed over him as he watched his brother slam the front door behind him, a sense that he was finally getting the chance to make something of himself, to show what he really could do.

The conversation with McSharry hadn't lasted long; once Rob had left the man was pure business.

"Leroy Tate" McSharry had said "The dickhead's a Caddock boy through and through. Now that his masters out of the way he thinks he's off the leash, sees himself going solo and making a name from himself, the stray thinks he doesn't need a new owner, but he's got another fucking thing coming"

The ferocity of McSharry's voice brought all of Rob's warnings back to the surface, this was a dangerous man, a vicious man, but that just made his friendship all the more valuable.

"The cunt needs to be knocked off his fucking perch" McSharry hissed, not giving Charlie a chance to respond "The problem is, we don't know where to find him, his fixed address is his mother's house but he hasn't set foot near that place since your brother jammed a knife in his bosses bowels. You help us find the prick and there'll be a sweet old reward in it for you, what do you say?"

Charlie hadn't needed more than a couple of seconds to betray the man who had supplied him for three years straight, Leroy Tate had never crossed the line from associate to friend, he was just a contact, and if the choice was between the man he knew and the man who stood before him, well the odds seemed highly stacked against poor old Leroy.

"He deals out of a boarded up council house in Litherland when he's trying to keep a low profile" Charlie had said enthusiastically, relishing the chance to use his expertise to a profitable end "He usually keeps a couple of guys with him but never more than three, niggers the lot of them, and smack heads to boot"

"You know where it is?" McSharry queried expectantly.

"I know where it is" Charlie confirmed.

From then on everything seemed to move in high speed, walking behind his desk McSharry dialled a number on the large phone, adjusted it to speakerphone and leaned back in his leather chair.

"Yeah?" a voice enquired after three rings.

"Yozzas off the radar?" McSharry enquired confidently.

"Fucking right they is!" the voice replied triumphantly "Left them behind bout ten minutes ago, we just traded the beamers in now"

"Change of plan" McSharry instructed "Meet us at the fallback point for the thing last week, we've got a guy who's going to take you to the problem in Bootle, says he knows exactly where the issue is"

"Bootle, eh? Looking forward to getting that one out the way. Vans all tooled up so we're ready to get to work"

"Fifteen minutes" McSharry said, hanging up before the voice could respond.

It wasn't long before they were in the car speeding across Liverpool with Begsy behind the wheel. McSharry spoke to him only once on the journey

"Don't mention your brother, under any circumstance" he had said, though the statement was simple enough there was more than a hint of warning in his voice, Charlie gave a slight nod and returned to looking out the window.

Their destination was a Matalan car park just outside the city centre. As they stepped out of the car Charlie took in the large, brick warehouses that stood between them and the river Mersey. He only had time to observe the buildings for a few minutes before the white transit van sped into the car park, giving a few midday shoppers a scare as they hurried towards their people carriers.

The van pulled up with a screech as the passenger door opened. A man jumped quickly from his seat and moved towards the three men with the kind of swagger that marked him out as a professional.

"Caffers" McSharry said with a nod towards Charlie "This is the lad that's going to help us nail Tate to the wall. Charlie, Caffers will look after you from here, go with them, back them up, make sure they get what they want, and we'll talk about your future when it's done"

Charlie nodded, anxious not to say the wrong thing, and watched as McSharry and Begsy returned to the blue Mercedes that had brought them there. Charlie turned back to the man McSharry had called Caffers, he was bigger than he'd first thought, and uglier too. A large, bulbous nose rested between two large sun burnt cheeks while his green eyes seemed too small for his large head, despite those defects the perpetual snarl that dominated his features gave him an air of authority that his looks never could.

"Where to, lad?" Caffers asked gruffly.

Looking up at the large, vicious face it took Charlie a second to find his voice "Mulbery Street" he said eventually, doing his best to sound confident "Litherland, by the Tesco"

Caffers gave a grunt, implying that he knew the place well, and led him to the back of the van. The rear doors creaked open and Charlie glanced inside, sat tightly along either side were five men, each wearing a different coloured tracksuit from the next, and sporting weapons from tools to crowbars, to baseball bats.

"Get in" Caffers ordered impatiently "We're in a hurry"

He climbed in without a word, the five men were spread out on two wooden benches running parallel along the length of the van, three men sat on the bench on the left, Charlie moved towards the right and took a seat.

It didn't take long to notice that they were all staring at him, some with interest, some with suspicion, some with both. Tentatively he nodded towards the five men, then lowered his head when he received no response.

"So who the fuck are you?" a voice eventually asked. Charlie looked to his right and saw that it was the man sat next to him who had asked the question, his tone was accusing as he scratched at a thick black beard that covered most of his face.

"Charlie Thomas" he told them, focusing on the man with the beard but speaking loud enough for the whole van to hear "I do some business with Leroy, so your boss asked me to come show you where he's hiding out"

The beard took a few seconds to exchange looks with the others before he returned his attention to Charlie.

"Does he trust you?" the man asked.

"Yeah, he trusts me" Charlie said confidently, trying not think what would happen if he was wrong "Too fucking stupid not to, isn't he!"

A smile appeared beneath the beard and the bloke let out a deep bellowing laugh from the bottom of his gut.

"Ads" the man said, slapping himself in the chest, lazily his arm moved to the man to his right, and continued, anti-clockwise around the van "This is Mercer, Sie, Rico and Nikolai"

Charlie nodded towards each man in turn and tried to memorise their names before they faded from his mind. Mercer was a large, bald man in his mid-thirties, a thin light brown goatee the only striking feature of his face. Sie was younger and less stocky than most of the others, even sitting down Charlie could tell he was tall, the confident look on his tanned face was in stark contrast to the unconcealed cruelty that was evident in the other men. He didn't know how he knew but he sensed that Sie was not a hardened killer like the others, it gave him comfort to know that he wasn't the only one. Next was the man Ads had called Rico, he was the largest of them all and the thick neck muscles that protruded from beneath his tracksuit suggested that he was in the best shape as well. He nodded in Charlie's direction and cracked his knuckles, a metal wrench discarded at his feet, as if he had no use for such a weapon.

The last of the five was the easiest to remember, it wasn't just that Nikolai was an unusual name for a Scouse gangster, but also the man it belonged to shared almost no physical features with the rest of his colleagues. Slight, with fair blond hair and glasses he was dwarfed by the overwhelming Rico who sat next to him, making him look almost childlike in comparison. The singular trait he shared with them was the cruel, malignant look that burned stronger and deeper in his small blue eyes. Charlie only needed to look into them for a few seconds to realise that this man unnerved him a lot more than the others, nodding slightly in Nikolai's direction he turned his head towards the conversation that was going on to his right.

"Not happy being stuck with this crowbar like," Ads was saying, swinging it gently in his hand "I can't get no fucking arch on the thing, give us the bat Sie, that's more my kind of tool"

"Get lost lad" Sie said, protectively drawing the bat closer to his chest "Last time we trusted you with a bat you nearly took out half our crew"

"Smashed a window and all, didn't you, soft lad?" Rico chimed in "One of them got past me while I was pulling shards of glass out my bloody arm!"

"You should have been paying attention then, you dippy bastard" Ads shot back.

Though there was banter in their exchange Charlie noticed that the men were hardening themselves, the excitement in the van was palpable as they moved ever closer to their destination, as he watched he found the sensation almost infectious.

He looked down at his watch, the drive would take ten minutes and so far they had done about five. Charlie could feel the sweat seeping through his pours as he sat amongst the hardened killers, each going through their own pre-battle rituals; Mercer rocking backwards and forwards in anticipation, Ads still gently swinging the crowbar and cursing in dissatisfaction, Rico cracking his knuckles. His mind drifted to Leroy Tate, something in his brain told him he should feel guilty for what he was about to do, but for whatever reason he just couldn't force the emotion. Leroy was scum, and if he was honest, Charlie had always resented being the man's subordinate. Sifting through his memories he recalled all the things he disliked about Leroy, his arrogance, his open hostility, his lack of loyalty, and used them to fuel the belief that what he was doing was justified. He remembered the people he'd known who had received a Leroy Tate beating and imagined their battered faces urging him on with what he was about to do.

"I can't wait to do this prick in" Rico said excitedly, there was hunger in his eyes as he slammed his right fist into the palm of his left hand.

Murmurs of agreement spread around the van, Charlie kept quiet as he took in the scene around him.

"He's had it coming" Sie agreed, though he was gripping the bat tightly Charlie still had trouble imagining the dark skinned youngster using it with any kind of violent intent.

"He should have been done last year, when he put Digger in the ozzy" Mercer said, with a rueful shake of the head "that shit should never have been allowed to stand. I don't care who was vouching for the prick, we should have put him away then and there"

Charlie lowered his gaze to the floor, he remembered Leroy bragging about how he'd done in a guy called Digger, another local dealer who had tried to move in on his territory. He remembered the story well; Leroy said he'd knocked the bloke unconscious with a larger bottle to the back of the skull, before slamming his head through the front window of a local pub. If he remembered right Digger had survived the incident with some brain damage and the loss of sight in one eye, he decided not to mention Leroy's delight at telling the tale, things were looking bad enough as it was for his old associate.

"We weren't going to war with Wayne Caddock and Tony Miller over Digger fucking Brown" Ads said contemptuously "Boy was a retarded smackhead who used as much heroin as he sold, if my house is getting firebombed it's going to be for someone worth a fucking lot more than that piece of shit"

"Good job Caddock's dead then isn't it?" Mercer said with a smirk, Charlie couldn't be sure but he thought he saw a few of the men glance at him suspiciously.

"Too right it's a good job" Ads replied, his face darkening "Any scenario that ends with me being able to take a crowbar to a gang of smack heads is sound with me"

Eventually the car pulled to a halt, silence reigned as the men looked around the van at one another, anticipation burning brightly in each set of eyes. Charlie suddenly realised that what Rob had told him earlier was right; these men were wolves, brimming with excitement for the hunt that awaited. He felt the adrenaline pumping through his veins as he embraced the craving to be one of them, a small smile crept to his mouth as he waited for someone to speak.

"So, is this it?" Mercer asked.

Charlie leaned forward in his seat to peek out the back window of the van "Yeah, this is it" he told them, pointing halfway down the street "Number 38, right over there"

A moment later the vans rear door opened and Caffers stood before them with another man, burly like the rest, but with a small, scrunched up face that reminded Charlie of a bulldog.

"The new lad says it's over there" Ads said to Caffers, pointing towards the boarded up house. Caffers glanced behind him for a second and nodded at the others.

"What was your name again, lad?" Ads asked.

"Charlie"

"Alright Charlie, here's what's going to happen, you're gonna go over there and knock on the door. If he asks what you want tell him whatever you need to to get him to open up, tell him you need more drugs, you owe him some money, you want to suck his dick, whatever you usually do to get the little prick to open the door, just do it. Make sure the door is open for about ten seconds and we'll take care of the rest, alright?"

Charlie nodded and climbed out, as he stepped onto the pavement he felt Caffers nudge past him as he and the other man climbed into the back of the van and closed the door behind them.

It only took a moment, as the doors slammed shut, for all of Charlie's excitement to rush from his body. Standing on the quiet street all he could hear was the sound of a group of kids playing in the park at the end of the street, and he suddenly felt very alone. He allowed himself another couple of seconds to stare at the back of the van as he tried to figure out what he would say when he reached the front door of number 38. He'd been to the house around seven or eight times, mostly when Leroy was keeping his head down while Wayne Caddock solved whatever local problem he was having, be it police based or otherwise. He wondered how different the reaction would be now that Wayne Caddock was dead, would he be seeing enemies in every face? If he wasn't then he really should start.

Slowly, he turned around and started walking towards the house, immediately he found himself worrying about what would happen next, had Leroy seen him exit the white van? Would he be suspicious that he couldn't see Charlie's car? Would he find it strange that Charlie hadn't called ahead like usual? Each possibility gave birth to a dozen more worries as he imagined himself being pummelled to death before McSharry's boys could get to the front door. Suddenly it became harder and harder to put one foot in front of the other. He ground to a stop in the middle of the street, before remembering what the people in the van would do to him if he failed, and then he continued.

The front gate opened with a groan and he stepped through into the small, overgrown patio that lay in front of the terraced house. The one window on the ground floor and the two on the second were all boarded up, though the door, with its badly chipped white paint job, was free of any such obstruction.

Using the sleeve of his jacket he wiped away at the beads of sweat that were building on his forehead and cursed his eagerness to help Stephen McSharry. Only a few hours earlier it had seemed like his ticket to a better life, now all he could see was at best a lengthy prison sentence, at worst a painful death. He glanced over his shoulder one last time towards the white van, it seemed so distant, so far away, if things went sour it may as well be a hundred miles away, Leroy Tate, for all his faults was no slouch, he knew how to hurt a man, and he knew how to do it quickly.

Taking a deep breath Charlie knocked on the door three times in quick succession, he tried to remember how many times he would normally knock but his brain refused to cooperate. The adrenaline pumping through his veins was making him more aware of everything around him, his heart was beating so loud he was certain Leroy would be able to hear it from the other side of the door.

Charlie waited a few seconds before he heard a sound from within the house.

"Yeah?" a deep voice asked.

"Alright Leroy, it's Charlie Thomas" he could hear his voice cracking under the pressure and swallowed hard to try and control it "I'm running low on supplies, any chance you could sort me out?"

There was no reply, the silence made Charlie's heart beat faster and faster until he thought it might explode in his chest.

"How'd you know I was here?" the voice came back suspiciously, the urge to run was almost unbearable but he steadied himself and tried to make his voice sound casual.

"You weren't at your place, I assumed you'd be here. More trouble with the busies?" Charlie asked, throwing in a small laugh at the end that sounded more nervous than casual to his ears.

This time the silence was longer, he imagined Leroy opening the door and firing a few shots into his chest, in that moment all Charlie could think about was seeing his little girls one last time.

But the shots never came, after what seemed like an eternity Charlie heard the sound of a lock snap out of place and slowly the door creaked open. Cautiously, Leroy Tate poked his head around the side of the door, he looked tired, a scraggly beard covered half of his dark face while his large, bloodshot eyes struggled to cope with the mid afternoon sunlight.

"I'm not selling right now, boy" Leroy told him gruffly, the term 'boy' provoked a wave of anger in Charlie's mind, it was a welcome distraction from the fear "Didn't you hear what happened? Half the city's on bloody lock down"

Charlie shook his head, trying to look slightly confused "No, what happened, is it the busies again doing one of those crackdowns? Must be an election or something in the offing, they only ever do that shit when they want some headlines"

Leroy looked at him with a mixture of surprise and contempt, he opened his mouth to reply but before he could speak his eyes widened at something over Charlie's left shoulder.

From then on everything seemed to move in slow motion, like some kind of dream. A push in his left shoulder sent him sprawling onto a patch of weeds to the right of the house, as he hit the floor he heard a loud snap, though it was only later that he realised the noise had come from the door as it was smashed from its hinges. Stumbling to his feet he turned to see Sie, the last of the men, piling into the house, without thinking he followed them inside. So much was going on at once, yet somehow his dazed eyes managed to take it all in. It was easy to tell who was on which side, the five men that seemed to be fighting with Leroy were all black, while McSharry's boys, with the exception of Sie, were white.

By the time Charlie had deciphered who was who the fighting had broken out into a number of small skirmishes. To his left he saw Caffers pin a man to the floor while Mercer began to stomp on his head. A groan towards the back of the hallway caught Charlie's attention and he eyed a young black man wearing nothing but a pair of jeans stumble out of the back room. The needle in his hand and the glazed look in his eye told Charlie that the man had just shot up, casually the junkie looked around the room, taking in the fighting as if he were watching it on television. At some point Ads had spotted the same man, and was walking towards him slowly, with a huge smile on his face. The man caught sight of Ads when he was only a few feet away and stared at him blankly until they were face to face. Charlie watched the two men with fascination, for a moment it seemed as though they just intended to stare one another out, then Ads dropped the crowbar that was still in his hand punched the junkie square in the jaw. The man stumbled backwards and a second later Ads had launched himself forward with a maniacal scream that echoed around the house. The two men landed with a

252

crash and even before Ads had a chance to adjust his body he was reigning on down punches on the opponent beneath him. The poor sod was too high to even protect himself, instead he just lay there while Ads fists connected with his face time and time again.

A guttural scream tore Charlie's attention from the fight towards a skirmish that was taking place in the lounge. Nikolai, the small man with the glasses, was tussling with a large brute who towered over him by at least five inches. Charlie noticed the two men were moving strangely, as if they were locked in some kind of weird dance, it took a few seconds for Charlie to realise it was because Nikolai had sunk his machete into the breast of the larger man. Slowly his movements became more laboured, like the dance was coming to an end and then he fell back, lifeless against the wall. A desperate, almost animalistic scream erupted as Nikolai yanked the blade from the dead man and turned around, running towards him and shrieking at the top of her lungs was a half-naked woman. The desperation of her cries marked her out as the lover of Nikolai's victim, she charged at him with vengeance in her eyes but Nikolai caught her easily, wrapping a hand around her throat and pressing her against the same wall where her man had just died. Her screams continued even though she was quickly running out of air, desperately she flung her thin arms at Nikolai who simply regarded her with a vague curiosity. She continued to scream and struggle for a few seconds longer before Nikolai sank his knife into her stomach, as her movements subsided and he wrenched the blade free Charlie was sure he saw a smile creep across the small man's face.

All around him the groans and curses continued, though he was only vaguely aware of them. Something heavy brushed against his foot and he looked down to see a metallic baseball bat lying on the floor. Slowly, he bent down and picked it up, to what end he wasn't sure, the fighting had been raging for a number of minutes now and seemed to be progressing quite well without his input, he looked back to his left and saw the man who was fighting against Caffers and Mercer was no longer moving.

A flicker of motion towards the back of the lounge caught Charlie's attention, Rico and Sie were trying to restrain one of the men by pinning him down. Amongst the jumble of arms and legs he saw a brick fly from a black hand and crack against Rico's temple. The big man fell backwards and a second later Sie took a knee to the stomach and was thrown through a glass coffee table. It was only when the man stumbled to his feet that Charlie realised it was Leroy. His old supplier surveyed the room for a new target before his eyes eventually settled on Charlie. Leroy's whole body began to shake as he started yelling curses in Charlie's direction, before he had a chance to respond the man was sprinting in his direction with murder in his eyes.

He barely had time to blink before Leroy Tate was only a few feet away, screaming inaudibly as he ran. Without thinking Charlie brought the bat up and with all his might swung it towards the onrushing black figure.

The metallic bat hit the side of Leroy's head with a sickening thud, projecting a red spray in all directions and right across Charlie's face, the next sound he heard was Leroy's body as it collapsed against the hard wooden floor. The impact forced him lose his grip on the weapon, and as it tumbled to the ground his hands went immediately to his face and wiped the blood from his eyes.

He sucked breath after breath into his lungs before looking towards the prone figure lying on the floor; Leroy's eyes had rolled into the back of his head as blood oozed from his left temple, the way his body was convulsing made his condition look even more severe. Nervously, Charlie took a step back.

Looking around the room, he suddenly realised that most of the noise had stopped. All of the men who had been present before his arrival were lying still on the floor, the only struggle that seemed to be on going was Ads continued assault on the junkie, though the topless man wasn't moving as Ads continued to rain punch after punch down on his face.

Glancing into the lounge he saw Sie and Nikolai sweeping a table full of ecstasy, cocaine, heroin and cash into a black bin bag. A few feet away Rico was stumbling to his feet, a deep cut evident on the left side of his head, the same side as Leroy's wound. Without thinking he glanced down to compare the two; Leroy wasn't moving anymore, and his eyes hadn't returned from the back of his head.

A short laugh erupted from the rear of the hallway shaking Charlie from his daze, the noise sounded alien, as if laughter could never exist in a place like this, a place so void of humanity. Charlie followed the sound to the rear of the room, Sie, bin bag slung over his shoulder was standing above Ads while he continued to beat the motionless junkie into the floorboards, Sie's laugh was care free as he watched the violence unfold.

"Easy does it Ads" Sie said in between laughs "I think the fuckers dead"

With his free hand Sie reached down and grabbed Ads collar, hauling him to his feet, he came easily, without resistance, looking around the room as soon as he was vertical like he had just been released from a trance.

Charlie took in the scattering of prone bodies and tried to comprehend what had just happened, what he had just been a part of, but before he could come to any kind of conclusion he found himself being hustled into the back of the van.

With a pang of disappointment he realised that his memories had caught up with reality, he looked around the van with the dazed expression of someone who has just woken up, and regarded the group of strangers he had just committed murder with. They all seemed happy enough, relieved faces and smiling faces surrounded him, making Charlie all the more aware that his current disposition probably wasn't in sync with the rest of the group.

Tentatively he returned his gaze to the splash of blood that had stained the back of his left hand, the urge to vomit returned but not as prominently as before, he took that to be a good sign. Wiping it on the side of his t shirt Charlie took a deep breath and tried to get to grips with what had just happened. He'd killed a man, that was what had happened, a man he'd known for years, who had trusted him, and he'd been murdered by Charlie's own hand. Somehow it didn't seem real, it didn't seem possible. Rob was the killer, not him, it didn't matter how many times he'd considered following his brother down that path, and it didn't matter that he'd committed his share of despicable acts over the years, the fact of the matter was that Charlie Thomas wasn't a killer.

Until now.

The realisation dawned on him, and with it, amongst the horror, came the smallest sliver of pride. Now he knew what it was like to take a life, he could understand what Rob meant when he talked about the guilt. Already it was building in his chest but not in the way he had expected, or at least not in the way Rob had described it. The weight was there, sure it was, weighing heavily on his lungs, but it wasn't all encompassing, it didn't cause everything else in his head to fade away like Rob always said it would, it was just another thing, another facet of his life to feel guilty about. When he thought of the regrets that weighed him down in the middle of the night he suspected Leroy Tate would probably only reach mid table, he certainly wasn't a title challenger.

Slowly, it dawned on Charlie that the van was no longer moving. He raised his head and wondered how long that had been the case, then a second later the rear doors opened and Charlie followed the others into the early evening rain.

It only took a second to realise they were back in the Matalan car park, it had seemed like an age since he'd been there last, staring into the unknown, though a quick glance at his watch told him that it had been just shy of an hour. Stood a few spaces down in front of the familiar blue Merc was Stephen McSharry and Begsy, both with faces like stone; cold and unreadable. Ads started off towards them with the drug filled bin bag wrapped tightly around his hand, Mercer followed a few steps behind but when Charlie went to join them he felt a strong hand grip his shoulder, looking behind him he saw that Rico had stopped him in his tracks.

"Not till you're told" the big man warned, seemingly showing no ill effects from the crack to the head. Charlie nodded once and the grip on his shoulder was released.

He continued to watch for a few more seconds until a stern glance from Begsy encouraged him to direct his attention elsewhere. Turning back he walked towards Caffers, Sie and Rico who were leaning against the side of the van, when he reached them the conversation stopped and three sets of eyes focused squarely on him.

"Was that your first time, doing someone over?" Rico asked him after a few awkward seconds, Charlie noticed there was a hint of derision in his question.

"Nah, not doing someone over, but it was my first time..." he searched for the right phrase "going to that level"

"Well you did alright" Sie told him with an encouraging nod of the head, he turned to the others "Should have seen him take out Tate with one swing of the bat, damn near took the bastards head clean off his shoulders, didn't you?"

Charlie nodded.

"Nice one, lad" Caffers told him "That boy needed to be put down a long time ago, you did half of Liverpool a favour getting him out the way"

Charlie swallowed hard and nodded again, he'd done half of Liverpool a favour, well at least that was something.

"Heads up newbie" Sie warned, nodding behind Charlie "Looks like you're up"

He turned around to see McSharry gesturing him to come over. Begsy, Ads and Mercer were watching him closely, he got the impression that the rest of the group were studying him too. He tried to get a sense for what they wanted, but all four men were impossible to read, nervously he looked around the car park, only a few shoppers remained, a lack of witnesses was unlikely to work in Charlie's favour.

He reached the four men and focused his attention immediately on McSharry, the light was slowly disappearing but not yet enough for the car parks floodlights to have been turned on. In the soft light it was almost impossible to see the flickers of grey in the older man's hair, and the wrinkles in his skin seemed less severe than they had in the bright afternoon, the way he looked now gave Charlie the strange impression that the man was getting younger.

"So," McSharry said, pausing a moment as his eyes flickered between Ads and Mercer "How'd it go?"

Charlie looked at each of the men in turn, he wondered if his initial hesitation had been noticed after all, not only noticed but reported back to the boss. From everything Rob had told him Stephen McSharry didn't seem like the kind of man who tolerated inaction from his employees. He focused back on McSharry before he had time to think about how such a disappointment might be punished.

"Yeah... good" Charlie said nervously "I mean, he was there, so your boys managed to get what they needed"

McSharry regarded him for a few moments before he continued.

"That they did, it's one less problem I need to worry about, and believe you me I have enough problems to last me a lifetime. Nonetheless the boys tell me I have you to thank for eliminating that particular problem?"

He looked towards Ads and Mercer who both had the smallest hint of a smirk touching their mouths, he felt the corners of his own mouth twitch upwards for a second before he remembered who he was talking to.

"I guess, I mean I didn't check to make sure he definitely was…you know…eliminated"

"He was" Ads said casually, before turning and spitting on the ground behind him, Charlie had suspected that was the case, but knowing it for sure still added slightly to the weight in his chest.

"Not bad for a first run out" McSharry told him, his face still a mask of neutrality.

Charlie nodded, still unsure what to say, he noticed that McSharry was staring at him quite intently, he wondered if they were waiting for him to say something but after a few seconds more McSharry extended a hand towards Ads, his eyes still locked on Charlie. Ads handed him the bag, and only then did he divert his gaze to look inside.

Holding the bag with his left hand he delved inside with his right and brought three bundles of cash out into the open. McSharry ran a finger through the bundles and Charlie noticed that they were all made up of twenty pound notes, probably totalling close to three grand each.

Having suitably scrutinised the money he handed two of the bundles to Begsy and dropped the third back inside the bag, before holding it out towards Charlie.

It took a few seconds for Charlie to grasp what was happening, it was only when McSharry raised his eyebrows and said "Go on, take it" that he reached out and took the bag.

He looked inside, there must have been about five grand worth of Cocaine in there, and probably the same again in Heroine and Ecstacy, not to mention the wad of cash that had just been dropped inside. He looked back up towards the four men and waited for someone to clarify the situation.

"You're the major player in Bootle now" McSharry said sternly "and you work for me. I take thirty per cent of anything you earn and when I need a job doing you drop whatever you've got on and you do it. Clear?"

Charlie wasn't sure where the enthusiasm he had possessed earlier in the day had been hiding but suddenly it was back, and in force. He glanced down again at the bag, the bag that was like a winning lottery ticket, a bag that could change his life.

"Clear?" McSharry repeated impatiently.

"Yes, yes sir" Charlie replied. He knew it was a meek answer but there was too much going on inside his head, he felt the adrenaline pumping around his body for what seemed like the hundredth time today and he fought the urge to break out into a huge grin.

"The boys will help you get set up, they'll make sure everybody knows that you're with us, and they'll make sure people know what will happen if they try to fuck with you. This isn't something you walk away from, you leave here with this bag and you're mine for life, you understand?"

"Yes sir" Charlie repeated "Absolutely"

If McSharry was pleased with Charlie's answer he didn't show it, instead he just stared at him for a moment longer, nodded and looked off towards the Mersey.

"The boys will drop you off at home, come tomorrow morning Bootle is yours to run, which means it's yours to lose. Don't screw up, and we'll be in touch"

McSharry didn't wait for Charlie to respond, turning on his heels he moved towards the rear door of the Mercedes and climbed inside, Begsy followed a moment later as Ads and Mercer made their way back to the van. Charlie watched the Merc speed out of the car park then turned to follow the others, a wide smile spread across his face as he walked, finally, after all the shit, his time had come.

As soon as Charlie stepped through the front door he knew that Vicky and the kids weren't home, there was a calmness about the place, a peaceful aura that filled the house when it was empty, that aura was impossible to replicate when his family were present. Automatically he breathed a sigh of relief, explaining the black bin bag wouldn't have been impossible, but it would have been tricky, this way he saved himself from what would inevitably turn into a fight.

With the bag locked firmly in his hand he flew up the stairs two at a time, the whole journey home he had been calculating the best location for his stash. The house wasn't big, it certainly wasn't big enough for a family of four and space was sparse, space for secrets was sparser still. He opened the door to Zoe's room, in the far corner was a small wardrobe, it had been a gift from Vicky's parents, a cast off that they no longer had any use for and Vicky, eternally anxious to play the role of unsupported wife, had accepted it with open arms. No wonder the old gits hated him so much. In time it would be Zoe's wardrobe, but for now the only use his one year old daughter had found for the faded wooden structure was to keep her spare quilt and a few of her older toys. After almost an hour of deliberation it felt like the safest place for his big prize, after all it was the only part of the house that wasn't ransacked on a daily basis.

Quickly, he opened the creaking doors, he didn't know where Vicky was but the night was ticking on, surely she wouldn't be gone for too much longer. On the top shelf of the wardrobe was a small, thin sheet that Zoe slept in during the summer. June was a far cry from November and Charlie was confident he would have all of the drugs offloaded by the time the warm weather came back around. Reaching inside he extracted the wad of cash and hid the bin bag behind the sheet in the corner of the top shelf. Carefully, he rearranged the sheet to ensure that the bin bag wouldn't be visible from any angle, once he was satisfied he slid the money into his coat pocket and made his way downstairs.

He was halfway down the stairs when he noticed the small metallic object resting on the carpet a few feet away from the front door. It was only when he reached it that he realised they were his car keys, preoccupied with hiding the bag he hadn't even checked to see if his car was parked outside, clearly it was and Rob had posted the keys through the door when he'd returned it. He wondered what Rob would make of the day's developments, he'd warned Charlie quite emphatically not to get involved with McSharry and his people but at the end of the day it was his life to live, not Rob's. Still, he suspected it would probably be more sensible not to go into details with his older brother, as far as Rob was concerned Charlie had helped McSharry out with a problem and that was the end of it. It wouldn't be in anyone's interest for the details of their new arrangement to come to light, at least not yet. Rob had enough on his plate without having to worry about what Charlie was doing, this way would be better for everyone.

He slid the keys in his pocket and was en route to the living room when he heard the lock click and the front door open, he turned to see Vicky trying to negotiate the pram through the front door, with Alexis a few steps ahead.

"Daddy!" she shouted excitedly, running towards him with her arms wide apart, Charlie caught her and hauled her up into his arms.

"Hey gorgeous" he said enthusiastically, throwing a cautious look in Vicky's direction, she was closing the front door having successfully manoeuvred the pram into the hallway. She regarded him with cynical eyes, a look that Charlie was all too familiar with by now.

"You're home, I missed you" Alexis told him, kissing his cheek and giggling. Charlie looked at his eldest daughter, it was one of his favourite things to do. He knew every father said it but she really was the most beautiful thing on the planet. Her big brown eyes were so full of love that it seemed sometimes like they might overflow, while her light brown hair, her mother's hair, bounced lightly as she giggled. He gave her a kiss on the cheek and squeezed her against his chest.

"Missed you too pumpkin" he said honestly, then he looked towards Vicky "Hey"

"Hello" she said coldly.

"Where've you been?"

She crossed her arms defensively "Suddenly you care?"

"For Christ's sake..." Charlie began before he felt Alexis flinch in his arms, smiling at his daughter he took a deep breath and tried to control himself "Look, I was just asking, ok?" he said, trying to put some softness in his voice.

"I was at my Mother's"

"How is she?"

"Same as always"

"Did you tell her I said hi?"

Vicky let out a small, bitter laugh "I don't think that would have gone down all that well"

Charlie narrowed his eyes while he looked at her, something was different from the last time he'd seen her "You've had your haircut?" he deduced after a few seconds.

"Yeah" she said, running her fingers through a light brown strand "I had it done yesterday, I needed something to cheer me up"

He studied her closely, for the last few months he'd only ever seen her hair wrapped up in a bun, the occasional strand falling down to frame her face, but now it was curled, and fuller, reminding Charlie of how it used to look when they had first started dating. It made her look a good five years younger, and though the perpetual frown was still etched upon her face she looked prettier than she had for quite some time.

"It looks good" he told her with a smile.

"Thanks" Vicky replied, regarding him suspiciously before lifting a sleeping Zoe out of her pram and taking her into the living room. He gave Alexis another kiss and dropped her onto the ground, watching as she ran up the stairs to her room.

"I need some money" Vicky called, Charlie stepped into the living room to meet her before she continued "We should start buying some of the Christmas presents for the kids before town gets too manic, I can't be arsed queuing for half a day in that bloody Disney store"

"Sure thing" Charlie said, reaching into the bundle of notes and pulling out just under half "But it's not just about the kids is it, what about you?"

"What about me?" she asked, placing Zoe in the baby seat and turning to face him for the first time. When she did Charlie was holding just over a grand out in front of her.

"I thought you might want to buy yourself something nice this year, I know it's been a hard one"

She regarded the money for a few moments before she looked up at him, Charlie was surprised to see anger burning brightly in her eyes "What the fuck is this Charlie? You think giving me money makes up for being an absent bloody father? And what are you getting yourself into when you can just walk in with that kind of cash?"

Charlie was caught off guard, he shrugged his shoulders "Work's going well, what the bloody hells the matter with you?"

"Works going well!?" she repeated angrily "I don't even know what that means? Does that mean you're doing more than just selling down the local? For fucks sake Charlie, you've got a family now, what in God's name are you thinking about? What happens if they lock you up? I'm just supposed to raise these girls by myself? With no income? You never fucking think things through do you?"

"Woah, woah" Charlie said, trying to get to grips with the situation "It's nothing like that, I just got a bit of extra cash coming in that's all, don't be so fucking touchy. I'm trying to do something nice for my family, I thought that's what a husband was supposed to do!"

"Since when have you been interested in what a husband is supposed to do? This is just a way for you to make yourself feel better about never being around"

Charlie pulled at his hair in disbelief, he tried to comprehend how the conversation had taken this perverted twist, but for the life of him he couldn't understand it.

"There's something seriously, *seriously* wrong with you!" Charlie said, he could feel his control over the anger slipping, he closed the living room door so Alexis wouldn't have to hear.

"This isn't what marriage is supposed to be about Charlie!" Vicky said, there was exasperation in her voice "You don't just come home and pay your family a couple of hundred quid so you can piss off again for another week without getting a bollocking!"

"Is that what I'm doing?" Charlie shouted back, he tried to keep what anger he could from escaping his mouth but he couldn't hold it all in "I just tried to come home and give you a nice surprise, to make things a little better and you've just got ruin it, poison it, like you poison every good thing that happens around here. I swear to God Vic, half the time I don't know why I bother!"

She took a step towards him and for a second Charlie thought she was going to spit in his face, but when she spoke her voice was low and fierce "You want to talk about ruined, my life was ruined the second I married you. If I could I'd take it all back, you, the house, the kids, all of it then I would, just to remember what it was like to feel happy"

If there was any chance of Charlie restraining what was left of his anger then it disappeared as soon as the words left Vicky's mouth, he felt a hatred wash over him that, even in their darkest moments, he had never felt for his wife before.

"You know what Vicky" he said slowly "You're a real fucking cunt!"

He took the bundle of rolled up notes that were still in his hand and threw them into her face, she knocked them away and let the notes scatter across the floor before she started yelling obscenities at Charlie that half the street would be able to hear, but he hadn't waited to listen to them, he was already out the door with his car keys in hand.

Twenty minutes later and the anger still hadn't subsided. Turning off the engine he climbed out of his car, he couldn't believe what the bitch had said, that she wished she could just eradicate their kids from the world, take it all back and live a completely different life. It had taken every ounce of self-restraint he had not to slap her in that moment, that was a line that she shouldn't have crossed, no matter what her issues were.

With a deep breath he knocked on the green door, he was imagining Steph's perfect face and already he could feel the anger beginning to melt, a few seconds later he heard footsteps making their way towards the door and his heart skipped a beat.

The door opened and just like always he found himself caught off guard by just how beautiful she was, the door was only open far enough for Steph to poke her head out and Charlie could see that her hair and make-up were immaculately prepared. She was going out.

"Alright hot stuff" Charlie said casually.

She smiled at him "Hey babe" opening the door the rest of the way she stepped onto the street and kissed him, Charlie breathed in her perfume as her tongue probed inside his mouth, the rush of blood made him feel faint.

A second later and the kiss was over, before Charlie could get his bearings Steph had already stepped back into the house and was climbing the stairs to her flat. It was only now that Charlie saw she was wearing a tight pink dress that barely reached her thigh with a pair of black high heels to boot. He followed her upstairs and into the flat doing his best to keep his tongue in his mouth, when he got inside she went straight towards the mirror to apply some lipstick.

"Off out somewhere?" he asked, trying to sound uninterested.

She looked at him through the mirror and smiled "Course, its Friday night, anyway I didn't think you were coming round tonight?"

"Change of plan" Charlie said, picking up a half drunk glass of white wine from the coffee table and downing it in one "Who you out with?"

"Yvonne, she had a pretty rough week and wants to find herself a man. I said I'd go along, you know, for morale support"

"Morale support? Right" Charlie said, picking up the wine bottle, pouring himself a glass and knocking it back.

"Ah baby, that's so sweet, you're jealous" Steph said, flashing him a cheeky smile through the mirror "Don't worry, you're the only married man for me. If you want to crash here I'll be back before you know it, maybe you can wait up for me, you know how horny I get after a night out!"

Charlie put the glass and the bottle back on the table and took a couple of steps towards her "Actually I thought you might want to stay"

"Oh yeah? Why's that?"

"I've got a surprise for you"

Placing the lipstick delicately on the mantelpiece she turned around and glided towards him, an inquisitive look sparkling in her eye.

"What kind of surprise?" she asked, tilting her head to the side as she reached him.

"Well, I noticed how tatty all of your clothes are looking" Charlie said, Steph pulled a face of mock shock and then smiled as he pulled the rest of

Leroy Tate's money out of his pocket "So I thought you might need to go on a bit of a shopping spree"

Steph's eyes lit up as he handed her the money, he suddenly realised she was even more beautiful when she was happy, he wondered how many more levels of magnificence she could reach before there was simply no higher she could go.

Her eyes were wide as she fingered the money "There's almost two grand here" she said, glancing up with a seductive look in her eyes "this is all for me?"

"Every penny" Charlie told her "I thought maybe we could spend tonight getting the last use out of this dress and then come tomorrow morning we can get you as many new ones as you want, you will have to model each and every one for me though, that's a non-negotiable condition"

Steph dropped the money onto the table and smiled her sweetest smile "I can do that" she said, leaning in close and pressing her lips against his.

Charlie wrapped his arms around her small body and fiercely returned the kiss, the smell of her perfume continued to make his head dizzy and the feel of her soft tongue against his was impossibly soothing. Moments later he noticed that her arms were no longer around his neck, his heart sped up when he realised they were unbuckling his belt. Steph broke the kiss as his trousers dropped to the floor, he looked at her expectantly and with a cheeky grin she dropped to her knees.

As Charlie closed his eyes and let the ecstasy wash over him his mind began to drift, ever so briefly, to the memory of Leroy Tate, at that moment he felt no guilt whatsoever for the things he had done. If these were the spoils of war, then he was more than ready to become a soldier.

Chapter 21

Rob took another gulp of lager. Slowly, he placed the pint glass back on the table as the alcohol coursed through his bloodstream; it was a welcome sensation, and one he'd strongly needed over the last couple of days. His cocaine relapse, however brief it may have been, had reawakened a craving in him that he hadn't known for a long time. Like any addict he had underestimated the strength of his compulsion and as the days passed by he could feel it gnawing away at his restraint with increasing ferocity. For the moment alcohol was doing an acceptable job of plugging that hole; a bottle of whisky here, a crate of lager there, but as a long term plan it wasn't without its flaws. He worried whether he could hold out long enough to kill Tony Miller and get his money.

He took another gulp and looked across the table, Matt was staring away into the distance, his small eyes looking at nothing in particular but yet strangely focused. After a few seconds he caught Rob staring at him and self-consciously lifted the pint glass to his lips.

It had been Matt's suggestion to meet straight after work, in a bar close to his office. Even over the phone his old friend had seemed a little off, and Rob wasn't surprised to see the same attitude present itself when they met. He had sympathy for Matt, Wayne Caddock had been a client of Buckland, Treadgold & Gardner for the last seven years, and although Matt had never been directly involved with the man, he had a lot of colleagues who had. Rob was sure that it would have been a lot easier for Matt to sympathise with his extracurricular activities had he not needed to kill a man whose death directly affected his workplace.

Matt's choice of bar was relatively busy, occupied almost exclusively by suit wearing twenty somethings, keen to forget their woes after another long day at the office, but even in such an environment Matt's grey Gucci suit still set him apart as a man of greater means than most. The flash cocktail bar wasn't the type of place Rob would have expected Matt to pick, but the more he saw of his hometown, the more he saw that such establishments were fast becoming the norm. Long gone were the days when a Liverpool night out was made up of an old pub and a pint of bitter, now it seemed more likely to be characterized by a place like this and a six pound mojito.

Rob finished off the last of his pint and surveyed his company closely, Matt had refused to meet his gaze for longer than a couple of seconds, and every effort he had made at small talk had been quickly snuffed out by brief, one word responses. There was a hostility in his old friend that reeked of both petulance and passive aggression, Matt was unprepared for the way in which this particular murder would affect him, and he blamed Rob for that reaction. Somewhere inside, he knew the best way to remedy the situation would be to show some patience and understanding, but Rob just wasn't built that way. Already he could feel the indignation at Matt's behaviour hasten the beat of his heart, he decided to tackle the situation the only way he knew how; head on.

"You got something you want to get off your chest?"

The bluntness of the question seemed to catch Matt off guard surprising considering he was a barrister. His boyish features gave his current attitude an air of immaturity, like a child pouting, it occurred to Rob that such bickering hadn't been present in their relationship since they left their teens.

"Not a thing" Matt replied evasively, pulling the tie from around his throat and undoing the top button.

"Not a thing?" Rob repeated sceptically "Alright, well if you don't have any worries you need to be rid of the least you can do is help alleviate a few of mine, how big of a stir has this Wayne Caddock thing caused at your office?"

Matt shook his head as a joyless smile touched the corners of his mouth "It caused a pretty big stir Rob, one of our most prominent clients was just murdered for Christ's sake, that kind of thing tends to have an impact on people"

Rob ignored the attitude and took another drink.

"What are they saying?" he asked, slamming the glass down onto the table.

"Who?"

"The people in your office, what are they saying about the murder?"

Matt shrugged his shoulders, for a second Rob suspected that would be it in the way of a response, but after a few moments he began to speak.

"They're saying the same thing as everybody else. They're asking how a lone gunman who can't be identified managed to butcher ten armed criminals, and they're asking who gave him the green light to do it"

Rob glanced around the bar, though it was busy the nearest table was ten feet away, well out of hearing range, even so he leaned forward onto the table and a second later watched as Matt begrudgingly mimicked the gesture.

"Who are they pointing the finger at?"

"It's a three way split at the moment. Some people are saying Tony Miller, others think its Stephen McSharry, a rumour seems to be gathering speed that it was a new player trying to make a name for themselves, but you know what this towns like, every other person seems to know a friend of a friend who's a small time dealer taking credit for the whole thing"

"That sounds about right" Rob replied, letting a small smile cross his face for the first time.

"So..." Matt began cautiously, he studied Rob with narrowed eyes, the anger fading to make way for something else "how did you do it?"

Rob let out a breath "Honestly mate, I couldn't tell ya"

"Try" Matt replied, his face was unreadable yet Rob still got the sense that the conversation was having a significant impression on him. He wondered how best to answer, and then decided that his friend deserved nothing less than the truth.

"I wish I could explain it, I get into this mindset where nothing else exists except me and my target, and when I do suddenly everything is simple, everything is clear. I just point and shoot, point and shoot, there's a focus that I've never known in any other aspect of my life, and when I come out the other side everyone is dead. That's the best way I can describe it, does that make any sense?"

"A little" Matt told him, there was a hint of sympathy in his face that told Rob they were getting closer to their usual dynamic "but do you enjoy it?"

Rob took another long gulp and realised that his glass was almost empty "No, I mean when I look back at what I've done, absolutely not, but when I'm there, when I'm in that place, and I see my enemies drop, one after the other, there is a buzz, no matter how much I try and tell myself I don't feel it, I do. It's difficult to understand unless you've been there, but its primal, it comes from a place inside that you don't know exists until that moment"

This time it was Matt's turn to put the pint to his lips, emptying its contents in a matter of seconds, when he turned his focus away from the glass his eyes were slightly glazed, though Rob suspected it had nothing to do with the alcohol.

"That's really fucking messed up!" Matt said after a few seconds, although there was concern in his words Rob sensed that his assessment was one of acceptance more than anything else.

"I know"

Looking up he saw Matt break into a smile, a second later he found his own face mimicking the action.

Rob raised the glass and finished his drink, as he returned it to the table he saw Matt gesture towards the waitress for two more. They sat in silence as their glasses were collected and their replacements brought over, it was only after Matt handed the waitress a ten pound note and told her to keep the change that the conversation resumed, Matt's face had regained a lot of its previous gravity, though with none of the hardness that had been there before.

"Caddock's wife came in today, something to do with papers for the will. The woman was a mess Rob, she was crying, gasping for breath, she was unsteady on her feet. I've never seen that side of what you do before, it's a grim place to be"

Suddenly, Matt's prior indignation seemed to make more sense, Rob regretted that he'd had to see that side of it, creating husbandless wives and fatherless children were the cornerstones of his self-loathing. He didn't want his best friend to be exposed to the horror that produced, trying to convince a law abiding solicitor to stay loyal to a cold blooded killer was a tricky enough prospect as it was.

"You don't know the half of it" Rob said bleakly, he recognised that it was an unsatisfactory response but he only had so much honesty in him.

"Probably not. So why not get the hell out of town while you still have a chance?"

It was a simple question, and one that Rob felt like he was answering on a daily basis these days, for a second his mind jumped to David Walker but he pushed the memory from his head, now wasn't the time.

"We've been over this Matt, I'm not going over it again" the tone of his voice brokered no further argument.

Matt nodded and glanced around the bar, the sound of rap music was barely audible over the murmur of the patrons, Rob took another drink and let the cold liquid slide down his throat, placing the glass back on the table he looked across to see Matt watching him with a guarded expression.

"You talk to your girl lately? What did you say her name was?"

Rob ran his index finger over the thickening hair on his chin "Jo" he told him cautiously "and not for a couple of days"

Matt nodded solemnly "Must be hard, being so far away from each other and all"

"What's your point?" he asked impatiently, he could feel a flicker of anger ignite inside of him, talking about his personal life evoked an uncomfortable feeling, he acknowledged the irony that he felt more at ease talking about killing people.

"No point, I'm just talking" Matt replied lightly, Rob got the impression that he was seeing the professional side of his best friend "how is she coping with all this?"

Despite himself, Rob felt the urge to answer the question honestly, whatever his gut instinct told him he knew that burying his head in the sand was unlikely to solve his problems, with a hint of resignation he did what Jo was always telling him to do, and spoke honestly.

"Not that well, she doesn't understand what I'm doing here, and she doesn't understand why I have to do it"

"She isn't the only one. Will she be able to keep it together until you get back?"

Rob shrugged his shoulders "Maybe, maybe not. When we talk... it isn't how it should be. I get the feeling this thing is taking a bigger toll on her than she's letting on"

Matt flashed him that rueful smile once again "Sounds like something you have in common!"

"You finished with the A Level Psychology routine?" Rob asked irritably, drinking the remaining half of his pint in one swift motion.

"For now. You want another pint before happy hour ends?"

"Can't" he stood up from his seat and grabbed the leather jacket from the back of his chair "I told Kelly I'd pop round"

"Kelly? Really? You're going back down that road?"

Rob shook his head dismissively "It's not like that"

"No?"

"No, I just like hanging out with her that's all, catching up. It helps take my mind of all this... madness"

"Catching up, ey?" Matt repeated mockingly "Is that what the kids are calling it these days?"

Rob tossed a ten pound note onto the table next to the empty pint glass "Finish your drink, nobhead" he said sliding on his jacket "I'll call you in a couple of days"

Rob made his way out of the bar and into the brisk evening air, he started down Wood Street towards the nearest taxi rank, noting the various bars and clubs whose bright lights illuminated the cobbled street.

There was no queue when he reached his destination, just three cars with three bored drivers waiting patiently for the citizens of Liverpool to drink their body weight in alcohol and demand passage home. Without breaking stride he approached the first taxi, opened the door and stepped inside.

He gave Kelly's address and settled into the back seat. The driver, a surly overweight man with a perm grunted in response and put the car into gear, clearly not the sociable type, but that was fine with Rob, he had enough on his mind to keep him occupied.

The car had only moved a couple of feet by the time Rob's thoughts drifted to David Walker. The man's presence in his head was almost a given these days, a constant niggling worry that hounded him whenever he was alone. It had been a surprise to see him again, but one Rob had always half expected, particularly after he'd hit Wayne Caddock and his boys. He had hoped, somewhat optimistically, that Walker was out of the picture by now, maybe he'd taken a desk job for more money, or gone down the political route, anything to keep him away from an active murder investigation and incapable of piecing together Rob's involvement in it. But now that his old accomplice had re-emerged he could see that theory for what it had always been; wishful thinking. Of course David Walker was still hunting down drug dealers, of course he was on the ball when it came to underworld hits. Back in the day the man had been single minded to the point of obsession, his commitment had at times boarded on the perverse, more than once his hunt for McSharry had reminded Rob of the stories you heard about deranged fans, obsessively basing their lives around celebrities they had never met. In a way he envied the man, having that one inalienable focus, a cause to base your entire life around, it was the kind of thing he respected. But at the same time Rob knew that that could never be him, he just wasn't that type of man.

His mind drifted back to their first meeting, even then he'd found himself surprised by the man's determination. The memory made him cringe, he'd been in a bad way when he broke into Walker's house at one in the morning, a twelve hour binge of coke, booze and whores had preceded the event, the fallout from the darkest thing he had ever done, and at the end of the twelve hours he had been sure of his next move. So he'd broken into the policeman's house and waited for him to come home.

The copper had been brave, stubbornly so considering he had had a Smith and Weston pointed at his chest, Rob had been too wired at the time to respect it, but now, as he thought back, that kind of nerve was to be admired. Still, it hadn't stopped the guys face turning a greyish kind of pale when Rob told him who he was, Walker no doubt thought that he was there to kill him, that Rob's confessions would be the last thing he would ever hear. But that was not the plan, and that was not why he was there.

Instead, Rob told Walker about Ploughman. About how the lawyer was on the edge, struggling to cope with being an accessory to murder. Ploughman was an Oxford Graduate, and as such he knew how to show his clients what they wanted to see. As far as Stephen McSharry knew James Ploughman was a trusted member of his inner circle, a man motivated by money who even had the added bonus of being empowered by the law to keep his secrets. But Rob Thomas knew desperation better than most, an even on the rare occasions when he had met the lawyer, one of the few associates McSharry ever allowed him to meet, Rob could sense his panic. James Ploughman was on the edge, all he needed was a push and he would flip, a push that Rob could provide.

All he asked for in return was that he be left out of the police investigation. Any mention of him would have to be buried before it could get any further than David Walker, and if Rob was allowed to walk free the ambitious young copper would get the chance to collar one of the country's leading figures in organised crime.

With a gun aimed at the man's head Rob had taken Walker's oath, an oath that he would never disclose where the information had come from. In normal circumstances a police officer may have had difficulty striking such a deal with a self-confessed murderer, but the mere mention of Stephen McSharry had brought a sparkle to Walker's eyes that Rob had noted immediately. The copper agreed unequivocally, and their collaboration had started at that moment.

The more years that passed, the more uncomfortable Rob had become with that collaboration. It wasn't that he regretted its outcome, far from it, McSharry was a vile excuse of a man, since Rob had first met him he had become an increasingly untouchable predator who, without question, needed to be stopped. What he regretted was how he'd gone about it, cooperating with the police, in secret, like some sort of grass. He'd never had any fondness for the police, not since being hauled into a riot van at the age of thirteen for fighting with kids from a rival school, but he'd never hated them either. Unlike most killers he was indifferent to the entity that hunted him, yet for all those years he had still existed in their world, he was one of their people, and in that world there was no greater sin than cooperation with the authorities.

But that cooperation had been a long time ago, a lot had changed in the ten years since he'd handed McSharry to David Walker. Rob was smart enough to know that Walker's loyalty to him was fuelled entirely by self-interest. The only reason Rob hadn't spent the last ten years sharing a cell with his boss was because it looked better for the new darling of the Merseyside Police Force to have taken down the head of a major crime syndicate by himself. Any mention of deal making, or bargaining with known criminals would inevitably bring with it another set of questions centring on ethics, credibility and transparency. These were the kind of questions that high price solicitors like James Ploughman made a fortune asking, and they were the kind of questions that could see an airtight case unravel in the blink of an eye. No, the best way forward for David Walker was for Rob to be a ghost, and Rob had recognised that fact before he'd even considered breaking into the man's home.

Now, it was different. The man who had stopped Rob on the side of the road wasn't the same man he'd dealt with ten years ago. Then David Walker had been an ambitious young detective, political, Machiavellian to the point that he was willing to do almost anything to facilitate his rise through the rank and file that blocked his path. Now that man had got his wish, the David Walker who threatened him on the side of the road was a different creature altogether, a successful, high ranking police officer who was considered to be personally responsible when an event like the Wayne Caddock hit captivated the public's collective consciousness. Which made the latter David Walker a much more dangerous animal than the former.

His success last time out had been based on his ability to manipulate Walker's ambition, with that ambition now fulfilled he no longer had anything the copper would need. All he had left was the threat of full disclosure, he may not be able to give Walker something that he wanted but they both knew that he could take away what he had. Yet even a threat as serious as that would only keep a man like David Walker at bay for so long, eventually his resolve would snap and he would take Rob down, regardless of the consequences, all he could do was trust in himself and hope that he would be long gone by the time that happened.

It took a few seconds for Rob to realise that the sound he was hearing was someone speaking to him, slowly he shook himself from his thoughts and reacclimatised himself to his surroundings. The taxi had stopped, glancing out the window he saw the familiar toy littered porch of number 38 that he remembered from his last visit, he only had a moment to take it in before the driver began talking to him again.

"I said, is this the place you're after, mate!?"

The impatience in the drivers tone told Rob that he had asked the question

270

at least twice already, sheepishly he met the drivers eye through the rear view mirror and nodded.

"Yeah, this is it"

He looked at the meter, seven pounds fifty. Taking a ten pound note from his breast pocket he slid it through the open square in the glass partition.

"Keep the change"

The driver responded with a grunt and a second later he heard the sound of the automatic locking system switching off. He climbed out of the cab and made his way across the street, once again feeling the palpitations in his heart as he approached.

Before he got to the door Rob stole a quick glance at his watch; 7:30, the kids should still be awake, no risk of getting in trouble there, the gate opened with a creak as he stepped onto the porch and rang the doorbell.

It was a few moments before Rob heard any kind of movement within the house, and a few moments more before he saw a figure shuffle across the living room. Slowly, the door opened, just a faction and Rob saw a small face covered with light brown hair peek through the gap and eye him suspiciously.

"Hello" Matilda said, it was more a question that a statement from the four year old, as if the word required an explanation as to what he was doing there.

"Hello Matilda, I'm Robbie, your mums friend. We met the other day, is she home?"

The child eyed him cautiously for a few seconds, as if she was debating whether or not to grant him access to her home. Rob suddenly found himself feeling very self-conscious, as if he was being scrutinised by an employer. He remembered hearing a story once that children were very good judges of character, he wondered in that moment whether Matilda could sense the terrible things he had done, and whether she was judging him for them.

A few more uncomfortable seconds passed before Matilda decided to admit him, swinging the door open the rest of the way she turned and walked away, Rob guessed her acceptance had more to do with a desire to get back in front of the television than anything else.

"Mum, your friend's at the door" Matilda shouted as she disappeared from his line of sight, Rob wondered whether he was expected to follow her inside but decided to stay where he was, polite was probably the best course of action as far as Kelly was concerned.

From his spot on the porch he saw Kelly exit the kitchen and walk towards him, cleaning her hands on a kitchen towel in the process. When she caught sight of her visitor Rob was sure he caught her try and repress a smile, when she reached him he raised his eyebrows and flashed her a grin.

"Well, well, he's back" Kelly said dramatically, leaning against the door frame as she flung the kitchen towel over her shoulder.

"Just like I said"

"You want to watch yourself Robbie, you keep behaving like this and someone might start to confuse you with the kind of guy who keeps his word"

Rob decided to ignore the passive aggressive criticism implicit in her comment, it wasn't as if he didn't deserve it.

"I thought those kind of men only existed in kids stories? Like leprechauns or fairies?"

"Well, I've always been something of a dreamer" she told him.

"Can I come in?"

"I suppose" she took a step back, holding the door open as he crossed the threshold. The living room seemed slightly more chaotic than the last time he'd visited, toys were scattered here and there across the room, yet the children remained in the exact same spot as when he'd last seen them; lying on the floor with their eyes glued to the TV.

"Kids, you remember Robbie, say hi"

"Hello" Matilda and Stevie said in unison, their tone existing somewhere between boredom and disinterest. This time they didn't even shift their gaze to acknowledge him, Rob suspected that was a rare privilege only received on a first visit.

Looking back towards Kelly he saw her gesture towards the kitchen, with a nod he fell in behind her, as they covered the short distance to the table and chairs. He noticed she was wearing the same light grey jogging pants and oversized white jumper he had seen her in on his last visit.

He sat down on one of the wooden chairs as Kelly leaned against the fridge and lit a cigarette. She looked him over for a few seconds, reminding Rob of the similar scrutiny he had suffered at the hands of her daughter, then she blew a mouthful of smoke into the air and readjusted her position.

"So, what prompted this unexpected visit?" she asked tentatively.

"I need a reason to come and say hello to an old friend?"

Kelly narrowed her eyes, as if not entirely buying his answer, slowly she moved towards the kettle and took two cups from a nearby cupboard.

"Coffee?"

"Please"

"No sugar, right? You're a changed man!"

Rob nodded when she looked at him, and watched as she heaped two teaspoons of instant coffee into each of the cups and doused them with milk. She waited a few seconds for the kettle to boil before filling each to the rim, and carrying them over to the table. Once she'd taken her seat across from him Rob began to speak.

"So, I just met up with Matty for a pint"

"Oh yeah" Kelly replied, her voice sounding slightly disinterested "Where'd you go?"

Rob tried to remember the name "Korva, or Korna? Something like that, just off Wood Street, you know it?"

With a wry smile Kelly shook her head "Nah, I don't really get out much these days. Any good?"

"Not really my scene, mood lighting, alternative art work on the walls, drinks that take so long to make they charge you by the hour, you know the kind of place, made for kids who don't know the difference between front and substance"

Kelly let out a chuckle with another mouthful of smoke "Lad, you got old"

"You're only a few months behind, skippy"

"There's a difference between being thirty five and acting thirty five"

"Says the mother of two?"

Kelly stubbed out her cigarette and pointed a warning finger in Rob's direction "Hey, I'll have you know I'm a very cool mum"

Rob wrapped his hands around the cup to gage its temperature, satisfied he took a first sip, appreciating the affect the caffeine would have on his tired brain.

"But do you remember what a night out used to be like?" he asked, placing the cup back on the table "Six or seven pints in the pub then we'd hit one of the late night clubs, throw back a couple of Class A's, dance like idiots, have a couple more pints, maybe a couple of shots. It was a classic system, from start to finish"

"Classic for you maybe. You didn't have to spend half your night being groped by teenage boys out of their minds on E. Nothing breaks up a flowing dance move like some skinny little schoolboy tapping you on the shoulder telling you you're his soul mate"

Rob thought back to the innumerable nights that time had blurred into one, he remembered how free Kelly used to look when she was on the dance floor. More often than not she would leave their group to go and sway to the sounds on her own, at times like that she had almost seemed at one with the music, it was no wonder so many pubescent clubbers fell in love with her.

"You loved it" he told her "No one who danced the way you did can claim to be shy about getting attention"

"It was your attention I was after" Kelly replied, sipping at her coffee and engaging him with those blue eyes he knew so well "Not some scrawny little nobody with an alcopop"

Rob looked away, feeling more than a hint of awkwardness, he didn't want her getting the wrong idea of why he was there.

"I never thought you were that picky" he said, smiling to let her know he was kidding, she smiled back and took another sip of coffee.

"Do you remember Joey Tartan's house party" she asked, taking another cigarette from her pocket and sliding it into her mouth "We drank straight through on the Friday night, did a few lines of coke, a couple of E's and went clubbing at the 051 on the Saturday, god how old were we then?"

Rob remembered the night well "Twenty one, it was Matt's birthday"

"That's right, God, he was so drunk, wasn't that the night he tried to take off all his clothes on the dance floor?"

The memory brought a burst of laughter from each of them, it took Rob a few seconds to find the breath to speak.

"He managed to get down to his boxers and socks before the bouncers tackled him"

Kelly lit the cigarette that was hanging from her mouth and let out another chuckle "That was a brilliant night" she said, inhaling her first breath of tobacco.

"He wasn't too impressed with us though, you remember? We left him outside in his boxers for an hour while we had another drink, when we found him he was curled up in the foetal position, semi-conscious and shaking. We were lucky his whole night was a blur or we'd have been creeping till his twenty second"

Kelly nodded as if she remembered, Rob noticed her eyes had something of a melancholy glint "We had some good times, didn't we?"

"We did"

A contented silence came over the room, Kelly's eyes focused on a spot on the floor. Smiling her sad smile, Rob wondered whether her thoughts were following the same path as his, whether she was trying to pinpoint exactly when their lives had started to spiral away from the care free kids they had both once been.

Rob took another sip of coffee and leaned back in his chair, the silence was serene, almost relaxing, only the faint noise of the television infringing on the otherwise perfect silence. In a flash the calm smile disappeared from Kelly's face and she jumped to her feet with a look of frustrated recognition etched upon her face.

"Shit"

"What is it?" Rob asked, suddenly on edge as he leaned forward in his seat.

"Lunches" she said in a distracted tone as she moved towards the fridge.

"Excuse me?"

"Lunches, before you got here I was just about to get started on the kids lunches. If I don't get them done before I go to bed it'll be chaos in the morning"

Rob stood up, grabbed his coffee and followed her to the work surface "Ok"

"I mean it, Matilda saw Babe last week and now she won't eat meat, Stevie's going through an anti-sandwich phase and neither of them will touch pasta, finding a meal for them to eat can take up half of my night"

He watched as Kelly hurriedly reached into the fridge, grabbing bags of things he couldn't even identify, with a sigh she nudged him out of the way and opened a cupboard where his legs had just had been, a second later she emerged with two plastic lunchboxes.

"So, what are you making?" he asked, peering over her shoulder as she worked.

"Tuna salad"

"Tasty"

Kelly turned on him with a mock stare "Shut up, it's healthy"

"Oh, I'm sure" Rob said, returning to the spot he had been expelled from moments earlier "You coping ok Kell, having to do all this on your own?"

For the briefest of seconds Kelly's movements seemed to slow down, from his current position Rob could only see the back of her head, he wondered how she was going to react but when she turned to face him there was a smile on her face.

"You worried about me Robbie? You don't need to be, I'm fine, years of practise relying on just yourself, eventually it becomes second nature, you know?"

The cynicism in her voice stung Rob, the sentiment was so far removed from the energetic girl he had known that it hardly seemed capable of coming from the same person.

"You can count on people" he said evenly, as soon as the words left his mouth he wondered whether he believed them himself.

"Not in my experience" Kelly replied, ripping at a lettuce head before dropping two handfuls into the lunchboxes.

"So, how long did it take? To become second nature I mean"

He sensed a change as Kelly returned the lettuce to the fridge, a few seconds passed before she picked up a knife and started slicing a tomato. Though her back was to him Rob caught a new edge to her voice, he couldn't imagine that she was smiling anymore.

"It took a while, when I first had Stevie, well, I was in a pretty bad place anyway, but I struggled a lot in that first year, but then I guess most new mothers do"

"It must have been hard" Rob said, once again feeling the same morbid fascination drawing him in as it had on his last visit, there was something about her life, something about her story that intrigued him more than it should have. Like a tragic novel he found himself thirsting for the next page.

"So, so hard. You know when you're pregnant, everyone wants to tell you how motherhood is instinctive, how it's the most natural, automatic thing that you will ever do, and that once you set eyes on your child you'll love it more than you ever imagined, but..."

"It's not true?"

"Oh no, it's true, to a point. But what they don't tell you is that suddenly you're responsible for this whole new life, for this tiny, vulnerable, fragile little thing. You're responsible for every aspect of this life and if you don't do a good job, or let things slip even just a little then this tiny life that you love more than anything else on the planet could cease to exist just as quickly as it appeared. It's a hell of a lot of bloody pressure, and I was never that good with pressure"

Rob took a step closer and considered putting a comforting hand on her shoulder, he was halfway through the motion when he changed his mind and returned the arm to his side. Letting out a long breath he took another sip of coffee and leaned backwards against the kitchen cupboards.

"That's not usually how you hear parenthood described" he said, trying to make the words sound light.

"Well, that's how it was for me" she said defensively "and my friends at the time, well, they weren't really big on supporting a single mum, god forbid it interfered with their social lives"

"But you coped, you got through it"

"Just about, I think in those first six months I cried almost every night, at least as much as Stevie did. In the end the doctor had to put me on Prozac just to get me through the days"

Rob knew that drug well, two of his earliest years in New York had been spent in a Prozac induced haze, to little effect "I always found whiskey a more effective stabiliser" he told her with a grin

"Ah well, you see, nobody told me about the whiskey, I could have been out the woods in no time"

"When did it start getting better?"

Snapping the lunchboxes shut one at a time Kelly placed each of them into the fridge and returned to her seat, she waited until Rob had taken his place on the opposite side of the table before she began to speak. Though there was a sad tint to her once bright blue eyes she seemed anxious to talk about her past, Rob suspected that living with two children didn't provide a great deal of opportunity for her to talk about her feelings. He could relate, being surrounded by people you couldn't open up to was a kind of loneliness that he had known for a long time.

"Probably a little after Stevie's first birthday" Rob noticed that she was focusing her gaze unrelentingly on his, as if she was as interested in his reaction as he was in her story "my mum finally started to click on to just how badly I was coping, and she started helping me out a lot more. She made a big difference, if it wasn't for her I'm not sure I'd have made it, and then a little while after that I met Jeff"

Rob remembered their conversation about Jeff, the sensitive club owner who had bolted as soon as things got too real. With a pang of self-realisation he reminded himself how he had departed Kelly's life and tried to put his anger in check, the only difference between the two of them was that Rob hadn't left her with a child, admittedly that made him the lesser of two evils, but it hardly absolved him of any guilt, with a self-conscious smile he nodded.

"Matilda's dad" he said.

"Yeah, it was nice having someone else around, someone to help share the load with. I don't think you realise just how lonely you are until someone comes into your life and shows you"

It only took a moment for Rob's thoughts to drift towards Jo, the pain in his chest returned as if it had never gone away, made all the worse when he realised that the only image he could conjure was the one of her crying as he walked out the door. He remembered her broken, lonely sobs and wondered how long it would take her to forgive him, he wondered how long it would take him to forgive himself.

"I agree"

Something in this tone must have betrayed what he was thinking, Kelly leaned forward in her chair as an inquisitive look spread across her face.

"Is there a special someone waiting for you back in America?"

Rob nodded, for a second he thought he saw a flicker of disappointment cross Kelly's face, though it could just have easily have been surprise.

"And how does she feel about you being on the other side of the world?"

Rob tried to smile but realised he wasn't quite up to the task.

"That's a long story" he said cryptically.

"Fair enough"

"So what's the deal with Stevie's father?"

Kelly looked him in the eye and Rob knew immediately that something had changed, there was a hardness in her face, complemented by the firming of her shoulders that told Rob their closeness had expired.

"That's a long story too" she said, with none of her previous warmth "and I think I've done enough sharing for one night, anyway, the kids still need their baths"

Rob regarded her change in mood as he gulped down the last of his coffee, setting the cup back down on the table he felt an idea blossom in his head and embraced it before he even had a chance to think it through.

"How much notice do you need to get a babysitter?"

She gave him a guarded look "I don't know, a couple of days, why?"

"Let me take you out for dinner, you look like you could do with a night on the town"

Kelly leaned back and crossed her arms "I don't know whether that's a good idea Robbie".

Rob shrugged his shoulders and smiled "Why not? It's just dinner, maybe a couple of drinks, for old times' sake, what do you say?"

Lighting another cigarette, Kelly took the time to take a long drag before she replied "Only if you tell me why"

"Why what?"

"Why you're so keen to take me out"

Rob didn't like the question, because he didn't know the answer. His feelings for Kelly didn't fall within the parameters of any discernible group that he could think of, they weren't romantic, he wasn't even sure they were feelings of friendship. With a sigh he did what he'd been trying to avoid and embraced the emotions that where so appealing in his ex-girlfriend.

"You have a soothing presence" he said, feeling more than a little ridiculous as the words escaped his mouth "and I could really do with that at the moment. Spending time with you keeps me from thinking about things I don't want to think about"

Kelly nodded as if she understood, it suddenly struck Rob that she probably understood a lot more about his problems than he gave her credit for, it worried him that he didn't know just how much of his secret life she may have pieced together over the years of their relationship.

"You're burying your head in the sand" she told him "why should I help you ignore your problems?"

Rob met her steely look with one of his own.

"Because you've seen what happens when I don't"

She took another drag from her cigarette and leaned back in the wooden chair, when she didn't speak Rob wondered whether the conversation was over, but eventually she dropped the cigarette into the ash tray and looked at him.

"I'll speak to my mother, see what days she can take the kids"

"Great" Rob said, slapping a hand on the wooden table "I'll call you Wednesday and we can sort out a date"

Kelly nodded and Rob took the movement as a sign to make his exit, as he reached the kitchen door something inside told him to turn around, moving back to face the kitchen he locked eyes on his ex, still perched on the wooden chair.

"It's good seeing you again Kel, really, it is"

The look of vague suspicion remained almost unaltered, only someone who knew her as well as Rob could translate the slightest twitch in the corner of her mouth as proof that his comment had touched her. Rob didn't need anything more than that, and he didn't expect it. He watched as she stood up and took two steps towards him, bringing the cigarette to her lips as she moved.

"Bugger off" she told him warmly "I've got a lot to do"

Chapter 22

Rob pressed the payphone hard against his ear, the sound of Jo's voice momentarily transported him to another world, far away from all of the worries and fears that clouded his mind. Yet even as the tranquillity washed over him he knew that all was not right, it had only taken a moment for him to sense the tension in his girlfriend's voice, but a moment was all he needed. Stubbornly, he refused to acknowledge it, the relief of hearing her voice had pushed all other thoughts aside and Rob had no intention of letting that change.

"So," he asked, trying to keep his tone jovial "how are things down at the bar?"

"Fine" Jo replied bluntly, the harshness of her tone pushed forward a mental image of her sitting with her arms crossed, cradling the phone between her head and her shoulder while she looked into the distance with a scowl. Rob wondered whether it was an image born from memory, or simply an interpretation of his current pessimism. His thoughts travelled back to his final night in New York and he remembered the altercation with the two Irish lads in McGlincheys, it felt like another life.

"Did those two Republican pricks ever show their faces again?"

"No"

"That's good" he did his best to ignore her less than subtle antagonism "They didn't seem like the kind of guys you want hanging around, especially drunk"

"No, I guess not"

Rob bit the bullet and grimaced "Is everything OK?"

"Yeah, everything's fine. I'm just not sleeping very well at the moment, that's all" she was defensive, Rob wished he could see her face to face before trying to gage her mood, picking the right tact in these circumstances without visual aid; he probably had a better chance of winning the lottery.

"I know, me neither"

Even through the crackly line Rob could hear the annoyed sigh escape from her mouth "You never sleep well" she reminded him.

"Fair point" he conceded, feeling his optimistic offensive beginning to crumble, "So you got any plans for this fine New York autumn Saturday?"

There was a pause before she replied "Yes actually, I took the night off work, I'm meeting up with some old friends for dinner and a couple of drinks"

"Oh right" Rob replied, hearing his own surprise "anyone I know?"

"No, I don't think so. I haven't seen them in a while, I used to hang out with them quite a lot before we met"

Rob wondered whether that was a trend he should be worried about, he shook the thought from his mind, he simply didn't have the room for jealousy or paranoia, not the relationship kind anyway.

"OK, listen Jo" he let his voice go a little bit softer "you're being careful right, you remember what I told you"

Rob thought he heard something smash from Jo's end of the line, he started to ask if everything was ok but before he'd gotten out more than a syllable he was cut off, she'd already started to yell at him.

"Oh for God's sake, Rob. You know you can worry about me or you can abandon me, it's a real testament to your stubbornness that you think you can do both at the same time. Yes, I'm being careful. I'm looking both ways before I cross the street, I'm anticipating danger from strangers and tourists every time I leave the apartment, I'm jumping out of bed in a panic whenever I hear a floorboard creak in the hallway. Is that what you want? Is that careful enough for you?"

Rob was taken aback by the sheer weight of hostility that she projected down the phone, it took him a couple of seconds to find his voice.

"I'm sorry" he said sincerely "I never meant for this to affect your life so much"

She scoffed and made a noise like she was fighting back the tears.

"No, of course, why would you think that leaving would have any effect on my life?" she asked bitterly.

Rob leaned his forehead against the cold metal of the phone box, it was becoming more and more difficult to believe that he did anything other than ruin people's lives. It was a bitter enough pill to swallow without adding Jo to that list, he refused to leave his destructive mark on her like he had so many others, she was the one he would fight for, he promised himself that.

"I didn't abandon you, ok? I'm coming home, I just have one more job to do in two days' time and then I'll be on the next flight back to New York, alright? Just try and stop me"

The tears were obvious now, it took Jo a few moments to compose herself before she was capable of speaking. Rob left his head where it was, allowing the cold to slowly numb his forehead while he tried to understand his capacity for corrupting people's lives. Even when he acted with the best of intentions it never seemed to work out like he wanted.

"Yeah, well, I've been thinking about that Rob" she said eventually "and honestly if you can't trust me enough to tell me what's really going on then maybe you shouldn't come back at all"

The words hit him like a hammer blow to the chest, he thought back to her comments earlier about her Saturday night plans and wondered whether she had already come to terms with a life that didn't include him. He pushed the thought from his head again, he wouldn't give up that easily.

"Listen, Jo. What you're asking, well it's a bigger conversation that this, please just trust me on that, but I promise you, I'm coming home and when I do we can talk it all through, ok? I promise"

"OK" Jo replied neutrally.

Rob felt his shoulders sag at the response, he'd hoped that his plea would go at least some way to bringing her round, but clearly the ice had a long way to go before it would thaw. He glanced at his watch, he didn't have much time.

"I have to go, there are some things I need to take care of, but Jo, honestly, I love you"

There was a pause at the other end of the line, a pause that was considerably longer than Rob was comfortable with, but eventually Jo replied.

"I love you, too"

Rob hung up the phone and stepped out onto the street, falling into step with the large crowd, all heading in the same direction. Sliding his hands into his pockets he listened to the one inalienable statement that was swirling around inside his head, repeating itself over and over; he was losing her. He realised suddenly that if she did move on before he got back then there would be no one to blame but himself. He'd asked too much of her, he had hidden too much. Even if she was waiting for him when he got back, he wondered whether or not he would be able to tell her the truth. It wasn't that he wouldn't, if he genuinely thought that letting her in would change things then he would do it in a heartbeat, but he knew it wouldn't be that simple. The fact of the matter was that Jo was a good person, a good honest person. And he was a killer, how could she ever absolve herself of that reality, how could she ever look at him the same way again, his chest tightened as the realisation hit home; he would lose her by keeping his secrets and he would lose her by sharing them.

Either way there was nothing he could do now about it now, and he needed to focus. For the first time since his return he felt ever so slightly grateful for the distraction of his duties, if for no other reason than it kept him from obsessing over Jo. With an effort he silenced the part of his brain that continued to dwell on her and instead focused in on the task at hand, just another small step on a very long journey, but it was a pivotal one, and having travelled so far there were only a few more steps left to take.

As Rob acclimatised himself to his surroundings he began to pick up snippets of conversation from the small groups in front, behind and at either side of him, unsurprisingly, as they walked through the streets of Anfield towards the stadium of the same name they all centred around the same topic: Liverpool FC. Rob listened where he could, the group to his left were discussing the team's ability to cope with the current injury to their star striker, to his right a debate was raging over whether they had the strength in depth to sustain a prolonged title challenge, and behind him he heard two men pondering the merits of the clubs various defenders, which ones they would keep and which ones they wouldn't. Rob smiled to himself, comforted by the knowledge that they were precisely the same topics that he had discussed on these streets twenty years earlier, and that others would inevitably be discussing in twenty years' time. Having seen so many changes in his home town since he had returned there was a certain relief in knowing that some things would forever remain the same.

The crowd turned right into a terraced street and Rob followed on auto pilot, listening closely as he tried to get to grips with all the intricacies of his team that he had missed in his ten year absence. As they continued to walk Rob noticed that all of the houses along the street were boarded up, just like they had been when he was young. It bothered him to think that for the thousands of opposing football fans who visited Anfield every year their impression of the city would be largely based on sights like this, doing nothing to distil the national stereotype of unemployment and poverty that had existed since Margaret Thatcher's days in Downing Street. Rob found himself surprised at the level of resentment the thought elicited inside him, though he knew he held little claim to Liverpool now, that New York was his home, the fact of the matter was that he still felt fiercely protective of his home town, and he knew that would never change. He felt pride when he thought about all the city had to offer; its warmth, its commerce, its culture, its two Cathedrals, its bustling city centre, its vibrant night life and its inspiring architecture. With a pang of regret his mind focused in on the Albert Dock, one of Liverpool's most famous landmarks, and now thanks to him its bricks were stained with the blood of its criminals. It was no longer a place of heritage or of culture, now it was a place of notoriety, a testament to the cruelty of the Liverpool people. Rob was once again reminded of his habit for polluting everything that he cared about, he felt his level of self-loathing increase by the second, which in turn only further fuelled the cravings for cocaine. A craving he'd been fighting since the night he killed Wayne Caddock.

Rob took a deep breath and pushed all of the jumbled thoughts to the back of his mind, *now's not the time*, he reminded himself, *there's a job to be done.*

The crowd continued to move at a steady pace, opinions and prejudices being passed back and forth amongst the faithful thousands, and after a few more minutes Rob finally set his eyes upon the grand old stadium. Looking up at the Kop he allowed his youthful memories to overwhelm him, he remembered the magical feeling he always felt in this place, accentuated by the distinctive aroma of burger vans and horse manure that lingered in the background of every memory. Slowly he walked over to the Shankly statue and watched as large groups of tourists took picture after picture of one another. As he watched he considered just how special a place Anfield was, admittedly being a Liverpool fan he was susceptible to bias but still, he'd been to Yankee Stadium, Giants Stadium and had watched the Knicks play in Madison Square Garden, but there was still nothing quite like this.

Glancing at his watch Rob muttered a curse under his breath and made his way towards the turnstile, he was running late. His plans had been accentuating at a faster pace this week, almost too fast for him to keep up with. Since visiting Kelly on Tuesday night it seemed as if his life had gone into overdrive, with a grimace he admitted to himself that he was definitely back in the thick of it now.

It was Wednesday night that had proved to be the catalyst for this sudden shift in gear, his first examination of the Old Oak pub had provided two very pressing insights. The first being that Charlie was right, if he could pin them into the cul-de-sac, cut off their escape and not allow them to surround him, then there was a chance he might just be able to get to Miller. The second was the realisation that this was by far the most difficult hit he had ever been involved in, just circling the pub he'd spotted more than double the amount of bodyguards to what Wayne Caddock had possessed, and that was before even going inside. Five men on the door, four in a black jeep, another four in a blacked out Fiat and an assortment of other individuals scattered around the vicinity whose efforts at subtlety were less than convincing to Rob's keen eyes. All in all a mammoth task that he was less than convinced he could achieve.

On the Thursday night he'd taken the next step and gone inside. The pub was a little less than half full, populated by considerably more men than women, and from the looks his entrance elicited Rob suspected the majority of the patrons conducted some kind of business with Miller's firm, and didn't take too kindly to strangers. Rob ordered a pint of bitter and took out a copy of the Mirror while he waited, a few moments later the bartender, a slim, humourless looking man in his thirties with small green eyes and greased back brown hair returned with his drink, before perching himself on the bar close to where Rob was standing.

The man's line of questioning was as direct as it was discourteous, he wasted little time in asking Rob why he was there, what business he had in the area and what he did for a living, each question more accusing than the last. Rob reeled off his pre-planned story with ease, telling the bartender that he was a salesman at a car dealership who had recently moved into a semi-detached house three streets away. His interrogator was either suitably convinced, or not as interested as his vigorous questioning had suggested, as a few moments later he moved away and began chatting to two men at the other end of the bar.

Rob took a seat at a small table, opened his paper and began reading, sporadically raising his head for a few seconds at a time over a twenty minute period, until eventually he was confident that his mental picture of the room matched the one in front of him.

He was surprised to find that the pub from which Tony Miller based the majority of his operations was unremarkable in almost every way; from the wooden furniture and faded floral wallpaper right the way through to the 90s jukebox and limited lager selection. The Old Oak was the mirror image of a hundred other local pubs scattered across the suburbs of Liverpool, or any other English city for that matter. If there was one difference that marked the small pub as something more than what it was, then it was the insidious quiet that seemed to hang like a veil over the entire room. Though there were at least twenty people scattered in small groups Rob could hear nothing more than hushed whispers over the steady drone of the jukebox. He wondered how much his presence had contributed to the reduction in sound, but as he glanced around at the various groups, talking quickly and gesturing with increasing enthusiasm Rob got the sense that this was simply the way business was conducted on Tony Miller's turf.

Folding the newspaper he leaned back in his chair and tried to find a face in the crowd that had been included in the dossier, but even after surveying each patron twice he found that no one in the pub matched his list of targets. Either he had found his way into the wrong pub, or the man firmly in possession of the dominating stake in the Liverpool crime syndicate was out of the office tonight, and he had taken his big guns with him. Rob wasn't sure what that meant, but he imagined it was unlikely to bode well for the current task at hand, or the man funding it.

Keen not to outstay his welcome Rob finished off the pint and made his way out of the pub with one thought at the forefront of his mind; to get the job done he was going to need some help.

Which brought Rob back to Anfield, and to an associate he hadn't seen in a very long time. As soon as he'd left the Old Oak in Wavertree, he'd made his way across the city to Anfield, and to another pub; the Albert, arriving half an hour before last orders. It had been a gamble, there was no way of knowing whether the system they had used over a decade earlier would still be in use, but Rob knew of no other way to get in touch with the man, and he didn't know anybody else who could get him what he needed.

In retrospect it was a risk Rob had been foolish to take, relying on a means of communication that was over ten years old was wrought with all sorts of dangers, the most prominent of which being that it was susceptible to interception from both the police, and potential enemies. Yet as it turned out it had been a risk worth taking, Rob had left a message with the barmaid, using the code he was surprised to realise he hadn't forgotten and took a seat in the corner with his second pint of bitter of the night. After fifteen minutes the barmaid had approached the table with his change and a ticket for Liverpool- Tottenham Hotspur game in two days' time.

So here he was, passing through the turnstiles and making his way towards row N of the Kop. From there he would wait for someone to make contact and hopefully tell him what to do next. As he stepped out of the tunnel and into the crisp autumn air Rob felt the hairs stand up on the back of his neck, the ground was more than three quarters full and the air of anticipation was prominent over the sound of music, but that wasn't why Rob's body was tense, it was tense because somewhere, amongst the thousands of people inside the stadium, he could feel eyes watching his every move.

Heading back down into the tunnel Rob bought a programme, and then spent five minutes queuing for a coffee in the hope of drawing out whoever was keeping tabs on him. It was a wasted effort, his shadow knew what they were doing and Rob got no greater hint than the vague impression at the back of his mind. If his senses hadn't have been right so many times before he may have even dismissed the feeling as paranoia, but as it was he kept his mind focused and his eyes on the crowd while making his way back into the stand and towards his seat.

His ticket led him to a row halfway up the Kop, to a seat that was the first one on its row. If the contact wanted to approach him then the seat gave them easy access to whisper something in his ear or pass him a note. Rob was equally aware of the alternative, if someone wanted to put a gun to his head, or slide a knife between his ribs he would be just as accessible, but that was a risk he'd already accepted. He kept a watchful eye on the crowd around him but as the seconds ticked closer to kick off their attention grew steadily more focused on the pitch below. Sitting down on the cold plastic chair Rob joined them, casually scanning the crowd every few minutes as he tried to fight the sickening feeling of impotence that rested in the pit of his stomach.

The game kicked off to a thick wall of noise as people all around him threw encouragement and criticism in equal measure at the twenty two men below. He tried to follow the game but before long his concentration started to wane, it was that feeling in his stomach, growing stronger and stronger with each passing minute.

The first forty five minutes sped by in a haze, focusing on the football became an increasingly difficult task as the implications of his potential meeting gained prominence in his mind. Only once, when Liverpool scored, did Rob allow himself to fully embrace the feelings of unity and passion that seemed to define the crowd, an experience that was complemented by the hug he received from the man next to him. It struck him as odd that football offered the only real exemption to the rule of physical contact among strangers, but he allowed himself to consider the oddity for only a moment before he slammed the door shut and returned his focus to the crowd.

It wasn't until the 78th minute, with the score still at one nil that a man stepped down onto Rob's row and settled in beside him, though his gaze remained focused on the match Rob could tell that the man was aware of every movement he made, this was the person who had been watching him, he knew it in his gut.

"Not a bad game" the man said, reaching into his pocket, removing a piece of chewing gum and sliding it into his mouth "they've played at a good tempo but they need to take more of their chances, a better team than this and we'd be drawing by now"

Rob allowed himself a few seconds to look at the man beside him, he was about the same height, though Rob suspected his new friend was close to ten years older. He had short, dark hair flickered with grey along with a thin layer of stubble that was a similar colour, his olive skin was heavily wrinkled as if years of bad weather and hard graft had taken its toll on his features. Though the man was in his forties he was in good physical shape and had the air of someone was not unaccustomed to physical violence. Rob responded with a grunt and returned his attention to the game.

"So you're Mr Smith, then?" the man said, turning to face him.

Rob mimicked the gesture and felt the man weighing him up "That I am"

"And you want to see the boss?"

"That I do"

The two men locked eyes, something happened on the pitch that caused a roar of outrage to spread around the stadium, but it had no effect on the man or Rob as they continued to hold one another's gaze.

"Boss says he hasn't heard from you in a while, says I'm to check you out, make sure you're on the level. When people go away they tend to go away for a reason, they come back they usually do that for a reason too, if you get my meaning"

Rob nodded "My reason for seeing Frank is the same as ever. He's always done right by me, I've got no interest in going down that road"

The man considered Rob's answer and turned towards the football, when he turned back his decision appeared to have been made.

"He reckoned you'd say something like that. He'll be expecting you in the Sandon after the game, you brought the money, right?"

Rob gave another nod as he subconsciously pressed his left elbow against the money belt around his waist. The man regarded Rob for another moment before turning away and making his way towards the exit.

Turning back towards the pitch Rob watched the final ten minutes, impatiently waiting for the game to end, at the sound of the whistle he fell in amongst the crowd and slowly made his way out of the ground. Around him people muttered satisfied appraisals, but Rob was already deaf to their observations, he had business to take care of.

Navigating his way through the crowd took longer than expected, every corner he turned he saw waves of people moving towards him and slowing his progress like a fish trying to swim upstream. Eventually he made his way out of the grounds and down the street to the Sandon, a small line of people were already queuing to get inside the pub, keen to augment their adrenaline with alcohol. He joined the back and waited, checking again that the money belt was still securely fastened around his waist.

It took a little over five minutes but eventually Rob made it inside, the pub was already full beyond capacity, directly opposite the entrance he watched as an overstaffed bar frantically tried to serve the throng of customers huddled all around them.

He squeezed through the crowd and made his way towards the back room, the further he got from the bar the easier it became to navigate until he reached a part of the pub that was considerably less congested.

Stepping into the back room he was greeted by the bellowing sound of football chants, close to twenty blokes were scattered around the room including the one who'd sought him out earlier, acknowledging his presence with only the slightest nod of the head. Despite their jovial mood they all gave the impression of being hard men, he assessed each one long enough to confirm they weren't who he was looking for, before moving on to the next. Eventually his eyes settled on a booth in the corner, at first it was difficult to tell specifics about the three men as they bounced up and down on the bench, but as they took their arms from around each other's shoulders he got a clear view of Frank Rowell singing along in full voice.

Rob crossed his arms and watched; Frank had always been a little plump but at some point in the previous ten years he had crossed the line into overweight. His blond hair had receded deep into his head leaving behind a much rounder face with large, red cheeks protruding on either side. The Liverpool shirt he wore was at least two sizes to small and failed to cover the flab around his midriff, Rob noticed that the shirt was inching higher and higher with every sway he made in time with the chorus. The appearance was even more striking in contrast to the hardened forms of the men around him, but then Rob knew that was no coincidence, Frankie Rowell paid them to look tough so he wouldn't have to.

When the song came to an end Frank patted backs all around and stepped down onto the carpeted floor, spotting Rob standing across the room he smiled, took three long strides to cover the distance and extended his right arm in Rob's direction.

"So it is you after all" Frank said, grabbing Rob's hand and squeezing it tightly.

"Too right Frankie" Rob replied, feeling a fondness for the large man that he hadn't quite expected "how you been?"

Frank flashed a cheeky grin and shrugged his shoulder "Me? Enjoying life fella, enjoying life. That's how I've been" he turned to face the others and raised his hands high in the air "OH WHEN THE REDS, GO MARCHING IN, OH WHEN THE REDS GO MARCHING IN..."

The chant ignited in the small back room, within seconds it had spread throughout the main bar, satisfied Frank returned his attention to Rob.

"So, I got your request..."

Rob cautiously glanced over each shoulder, aware that they were speaking in public, Frank had always been one for prudence, that was one of the main reasons why they had gotten on so well.

"Yeah?"

"Yeah" Frank repeated, a guarded look coming over his features "Bit of a surprise after all this time. You know a guy doesn't easily step in and out of your line of work"

Rob let out a cold laugh "I'd never make the mistake of calling it easy"

Frank wiped his brow with the back of his hand and looked around the room, finding what he wanted over Rob's shoulder he raised his right hand in the air "Trev!" Rob turned to see the man he'd spoken to at the game walking slowly over, when he reached them he put his arm behind his back and waited, Rob turned back towards Frank and gave a questioning look.

"Trevor's going to search you" Frank said matter-of-factly "No offence intended, it's not that I don't trust you, but a man has to be careful, you understand that. So let the man do his job without the aggro, let's not have any Johnny big balls today, alright?"

Trevor took a step towards him, there was a confidence in his eyes that said he would be ready if things got physical, Rob suspected he was probably hoping it would go down that road. He held out his right hand to stop Trevor in his tracks and used his left to unfasten the money belt around his waist. Pulling the belt free he held it out to the side, raising both arms in preparation of the search.

"Wouldn't dream of it Frankie" Rob replied, flashing the two men his best care free smile.

Frank gestured for his employee to begin "Good man"

Trevor stepped forward and padded Rob down, it was a thorough search but not one that was overly physical, after a few moments he stepped away and nodded towards his boss.

"Clean" the word muffled by the chewing gum in Trevor's mouth.

"Excellent" Frank gave a satisfied nod and began walking; it was only after a couple of steps that Rob noticed he was moving towards a door on the far wall. The realisation annoyed him, he liked to think highly of his own observational skills but he hadn't even noticed it was there "follow me to my office Mr Smith, and let's see what I can interest you in today"

Frank opened the door and stepped inside, holding it open as Rob passed through. The room was fairly small, no larger than fifteen feet in either width or length, but it had just enough room for a desk and a metal cupboard. Frank took a few steps back and leaned on the edge of the former, Rob stayed where he was in the middle of the room.

"I'd ask where you've been Rob, but to be blunt, I don't really care"

Rob rolled up the money belt and gripped it tightly in his left hand "Appreciate the honesty"

"As well you should. As long as you keep yourself away from the long arm of the law then as far as I'm concerned your business is your business, I'm happy to leave you to it. That said I'll be honest, on occasion I have missed your distinctive brand of violence around these parts. The majority of my clients are excessively boring, and excessively predictable. It's nice to work with villains who have a little bit more creativity, its brightens my day no end"

Rob smiled, though Frank Rowell was well into his fifties there was something almost childlike about him, that wasn't to say he wasn't dangerous, like all men in their trade he had more blood on his hands than he probably cared to remember, but he offset those shortcomings with a humour Rob wasn't used to. He liked dealing with Frank Rowell, he suspected the man would have been just as well suited to being an office manager as he was an arms dealer.

"I do like to keep you guessing Frank, how is business these days?"

Frank let out a short whistle "Good lad, very good, and it's been getting better and better since one of our major players got released from prison. Suddenly every two bit villain in town feels the need to tool up, the demand is absolutely ridiculous, the buggers are clearing me out!"

"At a fair price though, right?" Rob asked.

Frank threw Rob a savvy look "Well of course, but even my supplies have their limits. There's a hurricane on the way and the supermarkets down to its last few cans"

"Ain't that the truth" Rob said, feeling his mood darken, more weapons on the streets, more ripples in the pond. How many more people would he indirectly kill by finishing what he had started, "You got what I asked for?"

"Well..." Frank stood up and moved towards the metal cupboard in the corner, taking a key from around his neck he opened it and removed a black shoulder bag.

Bag in hand he walked across the room and handed it to Rob, putting the bag on the floor and dropping to one knee he began to unzip it while Frank returned to the cupboard.

Rob peered inside, he lifted up the contents surveyed it in his hand, slowly he placed it back in the bag; C-4.

"This isn't what I asked for" Rob said sternly.

Frank closed the metal door on the cupboard "What's wrong with it?"

"You know what's wrong with it"

"I really don't"

Rob tried to keep his composer, he was being messed about and he didn't like it "I need something more versatile"

"Why, you planning on eating it?"

Rob took a deep breath "Frank, I need a Primary Explosive, not Secondary" he tried to phrase his words carefully, Frank had always been a reasonable man but he was also a very proud weapons trafficker with twenty hardened men ready to kill for him on the other side of the door "I need my explosives to explode, one way or another, if your shit doesn't work then C-4 isn't gonna cut it, I'll be fucked and I can't let that happen"

Frank stepped away from the cupboard and folded his arms, his face was difficult to read and Rob found himself staring into the man's eyes waiting for a response.

"You know" Frank said slowly "A lesser man than me might take offence"

"Would a lesser man give me what I wanted?"

Frank nodded towards the bag on the floor "This is cheaper"

Rob shook his head "I don't care about the money"

"It's easier to come by"

"That never stopped you before"

Frank let out a nervous laugh "Well, it's like I said isn't it, I'm looking at a saturated market at the moment"

"Really?"

Frank shrugged his shoulders "It is what it is"

Rob took a step forward and stared into Frank's round face "You know what I think it is? I think it's that if someone comes around asking questions about C-4 then you can shrug your shoulders and send them on to another twenty people who might have supplied it, but if Acetone Peroxide suddenly hit's the streets then we're talking about a much smaller group aren't we? You and what, maybe three, four other guys? I know you're not worried about the police, they were coming after you ten years before I left and you're still here, so my only guess is that you're worried about the people I'm going to use it against, am I close?"

Frank looked at the floor for a moment while he considered Rob's words, he must have known who Rob's target was. Unless he'd been living under a rock for the last two weeks then Wayne Caddock's murder would have resonated loudly not only with Frank, but with each and every one of his clients. Frank was one of the few men who knew Rob's modus operandi, and though they'd never discussed it directly it was clear the weapons trafficker knew that it was Stephen McSharry who signed Rob's cheques. Were Frank's stonewalling attempts symptomatic of a lack of faith in Rob's ability to get the job done, or was he simply hedging his bets by keeping off the radar of the cities established criminal order? Either way he needed Frank's products, without them his chances of getting close enough to Tony Miller were almost non-existent.

After what seemed like an eternity Frank looked up from the floor and regarded Rob thoughtfully "I would have thought you of all people would appreciate a mans need for anonymity" he said ruefully "God knows I've gone above and beyond to protect yours over the years"

Rob recognised the truth of the words and felt an immediate pang of guilt for putting the man in the crosshairs of the Miller crew. The fact of the matter was that Rob's arrangement with Frank had made it possible for him to keep his identity secret from the whispering lips of the Liverpool underworld. Frank Rowell had gone to enormous lengths to keep that secret, to the extent that none of the man's employees had even heard the name of Rob Thomas, or dealt with him on more than one occasion. It was an arrangement that had worked out well for both of them; Rob managed to remain an unknown entity to those he hunted while Frank was able to avoid culpability in more than a few controversial gangland hits.

But as Rob was constantly discovering, this wasn't the old days anymore, things had most definitely changed. Making an enemy of Tony Miller was not on anyone's list of priorities, even amongst the most hardened of criminal elements. It was testament to the man's viciousness that such a city wide ethos had somehow managed to develop, he respected that kind of power but at the same time he resented the way it restricted his options. Tony Miller needed to be put down, that was all Rob needed to know, all he had to do was convince Frank Rowell of the same thing.

"You did go above and beyond, and I appreciate that" Rob began "but Frankie, I need that Acetone Peroxide, without it I'm a fucking dead man. We've done a lot of business together, so let me ask you a question; when have I ever let a loose end find its way back to you?"

Frank shook his head as if he was trying to shake a thought away, with a morose grin he moved off towards the metal cupboard and returned a few seconds later. He handed Rob another bag, this one slightly smaller than the first. He looked inside; Acetone Peroxide.

"Thank you Frankie" he said, "I really appreciate it"

"Don't thank me yet" Frank said, picking up the C-4 bag with his left hand and extending his right "Four grand"

Rob placed the money belt in Frank's outstretched hand and watched as he returned the first bag to the cupboard, counted the money and locked it inside with the explosives. Returning the key around his neck the big man returned to his perch at the edge of the desk, Rob surveyed his purchase, enough AP for two medium size explosions, precisely what he needed.

"You know Rob" Frankie begun, his body language was a little more relaxed but Rob could still sense a guarded edge to his tone "you make me curious, you really do. I'm tempted to ask what precisely it is you plan to use this for, and I probably would, if I wasn't so certain that I wouldn't want to know"

Rob smiled "Trust that instinct Frankie, you always were a smart man"

Frank nodded as if he agreed, then suddenly his face darkened "But for old time's sake I think I should warn you, be careful"

The tone seemed knowing, Rob felt a vague feeling of foreboding rise in his chest, and took a step forward "Be careful of what?"

Frank looked away, as if struggling to find the words, when he turned back there was a hint of anguish in his eyes "You know what this towns like Rob, people always planning, scores always being settled. The word in parts is that some plans are more in place than others. Be careful you're not doing what you're doing for the wrong people, the kind of people who might be dead before they get a chance to thank you"

Rob nodded in understanding "Appreciate it"

Pushing himself up Frank wrapped an arm around Rob's shoulder and led him towards the door. The large man seemed more at ease now that their business was drawing to an end, from Rob's perspective he found himself anxiously gripping the bag, this soon after the game the area would still be heavily policed and if he was discovered with a bag of explosives, well that would prove to be a spanner in the works even he couldn't overcome.

The door opened and the sound of chanting hit Rob like a wave, Frank raised his right arm in the air and joined in, his left was still draped over Rob's shoulder as he ushered them both into the middle of the room, finishing the chant he leaned in towards Rob's ear and shouted over the noise.

"You need anything else, you just let me know!"

Rob nodded and patted the arms trafficker on the back, using the opportunity to disengage from the man's grip, as he took a step backward Frank leaned in a second time.

"You wanna stay for some beers Smithy? This parties gonna be going on all night the mood these boys are in!"

Rob smiled and shook his head, tightening his grip on the bag.

"Can't Frankie, I'm late for dinner at my mother's"

Giving a quick thumbs up Rob backed out of the room and made his way out of the pub. The main bar was less condensed than it had been earlier, which was a blessing, Acetone Peroxide was a lot more combustible than C-4, he wasn't sure whether a stray cigarette or a hard bang would be enough to detonate it but he had no intention of finding out first hand. Stepping out into the cold evening air he started walking, he'd managed to solve one problem today, now Rob had to move on to the next one; his mother.

The walk from Anfield to his mother's house took a little less than half an hour, but diverting via his one bedroom flat in Bootle added nearly an hour to the trip, due in no small part to the post game traffic.

Rob briefly considered going straight there but decided against it, Vera Thomas was a curious creature at the best of times, any baggage that came with him was almost certain to be scrutinised with the same kind of vague distaste with which she judged all aspects of his life. On top of that Rob suspected that if he was forced to listen to too much of her criticism he might be liable to detonate the explosives right there in the middle of her dining room, just to be done with it.

So he took the long route, a route that got him to his mother's front door 45 minutes after she'd planned to serve dinner, knocking twice he suddenly wished he had brought the explosives after all.

The door opened with a creak and Rob looked down at the small, blond woman who had raised him. Physically there was little similarity between either of the brothers and their mother, where she was blond they were dark, and where she was short they were tall. Apparently both he and Charlie had taken the majority of their features from their father, a crime for which it seemed Vera had never entirely forgiven them.

"Robert..." Vera said, squinting and shuffling towards him, a cigarette held tightly between the fingers of her left hand "What time do you call this, you're an hour late. Come here and give me a hug"

Stepping over the threshold Rob leaned down and hugged his mother, it was only the second time he'd seen her since returning home and before the door had closed he was already feeling the need to escape.

"Yeah, sorry about that Mum" Rob said, giving her a squeeze and stepping away.

Vera shook her head and slid the cigarette between her lips, slowly she turned and began shuffling towards the living room.

"Sorry, he says. You were always late, even as a boy. Late for dinner, late for school, late getting to bed, late getting out of bed. It shows a lack of respect you know, but then you got that from your father, he had a sizeable selfish streak as well"

Rob was glad that he was facing her back, it gave him the opportunity to roll his eyes "I'll try and work on that" he muttered.

Vera led them into the living room and through to the kitchen. Charlie was already sat at the table, rocking a sleeping baby in his arms, with Vicky seated next to him. Sat on the floor with a colouring book in her lap and a half eaten plate of chips at her side was a little girl who the process of elimination told him was Alexis, she looked up eagerly when she heard Rob enter the room but, not recognising the new visitor, cautiously returned her gaze to the book.

"Sit down" Vera told him sternly "I'll bring dinner through. Cold now no doubt, but I'll bring it through nonetheless"

"Alright, lid!" Charlie said, as Rob took his seat on the opposite side of the table. His eyes met Vicky's and he smiled, a gesture that was returned instantaneously.

"Hello folks" replied Rob, shuffling closer to the table.

"What time do you call this? We're bloody starving over here!" Charlie said, keeping his voice low so as to not wake the baby.

"Sorry, got delayed coming out of the match"

His explanation seemed to impress his brother and Charlie gave him an approving smile "Good game then?"

Rob thought about his meeting with Frank Rowell.

"I think so yeah, all things considered"

The smell of food filled the room as Vera brought in two plates and set them in front of Charlie and Vicky, Rob eyed the roast dinners, with thick slices of beef dripping with gravy and suddenly realised he was famished. A second later Vera returned from the kitchen with two more plates, dropping one in front of Rob and sitting down with the other.

"Well, here we are. Took me most of the day to get this ready, but nothings too good for my family. The beef may be a little cold, but I think we all know why that is"

"Yeah, Rob!" Charlie added childishly, picking up a fork with his right hand while his left kept Zoe in place.

"This smells fantastic Vera" Vicky said politely. She was looking a lot better than the last time Rob had seen her. She was wearing her light brown hair down, in curls, and a thin layer of makeup made her look a few years younger, and a lot less tired, than on the previous occasion they had met. But more than that there was a pleasantness in her eyes, eclipsing the constrained hostility he had last seen, which made her face seem softer, Rob realised for the first time that she was actually quite an attractive woman.

"Well thank you dearie" Vera responded warmly.

"These potatoes are amazing" Vicky added excitedly, covering her mouth while he finished chewing "How do you get that golden colour?"

Vera leaned forward mysteriously, as if she feared who else might hear "Ah, a little secret of mine" she whispered "You soak them in goose fat overnight and it does absolute wonders"

Rob watched his sister in law raise her eyebrows in surprise and wondered if his mother could sense the polite insincerity behind the gesture. Probably not, Vera had never been the most intuitive of people, and her idea of a lively conversation probably wasn't the same as the other three adults around the table. He tried to imagine Jo sat here with his family, politely enquiring about cooking tips and trying to impress his mother. Somehow, the concept seemed too alien to envisage, though that wasn't an altogether bad thing.

"Goose fat, really?" enquired Vicky "I'll have to try that out the next time you come round for dinner"

"You have to use real potatoes mind" Vera warned, pointing her fork at Vicky "None of this frozen rubbish, can't get a proper taste with frozen potatoes"

Charlie shuffled Zoe closer to his shoulder, she responded with a murmur before drifting off back to sleep.

"No chance of that mar, Vicky's never cooked a meal in her life that didn't start out with a frozen centre, have you darling?"

Vicky playfully elbowed him in the arm "Get lost, you cheeky bugger"

Rob watched the exchange and smiled, it was hard to imagine his little brother as anything other than the consistent fuck up that he'd been as a kid, particularly after his little stunt at McSharry's house, but here he was playing the doting family man and playing it well. If cases were being made for the position of family fuck up, Rob couldn't deny that he was at least as likely a candidate as Charlie.

"Now, now children, no bickering at the table" Vera said reproachfully, she was clearly not as touched by their banter as Rob was "But really Vicky, children should be eating fresh food. How do you expect them to grow up big and strong if you keep feeding them this processed nonsense?"

Vicky nodded like a child who'd just been told off, which seemed to be how most people responded to their mother.

"I know Vera, I know. It's just finding the time" Vicky replied, wrapping herself around Charlie's left arm "Once my dearly beloved starts helping out a little more with the kids then I'll be able to experiment a bit more in the kitchen!"

"No, no, don't try and turn this around on me" Charlie told her "I'm the hunter, alright? The breadwinner, my job is to keep the fridge stocked, maybe to keep you in expensive jewellery as well"

Charlie looked down towards Vicky's neck, she responded with a bashful smile, her cheeks blushing. Rob followed his brothers gaze and noticed the shiny silver necklace half hidden under Vicky's collar. He didn't know much about jewellery but Rob knew expensive when he saw it. A wave of anger washed over him as he realised there was only one way Charlie would have been able to afford a necklace like that, a conversation with his brother was needed, and in private.

Vicky's face continued to blush "Yeah, well... whatever"

Rob focussed on the food in front of him and tried to suppress his feelings towards Charlie. Whatever his brother had done for the twisted old gangster it had been enough to get him a pretty sizeable pay off, but that conversation would come, and there was no use alerting Vera or Vicky to the fact that there was a problem. Stabbing another piece of beef with his fork he shoved it into his mouth and focused his rage on chewing the meat as fiercely as possible.

"So... Robert" Vera said after a couple of minutes of silence "how is this job of yours going?"

Rob and Charlie shared a brief glance across the table, Rob quickly turned his attention back to the food, slicing open a potato as he spoke.

"Quite smoothly so far, not too many complaints. There's still quite a lot to do though"

Vera looked at him suspiciously "But you're not making a mess of it? Getting yourself into trouble or anything like that?"

Rob suppressed a sigh "Not yet, no"

"I have to say I'm a little surprised that you're still here. I mean, going on previous experience, well I'd have thought you'd have been long gone by now"

Once again Rob met Charlie's gaze and he saw the look of amusement in his brothers eyes.

"Sometimes I surprise even myself" he told her, shovelling a fork full of potato into his mouth.

Across the table Rob heard Charlie let out a small laugh, which he quickly disguised as a cooing noise for Zoe. A moment later, Vera pushed the plate away from her and stood up from the table.

"Well, I think that's enough for me. The beef is much too cold, can't enjoy a roast with cold meat. I think I'll go into the back for a cigarette"

Rob watched his mother hobble into the kitchen, fighting the urge to respond to her little comments. When he returned his attention to the table

Zoe was awake and both of her parents had abandoned their dinner, trying to amuse her by pulling faces and making hand gestures.

"She's getting big, isn't she?" Charlie commented.

Vicky smiled at her daughter and tapped her on the nose "That's cos she never stops eating, like her father"

"You've got an appetite for life, haven't ya baby girl!" Charlie said, lifting her into the air until she laughed "You'll be talking soon, I can tell, my little princess has something to say, don't you? Let's just hope you do take after me, you talk as much as your mother and no one's going to get a minutes peace, are they?"

Vicky gave him another nudge in the arm.

"I don't know why I put up with you" she muttered.

"Because you're as patient as you are beautiful sweetheart" he spoke in a condescending tone that seemed to impress her "almost as beautiful as that necklace"

A moment later Vicky was blushing once again, a girlish smile spread across her face as she nuzzled into her husband's shoulder. Charlie turned his attention towards Rob and gave him a wink.

"So Robbo, listen up, me and the missus have been talking. We're thinking about maybe coming over to NYC for a week or two, probably in the new year. Let the kids spend some quality time with their auntie and uncle"

"Yeah?" Rob asked, his eyes darted towards Alexis, his niece who he was yet to be introduced to.

"Yeah, you know, we haven't been on holiday since Zoe was born and Vicky's always fancied going to New York. Besides, I wanna meet this bird of yours, make sure Jo isn't short for Joseph, or anything like that! So, what do you think?"

Rob paused, what he thought was that his brother was getting in deeper with Stephen McSharry than he'd initially suspected. Expensive jewellery and trips to America, his brother would have to be providing a valuable service to receive those kinds of reparations, and where McSharry was involved valuable usually meant risky, and it usually meant murder.

"I think it sounds like a pretty good idea" he said eventually "I know Jo will love to have you guys over, she always talks about how much she wants to meet the family"

The words caught in his throat but he forced them out anyway. He placed his odds at close to fifty-fifty as to whether Jo would be waiting for him when he got back, he didn't want to dwell on the possibility that she wouldn't, but the thought was a difficult one to keep out.

"Have you two been together long?" Vicky asked, evidently mistaking his look of dread for one of longing.

"Four years"

"Any plans to propose?"

Rob shook his head dismissively "We've got some problems we need to resolve. Some pretty big problems actually, but who knows, maybe"

Vicky looked at him sympathetically; he saw the hint of condescension in her eyes, like she was trying to explain something a child. The way women usually look when they explain relationships to men.

"There's always problems to resolve, sometimes you just have to get on with it"

Unable to think of a satisfactory response, Rob nodded and smiled at his sister-in-law.

"Bollocks" Charlie said, denting the serene atmosphere around the table "I think she needs her nappy changing, you wanna take her upstairs darling?"

"Not a chance Mr! I changed her this morning"

Charlie let out a sigh and stood up, adjusting Zoe in his arms "Fine, where's the bag?" he muttered petulantly. Reaching under the table Vicky grabbed a pink bag and placed the strap over Charlie's shoulder "I have to do all the bloody work, as usual"

"Enjoy" Vicky said, smiling as she watched him exit the room, once he was gone she turned her attention back to Rob, resting her head in her hands and smiling an apologetic smile "Sorry about before, putting you on the spot with the whole New York thing. I told him to mention it to you in private, and give you a few days to talk to your girlfriend, but you know what he's like once he gets an idea in his head, there's just no stopping him"

Rob nodded in agreement "He is an impetuous son of a bitch, no doubt about it"

"We don't have to come, if it's an inconvenience I mean" Vicky offered, her concern reminded Rob that they were still practically strangers, the rules of polite society could still not be ignored the way they could with family.

"No, don't be ridiculous" he said waving away her protest "It'll be great to have you guys over. Have you ever been to the states before?"

"Me? God no" she replied, as if it was the most ridiculous question in the world "I've only ever been abroad once, and that was when I was nineteen. Me and a couple of friends went over to Tenerife for a week. A few months later I met Charlie, and six months after that I was pregnant with Alexis"

Rob tried not to grimace at the sheltered existence Vicky had lived, to his mind being trapped like that was a fate worse than death, but he did his best to keep the emotions from his face and turned the conversation in a more positive direction.

"You'll love New York, it's another world. Compared to this place, to all of this, it's just a completely different world"

She leaned further forward, her head still resting in her hands as she examined him "You don't like it here much, do you?"

Rob smiled "Honestly, I'm not sure. Me and Liverpool, it's a love hate thing"

Vicky nodded in understanding "I feel the same way about your brother" she joked "So, do you think you want kids?"

297

The question made him think about all the fathers he'd killed, he pushed the thought back "I'm not sure I'm the paternal type"

"Men usually aren't before they have them" Vicky said reassuringly "I'm sure you'd be a great dad"

"Did you always want to be a mum?" Rob asked, it was the first question that came into his head, but having so many focused on him was becoming increasingly uncomfortable.

"Ever since I was a little girl. I can remember holding my baby sister when I was eight, and it just felt right, natural. It must be hard to understand but being a mum, sometimes I think it was kind of what I was meant to do, you know? I probably sound like a right loser"

"No, you don't" Rob assured her, he knew the feeling, more than he cared to admit "I understand. It's like my job, there are times I hate it, and there are times I wish to God I could do something else. But when I do it well, I get this feeling in the pit of my stomach, like this is what I was born for, like it's who I am"

Vicky was staring at him intently now, and Rob realised he was probably talking a little bit too much.

"What is it you do again?" she asked with genuine interest.

"Construction"

"Construction?"

Rob cleared his throat "Yeah, I work construction, for one of the big multi nationals"

"Oh, ok" Vicky said, a little taken aback "So you just compared my kids to building houses?"

"I guess so, is that a little odd?"

Vicky gave him a warm smile and nodded "A bit"

The sound of heavy footsteps thudding down the stairs tore their attention away from each other and towards the living room door. They watched as seconds later Charlie came marching through, shaking his head from side to side.

"There's something wrong with that kid, I mean Jesus, a healthy creature does not make that kind of smell. We're out of wipes darling, I'm going to run the shops and pick some up, you alright watching her till I get back?"

Vicky was up from her seat in a flash.

"You left her up there on her own? For fuck's sake Charlie!"

For a moment Rob was reminded of how he had seen their relationship when he'd first gotten back, the accusing tone he remembered from that day, though much fainter, had returned for a moment, and from the hesitant look on Charlie's face he hadn't missed it either. Rob glanced at the floor, half expecting a fight to erupt at any second, but it never came, Vicky had disappeared upstairs before there'd been a chance to respond, leaving Charlie standing in the doorway looking slightly confused.

"I'll come with you?" Rob offered, as keen to interrupt the awkward silence as he was to get a moment alone with his brother.

"Yeah? Alright"

The two brothers stepped out onto the dark street of their childhood home, the nearest shop was a five minute walk, as kids it had been owned by a likeable Indian man named Jatin who always gave them free sweets when they came to buy the paper for their mother. As Rob and Charlie got older their relationship with the older man soured as they delved deeper and deeper into their delinquent phase. Rob wondered whether Jatin still worked behind the counter, and if he did whether he would remember the two young punks who used to like to steal porn mags. Probably not, in a place like Kirkdale cheeky little shits were ten to the penny, he and Charlie had been nothing special, just two more rotten eggs in a derelict basket.

They walked a couple of steps in silence, the tension building as they went, eventually it was Charlie who snapped, refusing to look at Rob when he spoke.

"Alright then big brother, let's have it, I'm ready for my scolding"

Rob shook his head and kept on walking.

"You're a fucking idiot"

"You're just putting that together, Robbo?"

"What the hell were you thinking?"

"I dunno, it just happened didn't it? I saw an opportunity to make an impression on a powerful man-"

"A killer" Rob corrected, not giving Charlie a chance to continue.

"Whatever, a man with connections, with fucking money! I saw an opportunity and I took it!"

"You haven't listened to a god damn word I've said about these bastards, have you?"

"I listened. But maybe I'm not as sensitive as you, maybe I don't share this fucking military code of honour bullshit that you've been carrying around since you quit. It's a fucked up world Robbo, and you get ahead in fucked up ways. I deserve a piece of it as much as anybody else"

Rob had forgotten how much talking to his brother could resemble talking to a brick wall, he didn't know how many warnings he had left to give.

"You don't know what you're getting yourself into Charlie. They'll chew you up and spit you out, and I won't be there to protect you this time"

It wasn't difficult to tell when Charlie had taken offence, spitting in front of him he quickened his pace, bouncing as he walked like a gangster in a rap video.

"Fuck you and your protection lad, you have no idea what I'm capable of"

Rob saw through his brother's bravado as clearly as he had when they were kids, when Charlie would claim to have beaten the hell out of one of Kirkdale's hardest youths. He grabbed Charlie by the arm and swung him round until they were face to face.

"Explain it to me"

299

Charlie held his gaze for a good ten seconds, there was anger there as well as resentment, he didn't think Rob was giving him the respect he deserved, and it was a very bad sign if he already felt he had done enough to earn it. Despite his concern Rob kept his face like stone, matching his brothers' stare and not letting a hint of emotion touch his features. Charlie cracked first, looking down and walking away.

"You need to chill the fuck out, lad" Charlie said as Rob fell in a step behind "All I did was take them down to Bootle and point them in the direction of some people worth knowing. That was it, no big deal"

The words were clear enough, but Rob caught something in his brothers tone that sounded unnatural, a worried pause that told him more than any words could.

"You sure?"

For a few seconds Charlie didn't respond, but when he did his voice resumed its usual arrogance.

"Course I'm sure"

"And what do you get in return?"

"Well, if you need to know, they're giving me my own package. McSharry says they've got a shipment of pills coming in Thursday at Seaforth Docks. Says he's going to let me run point for the whole of Bootle, give it a month and see how I do"

Charlie selling drugs for Stephen McSharry, not an unexpected development but definitely an unwelcome one, he tried to think of a persuasive argument to dissuade his brother but as usual the same tired words came to mind.

"It's a fucking mistake Charlie"

His brother laughed "Nah, its fucking money big brother. This works out and I'm fucking made" Rob couldn't help giving Charlie a cynical glance that didn't go unnoticed "Just let me be, alright? I know what I'm doing"

"Fine, do what you bloody want"

"I will, anyway don't you think you should be worrying about your own problems right now?"

The rare valid point, the only thing that could stop Rob's indignation in its tracks.

"I am" he admitted.

Charlie looked at his brother, there was a hint of sympathy there, just a hint, the fire from their debate hadn't quite burnt out.

"You know what you're going to do?"

"I'm going to kill him. Tuesday night, I'm going to go to the Old Oak, and I'm going to fucking kill him"

"What about his people?"

"I'm going to kill them too"

"No, I mean how. The numbers aren't exactly on your side are they mate? You sure you don't need some help?"

Rob bit back a belligerent reply, Charlie might be trying to climb the criminal ladder as fast as he could, but he was also trying to help.

"I've got it covered"

"So what's the plan?"

Rob considered the question before he replied.

"Go in and start shooting"

"Elaborate. You all set?"

"I reckon so. Just need to make my peace with God and I'm good to go"

Rob looked up at the sky, not sure if he was being serious or not. It was a clear night and though the glare of the streetlights kept the majority of the stars hidden, a few still shone through, reminding Rob how insignificant his problems really were.

"You'll be fine" Charlie said, offering a reassuring pat on the back "You always are"

They walked in silence for a while as Rob considered Charlie's last words, he'd always done fine before, but wasn't that how these stories went? On the last job, when the finish line was in sight, that was usually when your luck ran out. A second's hesitation, one rushed mistake made out of eagerness and that was the game, Rob knew there was a poetic irony to his current train of thought, and that kind of thing could be more dangerous than a hundred loaded guns. He looked towards the sky one last time and then looked over at his brother.

"You and Vicky seem to be doing better?"

Charlie smiled, it was an honest, warm smile that he wasn't used to seeing.

"Yeah we are. Don't know if it's the extra money, or the easier hours or what but we've been getting on a lot better this past week. I'm starting to think there might still be something there; you know, in the long run, something worth saving. We'll see how it goes"

"Glad to hear it mate. You should try and stick it out, family's important. God knows raising kids on your own can't be easy, and there's enough single mums round these parts, more than there should be, you know?"

Charlie gave him a quizzical look "You talking about anyone in particular?"

For a moment he paused, whether it was out of some strange form of guilt or a lack of trust in his brother Rob couldn't say, but his hesitation surprised him. A gust of wind sent a chill down his back and he pulled his coat closer to his body.

"I've been to see Kelly Thompson a couple of times since I've been back, she's raising two little ones on her own, it looks like a tough life"

Charlie whistled through his teeth "Kelly fucking Thompson! I haven't heard that name in years. She was a tasty little tart, god knows what she saw in you. I had quite a little crush on her as a kid, you boning her then, or what?"

Rob repressed a sigh, he was getting pretty sick of answering that question.

"Not at all. She's good to talk to that's it, and there's a lot of history there.

Now my little brother's decided he fancies himself as a scouse Tony Montana its getting harder and harder for me to talk to someone outside the game, I need that real world shit with someone or I'm going to go crazy in this bloody place"

Charlie gave him a sceptical look.

"Alright then, you can pass her number on to me, I'll be sure to give the lady what she needs"

"Get bent!" Rob told him, eyeing the corner shop at the end of the street.

When they got within a few steps of the shop Charlie reached into his pocket to extract his wallet, almost without thinking Rob grabbed hold of his arm and pulled him to one side. He took in his brother's quizzical look and tried to speak but the words caught in his throat, they were words he desperately didn't want to say, but there was no use pretending he was stronger than he was.

"Listen Charlie, it's a big couple of days... I'm going to need a couple of grams"

Charlie nodded, his face suddenly serious.

"Not a problem, we'll finish up here, drop the kids off and I'll hook you up. Whatever you need Robbo. Thought you were trying to knock it on the head?"

Rob looked away, at that moment he couldn't look his brother in the eye.

"It's just a backup, that's all, I don't know how hard it's going to hit me"

"Say no more bro, Charlie's there for you, alright?"

Rob nodded "Cheers mate" he gestured towards the corner shop "Think I'll wait out here"

As Charlie disappeared inside Rob propped himself against a nearby wall, swallowing hard he looked up once again at the night sky, the stars seemed brighter now, more prominent, as if in response to his dipping mood they were trying to reiterate the insignificance of his plight. He looked downwards and focused instead on the cracked pavement beneath his feet, the cold, grey concrete captured his disposition considerably better, it was a sight that encapsulated a weak drug addict, or a killer.

One more week of luck, that was all he needed. Tony Miller was in his sights.

Chapter 23

It had been raining for almost seven hours, with only the briefest of pauses at around 10am, before it started back up again. David Walker watched from his car window, this wasn't normal rain, the kind that could be conquered by a sturdy umbrella or a baseball cap, this was the kind that soaked you through in thirty seconds, that stopped you from seeing further than five feet in front of you. It was the kind of weather that perfectly personified a Monday morning, David glanced at his watch, it was now Monday afternoon, the clouds obviously hadn't been notified.

Opening the car door he stepped onto the pavement and darted across the street, shielding his head with his overcoat as he ran. He reached the door of the greasy spoon café and pushed, it opened easier than he expected and the misjudgement caused him to stumble into the small room. Two men in fluorescent vests let out a small chuckle, David pretended like he didn't hear it, he had more important things to worry about.

He made a beeline for the table in the furthest corner of the small café, Chris Railton had been watching him as soon as he'd walked through the door but as David approached his focus shifted to the mug of tea he was nursing, his face held a dejected look, it was a Monday morning look. His deputy was wearing a leather jacket with a black t shirt underneath, the dryness of his blond hair told David he'd been sitting there for a while.

Draping his overcoat across the back of an empty chair David sat down, he gestured towards the window behind him.

"It's really coming down out there"

Railton nodded "I ordered you a coffee, and a bacon sandwich with-"

"Did you see him?" David asked, cutting him off.

There was a flash of annoyance in Railton's eyes, but by the time he'd looked away and took another sip of his tea it was gone.

"Yeah, I saw him. Young Ashley wasn't answering his mobile so I stopped by his house. We went for a ride, the little prick damn near pissed himself when he saw me. If he's this easily rattled by a possession and intent charge, I tell you Guv, I think he may need to start looking for a new line of work"

Ashley Tripp had been picked up eighteen months ago coming back from Amsterdam with a suitcase full of ecstasy. He was a small time drug dealer in his late twenties who was working a scam with the bouncers on a few of Liverpool's more popular clubs, but it was a scam that had some loose ties to the Caddock organisation, so David Walker had seen to it that he stayed on the streets. In exchange for his freedom he worked for the authorities as an informant, an arrangement Ashley Tripp was becoming increasingly uncomfortable with.

The waitress reached their table and placed a cup of black coffee in front of David, he smiled politely, waited until she moved away and leaned forward.

"The kids still green, thank Christ that he is or he'd never have flipped so easily. What did he have for you?"

Railton sighed and shook his head "Nothing I wanted to hear. The way the kid tells it our old friend is making some serious fucking headway. Ever since Wayne Caddock got himself shot McSharry's boys have been moving in and taking over, according to Ashley anyone loyal to Caddock has either taken up the McSharry colours, or been on the wrong end of a severe beating, and these guys aren't fucking about. He says there've been a few of the former but a shitload of the latter. It sounds like a war zone out there"

David thought for a moment about Ashley Tripp, the kid may have been reluctant but what he gave them was usually reliable, and it matched up with the conversations he'd been having that morning, all in all he was likely to believe it, but he couldn't make judgements on generalities.

"Did he give you specifics?"

Railton reached into the inside pocket of his leather jacket, a moment later his hand emerged with a crumpled up piece of paper. Flattening it out on the table with his left hand he used his right to take another mouthful of tea.

"Let's see..." Railton said, squinting at the illegible scrawl "A couple of the incidents were in Kirkby, one Caddock boy got his head smashed in during a lock in, and a house got shot up in Tower Hill, but there were no casualties. Kid says the house was used as a Caddock money drop, at least before Caddock got clipped, and the shooters got away with whatever cash was there. There was another incident in Bootle, McSharry boys raided the house of a local dealer, apparently the guy was Caddock through and through, they beat him to death with a baseball bat. Tripp thinks a couple of the dealers boys were murdered too, but he wasn't too sure on that one. One hell of a way to send a message, don't you think?"

David took a sip of black coffee; it was bitter but just what he needed. It had already been a pretty tough day, he'd spent the morning getting information of his own, just remembering it left a nasty taste at the back of his throat.

"Alright, check those incidents against the police reports over the last couple of weeks. See if our people picked anything up from the crime scenes that the kid couldn't give us. Did he say anything else?"

"Now this is the strangest part of all, he says he knows some people who have links to Tony Miller's crew and the word coming from their camp is that they're not to make a move against Stephen McSharry, or any of his people. They're just letting them get away with this shit, can you believe that?"

Railton looked at David expectantly, scanning his face for a reaction. David reached for his coffee and took another mouthful, he thought back to the morning he'd had and tried to figure out what was upsetting him more; the information he'd been given, or the means he'd used to get it.

"Hobbs gave me pretty much the same thing" David said, glancing over his shoulder before he continued "McSharry making his push, cons loyal to

Caddock either going to ground or fighting their corner. Only the way he hears it, there's more to this than Tony Miller just turning a blind eye"

"Like what?"

Greg Hobbs' words were still fresh in his mind, he sensed that the conversation would stay with him for at least a few weeks, not only because its content presented a number of problems to his plan to put Stephen McSharry back behind bars, but because Hobbs' desperation had given a weight to his words which would not easily be forgotten.

"He says it's all part of some arrangement Miller and McSharry have come to, he reckons the two of them met up sometime last week, diced up the Caddock interests like they were chips on a poker table, and went their separate ways. The guy wasn't there but he says that's the word he's hearing"

Had David Walker heard that statement from any number of people he would have been inclined to disregard it without a seconds thought, but Greg Hobbs was a man who'd been around long enough to know the difference between fact and fiction. It was only his second week out of prison having served every day of a six year stretch, and to look at him it wasn't hard to tell. The curly, dark red afro Hobbs had been sporting the day he went down was long gone, replaced by a greying crew cut with a fast receding hairline, his frame now carried an extra two stone of excess fat and his freckled features appeared both haggard and wrinkled. But despite his physical deterioration, when David had paid him a visit he hadn't been surprised to find that the man had lost none of his antagonistic disposition.

"That doesn't make any sense" said Railton, a puzzled look etched across his face.

"That's what I said"

"So you're Tony Miller, borderline psychopath, your long-time partner gets axed, leaving the monopoly on the cities drug trade firmly in your grip, and then you just go and hand it over to the same bastard who killed your boy in the first place? What the hell is that?"

"I was sceptical too, but I pushed Hobbs pretty hard, he was telling the truth"

Railton gave him a quizzical look and David found himself unable to meet the gaze. He knew the question wouldn't be asked, that just wasn't the way it was done, but it didn't stop David feeling ashamed of the implication that hung between them. The fact of the matter was that he'd pushed Greg Hobbs harder than he should have, harder than was necessarily legal.

Before being sent down the man had been muscle for a prominent procurer of cocaine, his boss had done a fair share of business with the major players in Liverpool, without being aligned to any particular faction. It was a business choice that made him a sizeable share of money, but also left him without the one thing more important in Liverpool: protection. It was that lack of allegiance which was behind his eventual murder, knifed to death outside a kebab house over a hundred quids worth of coke. Hobbs had been there when it happened, but had been too slow to react, after his boss was put in the ground Hobbs tried his hand at running the business, and six weeks later David Walker had him in chains.

He'd been belligerent then, sat in that fluorescent interview room having been caught trying to sell his product to an undercover police officer, and he'd been belligerent earlier that day, telling David that six years at her majesties service had done nothing to make him want to cooperate with the scum who had put him away.

David's patience with the stone wall that was Hobbs' response had lasted a little over ten minutes, after that he found himself doing something he'd never done in all his time on the force, pinning the larger man against a wall and threatening to plant enough drugs in his home to put him away for the rest of his natural life.

Hobbs reaction had been predictably unproductive; curses, retaliatory threats and the like, until he'd realised just how serious David was. He didn't know what it was that persuaded Hobbs of his conviction, but after staring into his eyes for a few moments, all of the cold, defiant aggression drained away, replaced by the desperate look of a man who could see his life disappearing in front of him.

After that, he gave up everything he knew, every word he'd heard since getting out, and while David eagerly digested every nugget of information, the unconcealed hatred with which Hobbs spoke did nothing to abate the growing sense of shame that was blossoming in his chest.

David Walker had never been that kind of police officer, while it was true his arrangement with Rob Thomas all those years ago had bordered on the unethical, he had never done anything quite as callous as threatening to steal a man's life, just for the sake of information. What scared him the most was that he knew it was not an idol threat, he meant every word of it.

He turned his attention back to Chris Railton, his deputy seemed to be playing something over in his mind, when he caught David's eye he began to speak.

"OK, so maybe this is a plan that's been in the pipeline for a while, Maybe the two of them have been working together to get rid of Caddock, maybe Miller was planning this with McSharry when he was still inside?"

David shook his head "I don't know, Caddock and Miller had their house in order, business was running like clockwork, why sabotage all of that to get involved with someone like Stephen McSharry, someone who can't be controlled?"

Railton tapped his right temple with his index finger "Miller's a fucking nutter, he's probably itching for all-out war, gives him a chance to rack up a body count, get his name back in the papers"

Taking another sip of hot coffee, David wanted to believe it, but his instinct told him otherwise, something was happening that they didn't understand, it

306

seemed like ever since he'd laid eyes on Rob Thomas again his world was slowly making less and less sense.

"It just doesn't feel right Chris, we're missing something big" he felt the frustration claw at his insides "chase up the reports on those attacks, have you got the name of that dealer in Bootle, the one they killed? I'll get the office to dig up a next of kin"

Railton reached for the crumpled piece of paper and tried to iron out the creases, scrunching up his face as he made sense of his own handwriting.

"Leroy... something, Tripp didn't know his full name"

"Alright, I'll look into it, get me the address where he was killed." David stood up, snatching his still wet overcoat from the back of the spare chair, he felt an overwhelming need to do something, to make some form of progress, or maybe he just needed the distraction "Call me if you get anything from the reports"

Wow" Railton replied, holding out his hands, palms upwards "what about your bacon butty?"

"You eat it, I'm not hungry"

"I've already had one"

"Have another" David told him, sliding on his coat he felt the wet fabric brush against the back of his neck "You're a growing boy"

"Where are you going now?"

"To find out more about these attacks"

Without waiting for a response David marched through the doors and out into the rain, pausing only once to nod at the waitress who was smiling as he passed. He walked briskly to his car, not bothering to run this time, the rain was going to have its way with him one way or another, trying to fight it suddenly seemed... futile.

David slid into the car and closed the door behind him, not bothering to remove his wet jacket. Before he knew what he was doing he was slamming his fists down into the dashboard, again and again, listening to the sound as it echoed around the interior of the car.

The base of his fist continued to pummel the plastic, over and over until a dull ache spread throughout his hands. When he finally stopped his breathing was heavy, and he could feel beads of perspiration forming on his forehead, sucking in as much air as he could he ran his hands through his hair and let out a grunt that was somewhere between anger and despair.

Nothing seemed to be making sense the way it was supposed to, Stephen McSharry and his gang of thugs were pushing their way towards the front of the queue, and the hardened criminals who'd spend the last ten years slaughtering each other in the man's absence, just seemed to be letting it happen. That McSharry seemed to be getting an easy ride was worrying enough, but what was even more concerning was the degree to which David himself was becoming emotionally compromised. He knew, somewhere deep down inside that he shouldn't care, that one drug dealer was just as bad as the next, but no matter how hard he tried to convince himself, he couldn't force the logic to resonate with his emotions. The fact of the matter was that Stephen McSharry was his collar, his crowning achievement. Putting him away the first time had separated David from his peers and brought with it a sense of accomplishment that was more addictive than any drug he'd ever encountered, but now that McSharry was back on the streets, what did that make him? Just another policeman trying to fight a never ending war on drugs, spending the next thirty years pushing the same rock up the same hill that coppers before him had done, and coppers after would follow. If Stephen McSharry made it back to the top, if the scumbags, the scallies and the crack heads ever again looked to him as the top dog, then it would be like nothing David had ever achieved would have mattered. He was ashamed to admit it, even to himself, but that meant more to him than anything else in this whole mess.

Walker slid the key into the ignition and eased out of his parking space, he didn't know where he was going, just that he needed to drive, to move, to get something done.

Almost subconsciously, he found his thoughts drifting back towards Rob Thomas, the man was the catalyst for the avalanche of problems that threatened to submerge him, he was the dark shadow in David's past, the killer his colleagues were searching for, and McSharry's secret weapon in the on-going war for control. It haunted him to know that McSharry's success, the steps he had already taken, couldn't have been achieved without Thomas's help, help David was enabling him to give, by not being able to stop him. The whole thing was fucked, from start to finish, standing between David Walker and Stephen McSharry was the one man who could bring his police career crashing to the ground, the killer, whose conscience had started this whole dance ten years earlier.

Try as he might, David could not comprehend why Rob Thomas had come back, the man had fought so hard, had risked his own life and the lives of others to help put Stephen McSharry away, and yet here he was, back at his side, killing once again. More than once the thought had crossed David's mind that maybe he'd been wrong about Rob Thomas, maybe after all this time he was finding out the truth, that he hadn't been dealing with a man who was filled with remorse, who was looking to right a wrong, maybe he had just been dealing with the same opportunist the whole time, a man who saw a chance to better his lot and took it, regardless of the consequences. Maybe that's what he was doing back here now, looking after number one, taking his chance on one last pay day, before disappearing back to whatever hole he'd been hiding in. David let out a long sigh, he just didn't know what to think anymore.

He stopped half way down a residential street and killed the engine, fishing his phone out from the inside pocket he considered his options, only one came to mind; stop Rob Thomas killing, stop Stephen McSharry's ascension.

It was that simple, in principle, he just wished he knew how to make it happen.

At first he considered redirecting the DST on to Thomas, he had the license plate number for the red Volkswagen golf, presuming he was still driving it, and so long as they were on his back, Thomas wouldn't be able to kill again. Wayne Caddock's bloated body pushed its way to the front of his mind, he didn't know if he could live with himself if Thomas killed again, these days the weight of Caddock's death rested so heavy on his shoulders that sometimes it felt as if David himself had slid the knife into the man's heart. He played with the idea for a moment longer before he let it slip out of his grasp, Thomas would spot a surveillance unit in no time, if David couldn't keep from getting made in a rented car then what chance did a bulky surveillance van have to keeping tabs on a slippery fucker like Rob Thomas. Besides which, explaining the reason for the tail would bring about all manner of questions, the kind of questions he still wasn't sure if he was willing to answer yet.

There was only one thing to do, follow the leads they did have, the concrete leads, the leads his colleagues were involved with, the kind that cases could be built on. He keyed in the number for the Intelligence Department and asked for the Detailed Surveillance Team when the dispatcher answered, a second later it was ringing. David and Chris had too much on their plates at this point, and since Roberts surveillance team had managed to acquire little information of note, the least they could do was help out with some of the leg work. After four rings a bright, female voice answered, he recognised it immediately.

"Rachel, it's David Walker"

"Oh, hi"

David saw her face as if she was standing in front of him, the beautiful warm smile, the perfect skin, the large brown eyes, it was testament to his mood that even that image didn't bring a smile to his face.

"Hi, I need you to run a check on all the hospitals in Liverpool over the last two weeks. We're looking for a murder victim, subject of aggravated assault, found in the Bootle area with wounds that could be attributed to a baseball bat. First name Leroy, second name unknown, you got all that"

David could hear the pen scribbling frantically at the other end of the line.

"Yeah, what specifically is it that you're after, sir?"

"When you have his full name run it through every database you can think of, we need a full history, next of kin, known associates, prior convictions, the works. We're also going to need the coroner's report, when you have it, check the time of death against the surveillance log, if we had McSharry I want to know which of his people were with him and which weren't, if we didn't, then I want to know how long we lost him for. And find out who were the officers at the scene of the crime, get hold of any statements they may have taken from any witnesses and any names for people in the area"

"I'll get it straight away" she said, he recognised the excitement in her voice, it was the sound of a person who built a life around their job, finding a contentment in their devotion that couldn't be replicated in the real world, David knew it well "When do you need it?"

Walker glanced at his watch, he felt a pang of regret at intentionally diverting his focus away from Rob Thomas, but that avenue was closed to him now, he just had to let it play out and hope the cards would fall in his favour. For now he had to concentrate on real police work, and if he could get his man that way, all the better for everyone. He started up the engine, finding a renewed sense of focus.

"I'll be in the office within the hour"

Chapter 24

A cold breeze, emanating from the Irish Sea, swept across the waterfront, mocking the illusion of warmth projected by the clear blue sky. Stephen McSharry took a final drag from his cigar and tossed it into the river Mersey, leaning forward on the rails before him he blew out a final puff of smoke and looked across the water towards the Wirral.

Today was the day. He could feel it, the blood in his veins, the hair on his arms, the taste in his mouth, it all told him that today was the day it would all change. The call had come through from Rob Thomas the previous evening, everything was set. For obvious reasons they couldn't get into details over the phone, but the boy had killed enough of McSharry's enemies to convince him that his preparations would be suitably thorough, if it paid off it would be the best hundred grand he'd ever spent.

Over the last few days McSharry had found himself thinking more and more about the conundrum that was Rob Thomas. Fate had tossed the boy into his lap and presented him with the perfect weapon; a stone cold killer without a hint of ambition. Ambition was a dangerous thing in their business, especially in someone that supremely gifted, but his complete disinterest, maybe even disgust, for the game combined to make him the most perfect kind of paradox.

During the long hours of reflection it hadn't escaped Stephen McSharry's attention that his success owed a lot to the Thomas kid. True, he was already established as a major force by the time he first crossed paths with him, but there was no denying that he'd found himself in a couple of nasty scraps since then, scraps he may not have gotten out of without him. Now he found another Thomas boy itching the climb into his back pocket, he couldn't help but think that if Rob's younger brother proved to be half as useful as his older sibling, then things were only going to get better from here on in.

Turning away from the river McSharry took in his surroundings, directly in front of him stood the large brick warehouses that made up the Albert Dock, a scattering of tourists were in view either side of him along the wide cobblestone walkway, but not as many as he would of expected. According to the local papers it had been that way since the murder of Wayne Caddock. The charms of the old docks it seemed, were not invulnerable to the scandal that had played out on its grounds, and bold claims were already being made that the city would lose millions of pounds of tourist revenue because of it. Stephen McSharry knew those claims were bollocks, fear might keep people away in the short term, but human nature being what it was, would draw them back in even higher numbers as time went by. Murder was an irresistible intrigue for the masses, as long as it was sufficiently removed from their reality to cease being threatening, such things added colour to their dreary little lives and gave them a window into a world in which they would never have the courage to live. In a few months the tourists would be descending on this place in droves to get a glimpse of the world McSharry had created, in their deepest, darkest fantasies he knew they all wished to be where he was, even if their morality did not permit them to admit it. He at least, knew it to be the truth.

Casually, he glanced to his left. Thirty feet away, leaning against the brick wall of the Albert Dock was Begsy. McSharry kept his eyes on the big man for a few seconds, when Begsy finally met his gaze he held it for a moment in acknowledgment, then quickly returned to scanning his surroundings. McSharry looked back towards the river, Begsys's presence was calming, like having a 12 gauge shotgun close at hand, the others were close too, he knew that, but it was their job today not to be seen. He was encouraged that they seemed to be succeeding in their task, but then it wasn't him they were hoping to fool.

A glance to his right told him that their target had arrived, the group was still around forty feet away but McSharry recognised the formation immediately; a normal sized man in a suit, surrounded by three larger men, one to either side and one in front. Turning back towards the river McSharry let a small smile creep onto his face, this really was feeling like his day.

Samuel Ho and his security advanced slowly, in no great hurry. McSharry liked that, it showed confidence, though from what he'd heard that was not an area in which the young man was lacking. It had been a difficult choice, deciding which of the two options to take. Since bringing the Drake brothers on board he had secured himself a significant portion of the North West ecstacy market, ecstasy was good, it was the party drug of the North, but for his plans to progress it simply wasn't enough. Heroin, that was the next step, control over the heroin trade would solidify his position and put pressure on his enemies, if a man was serious about running the table in Liverpool then he needed control of the H. Inevitably that was Tony Miller's backyard, the man had regular supplies coming in from a variety of locations, but those supplies were orchestrated by two specific men, each with their own contacts and each with their own agendas.

McSharry had looked closely at both men, weighing up each of their personalities and trying to decide which of the two to make contact with. He knew he was playing a risky game, the fragile peace with Tony Miller was unlikely to last if word got out of his intentions.

Eventually, he had settled on Samuel Ho, from everything he had learned the boy was pure business; financially driven, ambitious and calculating, just the kind of man who could embrace an opportunity when it came along. He glanced back towards Begsy, plans had already been put in place for Tony Miller's other supplier, he would be learning what the sharp end of Nikolai's knife felt like in the very near future.

McSharry glanced back towards the advancing crew, they were closer now, around twenty feet away. The call had been made via the appropriate channels a day earlier, McSharry had asked for a meet in the hope that the reverberations of the Caddock killing still had people acting a little erratically, an occurrence like that got people thinking, and it got people scared. It was a trick he'd learnt at the height of Rob Thomas' previous killing spree, men were a lot more receptive to your requests when they feared your next move, it was a trick he planned to use to full effect over the coming weeks.

Ho was close enough now for McSharry to get a good look at him, he was a young man, probably in his early thirties, of Asian descent and with a strong build. His hair was fashionably styled and he wore an expensive Armani suit that was probably a little too tight.

The group stopped, he watched as Ho dished out instructions to his entourage, each one nodded and listened intently. A moment later and all three were stepping back towards the docks, allowing their employer to approach McSharry alone. He was impressed to note that even without his entourage the man walked with a confidence and a certainty that few could maintain in his presence. He had no doubt it was a front, a collection of mannerisms carefully cultivated over a long period of dealing with sociopaths like Tony Miller, but still it was an impressive skill to possess, McSharry found himself liking the kid already.

He looked back across the Mersey, his forearms resting against the hard mettle barriers as he felt the cold air against his face, a moment later he sensed Samuel Ho fall in next to him, mirroring the pose and looking out across the water. For a moment the two men stood in silence, enjoying the view, after a few moments it was McSharry who decided to speak.

"You know when I was a kid this whole place was nothing but a bunch of warehouses, we used to make our way down in the dead of night, break in and steal whatever the fuck we wanted, and look at it now"

"When I was young the whole place was derelict" Ho replied, glancing behind him at the buildings they discussed "All the shit from the Mersey was seeping in and rotting the place, it was a piece of shit"

McSharry remembered those days, he nodded "It just goes to show; you might think you're finished, but this town, it'll always have a few surprises for ya" pushing himself up straight, McSharry turned to face Samuel Ho, the man mirrored the gesture and McSharry realised that they were almost exactly the same height "I appreciate you coming out and hearing what I've got to say, it showed a lot of balls. The way this games being played out, I was starting to think this whole fucking town was losing its mind. It's like that boy who got dumped in the Mersey was the first fucking villain to come to an untimely demise. You can't trust people to keep a cool head in times like this. A lot of pricks out there, they go into lockdown, no new meetings, no new opportunities, drives me fucking spare, I mean Christ, times of uncertainty are the best fucking time to expand, any prick with a business degree can tell you that"

Samuel Ho gave a slight nod, as if he was reluctant to agree with anything McSharry had to say this early in the discussion, but his demeanour was still calm, even when he spoke.

"I have a business degree"

McSharry glanced out towards the river, the Ferry was making its way back towards Liverpool, from where he stood it seemed almost deserted.

"I know you do, Liverpool Hope, right?" McSharry waited for Ho to nod before he continued "Good on you, not a lot of formal education about in this business, you've done well to get where you are. Most guys, you know, they see that kind of thing as a weakness, not me though, I know the importance of knowledge, in the right context of course. You need to have balls to use it in the right way mind, but there's too many of these pricks out there that think having a gun makes up for not having a decent head on your shoulders, guys like that are never gonna go far in this business, they just don't fucking get it"

"They usually get it in the end though, right?" Ho asked, pointing towards his temple with his index finger "just before you put the bullet through their skull. Natural selection at its best I suppose; the strong survive, the weak don't"

McSharry smiled at the man "Truer words never spoken. A few of my people, they were surprised you agreed to meet here today, one or two even tried to tell me it was a setup, a chance for one of your associates to settle an old score"

For the first time Samuel Ho's calm exterior showed signs of wavering, it was only for a moment, a slight widening of the eyes, but McSharry knew fear well enough to spot it.

"Look-" Ho began, his voice not betraying a hint of what had been caught in his eyes, but McSharry cut him off with a wave of the hand.

"Relax, I'm not fucking accusing you. You think I'd be here right now if I had the slightest hint that you were planning something? I pay my people to be suspicious, it allows me the luxury of being a little less cynical" Ho nodded, McSharry gave him a moment to settle before fixing him with a hard stare "Nevertheless, it does raise questions... why did you agree to come down here?"

Ho turned away for a moment, his eyes darting towards Begsy. From the look on his face it was a safe bet that he recognised his enforcer, he wasn't surprised, most people in the game knew the big man, that was why he was standing there.

"After I got your call, I spoke to some people. People who know their shit, who I trust"

"Miller people?" McSharry asked suspiciously, he heard the sternness in his own voice.

Ho shook his head, his eyes darted back towards Begsy as if he expected to see movement any second, eventually he tore his eyes away and focused back on McSharry.

"No, not Miller people. Guys on the street, from my older days. I asked them what they knew about Stephen McSharry, you know how it is, there's a lot of rumours going round these days, a lot of bullshit. They told me you're a serious player, that you shit up the Drake boys something rotten when they tried to take you for a ride. These guys, they made it clear to me that you are not a man to be disrespected, that's why I'm here. I'm a businessman, a very good one, but I plan to keep my nose clean, I sell a product and make some money, that's it. All the other shit just isn't for me"

For the first time McSharry found his eyes wandering towards the three men who had accompanied Samuel Ho. There was little to distinguish between the three of them, all were large men, all bald, he noticed one of them wore a thin layer of stubble, while another had a star tattooed on the side of his head. Aside from that they were almost identical, like they'd come straight off a production line. The thought tickled him for the briefest of moments.

"That's a sensible strategy" McSharry begin "Only a fool goes looking for trouble when it isn't his fight, unfortunately for you, its crap. You don't simply sell a product, you sell power, you sell control, and you put money in the pocket of the people who buy your product. You provide the ingredients that dictate who runs this town, that makes you more than a businessman. It makes you a weapon"

Ho's face suddenly seemed a little paler in the afternoon light, yet the confidence in his demeanour and the certainty in his tone showed no sign of wavering.

"I'm not a weapon" he said simply.

"Oh, you're a weapon, and you know it. You also know that if an enemy has a weapon that is better than yours then you have two options, you either steal it, or you destroy it"

Ho straightened up his back and looked over towards his three guards, each of whom immediately snapped to attention, *that was a mistake*, McSharry thought to himself. The movement from the corner of his eye told him that Begsy hadn't missed the gesture, and he'd bet that the rest of the boys wouldn't have missed it either.

"Assuming you can get to it" Ho replied sternly, though he managed to make the words sound vaguely threatening, McSharry couldn't help but be reminded of a teenage boy standing up to his father for the first time. The thought brought a smile to his lips that was still there when he began to speak.

"If you asked your little friends about me, then I'm sure you already know, I can get to anyone. That's why people in his town are afraid of me, that's why they fear me more than all the other little Johnny-come-lately pricks, pricks like Tony Miller. But I'm not here to threaten you Samuel, far from it. You're a valuable asset, with a good head on your shoulders. I want you to come into business with me"

If Ho was surprised by the proposition, he showed no sign of it. Instead he just slowly slipped his hands into his pockets and flashed an apologetic smile.

"I already have a business arrangement, and unfortunately it's the exclusive kind, so..."

"With Tony Miller?"

"That's right"

"You like working with that guy? He doesn't strike me as your kind of person. When I was inside I heard a story about the guy he bought his H from before you, Carlos something, right? I heard they had a disagreement and Miller killed the fucker, killed his wife and his two little girls as well. You hear that story?"

Ho nodded, the smile wiped clean from his face.

"Everyone's heard that story. The guy was skimming off the top, he pocketed close to three million by the time Miller got wise to him"

"So you agree with what he did?"

"I didn't say that" Ho muttered indignantly, there was a hint of urgency creeping into his tone "Everyone knows Tony's not all there, but isn't that all the more reason not to fuck with the guy? I'm sorry, like I said, I'm not trying to cause you no disrespect, but I've got an arrangement that works, I don't need to have a guy like Tony Miller coming after me trying to cut my fucking balls off"

McSharry felt his pulse quicken, he saw the cracks appearing in the kids resolve as clearly as he saw the river before of him, suddenly Samuel Ho was considering his options. It was hard not to love this part, but hadn't it always been that way? As a young man he'd always preferred the chase to the kill, nowadays this was as close as he came to reliving that sensation. He steeled himself for the final push, the importance of success weighed heavily on his mind, the levels of Heroin Samuel Ho was bringing in, the money that could be made, it was enough to make a star out of anyone.

"Wake up lad, Miller's time is done, this is my time now. You can see the way the winds are changing, that's why you're here, that's why I chose you. I was inside with a fella called Brian Whitter, he told me that when you first started out you were working with a few lads round Toxteth way, bringing in your drugs through your Russian pals and selling it on to these boys. These lads were a couple of well-armed muppets, am I right? They tried muscling in on a few smaller dealers on their turf. Whitter, he tells me that you saw something in one of these little crews, even though they were a fraction of the size of the outfit you were dealing with. But you jumped ship nonetheless, started doing business with this smaller gang, fucked off the people you were working with and damn near started a civil war on the streets of Toxteth. A few years later you and those boys are racking up a couple of million a year, and the dead ends you left behind are serving eight to ten in some prison in Belgium. Did Whitter get that one right? Is that the kind of man you are? Tell me the truth boy, otherwise we're all just wasting our time here"

Ho shrugged his shoulders "Like I said, I'm a businessman. That means anticipating my markets"

McSharry took a step closer "Then anticipate me" he growled "Your last shipment of H, how much did that Miller prick pay you for it?"

"Two million"

Just the answer he wanted, the answer he knew the ambitious little sod would give. McSharry fixed Ho with a cold stare, he held it for a few moments until the younger man became visibly uncomfortable, when he spoke he put as much severity into his voice as he could muster.

"Try again. How about one point two? The biggest shipment you ever gave him was one and a half, which was back in the winter of last year" McSharry watched as Ho took an involuntary step back, catching him out had been easier than expected, a little too easy for a supplier of his calibre "Don't look so surprised, you're not the only man who knows his market"

He watched the colour rise to Ho's cheeks, watched as his eyes dropped, darted left, then right, and rose again, he opened his mouth to speak but McSharry silenced him with a wave of the hand.

"No need to explain. I'd have probably done the same. You're a businessman right, you saw an opportunity?" McSharry gave Ho a few seconds to respond but the younger man simply held his gaze, his face impossible to read "I'm going to give you the two million for your next shipment, and for the shipment after that I'll give you another two million. I'm offering you this because I think you're undervalued, and because I think together we can make a lot of money for each other, but this offer comes with a warning. Don't ever lie, and don't ever bullshit me, ever. We go into business together and I expect a clear transparent relationship, a failure on your part to deliver on said expectations would bring about a world of trouble that even Tony Miller couldn't imagine. Am I making myself clear?"

In spite of the offer, Ho's poker face remained intact, his voice as even as before.

"What about Tony?" he asked "There's no way he'd let us just cut him out of his own operation, this is his baby, his fucking cash cow. He'll have half the city after us by the end of the day. I've worked with Miller for a while now, I know what he's capable of, he doesn't just kill the people who fuck him over, he tears them apart. Are you sure you know what you're suggesting?"

"You let me worry about Tony Miller" McSharry told him, reaching into his overcoat he pulled out a Nokia mobile phone and held it out "take this and get yourself out of town, find yourself a Holiday Inn or something down south, camp out and wait for my call"

Samuel Ho's eyes moved slowly down towards the phone, McSharry studied him carefully, he showed no sign of moving for it, and his poker face was still holding strong. Quickly, he stole a glance towards Begsy, his enforcer was watching the exchange closely and gave a short nod in response, he knew what would need to be done if the kid didn't play ball, and he knew it would have to be done fast. Just as he was about to return the phone to his pocket he caught Ho's right arm slowly rising from his side, he wrapped his fingers around the end of phone and looked McSharry firmly in the eye.

"What about my people?" he asked as McSharry relinquished control of the phone, sliding it into his pocket Ho straightened his suit jacket and let out a deep breath.

"If you trust them take them with you" McSharry replied "Do you?"

Ho stole a quick glance towards the three men.

"Yes, mostly. Two for sure, the other, well I can't be certain"

"Which one?"

"Mark, the guy with the tattoo on his face"

McSharry didn't need to look again, he remembered the man in question.

"Kill him. Today. This afternoon and then get straight out of town" The words were an order, not a suggestion, the nod of Ho's head told him he understood "Wait for my call, and when it comes you won't have to worry about Tony Miller anymore, when you get back you'll get that two million we discussed. You're making a smart move Sam, we're going to make a lot of money together"

Ho gave another nod "I hope you know what you're doing. I'm putting everything on the line for this"

McSharry gave him a reassuring smile "Wait for my call, everything will be fine"

Ho turned and walked away. McSharry watched as he joined up with his three men and made his way towards the car park, by the time they were out of sight Begsy had made his way over and was standing beside him.

"He's in?" Begsy asked, watching them leave.

"He's in" McSharry confirmed "Get Ads to follow them, one of his boys might be loyal to Miller, I gave him an order to put the fucker in the ground and I want to know that he follows it"

"Ads and Sie are already on it"

"Good"

"So, what now?"

The two men began walking in the opposite direction, Begsy kept his eyes on the surrounding area, allowing McSharry to take in the view of the river as they walked.

"Now, we celebrate" McSharry told him "We've done our part, it's time to sit back and let others do theirs. Call Francesca's, tell them I want my usual table tonight...and Begs, call the Thomas kid, tell him to come down and join us"

He could sense Begsy's questioning look before he even spoke "The brother? You sure?"

McSharry responded to the question with a reassuring smile "He's been doing well with the package, hasn't he? He needs to know his efforts are appreciated. Besides which, I want him close tonight in case things don't go according to plan"

The two men walked the rest of the way in silence, the end was in sight, all he needed was for Rob Thomas to give him one more moment of magic. He remembered the long hours of planning that had passed away the time, helping him forget that he was locked inside that cage. Fanning the flames of his revenge, giving him something to live for. Now that plan was almost complete, by the end of the night he would be king once again.

It was 10pm by the time he ordered his food. Begsy sat to one side of him, Charlie Thomas to the other. Francesca's was busy, it was always busy even during the week, but the proprietor could be trusted to find a table for Stephen McSharry when it was required. Though people were being turned away at the door the tables either side of them were both kept empty, that was how McSharry liked it that was how he demanded it.

The restaurant itself was nothing special; a basement Italian restaurant, dimly lit with sand coloured walls that were covered by pictures of Roman architecture. The food on the other hand was immense, and had been for over twenty years. The place had crossed his mind often over the last ten years, usually after a particularly repulsive prison meal. In those moments he would remember this place, and the taste of its Chicken Valdastana, it numbed the pain as he forced down whatever shit the prison kitchen was passing off as food.

It seemed only fitting that his first visit since getting out should be on this night, on the night when ten years of misery could finally be put to rest. A few nervous glances from nearby tables told him that at least some of the patrons recognised him. He gave a cold stare to one particularly interested middle aged man and a moment later the prick paid his bill and exited the building.

His guest seemed a little nervous, but then why wouldn't he be? Two weeks earlier the young lad had been stationed down his local, selling a couple of pills a night to bar flies and doleites, just scraping by in a life that was barely worth living. Now he was a major player in the Liverpool drug scene, if the people of Bootle wanted drugs they came to him, and they were coming in droves. McSharry watched the kid sip at his bottled beer, fidgeting with a silk sky blue shirt that clearly cost more than he was used to spending, so far the conversation hadn't gone very far, he wanted to give the kid a little time to settle.

Bringing Charlie in was a gamble he was feeling particularly proud of. He'd caught the look in that first meeting, the craving to get his name on the map, to be a part of the life, and McSharry had acted on it instantly. Undoubtedly there were perks to having a relative of Rob's on staff, but the kid was proving a useful little acquisition by his own accord.

Leaning forward, McSharry raised his eyebrows.

"So, how's my newest franchise shaping up?"

Another nervous sip of beer, followed by a nod "Been running like clockwork so far, Mr McSharry"

"And what about you kid, you liking the extra money?"

Another nod, this was decidedly more enthusiastic "Oh yeah deffo, its fucking boss! It feels proper good, you know, being a somebody, getting that respect. I appreciate the chance"

McSharry raised the glass of Cabernet Sauvignon to his lips and savoured the taste as it slid down his throat, a hundred pounds a bottle and worth every penny.

"You getting any grief from the locals?"

"Nah, not a sniff. After word got out about Leroy everyone's been on their best behaviour, even the junkies are showing a bit of respect"

McSharry wasn't surprised, junkies were a cowardly breed, the lot of them, show them a bit of violence and watch them scatter, like rats fleeing from the light.

"Enjoy it kid," McSharry told him "It won't last, and when they start getting above themselves, you know what you have to do, right?"

"Yeah, yeah, I know" Charlie replied, there was resignation in his tone.

"Don't give them a fucking inch, they'll have taken a mile before you have a chance to blink, they're animals, these fiends, so that's how you treat them" McSharry felt the bile clogging in his throat and washed it down with another gulp of wine "How's your supply holding up?"

"Actually..." Charlie began, shifting in his seat like he'd been waiting patiently to broach the subject "I've been starting to run a little low, mostly on the pills, the garys are a big favourite with these Bootle boys"

"Where've you been keeping your stash? Tell me it's not sitting in that terraced house with your wife and kids?"

Charlie scrunched up his face, like the insinuation was an insult "Nah, nah, I got a lockable garage up in Kirkby, I've been hiding it in there, in between a load of old boxes. No one's gonna go snooping around that place"

McSharry glanced towards Begsy, the big man hadn't said a word so far, he just sat there listening and weighing the kid up. Maybe they'd worked together for too long but McSharry only needed a second to interpret Begsys look, the man hated working with amateurs.

"You need to get yourself some people," McSharry said, turning back towards Charlie "guys you can trust. My name is only going to get you so far"

Charlie shrugged and leaned back in his chair "There aren't a lot of that type about Mr McSharry"

McSharry let the comment hang in the air, the statement was true enough, it made him thankful for what he had.

"Don't forget we've got the shipment from the brothers coming in Thursday" he kept his voice low. Johnny and Keith Drake had been the picture of professional cooperation since Caddock had been killed, and that relationship was only days away from coming to fruition "I want you down on the docks with a few of the others, make sure the whole thing goes down like it's supposed to. Once we get the stuff off the boat you'll have enough pills to see you through the Christmas rush and into the New Year"

Charlie's smile was from ear to ear "Sounds good"

McSharry suspected he'd already figured out how he'd be spending the money, but then that was how he wanted it. It was good for business to have his employees living on the edge, it made them that little bit more desperate for the next big pay day. He let the kid enjoy the carrot for a few moments, then he hit him with the stick.

"In return, you're gonna need to tool up with the rest of the boys on Saturday night. We've got a couple of cunts in Bootle, and a few more in Toxteth that require some attention. Mongrels, in the mould of your old dealer that need to be put down before they start causing problems." McSharry paused, took a sip of wine, and smiled "From what I hear we could probably just send you in with a baseball bat and have done with the whole fucking thing, but I'm thinking safety in numbers would probably be best. You'll be hitting four different stash houses, and in the morning I want to be reading about four dead low life's, we clear?"

The look of elation had faded, but the greed was still burning brightly in Charlie's eyes as he nodded "Crystal" he said firmly.

"Good," McSharry said, reaching over and giving him and firm slap on the shoulder "you're doing alright kid, proving to be a good little acquisition. You keep going on in this fashion and you'll be making some real fucking money. What you're taking home might look good now but in a place like this, with the plans that I've got, there's a hell of a lot more to be made"

Charlie smiled, it was a proud smile like he'd just brought his first A home from school.

"Cheers Mr McSharry, I'm loving the opportunity"

McSharry took another sip of wine and looked at his watch. Nothing brought out the carnivore in him quite like a nice glass of red, he tried to catch sight of their waiter but he was nowhere to be seen. A few of the others darted around the floor trying to keep control of their tables, he tried to catch an eye but to no avail. He felt a flicker of anger at being ignored maybe he should send Begsy over in response, no one made a point quite like he did. With a sigh he let the moment pass and refilled his glass.

"How's it going with that wife of yours? She liking the extra bit of cash you're bringing home?"

Charlie shook his head and pushed out a breath "You've got no idea, if I'd have known this was all I needed to do to keep her hassle free I'd have been robbing banks years ago, bitch has never been so bloody well behaved. Every couple of days I sort her out with a ton, send her down the shops and it's the quiet life for me. Proper boss, like"

For the first time in a while his thoughts drifted back to Julie, to what is was like to have a wife. At this point in his life he had little use for women, past the thrills of a quick fuck, but listening to the kid took him back to a place he had once been, that he sensed he might be forgetting.

"That's how it is with women," he said eventually, rubbing at his left eye and hearing the bitter twang in his words "they talk about love, about connections, about commitment, but at the end of the day all they're really after is a fat wallet and a fat cock. They'll try and chastise you when you lie to 'em, but they're no better, just more capable of lying to themselves. You ask me woman are for fucking and not a damn sight else, as soon as you give them a glimmer of something more your life won't be worth living"

He took another sip of wine and glanced towards Begsy, the conversation seemed to be of less interest to him than the goings on in the restaurant, he wasn't surprised, when your entire sexual history revolved around cheap, street whores who wouldn't complain too much when things got a little rough, you weren't likely to have too much to contribute on relationships.

"Sometimes they don't even need a glimmer" Charlie muttered.

"You got yourself a bit on the side, kid?"

"Course"

"Tidy?"

"Course, pure filth"

"And she isn't loving the money too?"

There was a pause, as if the kid was unsure whether to discuss such things with his boss. He looked at McSharry, then Begsy, and back again before eventually deciding to speak.

"At first she was, more than the wife to be fair, but to tell you the truth over the last few days she's really starting to get on my tits. When the money started coming in she was proper loving it, dishing out all kinds of nasty little surprises when I showed up with some jewellery or whatever. Then lately, I don't know, she's been getting a bit presumptuous, you know what I mean? I go round there without a present and she flat out refuses to give it up, says if she's not getting what she wants then she doesn't see why I should get what I want. How fucked up is that? And then, she starts demanding shit as well, telling me I have to take her here, I have to take her there, I tell ya, she may be fit as fuck but she's becoming a right little ball ache. Sometimes, feels like she's more hassle than the missus"

McSharry listened to Charlie's predicament, smiled in the right places and gave a sympathetic nod when it was appropriate. Truth be told he couldn't give any less of a shit about the kids domestic problems, but he knew it was important to make him feel wanted, Charlie Thomas was still green, and a green recruit needed to be handled delicately, to be eased into his new world, especially when he came with as many added bonuses as this one did.

"They all get like that at some stage son, stop giving and start demanding. That's when you know it's time to pack them in, there's plenty of other slags out there who know their place and shut their mouths. I was just thinking the other day your brother needs that type of bird, he gets himself wound up so bloody tight. He got one on the go at the minute?"

Charlie took a drink of his beer and swallowed harder than he needed to, his face took on a cagey look for a moment as he considered his answer.

"Rob?" he said eventually "Nah, don't think so. Not that the moody bastard couldn't do with getting his end away. I think he's been trying it on with his ex ever since he got back but the last I heard she wasn't having any of it. She must be warming up to the idea though, I can't see any other reason why he keeps getting himself round there. She was tidy mind, back in the day I mean"

A girlfriend, that rung a bell in McSharry's head, nothing much, just a mention but it was a piece of information he'd felt was relevant back in the day, sadly he'd never had a chance to find out how relevant. Rob Thomas was a closed book who had always played his cards extremely close to his chest, ten years ago when things had been running smoothly that hadn't been a problem but now, well he was always keen to possess some form of leverage on a man with a history of skipping out on his commitments.

"I remember him talking about her," McSharry began "they were together for quite a while weren't they?"

"A good few years I think, yeah, until he skipped out of town"

"Remind me, what was her name again?"

Another sip of beer, another cagey look.

"Kelly, Kelly Thompson"

McSharry gave a casual nod, ensuring out of the corner of his eye that Begsy had been alert to that section of the conversation. He had.

"That's right, well hopefully Kelly can spread her legs, do us all a favour and calm that brother of yours down. Men like him, they need distractions, I'm sure she'll give him one in the end"

Charlie ran a hand over the bristles of his hair and looked away "Christ, I bloody hope so" he muttered.

"What does that mean?" McSharry asked firmly.

"What? Nothing, I was just agreeing with you"

McSharry leaned in closer and fixed Charlie with a hard stare.

"You know he's doing a big job for me tonight?" McSharry waited for Charlie to nod, and then continued "If there's something wrong in his head, or something that's going to jeopardise my business then I expect to fucking hear it. Remember who you work for now"

He didn't know whether it came from uttering the firm words or watching the look of fear spread across the kids face, but McSharry felt his pulse quicken excitedly, it felt good.

"No, it's nothing; I'm just a bit worried about him that's all"

McSharry slammed his fist against the table and watched Charlie jump in surprise, around them he could feel people's attention diverting towards them, but he was too in the moment to care.

"Don't make me ask you again"

"He's started using again, that's all. Coke, a bit of coke to settle his nerves. Like I said, its nothing serious, it gets in my head a bit you know? He's my brother"

McSharry leaned back in his chair and let out a laugh, allowing the tension in his chest to escape like the helium from a hot air balloon. He looked towards Begsy and laughed again, Begsy returned the gesture with a crooked smile.

"He's going to make one hell of a bloody drug dealer this one, isn't he?" McSharry said to the big man, laughing as he spoke "Going grey over a couple of grams of coke"

Begsy nodded and let out a grunt, with another laugh he turned back towards the kid.

"Tell me you're not spouting this shit to your clients, boy? You'll put yourself out of business by the end of the month"

Clearing his throat McSharry noticed that the kid wasn't laughing, his face had taken on a sallow, pale look as he glanced off into the distance. McSharry began to speak but before he had the chance to get the words out Charlie had sprung from his chair and dived towards him.

He heard the sound before he felt the impact, the snap of the wooden chair, followed by the rush of pain in his chest as all the air was pushed out of his lungs, a second later he found himself on the floor and heard the familiar sound he'd been waiting for. Two puffs of air; gun shots, silencers. He waited to feel the pain from the shots Charlie had fired into his chest, waited, but the pain never came.

From the corner of his eye McSharry saw Begsy dart from his chair, the unexpected grace was there as ever, waiting to surprise its target, but instead of moving to protect his employer he charged in the opposite direction. McSharry watched him cover the three feet almost instantly, following Begsy he saw the man for the first time, the man he hadn't even realised was there. He stood in front of their table, dressed like any of the other black shirted waiters with a pistol aimed at the space where McSharry had just been sitting. He had only a second to take in his would be assailant; tall, well built, dark hair, the stereotypical look for a waiter in an Italian restaurant. A moment later the man was turning the pistol away from its original target, trying to intercept the onrushing Begsy. Unfortunately for the shooter he wasn't fast enough, the second he'd wasted considering what to do next had given Begsy enough time to make up the ground he needed, as the man tried to readjust his weapon Begsy was able to lock a large hand around his wrist and snap the bone, causing the gun to drop uselessly the floor. Before the man could even make a sound Begsy's other hand had clenched into a fist and connected with his jaw, McSharry watched as the shooter fell backwards, unconscious before he even hit the ground.

Suddenly everything was silent. McSharry pushed Charlie Thomas off from on top of him, the kid moved willingly, locking his eyes sheepishly on the ground as he dropped backwards and sat on the floor. Brushing himself off McSharry walked around the table and stood next to Begsy, staring down at the man who had tried to kill him. He gave Begsy a chance to speak but he knew he needn't have bothered, the big man kept his eyes trained solely on the unconscious assailant, his heavy breathing the only indication that anything had changed.

The face was unfamiliar, bore no resemblance to any player McSharry had ever known, but as the burning anger grew in his chest he knew for certain that soon enough the man's face would be etched in his brain for eternity. The urge to pick up the gun and unload the barrel into the man's chest was almost unbearable, but there was no danger of that until he had what he needed. Wiping a sliver of spit from his bottom lip he buttoned up his suit jacket and looked up at Begsy.

"Get him in the car. Now!"

An hour later and Stephen McSharry was still waiting for answers. That wasn't to say he hadn't learnt a lot, he had. He'd learnt that the perpetrator of his ill-fated assassination attempt looked a lot less like an Italian waiter when his black silk shirt was removed and the greased back hair was ruffled. On closer inspection the man's features were also less suited to his Italian environment than McSharry had first suspected. Now that he looked at him, really looked at him, McSharry could see the rough, common edge to the man that marked him out as a player. The bruises on his face and cigarette burns on his chest further heightened that impression, just a few tell-tale signs of his time with Begsy.

There was no getting away from the fact; this shooter was a tough bastard. After a beating, a burning and the systematic crushing of each of his fingers and toes they still didn't even know the man's name. The only sound he'd made other than screams and groans had been a muffled 'fuck you' moments before Begsy had took the hammer to the last of his toes.

At the very least the man had to be respected, had his crime been anything less severe than trying to kill him McSharry might have even considered offering the boy a job, but as it was there was only one punishment for that particular crime.

The room was quiet now, the only sound was that of their prisoner, hungrily gulping down breaths of air while Begsy took a brief respite from his interrogation. They'd needed somewhere quiet, somewhere quick, and the Drake brothers had needed to be reminded of their commitments to their new business partner. A brief phone call, that was all it took, the tone of his voice had left no room for misunderstanding and Keith Drake had quickly agreed to give them access to the dockside warehouse. When they approached the onsite security had simply nodded and opened the gates, paying them the slightest attention, no doubt on orders from their employer. The large warehouse seemed perfect for this sort of thing, the bright fluorescent lights highlighted every wound, bruise and decolourisation on the flesh that dared try to end the life of Stephen McSharry.

As he waited for Begsy to resume proceedings McSharry watched his victim closely, the only hint to the man's identity lay on his right bicep, three tattoos one above the other; Stacy 14/6/97, Emma 21/1/99, Luke 16/3/03, kids, no doubt, all of whom would be fatherless as soon as the fucker broke.

Turning away he walked a few steps, Charlie Thomas hadn't spoken since they'd entered the warehouse, quietly taking up a position to the side of the action. En route he had asked to be allowed to go home but McSharry wanted him to see how it ended, to remind him what would happen if he ever chose someone else's side over his. As he reached him Charlie looked up from the ground, his face had a green tint and he looked like he was struggling to keep his appetiser down, the kid had done all right, darting in front of him like that. He had a few men on the payroll who would have reacted a damn slight slower, had he been out with them he'd probably be dead by now. The two men locked eyes and McSharry gave him a firm nod, it was as close as he could come to actually thanking the kid, but over the next few weeks he'd be sure to find his actions rewarded. Charlie gave a small nod in return and looked back towards the floor, McSharry returned to the action.

His patience was starting to wear thin, he wanted answers and he wanted them now. He watched as Begsy slid a blade down the centre of the man's chest, not deep, just enough to make him feel it. As the blade made its way towards the abdomen he heard Begsy's gruff voice in the man's ear.

"Tell me who you were working for, and this can all be over"

The man growled in pain but refused to speak, his eyes focused on a patch of concrete floor in the distance. A small spasm made itself felt in McSharry's back, bruising from where he'd fell earlier. The pain was gone in a second but its impression lingered, taunting him, mocking his allusion of power. He stared at the man crying out and felt the anger rising in his chest. How close some greasy young fuck had come to ending his life, to destroying his legacy, to halting his plans on the verge of fruition. Suddenly, spurred on by his hatred, all patience had vanished. Marching forward he grabbed Begsy's shoulder and snatched the blade from his grasp. The big man took a step back and allowed him to work, McSharry leaned in close, the stink of fear on the man only spurred him on. He took the pricks chin in his left hand, raised it upwards and with the other he jammed the blade into his victims right eye.

The scream was barely human, desperate, pleading and maniacal all at the same time, pulling the blade away McSharry saw that part of the eye had come out with it. Keeping hold of the man's chin he held it in front of his good eye, drops of blood dripping onto his wounded chest.

"YOU SEE THIS? THIS IS JUST THE FUCKING START!" he screamed, spit spewing from his mouth "IF YOU DON'T TELL ME WHAT I WANT TO KNOW THEN YOU'LL BE BLIND IN ABOUT TEN SECONDS. BUT DON'T MISUNDERSTOOD ME YOU LITTLE PRICK, YOU'RE GOING TO BE ALIVE FOR A LOT LONGER THAN THAT. I'M GOING TO TEAR YOU APART, PIECE BY PIECE, EVERY PART OF YOU EXCEPT FOR THAT TOUNGE, YOU THINK YOU KNOW PAIN? YOU HAVE NO FUCKING IDEA, NOW TELL ME: WHO DO YOU WORK FOR?"

By the time he finished McSharry's own face was pressed tightly into the shooters, the blood from his eye wound was seeping onto his left cheek and dropping down onto his pant leg. The first thing he heard was the whimper, then the words catching in his throat as he tried to speak, then finally, the answer.

"Tony Miller" he mumbled between sobs, "I work for Tony Miller"

McSharry took a step away and turned around, Begsy was already walking towards him, a silencer at his side, McSharry nodded and continued towards the door. The sound of the shots echoed around the quiet warehouse. He didn't need to look behind him to know where they had gone; two in the chest, one in the head.

Chapter 25

The soft pitter-patter of rain helped Rob focus his thoughts as he sat behind the wheel of the stolen Honda Civic. So far he'd been sat there for two hours plus, watching the comings and goings of the Old Oak, in that time his thoughts had started drifting to a much darker place than he would care to go on a night like this, the sound of the rain worked like an anchor, drawing him back to the now, to where he needed to be.

Tony Miller and his entourage had arrived around ninety minutes earlier, not that they were hard to spot, the boss and his crew numbered seventeen as they entered the pub, and that was discounting the possibility that they were meeting more inside. The thought wasn't even worth contemplating, being prepared was one thing, knowing for certain that your next job was a suicide mission was quite another.

His left hand was concealed underneath a dark overcoat, he gave a reassuring squeeze to the grip of the Smith and Weston, as if the gun might protect him from the horde of criminals he was about to confront. Maybe the first few, but seventeen? It didn't bear thinking about.

Rob moved his hand to the passenger seat, released the gun and placed the overcoat on top. He'd stolen the car earlier than afternoon, finding it parked in a quiet residential street in the south of the city. With any luck the car wouldn't be reported stolen until there was nothing left but a burning heap, if the owner had reported it to the authorities he was still confident that they wouldn't be looking for it in this part of the city, from what he'd seen over the last couple of days this was Tony Miller's stretch of turf, even as far as the police were concerned.

He heard the ferocity of the rain increase against the roof of the car and took it as a sign to move. Reaching under the seat Rob took the two parcels of Acetone Peroxide and opened the door, Miller had only left one man outside the pub, four black jeeps were mounted on the pavement parallel to the Old Oak and that man was sat in the first car, watching what was going on in front of him. Cautiously, Rob crept from the Honda Civic five cars back and made his way towards the last of the jeeps, pressing the adhesive soaked side of the explosive against the rear bumper. Creeping back towards the Honda Civic he snatched the overcoat from the passenger seat, hid the gun in the glove compartment and straightened himself up, sliding on the coat he began walking towards the pub with the second bomb under his arm.

As soon as Rob got to within fifteen feet of the pub he heard the electric window of the jeep open and felt the eyes of its occupant burning into the side of his face. Fighting the urge to look round Rob buried his head in his overcoat, as if shielding himself from the rain and hurried towards the pub. As he reached the gates he made a show of searching for his wallet with his left hand, with his right he pressed the second explosive against the outside wall of the gate. He knew the soldier in the jeep would be unable to see the explosive as long as he was stood there, he could only hope that he'd attached it far enough back to be out of the man's line of sight once he moved. Lifting his wallet from his back pocket he took a deep breath and walked towards the pub. With each step he expected to hear the sound of gunfire and feel an explosion in his chest, but after three uneventful steps the fear began to subside. With a sigh of relief he hurried inside and made his way towards the bar.

Once he was in there was no mistaking where his target was. In the backroom, most of it just out of sight, he saw a number of large men pacing back and forth in the doorway. Rob ordered a pint and made a conscious effort to stay as far away from them as possible. Finding a small table on the other side of the building he drank quickly, feeling the Dutch courage alleviate some of this growing nerves, and left as fast as he could.

As he made his way outside he found himself locking eyes with Miller's man in the jeep, evidently the man had decided that whatever threat Rob may had posed on the way in had now long since passed, and held the gaze for the briefest of second before turning his attention back towards the street. Rob continued down the road past the Honda Civic before doubling back and returning to his look out post in the front seat. Dropping the jacket onto the passenger seat he leaned back and took a series of deep breaths. That was the hard part done, now all he needed to do was execute seventeen plus men.

The longer Rob waited, the more frayed his nerves became. Even by his own standards sleep had been in short supply recently, the nightmares that had plagued him in New York were becoming more and more frequent, even more so since he'd killed Wayne Caddock. Now he didn't even need to be asleep to see her face, it came to him in that hazy place between worlds, those amazing eyes haunting him constantly, waiting for a chance to take their revenge whenever his guard was down. On occasion the face would change, halfway through begging for its life it would become the face of Wayne Caddock, not the handsome man he had known from the surveillance photographs, but the gruesome desperate man he had known on the brink of death. In his dreams Caddock's face was always ghoulishly white, his skin leathery and decrepit, with drops of sea water sliding down his face and dripping into the nothingness below him.

Rob reached for the black and gold Smith and Weston for comfort, pressing the cold metal barrel against his forehead. The silencer was attached, making it bulkier and less agile than it naturally was, but the Old Oak was in a residential area and with explosives on the table he needed to embrace every subtle means of attack that he could.

Time dragged, the more tired he became the more his muscles began to ache in the confined space of the front seat, his back hurt, his legs hurt, his arse hurt, not what he needed in a situation where agility was going to be paramount.

He looked at his watch; 11:45, almost five hours since he'd first arrived. Reaching into the backseat he pulled the detonator from the shoulder bag he'd brought with him and fidgeted with the device, moving it around in his left hand as he watched the entrance to the pub. The distance from the main door, through the brick gates to the waiting jeeps couldn't have been more than twenty five feet, if they moved at normal speed Miller's people would have covered it within thirty to forty seconds, that didn't give him much of a window. He tried to keep himself from asking how he could possibly hope to kill so many men, but in its place he found himself thinking that even if he could there was a decent chance he might not come out on the other side of it. He didn't know if killing just wasn't in his blood anymore, or whether it had ever been, but if he lost as much of himself in this hit as he had with Caddock then scraping together enough pieces to take back to Jo was going to be difficult. He reminded himself of the kind of person Tony Miller was, of the terrible things he had done to the people of Liverpool. The file McSharry had given him was filled with a laundry list of crimes, almost every one deserving of a death sentence in itself. He knew McSharry had included the information for precisely this reason, to give Rob that final push, but it didn't matter, at the end of the day it gave him a small slice of justification for what he was about to do, and he couldn't ask for more than that.

"Just another gangster..." he told himself. He repeated the words four or five times until they started to sink in.

It was 12:30 when the waiting finally ended. Aside from the hammering rain the street was quiet, Rob had watched a steady stream of people leaving the bar over the last half hour and from the look of things Miller and his firm were the last ones to go. As the first two men stepped into the rain and made their way across the street towards the four jeeps Rob prepared himself for action. Sliding on his blue baseball cap he quickly wrapped his knuckles against the Kevlar vest, ran a hand over the extra clips that were bulging from the pockets of his trousers and moved himself closer to the two pistols waiting on the passenger seat. The detonator for the two Acetone Peroxide packs was still cradled in his left hand, he gripped it tighter and tighter as he watched Miller's soldiers pile out of the pub.

Ten of the men had already made it out on to the street by the time Rob laid eyes on Tony Miller, the jet black goatee was the first thing he noticed, and the way he bounced when he walked, like a man who thought he was untouchable. Rob felt a chill run down his spine when he realised how much he was looking forward to disproving that theory.

Another nine men followed Miller out of the pub, meaning that they had met people inside, Rob tried not to think about what that meant as he narrowed his eyes and watched the mans every step. His thumb hovered over the detonator as Miller took his first steps into the night air, Rob waited, feeling his hand shaking until his target finally stepped between the two brick gates, holding his breath he pressed down on the red button and waited.

Nothing.

Frantically he pressed the button again, and again, tasting the vomit as it rose in this throat. The explosion that should have been ripping through the night sky never came, with a curse he tossed the detonator to the floor and picked up the two Smith and Westons.

Opening the car door Rob stepped into the street and started walking towards the four jeeps. As his heart beat frantically in his chest he found himself suddenly thankful for small mercies, thankful that he'd seen this possibility coming, and steered clear of the C4. Tucking the second pistol into his trousers Rob took aim with both hands at the explosive on the back of the jeep, he was still just over fifteen feet away and the large group of men were yet to noticed him as they decided who was going in which car.

He fired the first shot, and heard it ping against the bumper just wide of its target. He heard a number of shouts in response to the noise but kept his focus on the small white brick attached to the back of the jeep. He let of a second shot, hitting the other side of the bumper, slightly closer than the first. As he took aim for a third time he heard the metallic clink of guns being drawn, the noises were louder now but Rob closed himself off to them, he kept his eyes locked on the jeep as he squeezed off a third shot. As soon as it left the chamber he knew it was good, turning away he dropped to his knees and covered his face.

The sound of the explosion was deafening, even with his arm covering his eyes he could see how the street around him was showered in light, Rob only allowed himself a second to shy away from the blast and jumped back to his feet, with both pistols trained in front of him. Quickly he assessed the situation, the explosion had taken out three of the four jeeps, two of which were burnt and overturned, the front jeep had been projected forward but the only damage he could see was that the rear view mirror was smashed. He counted six bodies on the floor, from the looks of things with various degrees of injuries, some were screaming and clawing at flesh, others were motionless.

The men who remained seemed to be caught between two possibilities, some were fleeing back towards the Old Oak while others were composing themselves and preparing to return fire. Without thinking Rob fired off three quick head shots towards three men who were raising their weapons, each one hit the mark perfectly, three small explosions of blood telling him they were out of the game. Spinning towards the pub he saw another four men scrambling over the gates towards the door of the Old Oak, he fired two shots at the second white brick and watched as the gates exploded, taking with it the door, the front windows of the pub and four more Miller soldiers.

Rob aimed the two pistols back towards the street, trying to get a sense for how many were left and whether Tony Miller was one of them. The second explosion had pushed two more men back into the centre of the street and Rob picked them off one after the other before they had a chance to react.

331

The rest of the crew had taken the brief respite that the second explosion had provided to regain some form of discipline, three were shuffling behind one of the overturned jeeps while two more were prying pistols from the hands of their dead colleagues. Rob marched towards the latter two men who were still exposed, but before he'd had a chance to fire one of them had squeezed off a couple of rounds, the shots were wild and anxious but they still forced him to dart behind a parked car and regroup.

By now the three men behind the Jeep had overcome the initial surprise and had started to return fire. Rob raised his head to scout their position and was inches away from taking one in the face.

"I want him alive! Fucking alive!" a voice screamed from behind the jeep, it was maniacal and half crazed, Rob knew that Tony Miller was still in play.

A moment later the shots stopped, Rob pressed his back against the side of the car and slid two new clips into the Smith and Westons, soon after he heard footsteps, footsteps that would usually be too light to hear but which were betrayed by the wet surface. Sliding onto his stomach he looked under the car and saw two sets of feet circling the vehicle, coming towards him from either side.

He didn't hesitate, aiming both weapons he fired three shots each at the feet of the two men, the simultaneous screams told him he'd hit his targets and before the other group behind the jeep had time to react he was running away from the car and darting across the street towards the what was left of the rear jeep. As he crossed the road he finished off the other two men, both of whom were too busy nursing their shins to see him coming.

Two shots rang out across the street but Rob was able to reach the cover of the jeep before he was hit, as best as he could tell there were only three men left and they were all huddled behind the Jeep two cars in front of the wreckage he was hidden behind.

Sucking in a series of deep breaths Rob lifted himself up and stepped around the other side of the wreckage, he aimed the two pistols towards the Jeep where Miller had just been but there was no movement, cautiously he started towards the car, taking one slow step at a time.

As he got to within a few steps of the vehicle there was still no movement, his eyes darted quickly around the surrounding landscape, trying to locate any possible escape routes the three men may have used.

Suddenly there was a flash of movement to his right and Rob turned just in time to see a dark haired man in a leather jacket sprinting towards him, letting out a scream as he raised his gun and started shooting. Instinctively Rob dropped, rolled to the right and lifted himself onto one knee, the shift of movement forced his attacker to readjust his body shape and by the time he had Rob's pistol was trained on the man's chest, firing off too quick shots he stumbled backwards and fell into the street.

It was then that Rob got his first real look at Tony Miller. Darting out from behind the front Jeep he aimed what looked to be a Glock and fired, the shot caught Rob in the ribs, ripping through the weaker part of the vest and piercing his skin. Grunting in pain he lifted himself to his feet and closed the distance between the two men, Miller went to fire again but Rob slammed the gun in his right hand against the Glock sending the two pistols spiraling towards the floor. The impact forced Miller to take a step back and gave Rob enough room to raise the gun in his left hand and fire three shots. All three hit Miller in the chest forcing him to stumble backwards until he was halted by the jeep. He kept his eyes trained on Rob as he slid down to the ground, leaving three bloody smears on the door as he fell, by the time he hit the floor his eyes were closed.

Cautiously, his gun still trained on the gangster Rob moved forward. Suddenly he felt two arms wrap around his upper body and launch him to the ground, the gun was out of his hand as soon as he landed and he had just enough time to adjust his body to see an overweight man in his thirties with fair hair and a receding hair line launching himself towards him. Rob was able to get to his feet before the man started raining down punches on him, he blocked them where he could but when one fist connected with his cheek and another with his temple he had to stumble backwards and drop to one knee. His attacker saw an opportunity and launched a vicious kick at Rob's head, dropping onto his back just in time he had only a second to gain his bearings before he was rolling away as the man attempted to stomp on his head. The pain in Rob's side was burning and his sight was blurry as he stumbled to his feet, still stepping away from the man. He willed his legs to move faster as his assailant closed in but they refused to cooperate. Rob saw the right hook coming but could do nothing to stop it as it connected with his jaw and spun him around, sending him spiraling onto his chest.

In his dazed state Rob thought he heard a grunt as if the man was bending down, as his eyes focused he saw Tony Miller's Glock lying on the floor in front of him.

Summoning the last of his strength Rob pushed himself towards the weapon and rolled onto his back, a moment later he had the gun trained on the large man who was holding Rob's Smith and Weston at his side. There was a look of resignation on the fat bastards face as he tried in vain to direct the gun, even with his vision blurred Rob saw the shot from the Glock blow apart a chunk of oversized chest.

Although he knew it was a mistake Rob let his head drop back against the floor and allowed the world to spin for a few moments. He tried to will himself to his feet but his body was battered and bruised. It was only when he heard the sound of the engine that he was suddenly aware again, pushing himself upright and scrambling for the two Smith and Westons.

Stumbling forward he saw light coming from the front Jeep with the smashed rear view windscreen. As he got closer and his sight began to clear Rob saw a man in the driver's seat leaning across and dragging Tony Miller off the floor into the passenger side. Rob fired off two shots as he moved forward but both were well wide, judging by the trouble the driver has having hauling Miller's prone body into the car it was difficult to tell whether he was dead or alive, but Rob had no intention of taking the chance. He fired another shot, this time smashing the glass in the rear door window, the proximity seemed to give the driver all the impetus he needed and with one final haul he dragged Miller into the car. Rob aimed both pistols and started firing but the jeep had already set off, a second later it had turned a corner and sped out of sight.

Suddenly the dark street was silent, Rob knew the sound of sirens would soon disrupt the calm, there were enough houses close by for at least one person to have called the police, letting the two guns rest at his sides he took in the chaos before him and tried to collect his thoughts.

The street was littered with dead bodies, some burnt, some shot, but the only one that mattered, the only one he needed had gotten away. Replaying the last few seconds over in his head Rob tried conclude whether or not Miller was actually dead, not that it mattered all that much. Without a body Stephen McSharry would not be convinced, and without a body Miller's men on the streets would still have something to rally around, which would make life harder for McSharry and his people.

Deciding it was time to leave Rob glanced one last time at the slaughter he had created and turned to head back towards the Honda Civic, that was when he saw him. A kid, seventeen, eighteen at the very most, he was wearing a blue tracksuit and sitting on top of a mountain bike less than twenty feet away, on the opposite side of the road. He was watching Rob with an intensity that was somewhere between fascination and terror, Rob's stomach lurched when he realised he was no longer wearing the baseball cap, it must have fallen off during the fight with the fat man. The kid was still staring at him, Rob stared back, swallowing hard as the realisation of what he would have to do struck home.

He didn't give the thought time to settle, he just followed his instincts and reacted. His right arm shot up and fired one quick shot towards the boy, he heard the grunt as the bullet struck and watched him fall back, the bike falling on top and trapping his legs. Rob walked over slowly, stepping over the bodies of two dead Miller lieutenants as he went, when he reached the teenager he saw that he'd caught him in the chest, probably high enough not be fatal, but he would certainly require surgery.

The kid's gaze was switching back and forth from the hole in his chest, to the man who had put it there. Rob stood over him and watched as he put a shaking hand over the wound and a second later pulled it away covered in blood.

Up close Rob could see that he really was just a kid, a scattering of pimples covered his cheeks and nose and there was a small layer of bum fluff on his bottom lip, what the kid no doubt thought was his first moustache and now it would be the only one he would ever know.

The boy was breathing heavily now, the wound in his chest forgotten as he stared up at the man with a pistol in his hand.

"Please...please....please" he muttered in between breaths "I won't tell anyone, I swear I won't, please..."

Rob called on every ounce of strength to keep his face from betraying the emotion behind it, he wished more than anything that he could give the kid what he wanted, but he knew deep down that it was impossible. He'd been made, and the kid, whether he knew it or not was a threat to Rob and to everyone he cared about, his rules had made him the best, his rules had made him a ghost, and now his rules dictated that he kill this child.

Slowly he shook his head, the kid started to cry in between breaths.

"There's no other way" Rob said, raising the gun "None"

He fired two shots in quick succession, both into the forehead of the boy. He waited for a second, making sure that he'd gone quickly, that there hadn't been any more pain than was necessary, and then he darted back across the road. Finding the blue baseball cap he shoved it under his arm and walked briskly to the Honda Civic. It was only after he'd started the car and put a few miles between himself and the Old Oak that his whole body began to shake.

He didn't need to be asleep to see the kids face, he knew he would see it wherever he looked for the rest of his life.

He drove for another fifteen minutes, in no particular direction, before stopping at a payphone on a dark, deserted, stretch of road. His body had shook uncontrollably for a few minutes and then his mind had begun to numb. Now he felt hollow, like his insides had been scooped out, like there was nothing left of him but a shell. Now and then he caught his eyes in the rear view mirror and they looked foreign to him, no, not foreign, alien. It wasn't that he couldn't recognise those eyes it was that he couldn't recognise their context, the context of everything just seemed beyond him. He saw the paleness of his face and realised suddenly that life itself was beyond him.

He climbed out of the car and stumbled towards the payphone. Taking the piece of paper out of his pocket he dialled the number he had been given, a familiar voice answered after three rings.

"Is it done?"

"I'm not sure"

"What do you mean, you're not sure?" Stephen McSharry asked.

"I got all of his people. Twenty I think, and I put three in his chest, but one of them grabbed his body and piled him into a car, I couldn't tell for sure whether he's dead. But I got the rest, his people are done"

"His people weren't the target" McSharry growled, the anger coming through clearly on the crackly line "He was"

"Even if he's alive he's going to be in bad shape, and all the guys I got were in that folder you gave me, his muscle is gone, his lieutenants are gone, even if he pulls through he won't be strong enough to keep you out. I've done my bit, I'm out"

The line went silent for a moment.

"Not yet. I need you to do one more job"

"Two hits, that was our deal"

"And you only gave me one and a half. One more job and then we're finished. I'll double your money"

"I don't want the money" Rob shouted "I'm done"

"You're done when I say you're done" McSharry warned, though his voice was low the weight of the threat was undeniable.

"Please..." Rob whispered, feeling all of his strength fading away "I'm done"

"You do what I'm telling you to do or you will be fucking done. This thing, its over when its over"

Rob ran a hand across his face, the blurred vision was still coming and going and there was a throbbing pain in his side where Miller had pierced the vest, he wanted nothing more than to drop to the floor and forget about everything.

"And when will that be?" he asked quietly.

The line went silent for a moment while McSharry considered his answer.

"When we bury the last of these pretenders boy, that's when"

"For Christ's sake, look around you. It's done, there's nobody left"

As Stephen McSharry spoke, Rob was sure that the old gangster was smiling.

"One more, just one more"

Rob was almost afraid to ask, but in a strange way he wanted to keep arguing, to keep the conversation going. It stopped his mind from settling on the kid, at this point, he was willing to do almost anything to keep himself from going to that place.

"Who?"

Again another pause, again, Rob got the sense that the man was smiling.

"Martin Cassidy"

Rob remembered him from the old days, remembered hearing his name in conversation all the time, McSharry's oldest associate, two organisations that had been working side by side for decades.

"I thought he was on board?" Rob asked.

"Things have changed. Tonight, a lot of things changed. This town is mine, and mine alone. One more hit, one last threat and then I'll let you go. Make sure you do this one right and I'll double your money. That's a cool two hundred grand. Considering how badly you fucked up tonight you should be grateful I'm being so generous, I hear another word about it and that generosity might just start to waver, you get me?"

Rob reached under his shirt and, between finger and thumb he gripped the

336

cross around his neck, the gift from Charlie, his twentieth birthday, when it had all started to go wrong. It symbolised nothing but misery to him but for some reason he just couldn't bear to throw it away, maybe it was because somewhere deep down he still hoped, still believed that a higher power could swoop down and save him, absolve him of all the mistakes he had made with that god damn free will, or maybe he had never been free in the first place, maybe that was the point.

By now there was nothing left but resignation, releasing the cross to fall back underneath his shirt he looked out into the dark night and accepted his fate.

"When?"

"Begsy will be in touch"

And then the line went dead.

Rob was in a daze as he stumbled back towards the car. It was a daze that kept hold as he drove out to an abandoned old factory on the edge of Kirkby, it kept its grip while he poured the petrol can first over the bonnet and then onto the roof of the green Honda Civic, and it was still there when he lit the match. A million thoughts were swirling around in his head but he found himself unable to connect with any of them, the daze led him onwards as he began the seven mile walk back to the flat in Bootle.

Chapter 26

The office was practically deserted when the call came through. David Walker had been working late, catching up on a mountain of paperwork; surveillance logs, requests for mobile phone records and a dozen other mundane tasks when the phone had started to ring. It had seemed like a god send, anything to get him away from the monotony of his administrative duties. How wrong he had been.

Ten minutes later he was behind the wheel, racing across the city at high speed. The post-midnight roads were mostly quiet, but going as fast as he was, he still found himself having to veer past the odd bus or taxi that threatened to slow his progress. As he progressed he couldn't help but prepare himself for what he was about to see, knowing that in a way he was as responsible as the shooter for the nights events. The call he'd received from dispatch had been brief, but it had been enough to let him know what he was dealing with; another shootout, several known affiliates of a criminal organisation amongst the dead, no ID on the shooter, it was Rob Thomas through and through.

David wasn't naive enough to have thought that his warning was going to do the trick, but he'd hoped there'd been enough humanity left in Rob Thomas to help push him on his way. Despite it all Rob had always seemed like he had something about him, something different from the people David crossed paths with on a day to day basis, he had always had the sense that the man had it in him to be a good guy, if he hadn't have been a homicidal murderer.

But that was all irrelevant now, another hit, this time on Tony Miller from the sound of it, was a step too far, something would need to be done. Ignoring the fact that another series of murders would inevitably destabilise the cities other drug traffickers the fact still remained that with each shot Rob took the more he jeopardised what they had achieved ten years earlier, and what David had achieved in the years since. A career built on a lie was always at risk of falling apart, he just wished the lie hadn't been quite so vast, a relationship with a known killer might do more than just jeopardise his career, it might end up putting him behind bars.

A black taxi tried to switch lanes in front of him and David swore as he found himself having to swerve hard to avoid a collision, pressing his foot down on the accelerator he left the cab behind, the sound of its horn lingering in his ears for a moment before it too disappeared behind him. He was getting closer now, closer to seeing exactly what his old accomplice had done in the Wavertree district of the city, closer to seeing just how much he had aided the cause of Stephen McSharry tonight. The bile burnt at the back of his throat whenever he thought about the gangster, the progress he was making was almost meteoric. With Rob keeping the focus squarely on the bosses McSharry was taking the opportunity to make massive strides lower down the food chain, stealing a supplier here, a patch of turf there, killing some small time up and comer, all while his ace in the hole was plotting the downfall of the famous faces, and so far it seemed like there was nothing anybody could do about it. Luckily David still had an ace or two left up his sleeve, and he was reaching the point where he might be ready to use them.

The congestion of police cruisers and yellow tape told him he had arrived at his destination, a sense of déjà vu came over him as he flashed his ID to the copper directing traffic, responding with a quick nod he told David to park up and head down the street.

The tension had brought a tightness to his chest by the time he'd gotten out of the car and started walking towards the crime scene, like his lungs were caught in a vice. Consciously he tried to take a deep breath as he caught his first glimpse of the chaos, an overturned jeep, still smouldering, the smell of burning metal caught in his throat as he continued towards the centre of proceedings.

White sheets covered at least fifteen bundles on the ground. His first thought was whether he was about to see a collection of smoking corpses akin to the overturned jeep, he'd viewed enough of Rob Thomas's victims in the past to know that he was likely to see more than his fair share of gruesomeness, but burning his victims alive, that was a step further than even David would have expected.

A small troop of police officers were scurrying around him as David started to walk amongst the bodies, there seemed to be little order to the chaos, bodies and burning cars were scattered across the street like leaves falling from a dying tree, across from him he saw the smoking wreckage of what had been a pub, from the look of it the structural damage was minimal but the front side of the building would need at least a couple of grand's worth of work.

It was then that he heard someone shout his name, turning he spotted Carl Drysdale walking towards him, the Detective Sergeant was shaking his head as he walked, scratching a notepad against his thick, dark grey beard.

"You caught this one, too?" David asked with surprise.

Drysdale pulled up next to him, he looked around the crime scene and shook his head again.

"It's been a bad bloody month" he complained.

A crowd was forming further down the street, David thought he spotted John Barry's white hair but his view was quickly blocked by another two police officers joining the huddle, dismissing it, he turned back towards Drysdale.

"Any leads on that Caddock thing?"

Another shake of the head "None worth mentioning, no one's talking and those that are know about as much as me or you. Still, god bless the 'pool, another day another dead scumbag, never get a chance to dwell on your problems in this city, am I right? Good job you're here, the natives are saying this public house here was a favoured haunt of one Tony Miller. Your team have been looking into him, right? Maybe you can help us ID some of these pricks?"

He'd expected the request, and although he wasn't looking forward to getting up close and personal with more of Rob Thomas's handiwork, the pull of his professional interest was too strong to ignore.

"No problem. Is Miller one of them? Have you found his body?"

"Not yet. A few of them got cooked pretty good, from the sound of it there were a couple of explosives involved, forensics are on their way to enlighten us. Hey, yo, Carter! Heighway" raising his hand Drysdale gestured towards two uniformed officers, both stopped what they were doing and jogged over "I want you to show Officer Walker here our collection, any luck he might be able to put a couple of names to our corpses. You come see me when you're done, ok?"

David agreed and headed off with the two officers.

Twenty minutes later he would have given the world to be back in the office going blind on paperwork. One rain soaked corpse after the next waited patiently for him as he made his way through the pack, the inconsistency of the kills told him how frantic the gun fight must have been, a head shot to one, two to the chest for the next, third degree burns for the one after, that one man could cause so much carnage was terrifying, fascinating and incomprehensible all at the same time. With each body that he passed he found himself becoming more and more convinced that Tony Miller was not going to be among them, he didn't know what made him so sure, maybe because Miller being dead would have made it all too easy, maybe because the fates seemed to be conspiring against him to prolong the bloodshed any way it could, whatever the reason by the time he dropped the sheet over the final corpse and made his way back towards Carl Drysdale, the certainty of what he would have to do next was already taking shape in his mind.

At the sound of his approaching footsteps Drysdale looked up from his notepad and raised his eyebrows expectantly

"Miller's not here, but these are all his people, every last one of them" a few more people had congregated around the area where David had thought he'd spotted John Barry, now he noticed they were all in suits. Locking eyes with Drysdale he nodded in the direction of the group "what's going on over there?"

Drysdale shook his head dismissively "Don't worry about it. What do you mean when you say 'his people'? lieutenants? Muscle? His fucking cleaning lady?"

"All of it. This is Miller's entire organisation right here. All you're missing is the man at the top"

Drysdale shook his head again and started writing frantically on the notepad "Anyone else?"

David mentally checked off each of the corpses against the dozens of files and reports from which he knew them, most of the dead men before him were men he'd never even met, never spoken a word to, and yet he felt as if he knew them better than almost anyone else in his life.

"Yeah, actually now you mention it I did count them one man short. His names Alex Kelly, he goes by Kel. I didn't see his face amongst the deceased"

"Maybe it was his night off?"

"Maybe" David said, making it clear from his tone that he didn't think it was likely.

"Fuck me!"

The first reporters were beginning to arrive on the scene, in the distance David saw the officer he'd first encountered calling for assistance to keep them back.

"What do you make of your crime scene?" David asked after a moments silence.

Drysdale flashed him a solemn look "It's pretty fucking familiar, isn't it?"

"Bullets?"

".45 Acps"

"Fuck!" David muttered, bringing a disapproving look from a lab tech close by.

"And now our guys added explosives to his arsenal" Drysdale said with a wry grin.

"What's he gonna have for us next?"

"WALKER" a voice shouted.

David turned to see John Barry emerging from the crowd across the street, the Regional Director gestured for him to come over, the surly look more firmly entrenched in his face than usual, if that was possible.

"I think you're about to find out Dave" Drysdale said, sliding the notepad into the pocket of his overcoat "I'll be seeing you"

David hurried across the road, stepping over two of the corpses on the way, by the time he reached Barry the regional director was already looking at him impatiently, his large bulbous face looked even redder in the glare of the flashlight. Before he had a chance to utter a word Barry grabbed him firmly by the arm and led him through the crowd, at its centre was another corpse, only this one wasn't covered by a white sheet.

"This one look like a gangster to you?" Barry asked, gesturing towards the body.

The first thing he noticed was the blue tracksuit, it was a bright blue, Lacoste, a tracksuit he'd seen on a thousand teenagers across the city, the only difference was that this one was stained with red, right across the torso. His eyes moved up towards the head as he saw the two bullet holes just above the eyebrows, even with the blood covering part of his face David could tell that the victim was just a boy, his stomach lurched when the pieces came together in his head, when he realised just what Rob Thomas had done.

"Jesus..." he whispered, more for his own benefit than anyone else's

"Looks like he walked straight into the middle of this mess"

The look of fear was etched upon the boy's face, not like the other victims, each of whom had died angry, determined or surprised, this one was terrified, scared out of his mind that someone was trying to do him harm, and he'd been right to be.

"He's been executed" David said, analysing the three shots, one in the upper chest, probably from a distance, two in the head from close range.

"No witnesses" Barry growled with contempt "Isn't that how these people operate?"

"Do we know who he is?"

"Billy Matteo, lives two streets away, we've just notified his mother"

David swallowed hard "How old?"

"Eighteen years, three months. Gunned down in a residential street. No way this mess is going to stay local, the national press are going to want a piece of it, maybe even the politicians. All this for one dead drug dealer"

David knelt down and examined the body, he tried to concentrate on John Barry's words, to process them but the ringing in his ears, telling him that he was as culpable for Billy Matteo's death as the man who pulled the trigger, refused to let him. Slowly, he stood up.

"Not even that sir" he muttered with regret "I did a quick run through with the MIT boys, and Tony Miller isn't amongst the dead"

Dragging his eyes away from the body he noticed that Barry wasn't even listening, his gaze was directed towards the mass of journalists and photographers forming behind the police barricade, and the numbers were swelling by the minute.

"What's that?" Barry asked distractedly, still staring at the crowd, like a rabbit eyeing a pack of ravenous wolves.

"Tony Miller." David repeated "he's not amongst the deceased"

"Not among the deceased? Officer Walker, how did it come to this? At what point precisely did you lose any semblance of control over the situation before us?"

David looked down at the body of the dead kid and asked himself the exact same question. When he didn't respond John Barry continued.

"What did I tell you? What did I say? How many times do I have to repeat myself? War on my streets will not be tolerated, what exactly are you doing to enforce this? Less than two weeks after these criminals, these pariahs, shoot up half the Albert Dock I find myself here, in the middle of the night, standing over yet another drug fuelled massacre. Only this one, just for fun, well it has the added bonus of civilian causalities thrown in. So Officer, I ask again, how exactly did it come to this?"

"If you're asking who committed these murders then I'm afraid you'll have to-"

342

"I'm not asking any such thing!" Barry cut in, this voice was loud now, and thick with accusation "MIT will find the culprit, that's their job. Your job, Officer Walker, SOCAs job is to get these drug traffickers off our streets before they have a chance to commit these kind of crimes. A task at which you have failed spectacularly. More murders, more crime, more publicity"

Once again his gaze was drawn to the dead body at his feet, Barry's reproach had barely scratched the surface, at any other time he would be seething with indignation, but not today. Today he knew there was no retort to the accusations that lay at his feet, Billy Matteo was the loudest critic he had ever known, and there was no comeback to his allegation, nor would there ever be.

"I'll get to the bottom of this, and quickly. You have my word on that sir"

Barry took a step closer, close enough for David to smell the brandy on his breath.

"Be sure that you do David, my patience is wearing very, very thin"

Without waiting to be dismissed David made his way past Barry and through the crowd of suits around him, as he crossed the street and started back towards his car he spotted Chris Railton walking towards him, his arms outstretched in a questioning gesture.

"What's the score?" he asked.

David didn't stop "Talk to Drysdale, write a full report of what went on here, I want it on my desk in the morning"

By the time he'd finished speaking Railton had been left several paces behind him, fishing the car keys out his pocket he quickened his step.

"Where are you going!?" Railton shouted.

David didn't respond.

Leaving behind the crime scene in Wavertree was like waking from a bad dream, the impact was still there, lingering somewhere in the background, reminding him that there was something profoundly wrong waiting to be embraced, but at least now he could think clearly. He put his foot down and fled the scene faster than he had rushed to it, with each passing mile that he put between himself and those bodies the reality of what he needed to do became clearer and clearer. Just one quick stop, to home, to the box hidden up in the attic and then he was on his way again.

The ace up his sleeve had presented itself to him two days previous, the first bit of unexpected, unanticipated luck that David had experienced in a long while. When he'd first flagged the licence plate number on the red Volkswagen the day after his conversation with Rob Thomas he'd done so more out of hope than expectation. The car was registered to a Mr Charles Thomas, from the date of birth he was most likely a brother or a cousin, no great surprise there, it was only when the car was spotted two days running by a foot patrol in Bootle, located outside an address that did not match that of its owner that David had started to get curious. It didn't take long to get the information that he needed, a quick call to his contact inside Bootle council confirmed that every property on the street was either abandoned, or council owned, the only one that wasn't had been purchased from the council in 1997 by a James Smith, the same Mr Smith who in 2002 and 2005 had been convicted of two possession charges, just the kind of man who might owe someone like Rob Thomas a favour. The more he thought about it the more it made sense, a rundown street in a rundown part of town was the perfect fit for a low lying killer looking to rest his head.

The first thing he noticed upon reaching his destination and killing the engine was that the red Volkswagen was nowhere to be seen. David looked at his watch, it had just passed one a.m, slowly, he opened the car door and stepped onto the street, it was quiet, quieter than he'd expected. He closed the door with as little sound as possible, the scattering of boarded up houses in and amongst the occupied ones gave the street an almost gothic sense, David got the feeling that, in and amongst the darkness and wooden boards, eyes were watching him. He knew it was his imagination playing tricks but the thought disturbed him none the less.

His gaze drifted across the street, before he knew it he was staring intently at the terraced house, his gut told him that it contained Billy Matteo's killer, contained the single greatest threat to his career, contained nothing but problems. He let his eyes fall to his right hand, to the black revolver that resided in it, he thought about what it would be like to kill a man, to be on the other side of it for once, the thought repelled him, made him sick to his stomach, but then so did the alternative. Sliding the gun into his belt he moved towards the end of the street, and into the alley way.

Try as he might, David seemed unable to keep his steps light, the souls of his shoes hit the wet cobbles and seemed to echo off the surrounding houses, he slowed to a snail's pace in an attempt to reduce the noise, and was surprised that it seemed to work. With each step closer he drew to the back of the house he found himself cursing his decision to come alone. Here he was, preparing to break in and execute a multiple murderer, a man who hours earlier had slaughtered twenty men without breaking a sweat, all by himself. He would have felt a whole lot better with an armed tactical unit at his back, and maybe a couple of bullet proof vests, he shook the thought from his head as soon as it had settled, he didn't have to remind himself why he had needed to come alone, he didn't need to think about anything at this juncture, all he needed to do was act.

Reaching the back of the house he pressed his shoulder lightly against the wooden door, locked. A purple rubbish bin rested against the wall, cautiously he climbed on top, his movements were slow, methodical, silent. Once he was perched on his knees David reached up and gripped the top of the wall, using it to steady himself he eased his way to his feet, the bin shook a little under his movement but the firmness of his hold kept it steady. Quickly, he looked around;, the alley was deserted and there was no movement in any of the windows, not wanting to waste another second he heaved himself over the wall and lowered his body down on the other side.

Landing lightly, David turned and surveyed his environment, the back yard of the property was as lifeless and derelict as the front, a small L shape patch of concrete was all that separated him from the back door of the house. The rear wall blocked his view of the windows, making his descent unnoticeable, taking the revolver in his right hand he gripped it tightly and stepped forward.

David peered out from behind the back wall and looked inside the house, a fragile, dirt covered window on the ground floor presented him with a brightly lit and sparsley decorated living room, and sitting within, sunk into an old brown couch was Rob Thomas.

The room was bright enough to ensure that David would be invisible in the shadows of the unlit back yard, despite that he moved cautiously, waiting minutes between steps as he made his way towards the back door. He used the time to examine the man he was about to murder, the sight was almost too difficult to bear; buried into the old couch like a beaten boxer slumped in his corner he held a half empty bottle of Jack Daniels in his right hand, in his left was a black and gold Smith and Weston. His face looked like it had taken a beating, purple bruises mixed with yellow bruises offset by a series of red cuts around his cheeks, jaw and forehead. David watched as he held the barrel of the gun against his left temple, slowly moving it around his face, under his chin and up to the other temple, in that moment any flicker of doubt he may have had over the identity of Billy Matteo's killer was extinguished.

Walker took another step forward, hoping desperately that Rob Thomas would do the job David had come to do for him, the glazed look in his eyes couldn't hide the despair that hid behind them, David gripped the gun tighter, telling himself that, if he had to, he would be doing Thomas a favour. For a few moments more he watched, Thomas continued to keep the barrel of the gun pressed against his face, moving it around slowly like he was in some sort of trance.

The back door was almost in reach as David took another step, for the first time he noticed a bag of what looked like cocaine sitting on the coffee table, from David's vantage point the bag looked like it was unopened, he hoped so, facing Rob Thomas when he was high was only likely to make the situation more difficult.

Gripping the handle with his left hand he gave the door a slight push, it opened without resistance and David was immediately greeted with the sound of the television turned up high, encouraged by the distraction he opened the door further and stepped inside. Closing it softly behind him he realised he was in the kitchen, his heart was beating fiercely in his chest as he raised the gun and aimed it forward, after three slow steps he was in the doorway of the living room, a step later and he could see his target, the pistol still pressed against his face as he drank from the bottle in his left hand. David took one further step forward and heard the floorboard creak under his weight, in that instant everything changed, Thomas was on his feet in a flash, his gun trained on David's upper body before the discarded bottle of Jack Daniels had even touched the floor. For what seemed like an eternity the two men stood in silence, staring at each other over the barrels of their pistols.

"You…" Rob Thomas said eventually "I probably should have guessed"

"Drop the weapon" David said firmly, his heart was pounding and his hand was slightly shaking, breathing through his nose he tried to remember his training.

"How did you find me?"

"Drop the weapon!" David repeated, hearing the firmness in his voice as he imagined the prone body of Billy Matteo.

"Not gonna happen" Rob told him, blinking three times in quick succession, trying to shake away the Jack Daniels.

David took another deep breath "Drop the weapon or I shoot"

Rob shook his head, there was disrespect in the gesture, contempt, that was almost enough to make David pull the trigger right then "Just turn around and walk away. You don't want any part of this"

"What the hell did you do?"

Rob didn't answer straight away, swallowing hard he let his gun drop a few inches, for a moment David thought he was on the verge of surrendering, then the gun was back in its previous position, trained on David's chest.

"I had to…" Rob said, certainty and regret tainting his words "there was no choice in it, no choice at all. It had to be done"

"Why?" David asked, horrified by his answer.

"He was a witness, he made me. One ID and that's it, I'm done in this game, I'm a liability. No witnesses, that's the rule, it's the only way I have value. The only way I have leverage"

"I'm a witness" David replied, tightening his grip on the gun "Why am I still alive?"

"You're…" Rob paused, trying to find the right word "compromised"

"Not anymore. I'm done keeping your secrets and watching people die because of it. You killed an innocent kid tonight, a civilian, there's no coming back from that"

"I don't need you to tell me what I can and can't come back from" Rob told him fiercely.

"I won't let you do it, not anymore. This kid is dead because I let you walk, it's not going to happen again, I won't let it!"

Rob considered his comments for a moment, David tried to guess what the man was thinking but his face was unreadable. He watched as, slowly, Rob Thomas lowered the gun to his side and tossed it onto the couch.

346

"So do it" he said eventually, his voice was even, resigned, though David could still hear a hint of a slur in his words.

Taking a step forward he raised the gun until it pointed at Rob Thomas's head, the man's sudden submission had caught him off guard, he hadn't been prepared for it.

"First tell me about Tony Miller" David said "What did you do with him? Hand him over to McSharry? Like a prize at a fair?"

Rob shook his head slowly "He got away. One of his boys hauled him into a car and sped off before I could get to them"

"Alive?" Rob didn't answer, just held his gaze, David took another step forward and aimed more carefully "ALIVE!?"

"I don't know. I put three in his chest but I got jumped before I could check, I don't know"

"So you gave him back his empire. After all that work, after everything we did to stop him, you just go and give it all back again. Why?" David waited for an answer but it never came, there was a look of almost boredom on the man's face, like he was asking about the weather "ANSWER ME!" he shouted.

Rob took a step forward, then another, David noticed a limp, he kept the pistol raised "Stay back!"

He continued to hobble forward, David took a step back, trying to give himself more time but a moment later Rob was upon him, he pressed his chest into the gun, pushing his torso further and further against the metal barrel until David was using all of his strength to keep his arm straight.

"No more talk" Rob said, looking David hard in the eye as he pressed himself against the revolver "Just fucking do it"

He felt the burn in his biceps as he pushed back, his grip tightened in an effort to keep the pistol in his hand, inadvertently pushing his finger down harder onto the trigger. David found he couldn't tear his eyes away from the intensity of Rob's stare, it was almost as if he was pleading, pleading for David to pull the trigger and end the whole thing.

"DO IT!" Rob shouted fiercely.

David's arm was going weak trying to maintain his hold, he felt his finger press harder on the trigger "You crossed a line. I won't let you do it again..."

He didn't know why he felt the need to justify himself, to explain his actions to the serial killer before him, he reminded himself that he was doing the work of the law, the work that needed to be done, even if people found it easier to pretend that it didn't. In spite of what he told himself he felt the pressure on the trigger reducing.

Rob looked down at the barrel, morbidly waiting to watch his chest explode, when it didn't come he looked back up towards David.

"Do you want to know why I left, back in the day, and why I came to you?" Rob swallowed hard "The night I went to your house, I'd been on the job, I'd been on a couple of days straight by then. You remember Julie McSharry, that tidy little model the old man had married a few years earlier. She got involved with one of the bosses soldiers, I don't even remember the guy's name, some small time muscle or such, he was supposed to be looking after her, carrying her shopping, watching out for trouble, that sort of thing. Well the stupid prick did a lot more than that, by the time I get the call they'd ran off together and no one had seen them for five days..."

Rob stopped talking, swallowed hard and looked down once more at the barrel of the gun, he glared at it expectantly, hopefully, as if he wanted David to put him out of his misery and keep him from having to go on. David remembered Julie McSharry, remembered the questioning when she disappeared. Her husband never gave away a thing, as far as he was concerned she'd ran away, left a note, it wasn't his job to give a shit, her note had made that quite clear. David had always suspected foul play, but then Rob had come along, handed him the lawyer, and the disappearance had taken a back seat. He didn't want to hear what was about to come next, but knew with every fibre of his being that he needed to.

"By the time McSharry called me they'd made it to Dover, dumb cow was still using a credit card. I found them in a little cottage just off the A20. If only she'd been a bit fucking smarter... if only he'd been a little more careful... the bloke, like I said I don't even remember his name. He put up one hell of a fight. You could tell he really loved her by how fiercely he fought in that little cottage, honestly, I was high as a kite and it was more than I was fucking expecting. That guy... he wanted to protect her so bad, so bad that it had to be love, you know? By the time I finally killed him both my guns were empty, I was getting cocky by then, so fucking arrogant that I didn't even think to bring a spare clip, just didn't seem worth it for two people... didn't seem necessary. No guns, no knives, so I did her with my hands. I put my weight on top of her, I wrapped my fingers around her throat and I squeezed the life out of her. I squeezed the air out of her lungs and she used every last breath she had to beg me to stop...and then I buried them..."

David fought to keep his hand steady, he didn't know whether it was shaking out of anger or disgust, maybe both. He tried to think of something to say, something to sum up the thoughts screaming in his head, but nothing would come, in the end all he could manage was a muffled "Jesus"

Rob looked down once more at the barrel, waiting, hoping, but David needed to hear more, needed to know exactly what had transpired before he could end his misery. When Rob looked upwards the anguish on his face was palpable, David reminded himself sternly that it was the mask of a vicious murderer.

"I see her face every night, I hear her voice. Now this kid..." he broke off, unable to continue, David pressed down on the trigger, prepared himself for the inevitable conclusion, Rob seemed to read his mind "Just do it man. End it now before it goes any further"

With the strength that was left in his arm he shoved the gun hard into

348

Rob's chest, causing his target to stumble backwards a few steps, the gun felt heavy in his hand as he carefully took aim. He focused just above the eyebrows, towards the same patch of skin that had been ripped apart on Billy Matteo's forehead. He felt the anger in the pit of his stomach, like a cancer it felt as though it was infecting his entire being, he understood suddenly how a man could become lost in it, how it could blend with pride and indignation to consume a life, or to end one. In that moment a certainty overcame him, an absolute truth that, once acknowledged, immediately made him feel better. He let out a long breath as he stared at Rob Thomas over the barrel of the pistol, he wasn't a killer, it just wasn't who he was. There was a small part of him, somewhere deep down inside that burned with frustrated impotence, but mostly, at that moment, he just felt relieved. Relieved that he knew who he was, and that he could be proud of that person in a way the man standing in front of him would never know.

With the gun still aimed in front of him he shook his head "No. That's not how this is going to go down. I'm taking you in, and you're going to answer to a court of law"

Rob narrowed his eyes, like a poker player trying to read an opponent "What about you man? You think if I start talking I'm going to suddenly just forget your name?"

David shrugged, the movement came naturally, the fears and worries that had plagued his every waking hour suddenly seemed inconsequential compared to what he had almost just become, in the cold reality that shone before him a career meant nothing when compared to a clear conscience.

"Maybe I'll have to answer to a court as well, but I won't lower myself by becoming the same as you, and I won't let you loose again. Hands behind your back"

Rob spat on the floor "Fuck that. I'm not going to no prison"

David stepped forward, with his left hand aiming the gun he used his right to reach for the handcuffs at his belt.

"Hands behind your-"

Before he could finish the sentence Rob's left hand had reached up and grabbed the gun in David's hand, as he twisted it backwards David had no choice but to release his grip before it broke a few of his fingers, as soon as he'd seized the gun Rob gripped David's arm with his free hand and launched him onto the couch, by the time David had landed and turned to face his assailant, the gun was already aimed at his face.

"I said I'm not going to prison" Rob repeated, there was a sternness and a certainty to his words that had not been present when he was unarmed.

David readjusted his body on the couch "So... now you're going to kill a police officer?"

Rob cocked the black revolver "Only if you make me"

"You're gonna have to. Otherwise I'm walking out of this house right now, going straight to the DS in charge of tonight's massacre and telling him everything I know"

"What if there was a third option?"

David pushed himself up from the couch, he waited for a response, a warning, a shot, anything, when that didn't come he spread his arms.

"Like what?"

"We kill the fucker." Rob's voice was ice cold, "We kill Stephen McSharry"

David sensed the opportunity in the proposal, even if he couldn't quite see it, he was suddenly struck with a severe case of déjà vu; the dead of night, a proposal from Rob Thomas, more secrets. There was logic to the suggestion, no question, but David knew immediately that making another pact with the devil would be too much for his weary soul to bare.

"No" he said with a dismissive shake of the head "No more murder. No more bodies"

"You think taking me and you out of the game is going to stop the bodies?" Rob asked incredulously "He told me two hits and that was it, I was done. Tonight he tells me one more; Cassidy. You lock me up and someone else will just move in and take my place. The only difference is that someone is going to be someone messier, someone less discreet-"

"You call that pub discreet?" David interjected.

"You know what I mean, the next guy can be hit back, and then you've got reprisal after reprisal to deal with. You know the bodies won't stop, not now that he is where he is"

David knew it was the truth but couldn't bear to acknowledge it "And whose fault is that?" he asked instead.

"You don't need to be involved, not with the killing, but I need your help to get me, my mother, my brother and his family out of the country"

David almost laughed at the absurdity of the situation; the man he had come to kill was now asking for a favour.

"Why would I even think about helping you again?"

Rob let the revolver rest at his side, the alcohol appeared to be wearing off fast, once again the mask of a psychopath that David tried to attribute to his face was slowly slipping.

"Cos this is the only way out, not just for me, not just for you, for this whole bloody city. You can't put the worms back in the can, not after this. You've seen the way the crazy old git is racking up bodies, do you honestly think that's going to stop? Do you think for one second that Stephen McSharry, the man we know, is ever going to run out of threats, out of fears? He'll always find enemies, and Liverpool's gonna look like a fucking war zone, like the days of Miller and Caddock was some 'garden of eden' type shit. Help me get my family out and I'll do what you can't; I'll end it!"

Listening to the words set his mind racing at a hundred miles an hour, he heard the sense to the argument, the image of Billy Matteo suddenly seemed less bright in his mind. What good would it do to take down Rob Thomas and for him to fall on his own sword, only to leave Stephen McSharry with the lay of land, carte blanche to kill as many innocent civilians as he wanted. Still, it wasn't as easy as all that.

"How exactly am I supposed to get you out?"

"Do whatever you have to. All I need is for you to put us on a flight under a fake name, so long as McSharry's boys can't trace me out the country I can do the rest myself. Call in some favours, feed the bosses some bollocks, I don't know, do whatever it is you police-types usually do, and me and Stephen McSharry are out of your world for good"

It was an appealing argument, without question, but the scolding reprimand from John Barry was still fresh in his mind, tolerance was in short supply amongst the authorities in Liverpool, the trail of death Rob left in his wake was seeing to that.

"It's not that easy," David said eventually, taking a few moments to phrase his response "my boss is trying to pin this whole mess down on me. My job, being what it is, means that I'm the first one to fall when people like you start tearing up the streets. The way things are at the minute I'm hanging on by a thread, calling in favours and using my influence won't go far at all with this knife hanging over my head"

Rob turned away in frustration, David felt for the handcuffs at his belt, he might not be planning to use them just yet but it paid to have options, he'd learned that much at least.

"What if I give you one of McSharry's shipments, coming in this week? Date, time location, think that'll be enough to get the bosses off your back?"

"It might do the trick, yeah" David said, trying to hide the excitement in his voice.

"This Thursday, at Seacroft Docks, I'll get the rest of the details to you later"

David couldn't believe how easily he was being sucked back in, but the promise of a headline arrest, the elimination of McSharry and the chance to save his career just seemed too good to ignore. He still hadn't made up his mind about the man in front of him, he wasn't an easy one to pin down.

"If this works, what are you planning to do for money?" David asked, it made sense to bleed him for as much information as possible, who knew when it might come in useful.

"I've got some put aside, and I've got an idea on how to get a little more. Does that mean we have a deal?"

Rob extended David's gun, handle first, towards him.

"I'm supposed to just let you get away with what you did tonight?" he asked, forcing the image of Billy Matteo to the forefront of his mind, ahead of the drug bust, of McSharry, of a glistening future. He tried to remember how he felt when he'd first laid eyes on the kid, already it was beginning to fade from his memory.

"There's no getting away," Rob replied bluntly "Not from any of it"

David took the gun from Rob and slid it into his belt, the two men looked at each other and David found himself wondering what Rob thought about his role in all this, the copper constantly snapping at his heels. Before he had a chance to ask he heard a hard banging on the front door of the house, Rob looked alarmed and reached for the gun that was resting on the ground.

"Get going, the way you came" Rob hissed urgently "I'll be in touch"

David nodded and darted out of the back door, it was only after he'd scaled the wall and ran to the end of the alley that he allowed himself a chance to catch his breath. He peered into the street from his hiding place, whoever had knocked was already in the house, without wasting an opportunity David ran across the street and climbed into his car. Two minutes later he was in motion, moving slowly out of the street so as to not attract too much attention.

He pulled the revolver from his belt and tossed it onto the passenger seat. The ramifications of their conversation suddenly seemed too complex to process, slowly he tried to remind himself of everything that had transpired since he'd walked into that house with murder on his mind. The more he thought about it the more it felt right, taking Stephen McSharry down within the parameters of the law had already failed once, maybe it was about time to try something else.

Chapter 27

Charlie had been walking around for a little over three hours by the time he made it to his brothers door, the nights events had left him with a lot to think about, despite that he felt as if he'd wasted the time trapped in some kind of daze, reliving rather than assessing the things that he'd seen, though god only knew what help that had been.

McSharry had insisted that he help Begsy dispose of the corpse, which had meant a long drive out towards Manchester, where they'd buried the body in an overgrown patch of woodland. The experience had been grimmer than he might have hoped, the number of wounds inflicted upon the body meant that blood had proved to be a considerable issue, on top of that the corpse had paled faster than expected and looked almost ghost like when they hauled it out of the van and into the moonlit woods.

Once the body was in the ground Charlie's spirits had lifted. Prior to that the process of digging a hole deep enough for their purpose, with the eyes of a dead man on his back had disturbed him more than he liked to admit. By the time Begsy dropped him off at home with a warning to keep his head down and his mouth shut he was more than ready to put some distance between himself and the entire incident.

He'd gotten as far as the front door, with his keys hovering just over the key hole, before he'd changed his mind and stepped backwards onto the street. There was something about killing, or at least being around death, that made him uncomfortable embracing his children. It was almost as if murder was contagious, that by hugging and kissing his two little girls he would somehow contaminate them with the things that he had seen, like a virus it would seep into their innocence, spreading and destroying until there was nothing pure left, just a cesspit of raw, ugly human emotion that they had no need to see.

The prospect of seeing Vicky had unnerved him as well, for all her faults she was still his wife, and like any wife she knew when something was wrong. She would flash him a look, raising her eyebrows while she twirled a strand of hair around her finger that said she knew he wasn't being himself. Lately she'd stopped following up that look with an actual question, it was almost as if these days she didn't want to know what he was getting himself in to, but the question hung between them nonetheless, unasked and unanswered. Sometimes he hated the fact that she knew him so well.

Those were the thoughts that were swimming around his head as he walked away from his front door, at first he'd contemplated a trip to the Stag and Bull, last orders were just about to be called but a stay behind was always liable to be on the cards. He had plenty of money in his back pocket, more than enough to get himself an invite, and a few stiff drinks might be just the thing to shake him from his current funk.

He wasn't far from the entrance when that idea had lost its appeal as well, suddenly the prospect of engaging in mind numbing chit chat with a bunch of pissed old men didn't seem like the best way to spend his night so, turning on his heels, he'd made his way towards Steph's place.

This time he made it past the front door, whether that had more to do with his desire to see Steph or his eagerness to get out of the cold was difficult to say, but either way, ten minutes later he'd wished he hadn't bothered.

Charlie hadn't been asking for much, a bit more warmth and affection, maybe a quick fuck from a woman who was supposed to care about him, a woman he was financially supporting with increasing regularity. Instead, what he'd got was a torrent of abuse the minute he'd walked through the door.

"I haven't heard from you in two days" she whined as she followed him up the stairs "you said you were going to buy me that Louis Vuitton dress, the one we saw in town last week. I told all the girls about it, I told them I was going to christen it tonight... are you even listening to me?"

Charlie took a can of lager from the fridge and collapsed on the couch "I'm listening" he mumbled.

"You haven't been answering my calls, what have you been doing?"

"Working"

"You didn't even have time to call me?"

"No"

Steph stormed into the bedroom leaving Charlie alone with nothing but the new Ibiza album in the CD player for company. He'd hoped that would be the end of it, but a minute later she emerged from the bedroom with a glass of wine in her hand and a scowl etched across her pretty, little face.

"I was supposed to be going out tonight" she said, pausing to take a large gulp of white wine "I was supposed to be going out in the new Louis Vuitton dress that you were supposed to have bought me. I've been looking forward to it all week, I had my hair done, my nails done, my tan done, and all for what? For nothing, you were nowhere to be seen and I've spent the night sat on my fucking arse watching Big fucking Brother!"

At least the beer was going down well, he blitzed half the can, rested his head against the back of the couch and propped his feet up onto the coffee table.

"Why didn't you just go out in a different dress?"

Steph kicked his left thigh hard, causing his feet to drop from the coffee table onto the floor, the only emotion that had time to register was shock before he realised she was screaming at him hysterically.

"I'm not going to go out in another dress! I'm sick of going out in all those shitty clothes I've been wearing for years, I wanted to go out in MY Louis Vuitton dress, not some shitty piece of crap I've been out in a thousand times before. Tell me Charlie, what is the fucking point of having a fella with money if he's never around to bloody spend it on you? I bet your wife's seeing plenty of it isn't she? I bet your wife's getting the fancy dresses she wants!"

354

She ended her tirade by aiming another kick at the side of his leg, despite the fact that his foot was now firmly positioned on the wooden floor. Never, in his life had Charlie been overcome with such an overwhelming urge to hit a woman, he leapt up, as if to do so, before the memory of the nights violence stopped him in his tracks; an empty eye socket, the whisper of the bullet as it passed through the silencer.

He pushed her roughly out of the way, hoping she understood just how much she owed to his restraint. As he made his way down the stairs and onto the street, he could hear Steph's voice bellowing from her bedroom window, screaming abuse and cursing his name with all the air in her lungs.

From there he just started walking, he had no particular direction, it didn't matter, snippets of what had happened in the warehouse continued to play over and over in his mind monopolising his concentration. It wasn't as if it frightened him, or scared him, that would have been easy, what was causing him the most distress was that he still didn't know how he felt about the things he'd seen, or how he fitted in to this new world in which he somehow found himself.

He understood Stephen McSharry's motivation, the dead man in question had gone to no small effort to try and kill him, he'd come close too, pretty much as close as you could come without being successful. That was how this world worked, when you gambled you gambled with your life, McSharry knew it, Begsy knew it and no doubt the guy in the restaurant knew it too. He knew it when he picked up the gun, knew it when he entered the restaurant and knew it when he fired those shots into an empty chair. It was the nature of the game that he was now a part of; high stakes, high rewards.

What didn't sit right with him was the brutality of the murder, killing was one thing, it was horrible, and it was ugly, but doing what they were doing it was necessary, no question. Torture on the other hand, that was something different, that kind of thing was meant for Marines and POWs, if it had a place in this world then it was in some cave, in a forgotten corner of Afghanistan, not in a warehouse on the Liverpool waterfront. If a guy was a problem and there was no other way around it, then putting him down was the only logical thing to do, but cutting a guy's flesh, bleeding him till he cried, making him beg for his life, Charlie just didn't know if he wanted any part of that.

He found, as he had a lot lately, that as soon as he started trying to justify murder to himself, an image of Leroy Tate would pop into his head. Most of the time he felt ok about what had happened, the guy had come at him with murderous intent after all, and the only way Charlie was ever going to break through that glass ceiling was by doing something unique, something the average guy on the street wouldn't. Thanks to Leroy and a baseball bat he'd done exactly that and he had no doubt it had been the reason why he was suddenly on the inside. Yet despite that, on occasion, he would suddenly see those events from a different angle, imagine someone describing the events from another point of view, and a tightness would take hold of his chest. At the end of the day he'd betrayed Leroy, he could try and dress it up and spin it in whatever way he wanted but when it came right down to it he knew that was the truth. Loyalty had always been important to Charlie, it was a trait that gave a man worth, he tried to tell himself that loyalty was to your family, to your friends, to your employer, not some two bit drug dealer who overcharged you every chance he got. He told himself that, but when those moments came, when he saw it from that different angle, those arguments suddenly seemed like they weren't worth shit.

He shook his head and tried to dislodge the image that was wedged within; Leroy Tate convulsing on his back, eyes rolled into the back of his head, blood seeping from his left temple. He shook his head again and spat onto the pavement.

The cold evening air was biting into his flesh when he realised he was heading towards Rob's flat, he glanced at his watch; nearly one in the morning, unless things had gone badly wrong his brother would be back by now. He wondered if someone had notified Tony Miller of his man's failure before Rob got to him, Charlie hoped so, he hoped that the bastard knew he'd failed before he died, that defeat was the final realisation to pass through his head when the end came.

Charlie spent the rest of the journey trying to untangle the conflicting lines of thought that were mixed up inside his brain, he soon realised that no matter what he thought about, no matter what issue he embraced, each train of thought led him back to that warehouse, to the guttural screams of a man who'd just had his eye ripped out of its socket.

By the time he reached the flat the cold had left his hands and ears practically numb. He rapped ice cold knuckles against the door three times in quick succession and drew them up to his mouth, rubbing them together and blowing whatever hot air was left in his body against the frozen appendage. Charlie waited for just over a minute before he heard any kind of movement, a few seconds later the door opened in front of him.

Charlie clocked the collection of bruises and cuts on his brothers battered face immediately, he was wearing a black shirt with a pair of denim jeans, Charlie found himself wondering whether it was the same outfit he'd done the job in. Rob opened the door as far as it would go, he gave a cautious look towards either end of the street before he settled his attention on his guest.

"Someone fucked you over good style didn't they? Mind if I come in?" Charlie made a show of vigorously rubbing his hands together against the cold.

Rob didn't respond, instead he just stepped aside and allowed Charlie to cross the threshold, he didn't suspect the silence was a very good sign.

Charlie kept rubbing his hands together even after the door closed, inside the flat wasn't much warmer than outside, a fact he was likely to reiterate to his brother once he'd gaged his mood. Stepping into the living room he spotted the bag of coke he'd given Rob a few days earlier, at first glance it looked untouched.

"Planning a bit of a party?" Charlie asked as his brother followed him into the living room.

"I was playing with the idea," Rob said, heading straight for the bag he snatched it up and dropped it into a small wooden cupboard on the opposite side of the living room "decided against it in the end, drugs are for losers, you know?"

Charlie let out a laugh and dropped onto the couch as Rob disappeared into the kitchen "I'm with you there, bro"

A moment later Rob returned with two cans of lager, Charlie watched him closely, he was acting strange, no question, but it was a different kind of strange than the night he'd killed the Caddock lot, that night he'd seemed like he was on the brink of losing it, like insanity was just a gentle push away. Tonight he was different; guarded, maybe a little more edgy, he could still hear the same trace of melancholy that had been in his voice that night, but the rest was different. Maybe his big brother was becoming reacquainted with his old ways, becoming desensitised again, Charlie wasn't sure how that made him feel, like a lot of things these days.

"What are you doing here, Charlie?" Rob asked, handing him the lager "It's like one in the morning"

Charlie opened the can and listened to the comforting hiss as the metal split, he always liked that sound, it made him feel safe, like he was home. If he really thought about it he could probably link it back to some childhood memory, maybe from when their father was still around, so he decided not to think about it.

"I didn't really fancy going home" he said after taking his first swig of lager "it's been a bit of a rough night. Spent the last few hours just wandering round to be honest, then I thought why don't I come visit my big brother, see how his night went"

Rob sat on a chair on the other side of the room and opened his can "I'd have thought you'd have already heard, what with being on the payroll and all"

The bitterness in Rob's tone annoyed him, it annoyed him that they weren't over this yet, that Rob couldn't just let it go, but that had never been his brothers way, and he saw no point in trying to make it so now. Taking another drink from the can he tried to make his voice as mellow as possible.

"There's no need to be like that lad, it's just a bit of extra dough in the pocket, that's it. Nothing to get worked up about, nothing that's gonna change anything"

"Maybe it will, maybe it won't"

"You alright?" Charlie asked genuinely "you seem a little off"

Rob flashed him an impatient look "Any idea why that might be?"

"How'd it go?"

Rob fidgeted in his chair and ran a hand over his short hair, "Not great. I got most of his people, but Miller got away, mind you I put three in his chest first, so there's a decent chance that whoever bundled him into the car isn't doing much more than lugging around a famous corpse, but that's not really the point is it? If the old man can't prove he's dead then people aren't going to believe it, which could make for a messy transition for those new friends of yours. After that it got worse, a young lad showed, got a look at my face... I had to drop him too"

Rob uttered the words calmly, but Charlie knew as soon as he heard them that it would be tearing his brother up inside, he wanted to know how young was 'young' but he couldn't find the heart to ask. Rob took another drink from the can, keeping his eyes glued to the floor, like he was afraid to meet his brother's gaze.

"Shit Rob," Charlie said eventually, unable to think of anything more comforting to say "You ok?"

Rob swallowed hard "What's done is done, right? No use crying about it"

He took his brothers hint and quickly moved the conversation on "You think McSharry's gonna feel the same way about the Tony Miller side of it?"

"Not my problem" Rob said, it sounded more like he was trying to convince himself than he actually believed it. Ideas were already swimming around Charlie's head, guesses on what the next move would be, predictions on how the entire game would play out, he took another sip of lager and felt an excited tingle pass through his body.

"Makes you wonder though, doesn't it?" Charlie said, speaking half to Rob and half to himself "What are the guys on the street going to think? On the one hand they hear the boss might still be kicking, on the other they know that all the muscle, all the players that kept it ticking have just been dropped. The boys who ran it on the street, who were the face of Miller's crew, just wiped out. I know I've said this to you before Rob but that's one hell of a fucking gift you've got there, Jesus fucking Christ! If that crew have the slightest chance of making it they're gonna need a lot of people to step up, fast"

Rob chose to ignore the compliment, although from the look he gave Charlie it didn't seem like he'd taken it in its intended spirit anyway.

"If they get the chance to step up" Rob said "If I know the old man he'll have Begsy and the others swarming all over those lads before they have a chance to settle. You probably want to turn your phone off for a couple of days Charlie, trust me when I tell you you want no part of that phone call"

"You think it's gonna be bad?"

Rob took another drink and nodded "Even if the Miller talk turns out to be just rumour, you're still going to have at least a couple of loyal boys who are gonna go to the matt for the guy. I reckon at the very least you're looking at half a dozen bodies for this kind of thing, and that's if only a few of them believe the rumours"

"There could be more?"

"There could be more!"

He thought about the guy McSharry had been telling him about a few hours earlier, though it felt like a hell of a lot longer. Hing or Ho or something, Tony Miller's Asian supplier although, maybe ex was more appropriate now. According to McSharry the guy had gone to ground, in hiding till he got the word that Tony Miller's influence had been wiped clean from the streets of Liverpool. Charlie hoped he'd found a comfortable hole to hide in, from the sound of it he'd be staying there a little while longer. His thoughts drifted towards Stephen McSharry and the kind of plans he must have been formulating at that very second.

"I bet you pissed him off good style with that one"

Rob responded by fixing him with an intent stare, he realised it was the first time since he'd arrived that he felt like Rob was really looking at him, but it was more than that, he seemed to be studying him, just as Charlie had done when he first arrived. He took another drink, finishing off the can, and dropped it onto the floor, the weight of his brothers gaze was beginning to make him feel a little self-conscious, he leaned back on the couch and returned Rob's stare in kind, whether or not he was trying to be defiant he couldn't say, but it had the desired effect, a moment later Rob began to speak.

"The old git is losing the plot, Charlie" he uttered the words wearily, like a man running on empty "he says he wants me for another job. The bastard swore I'd be done after two and now he says one more. What's he gonna say after that?"

Rob dropped his head into his hands, Charlie let the silence hang between them, he waited until his brother lifted his head, finished off the can and dropped it onto the floor.

"Well, I reckon that's probably got something to do with the guy who tried to kill him tonight?"

"What? Who?"

"Didn't get a name, but he was one of Miller's. Saw it with my own eyes bro, we were having dinner in some Italian gaff, shooter comes out of nowhere and starts firing, I just managed to get the old man out of the way"

Rob flashed him an angry look, it only lasted a second, before a shake of the head transformed it into something closer to inquisitive.

"How'd you know he was one of Miller's?"

"Begsy went to work on him afterwards. It was proper brutal like, he gave it up in the end. Sounds to me like this new job of yours is his way of making sure this kind of thing doesn't happen again"

"What? Kill anyone and everyone before they have a chance to become a threat? What kind of crazy shit is that?"

It was easy to see that his brother was getting agitated, but in spite of that fact Charlie couldn't help but defend McSharry against Rob's accusations.

Maybe it was because he'd spent so long playing both sides of the argument over and over in his head, that hearing one without the other felt like a lie, a lie he was too involved to ignore. He knew he was about to annoy Rob even more, but he started shaking his head nonetheless.

"It ain't that crazy. How else is he supposed to make sure that he hasn't got people coming for him the way he came for Miller?"

"Charlie, the guys a psychopath," Rob shouted back impatiently, he heard the condescension in his tone, like he was trying to convince his stupid little brother of the most obvious thing in the world, Charlie squeezed his hand tight to keep from showing the anger "he's buried all of his enemies and now he's looking to bury his friends. You know why? Do you? Because that's all he knows. For guys like him it's never enough, it's never over, there's always someone left to punish, someone left to beat, the old man doesn't know how to live any other way"

Charlie shrugged his shoulders and tried to dismiss the seriousness in Rob's tone, he let out a little laugh that felt forced even to him.

"Yeah well, what can you do?"

Rob waited for a moment before he responded, waited until he had Charlie's full attention.

"What if I told you I was going to kill him?"

Charlie let out another snigger, this one came a lot easier "I'd say you were out of your fucking mind. Wake up, you're not serious are you?"

It wasn't a question Charlie needed to ask, he knew the answer just by looking at his brothers face.

"He's losing it Charlie, he told me two hits and I was done, now he's demanding more. If I don't get out now you know he's going to have me kill every last dealer from here to Manchester"

Charlie leaned forward and pointed a finger at his brother "You're the one who's losing it Rob, you really think you could get through all his muscle, without the kind of background work you've usually got? I know you're good mate, but are you sure you're that good? There's some hard bastards in there, and at least one of them knows all about you"

"I don't need to get through them all" Rob replied quickly, quick enough to tell Charlie that he'd been giving it some thought "just enough of them to get sight of the guy at the top"

He'd seen that look in Rob's eyes before, that stubborn, pig headed look that said any criticism of his ideas would just fuel them that little bit faster, in that look he saw his world falling apart.

"And what about the rest of them? How far do you reckon you'll get before they track you down, how long before they track me down for Christ's sake!"

"I can get us out, all of us, trust me Charlie"

He knew they were both thinking about the same thing; Alexis and Zoe, Charlie felt a resentment building inside him that their uncle might jeopardise their safety just to settle an old score. The thought passed through his head that he would kill Rob where he stood before he let him endanger his little girls, he was embarrassed by the notion the second he'd thought it and passed it off as the fears of an overly protective father. Rob's sudden declaration had thrown so many aspects of his life into doubt, he stood up and started pacing across the small living room as he tried to put his thoughts in order.

"You need to slow down a minute, ok, cos a few seconds ago you and me were shooting the shit and now all of a sudden you've got me in a war with the people who pay my wages. You've got me fearing for my family's lives. I'm not going anywhere lad, you hear me? This is my home, this is my life"

"You have to come with me," Rob told him, Charlie heard that old condescension in his tone again, his big brother trying to tell him how to live his life "you all do; Vicky, mar, the kids, we all have to get out together. If I do this thing you're going to be the first person they come to ask, and they won't be asking gently"

Charlie saw himself back in that warehouse, he saw himself in the place of Miller's boy, Begsy, with tools in hand, standing over him. He heard himself making those terrible screams, imagined feeling his own eye being sliced out of its socket, he involuntarily took a step back, as if it would help him escape the images, Rob was watching him eagerly.

"Don't fucking do it then!" Charlie blurted out "You really are one cheeky bastard, you know that Rob? You just show up here, out of nowhere, after ten years, you get these fancy ideas in your head and you go and you fuck the lives we've been building here this whole time, lives you haven't got a fucking clue about! Liverpool is all I know, all right, this is my world, and you wanna tear it down all because you have trouble looking yourself in the mirror"

He knew the words had struck a nerve by the way Rob's face hardened, he took a step towards Charlie, the movement had more than a hint of aggression in it, Charlie mirrored the gesture, he was ready to take this as far as it needed to go.

"You know that's not why" Rob's voice was low, threatening.

"I'll tell you what I do know, you're jealous!" the words were spilling out of his mouth faster than he could think, he looked at his brothers angry face and felt an overwhelming urge to smash it in "You're jealous that your useless, fuck up of a little brother is finally starting to make a name for himself. That's what this is, isn't it? Isn't it!? I'm finally stepping out from under your shadow and you can't bloody well bare it. This is my big chance, right here, after all these years I'm finally getting some respect, I'm making a name for myself. This is my big chance and you don't know how to deal with it any other way than by trying to fuck it up!"

Rob took a step forward and pushed him hard in the chest, as Charlie stumbled backwards he readied himself to push back, but before he had a chance Rob was in his face, his voice thick with anger in a way that Charlie had never heard before.

"I had to kill a kid tonight!" he spat the words out like he was trying to expel the experience from his body "a fucking child, an innocent kid, and I had to watch him die. He died because Stephen McSharry put me there tonight, because I needed to keep my family safe. Do you know what that's doing to me? What that's doing to me right now? Nah, you haven't got a fucking clue. This is what happens when you let that man into your life, when you let his agenda dictate what you do, and you let his needs rise above your choices. Now I'm being told I have to kill again, where the fuck does it end Charlie? Ey, when is enough? Once you're in you don't ever get out from under this guy, that's a promise"

Rob shook his head and walked away, he moved towards the small wooden cupboard on the other side of the room, letting his hand hover over the draw that had the bag of coke inside. He seemed to consider it for a moment before he gave another shake of the head, walked back towards his chair and sat down. Charlie went back to the couch, they sat in silence for a few minutes, he thought about what his brother had said, he imagined a life of killing people like Leroy Tate, he weighed that against how good it felt to have money, to be somebody. Since he'd taken the bat to Leroy's head he'd felt different, he'd felt like a success, he told himself that was how a man should feel, that a life of feeling that good couldn't be ignored. But that was just one moment, one instinctive, defensive swing of a baseball bat, to do it every day was incomprehensible to him, trying to understand how it would make him feel was like trying to understand how it felt to walk on the moon. He looked at Rob, at how a lifetime of killing had left a weight around his neck he just couldn't shake. Charlie had always known who he was and what he thought, now everything was suddenly so muddled.

"I don't know Robo, I'm earning good money now..." he let the sentence trail off when he realised how stupid it sounded.

"Don't worry about money, I've got that covered. You remember when we were at McSharry's place, he had a safe behind his desk, I spotted a load of cash inside, a couple of mil easy. If we can get to that before we kill him we're made. It'll be more than enough to get us on our way"

A couple of million, Charlie looked down and saw that he was rubbing his hands together without even realising it. The money he was seeing now was pittance compared to that kind of cash, more money for less killing, Rob's plan wasn't without its logic. Still, there were a few pressing questions he had first.

"On our way where?"

"New York. Me and Jo have friends there, friends who'll help you guys get set up. It can be a whole new life for you Charlie, for Vicky, for Zoe, for Alexis. Don't you think you owe them more than this?"

He saw the iconic symbols of New York in his mind, imagined a life where Times Square, Central Park and the Statue of Liberty were daily realities for his two little girls. With that kind of money he could be the father he'd never been able to be here, the husband he'd never been able to be, with Rob keeping him on the straight and narrow he could be a better person. Just as the dream was starting to settle the sharp points of reality began to slice through it, he thought about Steph, whether he had it in him to leave her, she was as big a part of his life as anything he had, and to follow his brother he'd have to give her up.

"I have other commitments too you know Rob, it's not all just about Vicky and the kids"

The disappointed look in his brother's eyes told him that his efforts at subtlety hadn't been very effective, he felt the urge to shy away from that look, at the judgement lying within it, but he didn't. For everything his brother was asking of him, he had no right to judge the choices that Charlie had made.

Rob pointed his index finger at him, with that look still in his eyes "Fuck those commitments! Think about your family, that's all that matters. All the other bollocks, it doesn't mean shit. Your head needs to be with your family. You don't want to end up like the old man, do you Charlie? You're better than that, we both are"

It occurred to him that Rob must have felt strongly about the subject to invoke the memory of their father, since the old man walked out Rob had avoided acknowledging his existence to an almost obsessive level, as if by refusing to speak of him he could eradicate the influence he had had on their lives. Charlie understood why his brother would use that argument now, the thought of being like him, of inheriting that same cowardice made him sick to his stomach.

"My family?" he said with a small smile "In NYC?"

Rob leaned forward and returned the smile; he had the look of a car salesman on the verge of sealing a tidy little commission.

"You'll love it our kid, whatever you want, whenever you want it. Food, booze, entertainment 24/7. Your daughters will get the chance to grow up in the greatest city on Earth"

"I always thought that was Liverpool"

"Well now you can put that theory to the test"

They stayed up for the rest of the night drinking lager and planning out their future, Charlie asked every question he could think of and Rob answered each one with an enthusiasm he hadn't seen in his brother since they were kids. After that Rob started talking about all the things he wanted them to do together, he told Charlie about all of his favourite bars, the best restaurants, where they could catch the Liverpool games. When the sun came up they headed out of the flat and wandered the streets in search of a greasy spoon cafe, talk of New York had long since expired by the time they'd found somewhere that was open and they ordered a full English each. In its place they talked shit to one another, like they had when they were kids, bickering over football opinions, assigning blame for childhood misdemeanours and taking the piss out of each other, back and forth, back and forth, a natural bloody rhythm.

Charlie felt like he was twelve again, the difficult choices that would be waiting for them seemed a million miles away, neither of them acknowledged what they were going to have to do, neither talked about it, what was the point. Shovelling a fork full of bacon and sausage into his mouth he remembered a time when a post-nightout fry up had been a Thomas tradition, back when simple lives were filled with simple routines. He washed down the bacon and sausage with a mouthful of tea and imagined what it would be like to live the simple life again.

Chapter 28

The dimly lit study was peacefully quiet. A tumbler, half full of Johnny Walker Blue, rested on the 19th century mahogany desk. To the left of it was the day's edition of the Liverpool Echo, the headline jumped from the page, in bold, capital letters: NINETEEN DEAD IN GANG RETALIATION SHOOTINGS. As usual the civilians had it all backwards, the article tried to paint the entire episode as a response from the gang who'd been hit a week and a half earlier at the Albert Dock, sources inside the Merseyside Police department confirmed they were still chasing up leads for the initial attack and were confident that an arrest would be forthcoming, what a load of bollocks.

Stephen McSharry took a sip of whisky and continued to read, the article claimed that identification of the murder victims was still ongoing and that police were expected to go public with the names of the deceased by the end of the day. The article didn't mention anything about the boy caught in the cross fire, it appeared the police were hoping to buy themselves some time before that story broke, no doubt hoping they might have the man responsible in bracelets by the time the information leaked. The thought of their inevitable failure brought a smile to his face, he imagined them frantically scrambling for information and coming up short every time, chasing this particular ghost had already used up a whole lot of police manpower, and if he had his way it would use up a whole lot more.

It seemed information about the dead boy was in short supply at the moment, even the shooter responsible had decided to keep that piece of information to himself, luckily for McSharry his contacts within the Merseyside Police Force were a little bit more reliable when it came to the dissemination of critical information. Had he been forced to rely on the disclosure of certain well paid hitters he may have found himself as ill-informed as every other reader of the Liverpool Echo.

He reread the details, limited as they were, and allowed himself a moment to marvel at the kids talent. In all his years he'd never known anything like it, that instinct, that technique, that composure, it was unparalleled. During the boys early days he'd watched from afar when he'd killed for him; the speed and the accuracy was almost beautiful to behold, it was like he made murder into an art form. McSharry took another drink and used the details in the article as an outline, importing memories from hits gone by to fill in the gaps, a thing of beauty, without doubt.

But talented or not, Rob Thomas was doing nothing to appease his anxieties over the boys mental state. His partial break down over the phone, coupled with the killing of the kid and the fact that he chose to withhold the information, hinted to McSharry that Thomas Senior was reaching the end of his shelf life. It was a shame, no question, a talent like that didn't come along every day, but when push came to shove McSharry needed more than just talent to keep hold of what he'd taken back, he needed loyal heads on broad shoulders. Still the question remained; how much did the boy have left in the tank? He would have to think on that.

Readjusting his sitting position brought a sharp pain at the base of his spine, a souvenir from the night before, and the burning fury that had slowly been reducing raged back into life. He stood up and took a long gulp of the whisky, hoping to banish both the pain in his back and the memory of its cause, and started walking around the room. The very notion that someone would try to take his life had the blood boiling in his veins, he remembered the screams that followed after he removed the cunts eye, and it served to relax his growing anxiety.

Killing the bastard had felt good, there was no doubt about it, but it was hardly the end. Word had been put on the street; a five grand bounty for anyone who could provide further information about the man they had killed. Name, address, family, whatever they could get their hands on. McSharry intended to make such an example of him that no one would even consider crossing his path again, lest they suffer his wrath to the grave and beyond. Once they knew more about the man who raised the gun to Stephen McSharry's head then his house would burn, every member of his family would die and his name would become an omen to all those willing to test Stephen McSharry's patience. A message would be sent, and it would ring out through the streets of Liverpool and beyond.

A similar message would be sent to Tony Miller, if the bastard was still alive. When the call came through to say that Miller might not be dead McSharry had been livid, yet as the hours passed he began to see opportunity in the way that events had unfolded. Finding Miller alive would give him the chance to subject his enemy to a similar level of torture to that of his pup. Only this time it would be McSharry who got to have the fun, the very thought brought goose bumps to his flesh; cutting Miller apart one piece at a time until there was nothing left but a broken, bumbling mess, before firing the final bullet into his brain. The idea filled him with excitement, pure lustful excitement.

There was no doubt that the attempt on his life had altered the way he was seeing things, it highlighted just how vulnerable he was. It was a harsh truth to face but one he intended to confront nonetheless. As long as there were players out there who were working towards their own agenda, who answered to no one within the McSharry organisation and who didn't fear the name the way only those who had been up close could, then they were always liable to cause problems somewhere down the line. Military dictators had been doing it for centuries, and now it was time for Stephen McSharry to get in on the act.

That was why Martin Cassidy had to go, he'd been a friend for a long time and they had achieved some great things together, but that had been when McSharry was happy with a piece of the pie, now he wanted the whole thing. Friendship was ephemeral and it equated to little more than weakness, the only sure fire path to safety was dominance. In his time Martin Cassidy would have recognised that fact, but the tired old man who now bore his name had lost all concept of what it meant to be fierce, to a degree that made him toothless, but what about the next man to take the mantle, what guarantees could McSharry have that he would fall into line just as easily. No, it was safer this way, one power, one order, on some level he knew his old friend would understand the necessity behind his actions.

There was another reason to remove Cassidy from the equation; how sure could McSharry be that Tony Miller had been acting alone when he sent his man into Francesca's? He'd known friendships before that had amounted to little more than a long con, who was to say Martin Cassidy was any different. He finished off the Johnny Walker Blue and smiled, trying to convince himself of the validity of his actions was a wholly unnecessary act, Martin Cassidy would fall either way.

Things were moving quickly now, he had little time to second guess himself. A call had been made to Samuel Ho, the young entrepreneur didn't sound too pleased about having to hide out in a Midlands hotel for another three or four nights, but McSharry had convinced him easily enough. Until more was known about the fate of Tony Miller it was essential that Samuel Ho was out of pocket as far as any potential enemies might be concerned. All his new meal ticket had to do was keep his head down for a couple more days, give him and his boys the time to clean up Rob Thomas's mess and then he could return home to a new dawn.

McSharry poured himself a second glass of whisky and settled back into his chair. Plans were already afoot to begin utilising their new found supply, even for a city as drug hungry as Liverpool they were on the verge of finding themselves inundated with more product than they could shift. Feelers had gone out to Manchester, Leeds and Newcastle and the early responses were good, still McSharry knew any such expansion would have to be done carefully, not only would the local players need delicate handling but he also had a strong urge to keep his name of the lips off any additional coppers. Keeping a check on the gangsters and the busies in his own town was time consuming enough, he had no intention of multiplying those nuisances across the entire North of England.

His peace was interrupted by a knock on the door. McSharry rose and told his guest to enter, the door opened and Begsy marched in followed a few steps behind by Ads and then Nikolai. All three were breathing heavily, McSharry immediately noticed the pent up energy in Begsy, it was the way he always acted after a solid bout of violence.

"Well?" he asked, walking around the table and inspected the three men closer, a few drops of red on Ads white shirt, a twisted smile on Nikolai's face, and some bruising around Begs' right knuckles, though that could just have easily have come from the night before.

Begsy was the first to speak, pulling a grey pistol from his belt and handing it to Ads.

"Tips were good, both of them"

McSharry raised his glass to the three men and took a drink, since word of the attack on Tony Miller had spread, certain disreputable characters had come out of the woodwork, offering their services in the hope of earning favour with the new power. One such individual was Skip Demelweek, a small time con man and coke fiend. In spite of his obvious character flaws he was still a man who knew a lot more than most and when he'd called to tell McSharry and his people the location of the two remaining Miller safe houses they had been inclined to listen.

"Excellent news" McSharry responded before turning his attention to Nikolai "Talk to the snitch again. If you think he's holding something back; be creative. No sense in letting all that knowledge go to waste, is there?"

Nikolai nodded, flashing that same twisted smile that McSharry always found amusing he made his way out. McSharry waited until he'd closed the door behind him before focusing back on Begsy.

"No sign of Miller?"

"None"

He slammed his fist against the desk "So what did happen?"

"We hit them fast and hard, one after the other. Took a couple of kilos from each"

"Given what Ho told us that should be the last of their stash, shouldn't it?"

Begsy shrugged "More or less"

With no product to put onto the street McSharry wondered how long it would be before those still loyal to Tony Miller started looking for a new home, maybe if he'd seen McSharry coming a little earlier he may have had time to stock pile some supply, as it was the dominant force in Liverpool was running dry fast, but that was only half the battle.

"What about muscle?"

Begsy gave a derisive snigger and shook his head "Threadbare. A few pushers with 9 millimetres trying to step up. We took them down easy, there were a couple of junkies hanging about in the second place" Begsy nodded towards Ads "The boy here went to town on those two"

Ads scratched at his beard, flashed him his biggest shit eater grin and slammed his right fist into his left palm "Sent them to a better place boss" he said eagerly.

No drugs, no muscle. He considered how long the war may have dragged on if he hadn't had Rob Thomas to call on, the boy may have failed to get Miller but he'd succeeded in crippling his organisation, McSharry found it difficult to say which of the two he would have preferred.

He took another drink, slowly he could feel the alcohol making its way to his head "No casualties on our side?"

"Sie took a stray shot to the arm, we dropped him at the cockneys warehouse. Docs already on the way"

So far the Drake's waterfront warehouse was proving as advantageous an acquisition as the brothers themselves, he made a mental note to ensure that their contribution quickly started to increase. Their first shipment of ecstasy was due to arrive in a little over fifteen hours, perfectly timed to flood a weekend market going dry due to the wayward Mr Miller. If the brothers supply was as plentiful, and as potent as he had been led to believe then it would go a long way towards convincing those further down the food chain to get on board with the new world order. Dealers could keep selling the same drugs, users to keep hitting the same highs, all that would change was the man at the top, reaping the rewards.

It was a big week for the cockneys, a week that could very well define their future role, even more so now that Samuel Ho had fallen into line. With Miller off the map he was the only game in town and the Drake brothers would need to embrace that sentiment wholeheartedly. If they didn't, then he was willing to dish out a dose of the treatment their initial hospitality had warranted, but such thoughts were for another day.

"Ok, good. No muscle in their last two safe houses, that can mean only one of two things; either they've got no soldiers left after last night, or they've gone to ground with their boss"

Begsy's shrug suggested he was unconcerned by either scenario "Either way they're on their last legs. The more word spreads the more we're gonna get people like Skip trying to earn a favour with the new power. Dead or alive the prick won't stay hidden for long"

McSharry found his attention being drawn towards Ads, his eyes moved from Mcsharry, to the ground and back again in a continuous loop. He crossed his arms and watched, the soldiers urge to speak was unsubtle to say the least, and if he was shy about sharing then it could only be about one thing; the identity of their hit man.

Begsy had kept him up-to-date on what the boys were saying; they'd passed from mild curiosity to something resembling obsessive speculation. A few suspected Begsy to be behind it and the big man did nothing to distance himself from the rumour, McSharry could only wonder how that lie was intensifying his hatred for the boy, the rest of them were indulging in an endless stream of theories and predictions that were growing increasingly tiresome.

He fixed Ads with a cold stare, his voice close to a low growl "You got something you want to say?"

Ads looked away and shook his head "No"

"Good. Wait outside"

He slunk out the room without a word, McSharry waited until he'd closed the door behind him before lifting the newspaper from the table and presenting the headline to Begsy.

"Even when he fails he still puts on a show"

Begsy responded with an unimpressed shrug "He still failed"

"Not entirely"

"That's good enough for you?"

The thrill of the hunt was still fresh in Begsy's system, it made him bolder and more prone to rash comments, the kind of comments he knew better than to share in the cold light of day. McSharry dropped the paper onto the table and looked the big man square in the eye.

"Careful" he warned, he let the word hang between them as he reached for his glass and took another long gulp "I'll admit that when he called he didn't sound all there, we may struggle to get much more out of him before he cracks"

"You don't know what he's liable to do when that happens, he knows a lot"

Looking down at the front page of the Echo he nodded, once he could confirm that Miller and Cassidy were both out of the picture then the greatest threat to his control would be a loose mouth, it was the same thing that had cost him last time. The lawyer couldn't cope and McSharry wasn't wise enough to it, could he honestly tell himself that he didn't see the same kind of weakness in the boy.

"You think I need to put him down?" he asked, still looking at the headline.

"Always have"

He let his gaze wander down the article, picking out certain words along the way; *nineteen dead, no witnesses, gangland slaughter.*

"The kid is special" he pushed the paper aside and returned to his chair on the other side of the desk "See how he copes with the next job, we'll reassess from there. After everything that happened last night I didn't gage your opinion on the brother?"

Begsy took a moment to consider the question "Seems like a decent soldier, could have some value"

"He's stepped up twice already, killing the nigger, saving my life, not a bad start. Still, different mould from the other one isn't he?"

Begsy nodded in agreement "More heart. Less talent"

McSharry laughed "Well put. Keep an eye on him over the next couple of weeks, see how he develops. Down the line any attempt on the brother will have to be thought out very carefully, I'm not wasting my time grooming the kid now just to turn him into an enemy further down the road, you hear me?"

Begsy nodded again.

The knock at the door caused both men to turn, Ads entered a moment later with a sheepish look plastered across his face.

"You got a visitor boss"

McSharry leaned forward in his chair "Who?"

"Martin Cassidy"

McSharry shared a cautious look with Begsy, he'd expected some form of contact, but not this quick, and not this direct. The look in Begsy's eyes told him that he didn't think it was a good idea, but Stephen McSharry had never been afraid to face a problem head on. He stood up and moved towards the cabinet to pour himself another whisky.

"Send him in"

The two men waited in silence. It took Ads a few minutes to fetch Cassidy and bring him to the office, in that time McSharry could feel the tension radiate from Begsy in waves, he handed the big man a glass of Johnny Walker Blue and gestured for him to sit in the corner, Begs took the glass and obliged without a word.

Martin Cassidy knocked twice and stepped into the room, his leathery face wore the same familiar smile that McSharry knew so well, well enough to notice the twinge of nervousness that lingered as the two men shook hands. He looked towards Begsy and nodded a greeting; the big man responded in kind and took a sip of whisky.

"It's good to see you Martin" McSharry said, leaning against the desk and crossing his arms. He regarded Martin Cassidy as the old man looked around the room, he seemed to do so with an air of wonder, as if he'd never seen the room before, or he didn't expect to again.

"Afternoon my boy, I'm glad I was able to catch you"

"What do you need?"

"Need?" Cassidy asked, emphasising the word by pressing his right palm against his chest "Oh nothing. I heard about what happened last night, the regrettable incident in Francesca's"

McSharry noted his choice of words; 'regrettable' and allowed himself a moment to contemplate its meaning.

"How did you hear?" he asked coldly, he noticed the question caught the old man off guard.

"Word reaches me somewhat slower than it once did" Cassidy said, letting out a chuckle that sounded forced "but it reaches me nonetheless. Most of the city knows by now, at least those that matter"

"Did word of my assailant's affiliation reach you as well?"

"I'm afraid not"

"Tony Miller"

Cassidy gave a reassuring smile "Ah, well, I've also heard that you've taken care of that problem. I confess I was a little surprised not to hear that particular information directly from yourself, what with all our previous discussions and all"

The old man uttered the words with a smile, but McSharry could see the accusation behind the sentiment, he chose not to return his old friends smile.

"I suppose I was a little distracted by the attempt on my life Martin, phone calls and updates have dropped a little further down my to-do list, as I'm sure you can imagine"

Cassidy let out another chuckle, no doubt trying to pass of the exchange as a bout of friendly banter "Oh of course, of course. How are you holding up?"

He lifted up his glass and toasted it towards his guest "Top notch, all things

371

considered. It takes a lot more than a fool with a gun to knock me out of my stride"

Cassidy flashed that warm smile "I have no doubt my boy. I want to let you know that, with Tony Miller out of the picture I'm here for anything you need"

McSharry finished off the whisky and dropped the glass onto the table, he could feel the alcohol making its way towards his brain, he felt bolder, more commanding, and allowed himself to smile at the man he was preparing to kill.

"That's very kind of you"

"Not at all, merely an offer support from one old friend to another. You got what you wanted; the crown is yours. Now, tell me what I can do to help?"

McSharry smiled again, but he knew his didn't capture any of the warmness that his old friend's had; it was a cold, hard smile and he knew from Cassidy's face that it had projected its intended impression, it was the smile of the victor standing over his defeated adversary.

"That won't be necessary at the moment Martin, thank you"

The old man seemed taken aback by the snub, there was a much stronger sense of nervousness in his demeanor, when he spoke his voice was almost pleading.

"Surely there's something I can do? My people are at your disposal"

"Everything's in hand" McSharry replied coldly.

Cassidy tried to smile, but he couldn't hide the worry in his face, he looked over his shoulder to the seated Begsy, back to McSharry, and gave a resigned nod of the head.

"Well, you know where to find me if you change your mind. Take care my boy, I am glad no harm came to you last night"

The two men shook hands.

"Goodbye Martin"

McSharry watched him walk out the room, a few moments later Begsy moved towards the door and closed it. He waited until his enforcer had crossed the room and was only a few steps away before he spoke, his voice low and firm.

"Set the hit for three days time"

Chapter 29

The wind continued to build, for twenty minutes its speed had been steadily increasing, measurable by its growing noise as well as its increasing force, with the exception of the water, slapping against the brick walls of the Mersey, it was the only sound out there.

3.20 am, on a cold November Thursday, the Seaforth Docks were deserted, little surprise on a night like this. It was probable that even those intended to work had been paid to stay away, curious eyes would not be welcome tonight.

David stretched his left leg as much as his position would allow, cramp had started to set in a few minutes earlier, but he dared not move more than was absolutely necessary. Though the docks were dimly lit they were also eerily still, the slightest movement might be picked up by a keen observer, and he expected a few of those tonight.

He shifted his weight to his right leg, the concrete trench was only 4 foot deep, which forced him to squat uncomfortably to keep himself hidden. He glanced to his right, the two officers from the Armed Response Team were both a few inches taller and looked even more uncomfortable as they peeked over the concrete edge towards the dark red container.

It was the final container to come from the *Charlestown*, a ship that had docked from Amsterdam earlier that day. All of the others had been accounted for and moved on, only one remained; number 154, and it stayed untouched for nearly four hours. The information from Rob Thomas hadn't been quite so specific as to include a container number, but the details of its contents had been clear enough; thousands of tablets of ecstasy and a sizable amount of raw MDMA, if the dark red container was filled with any such content, then someone would come calling for it before long.

David whispered into his radio for an update, aside from him and his two tall friends there were two more teams spread out across the large, container filled shipyard. One was being led by Chris Railton, the other by a squad leader from the Armed Response Team named Taylor. David listened to the replies one after the other as they fed into the radio transmitter in his ear; nothing doing, not yet. Radio silence resumed as David rested some of his weight onto his left leg and continued to watch.

The tip from Rob Thomas had eventually come at the eleventh hour, or to be exact; at six am earlier that same day. David's regret over the deal he struck had been growing stronger with every hour that McSharry's triggerman didn't make contact, doubts had begun to surface in his mind that there was no shipment, and that there would be no attempt on McSharry's life. Instead, he allowed himself to believe that the whole thing had been one big con, an elaborate rouse, giving Rob enough time to put some distance between him and David, maybe even get himself out of the country.

Just as he was preparing to return to what he was sure was now an abandoned flat, the call had come through to his mobile; the time, the ship and its cargo, all the information he needed, except for the container details.

With so little time to get the resources he needed David had no option but to go straight to the Regional Director, which had also meant logging the details as an anonymous tip and falsifying documentation to have it confirmed by anonymous sources, who did not exist. The whole thing was dangerous, illegal and stupid but at this point it was in for a penny, in for a pound time, David could see no other way to play it.

His intention had been to keep the operation away from John Barry's desk for as long as possible, or at least until he had something tangible to report. Barry was still livid over the murder of Billy Matteo, which was easy enough to understand. So far they'd been successful in keeping that aspect away from the media, the mother had been accommodating enough, fed some nonsense that it would be easier to catch her son's killer if certain details weren't released, but that grace period was fast running out and an announcement would need to be made soon, an announcement that would confirm that so far the police had no concrete leads on the perpetrators of this horrific murder.

The response from the Regional Director had been precisely what David had expected, Barry was growing tired with David's lack of progress and their discussions left him in no doubt that if an armed raid on the Seaforth docks yielded no positive results then it would, in no uncertain terms, constitute the last of his nine lives as the lead for SOCAs war on crime in Liverpool. Barry was willing to give him what he needed one last time, if he succeeded maybe it would be the start of some genuine progress, if he failed then David had just requested the final foot of rope that he'd need to hang himself.

He gave a quick glance towards the two men at his right, and the assault rifles hanging from each of their shoulders. Taylor's team come highly recommended from contacts within the force and so far they had conducted themselves with the utmost professionalism and competence. He knew when it came down to it, that the success or failure of the mission was unlikely to be determined by the talents of his colleagues, but by the quality of his information.

Another cold burst of wind knocked him slightly off balance; he gripped the edge of the concrete wall and steadied himself. The darkness was almost peaceful, as he watched the red container his thoughts drifted back towards Rob Thomas, to Thomas and the deal they had made. The thought of letting a killer walk away still irked him, it was contrary to everything that he believed in as a police officer, everything he'd given his life for and yet at the same time he saw the logic behind it. Rob Thomas wasn't bad, or at least he wasn't all bad, that was plain enough to see, but what difference did that make when he was killing people left, right and centre, provoking gang wars and shooting children, at what point did a man's intentions become irrelevant against the weight of his actions?

He tried to look at the situation objectively, to decide whether his obsession with Stephen McSharry shaped the way he saw Rob Thomas, every time he came up with a different answer, every time he found another line of thinking that made the whole mess even more confused.

A movement amongst the shadows brought him instantly back to the now, he heard a crackle of the radio and a moment later heard Chris Railton's voice.

"Team 1 be advised, we have seven males moving towards your position"

David confirmed.

He brought up the binoculars that had been resting around his neck, the red container was 75 yards away, through the lenses he was able to make out the features of the seven men, he studied them one at a time, staring intently, focusing on every detail, every movement, every scrap of clothing.

By the time he let the binoculars drop back around his neck his heart was pounding, he took a long breath to steady himself and spoke into the microphone.

"Be advised, we have an ID on two of our guys. The suspect in the brown leather jacket and the blue baseball cap is Mark Mercer, suspect in the black t-shirt and brown khakis is Jeff McCoy, a.k.a Macca, both affiliates of Stephen McSharry, the others I don't know"

He heard some excited chatter go back and forth between the other two teams but David's attention was focused solely on the men, he watched as they moved to within fifteen yards of the container and stopped. Aside from Mercer and Macca there were two well-built men in expensive looking shirts, most likely suppliers of some kind linked to the shipment, and three men in tracksuits, David guessed they were soldiers, along to do the grunt work.

They spent the next few minutes talking, the men in the pricey shirts seemed to be leading the conversation. David watched as Mercer and Macca listened and nodded, from time to time their gaze would move away from the two men to survey the surrounding area. David knew they were well covered, from that distance their position would be impossible to see, but it still didn't stop his stomach from lurching every time they glanced in his direction.

After a few more minutes the conversation stopped, he watched as Macca called over the three guys in tracksuits and gave them their instructions. A moment later one of the men started jogging back the way they had come, Mercer and Macca took the opportunity to move away from the group, they walked fifteen feet to the closest container, he watched them light a cigarette each, lean back against the rusted metal and intently survey the quiet dock.

A couple more minutes past before the jogger returned behind the wheel of a black Renault Magane, he edged the car back, trunk first, towards the red container and killed the engine. David moved the binoculars back

375

towards Mercer and Macca, neither of the men had moved, the car held their attention for the briefest of moments before they continued watching, continued waiting.

David brought the microphone closer to his mouth "Railton, you getting shots on those two?"

"And the car" Railton replied.

David turned the binoculars away from the action, he focused on the area where he knew Railton and the two other officers were stationed, his motives were two fold; to get a better understanding of the angle of Railton's photographs, and to reassure himself that the three men were out of sight. Taylor's team were even further away, laid out on top of a container towards the gates at the rear of the compound. He scanned the area and saw no sign of life, when he turned the binoculars back towards the action the three track suited men were loading the car with boxes from the container.

The men spent the best part of ten minutes loading the car, during that time the duo in the pricey shirts left and returned in a dark red Mazda convertible, David suppressed a smile, hardly the kind of inconspicuous vehicle that would be difficult to track at three am on a weeknight. All the while Macca and Mercer continued to wait, smoking and watching as if the darkened dock yard offered the most fascinating sights on the planet.

The radio crackled in David's ear "Officer Walker, are we to intercept?"

It was Taylor's voice, the man was focused and straight to the point, it was those traits, as well as his thick Yorkshire accent, that distinguished his voice from the others on the radio.

"No, do not intercept" David whispered, "Whichever way they leave ensure that the unit waiting tails them to the drop off point, I want to know where these drugs are going, and who they're going to"

The affirmatives came in fast, from Taylor, Railton and both units waiting on the outside.

Once the container was empty the driver of the Mazda stepped out from behind the wheel, and walked over towards Mercer and Macca. The conversation was short and concluded with a handshake between the Mazda driver and the other two men, David tensed himself as Mercer and Macca flicked their cigarettes away and made their way to the rear doors of the Renault Magane.

The engines of both cars roared to life, the Magane led the way towards the rear exit with the Mazda close behind, David notified the two waiting teams, the cars were moving slow, cautiously easing down the concrete path.

From the corner of his eye he saw a flicker of light somewhere in front of the two cars, his stomach lurched as he realised it came from an area close to where Taylor's team had set up, the flicker suggested something reflective had just caught the light, a camera lenses maybe, or a pair of binoculars. He looked back towards the two cars, hoping they hadn't noticed, he saw frantic movement in the back seat of the Magane, they'd noticed.

He moved the microphone towards his mouth to utter a warning but before he could speak the sound of gunshots ripped through the night silence, he readjusted the binoculars and saw Macca, leaning out of the window unloading a pistol towards the top of a container, exactly where he'd left Taylor and his team four hours earlier. He heard the revving of the engine as the driver of the Magane put his foot down, the Mazda followed suit a moment later, more gunfire echoed around the docks, only this time he could see it was retaliatory, one of Taylor's officers was returning fire.

From the distance he couldn't hear the sound, but through the binoculars he saw the bullets rip through the windscreen of the Magane. It only took a second for the driver to lose control of the wheel, the car skidded left and slammed into the front of the container, it was the same container that the Armed Response Team were perched on.

The large metal structure shook, the driver slammed through the windscreen almost instantaneously, it took a couple of seconds for Taylor and his two men to lose their balance, and tumble off the top of the container fifteen feet to the floor below.

David was up and out of the bunker before he realised what he was doing, he shrugged off the radio at his hip and ran as fast as he could, he heard a shout from somewhere behind him but didn't have time to listen, he ran as fast as he could, his lungs burning in his chest as he tried to make up the 75 yards between him and the danger.

It wasn't long before his legs were aching, but he refused to slow down. Already he was close enough to see movement, the rear doors of the Magane were opening slowly, he saw Macca drop out, onto his knees, gasping for breath, blood dripping from his bald head, as he lurched to his feet David saw Mercer stumble around from the other side and help his associate up.

He couldn't be further than forty feet now, the realisation was encouraging and helped him pick up a bit more speed, in the back of his mind he was suddenly aware that he was unarmed, he didn't give himself the chance to think about what might happen when he got there, he just concentrated all of his energy on reaching the men before they could escape.

He noticed for the first time that the Red Mazda was stationary, a few feet behind what was left of the Magane, before he could determine the condition of its driver his focus shifted towards movement at the front of the container, the first of the officers was stumbling to his feet after the fall.

Urging his body on he felt the distance reducing rapidly, but he wasn't moving fast enough, he watched as Mercer pulled a gun from underneath his jacket and fired four shots into the chest of the police officer, he felt his throat burn as he shouted out in protest but the sound was swallowed up by the echo of gunfire.

The officer hadn't even hit the ground before Macca was moving towards the container and reaching to the ground, he emerged with another member of Taylor's team, gripping him by the collar, even from this distance David could see the blood on the young policeman's face. Macca gripped him around the neck and pressed his gun hard against the officer's temple, he couldn't hear the words but he could see the two gangsters shouting at one another, Macca shielded himself behind the body of the captured officer, constantly changing direction as he tried to determine where the next threat was likely to come from. With pistols raised the two men started walking backwards towards the Mazda, the rear door popped open as the two men got to within a few feet of the car.

David's lungs were burning, but he wasn't too far away, he urged himself on despite the protest of his muscles, McSharry's boys edged closer and closer to the Mazda, he knew what would happen to their hostage once they reached it.

He was only twenty feet away now, but it wasn't close enough, the two men had reached their destination, he saw the mocking smile on Macca's face as he cocked the pistol with his thumb. David saw him whisper something into the officers ear, the horror engulfed him as he realised that he was going to be too late, but the inevitability only made him run faster, fifteen feet now, fifteen lousy feet.

He heard the deafening force of the gunshot, maybe it was just his imagination but this one had seemed so much louder than the others, so loud that it brought him to a stop.

The shot had caught Macca clean in the face, forcing his head to snap backwards and dragging the police officer down with him, David looked back in the direction he had just ran, he knew where the shot had come from but he was too far away now to see it. He turned back and saw that Mercer had been looking in the same direction, only now his eyes had locked on David, with a snarl he raised his pistol and aimed it squarely towards David's chest. The thought passed through his head that this was the second time in a week someone had pointed a gun at him, he steadied himself for the impact, making sure to look Mercer in the eye for as long as he was able.

Three more shots rang out in quick succession, each one connected with a different part of Mercer's anatomy; the first caught him clean in the shoulder, the second high in the chest and the third pierced his stomach, sending him sprawling to the ground.

He knew where the shots had come from, their trajectory was the same as the shot that killed Macca, he didn't turn back, there would be time enough later to thank the men whose names he hadn't even bothered to remember, but right now there was still work to be done.

He covered the last twenty feet as fast as his weary body would allow him, by the time he got there the captured officer had taken Macca's gun and was ordering the two men in the Mazda out of the car, David paid them no mind, his business lay elsewhere.

Kicking the gun away from Mercer's side he dropped to his knees and inspected the wounds, the man was groaning in between heavy breaths but he was still in better shape than his accomplice, a quick glance told him that the bullet had passed straight through Macca's eye socket, most likely killing him instantaneously.

He examined the three bullet holes one at a time, the one in the shoulder seemed ok, the bleeding was controlled and from the look of the wound it may have passed clean through. The shots to the chest and stomach were not so neat, the chest wound was low enough to have almost certainly passed through the lung and the shot to the stomach was bleeding too fast to be anything other than fatal.

Taking off his jacket David pressed it against the stomach wound, Mercer grunted when he pressed down and he felt the man's hands pawing at his shirt, doing his best to grab hold but failing to find the strength. He continued to apply as much pressure as possible but it was doing no good, he tried to calculate how long it had been since the first shot, hoping that the ambulance would be well on its way by now. He looked away from the gunshots and realised that Mercer was staring at him, his eyes were wide and intense but it was impossible to tell whether the cause was fear or hatred, most likely both.

"Hold on" David said, he tried to make his voice sound reassuring "the ambulance is close, just hold on"

He needed at least one of them to live, if they lived, after the stunt they'd pulled tonight they'd be facing life, that is unless they rolled over on their boss. While there was still a legal avenue available to him David intended to pursue it, but that avenue closed the second Mark Mercer died.

A gurgling noise rose from somewhere in Mercer's throat, his whole body was shaking yet he still tried to take hold of David's shirt, after a few more attempts he somehow found the strength and, using his grip, he pushed himself upwards to bring the two men's faces closer together. He could see Mercer struggling to speak, but all that came out was the same gurgling noise as before, David leaned forward, straining to understand the words, he saw how the effort was taking its toll. He moved closer, heard one final groan and then the grip on his shirt started to loosen, a few seconds later it was all over.

Taking a deep breath he ran his hands down his face, it was drenched with sweat. His brown t-shirt stuck to his skin, when he looked down he realised it was caused by more than just perspiration; he was covered in Mark Mercer's blood from the waist upwards. Stumbling to his feet, he took in the scene around him, Chris Railton and his team had arrived from their station. Along with the officer Macca had almost killed, they were in the process of handcuffing the two men from the Mazda and one of the track suited subordinates, all of whom were on their knees. A quick glance towards the Magane told him why only one of the three was in custody, aside from the driver who'd taken a head first trip through the windscreen, the third man was still securely fastened into the passenger seat, with several bullets lodged into his chest.

Just behind the car he saw Taylor helping another officer to his feet, David was relieved to see that it was the same man that Mercer had fired at. From what he could see the four shots had been absorbed by the Kevlar vest. He watched for a few more minutes as the two men peeled the vest away, the officer was moving a little gingerly, perhaps suffering from a cracked rib, but aside from that the damage seemed minimal.

His eyes were drawn towards the back seat of the Magane, a bullet had shattered one of the rear windows giving him a clear view of the boxes stacked high in the boot. He wondered what the street value would be of the drugs inside, and the dent it would make in Stephen McSharry's master plan.

He was still surveying the damage when he felt the nudge against his right shoulder, he turned and saw a sombre looking Chris Railton standing beside him.

"You got a minute?"

David gestured in the direction of the concrete bunker, a few seconds after they'd started walking they passed the two officers from his team heading in the opposite direction. He considered thanking them, but all the words he could think of felt inadequate, in the end settled for an appreciative nod of the head, which one of the men returned in kind.

They walked for a couple more seconds before Railton abruptly stopped and turned to face him. His face was serious, more serious than David was used to seeing.

"I don't really know how to say this, so I'm just going to come out with it…" Railton paused, like he was gathering his nerve "I need to know where this came from"

David looked over Railton's shoulder, the first of the police cruisers were piling towards the crime scene, he wondered how long it would be before the bosses began to show themselves.

"I'm not sure I follow?"

He could sense Railton's agitation growing "You know what I mean Guv. This tip of yours, this information, it came out of nowhere, you need to tell me where it came from"

The insistence in Railton's tone seized David's full attention, he sensed another problem poised to join the queue. He scrutinized the features of his deputy, within the young face he saw fear, concern and determination, none of which encouraged him.

"I told you, it was an anonymous tip"

"Yeah, verified by a mystery informant. That's the part that just doesn't smell right, what Informant? Cause I've bloody well never heard of him. We've been out there for days and the last time I checked we were nowhere near this kind of info, I mean not even in the same league. I know it didn't come from Hobbs, Tripp's still scared out of his skin from the last visit I paid him-"

David raised his hand, palm first in a calming manner "Officer Railton-"

He was cut off before he had a chance to go on "What informant, sir!"

"The confidential kind"

He needed a moment to think, to halt the wave of suspicion, but the young officer had the scent in his nostrils and he wasn't letting up. That was what made him good police, it was why David had recruited him in the first place.

"Since when do you keep CI's from me? I'm supposed to be the number two on this"

David felt his own frustration rising, he saw the success of his plans jeopardised by Chris Railton's curiosity and he was angry at the young man for it.

"I do what I have to do to make sure that my investigation runs as smoothly as possible, that includes keeping certain sources of information off your radar, it includes a lot of things you haven't been privy to and have no justification to question"

Railton looked him dead in the eye "Respectfully Guv, I don't believe you"

"Just what exactly are you accusing me of, Officer?"

The younger man gave an exacerbated shrug of the shoulders and in the motion David saw the first signs of indecision, of confusion. Chris Railton had the instincts to sniff out a lie but he didn't have the experience to follow it through, it left a rotten feeling in the pit of his stomach to know that he was relying on that naivety to keep the young Officer away from the truth.

"I don't know, an illegal wiretap maybe? Something isn't right here, I know that much, and I know how quickly these things can start to unravel when someone pulls at the first thread. If I can see it, what makes you think someone else won't? I can't protect our case... I can't protect you Guv, not if you keep me in the dark"

More cars continued to arrive behind Railton, David saw forensics, detectives and a procession of uniforms.

"You're better off that way, trust me"

"I don't know what that means. What are you doing that you shouldn't be?"

He allowed himself a moment to consider what would happen if he told Railton the truth, the full unabridged account of what had brought him from the rank and file to the Seaforth docks over the last ten years. He tried to imagine how he would explain his deal with a multiple murderer, how he would justify the death of James Ploughman and how he would soon be an accomplice to a premeditated act of murder. He played it out in his head and realised that if Railton knew the truth there would be no way he would be able to just digest the information and then ignore it, if he was any kind of police officer at all then every instinct in his body would demand that he took action. It made David wonder exactly what kind of police officer had he become.

"It's complicated. There are factors in this that go way back, debts that go way back"

Railton looked intrigued, David saw the makings of a good detective somewhere inside that look.

"Debts? You mean like favours? Guv, are you blackmailing one of Stephen McSharry's men?"

David laughed and shook his head, yet as he thought about it he realised that the accusation was closer to the truth than he'd first thought.

"No, nothing like that, but you have to understand its complicated. Have you ever had to allow something bad to happen in order to avoid something worse further down the line?"

Railton paused, as if he was calculating all the possible meanings of David's words.

"I suppose"

"What if you started to lose track of what the worse crime really was? What if the lines started to blur into one?"

"Then I guess you'd have to draw a new line. Set your own limits"

David looked away as he thought about Railton's response, he saw the logic in the words, but the caveat came to him almost immediately. He was ashamed to utter the words, but he also felt like he needed to.

"Can you put a limit on an obsession?"

"I suppose that depends on the obsession" Railton replied, it was clear he only had a vague understanding of the nature of their conversation "Maybe you should give me more to go on?"

David looked back towards his deputy, he wanted to trust him, to let him in, but there was just too much to lose. He put a hand on the younger man's shoulder and looked him in the eye.

"I need you to trust me, and I need you to keep this to yourself for a little while longer. In a few days, I guarantee, this will all be over, and when it is we can have a real conversation, I'll tell you what you want to know. But until then I just need to give me some time, ok? No questions"

"What do you mean it'll all be over?"

"No questions"

He saw the confusion in Railton's eyes, saw his instincts pulling him one way and his loyalty another.

"Guv, I've got my career to think about, I don't want to get sucked into any kind of-"

David cut him off "There's nothing happening here that you could be made culpable for in any way, you have my word. Nothing here involves you. This whole mess, in a few days it will have run its course, you have to trust me on that, I just need you to give me a little more time"

He let his hand drop from Railton's shoulder and took a step back, he glanced again towards the crime scene and saw that a number of senior figures where pointing in his direction. Railton scratched at his head with his eyes locked on the floor, after a moment more he raised them and nodded towards David.

"Ok. I'll give you some time, but I want the truth, the whole thing"

David nodded and extended his hand, the two men shook.

"I appreciate that Officer Railton" he released his grip and gestured towards the container "We've got work to do"

It took the better part of two hours before he got himself away from the docks. The survivors of the drug deal were in the custody of the Merseyside Police Force and would be getting a full grilling way into the early hours, David would get his shot with them in the morning. He wasn't holding out much hope, the soldier would eat the charge, even if he didn't it was unlikely that he'd ever been in the same room as Stephen McSharry. The other two may have had more useful information, but he suspected that their superiors would lie outside the McSharry organisation, probably with some independent drug runners selling their product to the highest bidder.

For David's case Mercer and Macca had been the prize, and they were both dead.

Still, at least they had the drugs, it was the first meaningful disruption they'd managed since McSharry had resumed his campaign, and it felt good to have been the one to orchestrate it.

His time at the docks had been spent updating relevant divisional heads and talking through what had happened. There was always a song and dance when the Armed Response Team were required to discharge their weapons, but David was confident that their grounds were justifiable, and from the way his conversations had gone with various representatives of the Professional Standards Department, it seemed probable that they would agree.

Surprisingly there had been no sign of John Barry, it seemed the Regional Director was always the first on the scene when a reprimand was required, but not quite so punctual when a congratulations was the order of the day. He had called though, the early estimations were that the drugs seized had a street value in the region of over a million pounds and the Regional Director was keen to use that to his advantage. Barry had already outlined his intention to notify the press at the same time that he told them about the death of Billy Matteo. He also planned to link the seized drugs and the dead gangsters to Matteo's murder, claiming that the police and SOCA had 'strong evidence' linking the individuals to the attack that had resulted in the death of the innocent youth.

All in all Barry had seemed pleased, though he hadn't gone so far as to commend David for the success of his operation he had sounded considerably less hostile than in their previous conversations. If he needed to use some leverage to get Rob Thomas et al out of the country then he felt slightly more comfortable about applying it now that the Regional Director was seemingly back onside.

Once he was done with Barry and the PSD he'd been told to get himself home. His appointment with the smugglers and their lawyers was set for 10am and Barry wanted him well rested for the interrogation. He made it halfway home before deciding that he was too wired to sleep, and headed towards the office instead.

He heard a rustling of papers as he made his way into the DST bullpen and a moment later he spotted Rachel Saunders sliding sheets of A4 into a folder. She saw him and smiled, stopping what she was doing she stood up and crossed the room, the smile disappeared as soon as she saw the blood on his T-shirt.

"My god!"

David smiled and shook his head "Not mine, Mark Mercer's"

Rachel crossed her arms and gave a knowing nod. Her dark hair was tied back and she looked paler, as if she wasn't wearing any make up, it made her look a little more tired but David couldn't help thinking that she still looked like the most beautiful thing he'd ever seen.

"I heard about the bust" she said "I was just finishing up my shift when it came through, you ok?"

David swallowed the lump in his throat "I'm fine"

"What happened?"

"They got sight of one of our people, started shooting and tried to get themselves a hostage. There wasn't much else that could have been done"

There was genuine concern on her face, it wasn't a sight David was used to seeing, not these days anyway.

"You weren't hurt?"

He shook his head and smiled "No, a little cramp but that's about it, the boys from the ART did well. It's been a good day, I'm thinking maybe this is the change of luck we've been waiting for. It would have been nice to get to grips with those two though, I could have had some fun with that"

Rachel smiled. David realised it was the first real conversation they had ever had, somehow without a full room of eyes she was easier to talk to. It felt comfortable, natural even.

"There'll be more opportunities to get at his people," she said encouragingly "like you said; we just need that bit of luck"

The room went silent, David wasn't ready for the conversation to end.

"How've you been?" he asked.

"I'm good, like I said; just got off my shift"

"Pick up anything interesting?"

She uncrossed her arms and used them to lean back against a nearby desk, the movement increased the prominence of her breasts, he tried to act like he hadn't noticed, but the amused gleam in her eye told him that he'd failed.

"I don't know, maybe" Rachel said, ignoring his embarrassment "I just finished filling in my logs, they're in the file if you want to take a look. We got a few photos of one of McSharry's street level dealers meeting with Raymond Lester, they tell me he's got links to some of the clubs in town, supplies them with their narcotics"

David nodded, he'd arrested Raymond Lester seven years ago, but the charges had failed to stick, Rachel continued.

"We're still not close to any of the major players. Further down the ladder its getting interesting though, since they got to Miller there's been a lot of gossip, a lot of uncertainty too"

"What are they saying out there?"

"The latest one we're hearing is that Tony Miller is dead but his people have torched his body and dumped it in the Irish Sea, I guess they hope their guys will keep flying the flag until they get proof?"

From the resolution in her voice it sounded like she believed the rumour, David had seen too many come and go to give it any more attention than a fleeting acknowledgment, but he was reluctant to voice his doubts out loud through fear of offending her.

"Sounds like a desperate measure, if it's true"

She laughed, it had more than a hint of nervousness to it. It made her seem vulnerable, which in its own way, made her even more beautiful.

"I know" Rachel said.

"You guys are doing good work here," he told her "I know I don't say it a lot, and I probably should, but there it is"

She smiled that warm smile at him.

"Thank you" there was a pause "I was wondering; do you maybe fancy going for a drink, or something, next week?"

The question caught him off guard, it had been a while since the last time someone had asked him out.

"A drink?"

She nodded shyly, coming from a police officer it seemed a little too shy to be entirely real.

"Yeah. It would be nice to get a chance to know each other a little better, you know, outside of work?"

It suddenly dawned on him how ridiculous he must have looked; wearing a blood covered, sweat soaked t-shirt, in comparison to the way Rachel was used to seeing him. He wasn't used to feeling self-conscious in his place of business, but he found himself unable to hide from it now. She looked at him expectantly.

"A drink would be good"

Her face relaxed and she smiled, again he was reminded of how beautiful she was, a murmur of voices came from somewhere down the hall, Rachel stood up straight.

"I should probably get going, it's been a long night"

David gestured towards his desk "I've got some paperwork I need to get to"

She smiled again and walked away, he allowed himself a brief moment to enjoy what had just happened, and then it was back to work.

Chapter 30

There were a lot of places he would rather have been. In bed with a warm, young slut, in a warehouse with a sharp knife and another employee of Tony Miller, in his study reading a book, the list could go on and on, almost anywhere was better than a dimly lit industrial site car park at five in the morning.

He drew on the cigar and blew the smoke up into the air, it served a dual purpose; it distracted him from the cold and it calmed his increasing levels of anger.

McSharry leaned against the hood of the Jeep and surveyed the circle in front of him, almost everyone was here, everyone who was left anyway. He looked at his men one by one, as he had before the meeting with the four families so soon after his release. It seemed like an age ago, even longer when he considered the people who had been present that day; Wayne Caddock, Tony Miller, his unfortunate young nephew George. Now all that existed of those men were memories like the one he was currently reliving, and pretty soon they would all be gone too.

The faces of the men in the circle provided him with a range of emotions to consider, each one of which he clearly understood. Ads and Caffers looked angry, Sie looked concerned, Rico Wallace seemed cautious bordering on suspicious, Nikolai just looked bored.

It had been a hectic night for all of them, word had come through just over two hours earlier that the shipment had been seized, Mercer and Macca potentially killed, and since then it had all been go.

The first move was for McSharry to get out of the house. The proximity of the police to his dealings, coupled with the uncertainty surrounding Tony Miller made his presence there too much of a risk, he was too exposed. It annoyed him that such action was necessary, he loved his home, it was a symbol of his power, of his intent. The place he was at now was tolerable enough, a waterfront flat in South Liverpool, expensively decorated, untraceable and secure but the fact remained that he was being forced out of his home by the actions of others, a fact that did not sit well with him.

Still, he wasn't the only one who was having to relocate. Each of the men before him had gone to ground, it made little difference whether Mercer and Macca were dead or in custody, either way the police would come calling, and they would find themselves with a lot of questions to answer.

He glanced over his shoulder towards the driver's seat of the Jeep, part of the reshuffle had meant Begsy would no longer be driving him, like the others he would be going to ground, once business had been taken care of. In his place Begs had promoted some kid named Teller, he looked to be in his early twenties, with a slightly rounded face and a thick mop of fair hair. McSharry knew him by sight; lower level muscle used on the simpler jobs, on Begsy's recommendation he had scored himself a promotion; chauffeur the

387

boss around, prove your worth, maybe earn yourself a seat at the head table. So far the kid had done ok, he kept his mouth shut and he paid attention, McSharry had no doubt that there would be plenty of opportunity to impress in the coming weeks.

The glare of headlights caught everyone's attention, Begsy pulled up and jumped out of the black beamer like he was in a hurry . Of everyone tonight his job had been the most important, talking to their sources, directing their people on what to do while the major players were off the radar. It was a job that required Begsy's unique form of presence, people on the street needed to know that out of sight did not mean out of mind. McSharry watched his march towards the circle with interest, it was the speed of the big man's movement that really brought home the severity of the situation, Begs did not move quickly unless he had to.

Taking a final drag of the cigar he flicked it into the darkness and took a step forward to garner the groups attention.

"What do you know, Begs?"

The big man scratched at the scar across his cheek, let out an irritated sigh and shook his head.

"It's true, the bastards clipped Mercer and Macca"

He heard the reaction ripple throughout the group; shock, annoyance, anger, he felt them all.

"Shit" Sie grumbled, his left arm was in a sling courtesy of the bullet he'd taken at Miller's safe house the day before, McSharry was pleased to see the injury wasn't causing him to neglect his responsibilities.

"What about the drugs?" Ads asked.

"Coppers got them too" Begsy paused and looked at McSharry "We think it was that prick Walker again"

McSharry smiled through gritted teeth, an image of the smug, pointy nosed bastard popped into his head, he pulled another cigar from his breast pocket and lit it.

"Of course it was" he said, taking a first pull "Who've the police got in custody?"

"Two guys the Drakes sent over and one of our kids, busies killed the other two lads we sent with them, I got a sight of their bodies; one was shot to fuck, the other went headfirst through a fucking windscreen"

Whistles and shakes of the head went round, universal condemnation from the collection of murders, McSharry almost laughed.

"Fucking butchers!" Caffers muttered.

McSharry focused their attention with a click of his fingers "Ads, get word to the kids family. You let them know that if their son keeps his mouth shut and if he eats the charge then both him and his family will be well looked after. You make sure that message gets to him in double quick time, you hear me?" Ads nodded "Begs, I want you to speak to the cockneys, explain to them that there is an expectation for their boys to stand tall. Emphasise in the strongest way possible that there will be repercussions if they don't, for all parties, ok? Everyone just needs to keep their heads down for the next couple of days and we'll see how this thing plays out"

Nikolai was the next to speak up, hearing his voice caught McSharry a little by surprise.

"What about the drugs? Without that shipment we won't be able to hold onto all that new territory we've just took" his tone had a matter of fact evenness to it.

McSharry heard murmurs of agreement, Begsy was the one to articulate it.

"The lads right. We let those new lot go dry this quickly and there'll go looking somewhere else"

"Where they gonna go?" Caffers chipped in defensively.

McSharry rubbed his eyes in frustration "It doesn't matter where they go, they're fiends, they'll go to a friend of a friend of a friend, whatever, it doesn't matter. What matters is, once we lose that link, that control then we have to start all over again to get it back" he looked over at Begsy "Get Ho back into town, and do it quietly. Set him up with a place to crash and beef up his protection. I don't care how he does it but you make sure he gets his delivery moved forward, by hook or by crook Begs, we need those drugs!"

Begsy gave a slight shake of the head "He won't like those extra bodies, not this soon"

McSharry slammed his fist down on the bonnet of the Jeep "I don't give a fuck, just get it done!" he looked around the group "And where the fuck is the Thomas kid?"

There was a muted silence as the men exchanged a series of looks, eventually it was Caffers who spoke up.

"He hasn't checked in for a couple of days"

McSharry looked around the circle, they were all staring back at him blankly, he took a drag of the cigar to keep his anger in check, eventually his eyes settled on Begsy "So where the fuck is he?"

It was Ads who answered "People have been seeing him round town the last couple of nights, off his tits, surrounded by pussy, spending a shit load. Christ knows where he's going in the day, cos he isn't going home, but as soon as the sun goes down there he is, Concert Square, Matthew Street, whatever, but word gets to us the next day that he's been having it large"

He scratched at his eyes again and tossed the cigar away, this night seemed to be one problem after another and he was growing tired of it. Fast.

"Begs, get to grips with this kid will ya, get him back in line and put him to good use. He wants our money he can damn well work for it! What else?"

There was silence for a moment, long enough for McSharry to prepare to leave, and then Sie cleared his throat.

"I know no one wants to mention it" he said, a hint of caution in his voice "But how did the busies find out about the shipment?"

Almost without realising it McSharry assumed his poker face, that cold hard exterior that kept the world out of his head.

"I'm still pondering that one"

Ads was the first to offer his opinion "Do you think it might have been the Drake brothers? Maybe they aren't happy about getting involved with us?"

"Could be some Miller people?" Sie suggested "Maybe they got wind of it from their old Caddock associates and grassed us up to the filth?"

McSharry gave each theory a noncommittal nod, both were possible, but then so were other scenarios. He looked over at Begsy and knew they were both considering another possibility, though he had no intention of raising it here he couldn't help but ask himself the question; had he been wrong to put his trust in a Thomas? Was it going to be a mistake he would have to rectify twice over?

Before he had a chance to contemplate the idea any further Begsy's phone started to ring. The big man answered, uttered a few grunts and then listened. The group waited in silence, after a minute he crossed the circle and handed the phone to McSharry.

Putting the phone to his ear he listened to everything the caller had to say. At occasional intervals he asked for elaboration and very briefly he haggled over the price. At the end he thanked the caller for their information and hung up the phone. The content was interesting, very interesting indeed, but then when Chris Railton called it usually was.

"Change of plan boys" he said with a cold smile.

Chapter 31

The Friday night work crowd was just beginning to subside, in an hour or two they would be replaced by the Friday night party crowd, intermingled amongst both groups, as always, was the string of middle aged alcoholics, their crowd had a constant presence in this town. Any time, any place.

Rob sipped at his pint of Guinness. The sign outside Pogue Mahones pronounced it to be the 'The Best Pint of Guinness in Liverpool', it was the same sign that had been outside fifteen years earlier, and from what he could remember the taste didn't seem to have improved in that time.

It hadn't been the proactive advertising that had lured him in, back in the day Pogue Mahones had been the place where he and Kelly used to start most of their night outs together. In the latter years of their relationship those trips were broken up consistently by trips to the bathroom to feed their coke habits, just the sight of the faded ceramic sinks and cracked stained mirrors brought back a string of nasty memories that Rob had no desire to relive.

Despite all that it still seemed like a fitting place to meet Kelly for their first drink, for all the nasty experiences that littered the top of its memory there were still quite a few nice ones buried underneath, it had been a place where they'd gotten to know one another, where two young kids had sampled their first taste of an adult relationship.

He took another drink and inspected his surroundings; the inside may have had a refurb or two over the years but it still resembled every other Irish bar Rob had ever seen, in a way it reminded him of New York, of McGlincheys, and of Jo. It had been a while since they'd last spoken, nearly a week. He didn't have the heart to tell her that he wasn't coming home yet, that there was another job to do. Having to hear that disappointment and that anger in her voice was more than he could take right now, it was better to keep his distance and remember the woman who loved him, rather than be subjected to what he was turning her into; another embittered ex, another relationship in tatters.

He'd wondered how she would react if she knew he was meeting his ex-girlfriend for a drink. On the face of it, it looked bad, he could see that. But then there was very little going on in his life that would stand up against the slightest scrutiny these days, and he counted his relationship with Jo in that bracket. At the end of the day he knew he was pursuing no desire other than friendship with Kelly, and the way his life was drifting at the moment any form of human connection, romantic or otherwise, was worth all the money in the world to him.

He straightened out the afternoon copy of the Liverpool Echo in front of him and reread the main story. The words made him dizzy, he took another drink of Guinness to steady himself and read on. The story had finally broke, he didn't know how they'd managed to keep the information about the kid hidden for so long, but everyday he'd picked up the paper expecting the read about the horrific murder of a young boy and everyday he'd been left a little bit more confused. In his darker moments he had started to worry that he'd hallucinated the whole thing, but that would have been too easy, he knew he had done those things, and he knew he would have to live with them.

So the kid had a name; William Matteo. Billy. He knew all the details, they were etched in his brain now, but he reread them anyway. He read the details of Billy's life and felt his hand start to shake, he read the mourning statement from Billy's mother and felt it shake harder, he read the damning condemnation from the Echo columnist and he drained the full pint of Guinness, folding the paper away soon afterwards. Since Tuesday he'd been having a hard enough time trying not to relive it, but now that the news was out that task was proving even harder.

He closed his eyes and buried his head into his hands, he heard Billy's desperate panting, he saw the blood, he saw Billy's brown eyes, the fear in them, and then he saw that glazed look.

Sucking air into his lungs he raised his head and opened his eyes. Two elderly men on the next table gave him a strange look, Rob ignored it.

He was reliving this one more than the others, with the exception of maybe Julie McSharry. At least back then he'd had the coke to level him out, now there was nothing inside that fucked up head of his except him and his memories.

The bag of coke was still sat in the top drawer of his living room table, had he not been interrupted by David Walker and then Charlie there was a good chance the whole 3 grams would have been gone by now, as it was he'd somehow managed to hold out. It wasn't easy, the urge caught him at the strangest moments, sometimes it felt as if he was physically being pushed towards that draw like he was a puppet dancing slowly, against his will, en route to the inevitable.

Having a focus helped, there was no doubt about that. Ever since his two parallel plans had been put into place, first with the copper, then with Charlie, it had felt like he had finally taken back a degree of control in his life. The control made him feel stronger, gave him a determination that he'd been lacking since coming back to Liverpool, he was reclaiming what was his once and for all, righting a wrong like he should have done years ago. Whenever thoughts of Billy Matteo pushed in too close that was what he reminded himself, it was his rationale to push it away again. He could never push it away completely though, it lingered, like a shadow, always on the edge of him. He got the feeling that was how it would always be, he had no qualms with it, he deserved nothing less, and probably a hell of a lot more.

The two old men gave him another disapproving glance, Rob felt the urge within him, the urge to kill. It was growing, with each passing day. The more time he spent here the more he was starting to feel like his old self; untouchable, unchallengeable. It was an urge that left a sick feeling in the pit

392

of his stomach, he imagined it was akin to what a unfaithful lover would feel after they've strayed, a sense of repulsion at your own behaviour. Rob couldn't deny what he was any more than a cheating husband could deny that he was weak, but he didn't have to like it, and he could do everything in his power to try and ignore that dark, insidious part of himself that thrived on the kill. It was only a small part, that was what he told himself, only a small part.

Kelly was already ten minutes late, he headed to the bar, purchased another pint of Guinness and returned to his seat. He took out the paper again, making a purposeful effort to avoid any mention of Billy Matteo this time.

Rob read the story about the drug seizure that had taken place in the early hours of the morning. Four dead, a massive shipment of Ecstacy recovered and a number of key criminal conspirators in custody. At least there was some good news, Charlie's information had been good and Walker had pounced on it with what appeared to be complete success. He read through the names of the deceased, the first two he didn't recognise but the second two; Mark Mercer and Jeff McCoy, he knew those names from the old days, nasty pieces of work the both of them, Liverpool would be a slightly safer place with those two out of the equation.

He was pleased that Walker had been able to use the information he'd given him, if he was lucky maybe it would go some way to convincing the cop that Rob was still worth trusting. He understood the man's dilemma, it couldn't have been easy for him going against his own people the way he was, but at the end of the day they both knew that working together would be the only way that they would be able to get what they wanted. He just hoped that McSharry's people didn't trace the leak back to Charlie, it was unlikely, with all the upheaval that was going on there must have been a million ways for a piece of information like that to make its way to the police. Still, he found it hard to silence that voice in his head that told him Stephen McSharry was both intelligent and cautious, which made for a worrying combination when your little brother was within his reach.

He'd tried to call Charlie before leaving the flat but he'd had no luck, the call had gone straight through to voicemail. Rob left a brief but direct message, telling Charlie to call him as soon as he could, knowing his brother he wasn't expecting a swift response.

He watched as a young woman walked into the pub, it took him a couple of seconds to realise that it was Kelly, at least not the one he'd come to know recently. This one belonged to the past, to his half-forgotten youth. It was the hair that he noticed first, the last few times he'd seen her it had always been tied back, but tonight it was curled, strands of light brown hair fell to just past her shoulder making her look at least five years younger. It wasn't just the hair that caught his attention, she wore a tight cream dress that brought out the blue in her eyes, Rob stood up as she made her way towards him, from the delicate way she was walking he suspected she hadn't put on a pair of high heels in quite a while.

"You're late" he said, realising how underdressed he was in a black jumper, jeans and trainers.

Kelly smiled "Some things never change, do they?"

"You look… really fucking good"

She gave him a playful punch in the arm "No need to sound so surprised Robbie, Jesus"

They both sat down, Rob caught a couple of guys across the bar checking her out, further increasing his sense of déjà vu.

"Sorry, it's been a while since I saw you like this, its bringing back some memories, that's all"

Kelly gave an embarrassed laugh and lightly shook her head "Buy me a drink, nob head"

"You got it"

Rob returned a few minutes later with a glass of red wine and another pint of Guinness. Sitting down he folded up the paper and slid it under his jacket, Kelly was still fiddling with her mobile phone as she reached for her drink.

"So your mum was ok babysitting the kids?"

Kelly took a sip of wine and leaned forward, already she seemed a little giddy, like she was still trying to get used to her surroundings.

"Yep, she was fine. It's not like I impose on her a lot these days. She loves spending time with them, it's the only chance she gets to do the grandma thing"

"Chocolate and Ice Cream?"

"And fizzy drinks. At least she can deal with the sugar rush fallout. Usually she just loads them up and passes them back to me" she paused as she looked around the pub "So… this brings back some memories. I thought we were just going out for dinner? If I'd have known we were reliving our glory days I would have brought my glow sticks and my stilettos"

Rob laughed and checked his watch "We've got reservations in an hour. I just thought it would be nice to take a quick trip down memory lane. Just to be clear I am, in no way, trying to talk you out of the stilettos and the glow sticks"

"Understood" the smile faded and her face took on a more serious dimension "I expected to hear from you sooner, after what you were saying last time. Does that mean that you've been coping with those skeletons in your closet a bit better than you expected?"

He felt her eyes examining him, he suddenly felt a wave of self-consciousness wash over him, looking away towards the bar he took a drink.

"I don't really know how to answer that"

"You never did" Kelly said with a hint of irritation.

The comment put him on the defensive, leaning back in his chair Rob spread his arms and looked at her expectantly.

"Well, what is it you want me to say?"

"I don't know, something real. You asked me to come out to dinner with you because you said that being around me helps with the problems that you're in to; well do you not think it might help if I knew what the problems were?"

Rob's eyes involuntarily moved to the paper hidden beneath his coat, he forced them back onto Kelly as she took a sip of her wine.

"You never wanted to know before"

The wine glass slammed onto the table hard enough to draw a number of interested glances from nearby patrons.

"That is not true" Kelly said firmly, "You never wanted to tell me, there's a difference"

"Well, what if I still don't?"

Her face was neutral for a moment, and then she flashed him that disarming smile "Tough shit, I'm not your girlfriend anymore, it's not my job to care what you want"

Rob found himself smiling back "What, are you going to beat it out of me?"

"If I have to"

That self-conscious feeling came back and Rob repeated his trick of looking away, he felt the urge to talk to her, and he saw the value in it. Yet those old walls kept him in check, they whispered to him that safety and secrecy were one and the same. He looked up at those bright blue eyes and thought about all the things he'd put her through.

"To be honest Kell, I'm not doing that good. I think I've made some really bad choices lately. At the time, it didn't seem like they were choices but looking back I'm sure that there are different routes I could have taken. They're the kind of choices that weigh you down, you know? That are hard to get passed. I'm working on something that might go a way to putting some of it right, but when you've got my kind of luck... I'm not holding my breath"

She looked at him as if she knew exactly what he meant, and yet didn't have the slightest idea. There was sympathy in her face, Rob was amazed that she had any left for him.

"I can see it in you, that misery." Kelly said sadly, "You're better at hiding it than you used to be, but it's still there"

First Charlie, then Kelly. It was strange to once again be around people who knew him like they did. In New York he had made his past so hazy that he was almost starting to believe he didn't have one. To be around those who knew him, who had seen him happy and who had seen him broken; it was both comforting and terrifying at the same time.

"This place seems to bring it out in me" Rob said, raising the pint glass to his lips.

"How bad is it, compared to the old days?"

Billy Matteo's dead face flashed before his eyes.

"Pretty bad"

Kelly reached over and squeezed his hand. It felt nice, almost safe.

"But you're keeping off the coke though, right?" Kelly asked, he could hear her concern. He nodded "Cos that shit never did anything for you Robbie, for either of us"

She let go of his hand, Rob had to stop himself from reaching out and taking it back. He didn't want to tell her about his slip on the night Wayne Caddock was killed, she already knew more about his weakness than he was comfortable with, there was no need to add to that list. In spite of it all he still wanted to express his confusion, to justify it. If anyone understood the calling of addiction it was her.

"I know that Kell, but any distraction is better than no distraction at all"

Kelly let out a long breath, Rob watched as the sympathy seemed to drain from her face along with the air, it was replaced by that stubborn look she got when people tried to argue with her, he recognised it as the look she possessed when she knew she was right.

"You're wrong Robbie, trust me. I know what I'm talking about, if I hadn't gotten clean when I did I'd probably be dead by now, maybe worse. An addiction like that rips you apart, all that paranoia, the depression, the insomnia. It brings out the worst in you and then it projects it for the whole world to see. You can rationalise a hell of a lot in that place, I know I did and I'm pretty sure you did too. I don't know what your plan is for putting things right but it should start with steering clear of that nasty shit, that absolutely needs to be step one, or its all for nothing"

As she spoke Kelly's voice had grown steadily more agitated, she stopped speaking and glanced off into the distance, it took Rob a few moments to realise that she was staring towards the toilets. Her cheeks were flustered and her breathing was faster than normal, Rob had to call her name three times before she finally brought her attention back to the table.

"Do you mind if we get out of here?" she asked breathlessly "I'm not really feeling in a reminiscing mood tonight. Take me to that new bar you were telling me about, the trendy one?"

"Ok"

Kelly picked up what was almost a full glass of red and drank it in one long gulp. As soon as it was finished she walked out, it took Rob a moment to collect his jacket, he gave the copy of the Echo one last glance and decided to leave it where it was.

Stepping out onto the street he saw that the city was already starting to fill up. Large groups of leery teenagers and twentysomethings passed him left and right, squealing and shouting in celebration of another Friday night. He watched them go and wondered how many of the girls would end their night by fucking a guy they'd regret, he wondered how many of the guys would end up starting a fight they'd regret. The aging cynicism of the thought struck him immediately, he turned away from them, back towards Kelly.

It took five minutes to walk to the next bar, they made the trip in silence.

Kelly leaned on him for support, the cobbled streets were no friend to high heels, though he saw that every other woman who was out was suffering from a similar problem.

They reached the bar that Matt had taken him to a week earlier. It was busier this time, though they still managed to snare themselves a booth in the rear corner. Rob went to the bar and ordered a bottle of beer and another glass of red wine, the alcohol was already starting to help, that feeling of light-headedness kept the images of Billy Matteo at bay, he reminded himself to pick up another bottle of JD on the way home.

He returned to the table with the drinks and sat down on the opposite side of the booth, Kelly flashed him a slightly nervous smile, Rob returned it in kind and took his first swig of lager. The volume of the music made it difficult to have a proper conversation, a fact he was sure Kelly would be relieved about, he used the time who speculate what she had seen in Pogue Mahones to shake her up this bad.

By the time their drinks were finished she seemed more like her old self; the conversation had increased despite the handicap of the noise and her face had lost that flustered, melancholy look it had acquired in the previous pub. Despite her efforts Rob could still tell something wasn't quite right, though she was talking freely it was all polite, dreary conversation, it was as if she was on a first date, every word that left her mouth seemed designed for one of two purposes; to not give too away much, or to maintain the image that she was trying to project for herself. Rob went along with it, he answered her questions and asked similar questions back in kind.

When they finished their drinks they made their way deeper into the city, he'd booked a table at a Thai restaurant within the new Liverpool One shopping district. They made their way through the brightly lit complex, it was the first time he'd had a chance to assess it and Rob found himself quietly impressed by the style and the class of the place. There was a swell of pride in his chest as he thought about how far his city had come in the ten years since he'd left. He recognised that the change was only skin deep, and that a lot of work needed to be done to achieve something real, but still, it was a start. They approached the restaurant and Rob realised that it had been built on the site of an old car park, he remembered a particularly drunken night when he and Kelly had fooled around in one of its darkened corners, but decided that it probably wasn't the best time to rehash that particular memory.

A polite Asian waitress showed them to their seats and Rob ordered a bottle of red wine between them. The conversation resumed its previous polite tone and continued on throughout the starters, well into the main course. They talked about his job, about her house, about New York and about life in Liverpool, they talked about everything except the past that they shared. By the time their plates were being cleared away Rob found himself growing increasingly agitated, the bottle of wine was practically finished, he ordered a second while Kelly picked her desert.

As he refilled their glasses he caught sight of an elderly couple on the other side of the restaurant, he watched them for a few minutes, picking at their meals, never once raising their heads to one another, completely content in the silence that suffocated them. Something in the sight jolted him, placing the glass of wine in front of her he leaned forward as far as he could go.

"Can I ask you something?" Rob said, his voice low. He glanced towards the old couple once more and then back to Kelly "Earlier, when you were talking about getting clean, it sounded like you went through a pretty bad time. You know you can talk to me about it, if you want to?"

She flashed him an impatient look, something behind it told him that she wanted to talk about it, and that she wanted him to know what she'd been through.

"Is this you getting curious again, Robbie?" the sarcasm in her voice was biting, she picked up her glass and looked away.

"I just thought we were friends that's all. Isn't that what friends do, talk about this kind of bollocks?"

She gave him a 'what am I going to do with you' smile and shook her head, having quenched her thirst she leaned forward, mirroring his pose almost to perfection.

"There's not much to tell really. I had a problem, like you, I got over it, like you"

Rob came close to confessing his own fallibility on the matter, but suppressed the words before they had the chance to escape, this wasn't about him, it was about her.

"How long have you been clean?"

Rob caught a grimace, he saw that she couldn't look him in the eye.

"Five years"

It didn't take more than a couple of seconds to register that the maths didn't fit, Stevie was six. She finally looked at him, he tried to keep his face free of emotion, who the hell was he to judge.

"Yeah, I know" Kelly said, apparently his face wasn't quite as straight as he'd thought it was "Like I said, you can rationalise a lot"

Rob was surprised to see Kelly smile, it was nice, it said to him that she had learned to live with the mistakes she'd made, and that she'd found a way for forgive herself, he wondered how you went about learning a trick like that.

"What made you quit?"

Kelly took a moment to consider the question, knowing her like he did he knew she would have asked herself the same thing a million times over, probably producing a million different answers.

"I finally hit rock bottom" she said eventually, "It was the best thing that ever happened to me really. I don't want to think what might have happened to Stevie if I hadn't"

It occurred to Rob how different his life might have been if he'd have had an anchor like that, something he cared for so much that he was willing to change everything he knew just to keep it safe. For him rock bottom was a little like Liverpool, no matter how many times he left he just kept finding his way back.

"How did it happen?" Rob asked taking another drink, his own ears caught the slur in his words.

"I guess it was all down to Stevie's dad really. I met him about six months after you left. He was a bit of a local coke dealer. That was one of the things that hit me hardest when you left, all my supply used to come through my man, free of charge. When you left I went proper dry, proper fast. I had a little bit of a freak out actually, I guess that tells you a lot about my priorities back then"

Rob let out an unsure laugh. It made sense, for the last year before he left their involvement with one another couldn't have been described as much more than coked up fuck buddies, the money McSharry paid had been more than enough to keep them knee deep in powder, by that point he had nothing else to spend his money on; clothes and appliances had long since lost their appeal. He knew when he left that they were no longer in love, that was one of the reasons why he left alone, what he hadn't considered was that he had left her fighting an addiction as insatiable as his own.

"I was in the same boat," he muttered, hoping to validate her confessions "I know exactly what it's like"

"I don't think you know what this was like" Kelly replied, she looked like she was bracing herself, like someone on the edge of a cliff ready to jump "Without you I couldn't afford to keep up with my habit, I just didn't have the money. So once I used up all the cash that I had, and loaned as much as I could, I started paying him in sex"

Her face had the same flustered look as it had earlier that night in Pogue Mahones, when she caught Rob watching she put her head in her hands and buried her face with her hair.

"Don't look at me like that Robbie"

Rob reached over and pulled her hand away from her face.

"I wasn't"

"I know it's bad, but-"

"Kell, I swear; I wasn't"

She nodded and reached for the wine, Rob gave her a moment to compose herself. He wondered how many people she'd admitted that to, judging by her level of embarrassment it couldn't have been many. He felt the urge to match her honesty, to share with her all the terrible things he'd done, but once again that little voice in his head dismissed the notion without hesitation. He knew it was for vanity as much as it was for safety, he didn't want people seeing him the way he really was, in that respect he was a much weaker person than Kelly.

All it took was half a glass of wine and a deep breath before Kelly found the courage to continue.

"Anyway, after a while I ended up falling for the guy. I know, it's pathetic, but he looked after me, he showed me affection, and kept my addiction satisfied. Don't forget I was only a kid back then, a coked up relationship was the only kind of relationship I knew. I thought that was how everyone lived, that all marriage was about was fighting and fucking in between lines of snow"

Rob returned her sad smile "So what happened then?"

"For the first couple of years, nothing really. I moved in, we lived together for about eighteen months, I hung around with his friends, cut his coke, helped him make some money. Eventually I got pregnant, which I'm ashamed to say didn't change much, and then six months into it the bastard decided that it was time to go. Just packed up and fucked off, as men tend to do. He was still around Liverpool, the prick wasn't quite as ambitious as you Robbie. For a while I used to go looking for him, friends, clients, whoever I could remember. I found him a couple of times but whenever I did he'd just move on somewhere else, in the end it became a bit impractical for a heavily pregnant woman to keep chasing after her slippery ex, then, once I had Stevie it was the beginning of the end. I still tried to balance the two lives for a while but I think I knew that eventually one would have to go. It's funny, I don't think I ever would have quit to save my own life but I managed to quit to save his, isn't that weird?"

Rob tried to speak but the words caught in his throat, he took another gulp of wine and tried again.

"Not at all, you always put everyone else before yourself"

Kelly smiled a fresh bubbly smile, in an instant she was almost unrecognisable from the embarrassed young woman who'd just bared her soul.

"I need to stop doing that, don't I?" Kelly waited for a response, when it didn't come she sent a furrow browed look in Rob's direction "Say something, you're starting to freak me out a little"

He found his voice, there was a different kind of weight in this chest now, not despair, not horror, but guilt.

"I was just remembering something. I was thinking back to a night out we went on when we were about 22. We were out with some of the people you worked with in the bar, do you remember? It was during that summer when I was in a foul mood for pretty much the whole 3 months. We'd been to a bar with all your friends and I started fighting. You left with me to get a taxi home and I ended up brawling in the cab queue as well. In the end we had to walk, it started pouring torrential rain in the middle of August. Do you remember, when we got back we stayed up for the rest of the night in front of the fire trying to dry off?"

Kelly narrowed her eyes and gave him a look like she was unsure where he was going.

"Vaguely" she said, picking up her glass, "Why?"

Rob realised that what he was about to do felt worse than confessing to the murders, he braced himself, stood at the edge of the cliff, and jumped.

"Because that's the night I first got you to try a couple of lines of coke. You didn't really fancy it, you said it wasn't your thing, but I was just starting to get hooked and I didn't like doing on my own. I shouted at you, and I told you to just do. And you did"

Kelly reached out and took hold of his hand, she gave a gentle squeeze, he saw the sympathetic look on her face and it made him hate himself even more.

"Robbie…"

"I'm sorry Kel," Rob said, the words felt meaningless when measured against the bar of his actions, but he had nothing else to offer her "I never brought anything other than trouble into your life, this whole time"

She gave his hand another squeeze "You didn't bring anything into it that I didn't let you, you've got nothing to apologise for"

His head spun with all the possibilities that he'd stolen from her, he thought about the million different lives she may have led if he had never stumbled into her life, he thought about all the things she could have been if he hadn't have turned her into a coke fiend.

"I'm sorry Kel, you deserved better" Rob muttered.

Another squeeze "I know, but I chose to settle for you"

From then on Rob struggled to find the heart for sustained conversation. The realisation of what he'd done summoned a string of emotions to the surface, emotions he was only used to feeling post-kill, though in a sense that was precisely what he'd done; he'd murdered Kelly's future, he'd executed all the possibility that lay before her.

They left the restaurant and made their way back through the city. Kelly led the conversation, telling him funny stories about the kids, rehashing memories from their youth, trying anything she could to cheer him up, but her efforts just made him feel worse. They'd been walking for a few minutes before he felt her fingers slide in between his own, he squeezed her hand and carried on walking, the intimacy felt nice, it was a feeling he was beginning to forget.

By the time they reached the taxi rank she'd almost given up on raising his spirits, for her part Kelly seemed to have settled on a perch somewhere close to his melancholy state, talking absentmindedly about the world around them.

Rob opened the door to the first waiting taxi "You take this, I'm going in the opposite direction"

He saw the sad look in her eyes as she leaned in and kissed him on the cheek "Don't do it to yourself Robbie, you've got nothing to feel bad about, ok?"

Rob nodded and gave her a hug, closing the door he watched the taxi pull out and drive away. For a few moments he stood on the side of the road, watching the world go on around him, then he wandered back the way he'd come in search of the nearest pub.

It was a little after midnight when Rob finally made it back to the flat. One shot of whiskey to quieten his guilt had quickly turned into four, after that the urge to walk had taken him, he must have wandered for about two miles before he finally got bored and waved down a passing taxi.

He turned on the light in the living room and dropped onto the couch, in a depressing way the one bedroom flat was already beginning to feel a little bit like home. More often than not the tattered furniture and grim fixtures reflected his mood and reminded him of who he was, there was a correlation between him and the dull flat, an understanding that neither tried to be more than what they were. Good homes were meant for good people, Rob understood that his place was here, or somewhere just like it.

Kelly's words were ringing in his ears, he saw flashes of the life she'd made out of the mess he'd left behind. In his mind he saw Kelly selling her body to maintain the habit that he had forced upon her, he saw her falling for a low life prick because he was the only one who could give her what she needed, he saw a broken woman alone with a child, teetering on the edge of suicidal depression. He connected the dots like a kid with a colouring book, always coming back to the same starting place; him, the original low life prick who instigated a routine spanning fifteen years and counting.

Rob's eyes found their way towards the set of draws in the corner of the room. He lifted himself from the couch, the nights revelations had left him feeling hot and sticky, the scent of his own sweat was thick in his nostrils, lifting up his arms he pulled the jumper over his head and tossed it behind him as he moved across the room. Reaching his destination he opened the top draw and pulled out the bag of coke Charlie had given him, it felt heavier than usual, as if the weight of Kelly's admissions were hidden somewhere amongst the tiny grains of white powder, gripping the bag tightly in his hand he walked through the kitchen and into the bathroom.

The light was bright, bright enough to sting his eyes. He walked towards the mirror, rested the bag on the edge of the sink and looked at his own reflection. He looked old and tired. The lack of sleep was making everything worse, coupled with the constant stream of alcohol it gave him a washed out, half dead look. He ran a hand over the bristles on his head, his hair was slowly starting to grow back, this batch looked greyer than its predecessors, that was obvious already.

Rob took in the sight of himself, he watched the cross around his neck dangle ever so slightly backwards and forwards, it told him he was shaking. Rob glared at his own reflection with disgust. The shaved head made him

402

look like a thug, for so long he'd tried to convince himself that he was more than that, that it was just a disguise, but the truth was clear to him now, it was all he had ever been, and all that he could be. He measured his intentions against his actions and came up pathetically short every time, for every regret he had, for every well-meaning deed he found a dozen transgressions like the one he'd stumbled across tonight.

He tried to understand how he hadn't seen this coming, when he left he thought he'd been doing her a favour, cutting her loose, helping her get away from a bad influence she didn't have the strength to escape from herself. He'd never even considered that the addiction he'd encouraged would drive her right back into another equally destructive relationship, in retrospect it seemed so obvious, but the rose tinted view of his sacrifice made it impossible to see until now.

Lifting the bag of coke and feeling the weight with his hand, he asked himself if he'd ever brought anything construction to another person's life. The answer came back to him as a resounding no. He thought of Kelly, of Jo, of Charlie, Matt, Vera, James Ploughman, Billy Matteo, Wayne Caddock, Tony Miller. A million forgotten names, a million dead faces etched into the wall of his skull, he was nothing but an angel of misery, infecting all those around him with his curse. He gripped the bag tighter, noting the irony that it was thinking like this which got him hooked onto the coke in the first place.

Rob looked back at his reflection and made a decision; there would be no more. No more pain, no more misery, no more guilt. He was done with this life and with his role in it, he had one job to do to and then he would be free. Good people would stop paying the price for his debt to Stephen McSharry and he could leave knowing that he'd finally done something constructive with his life. Stephen McSharry dead, that was all that needed to happen, and it would happen tonight.

Letting out a deep breath Rob opened the bag of coke, the shit might not have been the cause of all of his wrongs but it was definitely a facilitator, he had no need for it now, his life was not going to be about regrets, it was going to be about redemption. He tipped the bag towards the sink, watching as the first few white grains trickled out and into the waiting abyss below. The mobile phone in the living room started to ring, Rob froze, only two people had that number, the second had demanded it a couple of days earlier as a necessity for their on-going business. He looked at the tilted bag of coke and then up to his own reflection and wondered what to do. The phone rang twice more, Rob placed the bag back on the side of the sink and made his way into the living room.

He lifted up the mobile phone and checked the screen, he didn't recognise the number.

"Hello?"

He heard a voice at the other end of the line, it wasn't the voice he wanted to hear.

"Good evening, my little poisoned arrow"

Dead man walking. The thought gave him strength and calmed his nerves, it was the first kill he had ever looked forward to.

"What is it?"

"Don't you think you should show a little more courtesy to the man who's making you rich?" McSharry's tone was light but there was a hard edge to it.

Rob was in no mood for games "What is it?"

"I need to talk to you about your next job"

Rob eyed the details on his living room table, two sheets of folded, handwritten A-4 paper, a far cry from the detailed dossiers he'd been given for the first two hits, bare details about the man's address, one old picture, McSharry's plans were becoming disjointed and rushed, they couldn't keep up with the wave of his ambition.

"Begsy dropped off the Cassidy details, I know where he lives, where he works and when you want it done" Rob could hear that he was being short, he tried to soften his voice, there was no sense in giving McSharry a sense of what was coming "So what else could you want?"

Rob thought he caught a snigger at the other end of the line.

"No, you misunderstand me. Martin Cassidy will be the job after, I'm talking about your next job"

He felt that sick feeling in the pit of his stomach "I don't understand"

"Well, there's been a complication. An old enemy has made his way back onto my radar, my information is a little sketchy at this stage but I'm led to believe that he intends to do me harm at some point in the immediate future. I need you to get to him before he has a chance to do so"

Rob's mind was working overtime, maybe this would be a good thing, if he could get close to McSharry tonight, under the pretext of this new job, it might give him the window he needed to end this whole thing, once and for all.

"Who is he?" Rob asked.

"His name is David Walker, he lives alone in Childwall and he has no security whatsoever. Compared to the other jobs you've been doing lately it'll be a walk in the park"

Rob felt his legs go weak, he stumbled towards the couch and sat down. David Walker, his way out, the alcohol was slowing his brain, he needed to think, he needed more time.

"But... I mean, who is he?" Rob bumbled as he tried to understand what he needed to do.

"He's a man who is causing me problems, that's all you need to know"

"That's bollocks" Rob exploded, the old man was playing him. He didn't understand why "He's a copper. You want me to walk into the house of a police officer and execute him? Are you out of your fucking mind?"

There was a pause, he realised how badly he'd just fucked up, the alcohol was making him sloppy.

"Now how would you know that he was police?"

Rob's weary brain scrambled to keep up with the conversation "I remember from when they sent you down, wasn't he the main one behind the case?"

"All the more reason for the cunt to get taken off the board" McSharry told him, he wasn't dwelling on Rob's slip, for that he breathed a small sigh of relief "His profession is irrelevant to you. The only relevance you should concern yourself with is that I'm giving you an order and I expect you to follow it"

"Do you know the kind of shit storm you'll bring down on yourself by killing a busie?" the concern felt natural, he'd found the best way to play it, killing police was bad news in any circumstance, he'd refuse to do it on those grounds, His anonymity couldn't afford the risk.

"Let me worry about that"

Rob ran through the possibilities, how could they know about what Walker was planning, and did they know he was involved? Was it all a set up to get them both in the same place at the same time? Every question gave birth to five more, their plan was so close to coming together, why did McSharry have to get wind of it now.

"Not a chance. Killing gangsters or drug dealers is one thing but what you're talking about is a whole other level, I want no part of it"

He caught another snigger "Come on now, is it really that much worse than killing a teenage boy?"

"Fuck you!" Rob spat, his hand closed around the phone and he heard the corners of the plastic start to crack.

"Watch yourself boy" McSharry warned, "My patience has limits"

The threat didn't come close to extinguishing his anger, he felt his heart going a hundred beats a minute in his chest, never in his life had he felt hatred like this.

"So does mine old man, and I'm telling you no, there's not a chance in hell that I'm doing this shit for you"

Somewhere in his head a voice warned him not to antagonise the man, that he needed to keep up the illusion if he wanted to get close enough to kill him, but the voice was drowned out by the roaring hatred that had taken over.

"You know Robert," McSharry began, his voice sounded calm and controlled, that worried Rob more than if he'd been shouting "this is a stressful time for me, among other things I've had to move out of my home and go into hiding, I don't appreciate leaving my home, I don't appreciate compromise. Now, I don't know whether you're the type to read the paper but you may have heard that two of my boys were killed last night, courtesy of the police. They were good boys, loyal boys. What I'm getting at is; at a time like this I really need to be relying on my team players, on the people I can trust. A man in mourning can be prone to some pretty irrational acts. I advise you not to test me today or there will be repercussions, I promise you"

Rob slammed his foot against the wooden draws, they fell to one side, collapsing as they hit the floor, he felt a little better.

"Yeah, I remember how this goes, you threaten me, when that doesn't work you threaten my family. Well here's what I think, I think I can get to you and put two bullets in your fucking brain before you get anywhere near my mother or my brother. If you want to go down this road then I'm all for it, but I will bury you and your yobs before you get anywhere near my people"

The words just spilled out of his mouth, he was only partially aware that he was saying them. A part of him knew that it was stupid, that he should be doing what he always did; keeping his mouth shut, but tonight was the night for change, he refused to live in that endless circle anymore.

"Kid, calm the fuck down" McSharry said, that same calm tone. His sense of foreboding grew stronger "I wouldn't dream of hurting an old woman, what kind of man do you think I am? And your brother? The boy works for me, I have no intention of threatening him. But that girl of yours on the other hand, that tidy little slag Kelly Thompson, well, that's another matter"

Rob's knees went weak, it was worse than before, he leaned against the wall for support, how did they know about Kelly? How could they possibly know?

"You fuck" Rob whispered into the phone, it was a pathetic response, it told McSharry everything he needed to know; that he had him.

The calm tone had turned to smugness "My boys just told me she's looking pretty fit tonight, all dolled up in a tight little white dress. She got home a couple of hours ago, out with you I assume? My guys are itching to get in there and have a little fun before they kill her. I've got them on the leash, for now. There are two little kids inside after all"

His world spun, after everything he'd brought to Kelly's door now he was bringing this. He struggled to find an argument to retaliate with, but he had nothing, nothing to offer and nothing to threaten. He pressed his forehead against the wall, gripped the cross around his neck and prayed for an answer. No help came, the desperation closed in.

"I'll fucking kill you"

McSharry laughed off Rob's threat "So you've said. But are you still confident that you can get it done before my boys move into that little terraced house and paint it red?"

He punched the wall, the pain helped, it focused his mind "You go near that fucking door and I'll spend the rest of my life hunting down you and everyone you've ever met"

"Yes, I've heard your threats, you little prick" McSharry shouted back, he was losing patience, Rob was suddenly fearful that it might cost Kelly her life "but none of them change the fact that your slag and those two little kids will be dead in five minutes flat if you aren't on your way to the coppers house"

Rob tried a change of tact, anything to give him more time to think "Why this guy? Why does he need to die? Do you even know what he's got on you?"

There was a pause, when McSharry spoke there was no sign of the calmness, or the irritation, just cold, hard conviction "I know enough. I know he's going to die tonight whether you help me or not. The only difference is how many other people go with him, it's your call boy, so, what's it going to be? Dead copper, or dead girlfriend?"

Rob dropped to his knees, his upper body was caked in sweat.

"Fine. I'll do it"

"Begsy's waiting outside"

The line went dead. Rob dropped the phone onto the floor.

Chapter 32

Unsteady legs carried him into the bedroom. Rob flicked on the light and stumbled towards the wardrobe, from the rail he took a grey hoodie, slipped it over his shoulders and zipped it up. From the bottom draw he took the two black and gold hand guns.

One by one he checked the clips, both were full, after a few moments deliberation he decided to leave the second gun in the draw, killing one man wouldn't require both, and he was cautious to put all of his eggs in one basket while Begsy was around. The more he thought about it, the more unnerved he was by Begsy's presence in this latest development. It was no secret that the two men didn't see eye to eye, so if McSharry wanted him along then there could only be two reasons why; either he didn't trust Rob, or he had something in store for him. Neither one boded particularly well in the long run.

Sliding the pistol into the back of his belt he made a conscious effort to direct his thoughts away from predicting future problems, and towards the one directly in front of him. How could he avoid killing David Walker without getting Kelly killed in the process? He made his way towards the door, as far as he knew wasting time here was just as likely to get her killed as anything else, but at least he had the reprieve of the car journey to think of a way out for himself.

Rob caught sight of Begsy as soon as he opened the door, the enforcers large, overwhelming figure was leaning, arms folded, against the bonnet of a black Range Rover directly outside Rob's flat. As he moved towards the big man he noticed that sick, sadistic grin on his face, Rob's fingers twitched as he felt the urge to pull the Smith and Weston and rid himself of the bastard once and for all.

Rob stopped a few feet away, he waited while Begsy gave him a derogative once over; contemptuously looking him up and down with that same sadistic smile plastered across his face, taunting him, goading him to start something. Rob kept his calm, there were already too many variables in this situation without throwing another one into the mix. He tried to focus on how to get out of this current situation but his attention was constantly drawn back to that cold smile, and those dead, grey eyes.

"You carrying?" Begsy eventually grunted.

Rob nodded, a second later Begsy's arms had unfolded to reveal a grey 9mm in his gloved right hand, the gun was firmly pointed at his midsection, Rob hadn't had the slightest chance to react.

"Hand it over," Begsy demanded "Slowly"

Raising his left hand into the air he reached around slowly with his right and lifted gun free from his belt, he held it out in front of him, Begsy snatched it with his free hand and slid the weapon into his jacket pocket.

"What now?" Rob asked

Begsy spun the 9mm 180 degrees and presented it, handle first, to Rob. There was a moment's hesitation before he reached out and took it, as soon as he had Begsy flashed another smirk and walked around the Range Rover towards the driver's door. Rob checked the clip and made sure the gun was loaded, it was. Sliding it into the same place the Smith and Weston had been a few minutes earlier he opened the passenger door and followed Begsy into the car.

They travelled in silence, that suited Rob just fine, he urged his brain into overdrive and desperately tried to think of a plan to keep both his accomplice and his ex-girlfriend alive. The key to the whole situation was the man driving the car, he knew that much for certain, if he refused to kill Walker then Begsy would notify McSharry immediately and Kelly would be dead. If he tried to stall then Begsy would be onto him in a flash and Kelly would also be dead, and in both situations the odds were fairly high that he would join her.

So what options did that leave him? He pressed his back against the seat and felt the cold metal of the 9mm against his skin, if he moved quickly he could have the gun free in a couple of seconds, and Begsy would be dead in a couple more. With him out of the equation he could drive to Kelly's, kill McSharry's men and get her somewhere safe before the old man had a chance to react. He caught a street name out of the window and reluctantly let the idea out of his grip, even if he turned the car around now he was still fifteen minutes away from Kelly's place, he knew McSharry well enough to know that he'd have a system in place to keep him constantly up-to-date. Rob could only guess at the specifics but he was sure that anything over a few minutes of radio silence from Begsy would be enough to convince McSharry to send in the boys, kill Kelly, and get out again before Rob was anywhere near the place.

So killing Begsy was out, at least in the short term. He considered pulling the pistol and forcing the big man to call McSharry at gunpoint, if he could coerce him into telling the old man that Walker was dead maybe he'd have enough time to get to Kelly before his ruse was discovered. Out of the corner of his eye he caught a smirk creeping into the corners of Begsy's mouth, he got the feeling that they were both thinking along the same lines, that Begsy's smile was an invitation, a challenge to see if he could break him fast enough to save his woman. Rob weighed up everything he knew about McSharry's top enforcer and decided that any attempt at persuasion would be useless; Begsy would rather die than yield the slightest concession to Rob, something in the smirk told him that for certain.

He switched to other potential solutions, maybe if he just pretended to kill Walker then that would be enough, though with Begsy hanging on like a shadow he wasn't sure precisely how that would work. One thing he did know was that it was imperative that he kept Begsy out of the house. If Walker gave even the slightest hint that the two men knew each other then any chance Rob or Kelly had of surviving would evaporate in that instant. If he could get into that house alone then he still had options, if Begsy went with him there was only one course of action left; kill David Walker on sight.

The car made its way into Childwall, Rob tried to steady himself, game time was fast approaching. He kept his exterior calm but in his head he continued to frantically run down dead ends streets, every option he considered culminated in the death of at least one of him, Walker or Kelly, and in most cases all three. His hatred for McSharry and Begsy continued to bubble away but Rob did his best to push it to the back of his mind, there would be plenty of time for hatred later, right now he needed a solution.

The car pulled to a halt and Rob recognised the house he'd broken into more than a decade ago, he acknowledged his return as the culmination of that agreement all those years before, he fought back a wave of sickness when he considered that the outcome of that agreement would be David Walker's death, at his hand.

Rob followed Begsy's eye line towards Walker's house, he looked left then right as if he was trying to get his bearings before focusing his attention on the same building.

"Is this it?"

Begsy nodded and opened the door on his side "Let's go"

Rob moved his left hand behind his back "You're not coming"

The big man regarded him with an almost amused look "What's that?"

"I don't do well with an audience. If you people want me to do this then you'll leave me to do it my way"

That same smirk, Rob watched the scar across his right cheek change shape "Listen to me carefully you little fucking pussy; I don't want you to do it, not in a million bloody years"

Rob's left hand moved closer to the gun, he kept his face calm "But your boss does, and there's no way that I'm going in there with a sneaky little shithouse like you at my back. I know exactly how your kind work, a sly shot when I'm looking the other way, you go back and tell the old man I stumbled in front of a shot meant for the copper? Fuck that shit"

Begsy grunted, it sounded something like a chuckle. He gave him another condescending inspection, up and down, as if he was deciding whether or not to grant his request, then closed the door and settled back into his seat.

"You've got two minutes" Begsy said, looking straight ahead.

Rob stepped out of the car, pulled the grey hood over his head and darted around the side of the house. That first small victory had encouraged him, but he was still no closer to knowing what he was going to do once he got inside.

The wooden fence separating Walker's garden from the side of the house stood two metres tall, he hopped it and landed on a patch of unkempt grass, dropping onto one knee he settled into the shadows of the fence and pulled the pistol from his belt, inspecting the house in front of him as he did so. It was a large, semidetached property, though the house itself looked expensive it was clear to see that it needed some attention. The place like everything else about David Walker seemed to scream 'workaholic', Rob admired that in him, he maybe even envied it a little too.

Keeping the 9mm at his side Rob darted across the grass and into the shadows that covered the rear of the house. There was no light or sound from within, not overly surprising for 1am on a Saturday morning. He made his way towards the back door, stopped and listened again. Nothing. The bottom half of the door was all wood, further up were a series of frosted glass tiles, Rob took the butt of the pistol and popped the tile closest to the handle, the first hit cracked the glass, the second sent the tile tumbling to the kitchen floor, Rob quickly put his hand through the gap, unlocked the door and made his way inside.

It was difficult to tell just how much noise the dislodged glass had made when it landed, but Rob trained the weapon in front of him and assumed the worst. The darkness was thicker than he had expected, for a few moments he looked ahead nervously into the abyss while his eyesight adjusted. Starting with the kitchen he made his way through each of the rooms on the ground floor, taking in the outdated furniture, the bundles of paperwork and the occasional dirty plate, his movement was slow, light and intended to make as little noise as possible. He kept his ears sharp, whenever he heard the first creak of a floorboard underneath his feet he halted the pressure in his step and moved backwards, by the time he'd covered the kitchen, the dining room and the living room he was still yet to hear a creak of a floorboard anywhere else in the house.

Once his sweep of the ground floor was complete Rob made his way towards the staircase, he took a couple of deep breaths to try and slow his heart rate, aimed the pistol upwards and slowly started his ascent.

With each step he became more convinced that the next would bring with it an attack of some kind, he remembered from David Walker's previous visit that the man had access to a pistol, in this darkness, in this kind of situation Walker had every chance of shooting him dead before he even realised who his intruder was.

Rob reached the top of the stairs and took in his new surroundings. There was a bathroom straight ahead, easing his way in he quickly added it to the list of vacant rooms. From there was a long, narrow corridor with four doors, two on either side of hallway. If David Walker was home then he would either be sleeping, or waiting, in one of those four rooms.

Slowly, Rob moved forward. His heart beat so fiercely that he was sure it would give away his presence, he breathed in through his nose and urged it to slow down, but all that accomplished was to make it go faster.

He approached the first door on the right and steadied himself, he was still yet to hear a single flicker of movement since he'd entered, he hoped beyond belief that the house would prove to be empty, but knew he still had a long way to go before he could breathe that particular sigh of relief.

Rob eased the first door open with his right foot, it let out a low creak as it moved, slowly showing him the inside of what appeared to be a darkened storage space. The door had opened halfway when he caught a flicker of movement out of the corner of his eye, instinct forced him to turn towards it, as he did so he realised it was a baseball bat, moving at a high speed towards him. The alcohol slowed his reactions, as it was he managed to move his head a split second before the bat would have connected with it. The movement caused him to stumble off balance, by the time he'd steadied himself the bat was swinging back for another pass, this time he wasn't fast enough, the wood smashed against his knuckles sending the 9mm sprawling from his grip.

Rob felt the pain shoot through his hand, he immediately took a couple of steps back to establish some distance between himself and the bat. It was only then that he got a first look at David Walker, the police officer was wearing a green t-shirt with a pair of black tracksuit bottoms, the dishevelled state of his hair confirmed that he hadn't been awake for very long, though you wouldn't know by the wide eyed, crazed look he possessed as he slowly stalked forward. Rob knew the darkness combined with the hoodie concealed his identity, though he didn't know whether it was a good thing or a bad thing at that particular moment.

Raising the bat above his head Walker charged ahead. Rob took a step forward to meet him and caught Walker's arm as he brought it down in an arching swing. The move caused Walker's arm and the bat to halt in mid-air, Rob used the moments reprieve to force his knee upwards into the other man's groin. He heard a grunt of pain as his knee made contact and followed it up by twisting and launching Walker head first towards the wall with as much strength as he could muster.

The policeman hit the wall hard but was already turning back to face him before sound of flesh on plaster had faded from their ears. Rob covered the distance in an instant, balling his right fist as he moved. A second later it connected with Walker's jaw, this time it was the back of the coppers head that slammed against the plastered wall.

A shot like that took a moment or two to recover from, Rob used the time to grab Walker's left arm with both hands and slam it against the wall repeatedly until the bat fell to the ground.

The sound of the wooden bat hitting the floor brought the copper back immediately. He responded by connecting with a right fisted shot of his own, straight into Rob's cheek. The shot turned his head towards the ground and Rob caught the glimmer of a grey piece of metal a few feet away. Using the momentum of Walker's punch he let himself fall to the ground and rolled towards the glimmer. In one swift motion he was up on one knee, with the 9mm in his hand trained squarely on the shape of David Walker.

Seeing the weapon aimed at him Walker responded by slamming his fist against the wall, a moment later the entire hallway was bathed in light and Rob's anonymity was instantly a thing of the past.

"You!" Walker growled, peering into the hood "What the hell are you doing?"

With the gun aimed at Walker's chest Rob pulled back the hood and sucked air into his lungs. He saw the look of confusion on the man's face and suddenly his throat was dryer than it had ever been. It took a couple of moments for him to find his voice.

"I'm sorry. I didn't want to do this, but they have someone I care about"

The look of confusion gave way to hardened understanding, Walker didn't look at the gun, not once, he kept his eyes focused exclusively on Rob.

"What are you talking about?" Rob noted the hostage negotiator tone in his voice, training on how to deal with an armed suspect, it had probably kicked in before Walker had even realised it. If only he was a kidnapper, a man with demands, capable of being talked down. But unfortunately for the one without the gun, that wasn't what this was.

"I don't have a choice" Rob said. Every murderous instinct in his body told him to pull the trigger, to not get bogged down in conversation, but he couldn't do it, not yet. He needed this victim to know why he was there.

"Just wait," Walker said, raising his arms as if he was surrendering "just slow down, talk to me. Of course you have a choice"

His chest was so tight it was becoming difficult to breathe, he used every ounce of strength in his arm to keep it from shaking. He tried to remind himself about Kelly, about what would happen to her if he failed, but all he could see was the man in front of him, the copper who wanted the exact same things that he did.

"No," Rob replied, shaking his head. He tried to harden himself to what he was about to do, he'd done this more times than he could remember. So why did this feel so alien?

"Just calm down"

"It's over. They're waiting outside. If I don't do it they'll come in here and do it themselves. Then they'll kill my friend, I can't let that happen"

Walker took a step forward with his hands still raised, Rob refocused his aim at the coppers head.

"Just slow down. Let me make a call, this place will be swimming with police in five minutes flat. We can get to the people pushing this, and we can get to your friend too"

Rob gave another shake of the head "It'll be too late. I need to do this now or she dies"

He saw the cracks start to appear in David Walker's performance, he caught a glimpse of fear, of blind panic poking its way through the disguise of his training.

"What about everything we've done?" Walker said, there was a hint of pleading to his voice "What about everything we've risked? If you kill a police officer you're going to spend the rest of your life in prison, and what happens then? Stephen McSharry goes on killing, how many more people like me, you and James Ploughman are going to die trying to stop him? You can't do this, what we're doing is too important"

Rob heard the argument, it was an argument he'd been making ever since he'd gotten the call, but it wasn't enough. Not when he considered the alternative.

"You don't understand" Rob told him, the urge to explain himself was almost overwhelming. A part of him screamed at him to recognise the futility of it all, but he had to at least try "I can't just sit back and let him kill her. After everything... I can't let it happen"

Rob could see the fear clearly now in David Walker's eyes, the sweat was already starting to seep through his t-shirt.

"What is it that makes her life worth more than mine?"

"We chose to be a part of this. She didn't"

Walker swallowed hard "I can help you" his voice full of emotion.

"No," Rob said, cocking the 9mm "Not anymore"

There was silence for a few seconds, Rob tried to find the courage he needed to complete the job. After a while David Walker took a deep breath and stood as tall as his frame would allow. Rob acknowledged the bravery in the move, he hoped he'd be able to act the same way when his time came.

"I was wrong about you," Walker told him, hatred fuelled by panic, it took Rob to a place he was much more familiar with "I wanted to believe that underneath all this you were a good man, that we were the same. But the truth is you really are nothing more than a murderous thug. You're a killer, no better than the bastards pulling your strings"

"I know, and I'm sorry"

As they stood in the narrow hallway, staring into each other's eyes, he suddenly heard a voice, somewhere in his head, it took him a moment to realise that it was his own.

"I'm sorry Kel, you deserved better"

Her voice came back, almost instantaneously.

"I know, but I chose to settle for you"

In that moment he knew; he could never let that choice bring her to harm again.

David Walker steadied himself "You won't get away-"

Rob fired.

Once, twice, three times in quick succession.

The first shot hit the chest, so did the second. The third one caught him in the face. David Walker tumbled backwards. The hallway wasn't quite long enough, he fell onto his back, his head and neck were propped against the wall at an unnatural angle.

Walker's body had barely hit the floor before Rob's had started to react. A wave of terror overcame him in an instant, it made the walls spin and his stomach try to force its way out of his mouth. His legs turned to jelly, dropping the gun he stumbled backwards towards the floor and slid to the ground, face to face with man he'd just killed.

Everything seemed to unravel in that one instant, the world continued to spin, the urge to throw up was almost overpowering. Walker's eyes were open, Rob stared into them, it felt as if they stared back. He felt condemned by those eyes, for all Rob knew they were the eyes of The Lord Himself. He touched the cross at his neck, as if for protection. It brought none.

Staring into those eyes Rob lost all track of time. The severity of what he had done seemed to increase with each passing moment. He'd killed an accomplice. He'd killed a police officer. He'd killed an innocent man. He'd killed a good man.

Somehow, at some point, it occurred to him that this was the first time he'd ever killed someone he knew. Someone who had trusted him. The realisation brought a wave of vomit up his throat but Rob kept his mouth shut and forced it back down again. His eyes remained locked in togetherness with Walker's. He could still see the panic, the fear, the shock and the pain in them. He was used to that look, but not in faces he knew, not in people he could recognise before he'd brought that look to their faces. Something clicked in his brain; he suddenly saw the same look on Charlie's face, on Kelly's, on Jo's.

Rob continued to sit, staring at what he'd done. It felt like a single second, and it felt like a million years. At some point he became aware of another presence, he heard the heavy movements and caught flickers of the hulking shadow but still his eyes remained locked with those of David Walker. It was only when Begsy leaned down and checked Walker's pulse, severing the connection of their eyes, that Rob came back to the world.

All he could do was sit and watch, exhaustion had drained him of the capacity to do anything else. He watched Begsy confirm the kill, the big man studied Walker's body with interest, he pressed his face close, inspecting the wounds and taking in the dead man's final emotions with a sordid fascination.

The smug, victorious look on Begsy's face brought a fresh wave of loathing to the forefront of Rob's mind. The choices he'd made had brought him to this place, the lines had been drawn and this was where he stood; next to the likes of Begsy and Stephen McSharry. He watched Begsy's gloved hand pick the 9mm from the floor and slip it into his pocket, even without looking he could feel the dead man's accusing stare, he found himself wishing that Walker had found the courage to kill him when he had the chance. Things had been allowed to go too far, with David Walker dead he was clueless as to where they would now go.

Begsy grunted, it took his dazed brain a couple of seconds to decipher the sound as an order to move. Rob stumbled to his feet, the dizziness got worse, he grabbed hold of the wall for support and slowly followed Begsy down the hallway.

Reaching the top of the staircase he turned back and studied Walker's prone, crumpled figure. Away from the focus of those eyes he was suddenly able to see so much more, like how the blood had soaked through the green t-shirt making it look almost black, and how the impact from each shot had left a light spray of blood on the beige wall above the body. The weight of what he'd done continued to build in his chest, he spent one, final moment staring at the chaos he had created, and then continued on down the stairs.

By the time he caught up to Begsy they were within a few feet of the car, Rob climbed into the passenger seat, fought the exhaustion that was infecting his body and tried to take stock of the situation. With the house behind them his brain was slowly starting to kick into gear. As the wheels began to turn it brought with it the flood of reality that had so far been kept at bay.

The car pulled out quietly, picking up speed as soon as it got out of the street. The acceleration made his world spin that little bit more, Rob stared out the window and tried to breath but no matter what he tried he just couldn't seem to steady himself.

Repercussions were coming to him quickly now, a dead policeman would not be accepted lightly, such events were rare but when they did happen they were inevitably followed by a mass show of police force. Within a few hours officers of the law would be coming down hard on anyone and everyone who might be able to shed some light on the killing, pesky inconveniences like suspects rights and fair treatment were unlikely to apply when it came to this kind of situation. Finding him would be their top priority, it would be their only priority, and to say that Rob was less than convinced about the reliability of his co-conspirators would be something of an understatement. Now Begsy had the murder weapon, with Rob's prints all over it. Had he been more alert at the time he would never of let that happen, as it was there would be no way to retrieve the gun without resorting to a bout of physical violence, and with David Walker's corpse still fresh in his mind Rob was far too exhausted to consider any such action.

Not only would Walker's execution bring with it a shitstorm to anyone who made their living within the parameters of organised crime, it also eliminated all of Rob's serious options for getting away clean. Without Walker's contacts there would be no way for him to get out of the country undetected, that meant a lifetime of running with his mother, brother, wife and kids in tow. That was assuming he could even get to McSharry, the revelation that the old man had gone to ground had seemed insignificant in the context of the wider conversation, but now that his brain was beginning to function he realised that even getting sight of Stephen McSharry had suddenly become a much trickier concept. He replayed the conversation in his mind and began to grasp just how difficult that was going to be, he'd threatened to kill the old man more than once, that wouldn't be taken lightly.

On top of that he was due to take out Martin Cassidy in two days' time, the job that he'd never intended to carry out had suddenly become intrinsically necessary. McSharry needed to be indulged and Rob needed to stall. No matter what, the old man would know that Rob was still dangerous, and that might buy him enough time to figure out his next move. A quick and clean hit on Martin Cassidy might just buy him a little more, Stephen McSharry didn't forgive easily, but nor did he throw away assets needlessly.

Rob consoled himself with the knowledge that at least Kelly was safe. He told Begsy he wanted dropping at his friend's house, a disinterested glance was all he got to tell him that his request had even been heard.

Ten minutes later they pulled up outside her house. Begsy was out of the car instantly, Rob followed a couple of seconds behind. He watched McSharry's first choice thug walk in front of the car and scan the street, Rob stood beside him and followed his eye line; four cars down, on the opposite side of the road was a blue Ford Mondeo. The car was parked under a broken streetlight, in the darkness it was difficult to tell whether it was occupied or not, but as soon as Begsy pointed away from the house he heard the engine roar to life and saw flickers of movement in both of the driver and the passenger seats. As the car drove past them and away into the night a disturbing thought played its way across his mind; they'd just allowed at least two of their men to see Rob's face. It was the clearest indication yet that his future looked bleak.

Rob turned to face the larger man.

"I want my gun back"

For a moment Begsy looked as though he was going to refuse. That smug, cruel smile playing on his lips as he considered which way to play it, with a dismissive snigger he reached behind him, pulled the Smith and Weston from his belt and handed it to Rob.

"Don't forget. Sunday night, that's when we want Cassidy done. Once we know he's dead that's when you get the money. You got a problem with that arrangement you talk to me, clear?"

Rob slipped the pistol into his belt and nodded. He watched as Begsy walked back to the car and got in. Rob waited, once the car was out of sight he gave the street another once over, when he was as sure as he could be that McSharry's boys had split he turned around and walked towards Kelly's front door.

He banged hard on the door four times. A quick look at his watch told him that it was pushing 2am, he wrapped his knuckles against the door twice more, a few seconds later he saw light fill one of the first floor windows.

It took another couple of minutes for Kelly to make her way downstairs. Even from outside Rob could hear the creek of floorboards as she stumbled down the staircase, through the glass panes he saw her check the peep hole, pause, and then open the door.

Kelly still looked half asleep as she leaned against the frame of the door. "Miss me already?"

"Can I come in?"

Rob caught a cautious look "I don't know, what's this about?"

"It isn't that," Rob assured her, sex was just about the last thing on his mind at that moment "but I really need to come inside"

Kelly opened the door the rest of the way, Rob gave the street one quick check and made his way inside, she closed the door behind him, he saw she was wearing blue pyjamas two sizes too big.

"Is everything ok? You look a little pale"

Rob went and stood next to the fireplace "I'm fine"

"And you're shaking"

He tried to ignore the concern in her voice, sympathy burned worse than boiling water, he didn't deserve it and he didn't want it.

"Kel, I need you to pack up your stuff, take the kids and get out of the house. Go and stay at your mothers or something"

Kelly crossed her arms and leaned back against the door "What the hell is this about?"

"You need to listen to me," Rob heard the panic creeping into his voice "you need to get the kids and go to your mothers now"

She walked towards him, half worried, half sceptical "My mother lives in a one bedroom, supported living bungalow, we can't stay with her. What the hell is going on Robbie, you're starting to scare me"

Rob looked away, the shame was too much. He tried to understand how she could accept everything he'd done to her and still stand her with concern and compassion, it was beyond him to comprehend.

"You have to know, I never meant to bring this on you, especially after..." words failed him, he switched tact "but some very nasty people know that we have a relationship. If you stay here you're going to be in danger, these people will hurt you if they think it'll help them get to me"

Her eyes went immediately to the top of the stairs. A mother's reaction. Her face lost some of its softness, she shook her head at him "What have you gotten yourself into?"

"I don't have time to get into it Kel, just listen to what I'm telling you. You need to leave and you need to leave now"

"I'm not going anywhere." she said defiantly. That old stubbornness showed itself, Rob had expected nothing less "this is my home, my children's home, it's where they live their lives, where they've grown up, I won't be chased out of it by some gang of thugs"

Rob felt frustration mingling with panic, it made the dizziness even worse.

"Kel, these are dangerous people. I can't protect you if you stay here"

He could see she was getting angry, in no way was that likely to help his cause.

"I don't need protecting, and I don't need to leave. I'll tell you something else as well Robbie, I don't appreciate you coming round here in the middle of the night and scaring me half to death. I've dealt with dangerous people before, and if they come round here looking for trouble I'll give them plenty to take back with them. But right now, the only dangerous person I can see causing trouble is you. I'm not leaving my home because of some mess you've gotten yourself into and you've got a lot of cheek asking me to"

Her response didn't come as much of a surprise, one of the things he'd loved most about her was that strong minded determination, it was also one of the things that drove him up the wall.

"There's nothing I can do to change your mind?"

She crossed her arms and glared at him "Look at my face"

On to plan B. Rob reached behind him and pulled the pistol from his belt.

"Fine, then at least take this"

Kelly took a step back "Jesus Christ"

The realisation hit him, it was the second time in a month that he'd presented a woman with a gun. The reason; to offset the danger he'd brought to them. The disgust he had for himself moved up another notch.

"Just take it"

Kelly glared at him incredulously "I have kids in the house, are you out of your mind?"

Rob held the gun out further "So keep it somewhere safe. But I'm not leaving until I know you can protect yourself"

He stood there for a while with the gun in his hand, eventually she sighed and stepped forward "Fine, but I'm not happy with you, and I don't like this shit in my house"

Rob followed her towards the back of the living room, she reached a set of large wooden draws, and took a key from the top shelf. Kneeling down he watched as she unlocked the bottom draw, gently rested the gun inside and locked it again. Returning the key to the top shelf she walked towards him, crossed her arms and gave him a cold stare.

Rob tried to smile and touched her lightly on the arm "I understand you're upset, but Kel you need to listen to me; be careful and pay attention. If you see something suspicious, even just a little odd, you call the police. If you see something really suspicious you call me, you got it?"

She peered at him curiously, Rob felt a wave of dizziness nearly knock him off his feet, Kelly grabbed his shoulders to help steady him.

"Do you need to sit down? You don't look so good"

Rob pushed himself away and stumbled towards the door, there was only one thing he needed, and it wasn't here.

"I have to go" he said, reaching the door he opened it, turned back, and faced her "Remember what I told you. Be careful"

Rob got back to the flat and made his way straight to the bathroom. Cupping his hands underneath the tap he splashed cold water against his face again and again until his fingers were numb. The process woke him up, but did nothing to halt the ever increasing sense of panic in his chest. Looking down he saw the bag of coke, on the edge of the sink, just where he'd left it. He picked it up and felt the weight in his hand, it felt lighter than it had before. Rob gently shook it and watched the coke move, the way his world was spinning made the little white grains dance. He gripped the bag tighter and felt some of the powder slip between his fingers, wandering back into the living room he dropped the bag on the wooden table.

Taking a credit card from his wallet Rob poured out the contents of the plastic bag and got down to it. Dizziness made splitting it into lines hard work, even with so much coke in front of him. More than once he had to stop to catch his breath, pushing Walker's dead face from the front of his mind and resuming the job at hand.

Eventually, it was done. 3 grams of coke split out evenly in front of him, just the sight of it seemed comforting, like a caring parent promising to banish away the nightmares of a child. Rob dropped the credit card and retrieved the small straw from his previous cocaine relapse. He held it out in front of him, surveying his handiwork, panic had raised his heart beat to an alarming level, he needed a rest, a reprieve, something to change the record from this endless loop of fear and self-loathing.

Lowering his face to the table Rob took a first line, then a second, then a third. The high hit him fast, it knocked him out of his loop and brought fresh views of similar terrain. Rob didn't stop to enjoy it, he kept going; fourth, fifth, sixth. He started to lose count. With each line the world seemed to settle that little bit more, it calmed his world, shored up his footing and regulated his thinking. He took a little walk around the living room to get the blood pumping, he marvelled as dead faces mingled into one and then slowly faded away. The tightness in his chest began to subside, he checked his pulse, it was still beating fast but not in that panic attack, can't breathe kind of way, this was like an enthusiastic, excited beat, like an eager puppy anxious to play.

He left behind his regret and started to think proactively, what's done is done, what's next? Taking another line he recounted everything that had happened. Somewhere along the course of his memories guilt started to make way to anger. By the time he'd caught up with the present he felt an overwhelming urge to assign blame, it called to him and demanded to be satisfied, Rob took another line and laid it all out in front of him. Every action had brought a reaction, in amongst the tangled mess, somewhere, was culpability. Another line of coke disappeared as Rob started working backwards, it was a few minutes before he got to a place that made sense: Kelly. It was her exposure which had blown the whole situation out of control. His mandate had been clear, and it had been working. The old man's days were numbered, Rob had everything planned and all the means he needed to carry that plan out. Then Kelly's vulnerability had been brought into the mix and it had pushed Rob to a place that he never should have found himself.

So how did the old man know? He'd been careful, he was always careful, but it must have come from somewhere.

Rob sat on the couch, leaned back and allowed his mind to work. It raced ahead, chasing down theories and ideas with the speed of a formula one race car, all he could do was hold tight and go along for the ride. His brain worked through every possible explanation, dismissing one after another until there was only one left. He considered it. His gut confirmed it. A wave of anger brought his speeding brain to a halt, it whispered retribution and forced him to his feet. Rob looked down at the wooden table, only a few lines remained. He moved into the bedroom, retrieved the one gun he still had, came back and devoured what was left.

His fist hammered against the door again and again without pause. In time it developed a harmonious rhythm with his heartbeat. He kept going even when he heard movement, it was only when the door opened, and moved out of his reach that he halted. He saw the door open halfway and Vicky's face appear behind it, he didn't wait for an invitation, pushing it open the rest of the way he bundled past her and moved towards the living room.

He looked around the room and saw no sign of Charlie, Vicky was a couple of steps behind him.

"What do you think you're doing?" she hissed, her voice low and threatening.

"Where is he, Vicky?" Rob demanded, he peered into the kitchen; empty "I need to see him now"

She took a step toward him and stared "Bloody hell. It's 4.30 in the morning, I think you need to leave"

She was wearing a pair of pink, satin pyjamas. They looked new, and expensive, another purchase funded by Rob's enemy, and by Charlie's betrayal.

"Where is my brother?"

Her dark hair was curled and messy, she impatiently brushed a strand away from her face and gestured emphatically towards Rob.

"He isn't here. He hasn't been here for going on three days now. He does this, now sometimes, I learnt a long time ago that I was better off not asking any questions, it saves us both the bother of having to listen to his lies"

Rob's brain moved back into overdrive, it took in the words and dissected them, was she lying? Was she trying to trick him, to protect her man?

"You're telling me you haven't seen your husband for three days and you don't know where he is? You expect me to believe that?"

"Believe what you want" she said aggressively "He's your brother, why don't you tell me where he is?"

"I need to see him" the anger inside needed a release, Rob turned and smashed his fist into the wall, he didn't feel the pain but he saw the dent in the wall "I need to see him right now!"

Vicky's face went from angry to fearful and back again all in the space of a few seconds.

"You really need to leave. I have children in this house, your nieces. Your brother might not give a shit but I do, and I won't allow them to hear this. Get out."

Rob took a step towards her, their faces were close.

"I need to see him now, we have something very serious to talk about"

She peered into his eyes "I don't know what you're on but you've had way too much of it. If you won't leave by yourself I'll get the police to come get you"

Vicky grabbed him by the arm to lead him out, Rob reacted without thinking, his hands gripped her shoulders and pushed her backwards, pinning her against the wall. He moved his face close to hers, close enough to smell her scented shampoo, impatience guided his actions.

"You seem like a nice girl, and a good mum, but I'm not going anywhere until you tell me where I can find my brother"

"I don't know where he is" Vicky said, looking down to where he gripped her shoulder "You're hurting me"

Rob let go and punched the wall above her head, Vicky flinched but didn't utter a word.

"I killed a police offer tonight" Rob said, words started tumbling out of him without his consent "I shot him three times in his own home, he was a good man and he deserved better than that kind of death, the forensics and the police tape, the reporters and the investigators, he didn't deserve it. He died because that worthless fuck you call a husband sold me out, and put a friend of mine in serious danger. She's a mother, with two kids, just like you, and to save her life I executed a fucking police officer!"

He saw the horror spread across his sister-in-laws face, he didn't know whether it was horror for what he had done, or what Charlie had done, in the end it didn't really matter which.

"My God" she whispered.

"My God is right. So I need to talk to my brother tonight. I need to know where he is"

"I told you, I don't know"

He moved his face closer she stared at him with a strange mix of fear and wonder. He felt impatience begin to give way to something else.

"Would you tell me if you did?"

"I don't know"

"What do you know?"

She stared at him with wide eyes and slowly shook her head.

Something came over him. He pressed his lips against hers, she reacted instantly, pushing him away with all of her strength.

"What the hell are you doing?" she shouted

"I don't know" Rob muttered, his brain raced away once again, showing him different ideas, different perceptions.

He moved forward once more and pressed his lips against hers. This time she didn't push him away, this time her hands moved around his neck. He lifted her up against the wall and felt her legs wrap around his waist. He was lost instantly, in the sensation, in the possibility. Her body pressed naturally against his, it felt warm, safe, a desperate craving awoke in him from nowhere, he hadn't felt like this in years. Once again time seemed to evaporate before him, everything disappeared except for her. His eyes were closed and his mind was clear, nothing existed but the moment, the embrace. Eventually they made their way towards the couch, Rob dropped her without breaking the kiss, they hungrily tore at each other's clothes, her fingers scratched at his flesh, first around his neck, then lower, all the way to the base of his back. He ripped her clothes apart until she was naked beneath him, pressing his face against her neck he inhaled the scent. He felt her panting, at that moment his mind stabilised and he somehow managed to stay locked in the moment.

He felt peace, a peace that was almost forgotten. Somewhere in the back of his mind he was aware of its transient nature, but right then, in that bubble, it felt like the most impenetrable place imaginable.

Chapter 33

November was drawing to a close, and taking with it all manner of things. Even Mother Nature seemed keen to get in on the act; England was blessed with its first snow fall for nearly two years, a white blanket that offered a potential clean slate to any and all who needed it.

Stephen McSharry sat in the back seat of his BMW and watched the snowflakes tumble across the quiet, darkened car park. It was still too soon to tell whether it would stick, the wet ground threatened to thwart the transformation before it had even begun, but like most things in life, all that was needed was a little persistence.

The heating in the car was turned on full blast, yet still McSharry suppressed a shiver. He remembered what it was like to feel cold, real cold at least. Prison cold. Ten years of that incarcerated chill was still fresher in his mind than he cared to admit, times like this brought it back to him. It made him thankful for the luxury he had, and hungrier to ensure that it lasted.

There'd been a spring in his step for most of the day, finally being rid of the pointy nosed copper brought with it a freedom almost exhilarating as being released from prison. It felt so good he didn't know why he hadn't done it years ago, his only regret was that he hadn't been there to see the little prick die, though he'd been sure to make Begsy talk him through it several times in detail.

That was why he was here now, meeting Chris Railton in person was a bigger risk than he necessarily needed to take, but the thrill of extracting one final victory over David Walker was too strong to ignore. He wanted to be the one to hand over the money, to personally thank the pricks trusted sidekick for his contribution.

It was the perfect remedy for his on-going agitation. Ever since the attempt on his life he'd felt an overwhelming need for action, compromise had suddenly become the word that sickened him more than any other in the English language. The very concept had him seething, a state of mind that was aggravated further by the death of his boys and the confiscation of his drugs. Combined, the two events showed just how far he still had to go until his rightful place was restored, until no man, within or without the law, dared to fuck with his plans.

The whole concept of laying low ran completely parallel to everything he was trying to do. It was Begsy's idea, and he saw the necessity behind it, but that didn't change the fact that it went against every instinct in his body. The way the city was changing, the speed with which it evolved, it felt foolish to have his people out of sight so soon after taking back control. He could practically feel the vermin, scurrying around his city, using this downtime to plot their moves against him. How he longed to wipe them all out, to kill every last man who might one day prove to be a problem for him or his people. It was long overdue, like an unkempt garden Liverpool had become riddled with wild weeds that soured everything around them. They needed to be ripped out by the root, or his garden would never be able to properly flourish.

McSharry pulled a cigar from his breast pocket and breathed in its scent, one thing at a time he reminded himself, looking out the window he focused on the evening at hand.

The car park was deserted, the Southport beach front was unlikely to draw many spectators on a Saturday night in late November, even less so in the current weather conditions. Still, they'd been careful to pick a spot void of security cameras, word was already starting to filter down that the Merseyside Police authorities were cracking down hard on anyone they could get their hands on, being caught in conversation by the wrong pair of eyes would undo a lot of good work in very little time.

A blue Ford parked up on the opposite side of the car park. A moment later there was movement, McSharry lit the cigar and watched Chris Railton stroll across the tarmac, burrowing his chin into the collar of a black leather jacket as he walked. Begsy opened the driver's door, got out and took a few steps forward to meet the young rat half way. Begsy led the copper around the car and to the rear door, McSharry lifted the bag from the empty seat beside him and rested it on his lap.

Railton opened the door and sat down next to him. McSharry watched the kid rub his hands together and brush a couple of snow fakes off the shoulder of his leather jacket.

"You're late"

The kid gave him a look, a cocky double-take, it was only the second time McSharry had met him face to face.

"It was a little tough to get away" the copper said, keeping his eyes on Begsy as the big man circled the car, opened the driver's door and resumed his position behind the wheel "I don't know if you read the papers but we're in a little bit of a crisis: a prominent police officer was murdered last night, the bosses are calling for all hands on deck"

McSharry smiled and pressed his hand, palm first, against his chest.

"My heart bleeds"

Railton flashed him his young, confident smile "It's a big day, all the overtime will kick in just in time for Christmas"

McSharry patted the bag on his lap "I don't think you need to worry"

"Have to keep up appearances though, don't I? My boss was just killed after all" the kid kept a straight face as he uttered the words, he was a better actor than McSharry had given him credit for.

"You seem to be coping well with your choice" McSharry remarked. He watched him more closely, interested to see if any emotion existed behind that convincing mask.

Railton shrugged his shoulders "He got in the way, didn't he?"

"Of what?"

The little rat nodded towards McSharry's lap.

"Me and that bag"

McSharry let out a hearty laugh and tossed the bag towards him, Railton caught it in both hands and quickly looked inside, he let the kid have his moment and gazed out the window at the falling snow.

"It was a long time coming for that cunt," McSharry said, pausing for a pull on his cigar "Begsy tells me he died with a piss scared look on his face. I picked him out for a bitch the first time I met him. I have to say, I was beginning to doubt whether you were ever going to come through for me. You made me wait long enough before this new job or yours paid off. Too long to save my shipment, or two of my guys"

The rat kept his face calm, but McSharry caught him grip the bag that little bit tighter.

"I had to be careful, you know, save it for when it really mattered. I didn't get what he had but I could see it; he was gunning for you BIG time"

McSharry didn't doubt it. He watched as the snow fall increased outside, it was a problem he didn't intend to consider for long, Rob Thomas and a 9mm automatic had already solved it. Better to spend his time on the ones that still needed resolution.

"I have a few ideas. Don't worry Officer, you've earned your pay day"

The rat let his grip loosen on the bag, he went to speak and then stopped. A few seconds later he tried again.

"Now I need you to lay low for a while. My people are going to be out for blood, and given your history with the dead officer, there's obviously going to be a lot of interest in you. The best thing you can do is keep out of their way and don't make any waves. At least until the clamour on this thing dies down"

Another advocate for inaction, he felt their incessant gnawing at every turn. This time from a copper, if he ever felt the need to start wiping them out, he knew where he would begin.

"I'll consider it"

The rat leaned in closer "You need to do more than that"

"I said I'll consider it" McSharry returned loudly, he saw Begsy shift an arm towards his weapon, the rat saw it too "That's as much as I'm going to give you. Now, if you don't mind, I have more business that requires my attention"

The rat wrapped the straps of the bag tightly around his left hand, reaching for the door handle with his right.

"You won't hear from me for a while. In six months, if something comes across by desk I'll let you know. Are we good for the same price?"

McSharry considered it. Two hundred and fifty thousand to be rid of David Walker was a steal, but in six months' time his need for the kid could long be expired.

"If the information warrants it"

The rat nodded and opened the door, a gust of cold wind nearly extinguished his cigar.

"I'll be seeing you"

The door closed, and then he was gone. They watched until he'd crossed the car park and departed in his blue Ford. It was McSharry who broke the silence as he tossed his spent cigar out of the window.

"I fucking hate rats"

His eyes met Begsy's in the rear-view mirror.

"Only breed fouler than coppers"

McSharry laughed. He readjusted his position and made himself more comfortable, the snow seemed to be getting worse, the warm beamer felt more like home than his new apartment.

"He is useful though. We seem to have developed a habit for acquiring these valuable little vagabonds, don't we Begs?"

Begsy scoffed. "Too many for my liking boss"

That brought them back to another problem, the nights events had left them with little time to take stock, had Walker's death not brought him so much delight McSharry might spend a little more time seething over Rob Thomas's tirade. The insolent little ingrate had crossed a line, McSharry was half tempted to kill his bitch and her pups simply out of principle.

"Speaking of which, how did he handle it?"

"Quiet, subtle" he could tell by Begsy's tone that the big man was disappointed with what he was reporting "the little bitch did have a bit of a post-kill breakdown though. I found the fucker sitting on the floor staring at Walker's body, I swear the piece of shit was seconds away from filling up"

McSharry took in the words and formed the image in his mind, something about it struck him as off. The boy might not have the lust, but he'd never heard of him being quite so sentimental. In and out was always his mantra, it was one of his more reliable habits. Unless Rob Thomas held some deep seated admiration for police officers there was something not right with that picture"

"You heard about our conversation beforehand? The little fucker threatened to kill me"

He caught Begsy's eye in the mirror, now there was the lust for the kill.

"Just give me the word boss, he's one more problem we don't need"

Disputing that claim was becoming more and more difficult, and there was something else that was bothering him; an idea hovering near the back of his brain since the night Macca and Mercer died. It lingered, like a moth near a flame, bringing forward the same questions over and over again.

"I keep coming back to the docks. How did those pricks find out about our shipment? I've ran through all the people who knew, and I've ran through them again, I don't see a lot of weak links in there. The kid lost it bad when I told him to kill the copper. He knew who Walker was before I told him. Did you get anything when you were with him? A vibe, anything that said that he knew the busie?"

He saw Begsy shaking his head from the back. "No" the big man paused, McSharry heard him tighten his grip on the steering wheel "But now you mention it , he was dead set on going in there alone. Said that was how he worked, that he didn't like an audience. But the bitch looked scared boss, he didn't want me in there"

Pieces seemed to come together and merge, he didn't know where intuition ended and paranoia began but he did know that he was quickly running out of justifiable reasons to keep his top shooter around.

"I'm developing some serious concerns about this kid, Begs. At best he's immensely unstable, at worst..."

The sentiment hung between them for a moment. It didn't take Begsy long to push his recommendation.

"We need to kill him. At a time like this we've got no room for risks"

His enforcer may have been biased, but there was truth in what he said. Caddock, Miller, Walker and Cassidy had all posed a risk, and he'd done what needed doing. He thought about James Ploughman, the weak link he'd missed. The weak link that cost him ten years.

It was true he appreciated the gifts Rob Thomas possessed, and he'd be loath to lose them from his arsenal, but when he was honest with himself, he knew the situation; the kid was nothing more than another wild weed in need of culling. Like the rest of them he would fall, before he brought everything down.

"Give me a day or two to think it through," McSharry said, watching the snow as it tumbled from the sky "I want to make sure we do this right"

Chapter 34

Light flooded in, bringing with it a headache capable of splitting rock. Charlie closed his eyes but it was too late, the hangover had already found its way into his skull, he pressed the palms of his hands against his temples and gave a loud groan. It didn't help, the pain remained, working its way through his brain until he could feel it just behind his eyeballs.

He pressed his head into the pillow and tried to go back to sleep, it wasn't doing. He rolled over onto his back and faced the inevitable; he'd have to see this hangover through.

Slowly, he started to make sense of his situation. The first thing that he noticed was the fact that he was naked, the room was bright and he was above the covers of a bed that seemed familiar. A glance to his left told him why; Steph was passed out next to him, lying naked on her stomach and snoring lightly. He tried to remember how he'd gotten there but it was too soon, lightly he ran his index finger down Steph's bare back, she didn't stir an inch.

A wave of sickness hit him and Charlie moved to prop himself up against the headboard. He spent the next few minutes taking deep breaths, trying to will his body back to normality, in that time snippets of the last few days started to come back to him.

He remembered meeting up with Benny and Glen on Thursday night. He was still buoyant over the fact that he'd soon be heading to New York with a couple of million in the bank, the urge to hit the town and blow off a little steam had been stronger than he'd known it for many a year, he had so few opportunities left after all, it seemed a shame to waste a single one of them. Benny and Glen were up for it, as they always were. Their enthusiasm only increased when they found out that Charlie had a deep enough supply of coke and ecstasy to last them through a small war.

Somehow, that had been the start of a three day binge. The excitement over his impending emigration, coupled with his enthusiasm for one, final massive blow out had pushed them through almost the entire weekend.

More than anything it was Charlie's stash that had proved to be the key, it kept their high going non-stop and attracted plenty of female attention once they were inside the clubs. Such a good time was being had by all that suddenly, one night had turned into three. At least, that was true if today was Sunday, his head was so mashed up he couldn't be certain.

The outline of the last few days felt increasingly solid, but as Charlie sat there, taking long deep breaths in an effort not to be sick, the details of each night slowly started coming back to him.

He remembered the first night clearest of all, Thursday nights in Liverpool were always littered with student types, and it hadn't taken long for them to meet a group of nineteen year old posh birds from somewhere down south. Charlie sussed them out straight from the off; they were experimental rich kids looking to do two things: go slumming and score some free snow, he was happy to oblige them on both counts.

They'd spent the next few hours hanging out with their new friends in a couple of bars, after that it was back to the girls four bedroom flat in Sefton Park. That was when the fun had really started, the boys had taken turns, fucking each of the slags one after the other and then swapping round. The memory brought a smile to his face, all four were vintage, A star knockouts, he'd been having so much fun that by the time Charlie stopped to catch his breath it was Friday lunchtime and the rest of the flat was silent. They left without saying goodbye, leaving the girls scattered, half conscious around the flat. Charlie left with his stash of coke a good few grams lighter.

After that they'd made their way back to Benny's. A fresh supply of coke, a couple of E's and a helping of vodka and red bull had carried them through to the Friday night without pause, when the whole thing had started again. Bulging pockets and his growing reputation as an associate of Stephen McSharry got them straight into a couple of the top clubs. Once inside it was the same old story; more impressionable slags who digged his reputation and the product he was offering, this time it was two sisters and a couple of their friends on a birthday night out, not quite up to the previous night's standards but still impressive nonetheless.

Once they were done with drinking and partying everyone had piled back to Benny's house. On their way to the taxi Charlie thought he'd caught sight of his brother, but then he'd been distracted by the birthday girl nibbling on his ear, and by the time he'd shook her off the man was out of sight. She started nibbling on his ear again and Charlie had forgotten all about it.

The girls skipped out in the early hours and sleep had finally come on Saturday morning. By Saturday afternoon they were back up. A couple of pizzas and a few beers resettled them and, spurred on by Charlie's enthusiastic urge to enjoy the time he had left, they hit the town again.

They hit the same clubs as the night before, the bouncers remembered and let him through without a seconds hesitation, it depressed him to think that soon he'd have to queue with the six million other inhabitants of New York to get into somewhere similar. A couple of lines and a few shots refuelled his buzz, and within the hour he'd crossed paths with Steph.

It was the first time he'd seen her since she lost the plot at him for not buying her the dress she wanted. When she saw him she feigned surprise, but Charlie didn't buy it for a second. Most likely she'd been hassling one of the lads for his whereabouts, if he'd had to guess he would have said Benny, the lad couldn't say no to a pretty face, and who could blame him.

Before they had a chance to get into it she told him that she was sorry, and that she'd acted like an idiot. The words hadn't meant much to Charlie, it was the blowjob in the club toilets that sealed the apology for him. After that they'd all spent the night together, her friends and his, hitting a couple of VIP rooms aided by a constant stream of coke and champagne.

When they got back to Steph's flat they'd enjoyed the best sex they'd had since they first met. Make up sex was always something special, but with Steph it was out of this world. He made a mental note to fit in as many fights as he could before he left, he was even considering the feasibility of flying her out to NYC now and then for a cheeky weekend.

For now, his body was crying out for a rest. Stumbling out of bed he made his way across the bedroom, picking up randomly tossed items of clothing whenever he came across them. By the time he'd reached the kitchen sink he was almost fully dressed, all that was missing was a left sock and his watch.

Charlie poured himself a glass of water and downed it in one, the liquid did its best to come straight back up again but he stayed strong, kept his mouth shut and waited for it to pass. A few minutes later he tried again with pint number two.

Dropping the glass into the sink he started the post-night out process of checking his pockets. His wallet was empty but for a couple of pound coins, and there was no sign of either the pills or the coke he'd been carrying with him the night before. He scrunched his eyes shut and tried to think back to the end of the night, after a couple of seconds the images came to him, finishing off the cocaine with Steph, giving away his last few pills to a couple of girls who showed him their tits.

He stumbled to the couch and tried to will his brain into doing some basic calculations. He didn't know what he'd spent but he knew what he had pre-Thursday. Assuming he'd blown at least four or five hundred quid, which his memory assured him he easily had, he was also down around two and a half grand from his Leroy stash. Two and a half grand for which he owed Stephen McSharry thirty percent. Killing McSharry had suddenly become even more of a necessity, if they didn't Charlie was going to be spending the next couple of weeks hustling drugs and seeing nothing of the profit.

The thought took him to another place he should have gone to first. He stood up and went to the table in the corner, there was his mobile. He picked it up and pressed down the picture of the green phone. Nothing. Dead. Memories came back to him, he left it at Benny's before they went out on Thursday, by the time they'd come back Friday afternoon the battery had packed in, he'd been too high to care.

It suddenly hit him that he hadn't checked in with Rob or McSharry for a good couple of days, he wondered who'd be more pissed. Surely he wouldn't have missed too much, Rob's plans weren't going ahead just yet and he'd only been out of the loop for three and a half days.

He decided to stop off at Rob's flat on his way back, make sure everything was kosher and then head home to recharge the phone. If McSharry wanted a meet then he'd go over hat in hand and promise it would never happen again. He told himself it wasn't a big deal, he could tell McSharry he was sorry and promise him whatever he wanted, it wouldn't matter anyway. Once Rob was through either McSharry would be dead, or he'd have failed and the both of them would probably be on the run. Whichever way it went no one was going to remember a couple of days when he forgot to pick up his phone.

Charlie spent the next five minutes searching for his misplaced sock, finally he found it under a chair in the bedroom. Steph still hadn't stirred, he walked over and planted a gentle kiss on her bare shoulder. He told her he had to go, that he had business to take care of, and that he'd call her later. She responded with a small groan and buried her head deeper into the pillow, Charlie slid on his sock and then his shoes, that was all the goodbye he was likely to get.

The first thing he noticed as he stepped out of the flat and on to the street was the snow. There wasn't much of it, at least not anymore, sporadic white chunks were scattered around the street, covering the odd car roof or patch of pavement. The sight brought more memories back to him, when they left the club the night before the snow had been falling hard, the girls were complaining and he'd made a couple of stupid jokes about not needing to worry that his stash was all used up.

Even though it was cold the sun was shining brightly in the sky, Charlie gave it another couple of hours before all sign of the snowfall had been eradicated completely.

He walked ten minutes to the nearest set of shops, which was about ten minutes more than his body could handle. He withdrew thirty quid from the cash machine, his new found affluence meant that his dole cheques were going unnoticed and undisturbed. There was a tidy little sum waiting for him, he considered blowing it all before he'd need to abandon the account.

The greasy spoon café next door was open and half full, Charlie stumbled in and ordered himself a bacon butty and a cup of tea. The food gave him energy, the caffeine made him more alert, he brought a second cup and asked the old woman at the till to call him a taxi, he was only halfway through his tea by the time it arrived.

The taxi driver was jovial and chatty, unfortunate considering Charlie's brain was still taking its time to work through the gears. Luckily the man led the conversation quickly towards football and Charlie was able to settle into a predefined conversational structure that required the minimum amount of effort. He expressed the same opinions, told the same jokes and slated the same players as he always did when talking to a stranger about the beautiful game, only half listening to the responses and reactions that came back to him.

It didn't take long to get to Rob's flat, Charlie tipped the driver a couple of quid and hopped out. He got close and saw that the front door was ajar, nudging it open he walked through the hallway to find his brother perched on the edge of the old couch, surrounded by discarded cans of lager. He took another couple of steps further into the room and noticed that the table was covered with coke residue, he was pleased to see that at least some of his supply wasn't going to waste on strangers.

"There he is!" Charlie said, leaning against the wall "I'm liking the set up you've got here, but I'm feeling more in the mood for an aspirin. If you've got one lying around that would be ace"

Rob stood up. He was looking forward, offering Charlie a side view of his face. It was only when his brother started walking towards him that Charlie was able to see the severely pissed off look that dominated his brothers features.

Before Charlie had a chance to ask what was wrong Rob had swung his first hard, catching Charlie hard on the base of the jaw. He stumbled, but didn't go down, before he could respond Rob had grabbed him by the neck and slammed him up against the wall.

"What the hell are you doing?" gasped Charlie, a second before Rob's hands closed tight around his windpipe.

"Where've you been, Charlie?" he heard the slur in his brothers words, it mixed with his anger and reminded him of their father.

"Settle down"

Charlie tried to push Rob away but there was no budging him, he felt the grip pull him away from the wall then slam him hard against it. Rob's grip loosened, enough to let him breath, not enough to let him move.

"Answer me!" Rob demanded.

"I've been partying with a few of the lads. Just a bit of an impromptu send-off that's all, what's the problem?"

Charlie noticed for the first time that although Rob was looking at his face, he wouldn't look him in the eye. It happened for the briefest of moments, in that moment Rob's grip slightly loosened then he immediately looked away.

"The old man knows about Kelly, Charlie, he knows I've been seeing her. He put two guys on her house, he called me up and he told me he was going to kill her and her kids unless I took on another ad hoc hit for him. Now you tell me Charlie; how the fuck did that happen?"

Charlie struggled to imagine McSharry making that threat, try as he might he just couldn't hear him saying those words. Suddenly his mind flashed back to the warehouse, he remembered that crazed, vicious look as he went at the hitter with the knife. The screams came back to him again, in that instant he could hear the threat being made, more than that, he could imagine McSharry killing Kelly and those kids himself.

He didn't remember ever mentioning Kelly, why would he? He scanned his brain for any time his conversations with McSharry had encompassed Rob, it didn't happen often, his older brother was almost taboo when it came to his relationship with the gangster. It was a dynamic that Charlie was already too familiar with; Rob was where his loyalty should have been, McSharry his bit on the side. The less it was mentioned the better.

He'd recapped most of his conversations when it came to him. The night at the Italian restaurant, just before Millers hitter appeared on the scene,

McSharry had been asking questions. He closed his eyes instinctively, Rob's grip tightened.

"Ah, shit" Charlie muttered.

The grip around his neck lifted him forward and slammed him back again into the wall. The back of his head smacked the plaster, the room spun for a couple of seconds then settled.

"You're going to have to do better than that Charlie. You sold me out to the old man, didn't you? I swear to God if I'd have found you last night I'd have put two in your head without a second thought"

Charlie didn't doubt it, Rob had always been highly strung but this was something else. He was cracking right in front of him.

"Just calm down, lad. I didn't sell you out"

"No? What would you call it?"

Charlie pressed his hand into Rob's chest and tried to gently eased him back. His brother flashed a look telling him not to even try.

"I was just talking to him. He seemed worried about how stable you were, thought you'd be better off if you were getting laid. I just told him you'd hooked up with an ex, that's all, I was trying to get him off your back. How was I supposed to know this would happen, is she ok?"

Rob released his grip and walked away. Charlie rubbed at the flesh around his neck and sucked in the air he'd been deprived off, his heart slowed down and his hangover returned. He watched his brother go to the table and retrieve a can of lager. A couple of swigs later Rob turned back to face him.

"She's fine" he crushed the can in his hand and tossed it at the wall "what were you thinking talking to him about my life, Charlie? Are you a fucking retard? Haven't you been listening to a single word I've been saying to you?"

Charlie wasn't seeing it. He knew why Rob was upset, but not enough to justify all the dramatics. If an unfulfilled threat was able to cause this much damage to his brothers somewhat fragile mental state, what was going to happen when they actually tried to kill Stephen McSharry? He considered leaving the question unasked, but even in Rob's drunken state Charlie needed to hear his answer.

"What's the big deal? So he threatened her, you said yourself she's fine. Just give her a chunk of our McSharry cash and when we skip out tell her to lie low for a while"

Rob let out a sigh, reached into a box of lager and pulled out another can.

"There isn't going to be any skipping out," he said accusingly "there isn't going to be any big pay day and there isn't going to be any getting out from under the old man. You made sure of that when you started running your mouth, you fucking idiot"

The words lit a flame in Charlie's head, the tone stoked the fire. The headache thumped against his skull like a war drum and challenged him not to take the reproach lying down. He wasn't a child anymore, he wouldn't have his drunk burnout of an older brother talking to him like one.

434

"Watch it lad," Charlie warned, his jaw still hurt from the punch, the flames grew higher "you're really starting to piss me off"

Rob was unmoved by the threat, he was agitated, on the edge, Charlie wasn't sure who he was talking to but it didn't feel like the Rob he knew.

"You don't get it do you? You've fucked everything up, just like you always do. You don't think, you just do whatever comes into your little head and suddenly everything goes to shit"

Charlie took a step forward, feeling the urge to swing for his older brother. The instinct almost made the decision for him, then he remembered how dangerous Rob was, and how drunk. He thought better of it.

"Maybe you should stop your bitching and tell me what the problem is?"

"McSharry's gone. He's in a safe house somewhere, if we don't know where he is how are we supposed to kill him?"

Charlie shrugged his shoulders "So we find him. He's a millionaire gangster with a taste for the flash, and this is hardly London, is it? We can get to him, it's not the end of the world"

Rob swallowed hard and shook his head. He looked like he was on the verge of tears, Charlie took another step forward, this time it was more out of interest than aggressive intent.

"It's more than that. I had a link that was going to get us abroad under false names, a copper I was working with. When the old man found out about Kelly he used her to make me kill him. That was our only way out, we needed that help to sever the trail. With the old man's money, with his connections, he'll trace a travelling family of six in no time"

The look of disgust came to his face immediately, Charlie saw no reason to hide it.

"You've been working with the filth? What the fuck, lad?"

Rob made a dismissive gesture with his hand "It was the only way"

Charlie shook his head, that wasn't good enough. He'd known a few guys over the years, decent blokes who'd squealed to the police to get themselves out of a tight spot or two. When word of what they'd done got out their reputations in the community dropped somewhere close to that of a paedophile or a crack head. He'd seen grasses walk into a pub where they spent half their lives and get a beat down from guys they'd drank with for ten years. More than that they'd deserved it, every last one of them. In that moment he felt a lot of the respect he had for his brother drain away, there weren't too many things that you just didn't do, but this was one of them. He looked at Rob and realised that for all his experience that was something he had never understood.

"That still ain't no excuse. You don't grass, not ever"

The animosity between the two of them seemed to grow, Rob was pacing, he had an energy that was both angry and remorseful, without ever committing to either. Just having to be around it made his hangover feel worse.

435

"Don't talk to me like you know what this is!" Rob shouted back, "You might be having a good little time playing gangster and getting paid but you haven't got the slightest clue of what I'm trying to do here, what I'm trying to do for us. The old man will bring us down Charlie, he'll bring us all down. You get into bed with anyone you can who can help you get away from that. If you had a bit more fucking sense on your shoulders you'd be trying to do the same"

All Charlie heard were excuses, inadequate justifications delivered in an angry tone to try and make them sound defensible. He was starting to see just how much of his brother he genuinely understood, and how much was self-righteous bollocks.

"I've got sense enough to know you don't go talking to no police" Charlie shot back "You'll bring a world of trouble down onto you, from both sides"

Rob stopped pacing and dropped onto the couch, the urgency in him seemed to quickly disappear, Charlie felt the anger inside him do something similar.

"My worlds pretty full as it is" Rob told him.

His brother seemed to disappear inside his head, Charlie gave him a couple of moments before he decided to speak.

"So what now?"

Rob took another drink and watched the floor "Just get the fuck out of here Charlie," his voice was resigned rather than angry, it made the words sting even more than they might have "you did what you did and now this whole mess is spinning well out of control. Tonight I have to go and kill Martin Cassidy, just to keep on top of it all, once that's done I'll decide what our next moves going to be"

He could see his brother wanted him gone, his first instinct was to stand his ground and argue, but something in Rob's demeanour told him that it wouldn't be a wise choice. He glanced towards Rob one last time, his brother still wouldn't look him in the eye, then turned and headed for the door.

"Fine"

"Hey, Charlie?"

He turned as he got to the living room door. Rob was still staring at the carpet.

"What?"

"You nearly got Kelly and her two kids killed. Instead you got a copper killed, he didn't deserve it, he shouldn't have gone that way. Wise up, ok? Fast. The next dumb move might kill someone you really care about"

Charlie left the flat with his brother's words still ringing in his ears. He had no love for coppers, but he regretted that Rob had needed to kill one because of something he'd said. More than that he felt bad about Kelly. She'd always been good to him, he recalled the crush he'd had on her as a teenager, putting her in the middle of Rob and Stephen McSharry had never been his intention.

He walked half the way home then flagged down a passing taxi. He reflected on how quickly a classic weekend could make way to a shitty week, and he still had Vicky and McSharry to face. Talk about a bitch of a comedown.

As he sat in the back of the cab and thought about everything that Rob had said, he recognised the part of himself that felt relief at the possibility of the New York move falling through. The weekend had reinvigorated his love for the city, it had brought home just how much of him was inseparable from Liverpool. It defined who he was, without it, he didn't know what his identity would be, or how he would find it. His plan had been to break the news to Vicky today, maybe even use it as a means of explaining away his busy weekend, but the conversation with Rob had him thinking twice. Maybe it was better to wait until he knew more about their plans, or until he had decided whether he was genuinely willing to go through with them.

His thoughts went back the busie. He had no idea who the guy was, in his mind he was just a uniform without a face, but at the end of the day it was another dead body to add to the list. After tonight it would be a couple more, he'd never met Martin Cassidy either but he knew enough about his reputation to know that his murder would be another big deal, akin to the likes of Wayne Caddock and Tony Miller. The growing body count affected him in two ways; he thought about Stephen McSharry, and how every execution brought him, and by association Charlie, a little bit more power. Then he thought about Rob, the reluctant assassin, and how every execution seemed to be breaking him apart that little bit more. He was connected to them both, and he was affected by them both, yet in a lot of ways the whole concept was alien to him. He didn't know the targets, he didn't see them die, he just sat back and watched the repercussions go on around him, like ripples in a pond, he viewed them safely from his boat, watching the ripples pass by.

As he stepped out of the taxi he felt his headache sharpen in the face of what was coming. Vicky wouldn't be happy, she never was when he didn't call, he just hoped she hadn't dropped the kids off at her mothers, if his aching head was going to make it through he needed the shield of their innocence to keep her from screaming the house down.

The first thing he noticed when he entered the house was how quiet it was, something told him that wasn't likely to be a good sign. He found Vicky in the kitchen packing a lunch, she was fully dressed like she was planning to go out, he felt hopeful that an afternoon nap in an empty house might be on the cards.

"Hey hun" Charlie said as he stepped into the kitchen.

He walked up behind her and planted a light kiss on her neck, she flinched and moved away, Charlie pretended like he hadn't noticed.

"Where are the girls?"

Vicky slammed a cupboard hard. "Upstairs"

Charlie grabbed a glass and filled it with water, the hangover sapped at his energy, making it so much harder to find the enthusiasm for creeping. He drained the glass and gave it a go anyway.

"You ok?"

"I'm fine"

He tried to keep his voice light as he talked to the back of her head, like he hadn't noticed her mood.

"I'm sorry I didn't call. A night out with the boys got a little bit out of hand, ended up turning into a full weekend. I would have called but my phone died Thursday, you know what I'm like trying to remember peoples mobile numbers. I was technically working though, got talking to a few guys in the clubs, put my name about, made some connections. Could be some real money to be made, on top of what we're seeing already"

"Great" she muttered, refusing to divert her attention away from buttering bread.

His head thumped, Charlie got another glass of water, he could feel his patience waning already.

"You're pissed. Why? Because I didn't call? I already said I'm sorry"

Vicky dropped the knife and turned angrily to face him, Charlie noticed for the first time that she was a little pale. He saw a red tint around her eyes, as if she'd been crying.

"I heard you. A couple of empty words, do you think that makes everything ok?"

He knew her complaints by heart, it was always the same, all they ever accomplished was to annoy him, today they went a step further and made his head bang twice as fast.

"This again?" Charlie asked, dropping the glass into the sink "Look I was just blowing off a little steam, ok? You've been having plenty of fun with all this extra money I've been bringing home. Don't you think it's fair that I get to enjoy a little bit of it too?"

She looked at him like he was speaking a different language, he thought he saw the glint of tears in her eyes, it caught him off guard. His wife responded to arguments by closing down and becoming cold, that kind of emotion hinted to him that something else was going on.

"You think that's what this is about, that I don't want to see you spending your own money?" she asked the question in a tone verging on disbelief "Your daughters haven't laid eyes on their father for four days, without so much as a text or a phone call for comfort. I could have been sitting here worried sick, I could have been thinking you were lying dead in an alley somewhere. Lucky for me I'm not that naïve anymore, I guess I can thank you for that"

Vicky turned around and went back to the sandwiches, Charlie started to lose control of his temper. He'd already suffered his brother's abuse today, taking it from his wife as well was too much for this thumping head to handle.

"Don't be so dramatic" Charlie told her, there was a bite to his words that was intended as much for his brother as it was for her "You knew I'd come back after a couple of days. I always do, don't I?

Vicky turned back to face him, this time he definitely saw tears.

"So that makes it ok? You push me away Charlie, you push me into being someone that I don't want to be, I can't stand it anymore. I'm sick of waiting for you to grow into the man I thought you could be. Marriage didn't do it, being a father hasn't done it. I could stand here and ask you what kind of husband just goes out and doesn't come back for more than half a week, but what would be the point? We've been here a thousand times before and you've never once given me a real answer. I'm not even sure that this is a real marriage anymore, now I think about it I'm not sure that it ever was"

It took a while for Charlie to digest the words, he felt a little stunned as he watched his wife wrap the sandwiches in tinfoil and toss them into a plastic bag. They fought all the time, it's what they did, but something about this felt different, maybe even final. It was as if something had been broken and they were both trying not to get cut on the sharp remains that surrounded them. He couldn't see her face but he heard the sniffing of stifled tears, it brought a lump to his throat and a guilty feeling to this chest.

"Come on, don't talk like that. Of course it is, you're my wife for God's sake, haven't I said I'm sorry. Just tell me what I need to do to make this better?"

Vicky turned to towards him again, it hurt to see just how little love she had in her eyes.

"Maybe you should go back out again for a couple more days," Vicky told him "I don't think I can stand to be near you right now"

Charlie took a step towards her, Vicky took a step back and raised her hands. He tried to look into her eyes and make a connection, but there was nothing there, just an empty space where her love used to be.

"I'm not going anywhere. Let me take you out for dinner and we can talk this through" Vicky shook her head and wiped a tear from her eye "Then let me take you shopping, or we'll book a trip. Come on, there must be something I can do?"

She picked the sandwich bag off the table and wrapped it around her hand.

"I'm taking the girls to my mother's house for the day. You just do what you want to Charlie, you always do"

He tried to respond but she'd already stormed out of the kitchen on her way upstairs. Charlie drank another glass of water and tried to reassure himself that this was just another angry fight that would die down after a couple of days. He was still trying to convince himself that it was more than just positive thinking when he heard 3 pairs of feet pattering down the stairs, he made his way into the hallway to meet them.

Alexis screamed with delight when she saw him in the doorway, she tried to run towards him but her mother held her back. She didn't try a second time, his little girl knew the drill well enough by now, she just smiled at him behind Vicky's back, the little code she had with her father when mummy and daddy were fighting. Charlie tried to return the smile, he could tell from the way Alexis looked back that it was a poor effort.

He tried pleading with Vicky one last time while she struggled to get the baby bag over her shoulder with Zoe in her other arm. He offered to help but she shook him off without a word, Alexis just watched, smiling up at Charlie trying to get his attention. He stroked the side of her face and told her to be good for her mother.

"Victoria, come on. Don't be like this, can you just stay and we'll talk it through?"

She left without another word. Charlie watched the door slam shut behind her, the quiet he'd been yearning for earlier in the day suddenly felt hollow and meaningless, he could hear Alexis talking as they made her way down the street. He stood where he was and listened until her voice finally disappeared, then he wandered back into the living room.

In the corner of the room, next to the television he caught sight of his phone charger plugged into the wall, he attached his phone and waited for it to come to life, it took a couple of seconds and then he saw the screen flash white.

It was worse than he'd thought, 23 missed calls, no wonder his battery had died so fast. He had 9 voicemails, all from the same number, he checked the first couple, it was Begsy, they started off with simple instructions.

"Call"

The further down the list, the more colourful they became.

"Call now fuck head, don't keep me waiting"

Charlie tried calling the number back, it rang six times then went to a generic voicemail service, he decided not to leave a message.

The phone had given him another bad feeling, it looked increasingly likely that he was going to be in the shithouse three for three by the time they called him back, it wasn't often he found himself missing the carefree days of dole queues and *the stag and bull* but this was definitely one of those rare moments.

The headache continued to thump harder and harder against the inside of his skull. He lay down on the couch and closed his eyes, though his body was exhausted the excessive thumping refused to let him sleep. After a while it even starting beating in time with Rob and Vicky's accusations, as they reverberated around his head.

He felt a sharp pain in his back and moved onto his side. As he tried to find a comfortable position something caught his eye, it was only there for a split second, something reflective catching the sunlight at the right angle, hidden somewhere between the cushions.

Charlie buried his hand in the gap and touched something sharp. Pulling it free he realised it was a cross, a silver cross. It was his brothers silver cross.

Holding it closer to his face he examined it, it was definitely Rob's, he knew because he'd bought it for him on his twentieth birthday.

The first thought that crossed his mind was how his brother's chain had made it between the cushions of his coach. He thought back, Rob hadn't been there since the day Charlie picked him up from the airport, if he remembered rightly Rob had barely even sat down that day.

His heart started to beat in time with his head, he turned the chain over in his hand and examined it again. One of the links where broken, snapped off. Charlie held it right up to his eye, it looked like it had been ripped, like something had pulled at his brothers neck to sever it.

Thoughts came to his head, they had a hint of coke charged paranoia. Images that forced him to close his eyes and made his heart beat fast enough to forget the headache. Charlie tried to rationalise, he told himself that Rob may have come round to see his nieces, it may have happened playing with Alexis. But that didn't explain why Rob couldn't look at him, why Vicky flinched when he tried to touch her.

An overwhelming sense of sickness came over him, Charlie jumped up from the couch as his mind began producing images of his wife and his brother fucking on his couch. He stepped backwards and tripped on one of Alexis's dolls, he fell hard onto his back but kept his eyes on the couch. His mind taunted him with increasingly graphic images, he heard his wife moaning in his brothers arms, he saw him caressing her. His world began to fall apart as he saw the mother of his children betraying him with his own brother.

Charlie tried to convince himself that it wasn't true, that he was jumping to conclusions. It didn't work, his mind kept taking him back to one place, to the one damning sentence his wife had uttered.

You push me into being someone that I don't want to be.

That was it, that was her confession. The broken look suddenly seemed to fit, everything suddenly made sense in the most horrific of ways.

His whole body started to shake, the images continued to torture him. He made his way into the kitchen and threw up in the sink.

The mobile phone started to ring, he walked towards it in a daze. Charlie lifted it up, his hand was still shaking. It made sense to answer it, any distraction that might stop his brain from conjuring more of these images had to be worth a shot.

He places the phone at his ear, he heard Begsy's voice.

"Where are you?"

Charlie opened his mouth, his breath caught, he tried to concentrate.

"I'm at home"

"Stay there. A car will be over in twenty minutes"

"Ok"

Begsy hung up, Charlie gently put the phone back down. He looked around his living room in disgust, he wanted to burn it, to burn the whole place down. He wanted that cheating bitch to be inside when he did.

A wave of nausea forced him back into the kitchen to throw up again. He tried to comprehend how they could do that to him. He wondered how long it had been going on, whether his dear old brother was planning to take them with him when he left, leaving Charlie alone to face the rap. He wondered whether they laughed about him, whether they talked about how clueless he was, whether Vicky came harder when she fucked his brother. He darted back to the sink and threw up again.

There was a knock on the door. Charlie looked at the clock on the wall, it had been twenty five minutes since the phone call to Begsy. Where had it gone? Betrayal and distorted images were fucking with his sense of time.

He stumbled towards the front door, opened it and saw a chubby guy with messy blond hair that he didn't know.

"Charlie Thomas?"

"That's right. Who the fuck are you?"

"Teller. I'm the bosses new driver"

"What happened to his old driver?"

"Begsy's got a lot of his plate right now. Boss wants me to bring you to see him"

Charlie followed him out the house without question. As they got to the jeep he realised he hadn't brought his keys, wallet or phone. It didn't really matter. He didn't know what did anymore.

Teller didn't really speak while he drove. A couple of times Charlie saw him glancing his way with a look of mild distrust, he didn't know what that was about, he didn't care. He just hoped McSharry had something for him, something to get him busy and take his mind off the images that continued to swirl around his head. More than once he thought he'd need Teller to pull over while he threw up, but he managed to hold it in.

Their destination turned out to be a hotel bar on the edge of the city. Teller told Charlie that the boss would be waiting inside, he said he'd stay where he was to drop him off at home once he was done. Charlie told him that wouldn't be necessary, he wasn't planning on going home.

He made his way into the bar, a few couples and families were scattered amongst empty tables, enjoying their Sunday lunches. Charlie spotted McSharry sitting alone at the bar, a couple of seconds later he noted Begsy sitting at a table with Ads, and Nikolai sitting on another table alone.

Charlie stumbled towards the bar and waited for McSharry to notice him, there were two glasses of whisky sat in front of him, he was sipping at one. It made him think of Rob with his bottles of JD. Which led him to the two of them fucking on his couch. A wave of nausea came over him, he was getting better at controlling it.

"Take a seat" McSharry said without turning to face him. Charlie sat down and waited, McSharry nudged the second glass of whisky in front of him and flashed a stern look "you've been off the reservation for a good couple of days now kid, you mind telling me where you've been?"

Charlie took a sip of the whiskey, his hand was shaking, he put the glass down quickly.

"I was..." words caught in his throat, he took a second to breathe and tried again "I was drinking...with some friends"

"Drinking? This whole time?"

Charlie tried to focus. He reminded himself that he was talking to a dangerous man, that he had explaining to do. He was grateful for the opportunity, the risk opened up the slightest gap in the fog that was consuming him. He focused on that gap, he tried to tell himself that it was important to appease the top gangster in the city, that there was importance in the world outside of the images he was seeing. He didn't really believe it, but he said it to himself nonetheless.

"That's right. My phone died on Thursday, I didn't get your messages until just before I called. I fucked up, I know that. It isn't going to happen again"

McSharry looked over his shoulder, Charlie guessed that he was looking towards Begsy but he didn't have the desire or the will to check. He focused on trying to steady his hand and lifted the glass of whiskey. The first sip made him want to vomit, the second brought a warmness to his stomach that came close to being soothing.

"While you were MIA we lost Mercer and Macca. They were gunned down by the police trying to retrieve our shipment a few nights ago"

Charlie looked at McSharry with surprise, the news made him forget for the briefest of seconds, then it returned. It came to him in that instant that work would be the only way to keep himself sane.

"They're dead? Just like that?"

McSharry smiled at him "Don't worry, we got the prick copper behind it all. Your brother took care of that one for us. Have you seen your brother lately?"

Charlie looked down at the bar. He thought about how Rob had found the nerve to hit him after what the bastard had done, it was hatred he'd never known, that he never knew existed.

"I've seen him"

"So you know he's killing Martin Cassidy tonight?"

Charlie nodded "He told me this morning"

McSharry called over the barman and told him to leave the bottle of whiskey. When the barman left McSharry refilled both their glasses.

"It's been a big couple of days. I needed all my hands on deck and you weren't around. You picked a bad time to go missing, the police got a line on our shipment, people start talking about rats, it doesn't look good for the guy who suddenly stops showing up"

Charlie got the implication, he realised in that moment that he wasn't afraid for his life, but he couldn't bear the thought of dying and leaving his wife and his brother to continue their affair. He pictured Rob moving in and becoming a father to the girls, he imagined his baby Zoe having his traitorous brother as the only father she'd ever know.

"I haven't talked to anyone" Charlie said, he heard how desperate his voice sounded and knew it wasn't a good sign "I swear, I've just been out drinking. I can get plenty of people to verify it, friends, bouncers, bar staff, whatever you want, I swear to you they'll back it up"

McSharry regarded him with an amused half smile.

"You've been around for a little bit. I see you watching, taking things in. How do you think I usually react when I suspect someone of talking?"

Charlie knew the answer. His mouth went dry. It seemed best to lie.

"I don't know"

"There's only one thing you can do. If you think someone's talking then the decision is already made. They have to die. No man is worth risking the entire business for. You understand?"

Charlie's palms became sweaty. He saw the two of them holding hands at his funeral.

"I didn't talk. I swear"

McSharry gave an exasperated sigh, like he was trying to explain it to a child.

"It doesn't matter if you did. I just need to believe that you might have. That's more than we can afford to risk. I want you to understand that"

He saw Alexis at eighteen. She spoke with an American accent. She called Rob 'Dad'.

"Please, I didn't..."

McSharry laughed and gave him a firm pat on the back.

"I know, relax. Luckily for you your presence didn't go unnoticed on the Liverpool club scene, you can thank your newly enhanced reputation for that particular reprieve"

McSharry flashed him a smile, Charlie breathed in and felt a little dizzy. McSharry topped up his whiskey.

"Thanks, boss" he muttered, he drank half the glass in one gulp, he felt stretched thinner than he ever had before.

"I trust my instincts Charlie, and they tell me that you're no grass, but I'd like to talk a little bit more about that brother of yours. Did he know about the shipment we had coming in?"

The question caught him off guard. He didn't want McSharry involved in what was going on. He needed time to think, and if he decided to do something he wanted it to be him who did it. He looked the gangster in the eye and realised there was still some semblance of loyalty for family, not much, but a flicker. He took heart in the fact, that it made him a better person than the two who had betrayed him.

"Rob?" Charlie shrugged his shoulders "I don't know"

McSharry seemed to think about it.

"How'd he seem to you, when you saw him this morning?"

Like a traitorous little bastard, a piece of scum that couldn't look me in the eye.

"He seemed the same as always"

McSharry leaned in a little closer "Did he seem upset?"

A lump made its way up Charlie's throat. He saw Rob and Vicky on his couch, he wondered if they'd made it up to his bed. He felt the emotion begin to overwhelm him, he took another sip of whiskey to keep it at bay.

"Yeah, a little. I mean, he'd just killed a copper, right? I think that was playing on his mind, doing things to him maybe. I don't know... I just don't..."

The words trailed off, Charlie swallowed hard and forced back the tears he could feel welling behind his eyes.

McSharry moved in closer, he could smell blood. Charlie knew he was doing a piss poor job of hiding his emotions, he tried to drink more whiskey to settle himself but it just wasn't working, it all felt like too much.

"You care to elaborate on that sentiment?" McSharry asked.

Charlie pushed the whiskey away, images were appearing at an increasing rate, it was like someone was playing a slideshow in his brain.

"Not really. I'm just talking, thinking out loud, you know? I think maybe I should go"

He pushed the stool out and stumbled to his feet, McSharry's hand grabbed his shoulder, it was strong and firm for an older man. He pushed Charlie down hard, he hit the chair was a thud, families paused their conversation, McSharry sat and refilled their glasses, the conversations resumed.

"Keep talking. Whatever you think you know about your brother, you work for me now, your allegiance is to me, I'm your family. Whatever's going on in your head you pass it on to me, I decide if it's worth keeping"

Charlie shook his head. He felt the first tear drop from his left eye, he pretended to scratch his cheek and wiped it away.

"It's nothing, it's not business, nothing to do with business"

"What then?" he heard the impatience in McSharry's tone, he tried to think of something to say, a lie to get him off his back. Nothing came, the slide show was moving at supersonic speed now, he still saw every image. He took in every detail.

"I think, I think he might be..." the tears burst through, he put his head in his hands and mumbled the rest "I think he's fucking my wife"

McSharry didn't speak for a minute, he waited for Charlie to compose himself. After a while the first wave of tears began to subside, he raised his head and sniffed away the remnants of emotion.

"You sure?" McSharry asked. There was no warmth or concern in his voice, he was a man who was only interested in facts.

Charlie wiped his nose with the back of his sleeve "I found his chain, down the side of my couch. When I saw him he couldn't look me in the eye. Vicky, the bitch, she flinched when I tried to touch her"

McSharry was quiet for a moment. He took a sip of whiskey, Charlie followed. He felt more under control now, the eruption left him embarrassed but at least it was out. He felt able to function again, but the images continued.

Charlie watched McSharry refill their glasses, the gangster seemed to be deep in thought.

"It takes a certain kind of man to sleep with his brother's wife" McSharry muttered with contempt "A man like that doesn't understand loyalty. I've been where you're sitting now Charlie, I know how it feels, it might just be me, but I made damn sure the prick died for what he did. Guys like that deserve nothing less"

Charlie looked around the room. None of the boys were watching, they all had their eyes sharply focused on the exits, he hoped they hadn't been watching earlier.

"He's my brother" Charlie told him. Somewhere inside that still meant something, he thought of their mother.

"And he betrayed you. How long till he betrays the rest of us? If you can't trust a man to keep his hands off your woman how do you trust him to keep your secrets?"

Charlie nodded in agreement. He felt the hatred rise up inside him, he saw the face of the man he'd know his whole life, all he could see now was the face of his enemy.

"You don't" he said, looking McSharry in the eye "After the Cassidy hit he's making plans to kill you. He thinks that if he can get to you, and the money in your safe that he can get out of town before there are any reprisals"

For a moment there was silence. Charlie didn't know what kind of reaction he should expect, he was surprised when McSharry turned to him and saw that his face was deadly calm. There was something in his eyes though, something fierce that he remembered from the warehouse.

"Is that right?" he asked evenly, "May I ask why he told you this?"

Charlie took a sip of whiskey, it helped his overwhelming need to swallow the lump in his throat.

"He wanted me to help. To let him know your whereabouts. I told him I wasn't interested"

"Smart choice. But here you are telling me now. I can only assume that by telling me you know that there is only one way that I can possibly react"

Charlie held his gaze and nodded. "I know"

McSharry gave him that amused half smile and put a hand on his shoulder. A second later his face was grave, he leaned in a little closer and whispered.

"The prick fucked your wife, most likely while your kids were asleep

446

upstairs. He's your brother, you're flesh and blood and he did that to you, God knows how many times. I'll pay you a million quid to help me kill him"

From somewhere deep inside him, he found the will to smile. It was a cold, angry, hate filled smile that was fuelled by something sinister, but it was the only smile he had left.

Chapter 35

The view from the top level of the multi storey car park gave a clear picture of the Centurion hotel, and the private car park that surrounded three sides of the large, white building.

Rob stared through the binoculars he'd purchased earlier that day, not only did they give him clear sight of Martin Cassidy's muscle lingering subtly in the car park, they also provided him with a glimpse of the penthouse where Cassidy was staying. They'd been up there for a little over ninety minutes, aside from his target Rob had only caught sight of two other villains.

Twice already he'd left his perch and conducted a quick sweep of the area, the first one verified the two guys in the car park and also alerted him to the one man sat in the hotel reception area, the second trip merely confirmed what he'd learnt on the first.

Rob placed the binoculars on the floor and rubbed his hands together. He'd been surveilling the hotel for nearly three hours, one hour into it Cassidy and his men had shown up. Wherever they'd been Rob wasn't the only one expecting them, as soon as their car had parked up they'd been approached by four police officers waiting in a van on the other side of the car park.

Rob watched the exchange with interest, two of the coppers were in uniforms, two were in civilian clothes. The latter two were probably detectives, though Rob was quick to note that they both seemed a little too young and a little too pretty to be of the D.C rank. He'd focused the binoculars on those two and studied them as best he could. The man in the leather jacket seemed to be leading the conversation while his wild blond hair blew in the wind, to his right a pretty little brunette was taking notes. Rob thought he caught her pausing on a couple of occasions, as if she was either having difficulty understanding or she was struggling with the requirements of her role.

The conversation lasted around fifteen minutes, after that Cassidy and his two guys headed straight for the elevator and made their way up to the penthouse. Rob kept watch on the group of police, he saw the two uniforms go back to the van while the pair of prospective detectives held a conversation at the entrance of the hotel. A few minutes in he saw the brunette drop her head and watched as she wiped her eyes with a tissue. The blond man put a comforting hand on her shoulder, a moment later she reached up and gave it a squeeze.

They hadn't lingered for long after that, Rob waited half an hour to make sure they were gone before he conducted his first walk around. He'd kept a vigilante watch on the surrounding area ever since, from what he could tell the coppers didn't look like they were coming back.

It was nearly time to move, he could feel it in his bones. A flicker of the old apprehension returned, Rob responded by reaching into his pocket. Just touching the coke gave him comfort, it reassured him that a reprieve from such emotions was possible.

Getting a new supply had proved trickier than first expected. He couldn't go back to Charlie for obvious reasons, at the same time the prospect of conducting another kill sober, with everything that was going on in his head, just felt like too much to handle. The upcoming execution had forced him to stop drinking as soon as Charlie had left his flat earlier that morning, he had no intention of letting slow reflexes cause his downfall but at the same time he needed something, from somewhere, to keep his head straight.

That hadn't left him with a whole lot of options, the one he'd eventually chosen was to return to a few of his old haunts in the hope that business was still booming. The first place was a dead end, the seedy old man pub he knew from his youth had, at some point over the last ten years, been converted into an expensive cocktail lounge. Rob made his way inside on the off chance that a few of the old patrons still remained, but it didn't take long to realise that the flower covered establishment was unlikely to have an in house coke dealer.

His second attempt was much more fruitful. Not only was The Stanley Arms exactly where he'd left it, it looked exactly the same as it had ten plus years ago. Rob ordered a lemonade, sat in the corner, and got a feel for the place.

He clocked his man within the first ten minutes; a scrawny, spotty skin head who possessed about as much subtlety as a tornado. His would be supplier couldn't have been any older than twenty two or twenty three, yet he carried himself like he was the little king of everything. Rob watched him talk to prospective clients, take their money and send them into the toilets. A moment later he would slam his pint glass onto the bar, as if to alert the entire pub to his intention, and then swagger off to distribute his product in the privacy of the men's room.

Rob watched the routine five times, on the sixth he waited until the spotty kid had been gone for a couple of minutes and then he followed him into the toilets. He got the timing spot on, just has he pushed open the door the kids client, suitably rebuzzed, was making his way out of the toilet and back into the pub.

The punk looked in his direction and tried to stare him out, Rob took a couple of steps towards him, pulled a wad of twentys out of his pocket and waved it in the air.

"I want to buy some coke, whatever you've got on you now will do"

The kid was snarling, he looked Rob up and down before he started to rub his hands together.

"Sorry lad, I don't know what you're talking about" he nodded towards the door "Run along"

"I'm not a busie. Just take the money and give me the coke"

He noticed the kid was starting to breathe heavily, he seemed caught between wanting to start something and hedging his bets against a possible copper.

"Like I said, don't know what you mean. Now why don't you fuck off before you get yourself into some real trouble"

His new friends obstructive attitude snapped Rob's remaining patience into pieces. He pulled his Smith and Weston free and took a step forward, pointing the gun square in the kids face.

"Give me the coke now, I haven't got all day"

Rob enjoyed seeing the look of shock almost as much as he enjoyed seeing the bag of coke appear from within the kids pocket, he snatched the drugs and replaced it with the wad of twenty pound notes. The look on the kids face had evolved to hatred by the time Rob was halfway towards the door.

"Do you know who I am?" the kid started to shout, Rob stopped dead in his tracks "I'll have you done, lad! You can say goodbye to your fucking kneecaps!"

The threat set Rob off before he had time think, it took barely a second to cover the ground between them and another second for Rob to draw back the gun and pistol whip the little bitch right across the face. A couple of teeth spilled out of his mouth as the kid tumbled towards the floor. Rob followed him down with a string of punches, when his hand started to hurt he lifted himself up and slammed the soul of his shoe into the kids face seven or eight times. By the time he'd calmed down there wasn't much left to see of The Stanley's resident coke supplier, a thick layer of blood concealed almost all of his features. It was an improvement as far as Rob was concerned. Sliding the gun into his belt and the coke into his pocket he made his way out, not bothering to check whether the little bastard was still alive.

The incident hadn't crossed his mind since, until now anyway. Rob genuinely didn't care if he'd killed the boy, the way he saw it, if he had to be complicit in the deaths of people like David Walker, decent men who were trying to seriously do some good in the world, then killing little pricks like that simply served to balance up the score. Reaching into the bag Rob heaped as much powder onto his little finger as he could, giving the car park a quick once over he lifted the finger to his nose and sniffed. The affect was instantaneous. It refocused him, kept his mind on the job and made him more alert.

It was time to move, another night's work that he needed to get over with. He lifted the gun from his belt and checked the clip, fully loaded. Just the one gun tonight, he reminded himself of the need to adjust his movement to compensate, there was concern at the back of his mind that it would disrupt his rhythm. He pushed the thought aside, compared to Tony Miller's entourage Martin Cassidy was practically unprotected. If he could get through that with two guns and a few explosives then surely one would be enough to eliminate an old man and his five thinly spread soldiers. The old confidence was coming back, with it came the itch, that part of him which yearned for the next kill. Its voice grew louder, the coke made it louder still, he steadied himself and took the lift down to the ground floor, he knew what he had to do; maintain your focus, maintain your composure. Silence the voice.

Rob stepped out of the car park and walked across the street. He walked behind the blue car and kept himself out of line with its mirrors. The route gave him enough time to study inside the reception area as well, he saw Cassidy's other man sat in a leather seat on the far left, his eyes were focused solely on the door, he was paying no attention to what went on beyond it.

Rob reached the bench that he'd picked out earlier, the bushes separating the hotel car park from the street hid him from the man on reception duty, it also gave him an eyeball on the back of the blue car. He settled down and waited for something to shift, the coke kept him alert. He watched the back of the two men's heads through their rear mirror, every few minutes peering through the bushes to confirm his other target was still in pocket.

After a while his mind started to wander, it kept coming back to the conversation with Matt earlier that day. It was pre-Stanley Arms, he'd needed to talk to someone, anyone who he was capable of having a real conversation with. The night before had left him feeling dislodged, detached somehow from everything that was going on around him. He felt an overwhelming need to connect, to speak to someone who still had a stake in the world beyond all the craziness. His first instinct had been to speak to Kelly, he even got as far as her front door, but then a feeling that he later interpreted as guilt drove him back, and he went to Matt's house instead. He hadn't gone inside, Matt hadn't offered, he'd just talked from his doorway while Rob stood in exile on the front steps. It seemed to him like a fairly apt metaphor.

The conversation still grated on him. He'd known, as soon as he caught the look on Matt's face, that it wasn't going to be the reassuring pep talk he'd been hoping for. The look captured the disappointment and the horror that he carried around inside himself, it was the look of someone from the outside looking in. Rob stood on Matt's front step and embraced it, being judged felt vaguely comforting, it validated him and condemned him all at the same time. It reminded him that there was a world of acceptable moral absolutes, he simply wasn't a part of it.

"You don't seem too pleased to see me"

The disappointed look hardened.

"Is that supposed to be funny? Tell me it wasn't you"

Rob looked away "It was"

"Fuck Rob. A copper? That's a whole new level, even for you. He wasn't just any old policeman you know? This guy was handpicked by SOCA, he had clout, they knew his name down South. The guy was being groomed, I can't believe you did it"

He had listened to the accusations of his best friend and considered all of his relationships, as he did so it dawned on him that this was the closest he came to transparency. Everyone else knew snippets, aspects, he'd kept them distant for their own good, there was only his best mate who he'd let in all the way. He realised that was why he'd come here, for the chance to be honest.

"They were going to kill Kelly Matt, what was I supposed to do?"

The statement shifted Matt's perspective, he looked at the ground and deliberated the words for a few moments "They were going to kill her?"

"Had guys waiting outside her house"

Matt shook his head, the ensuing sympathy Rob had hoped for never came, instead it was despondent apprehension that looked back at him through his best friends eyes.

"What have you gotten us all into?"

The words hit him harder than they should have. He hadn't anticipated self-preservation being a factor for Matt in any of their conversations before. He understood it, and he didn't judge Matt for voicing it, but once again he felt the pain of letting someone down. He was losing count on the number of times he thought he'd hit rock bottom, no matter how far he fell there always seemed to be further to go.

"I really don't know how it came to all this," Rob told him "I came by because I just needed to talk to someone. Anyone who cares about me whose life I haven't fucked up. Thinking about it, you might be the only person left who fits that description. That says it all really, doesn't it?"

He had tried to smile but it wouldn't come. Matt managed it, it was a smile that showed Rob all of the old honesty and goodness that made his best friend the better man.

"You've still got time Rob, my happiness is pretty fragile"

He managed something close to a snigger "Yeah"

Matt opened the door a little wider "Listen, I've got people coming round later but do you want to come in for a quick drink or something?"

Rob shook his head and took a step backward "No. I've got somewhere I need to be. Thanks for the chat mate, I didn't mean to bother you"

"You didn't. Take care Rob, you hear me? I don't want to pick up the paper and see your name plastered across the front page"

Rob took a few more steps backwards "You don't need to worry there Matt, I'm nothing more than a figment of your imagination"

The memory faded, Rob returned to the job at hand. The conversation left a bad taste lingering in his mouth. He looked at his watch, it was nearly 9pm, business was dwindling in the hotel reception, the rush had passed. He saw a few people perched at the bar on the fifth floor. Rob scanned the car park, aside from his two friends there were only a handful of other cars, all empty, as hit spots went this one was looking better by the hour.

Matt's words refused to leave, *what have you gotten us all into?* he took another hit of coke, it sent the words scurrying away into the darkness, he felt the pistol in his belt and continued to watch; first the car, then the reception, now and again he checked the surrounding area. He raised two fingers to his neck and checked his pulse; it was racing.

He waited a little while longer before he finally got the movement he wanted. Something passed between the two men in the car, a moment later the passenger door opened and out stepped a large man in his thirties with a square jaw and jet black hair. He had a phone pressed to his ear, he turned towards the hotel and a moment later Rob saw Cassidy's man in reception step into the night air talking on his own mobile. The two men looked at each other over a distance of forty feet throughout their conversation, Rob caught a few nods of the head from the muscle on reception detail. Their discussion lasted for forty seconds, when it was finished the man at the car slid on an overcoat, took a few notes from his pocket and walked out of the car park, his counterpart flashed him a thumbs up and returned to his position inside the hotel.

Rob checked the clip one more time and waited, his instinct said food run, the hotels location on the edge of the city centre meant the trip wouldn't take long, he knew he needed to be ready when his target returned.

His phone vibrated in his pocket, the suddenness of it almost caused his heart to jump out of his chest. Rob quickly checked his surroundings before lifting the phone free; it was a text from Charlie.

I got a line of where McSharry's at. Meet me at midnight, I'll pick u up outside Bootle strand!

Rob responded with a simple *OK*, he considered abandoning the job but quickly thought better of it. This might be his only chance to get to McSharry, the old man might bolt if something went wrong with the hit, who knew what was going on in that crazy, old head of his.

He slid the phone back into his pocket and tried to settle his mind. Charlie was the last person in the world he needed to hear from at a time like this, his efforts to keep his brother out of mind had been largely unsuccessful, it was only the coke that kept him from settling on the events of the night before. He felt himself cringe for what must have been the hundredth time that day.

In the cold light of day it ranked as probably the worst thing he'd ever done, but in that moment, in that place, he still knew that he'd had little choice in his actions. Killing David Walker had pushed him closer to breaking point than he'd ever been before, with the horror of Billy Matteo still fresh it had felt like more than he could take. It was only that unexpected period of intimacy that had managed to balance him out and bring him back. He'd almost forgotten what positive human interaction was, had it not shown itself when it did he wasn't sure what he would have been liable to do.

He knew for her part that Vicky was working through her own issues. It would have been the height of naivety to assume that what happened was anything more than the actions of two desperate people craving something emphatic to break the cycle of their misery. Like him he was sure that she would be riddled with regret, but a part of him at least hoped that she saw the value of the moment, in spite of how misguided it may have been.

All he could do was hope that Charlie didn't find out. He knew he could live with the secret, the anger he still felt over his brothers part in David Walker's death made it easier. Rob's mistakes hadn't absolved Charlie of that blame, in a strange way it almost justified his actions, as far as he was concerned he didn't consider his betrayal of Charlie any greater than Charlie's betrayal of him. It was a sad fact that spoke to the depths of which their bond had sunk, but at the same time it made the weight he had to carry that little bit lighter.

He forced himself to take another hit, the coke was a god send, it kept him from dwelling on everything around him. He was starting to worry that if he ever started to analyse the shit in his head he might not be able to stop himself putting a bullet through it.

It was in that moment that Rob caught sight of target number one, he waited for the large man to enter the car park, he had two pizzas locked tightly in his grip. He must have been hungry, he was keeping a fast pace as he made his way towards the car.

Rob stood up from the bench, he tried to time it, he started walking once the big guy was halfway there. He walked fast, fast enough to make up ground, not so fast as to draw attention to himself. He stayed on the street for as long as possible where the bushes obscured his presence. The route kept him out of sight of the reception area for almost the whole way, the only time he would be visible would be for around ten seconds between entering the car park and reaching the car. If everything worked out that would be the only window the next guy got. The ground sped by beneath his feet, he was close, he stepped into the car park. Overcoat bundled the pizzas under one arm as he prepared to open the door, Rob pulled the gun from his belt and took a deep breath.

He watched the man pull at the door. Rob covered the last few feet in a sprint, raising the gun as he did so. He fired the first shot as soon as the door was open, the silencer muffled the sound, the quiet night air carried it further than he would have wanted. The shot hit his man square in the back and pushed him against the frame of the car. Rob fired again from close range, this one hit him a little higher, he heard the crack of metal that told him the bullet had passed right through.

Target number one dropped, Rob followed, using him as a shield. The big man landed on his knees, Rob raised his head above the man's shoulder, his gun already raised. The driver was still trying to pull his own pistol from the confines of his belt. Rob fired twice more, the fingers of target number two had barely touched the grip before he died.

He stayed perched where he was for a few seconds and waited for some

454

kind of response. There was none. He lifted his head and peered over the roof of the car towards the hotel; the remaining soldier was trying to get the attention of a young receptionist. Rob dropped back behind the car and got to work.

It took most of his strength to peel the overcoat off the first man and bundle him into the passenger seat. He tried to work quickly, the car park may have been deserted but the bushes that separated it from the street wouldn't protect him from the eyes of any pedestrians passing by. Once that was done he grabbed the collar of the driver and hauled him downwards until he was almost horizontal. He pushed the two men as far down as they would go until they were both laid out across the front two seats and the leg room below it. He had to go through all of the first man's pockets before he found the mobile phone, once that was done he grabbed the overcoat and laid it over the two corpses, concealing them as best he could. When he was happy with the results Rob closed the passenger door and circled back around the car park, out of view of the reception area.

Navigating his way through the phone took a little longer than expected but Rob eventually found his way to the list of called numbers. The last call was the one he wanted, the number dialled belonged to someone called Jomo, it had been made fifteen minutes earlier.

Rob pressed call, dropped the phone into his pocket, slid his blue baseball cap onto his head and started walking towards the hotel reception. The phone must have rung three or four times before Jomo reached into his pocket to answer it. The receptionist, relieved at the interruption, darted into the backroom away from his ongoing attempts of engagement. Rob veered to the left and came towards the hotel entrance from the side. He watched as Jomo talked into the phone, when he got no response he stepped up and walked towards the main doors to try and eyeball his caller. Rob slowed down and waited, Jomo was peering left and right through the glass front of the reception trying to locate his two colleagues in the blue car. After a couple of seconds he stepped out through the electric doors for a better look. Rob pounced, pulling his pistol free he approached his target from the side and pressed the Smith and Weston into the man's ribcage before he had a chance to react.

"Hello Jomo" Rob said calmly, he nodded towards the side of the hotel "That way. No sudden movements"
Jomo cooperated without a word. Now that they were close Rob was able to see that the man was younger than the other two, maybe in his late twenties. He had a dark brown crew cut and a clean shaven face, something about him said ex-armed forces.

They continued on passed the end of the car park until they reached the alley, once Rob was convinced that they were beyond the view of spectators he grabbed Jomo by the neck and pressed him hard against the wall of the hotel.

Rob raised the gun and rested the barrel against the base of Jomo's jaw. He remembered the scant surveillance details on Begsy's scrap of paper.

"I know there's a code for the penthouse. Give to me before I hurt you"

Jomo spat in his face "Fuck you"

Rob lowered the gun and fired into Jomo's left kneecap. He clamped his hand quickly against the man's mouth and muffled the screams, he waited until they turned into whimpers and then he pulled it away.

"The code?"

Jomo took a couple of deep breaths and tried to compose himself. Rob saw the fear, he could feel the heartbeat through his grip around Jomo's neck. Green eyes studied him, they were trying to understand the man before him threatening to kill, Rob knew that all they would see was a cold, straight face.

"2579"

Rob lowered the gun and shot again, this time into the right kneecap. He kept Jomo upright by maintaining the grip around his neck and pressing him against the wall. They followed the same routine; he muffled the screams, he waited for them to subside.

"The next one goes through your balls. Birds like that receptionist will be a thing of the past for you Jomo, a thing of the past if you lie to me again. The code?"

Jomo sucked in breaths of air and nodded frantically. He looked more like a scared child than he had before.

"8985... I swear, please, believe me"

Rob searched Jomo's eyes for the truth, he must have stared for well over a minute before he was sure he believed the words.

"Thanks"

Rob took a step back and fired once into Jomo's forehead. The shot sent a spray of blood across the white wall of the hotel. He kept his grip around Jomo's neck for a few minutes while he searched his pockets. He found a mobile, a wallet, a small silver pistol and a key card. Dragging Jomo's lifeless body to the large industrial bin a few feet away Rob lifted it up and tossed it inside. A moment later it was followed by the two mobile phones, Jomo's wallet and the silver gun.

As he replaced the clip in the Smith and Weston Rob gave himself a quick once over; aside from a few drops on his shirt and a few more on the back of his right hand he was clean of any tell-tale signs of blood.

Returning the gun to his belt he zipped up his black jacket and slid his right hand into the pocket. He lowered his head as walked towards the front of the hotel, the baseball cap hid the majority of his face, too much for an ID even if someone was paying close attention to him. He passed through the automatic glass doors and headed straight for the elevators, he could feel the eyes of the receptionist burning into him, he tried to keep his movement confident and at ease, just another local goon coming to see the boss, no big deal.

Rob reached the elevator and raised his head. He could see the receptionist still watching him through the refection of the elevators brass doors. He watched her lean forward toward him.

"Excuse me"

Rob felt his left hand move instinctively towards the gun, the disgust at the concept hit him a moment later. Relaxing his hand he leaned his head ever so slightly towards her.

"Yes?" he said in a gruff tone.

"You're going to the penthouse?"

"That's right"

"You need to use the next elevator to your left, it's the only one that goes up there"

Rob let his eyes close for a brief second and let out a slow breath, making sure to keep his head facing forward he took two steps to the left and pressed the upward arrow on the wall.

"Thanks"

The ding of the elevator signalled its arrival, Rob stepped inside and waited until the doors had closed before he turned around to face them. The card slot and the keypad were head height high, he took the card from his pocket, slid it into the slot, held his breath and typed the code: 8.9.8.5.

Rob held his breath for a nervous moment before the elevator came to life and the small P above the floor list lit up. He kept his right hand close to the bottom of his back, close to the gun. It was too soon to have it in hand, no matter how reassuring it may have been, not when he didn't know where the elevators security cameras were feeding into.

The elevator opened and Rob stepped out cautiously. He was greeted by a small hallway with one door, it was deserted. With the key card still in his left hand he withdrew the pistol with his right and stepped slowly towards the door. There was no sound coming from the other side.

He pressed the card into the slot as lightly as he could. When he pulled it free and caught the green light he flicked off the safety on his weapon, turned the handle and walked into the room.

Three light steps were all he got before a fragment of the door exploded above his head. Rob rolled and shielded himself in the doorway of a bathroom, it gave him a moment to reassess. He'd walked into a large, open plan room, part living area, part bar, part kitchen. Before he'd hid himself he'd had time to catch two separate flashes of movement. He felt ill-equipped with just the one gun, he regretted ditching Jomo's silver pistol, it might have come in useful.

Pushing himself up he stepped out of the bathroom and aimed the gun towards the area where the movement had been a few moments before, he got nothing. The position gave him a clear view of the room, he noted four pillars; perfect enemy cover.

One step forward brought a response. He saw a skin head lift himself from behind a couch at eleven o'clock. They both aimed at the same time, Rob got his shot off a fraction earlier, it ripped through the man's head and separated a chunk of the skull from the rest of him.

Movement came again, this time at two o'clock, from behind one of the pillars. Rob couldn't move fast enough to stop this one getting a shot off. It was so close he heard it whistle past his ear, there was no time to stop and count his blessings, he stepped forward and fired twice; two in the chest, he hadn't even gotten a glimpse of what this one looked like.

Suddenly it was silent. He circled the room, paying particular attention to the four pillars. Once he'd cleared all four he studied the rest of the penthouse, in the corner, next to the large ceiling high window Rob caught sight of an old man sat reading a newspaper. He seemed unperturbed by the events going on around him, blocking them out as easily as a noisy television. It was only when Rob stepped closer, with the gun still aimed at the old man, that he folded up the paper and looked at him. The photograph Begsy had given him must have been at least five years old, the Martin Cassidy Rob saw before him was a much frailer creature.

"I've been waiting for you," the old man said with what was almost a warm smile "So you're him? Stephen McSharry's infamous hidden weapon? His ace in the hole? I've wanted to meet you for quite some time. I must say you're not what I expected, you must know what you're doing though. My men downstairs?"

Rob's heart pounded in his chest, the coke left him with nothing but the kill. He yearned for it, the others had simply wetted his appetite, this was the target, this was the main event. He tried to control himself, to give the man his final moments.

"The two in the car and the one downstairs?"

Rob thought he caught a flicker of disappointment in Martin Cassidy's face "That's correct"

"Dead"

Martin Cassidy shook his head sadly. Rob struggled to see the killer inside, Caddock and Miller had been men who were defined by their lifestyles, they showcased their rank for all to see, his man was subtler. In a strange way it reminded Rob of himself.

"They were very talented men, killers you know, each and every one of them. They'd all lived The Life for a long time, and the final word on each of their journeys is from you; muttering the word 'dead' like you've just swatted a fly. You're a man with a true gift for death. Having lived the life I have I can think of no more fitting way to go"

The candid fearlessness caught him off guard, of all the terrible things he'd seen in moments just like this Rob thought that he had lost the ability to be surprised by the turns they took. He was wrong, he felt a growing respect for the elderly man sat before him, the man he was going to execute.

"You don't want to live?"

Cassidy flashed him a patronising smile, it was a smile that said *one day young man, you'll understand.*

"Would you prefer it if I begged for my life? If I swore revenge? You've managed to find your way past five killers in their prime, what chance does an old man have of stopping you? Did my old friend at least tell you why he wanted me dead?"

"I didn't ask"

Rob glanced towards the door, he saw the hole where the first shot had ripped through it just above his head, people may have heard the shots. He needed to move, but he wasn't sure if he could, not yet. The old man was fascinating, Rob wanted to take his wisdom before he killed him, something inside said he needed it. That it might save him further down the road.

"Of course not, you're just a loaded gun, following orders, void of responsibility. Is that what you tell yourself?" Martin Cassidy scrutinised him while he waited for an answer, when it didn't come the old man looked away and let the question disappear into the night air "He didn't tell me the reason either. I would liked to have known, the betrayal of a friend has caused me much more pain than any form of punishment you can offer. I suspect Mr McSharry has transcended the period of his life where friends are considered necessary. Being surrounded by enemies and subordinates must be a much simpler way to exist, though extremely lonely, don't you think?"

He was running out of time, he pulled back the hammer on the pistol and let the itch wash over him.

"If it makes this any easier, he won't be alive for long"

Cassidy made a dismissive gesture with his right hand "It makes not the slightest bit of difference young man. What interest do the dead have in the world of the living? My only hope is that you make it quick and painless, for the both of us"

He took a step forward "I can promise it for you, not for him"

Martin Cassidy gave him a grave look "Don't underestimate him. He's buried smarter and deadlier men than you"

"I did most of that burying"

Rob caught the look, it was the look the old saved for naïve young men who thought they ruled the world, it was experience encapsulated. Rob felt the force of the look and shied away from it instinctively.

"You did a fraction, no more" the old man told him seriously "Now let's get this over with, I see Death lingering impatiently over your shoulder"

Rob shot two bullets into Martin Cassidy's chest. The old man made a quiet groan and died an instant later. Sliding the gun into his belt Rob quickly checked the man's pulse, confirmed the kill and made his way out of the penthouse.

The elevator hit the ground floor. Rob stepped out and marched through the reception area with his head down. He heard no screams and he heard no warnings, five minutes later he was lost within the city when he caught the first trace of sirens in the distance.

Rob got to Moorfields just as the five past ten train to Bootle was pulling in. He climbed on and took a seat in the corner, the train was Sunday night quiet, it gave him the peace to think things through.

It was all drawing to an end, he could feel it in his bones. Almost all the major players were dead, on both sides of the fence, and in a little under two hours he and his brother would get their shot at the puppet master. One way or another it would all be over soon enough.

Rob stepped of the train and made his way out of the station, he saw a gang of teenagers verbally abusing passers-by, their way of mourning the end of another weekend, they ignored Rob as he passed.

He was close to the flat when the phone in his pocket started to vibrate. He didn't recognise the number, when he pressed the phone to his ear all he heard was heavy breathing. He stopped dead and waited for the caller to speak.

"Rob?"

He recognised the voice immediately, it brought a string of confused emotions to the surface.

"Vicky? What is it? What's wrong?"

Rob listened to a few more moments of heavy breathing before she answered.

"Rob, he knows, Charlie knows" he heard tears in her voice.

"How?"

Vicky sniffed back the tears "He found your cross, He was so high, he just started hitting me, he kept going until I admitted it"

Rob's free hand immediately moved to his neck, it was gone, he hadn't even realised that it had been lost. He'd been too preoccupied. Too high.

"Fuck. Are you ok?"

He thought about his brother, about the text message he'd sent. Charlie had a line on McSharry, because they were working together. The plan came to him instantly, back to the flat, as much as he could carry and get gone. If he stole a car tonight there was a good chance that it wouldn't be found until morning. Rob could put a lot of miles on the clock by then.

His mind tried to imagine what Charlie must have been going through, shame and guilt hit him like a tidal wave, he took another hit of coke to try and delay it. *Time and place Rob, there'll be a time and a place.*

"There's something else" he heard Vicky say "I heard him talking to some people on the phone. They were arguing about what to do with your girl, I don't know what that meant"

His stomach tried to lurch out of his mouth. Rob was running by the time Vicky had finished the sentence, he kept the phone pressed to his ear and tried to organise his thoughts as best he could.

"Vicky get out of the house now. Go somewhere safe, a friend's house, someone that Charlie doesn't know about and don't answer this phone for any other number except this one, you understand? It isn't safe"

"I'm not afraid of him"

Rob ran as fast as his legs would carry him, he felt the pistol becoming dislodged from his belt and gripped it with his free hand.

"He already beat you didn't he? And it's not just him you have to worry about. Go somewhere safe, I'll come talk you through it as soon as I can, ok?"

Vicky agreed and hung up. Rob put the phone away and sprinted towards the flat.

Once he reached his makeshift home Rob didn't spend much time inside, just enough to reload his gun and grab a couple of spare clips. Ninety seconds after he'd walked through the door he was on his way out again, lightly jogging for a couple of streets until he found what he was looking for.

The dark brown Vauxhall cavalier had caught his attention just over a week ago, he saw it parked in the same place every night and every time it brought a smile to his face, except for tonight.

When Rob and Charlie were growing up their next door neighbour had owned the exact same make and model. As teenagers the brothers would break into it every couple of months and liberate it from the clutches of its owner, a foul tempered BNP psycho who would keep the whole street awake on the frequent nights that he chose to beat his wife. Despite his best efforts the Nazi scumbag had never managed to prove who was behind it, even in the end when they drove the car to Anfield car park and set the thing on fire. Joyriding around the city in the rusted shed had produced some of the best memories Rob and Charlie had ever shared together, the kind of memories that were categorically beyond them now.

Rob fired one shot into the side window and unlocked the door. His delinquent youth came back to him in seconds and it wasn't long before the engine came to life, it was easier than he'd expected, but Rob didn't have time to congratulate himself. A moment later he was pulling out the street and speeding towards Kelly's house as fast as the old shed would take him.

Rob killed the car halfway down the street and covered the rest of the distance on foot. When he reached her house he saw that the front door was slightly ajar, it confirmed all of the dark thoughts that had harassed him on the way over.

Slowly he eased the door open and stepped inside, the room was dimly lit, two lamps bounced off the beige walls and gave it an orange tint. He closed the door behind him, it creaked as it locked, Rob grimaced at the sound.

The living room appeared to be clear, the kitchen was almost entirely visible from his vantage point on the threshold, but it made sense to check it regardless, he saw no reason to leave any stone unturned.

He'd crossed half of the living room when he saw it. From his initial position it had been hidden behind the couch, but from the centre of the room he was able to lay eyes on the sight that had haunted him since Vicky had called.

The body was lying flat on its stomach, a couple of feet away from the large set of wooden drawers in the corner. Rob saw two red holes in the back of her dressing gown, a layer of dark red blood pooled underneath her midsection. Rob recognised the light brown hair instantly, he knew when he turned her over that he would recognise the eyes.

The old instincts kicked into gear instantly. He knew he couldn't go to Kelly, whoever was responsible might still be in the house, they could be waiting for him. He stormed into the kitchen and confirmed it was empty, a moment later he heard the voice in his head reprimanding him. *Emotion is no excuse. Be careful. Be clinical.*

He raised the gun in front of him and crossed the living room again, this time making his way towards the staircase across from the front door. His movement was slow and silent. It occurred to him that he couldn't hear any noise coming from upstairs, considering there should have been two children up there he knew what that was likely to mean. He dismissed the thought and refocused, he strained his ears for a single sound that might give him the edge. He heard none.

The stairs disappeared beneath his feet, before he knew it he was at the top with no clue what to expect next.

The space between the top the staircase and the landing curved sharply to the left. Rob shifted his body and moved forward, there were three steps ahead of him, passed that all he could see was darkness. A figure came at him from nowhere, he caught a glimpse of a snarling face and a harsh scar, an instant later he felt a knee cap connect with his hand and send his gun spinning into the darkness.

Begsy wasted no time in bringing his own weapon into focus, Rob was able to grab the barrel and force it upwards a second before it went off, the shot was deafening as the bullet buried itself harmlessly in the ceiling.

Both men kept a firm grip of the gun and tried to wrestle it from the others grasp. Rob moved to bring his knee up and into the other man's groin, but Begsy was smart to it. He raised his own knee and slammed it into Rob's thigh knocking him off balance, it was only his grip on the gun that kept Rob upright.

Begsy readjusted his feet and slammed the gun hard into the wall. Rob knew he was out powered by the larger man, he did his best to halt the guns trajectory but did little more than disrupt his own balance. His right hand smashed against the brick, he felt his grip loosen, Begsy pulled back and slammed the gun again, this time Rob lost his hold altogether.

The reverberation of hitting the wall almost knocked Rob off his feet, the terror hit him as he suddenly realised he was balancing precariously on the edge of the staircase.

A moment later he was falling, he felt the weightlessness and the numb shock that he remembered from childhood. Frantically, he tried to grab at whatever he could, his left hand managed to get a chunk of Begsy's shirt, he saw the shocked look on the big man's face when he realised he was being pulled down with him.

Rob felt a series of sharp pains as he tumbled down the stairs, it hit him first in the back, then in the head and again in the back. He landed on the wooden floor sending a sharp pain right through his spine, a fraction of a second later Begsy landed on top of him, he heard one of his ribs snap on impact and felt the pain engulf his chest like a flame igniting a puddle of oil.

Somehow he managed to push himself out from under Begsy. Rob was the slower of the two to get to their feet, he managed to take one step backwards before a fist connected with his face and sent him tumbling back to the ground.

For a moment the pain in his chest was gone. Darkness spread around the periphery of his vision and Rob suddenly found himself unable to make sense of the spinning objects around him. He only had a moment to embrace the feeling before he was being pulled up by the neck. As soon as he was on his feet Begsy delivered a fierce punch to Rob's midsection, in that instant all the pain of the cracked rib returned and intensified tenfold.

Rob tried to push himself away but he was powerless against the larger man's strength. Begsy used his grip on Rob's neck to pull their faces closer together, he saw the cruel vicious smile spread across his enemies face.

"This is like fucking Christmas" Begsy spat.

Before Rob could respond he felt his head being forced forward, Begsy's forehead smashed against his nose, Rob somehow heard the crack before he felt the pain. When Begsy let go the world seemed to plummet, Rob dropped to his knees and then collapsed face first against the wooden floor.

Rob wheezed, every breath burnt like hell. He tasted blood in his mouth, somewhere above him he could hear a mocking snigger. The sound fuelled him, it forced his hands to brace the floor and push, even though every muscle in his body was begging him to lie still.

Begsy waited patiently while Rob struggled to his feet. Rob caught a glimpse of that sadistic grin, he felt the urge to lunge, he stifled it. Begsy took a step forward, he raised his right hand and then hesitated. Rob took the chance when it came, he threw his right fist forward, blocking out the pain it caused in his chest. He caught Begsy on the side of the jaw, the large man stumbled backwards, shock replaced that grin and spurred Rob on. He took his own step forward and swung, Begsy read it with ease and stepped out of the way, Rob's own momentum sent him stumbling forward, before he could find his balance Begsy had gripped the back of his head in one giant hand and sent Rob face first into the mirror. Glass shattered, ripping through his forehead and his cheeks, the only thought that passed through his head was the amazement he felt when he opened his eyes and realised he wasn't blind.

Rob stumbled forwards, he felt a hot sensation moving down his face, he tried to get his bearings but a vice like grip locked around the back of the neck and tossed him like a doll into the set of wooden cupboards. Rob landed with a groan, it took a couple of seconds for him realise that he was lying next to Kelly, it seemed like a fitting place to die.

Every breath burnt more fiercely than the last, he watched the blood dripping from his face onto the wooden floor and wondered just how badly he was injured.

Above the sound of his wheezing Rob could hear footsteps, they sounded like they were moving away from him. Even in his dazed state he knew what that meant; Begsy was looking for his gun, he was preparing to finish Rob off.

The idea came to him in that instant, he forced himself to look at where Kelly had fallen. Against the objections of every muscle in his body he leaned forward and lifted Kelly's hands, underneath her right was a key, a key for the set of drawers.

Rob gripped it in his right hand and dragged himself towards what remained of the wooden drawers. He saw two lockable cupboards on the bottom shelf, he tried to remember which one Kelly had used but his brain refused to cooperate.

Lifting himself as high as he could he saw the back of Begsy as the large man dropped to one knee and collected his gun. Rob eased himself back down and tried to slide the key into the left hand cupboard, he would only be hidden by the couch for a few more seconds, after that Begsy had a clear view of what he was doing, and a loaded gun to stop it.

The left hand cupboard was no good. He tried the right, his hand was shaking, the key wouldn't go into the whole, no matter what he did he couldn't make it fit.

With all the energy he had left he pushed the key in, it clicked into place, it was the sweetest sound Rob had ever heard. Turning the key he pushed the door open and thrust his hand inside, it settled on the barrel of his Smith and Weston, Rob could have cried.

Pulling the pistol clear he rolled onto his back and aimed it into the air. Begsy was halfway towards him when they locked eyes, Rob saw fear in the enforcers face, it only lasted a second, replaced by a scowl as Begsy brought his gun up to aim.

Rob shot once, so did Begsy. The big man's shot ricocheted of the wooden floor inches away from Rob's head, his caught Begsy high in the left lung. He watched as the huge, hulk of a man stumbled from the impact and dropped to his knees. Their eyes remained locked, even when Begsy found his way to his feet and carried on walking forward.

Rob fired again, this time in the centre of the chest, Begsy took the shot but didn't stop, the gun slipped from his hand but his eyes remained fixed as he carried on walking. Rob hit him again, in the same area, Begsy dropped to his knees and lurched forward. Rob tried to keep the gun trained but his arm was growing heavy, it was shaking more and more with every passing second.

For a few moments Begsy didn't move, then Rob saw his left hand curl around something on the floor. It was only when Begsy had lurched to his feet that Rob saw it was a piece of glass, the sharpness had already pierced Begsy's hand but the big man didn't seem to have noticed the bleeding. Rob saw determination in those eyes, he saw Begsy's mouth twist into that vicious smile once again as he carried on walking. Rob fired too more shots but he couldn't stop his hand from shaking, they both flew well over their targets head. Begsy was only a few feet away now, he raised the piece of glass high above his head, Rob knew he only had one more shot before McSharry's enforcer sank it into his heart.

He waited, Begsy took another step closer. The gun shook incessantly in his hand, he used all of his strength just to keep it upright, Begsy took another step, the sharp shard of glass glistened with blood, he watched the man's eyes as he prepared to bring it down with all his considerable force.

Rob took the shot.

It flew right between the lips of that cruel smile and exploded the back of Begsy's head. Rob kept the gun aimed, he waited until the shard of glass had hit the floor, and he continued to wait until Begsy's large frame had fallen backwards and the sound of him smashing against the hard ground had echoed around the room, and then he dropped it.

And then he found the strength to cry.

Rob spent ten minutes cradling Kelly's lifeless body. He stroked her hair and thought about all of the things he could have done differently that would have saved her life. If he'd let McSharry kill him in the cemetery, if he'd been less belligerent to the old man, if he'd managed a clean kill on Tony Miller, if he hadn't been so honest with Charlie. He looked down at her pale face and asked himself whether a single one of those changes would have been enough to keep her alive.

A drop of blood fell from the cut on his cheek and landed on Kelly's forehead. As he wiped it away with his sleeve Rob arrived at one absolute certainty; if he hadn't of come back, she would never have been in danger.

He felt more tears, they mixed with the blood, he turned his head to the side to avoid contaminating her any further.

I'm sorry Kel, you deserved better
I know but I chose to settle for you

His choices had robbed her of so much over the years, now they had taken everything that was left. Rob squeezed her body tightly against his own and prayed for her forgiveness. He didn't deserve it, and he knew she could no longer give it, but he asked for it nonetheless. What other choice lay in front of him?

After a while Rob let go of her body and willed himself to stand up. The police wouldn't be far behind, for the second time that night he needed to make sure he was long gone by the time they arrived.

As he stumbled to his feet Rob felt an intense pain with every breath he tried to take. He ignored it as best he could and began the process of rounding up potential evidence. He started with the Smith and Weston, flipping the safety on he slipped it into his pocket and stumbled towards Begsy's corpse. Kneeling down to pick up the gun, he realised it was the same weapon that had killed David Walker. Rob glanced back towards Begsy's body and noticed for the first time that McSharry's enforcer was wearing gloves. So that was their plan, frame Rob for Walker's death, throw in a dead ex-girlfriend for the hell of it, send him into a trap and put him down. Everything would be wrapped up in a nice little bow and with Walker out the way Stephen McSharry could get back to distributing drugs against a backdrop of the same lethargic police interest that he'd exploited throughout his career.

Rob slipped the silver 9mm into his back pocket and climbed the stairs to retrieve his second gun.

He saw it lying in a doorway, as Rob lifted the weapon from the ground his eyes were drawn towards the two beds on opposite sides of the room, he saw Stevie and Matilda lying still, they could have been sleeping, had it not been for the single bullet hole in each of their skulls. Their eyes were closed, Matilda held a bunny rabbit tightly against her chest.

The sight was too much for Rob to bear, he quickly closed the door and stood still in the hallway, his stomach threatened to project its contents in all directions. He tried to take a breath and remembered the pain, he tried to take an even deeper breath, the cracked rib did its best to propel his focus away from that image. Rob knew it would be lodged in there forever; right alongside Julie McSharry, Billy Matteo, David Walker and countless others, he asked himself how much room could be left for new atrocities. The answer came back; he hoped he would never find out.

Death smothered him, it surrounded him from every angle and sought to drag him down into the depths of decaying flesh and blood curdling screams. He felt it ripping his insides apart every day, infecting and polluting everything that he had been before all this began. He questioned how much of that person he had left inside of him, it couldn't have been much, the years of slaughter had sliced through that boy like a scythe through grass. He was desperate to know when it would all be over, and even more desperate to know whether it could be.

In the darkness, a bright flicker caught Rob's eye. He stepped towards Kelly's room, in the corner he saw a set of drawers, covered on the top by a cluster of framed photographs. A silver frame reflected the moonlight, Rob flicked on the light switch and walked towards it, when he got close he saw his own image trapped behind the glass. Carefully he lifted it out from amongst the others and studied it. The picture wasn't just of him, Kelly and Charlie were squeezed into it as well, he saw the edge of Kelly's arm where she held the camera above them, he saw the sand in the background.

He remembered the picture. He knew it in an instant.

It was taken on his twentieth birthday.

Chapter 36

The flash went off.

Rob tried to blink away the orange sphere that had burned itself onto his retina, he felt Charlie's head leaning on his shoulder, he pushed his little brother away and digged him hard in the right arm.

"A little thing called 'personal space', dick" Rob told Charlie as he stumbled backwards.

He felt the suns warmth against his face, it was perfect birthday weather, town would be banging, everyone would be in a good mood, it had all the makings of a quality night. The first part of June had been practically tropical, he only hoped that it lasted for another couple of months, six weeks left to serve and then he was free, his days in Her Majesty's Armed Forces would be over.

The thought filled him with optimism. Joining the army had been a mistake, he recognised that now, it had just been a way for his sixteen year old self to escape from a turbulent home life.

The Cheshire Regiment had been good to him, his time with the Old-Two-Two's had turned him into a man, and shook loose a lot of the immaturities of childhood. But Bosnia had been a turning point, the thing with the farmer still gave him nightmares, even if their guys told him that he had nothing to feel bad about. They were good blokes, and he was glad he'd gotten to know them.

He didn't regret signing up at all, he'd learned some important things, met some important people, but in his heart he knew it wasn't what he was meant to do, the violence wasn't really him, he had no thirst for it. This way would be better, maybe he could even go back to school.

Meeting up with Matt O'Neil had really inspired him, while Rob had high tailed it to the army at the first chance he got. his old mate had stayed on at sixth form, got his A Levels and just finished the first year of his law degree.

Seeing Matt in his new surroundings had opened Rob's eyes to a life he'd never considered before. His old school mate seemed more confident, more at ease, and he noticed something else about him. He had an energy, something that said he was learning, bettering who he was and adding attributes to himself that kids from their neck of the woods had never had the chance to embrace before. Rob thought maybe he could take a piece of that, maybe he'd sign up for his A Levels in September and take it from there.

"Don't pick on your little brother" Kelly said as she wrapped her arm around Rob's waist.

She gripped her sandals lightly in her free hand and squeezed herself into Rob. Both he and Charlie had tried to warn her about the dangers of walking barefoot along Crosby Beach, but she refused to listen. Their warnings of glass, needles and the like fell on deaf ears, Kelly simply smiled and continued skipping across the sand like she was sunning herself in Ibiza.

"Yeah, listen to your bird" Charlie muttered while he rubbed his arm back to life "This is what I get for buying you a present, if you're gonna beat me up either way I may as well take it back"

Kelly drew her arm back from around Rob's waist and thrust her hand down the top of his shirt.

"No Charlie, you can't do that" she said, emerging with the silver cross "I really like it, it's well fit"

"It brings me closer to God," Rob said, sliding his hands around Kelly waist "Which won't bold well for you, he doesn't like all that sin you've been throwing at me"

Kelly flashed him that tight smile and pressed herself closer to him "He can watch if he wants"

With that she pushed herself away and skipped off into the distance. Rob caught Charlie's eyes following her ass.

"Eyes front and centre there, chief" Rob said as he fell in alongside his brother.

Charlie blushed and looked towards the sea. Rob stifled a laugh, he felt for Charlie, seventeen had been a rough year for him so far, the lad was little more than a walking hard on, and having to listen to him and Kelly shagging in the next room for the last four nights couldn't have done much to help. He just hoped Charlie didn't embarrass him when they went out clubbing later that night. Getting him in wouldn't be a problem, he was passable for eighteen, it was how he behaved with the girls inside that worried Rob.

Charlie sighed and glanced at his watch "This beach bollocks is getting a bit boring. Its half 6 already, why don't we go into town and get a couple of pre-night out birthday drinks in ya?"

"I like your thinking there, young'un" Rob told him.

Kelly skipped back towards them. Rob watched her move, she had the most amazing figure he'd ever seen, it was the first thing he thought of during the weeks away when all he had was his imagination. She'd offered to take a couple of naked pictures of herself to keep him amused but Rob had refused, a few of the guys in the barracks had made that same mistake and after a quick trip to the photocopier those girls had become the wanking aid for most guys in the unit. Kelly was his, all his, he had no desire for anyone to see that body but him.

She stopped just in front of them, Charlie told her their plan, Kelly wrinkled her nose and shook her head.

"I can't go into town, I need to head home and start getting ready" she lifted Charlie's arm and looked at the time "I'm probably going to be late as it is"

Charlie looked to Rob as if he wanted him to say something, his shrug of the shoulders didn't seem to satisfy his little brothers requirements.

"How can you need to get ready now?" Charlie asked her "We aren't getting the train into town till ten, that's three and a half hours away"

Kelly dropped her shoes onto the floor and slid them on, counting on her fingers as she did so.

"I need to do my hair, do my makeup, pick my outfit, do my nails, I'm thinking we might need to get a later train"

Rob stepped forward and wrapped his arms around Kelly's waist "You look perfect to me as it is, love"

"Ah, aren't you sweet" Kelly said, leaning in to kiss him.

The kiss couldn't have lasted for longer than twenty seconds before a splash of cold water hit the side of their faces, Rob tasted the salt turned instantly to face Charlie, his brother had his hands cupped together and was laughing like a child.

Rob darted forward and tackled Charlie to the ground. Straddling his little brother across the stomach he used his knees to pin down Charlie's arms and proceeded to grab handfuls of sand and dump them into his little brothers unprotected face.

"Exfoliating's supposed to be good for you Charlie," Rob said in between his brothers protests "We'll have you looking gorgeous for tonight"

Charlie spat out a mouthful of sand and thrashed around as much as his restricted position would allow "Fucking get off me Rob, this ain't funny!"

Rob grabbed another load of sand and bundled it into his brothers mouth, Charlie frantically tried to fight his way out but Rob just pressed his knees down harder onto his brothers arms and laughed.

He heard a sigh behind him.

"Urghh, boys"

Rob turned and saw Kelly walking away, across the beach towards the car park.

"Babe, where you going?"

"I haven't got time to watch you two dicking about like a couple of five year olds, I'm driving home"

Rob heard Charlie brushing himself, a few seconds later he was standing beside him watching Kelly go.

"Can't you drop us off into town on your way?" Rob asked.

She sent back a dismissive wave without breaking her stride.

"It's in completely the opposite direction, get the bloody train you lazy bugger!"

A second later she disappeared over a sand hill. Rob looked at his brother and shook his head.

"Nice one, Charlie"

It took them nearly forty-five minutes to get the train into the city centre, had it not been such an effort to get in they would have headed straight back out again. As it was they agreed on one quick pint just to justify their efforts, before heading home to get changed for the night ahead.

They settled on a pub close to Moorfields train station. Neither of them had been inside before, but from the exterior it looked cheap enough. Considering both Charlie and Rob were both planning for a heavy night it seemed a perfect fit for a quick 'one and out'.

He should have noticed that something was wrong as soon as they stepped through the door. The pub was dark, almost gloomy, it was a large, narrow room with only one frosted window next to the entrance capable of providing natural light. The barman regarded them suspiciously, Rob just assumed it was because of their age, he withdrew his driver's license and thought no more about it, it was only later that he recognised the flicker of fear that had crossed the man's face as well.

The two brothers walked towards the bar, Rob heard their footsteps sound against the stone floor and echo around the room. For a brief moment he thought they were the only two customers in the place, then he caught movement, in amongst the shadows against the far wall was a table, his eyes took a couple of seconds to adjust before he spotted the four serious looking men deep in conversation.

Rob got to the bar and ordered two pints of lager. The barmen looked them both up and down, he let a moment pass before deciding it wasn't worth the trouble, and wandered off to pour their drinks.

A strange feeling had taken hold of him ever since they'd walked through the door. He felt the eyes of the men at the table gravitating towards them, something primal told him not to look back, by the time the drinks were placed on the bar he found himself wishing that Charlie had been ID'd.

Whatever the uncomfortable vibe that afflicted him was, it had zero effect on his brother. He half listened as Charlie rambled on about some girl he was trying to screw, his only pauses coming when he stopped to laugh at his own jokes. Rob became cautiously aware of the volume of his brothers speech, aside from his voice the room was deathly quiet, an overwhelming self-consciousness came over him. Rob began to drink his pint as fast as possible.

After a while he noticed that Charlie's gaze had started to drift towards the table of men. Rob tried to catch his eye and subtly discourage him from the process, but a moment later his brother was shaking his head and leaning in towards him.

"One of those lads over there won't stop staring at me, he wants to be careful, I'll go over there and beat the shit out of him if he keeps eyeballing me like that"

Rob rolled his eyes, two drunken fights in the last six months and his little brother suddenly thought he was Lennox Lewis.

Rob lowered his voice "Charlie, don't start I mean it, alright, not on my birthday"

Charlie glared back at the men, a few seconds later Rob's words seemed to register and he snapped out of it, flashing his older brother a smile he leaned onto the bar.

471

"You're right Robbo, soz lad. It is your birthday, so let's get you in some birthday shots"

Rob raised his hand to protest but by the time he had Charlie was already calling the bartender over and asking for two shots of tequila. A shot wasn't going to help them get out any faster, Rob gave a cautious glance towards the group of men and saw that one of them had stood up and was making his way towards the bar.

As the man got closer Rob could see that he was in his mid to late thirties, his short dark hair was greying, which made his bushy, dark eyebrows even more prominent. Below them Rob saw a morose, bad-tempered face, the man glared at him for a second as he passed, before focusing his attention onto the bartender.

"Four whiskeys, kidda" the man grunted. It was an order, not a request, Rob got the immediate impression that the man conducted most of his exchanges in that manner.

The barmen stopped halfway through pouring their tequilas, nodded and collected four glasses from above the bar. As he started to pour the whiskey Rob felt Charlie move around him towards the morose man standing further down the bar.

"Wow, what's that all about?" Charlie demanded belligerently, Rob tried to grab his shoulder to quieten him but his little brother just shrugged him off "Wait your turn nob head, we ordered ours first"

The man turned, Rob noted the thick shoulders, the posture said it all; not a hint of concern, not a hint of surprise. This fella was a man of violence, Rob knew it instantly, he served with enough of them day in and day out to know the type.

The man glanced towards the bartender "Who is this scrawny little shit?" he asked, when the barman gave him nothing more than a nervous shrug of the shoulders he turned back to Charlie "I think it's time you two faggots moved on, this isn't that kind of pub. Just looking at you is putting me in a foul bloody mood"

Charlie needed to read the signals and move on, Charlie needed to know trouble when he saw it and step out of its way. Charlie was seventeen, Charlie didn't know shit.

"Who the fuck are you bell end?" Rob heard his brother shout, he reached forward again and tried to pull him back by the shoulder, Charlie shrugged him off for the second time "Nah Rob, get off me. I'll knock him out if he thinks he can talk to me like that"

Rob reached forward again and this time pulled him back before his brother had a chance to move.

"Charlie, let it go" Rob turned to the man at the bar, he looked ready to pounce "It's ok, we're leaving"

Charlie strained against his grip, being held back seemed to spur him on even more "You think I'm walking away from this knob jockey? Go fuck

472

yourself mate, you want a go? I'll beat the shit out of you right here"

Rob watched as a second man wandered over from the table, he was bald, of a similar age and with a similarly violent edge to him. Looking passed the man Rob saw the remaining two stand up and take note of proceedings, one was a well-dressed man in his forties, the other was a huge, vicious looking brute with a thick scar protruding from his right cheek. Rob saw something primal and cruel in the large man, every instinct in his body urged caution, his attention was redirected as the bald man took his place a couple of steps behind his colleague. The whole mess required caution.

"Charlie.." Rob's voice was low and serious, he hoped his brother got the warning behind it.

"Last chance" the man said, the arrival of his back up had significantly increased his appetite for violence, Rob could see it in the eyes "Fuck off"

If they had one chance left to get out this was it, he willed his little brother to show some restraint, his eyes drifted back to the large man, he didn't know how bad it might get if that fella got involved.

Charlie took half a step forward "Fucking make me, you cunt"

A crazed look erupted on the face of the man, Rob saw him reach behind his back, he felt awash with terror as the hand reappeared holding a black pistol.

"No!"

It took a second for Rob to realise the voice was his own, without thinking he gripped his pint glass and launched it at the man's head, it connected with the bridge of his nose and smashed across his face.

The man screamed and stumbled back, the gun went off, it was a wild shot that smashed against the mirror above the bar. Rob darted forward and forced the man's wrist upwards, a second shot went off, this time into the roof.

From the corner of his eye he saw the bald man reaching for a weapon of his own. Instinctively Rob twisted and pulled the arm he was gripping down, as he did so he locked his right arm around his opponents bicep and directed the gun towards the bald man.

He felt the man trying to free his arm from Rob's grip, before he had a chance to do so Rob's left hand darted towards the gun and pressed down hard on the man's trigger finger. He heard the shot go off and saw the bald man stumble backwards as the bullet buried itself deep into his chest.

There was no time to think about the shot, Rob felt the other man's breath on his neck as he tried to free his arm. Keeping a firm hold on the gun with his left hand Rob released his grip and slammed his right elbow into the other man's face; once, twice, three times.

On the third hit the man was forced to release his hold on the gun as he stumbled backwards. Rob swivelled, to face him, even as the man staggered he was pulling a flick knife from his pocket, a second later, covered in blood he was charging forward. Rob raised the gun and fired without thinking, three shots, each one hit high in the chest. The man flew backwards and smashed into a nearby table.

A moment later he felt like he was falling, overcome with a blinding panic that he hadn't known since that day in Bosnia. He swivelled and was suddenly faced with two guns pointed squarely at his chest. The well-dressed man and the oversized goon were stood a few feet away, their weapons trained carefully as they regarded the boy in front of them. Suddenly everything was quiet, all Rob could hear was the sound of his own breathing, he kept his gun aimed at the middle aged man, something in their body language said that he was calling the shots. To his right Charlie was squatting on the floor with his hands over his ears.

The large man was the first one to speak "Shall I take him?"

The urge to pull the trigger was plastered across the goons face, but when Rob looked at the older man he saw something different, Rob thought it looked something like amused curiosity.

"Not yet" the older man said with a shake of the head, he looked at Rob and raised his eyebrows "you just saved me forty grand, lad"

Rob allowed his eyes to rest on the corpse of the bald man for the briefest of moments.

"I didn't mean to kill them"

"Oh, I wouldn't worry about that, you can be sure they meant to kill you. No, the problem you have is that I just hired these gents to take on a very important and a very pressing job, now you've just knocked me right back to square one. What you've also got working against you is the fact that I get very upset when someone points a gun at me, so why don't you drop that piece on the bar and we'll all have a nice little chat"

The big man was glaring fiercely at him, Rob looked down and saw that Charlie still hadn't moved, he was watching the exchange with wide eyed terror.

"Let my brother go, and I'll do whatever you want"

The well-tailored man let out an amused laugh "Kid, you havent got the strongest bargaining position"

Rob tried to keep his voice firm, he felt the contents of his bowels turning to water "I have a gun"

"We have two"

He swallowed hard and tried to remember his training "So I'll take one of you with me when I go"

A low growl emanated from the throat of the big man, Rob saw pure hate staring back at him "Say the word boss, I'll do them both"

'The boss' gave Rob another confident smile "Let the kid go" the man looked down at Charlie "Go on boy, on your bike, before I change my mind"

After a moment's hesitation Charlie rose to his feet, Rob caught a wet patch around his brother's groin, he didn't acknowledge it.

"Charlie, go"

His brother frantically shook his head "No way, I'm not leaving you"

"You need to go now, Charlie. Head home and don't say a word to anyone. I'll be home soon"

Rob knew it was a lie as soon as he said it, but he didn't care. He was willing to do whatever it took to get his little brother out of harms way. If it transpired that these men had to kill him then Charlie could spend the rest of his life hating Rob for that final lie, all that mattered was that he would get to live it.

Charlie nodded and hurriedly walked out of the dark pub. Rob waited until the door had closed behind him before he dropped the pistol onto the wooden bar. The two men kept their guns focused on Rob's chest.

The boss watched him for a few more seconds before he began "Those two men you just dispatched, they're well known killers around these parts. They have a lot of dangerous friends who are going to be very pissed when they hear of their untimely demise" he nodded towards the big man "Begsy here will have to bury them or we'll end up answering a lot of awkward questions ourselves, Begsy hates burying people"

Rob didn't see a way out, he tried to stay brave and hold his nerve.

"I didn't mean to kill them"

"But you did" the boss said, in a dismissive tone "and now I'm left with a job that needs sorting as a matter of absolute urgency. You see, I have a few unsavoury characters hanging around my turf and disrupting my business. I need them killed quickly and quietly, the problem is, we share some friends, me and these headaches, so I need them killed by someone who can't be linked back to me. The way I see it, you've got yourself two choices; either we put you down right here and bury you with your two victims, or we let you live and you take a crack at the job you so thoughtlessly made vacant"

The big man he'd called Begsy glared at the boss with disgust "What?"

The boss kept his eyes on Rob, he could see the wheels turning in the man's head "We need someone who can't be linked to us Begs, he took down these two pretty well. I'm going to give him a shot"

Rob shook his head. He felt the beads of sweat dripping down his face, this whole situation was unreal, the panic in his chest told him it was a nightmare but he knew he wasn't that lucky.

"I'm not a killer"

Begsy grunted "You send him against Mick's boys and he'll be dead inside of two minutes"

The boss shrugged "Probably, but we haven't got the time to go fishing for another hitter. What's your name, kid?"

He swallowed hard "Rob"

"Alright Rob, you seem like a smart lad, this is very simple: you say no to my offer and you're dead right here, right now, no two ways about it. You accept and at the very least you'll get to live for a few more days, who knows, if you pull out another move like you did with these two you might just live a little

while longer than that. You picked the wrong bar to walk into son, it's a bitch
but there it is. So, what do you say, you want to help us out?"

The terror of what was being asked mingled with the relief that they might
not kill him, the combination made him feel faint. He tried to think but in the
back of his mind he knew he didn't really have a choice, eventually he gave a
slow nod.

"Ok"

The boss gave a hearty laugh "Take a seat. Bobby...?" after a few moments
he saw a head emerge from behind the bar "Get the kid a whiskey"

Rob returned the silver frame to where he found it and hurried down the
stairs. The pain in his ribs increased with each step but failed to slow him
down. When he reached the bottom he allowed himself to look at Kelly one
final time, a moment later he was out the door.

Climbing into the stolen Vauxhall Cavalier, Rob dropped the three guns
onto the passenger seat and checked his watch. Ten past Eleven, fifty
minutes before he was due to meet Charlie.

Starting the engine Rob drove carefully, his eyes scanning the quiet street,
alert for any sign of approaching police. Once he'd put a reasonable distance
between himself and the house he steadily increased the speed.

Only one option came to his weary mind, he knew it was the only choice
available to him, just like he'd known the first time he met Stephen
McSharry. Rob put his foot down as far as it would go, he had a lot to do in
fifty minutes.

Chapter 37

Taking a deep breath was hard. The cold air made it even harder.

Rob waited at one of the bus stops outside the front of Bootle Strand, it was a four minutes to midnight. The last pedestrian traffic from a few nearby pubs seemed to be long gone, the Sunday night crowd had packed in a while ago, preparing themselves for the week ahead, only one solitary teenager had crossed his path in the ten minutes Rob had been waiting.

On the other side of the road there was a side street, halfway up he saw a darkened car with its engine running. The street was too dark for Rob to even tell its colour, green maybe, or blue, he let his eyes linger on it for just a moment and then returned to surveying the main road.

Every movement caused an eruption of pain in his chest, he'd seen plenty of scraps in his day but none quiet as debilitating as the encounter with Begsy. At least the vicious bastard was dead, after what he had done, Rob's only regret was that he couldn't go back and kill him again.

Eventually his attention drifted towards the large indoor shopping centre behind him. Bootle Strand, Rob had been seventeen when the eyes of a shocked nation turned to this place in horror. He remembered watching the events unfold on TV from the army barracks in Catterick, he remembered the shock and the outrage as word spread of that poor little boy. A little boy brutally murdered, by two youths who were nothing more than boys themselves.

It had been a dark day in Liverpool's history, one of the darkest he had known. Now Rob's own tale included two dead children, he wondered if anyone out there would ever put all the pieces of his story together, and if they did whether the eyes of a shocked nation would once again turn to his part of the world and judge its people.

The wind caused a scattering of rubbish to tumble noisily in front of him, it caught Rob off guard, an instinctive anxious breath sent a fierce pain shooting through his chest.

His hand went instinctively to his belt, and then he remembered, he was unarmed. It felt almost unnatural, without his guns he couldn't shake a sense of nakedness that kept him on edge. Still, at least he knew that his two guns were safe, and it was better this way. Going in shooting was never going to be an option, not with his brother caught in the middle of the whole thing. Rob had taken responsibility for a whole heap of terrible things lately, but accidentally killing his brother would be more than even he could take. He knew, if it ever came to such a choice, that he would put a bullet in his own head before he allowed himself to hurt Charlie.

Even if his little brother hadn't been thrust into the centre of McSharry's scheme, Rob still doubted whether all guns blazing would have been the best way to go. The broken ribs were just the start, Begsy had left his entire body aching and there was an unfocused, dizzy sensation in his head that felt something like a concussion. Every movement took twice as long, in a tight spot he knew that his battered body would be unable to react in anything like the time it usually did. In this state he didn't fancy himself in a one on one gun fight, let alone the stacked deck that Stephen McSharry no doubt had waiting for him.

As if on cue Rob heard the sound of a struggling engine gunning its way towards him, as the sound got closer it began to mix with the deep thumping of an R'n'B track at full blast, a second later he caught sight of the red Volkswagen, watching as Charlie pulled into the bus stop and skidded to a halt.

Rob walked towards the car and climbed in, the sound was almost deafening. A cold stare greeted him as he sat down, he could see in his eyes that Charlie was high, they looked wider, more suspicious, and more unpredictable than usual. Rob waited as Charlie took in the bruises that covered his brothers face, he looked for a moment as though he might question their cause, before he thought better of it. Without a word he pulled away from the bus stop and turned the car into a sharp U turn, heading back in the direction he had just come.

The music continued to fill the gap between them, it took Rob a song and a half to find the nerve to speak. He flicked off the radio, the tension was instantly evident, the distance that was now between them physically hurt him, it hurt so fiercely that Rob found it difficult to speak.

"So where are we going?"

Charlie kept his eyes on the road, hatred was radiating from his brother in waves, his hands gripped the wheel so tightly it looked as though it might break.

"The docks" Charlie replied evenly, a second later his hand was at the radio and the thumping bass was once again vibrating against Rob's skull.

A few more moments passed before Rob found the nerve to switch off the radio for the second time.

"Charlie..."

The words caught in his throat, the courage to continue alluded him, it was hidden somewhere, in the depths of his stomach, but it refused to surface.

Charlie turned the radio back on.

Rob rested his head against the window and tried to locate a single proactive thought inside his muddled head.

A little over five minutes later the car came to a stop. Rob took in his surroundings; a dark, dimly lit street, a little further down he saw a collection of warehouses. He knew the Mersey would be just behind them, it was likely that whatever fate awaited him would culminate with his corpse drifting across that body of water, or resting beneath it.

On the drive in he'd noticed the area was a combination of more warehouses, low rent housing and abandoned buildings, whatever happened here he didn't expect a quick response from the Merseyside police force, the few people that did still inhabit the area were unlikely to be the 999 type.

Charlie climbed out of the car without a word and began walking towards the warehouses. He'd reached halfway when he turned around and realised that Rob was still standing next to the car, anger and impatience dominated his face as he made his way back up the street.

"Let's go" Charlie instructed when he was only a few feet away.

Rob stood his ground and struggled to settle his nerve. He knew if he was going to speak then it needed to be now, there was every chance he wouldn't find another opportunity.

"I..." once again the words caught in his throat, taking a deep breath he urged himself to push through "I need you to know that I'm sorry, I really am. You're my brother Charlie, I never wanted to hurt you"

For a few moments Charlie's face was unreadable, then, piece by piece, the mask began to crack. First his eyes, already coke-induced wide, seemed to expand to an almost inhuman extent, a second later his face turned a dark shade of crimson, and soon after that his whole body began to shake.

Rob was still thinking about what else he could say when Charlie pulled the pistol from his pocket and smashed it across Rob's face. His head smacked hard against the roof of the car, the dizziness came flooding back, as he tried to compose himself he felt Charlie padding him down. He tried to speak but the taste of blood kept his mouth closed, Charlie finished the frisk and spun him round, pushing him hard against the side of the car. Rob looked away from the gun aimed at his face and spat a tooth onto the pavement, along with a mouthful of blood.

"How could you?" Charlie asked with tears in his eyes, Rob felt his heart breaking as he listened to his brothers voice descend into a shrill scream "How could you do that to me!?"

The sound echoed down the silent street, as if the very buildings surrounded them demanded an answer. Rob wished he had one, he wished he had anything to sustain him, but after everything that had transpired he had nothing left, nothing but the truth, and when was that ever enough.

"I never meant..." the words faded as he realised where he was going, he paused, spat out another mouthful of blood, and tried again "It wasn't planned. Killing that copper hit me hard. I'm not making excuses, but I was high, I was confused. You don't know what it's like to kill a man Charlie, it does things to you, things you wouldn't understand"

The moment he stopped speaking Rob realised that his words were doing nothing to appease his brothers rage, if anything, he seemed to be making it worse. Charlie took a step forward and pressed the gun hard against Rob's forehead. He continued to apply pressure until Rob felt the wound from earlier begin to bleed. The look of hatred on his brothers face was so intense, and so absolute, that there didn't seem to be any way back for the two of them.

"You sure about that?" Charlie snarled, continuing to exert more and more pressure against Rob's wound. In that moment he caught something else buried in amongst the hatred, he saw the arrogance in what Charlie was saying, he was a killer now, Rob had let him get too close to the old man and now he'd crossed that line. His brother seemed to read his thoughts, he flashed a cold smile and nodded his head "Yeah, that's right, and tonight I'll do it again. I looked up to you my whole life, we were family"

Rob felt his eyes well up.

"We still are"

Charlie shook his head "No, not anymore. Family would never do what you did, family would never fuck the mother of my kids in my own home. Was it good? Was she a good fuck? Did I cross your mind once?"

He could see Charlie holding back the tears, he could see everything that was going on inside him, every little tick that came from a lifetime of knowing one another, of growing up together. Rob could see everything, but like a watchmaker looking at a terminally broken clock he knew that there was nothing he could do to repair it.

"Charlie-"

The gun was driven harder against the wound, slamming the back of Rob's head against the roof of the car.

"Answer me!" Charlie screamed.

The world spun. He tried to focus on the figure in front of him but it refused to stay still long enough for Rob to get a clear sight. He waited until it started to settle, until he could see his brother, red faced and broken, on the edge of something sinister.

"No"

The pressure remained for a moment longer and then it was gone. Charlie took a couple of steps backwards, the gun still aimed forward, as Rob struggled to his feet.

"Then we've got nothing left to talk about" Charlie told him, the finality of the statement scared Rob, it told him that the final ship had set sail, and that his brother was lost forever.

Charlie wiped his nose and composed himself before he continued.

"You're nothing more to me now than a problem that's about to be solved"

Rob nodded and took a step forward, Charlie moved in harmony, taking a step backwards at precisely the same moment.

"I understand," Rob said, wiping the water away from his eyes "but you'll always be my brother, and I'll always love you"

Charlie gestured down the street with his gun.

"Fucking move"

Rob started walking, he heard Charlie follow a few steps behind. As he passed the first of the warehouses he recognised a grim truth; it was over for him, there would be no great escape this time. The only thing he could hope for, the only thing he had left, was to make sure that Charlie wasn't the one who had to kill him. He'd done enough damage to his brother, to everyone he cared about for that matter, he wouldn't permit Charlie to suffer the burden of killing his flesh and blood. Even if Charlie thought he wanted it, he wasn't a killer yet, not a true one anyway, and Rob knew enough about the passion of murder to know that it dwindled over time, dwindled until there was nothing left but regret and self-loathing. He wouldn't make Charlie live with that choice, it was the one decision left that he had any say in, and for his brothers sake he would do everything he could to make sure that he died the right way; at the hands of an enemy, not at the hands of his family.

Charlie directed him towards a set of open gates leading straight into a fenced off car park. Rob noted four black cars in the far corner, as they passed through the gates he realised that the large white building surrounding the car park was actually five separate warehouses. A nod from Charlie told him to head towards the four cars, behind them he saw a warehouse with a thick blue door, even half concussed he sensed that would be their destination.

As they got closer Rob spotted movement, to the right of the door he saw a man. His outfit was pure black, giving him something of a bouncer look. The way his right hand rested within the confines of his black bubble jacket told Rob, and anyone else who came too close, that he was armed.

Charlie kept his distance, always five paces back, never close enough to get caught off guard, his little brother was learning fast.

They reached the door and Rob was able to get a good look at the man guarding it. He seemed young, younger than him or Charlie at least, with straggly blond hair and a round face. He surveyed Rob with all the confidence of a man carrying a loaded weapon, when his gaze drifted towards Charlie he gave a familiar nod.

"Alright lad, this him then?"

Rob felt the barrel of the gun press hard against his lower back.

"What do you think Teller? You wanna tell the boss we're here?"

Teller stepped backwards towards the blue door and knocked. The first two knocks were wrapped against the top of the frame in quick succession, there was a pause, and then he knocked once more against the lower section of the door that was level with his knee.

An uncomfortable silence descended over the three men as they waited for a response. Rob took the opportunity to turn and steal one last look at his brother, he tried to make eye contact but Charlie looked straight past him like he wasn't even there, his eyes poised on the thick blue door ahead of him. Over Charlie's shoulder Rob caught sight of a car labouring slowly up the street, on the other side of the metal fence. Its headlights were turned off, only when it passed underneath the beam of a streetlight was Rob able to see that it was dark blue in colour.

The door made a low, dragging noise as the metal bolt was pulled free, he turned his head towards the sound just in time to see three heavily armed men standing in the open doorway. Another sharp prod in the back told Rob to step forward, the three men parted ahead of him, the cold look each man gave him betrayed just how keen they were to start shooting. The bright lights of the warehouse burnt his eyes as he and Charlie stepped inside, the door slammed behind them and the heavy bolt was dragged back into place.

As his eyes adjusted, Rob spotted a group of men huddled in the centre of the large room, behind them was eight rows of boxes, each stacked four wide and thirty or forty deep, reaching right up to the white brick wall at the far end of the warehouse. Another prod in the back told him to make his way towards the huddle, as the men began to adjust their position to take in the new arrivals Rob caught sight of Stephen McSharry standing in amongst them. He had the same shit eater grin that had been plastered across his face the first time they had met.

Rob approached the group without a word. His count totalled thirteen, not including the old man or Charlie, safety in numbers was clearly the order of the day; no risk, no mistake. He tried to scan for familiar faces, McSharry had done his level best to keep his crew and his shooter as separate as possible, but Liverpool was a small town, he fancied he'd know a few faces from around the way.

He drew mainly blanks, most of the more heavily armed players were young guys in their mid-twenties, muscle no doubt, in to beef up the lines. Whoever they were, their time was post-Rob's time, they could be the toughest bastards in the whole country and Rob would be as oblivious to them as if they were European politicians.

In amongst the older faces he got a couple of nudges of recognition, not so much from their faces as from their reps. The funny looking guy with the blond hair and glasses had to be Nikolai, the shady knife merchant who inspired almost as many horror stories on the streets of Liverpool as Begsy or McSharry. One of the big men also flashed familiar, it took Rob a couple of seconds to click that he used to go watch the guy fight semi-pro; a couple more seconds got him half a name; something Wallace.

Aside from that the group gave him nothing but blanks, yet what they lacked in familiarity they more than made up for in viciousness. The old man's rapid ascension suddenly seemed to make even more sense, standing in front of this group of killers made Rob's own contribution feel a little less decisive. It was a nice feeling, at least until he thought about what he'd helped to leave behind for the next guy who took it upon himself to try and kill the old man. From where he was standing it didn't look like an easy monopoly to break.

"Did you search him?" McSharry asked, his voice echoing off the walls.

Charlie nodded "He's clean"

McSharry considered the answer, his eyes passed over the two brothers, lingering over Rob for a brief moment, before they settled on two of his men.

"Search him again" McSharry ordered, his face didn't betray a hint of emotion.

The two men marched over and roughly patted Rob down, as they did so he stole a glance at his brother, it was subtle, but he caught it, the flicker of annoyance that flashed in his eyes. When they were finished one of them slapped Rob in the back of the head and signalled the all clear to the boss

McSharry took a couple of steps towards him, as he did so the rest of the group spread out and formed a circle around the two men. Rob turned and saw that Charlie had already dropped back into the group, the pistol resting at his side, shaking ever so slightly in his hand.

The old man reached up and backhanded Rob hard across the face. The blow caught the side of his mouth still red from Charlie's pistol whipping, causing him to wince, he heard chuckles of laughter as his head snapped to the side.

"That," McSharry said, pointing a finger into Rob's face "is for conspiring to kill me you little prick. I'm disappointed, after everything I've done for you, I'd have thought you would have shown a little more loyalty than that"

Rob spat out a mouthful of blood.

"To you? You've been a cancer on my life for the last fifteen years"

"Thanks to me you were rich"

"Thanks to you I was condemned"

McSharry reached out, one of the men handed him a gun, Rob felt the anticipation in the crowd go up a couple of notches.

"I put your talents to good use" his words were slow and methodical, the glibness was suddenly gone "I gave you a chance to make a difference, but you've never been man enough for this life have you? Take a look at yourself; burnt out, broken, you've served your purpose and you never once saw the value in it. Stronger men than you would kill for the life that I offered"

"Not me. I never wanted any of it, and I don't owe you a thing, least of all my loyalty"

He saw the arrogant smile creep back onto the old man's face, it made his skin crawl.

"So who do you owe it to, then? Your brother? Your own flesh and blood? I don't know, screwing another man's wife is low enough, but to do it to your own brother? If I didn't plan to kill you already you can be sure that I would have buried you for this. Makes me sick, you remember how I feel about adulterers don't you?"

Rob felt his brothers eyes burning into him, he dared not look through fear of setting him off. Rob's focus moved towards the gun in McSharry's hand, he had to get him to fire first, before Charlie lost his temper, it was the only way he could save his brother.

"I remember that you couldn't even keep your own wife satisfied. That you needed me to come in and clean up the mess when she skipped out on your wrinkled arse"

No one spoke, not even a gasp, but he could sense the tension fill the warehouse in an instant. McSharry reached up and backhanded him again, he looked into the old man's eyes and saw that the provocation had failed, he was too smart for it, he knew exactly what Rob was trying to do.

"I wouldn't expect a man like you to understand the sanctity of marriage" he sniggered and looked over Rob's shoulder "would we, Charlie?"

"Let me kill him" Charlie pleaded, it was a guttural plea, like an addict begging for one more hit.

McSharry shook his head and smirked at Rob.

"Not yet. We haven't even got round to the introductions yet," McSharry looked around the group "boys, satisfy your curiosity, this is the man you've all been so interested in: Rob Thomas, natural born killer and disloyal dog, my own personal poisoned arrow. Right?"

McSharry asked the question with a smirk, Rob looked around the group of killers, each one looked back at him with more contempt than the last.

"No more than the rest of your thugs"

McSharry's laugh echoed around the room and bounced off the walls.

"I suppose you're right, I'm surrounded by my collection of poisoned arrows, righting the world one dead scumbag at a time," McSharry pulled back the hammer on his pistol, to Rob's ears the sound was a million times louder than the laugh had been "starting with you"

"He doesn't look like much to me, boss"

The sound came from Rob's right, he looked and saw a well-built man with a thick black beard glaring back at him.

"Give me one round with him and I'll show you a natural born killer" said the ex-boxer, a few sniggers spread around the group as the large man cracked his knuckles and raised his eyebrows invitingly.

"Don't be fooled lads," McSharry told them "this one's a vicious little bastard. Many a complicated problem has found itself untangled via his hand. Speaking of which, I must thank you for coming through on that final job. I appreciate a man who keeps to his word, even if it is simply as a means to meet his own traitorous ends. I am curious, was it my old friend who inflicted all this damage, or one of his girls maybe?"

Another scattering of chuckles. Rob saw his chance, this time it was his turn to flash a glib smile.

"What this?" he asked, pointing towards his battered face "No, this was your pet goon. He fucked me up pretty badly, right before I put a bullet through his mouth. It's funny about these big guys, you know they look indestructible but they die just as quickly as the rest when you blow their heads off. Except they make a cooler noise when they drop"

Rob watched with delight as the colour drained from the old man's face.

"You're lying to me"

"Am I?" McSharry stared at him, Rob stared right back, he'd keep their eyes locked together for as long as it took for McSharry to see that there was nothing but truth in his words. He raised his voice as McSharry continued to scrutinise him "He sent Begsy to Kelly's house Charlie, did you know that? He killed her and her two little kids before I shot him. These are the kind of people you want to give your loyalty to?"

Rob took a risk and glanced over his shoulder, he saw the look on confusion on his brothers face, it was the first ray of genuine hope he'd felt since before Kelly had been killed.

"Is that true?" Charlie asked, looking passed Rob to McSharry, his brothers tone was respectful but firm "you said you'd leave her out of all this?"

Rob heard the gunshot first. It took a fraction of a second for him to feel the pain erupt in his right thigh. A second later he was on the floor, wrapping his hands tightly around the wound in an effort to stop the blood from pouring onto the concrete beneath him. He heard a deep, rough scream filling his ears, it was only when he saw the smoking gun in McSharry's hand that he realised it was coming from his own mouth.

"Pick him up! Now" McSharry barked.

Rob felt rough hands gripping his arms and hauling him to his feet. The pain was excruciating, he tried to rest some of his weight onto his right leg and felt the pain multiply by a thousand.

McSharry pressed his face close to Rob's. The two men holding him up had a firm grip on each arm to keep him from lashing out, he was breathing heavy, he could hear it, but he couldn't stop it.

"You're lying to me, aren't you?"

The pain in his leg made it difficult to speak, when he finally managed it the words came out in a low growl.

"Go and see for yourself. I got the 9mm too, you can forget about pinning that cop killing on me. You'll have the police on your back long after I'm gone, boss!"

McSharry was so angry he was beginning to shake, Rob watched him raise the gun high enough for Rob to see it.

"That isn't going to be long at all, you fucking runt-"

The two-knock-pause-one-knock at the door cut McSharry off mid-sentence, the old man turned his attention towards the sound, Rob tried to use the distraction to grab the gun but the grip of the men holding him was too strong to get his hands free.

"What!?" McSharry screamed impatiently.

The door slid open and Rob saw the blond, slightly chubby face of Teller looking expectantly towards them. He only saw the face for the briefest of moments before it was obscured by a red mist, after that all he saw was the blond head of hair falling to the floor as the door swung over and rapid gun fire began to echo around the warehouse.

The men either side of him released their grip as three rifle wielding guys forced their way inside. He recognised the final man through the door; he wore some kind of brace on his arms to help keep the rifle in place. Though his figure was pale and thin Rob recognised the fury instantly; it was Tony

Miller.

With all the energy he had Rob flung himself towards his little brother. The leg wound significantly reduced the distance, but somehow he managed to get enough push on his left leg to tackle Charlie by the waist and cover him as the gun fight erupted rapidly around them.

Charlie struggled beneath him. In those first few seconds Rob took in nothing but the sounds erupting around them; rapid gun fire, the thud of bullets embedding themselves in flesh, the low groans of the dying.

Matt had come through. Rob didn't know why he was surprised, his old mate always did. The shot had been a long one; use your Caddock connections at work to get a message to whatever was left of the Miller crew, tell them to be at the Bootle strand for midnight, from there he would lead them to the man they wanted. He was both relieved and terrified that his final play had yielded results, at this point he still had no idea what those results were going to be.

Rob used his weight to pin Charlie down, like he had when they were kids. With his free hand he pried the gun from his brothers grip and took a quick look at the chaotic scenes unfolding around them.

The entire warehouse was disorganised anarchy, the first thing he saw were the bodies of the four dead McSharry boys scattered across the floor in front of him. After that he tried to take as much in as 360 degree turn would allow him. He saw McSharry and the boxer crouched behind a desk in the far corner as Tony Miller stumbled towards them firing shot after shot into the wooden furniture. One of Miller's shooters had already been forced back outside, two men had gone into the evening air after him while two more lingered on the inside of the door, leaning out to fire an occasional shot.

Behind him he saw three more McSharry goons fleeing down one of the aisles with a rifleman in hot pursuit. A moment after all four had disappeared Rob caught sight of Nikolai following them, fluorescent light reflected off the blade in his hand as he stalked silently forward.

Charlie tried to move again, Rob looked down and saw the same terrified look that he'd seen on his brothers face the day they first met Stephen McSharry. A bullet ricocheted off the floor inches away from Charlie's head. Rob pulled his brother upwards, shielding Charlie behind him. The two men next to the door had turned their attention away from the fight in the car park and focused it on them, Rob recognised one of the two as the thick bearded loudmouth from earlier.

Another shot fizzed just past him, Rob felt movement from behind and realised that Charlie had flung himself towards one of the dead bodies. The beard followed the movement and fired, Rob raised his gun a fraction later and squeezed twice; both the beard and his accomplice left a red spray on the wall behind them, before sinking to the ground.

When Rob turned and saw the blood begin to seep through his brother's shirt he felt the air instantly evaporate from his lungs. The shot seemed to be high and to the left of the chest, Charlie saw the blood and started to hyperventilate. Without thinking Rob grabbed his brother under the arms and dragged towards the wall, five feet further down from where the beards body had fell, a few boxes gave them a limited amount of cover.

Charlie was conscious, but pale, he kept staring at the wound and then staring at his brother as if he couldn't comprehend what was going on.

Rob inspected the gunshot, it was bleeding faster than he would have liked, but it was too tight to tell whether it had caught the lung or not.

"You're fine Charlie," Rob lied, "It caught you high, but you're going to need a doctor"

Charlie shook his head like he didn't believe a word of it.

"I don't want to die, Rob"

"We'll get you out of here"

"I don't want to die"

Rob looked around, the sound of gunfire continued to echo through the air. They weren't going anywhere until this fight had been won, if McSharry managed to win it with a few men to spare then they wouldn't be going anywhere at all.

He looked down the nearest aisle and saw a gap towards the end, it led to the same aisle that Nikolai et all had disappeared into earlier, taking them out would cut the number of his remaining problems in half. One look at his terrified brother urged him to rethink his strategy, but it was the only way he knew to get them out.

"Wait here Charlie. Once we've got a clean run through I'm going to get you out of here, but we can't go anywhere while these bastards are running around shooting everything that moves. Just wait here and keep quiet, ok? I'll get you out, I promise"

Behind the fear Charlie seemed to understand the logic, his face was pale and his breathing was ragged but he still managed to nod and smile. Rob planted a kiss on his brothers forehead and stumbled towards the gap in the boxes, as he moved he checked the clip in the gun, ten shots left.

He stepped into the aisle and made his way slowly forward, the wound in his leg had him hobbling at a snail's pace, though gladly the adrenaline had numbed some of the pain. The first thing he saw was a dead McSharry thug, face down on the hard concrete. As he made his way further up the aisle he saw Nikolai and another man standing over something, as he got closer he realised it was the body of Miller's rifleman. Another couple of steps put the scene in focus; Nikolai was leaning over the other man as he pressed his blade deeper and deeper into his adversaries chest. His accomplice stood by watching with interest, he seemed like one of McSharry's younger guys, in his twenties, tall and thin with darkish skin.

Rob raised the gun, neither man was looking in his direction, that gave him time. As he pressed down on the trigger Rob felt something hard slam into him from behind. He had just enough time to see the bullet bury itself harmlessly into one of the boxes as the tall, skinny man bolted from the aisle.

The hit from behind gave Rob the space he needed to turn and face his attacker, he cursed as he realised it was the man he'd presumed dead further down the aisle. The man might have still been alive but he was also badly wounded, he stumbled forward in an effort to slam his body once more into Rob's, but the distance was too great, there was enough time to raise his pistol and fire once into his attackers forehead. This time when he dropped Rob was in no doubt that he was dead.

Turning around Rob caught sight of the blade as it was inches away from his face. Stumbling backwards he managed to get out of the way just in time, but the loss of balance forced him to put his weight onto his injured right leg, which sent him hobbling backwards a couple more steps and allowed Nikolai to close in.

Rob tried to raise the gun but the knife slashed at his right hand, sending the pistol tumbling to the floor. It came at him again a second later but Rob was able to grip Nikolai by the wrist and direct the blade left away from them both.

The two men locked eyes for the first time and Rob saw that behind those glasses the little blond man was smiling. He only had a second to consider the oddness of the gesture before a flash of movement told him that Nikolai had pulled a second knife free with his other hand.

Rob released his grip and stumbled back a couple of more steps until he was out of reach of the blades. Nikolai stalked towards him with that same grin, his arms spread wide with a glistening blade at the end of each. Rob tried to think of a means of regaining the initiative but his mind was blank, all he could do was react as the blades slashed down towards him. He managed to intercept the first one, slamming his left fist into Nikolai's wrist with enough force to knock it free, but the focus left his right side exposed and he screamed as he felt the blade slice through his side.

Nikolai brought the blade up for another pass, somehow Rob was able to reach up and wrap both his hands around the moving wrist. Before Nikolai had a chance to react Rob slammed his head into the little mans, breaking both his glasses and his nose in the same instant. The momentary disorientation gave Rob all the time he needed, using his strength advantage he twisted Nikola's hand inwards and thrust the knife into the man's chest.

Nikolai gave a small cough before his body went limp and he dropped onto the floor.

Picking up the gun Rob continued to hobble up the aisle as fast as he could. As he made it towards the top he saw McSharry stand from behind the desk, raise his gun and fire once, when Rob got a few steps closer he managed to catch sight of a heavily plastered arm as it swayed, dropped its rifle and collapsed on the ground.

Rob hobbled as fast as he could, there was nothing but silence now, for the first time he could hear his own frantic breathing.

488

McSharry darted from behind the desk with the boxer only a couple of steps behind, Rob tried to take a shot but by the time he'd raised the gun they'd disappeared from the thin line of sight that the aisle offered him. Lowering the gun he stifled a curse and continued as fast as his battered body would allow.

Finally, he reached the end and stepped back into the jumble of bodies where the whole thing had started, his eyes rested on Tony Miller, a bullet hole where his left eye should have been and the same fierce snarl etched eternally on his lips. The thick door stood wide open and through it Rob could hear the two men racing towards the four cars that were parked close by.

The gun felt heavy in his hand, Rob took a couple of steps forward and looked towards the boxes where he'd left his brother, he saw Charlie's pale face poking out and flashing him a relieved look.

Rob's gaze moved back towards the door, he involuntarily squeezed the grip of the pistol, it was so close to being over, he could end the whole thing with two more shots.

He looked back towards Charlie, he could tell that his brother knew exactly what he was thinking, and the slow solemn nod was Charlie's way of telling him to go for it. Rob returned the nod, raised the gun and hobbled towards the open door.

Chapter 38

Rico Wallace had the keys in his hand as he fumbled at the driver's door, McSharry was in no mood to wait, he fired two shots into the passenger window and unlocked the door from the inside, he was in his seat with the door closed by the time the big lump had gotten his open.

"Get us the fuck out of here" McSharry ordered briskly.

Rico didn't respond, a few nervous moments passed before the key was in the ignition and the engine came to life.

Rico put his foot down and the car jerked forward, it had just started to build speed when Stephen McSharry saw the last thing he wanted to see on this earth, Rob fucking Thomas emerging through the doorway with a gun in hand.

He tried to shout a warning but the gun totting prick was too fast, he raised his weapon and fired before McSharry could get a word out. Two shots flew through the side window and hit Rico in the side of the head, McSharry lunged for the wheel but the big man's heavy grip pulled it sideways as he died, the wall of the warehouse came into view a second before the car slammed into it.

He felt pain shoot up his side, right the way from his hip to his shoulder. His head had smashed against the dashboard and he could feel the warm sensation of blood running down his face.

In between Rico's head and the steering wheel McSharry could see Rob Thomas hobbling slowly towards the wreckage, with his gun focused unerringly at the car. McSharry fumbled around on the floor in search of his gun, eventually he found it, his aching arm tried to lift it upwards, it took two attempts to succeed.

The prick was less than ten yards away when the shout came from inside the warehouse.

"Rob!"

It was a weak, gasping shout but McSharry still recognised it as the voice of Charlie Thomas. He watched the older brother spin around to see a bloodied Nikolai leaning against the doorframe.

The opportunism inspired a burst of energy, pushing the door open he stumbled out into the car park just as the rat raised his gun and fired three shots at Nikolai. He was too late to save the last of his boys but the distraction gave him enough time to lift his own pistol and fire one shot; it hit the bastard high in the back and he collapsed forward with a groan.

McSharry walked over slowly, he heard heavy breathing as he got close and kicked the gun away from Thomas's hand, a rage suddenly overcame him and he found himself kicking the traitorous little prick again and again until he'd rolled over onto his back.

McSharry lifted his head by the collar.

"You thought bringing a cripple to my door would be enough? You thought

I'd fold that easily? Look at me!"

Rob Thomas's eyes finally managed to focus and McSharry brought the base of the gun down onto his face over and over until his features were soaked in blood.

"I am this city!" he shouted as he released his grip and watched Thomas's head smack against the ground "What right do you have to even think of separating me from it?"

Rob Thomas slowly rolled over, he tried to raise himself up and collapsed back down. A few seconds later he tried again, he'd managed to get onto his hands and his knees by the time he spoke.

"What right did you have to bring me back?"

McSharry almost laughed. He pulled the hammer back on the gun, the talk and the games were beginning to tire him, he wanted the peace that only victory brought.

"That was my mistake" he said, raising the gun to the battered man's head "lets rectify it"

As he pressed down on the trigger a hand darted upwards and palmed the gun away. The speed of the movement caught McSharry off guard, a moment later the other hand came up and knocked the gun from his hand altogether.

McSharry took a step backwards but Rob Thomas was up and chasing him in a heartbeat. A right fist connected with his jaw, a left slammed against his ribs, a knee forced its way into his balls, before McSharry knew what was happening he felt fist after fist connecting with his face and cracking bone after bone. When it finally stopped Thomas gripped his hair and slammed his head first into the driver's door of the smashed up Jeep. As he slipped downwards he tried to hold onto something and inadvertently opened the door. He fell on his face dazed as the sound of footsteps filled his ears, when he finally regained his senses he looked up to see Rob Thomas standing a few feet away with a gun in his hand.

Rob Thomas raised the weapon, McSharry crawled backwards, pressing himself as close to the car as he could. As his eyes darted from the vehicle to his attempted murderer they caught something black and shiny; a gun, on the floor of the car next to Rico's feet, just within reach.

He told himself to be smart, younger and fitter men than him had lost out to Rob Thomas in a battle of reflexes, if he reached for it now he was a dead man. The black piece of metal called out to him, it offered to save him from the subordinate position in which he was currently stranded, but he ignored it, there would be time for pride, it would come after victory.

McSharry waited as Rob Thomas continued to stare him down, he waited for the gun to go off, he saw the cold look in the man's eyes and finally understood what it must have felt like for all the people who had died at the man's hand, deaths that he had sanctioned.

"This ends" Rob told him.

McSharry waited. Every breath brought with it a wave of horror, as if each one was likely to be his last.

Rob Thomas lowered his weapon.

"But not your way. I'm done killing for you"

McSharry couldn't help but smile, his hand crept closer and closer to Rico's gun, *keep your eye on the target* he told himself, *keep him distracted.*

"You never wised up, did you?" McSharry asked.

Rob Thomas craned his neck as if he was listening for something, a moment later McSharry caught it too, it was the distant sound of sirens.

"I think maybe I finally did"

His hand was only inches away now, the excitement took hold, he reached out and pulled the gun free. He caught the look of surprise on Thomas's face, he'd only got his weapon halfway up when McSharry squeezed off a shot. It caught the prick right in the throat and sent him tumbling backwards, gasping for breath.

McSharry finally found the calm to breathe normally, without the panic. Dragging himself up he walked slowly over the prone body and took a closer look; Rob Thomas was gasping for air, dying slowly, but dying all the same. The shocked look he'd possessed a moment ago was suddenly magnified, his eyes were wide with both fear and confusion, McSharry heard a small laugh escape from his own mouth.

Slowly the shocked look began to subside, and Stephen McSharry was amazed to see it replaced by a smile. The boy continued to gasp for air but he did so with none of the desperation of before, the wideness in his eyes began to appear enthusiastic and childlike. He looked relieved; the wrinkles etched into his forehead seemed to disappear as his mind stumbled closer and closer towards death.

McSharry could do nothing other than shake his head.

"Stupid fucking boy"

Dropping to on one knee he pressed the pistol down hard over Thomas's heart, he waited for a reaction, to see that look of fear return, but it didn't, just that same god damn grin staring back up at him.

Stephen McSharry pulled the trigger and felt the body convulse beneath him. The bullet pierced his heart and killed Rob Thomas within seconds, the little prick died with that same contented smile plastered across his face.

McSharry raised himself to his feet as the bright lights and police sirens flooded the car park. He dropped the gun on the floor and raised his hands above his head.

He looked down at the body of his dead enemy. Victory had come.

He tried to smile, but his attention was diverted towards the masses of police officers that were flooding forwards. They locked onto him with hungry, blood thirsty eyes, like an angry mob rampaging in the dead of night. He was suddenly very aware of the pistol that resided at his feet, the smile refused to come as he allowed himself to consider for the first time; just what the cost was going to be.

Epilogue

December first and already New York was covered in three feet of snow. The tourists loved it, they skated in Central Park, wrapped up warm in Times Square and hugged hot cups of coffee on the subway, Jo Boyd found it little more than an annoyance, particularly when she was trying to lug a week's worth of groceries back to her apartment.

One of the bags dug into her wrist as she keyed open the door to her building. Jo's mind was already drifting towards the eight hour shift that was due to start in a little under two hours, McGlincheys was going to be the end of her, she needed to find some proper work before she ended up a fifty year old barmaid like her mother.

She was halfway up the stairs when she paused to look behind her. A thick trail of watery snow followed her right the way from the door, untouched to the right was the buildings new doormat with the hastily written warning "Please wipe your feet!!!". Jo had felt the three explanation points added a slightly too brazen element to the message, but like most of the residents she was easily cowed in the face of such overbearing domestic authority.

Hurrying the rest of the way seemed like the best plan of action, if she was lucky perhaps she could reach her apartment door before she was spotted at the scene of the crime and no one would be any the wiser.

She stepped from the staircase and into the hallway at a brisk pace while she fumbled around inside her bag, when she finally raised her head and saw the man lingering outside her door something between a gasp and a scream escaped from her mouth as she stumbled backwards into the wall.

The man raised his hands, as if to indicate that he meant no harm.

"Wow, sorry. Is your name...are you Joanne Boyd?"

All of Rob's words came back to her, in an instant paranoid ramblings suddenly felt like stone written prophecies. She heard the scouse twang and the recognition brought a stab of pain that reminded her just how badly she missed him. The man before her didn't look dangerous, he was handsome in a boyish kind of way, with a warm yet sad smile, in a different situation she might have been inclined to trust him, but Rob had been very clear on the subject. She reached into her bag and searched for the pistol, she always carried it with her, that was one of the things he had insisted on.

The man in front of her seemed to sense what she was about to do, he raised his hands even higher and tried to smile, though the worry on his face made it look less charming than it had a moment ago.

"You don't have to reach for that, I'm a friend of Rob's, my names Matt, he asked me to come and see you. He said you might be a little... on edge"

Her hand had found the gun but she decided not to pull it free just yet. The man was still a good few feet away, she liked her chances of drawing it before he could get to her, though something about him made her feel like that wouldn't be necessary.

"Why should I believe you?"

The man lowered his hands slightly.

"Rob said you'd ask me that. I'm supposed to tell you that you can trust me because you know that scousers are practically Irish, he said you'd know what that meant?"

An involuntary smile crept to the corner of her lips, it was the line he always liked to pull when he met people from Ireland, it had been one of the first things he'd said to her when he was trying to chat her up. Jo's hand relaxed, the gentle memory quickly evaporated when she realised that something would have to be seriously wrong if his friend had needed to come in his place.

"What's wrong? Did something happen? Is Rob ok?"

First the sad smile, then it was replaced by a look of plain sadness, a moment later Jo thought she saw a tear drop from the man's eye, she got a terrible feeling in the pit of her stomach as she watched the man struggle to speak.

"A couple of days ago he was killed. He came to see me a few hours before he died, he asked me to store a couple of things for him, and if things went badly he made me promise to come to this address and give something to you"

Jo tried to breathe and realised that she couldn't. Her legs felt weak and she leaned against the nearby wall to keep from falling. The man reached inside his coat, she was motionless as she watched him, vaguely aware that he could be about to pull a gun, or a knife. His hand emerged holding an envelope, he reached forward and held it out to her, the closer he got the easier she could see his tears, it spurred on the counterparts that were building behind her own eyes.

For a few moments she simply stared at the outstretched hand, afraid to accept what was being offered. Eventually she found the courage, reached forward and took it. The envelope wasn't sealed, it opened with ease. She recognised Rob's handwriting immediately.

Dear Jo

If you have this letter then it means that things didn't work out too well, and I didn't make it. Or maybe it means that things worked out the best possible way they could have, I don't know, I look at things now and I'm not sure I understand what counts as a win or what counts as a loss anymore. I know I'm being obscure, I apologise, obscurity is something you've had to live with since the day we met and that should never have been the case. I should have trusted you enough to tell you the truth, the problem was that the more time I spent with you the more I loved you, and the more I loved you the more I couldn't stand the idea of losing you. So I kept quiet and forced you to live a lie, for that I have no excuse, and I hope that one day you will come to forgive me for than naïve selfishness.

The truth is this: before we met my job was to murder people. As I write this I think about how smart you are and it strikes me that, on some level, you probably already know everything that I'm telling you. Could you still have loved me if we'd put these things on the table and lived with them day in day out? I guess that's something that only you can answer, and that I can never know. What I do know, and what I wish I'd known earlier, is that leaving you was the worst mistake I ever made. Since I came back here I've done some terrible things, things that I would be ashamed and horrified for you to know, I wish I could take them back, but I can't. If this is how it ends then maybe it's fitting, maybe I don't deserve to make it back to you, maybe after everything that I've done this is how it needs to end. I wish more than anything that I could tear up this letter, hop on a plane tonight and not have to face these horrible things that I suspect are waiting for me, but the truth is that I can't leave this place without first trying to fix the mess that I've made.

I'm babbling again, it's stupid I know but if this is the last message that I ever get to give you then I want it to try and encompass everything that I am. I know that's impossible, and after all these ramblings I still haven't told you the most important thing, so here it is:

You made me into more than I ever thought I could be. It was by trying to be the man that you thought I was, and to return the love you gave me, that I was somehow able to become more than just a killer. I owe you everything for that, and my biggest regret is that I have no way to return your gift. My only hope is that someday in the future, you find someone better to love than me. Someone worthy of everything you have to give, it breaks my heart that I couldn't be that person for you.

Every day before that and every day after I'll always be with you, you were the only thing in my life that ever truly meant anything.

Yours forever

Rob

The letter dropped from her hand, her legs managed to hold out for a moment longer before she collapsed onto the floor in tears. He couldn't be dead, he just couldn't be, he'd promised to come back to her.

She cried and cried until her throat was hoarse, at some point the man knelt down and wrapped his arms around her. She buried her head into his chest and continued to sob. Her hand reached out for the letter and gripped it tightly, it was all she had left.

A letter and a hole.

CPSIA information can be obtained at www.ICGtesting.com
Printed in the USA
LVOW042248250412

279151LV00017B/131/P